W.i.t.c.h.

Will   Irma   Taranee   Cornelia   Hay Lin

Part I. The Twelve Portals
Volume 3

W.i.t.c.h.

Will Irma Taranee Cornelia Hay Lin

Part 1. The Twelve Portals
Volume 3

CONTENTS

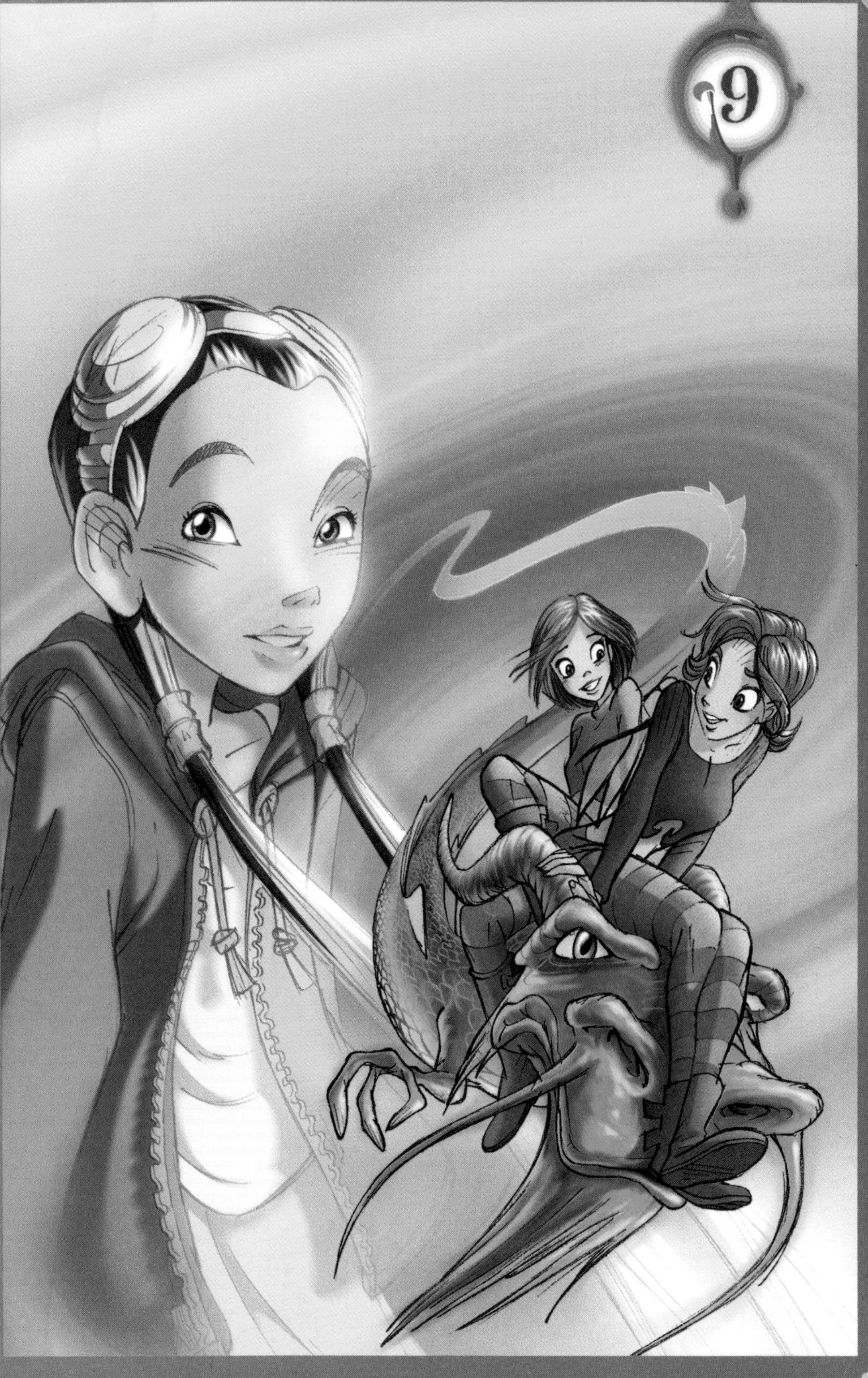
9

THE FOUR DRAGONS

"That's how Xin Jing, the Nymph, soared above the world..."

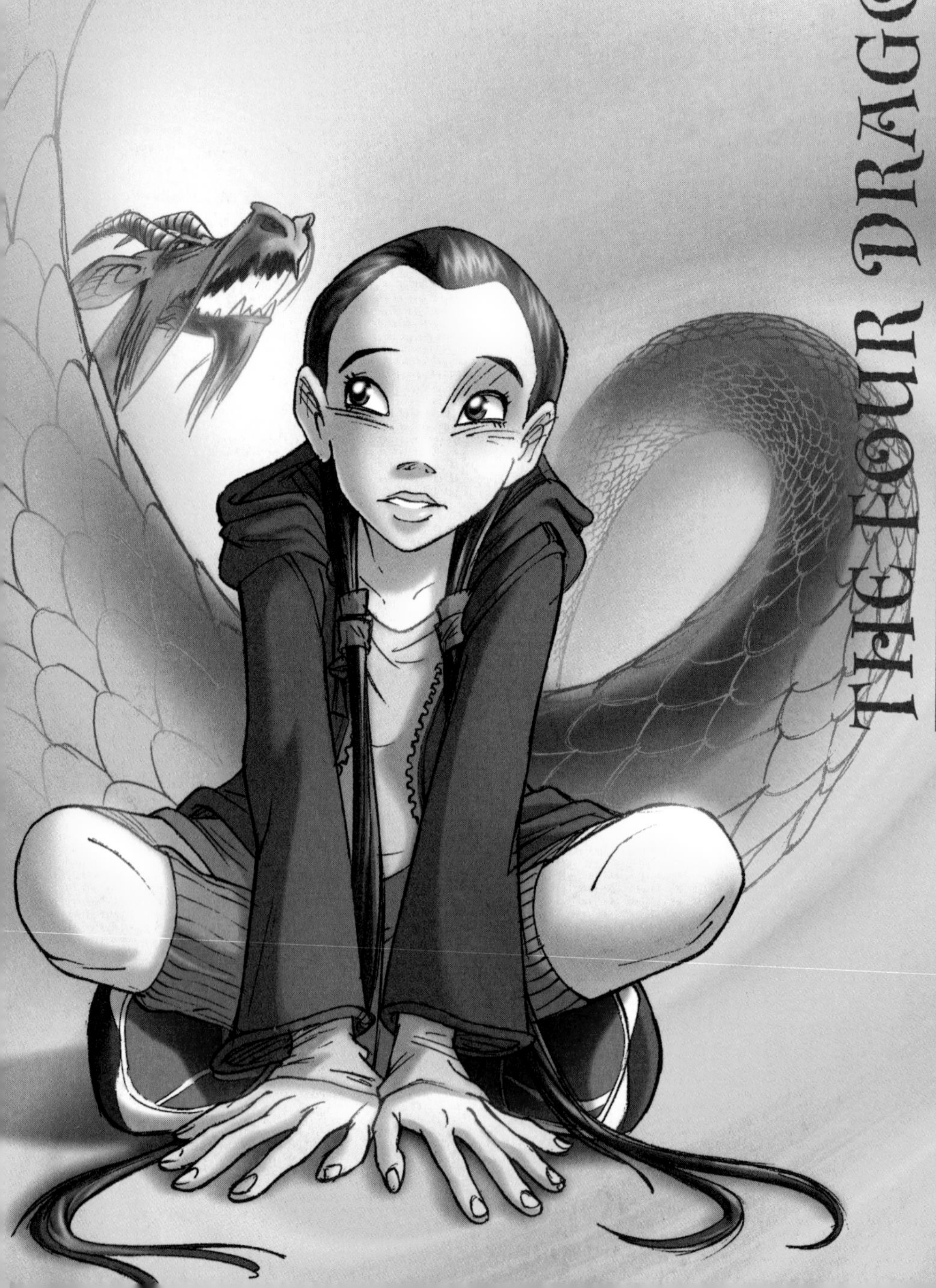

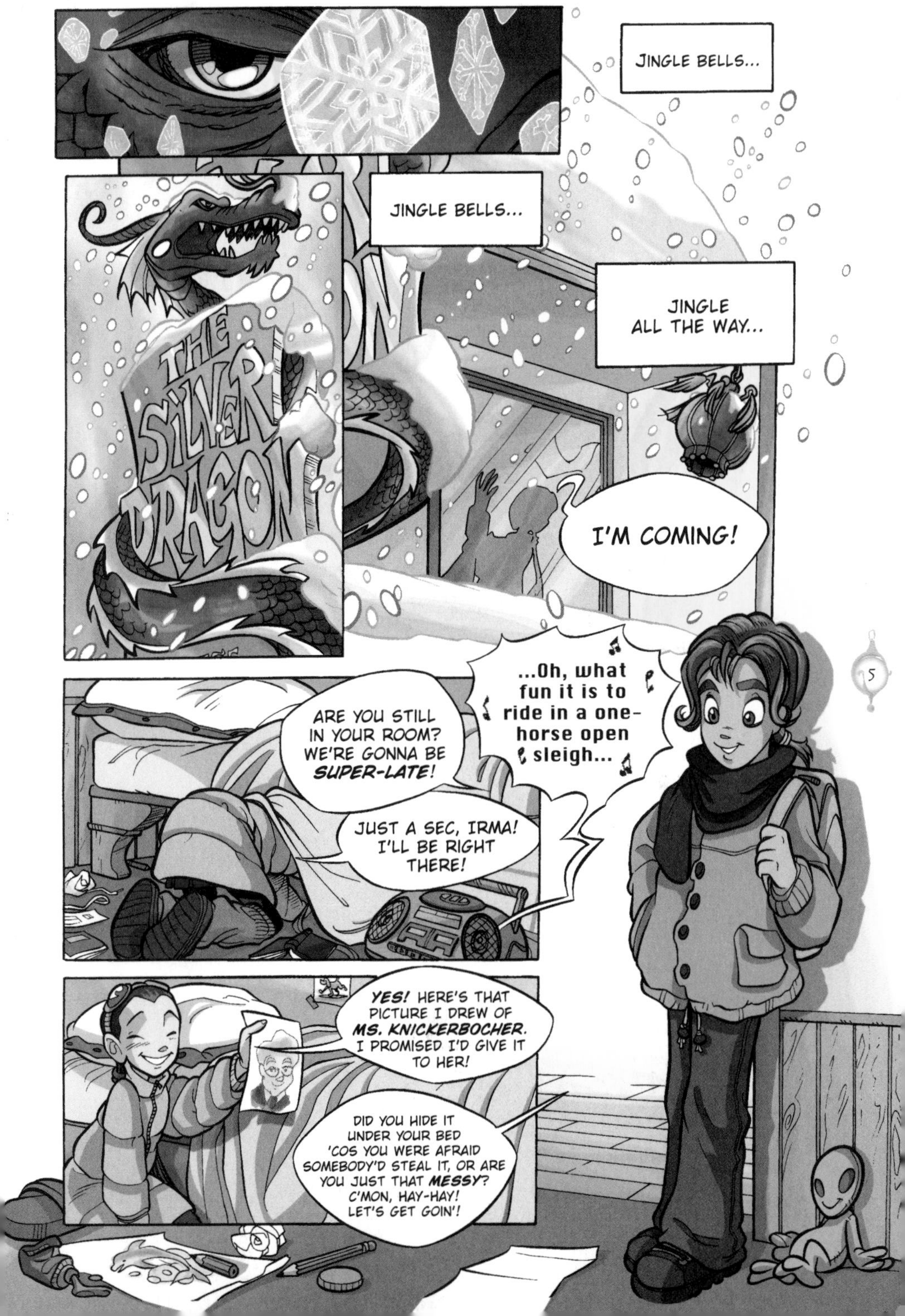
JINGLE BELLS...
JINGLE BELLS...
THE SILVER DRAGON
JINGLE ALL THE WAY...
I'M COMING!
...Oh, what fun it is to ride in a one-horse open sleigh...
ARE YOU STILL IN YOUR ROOM? WE'RE GONNA BE *SUPER-LATE*!
JUST A SEC, IRMA! I'LL BE RIGHT THERE!
YES! HERE'S THAT PICTURE I DREW OF *MS. KNICKERBOCHER*. I PROMISED I'D GIVE IT TO HER!
DID YOU HIDE IT UNDER YOUR BED 'COS YOU WERE AFRAID SOMEBODY'D STEAL IT, OR ARE YOU JUST THAT *MESSY*? C'MON, HAY-HAY! LET'S GET GOIN'!

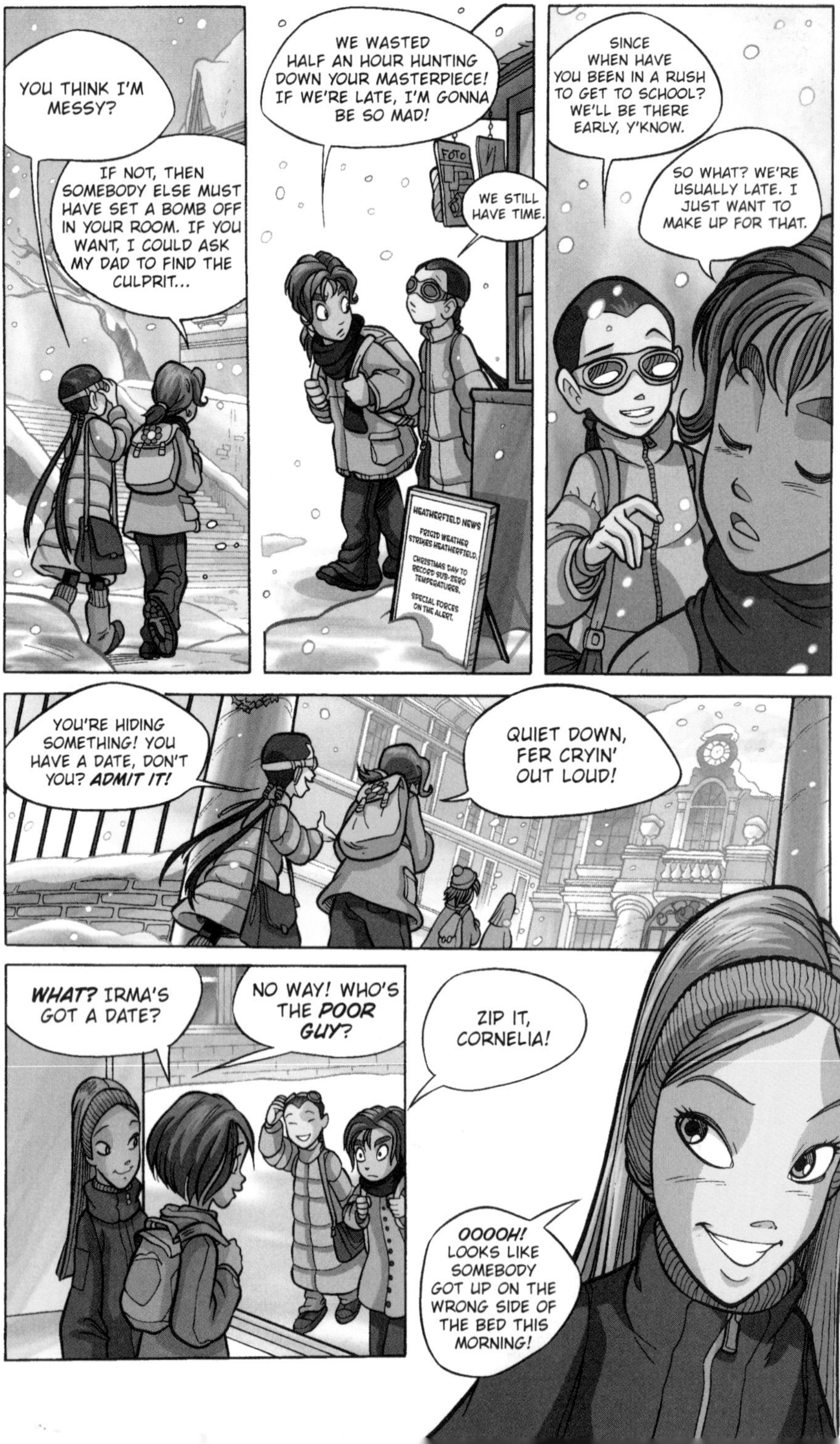
YOU THINK I'M MESSY?
IF NOT, THEN SOMEBODY ELSE MUST HAVE SET A BOMB OFF IN YOUR ROOM. IF YOU WANT, I COULD ASK MY DAD TO FIND THE CULPRIT...
WE WASTED HALF AN HOUR HUNTING DOWN YOUR MASTERPIECE! IF WE'RE LATE, I'M GONNA BE SO MAD!
WE STILL HAVE TIME.
FOTO
HEATHERFIELD NEWS
FRIGID WEATHER STRIKES HEATHERFIELD.
CHRISTMAS DAY TO RECORD SUB-ZERO TEMPERATURES.
SPECIAL FORCES ON THE ALERT.
SINCE WHEN HAVE YOU BEEN IN A RUSH TO GET TO SCHOOL? WE'LL BE THERE EARLY, Y'KNOW.
SO WHAT? WE'RE USUALLY LATE. I JUST WANT TO MAKE UP FOR THAT.
YOU'RE HIDING SOMETHING! YOU HAVE A DATE, DON'T YOU? ***ADMIT IT!***
QUIET DOWN, FER CRYIN' OUT LOUD!
WHAT? IRMA'S GOT A DATE?
NO WAY! WHO'S THE ***POOR GUY***?
ZIP IT, CORNELIA!
OOOOH! LOOKS LIKE SOMEBODY GOT UP ON THE WRONG SIDE OF THE BED THIS MORNING!

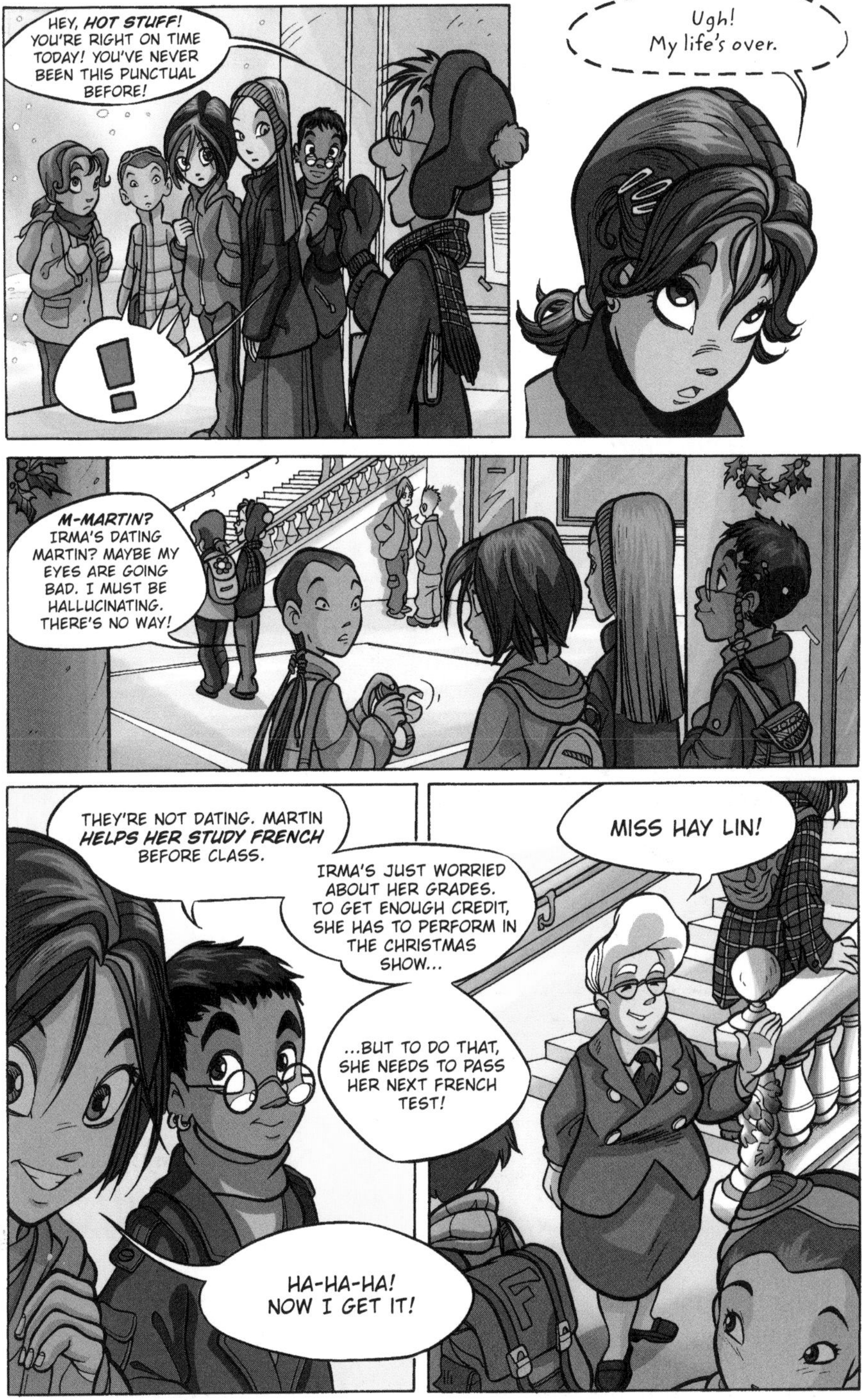
HEY, HOT STUFF! YOU'RE RIGHT ON TIME TODAY! YOU'VE NEVER BEEN THIS PUNCTUAL BEFORE!
!
Ugh! My life's over.
M-MARTIN? IRMA'S DATING MARTIN? MAYBE MY EYES ARE GOING BAD. I MUST BE HALLUCINATING. THERE'S NO WAY!
THEY'RE NOT DATING. MARTIN HELPS HER STUDY FRENCH BEFORE CLASS.
IRMA'S JUST WORRIED ABOUT HER GRADES. TO GET ENOUGH CREDIT, SHE HAS TO PERFORM IN THE CHRISTMAS SHOW...
...BUT TO DO THAT, SHE NEEDS TO PASS HER NEXT FRENCH TEST!
HA-HA-HA! NOW I GET IT!
MISS HAY LIN!

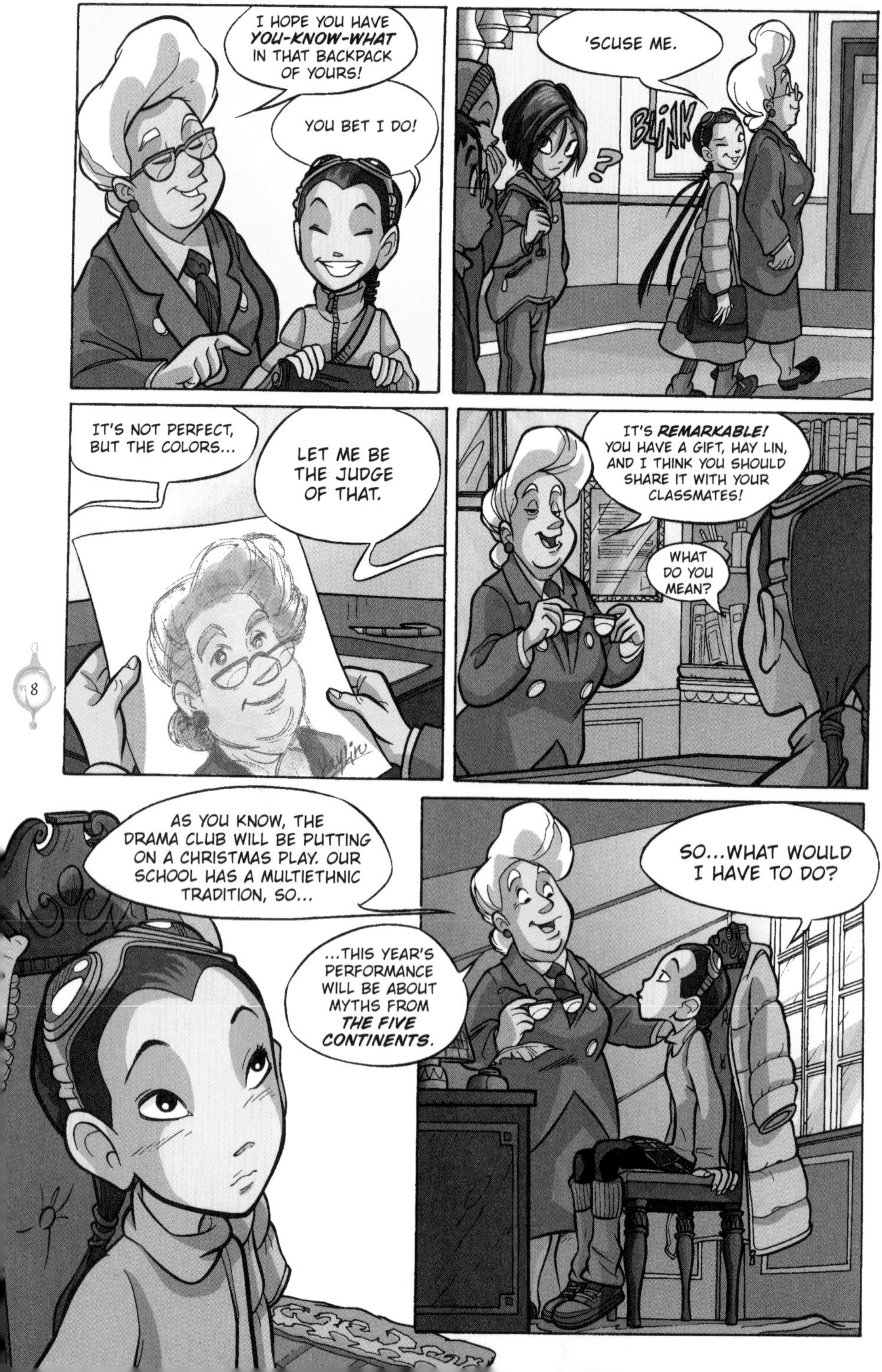
I HOPE YOU HAVE YOU-KNOW-WHAT IN THAT BACKPACK OF YOURS!
YOU BET I DO!
'SCUSE ME.
BLINK
IT'S NOT PERFECT, BUT THE COLORS...
LET ME BE THE JUDGE OF THAT.
IT'S REMARKABLE! YOU HAVE A GIFT, HAY LIN, AND I THINK YOU SHOULD SHARE IT WITH YOUR CLASSMATES!
WHAT DO YOU MEAN?
AS YOU KNOW, THE DRAMA CLUB WILL BE PUTTING ON A CHRISTMAS PLAY. OUR SCHOOL HAS A MULTIETHNIC TRADITION, SO...
...THIS YEAR'S PERFORMANCE WILL BE ABOUT MYTHS FROM THE FIVE CONTINENTS.
SO...WHAT WOULD I HAVE TO DO?

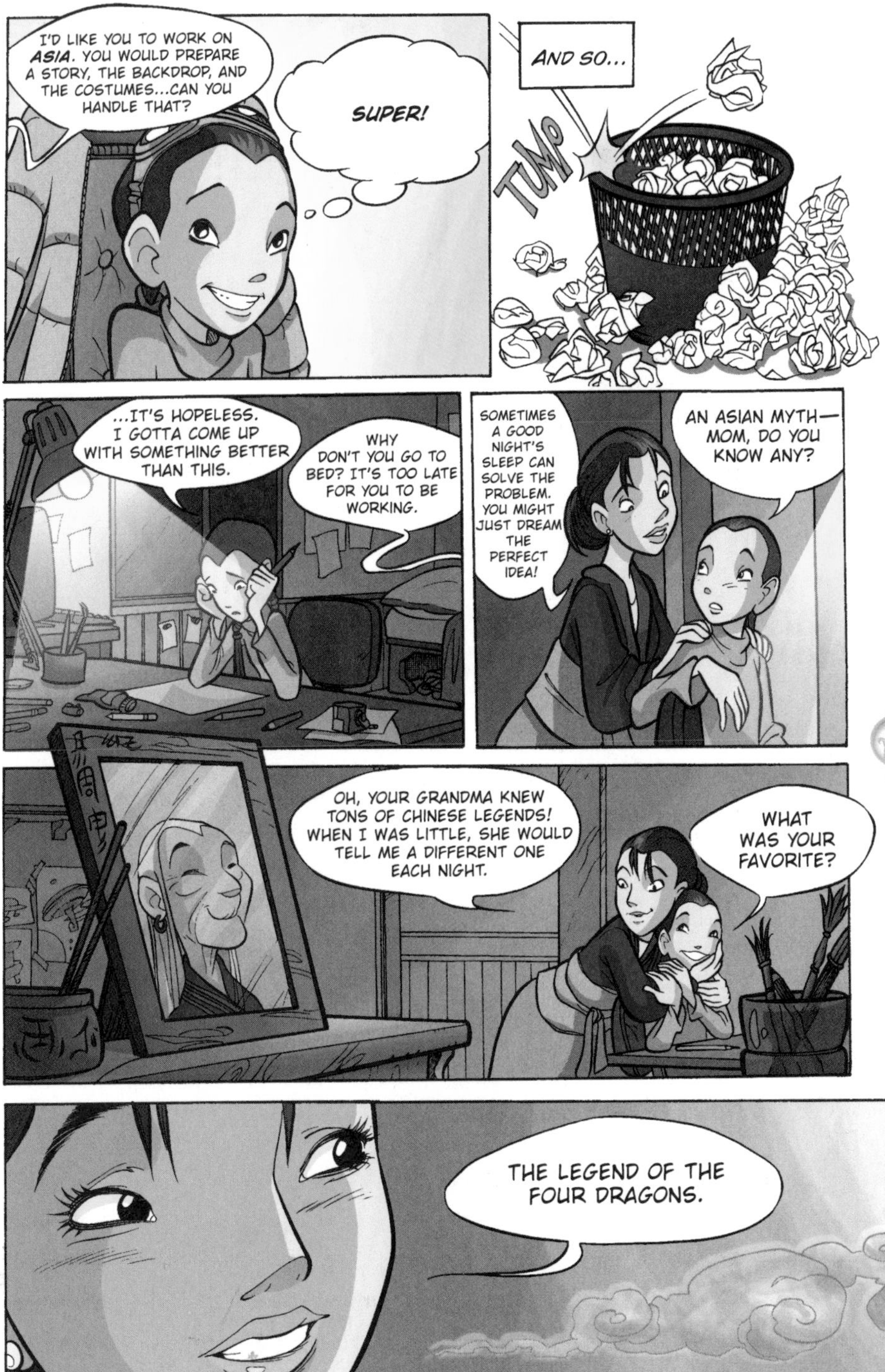
I'D LIKE YOU TO WORK ON ASIA. YOU WOULD PREPARE A STORY, THE BACKDROP, AND THE COSTUMES...CAN YOU HANDLE THAT?
SUPER!
AND SO...
TUMP
...IT'S HOPELESS. I GOTTA COME UP WITH SOMETHING BETTER THAN THIS.
WHY DON'T YOU GO TO BED? IT'S TOO LATE FOR YOU TO BE WORKING.
AN ASIAN MYTH— MOM, DO YOU KNOW ANY?
SOMETIMES A GOOD NIGHT'S SLEEP CAN SOLVE THE PROBLEM. YOU MIGHT JUST DREAM THE PERFECT IDEA!
OH, YOUR GRANDMA KNEW TONS OF CHINESE LEGENDS! WHEN I WAS LITTLE, SHE WOULD TELL ME A DIFFERENT ONE EACH NIGHT.
WHAT WAS YOUR FAVORITE?
THE LEGEND OF THE FOUR DRAGONS.

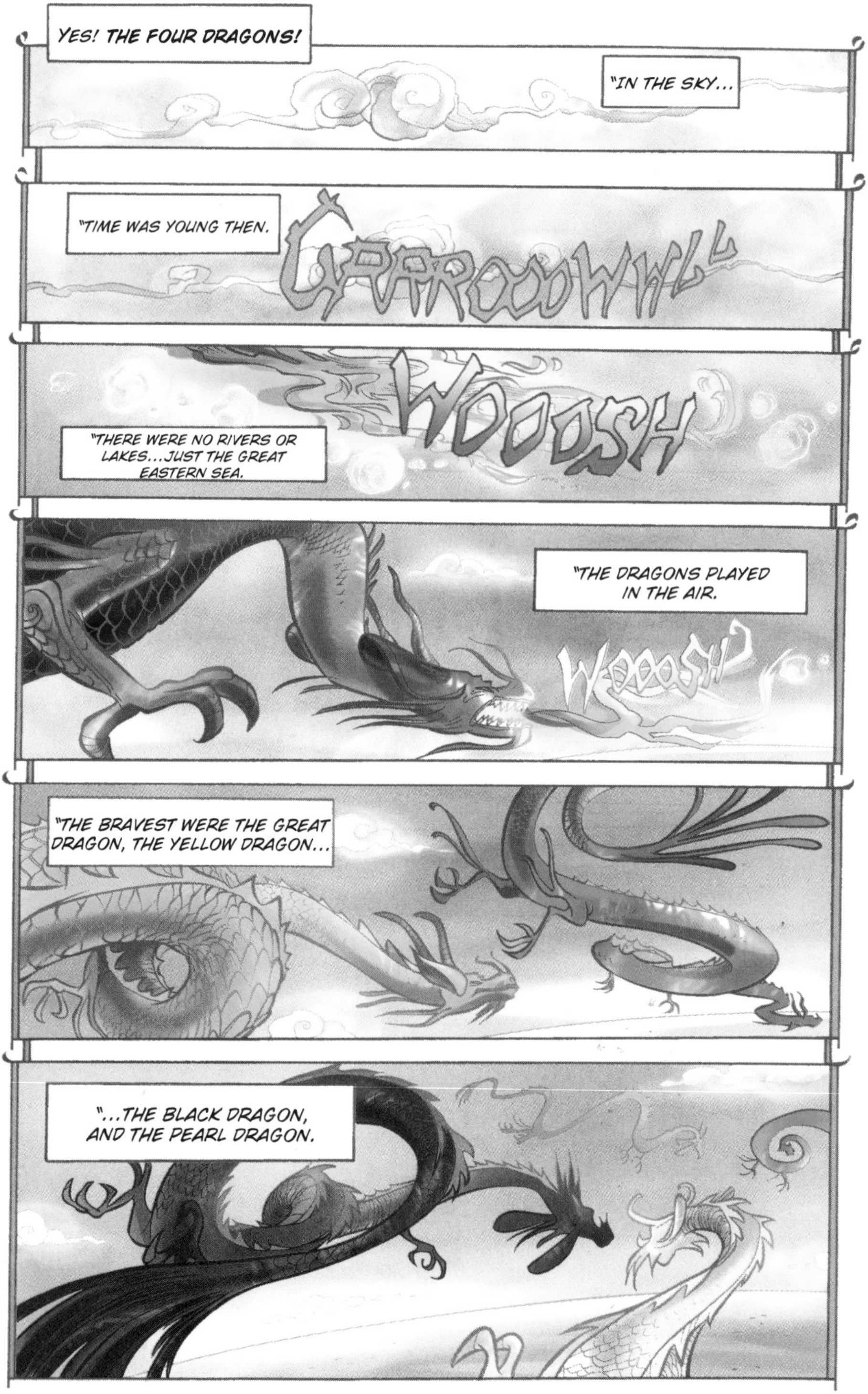
YES! THE FOUR DRAGONS!
"IN THE SKY...
"TIME WAS YOUNG THEN.
GRRROOOWWL
WOOOSH
"THERE WERE NO RIVERS OR LAKES...JUST THE GREAT EASTERN SEA.
"THE DRAGONS PLAYED IN THE AIR.
WOOOSH
"THE BRAVEST WERE THE GREAT DRAGON, THE YELLOW DRAGON...
"...THE BLACK DRAGON, AND THE PEARL DRAGON.

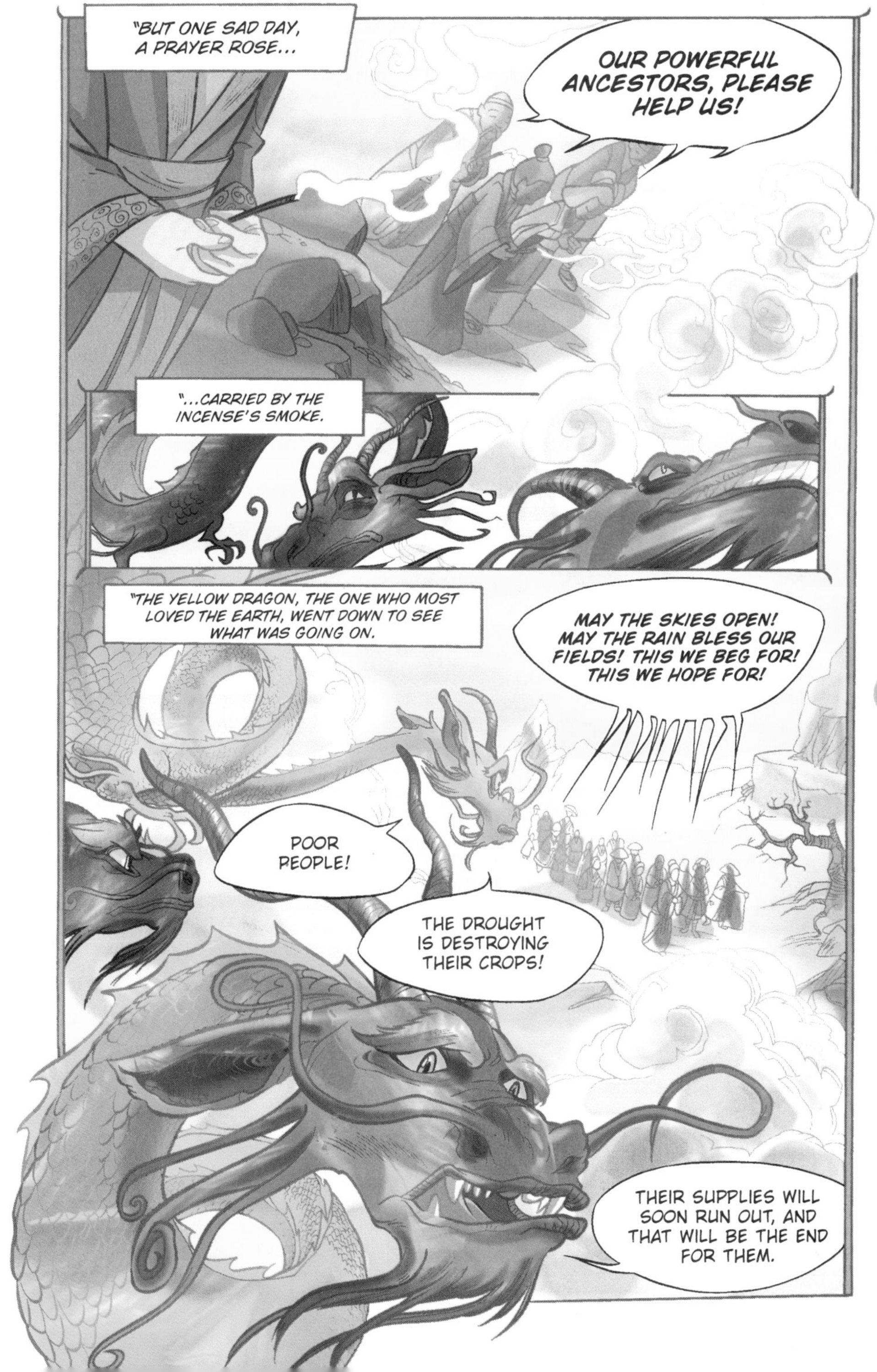

"BUT ONE SAD DAY, A PRAYER ROSE...
OUR POWERFUL ANCESTORS, PLEASE HELP US!
"...CARRIED BY THE INCENSE'S SMOKE.
"THE YELLOW DRAGON, THE ONE WHO MOST LOVED THE EARTH, WENT DOWN TO SEE WHAT WAS GOING ON.
MAY THE SKIES OPEN! MAY THE RAIN BLESS OUR FIELDS! THIS WE BEG FOR! THIS WE HOPE FOR!
POOR PEOPLE!
THE DROUGHT IS DESTROYING THEIR CROPS!
THEIR SUPPLIES WILL SOON RUN OUT, AND THAT WILL BE THE END FOR THEM.

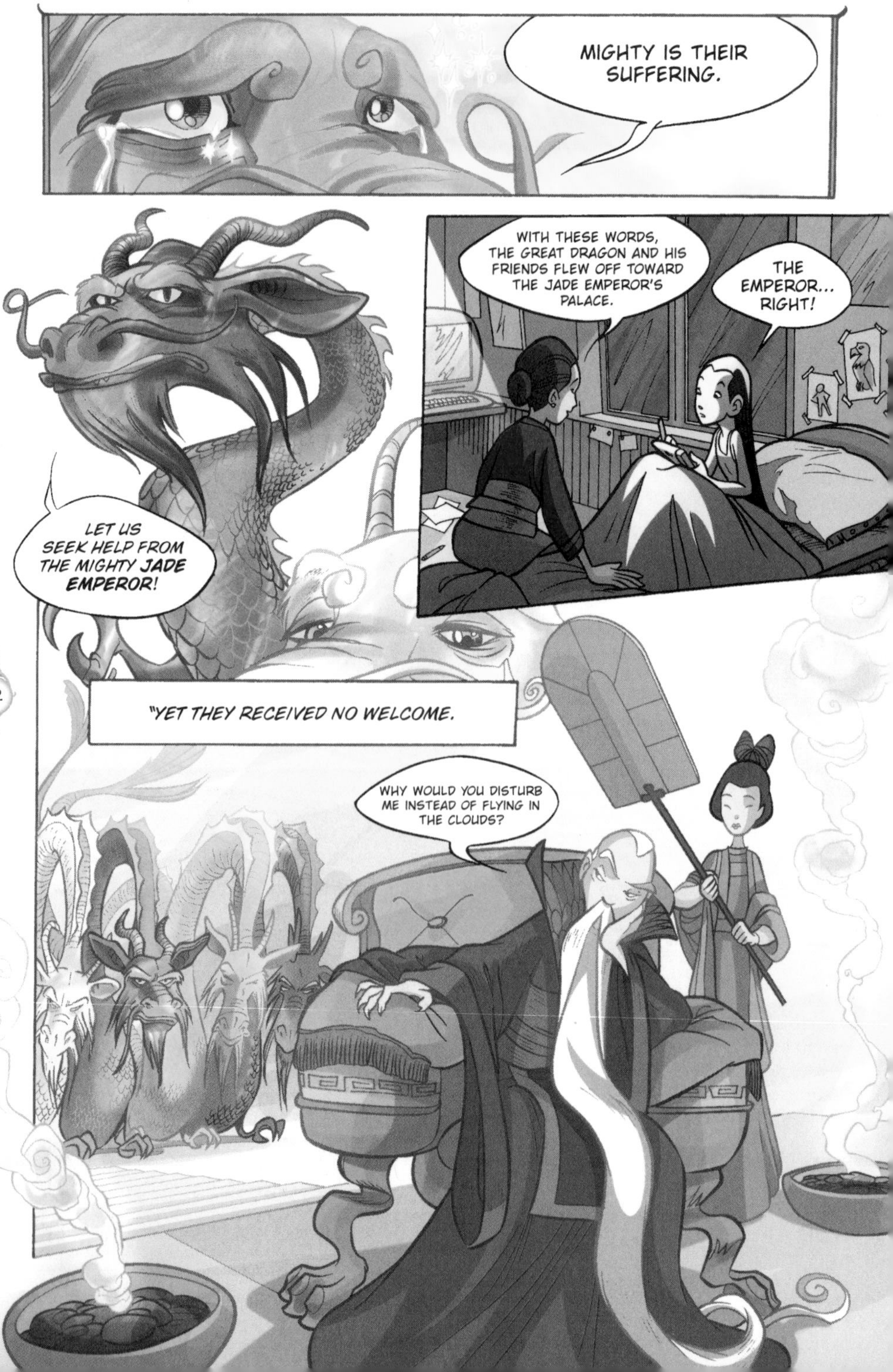
MIGHTY IS THEIR SUFFERING.
LET US SEEK HELP FROM THE MIGHTY JADE EMPEROR!
WITH THESE WORDS, THE GREAT DRAGON AND HIS FRIENDS FLEW OFF TOWARD THE JADE EMPEROR'S PALACE.
THE EMPEROR... RIGHT!
"YET THEY RECEIVED NO WELCOME.
WHY WOULD YOU DISTURB ME INSTEAD OF FLYING IN THE CLOUDS?

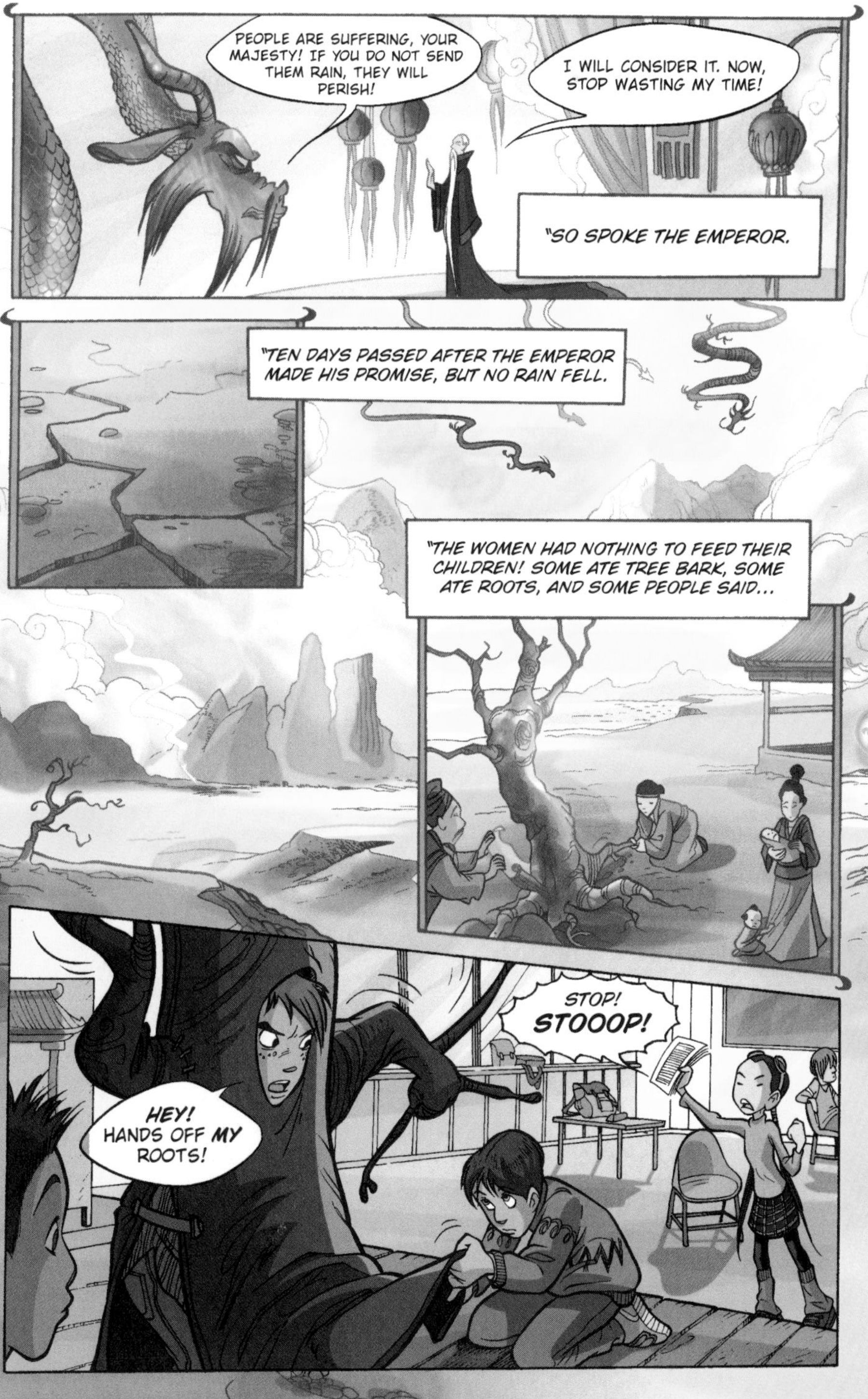

PEOPLE ARE SUFFERING, YOUR MAJESTY! IF YOU DO NOT SEND THEM RAIN, THEY WILL PERISH!
I WILL CONSIDER IT. NOW, STOP WASTING MY TIME!
"SO SPOKE THE EMPEROR.
"TEN DAYS PASSED AFTER THE EMPEROR MADE HIS PROMISE, BUT NO RAIN FELL.
"THE WOMEN HAD NOTHING TO FEED THEIR CHILDREN! SOME ATE TREE BARK, SOME ATE ROOTS, AND SOME PEOPLE SAID...
STOP! STOOOP!
HEY! HANDS OFF MY ROOTS!

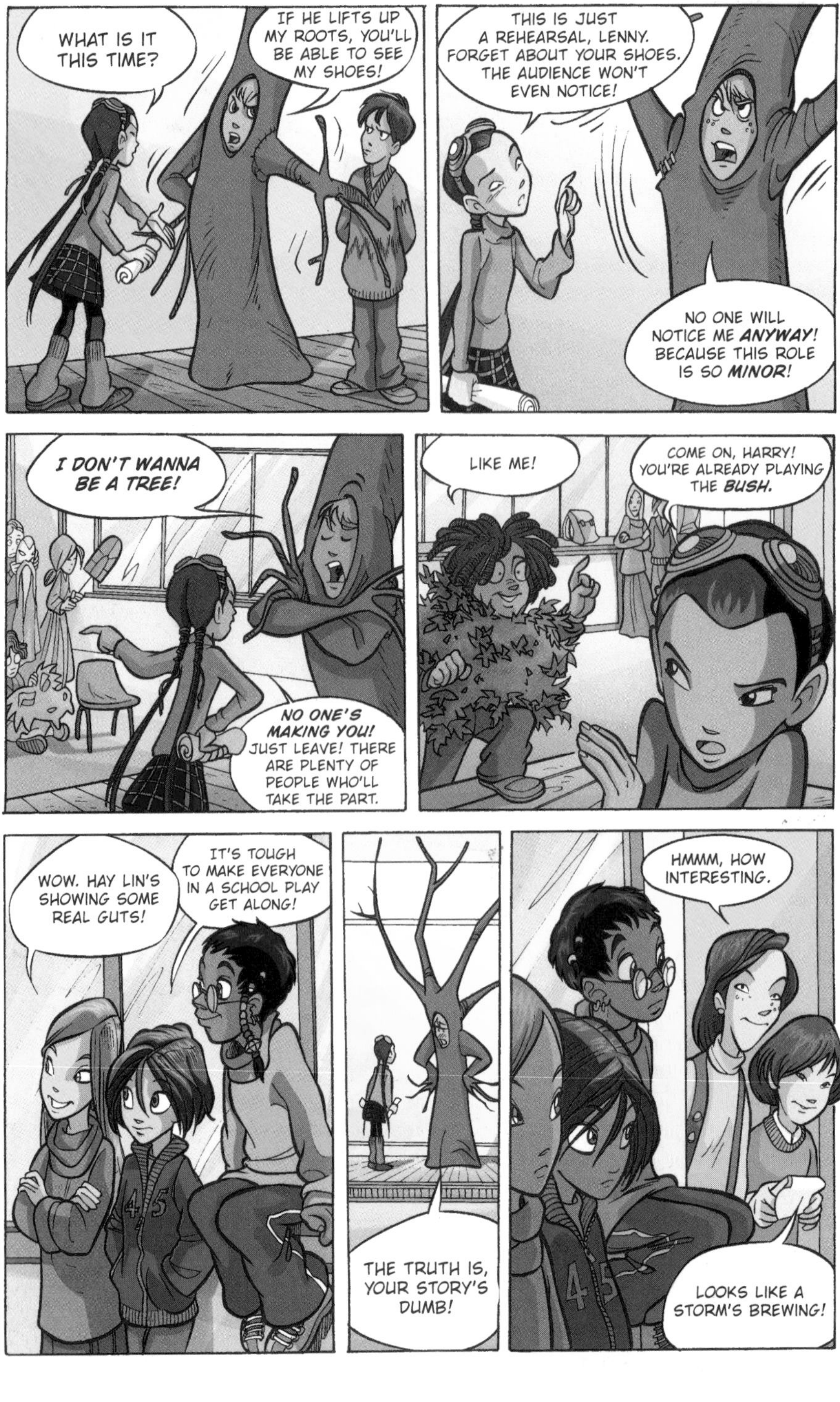
WHAT IS IT THIS TIME?
IF HE LIFTS UP MY ROOTS, YOU'LL BE ABLE TO SEE MY SHOES!
THIS IS JUST A REHEARSAL, LENNY. FORGET ABOUT YOUR SHOES. THE AUDIENCE WON'T EVEN NOTICE!
NO ONE WILL NOTICE ME ANYWAY! BECAUSE THIS ROLE IS SO MINOR!
I DON'T WANNA BE A TREE!
NO ONE'S MAKING YOU! JUST LEAVE! THERE ARE PLENTY OF PEOPLE WHO'LL TAKE THE PART.
LIKE ME!
COME ON, HARRY! YOU'RE ALREADY PLAYING THE BUSH.
WOW. HAY LIN'S SHOWING SOME REAL GUTS!
IT'S TOUGH TO MAKE EVERYONE IN A SCHOOL PLAY GET ALONG!
THE TRUTH IS, YOUR STORY'S DUMB!
HMMM, HOW INTERESTING.
LOOKS LIKE A STORM'S BREWING!

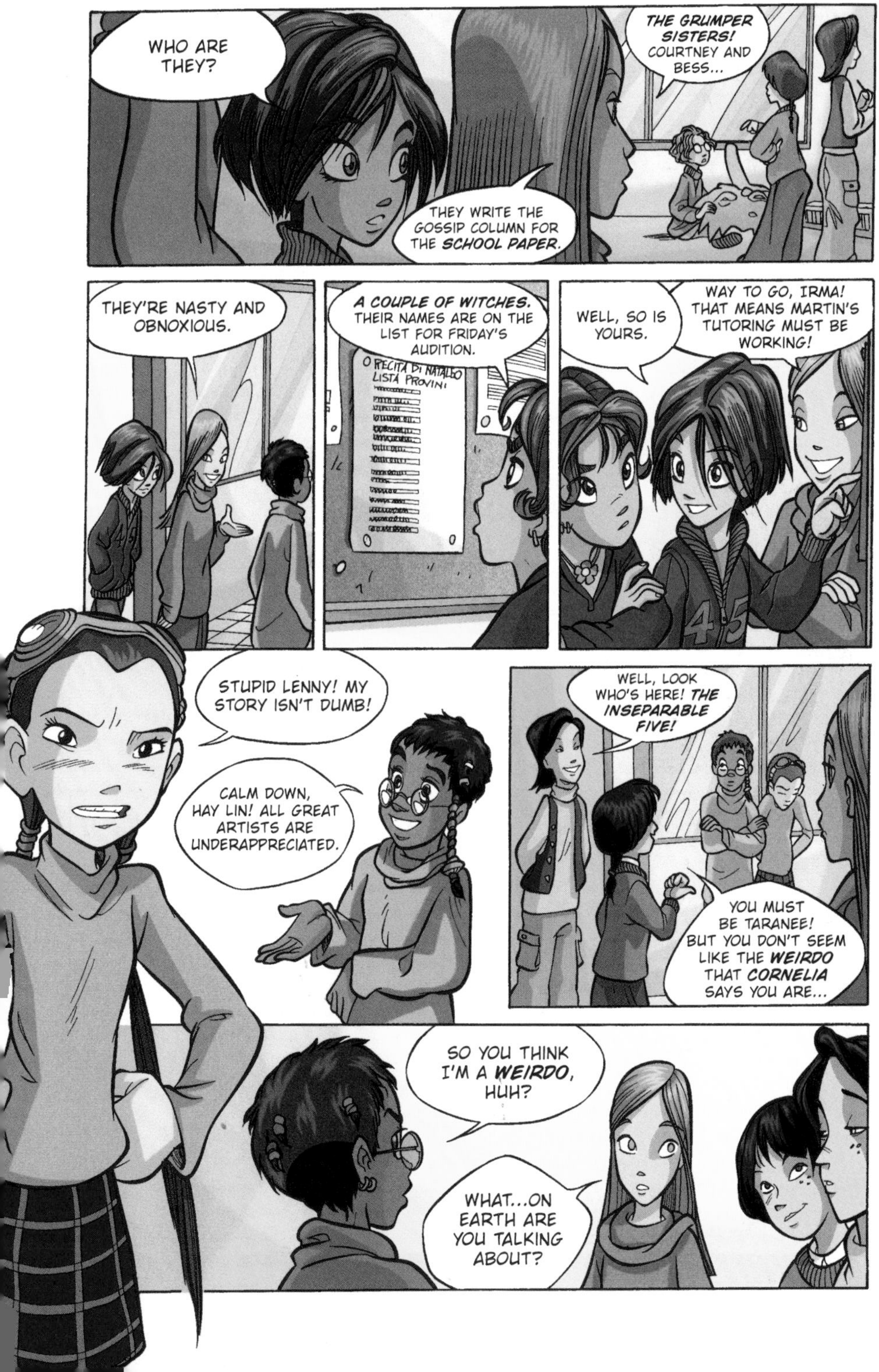
WHO ARE THEY?
THE GRUMPER SISTERS! COURTNEY AND BESS...
THEY WRITE THE GOSSIP COLUMN FOR THE SCHOOL PAPER.
THEY'RE NASTY AND OBNOXIOUS.
A COUPLE OF WITCHES. THEIR NAMES ARE ON THE LIST FOR FRIDAY'S AUDITION.
RECITA DI NATALE
LISTA PROVINI
WELL, SO IS YOURS.
WAY TO GO, IRMA! THAT MEANS MARTIN'S TUTORING MUST BE WORKING!
STUPID LENNY! MY STORY ISN'T DUMB!
CALM DOWN, HAY LIN! ALL GREAT ARTISTS ARE UNDERAPPRECIATED.
WELL, LOOK WHO'S HERE! THE INSEPARABLE FIVE!
YOU MUST BE TARANEE! BUT YOU DON'T SEEM LIKE THE WEIRDO THAT CORNELIA SAYS YOU ARE...
SO YOU THINK I'M A WEIRDO, HUH?
WHAT...ON EARTH ARE YOU TALKING ABOUT?

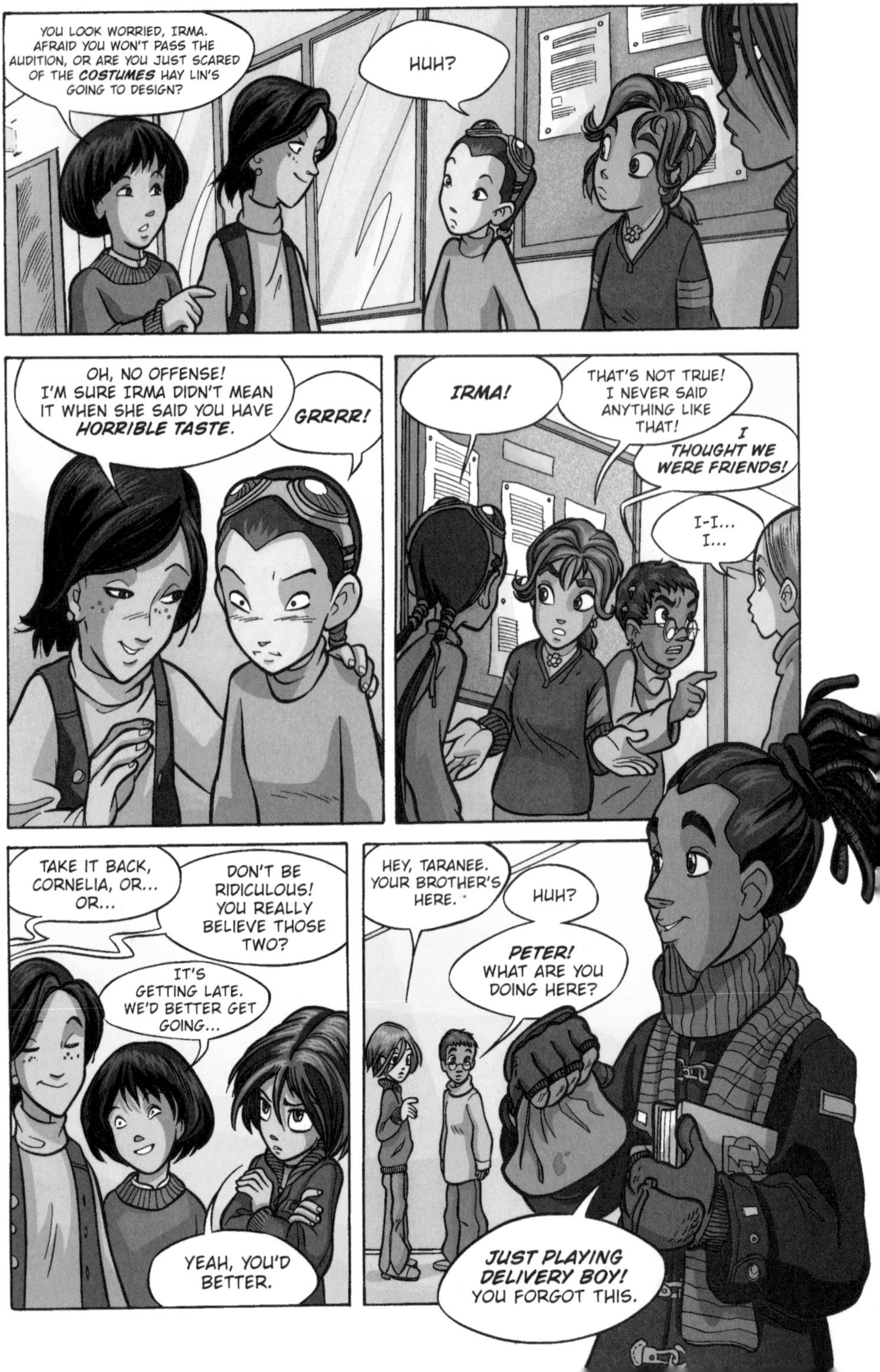
YOU LOOK WORRIED, IRMA. AFRAID YOU WON'T PASS THE AUDITION, OR ARE YOU JUST SCARED OF THE COSTUMES HAY LIN'S GOING TO DESIGN?
HUH?
OH, NO OFFENSE! I'M SURE IRMA DIDN'T MEAN IT WHEN SHE SAID YOU HAVE HORRIBLE TASTE.
GRRRR!
IRMA!
THAT'S NOT TRUE! I NEVER SAID ANYTHING LIKE THAT!
I THOUGHT WE WERE FRIENDS!
I-I... I...
TAKE IT BACK, CORNELIA, OR... OR...
DON'T BE RIDICULOUS! YOU REALLY BELIEVE THOSE TWO?
IT'S GETTING LATE. WE'D BETTER GET GOING...
YEAH, YOU'D BETTER.
HEY, TARANEE. YOUR BROTHER'S HERE.
HUH?
PETER! WHAT ARE YOU DOING HERE?
JUST PLAYING DELIVERY BOY! YOU FORGOT THIS.

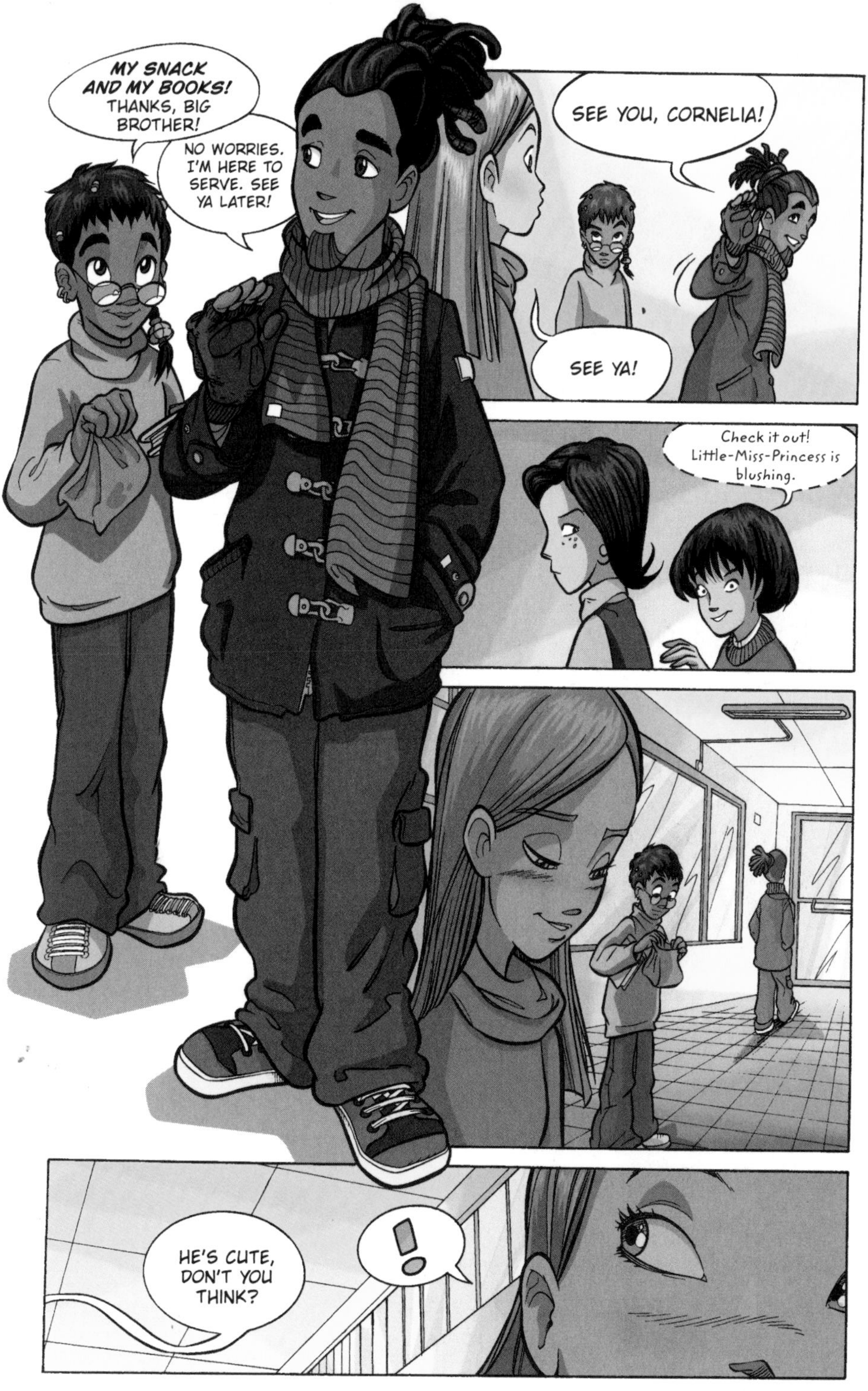

MY SNACK AND MY BOOKS! THANKS, BIG BROTHER!
NO WORRIES. I'M HERE TO SERVE. SEE YA LATER!
SEE YOU, CORNELIA!
SEE YA!
Check it out! Little-Miss-Princess is blushing.
HE'S CUTE, DON'T YOU THINK?
!

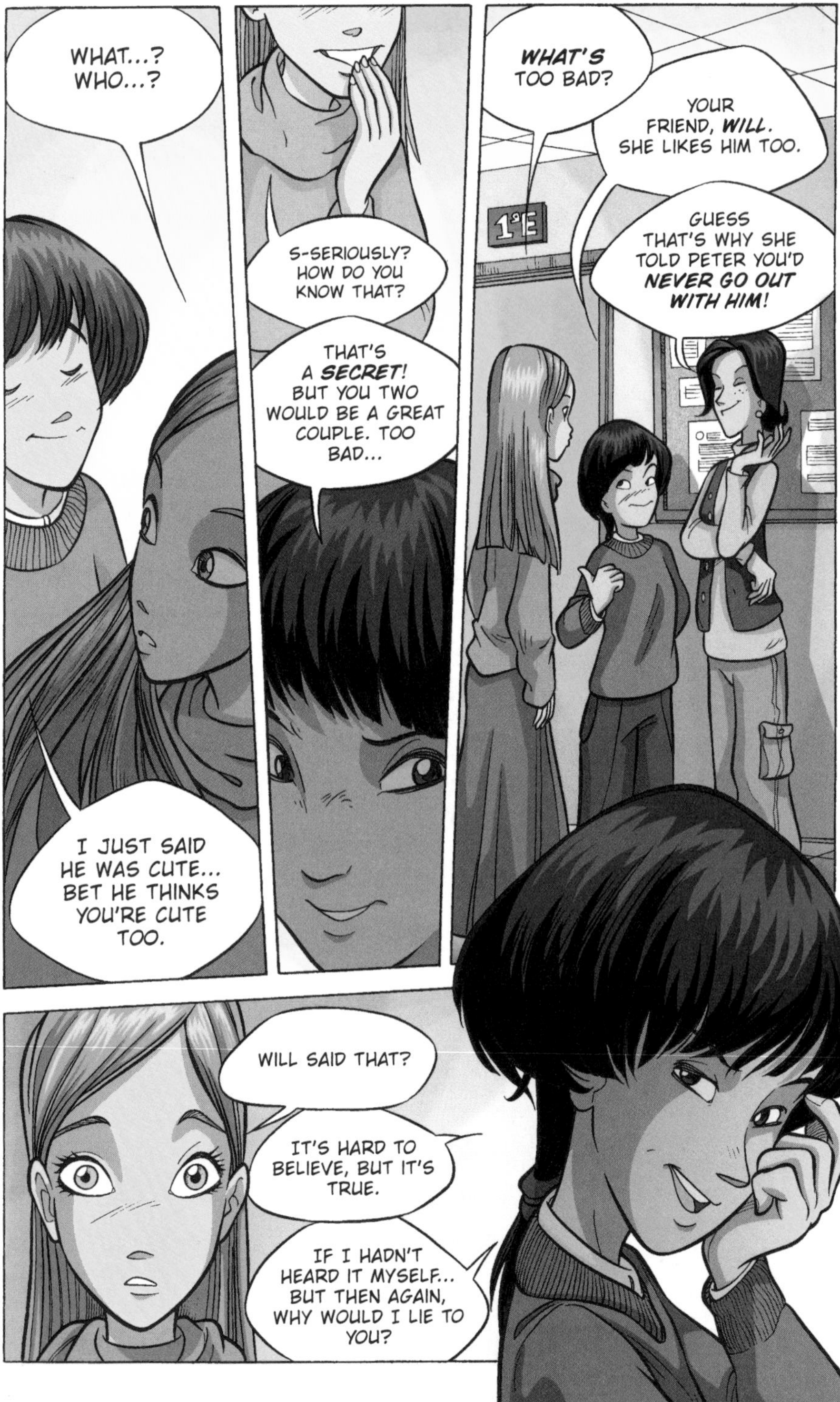
WHAT...? WHO...?
I JUST SAID HE WAS CUTE... BET HE THINKS YOU'RE CUTE TOO.
S-SERIOUSLY? HOW DO YOU KNOW THAT?
THAT'S A **SECRET**! BUT YOU TWO WOULD BE A GREAT COUPLE. TOO BAD...
WHAT'S TOO BAD?
YOUR FRIEND, **WILL**. SHE LIKES HIM TOO.
GUESS THAT'S WHY SHE TOLD PETER YOU'D **NEVER GO OUT WITH HIM**!
1°E
WILL SAID THAT?
IT'S HARD TO BELIEVE, BUT IT'S TRUE.
IF I HADN'T HEARD IT MYSELF... BUT THEN AGAIN, WHY WOULD I LIE TO YOU?

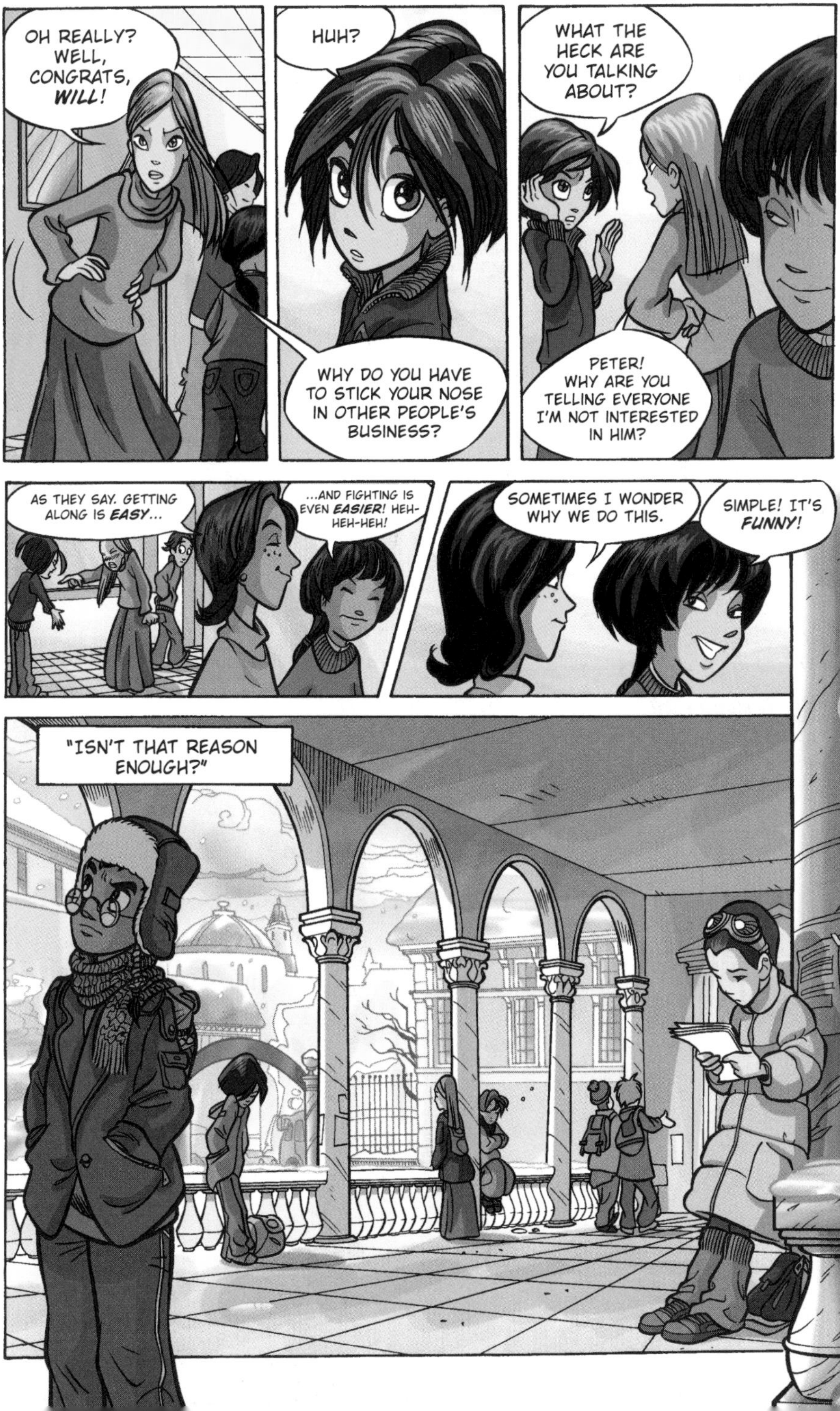
OH REALLY? WELL, CONGRATS, WILL!
WHY DO YOU HAVE TO STICK YOUR NOSE IN OTHER PEOPLE'S BUSINESS?
HUH?
WHAT THE HECK ARE YOU TALKING ABOUT?
PETER! WHY ARE YOU TELLING EVERYONE I'M NOT INTERESTED IN HIM?
AS THEY SAY. GETTING ALONG IS EASY...
...AND FIGHTING IS EVEN EASIER! HEH-HEH-HEH!
SOMETIMES I WONDER WHY WE DO THIS.
SIMPLE! IT'S FUNNY!
"ISN'T THAT REASON ENOUGH?"

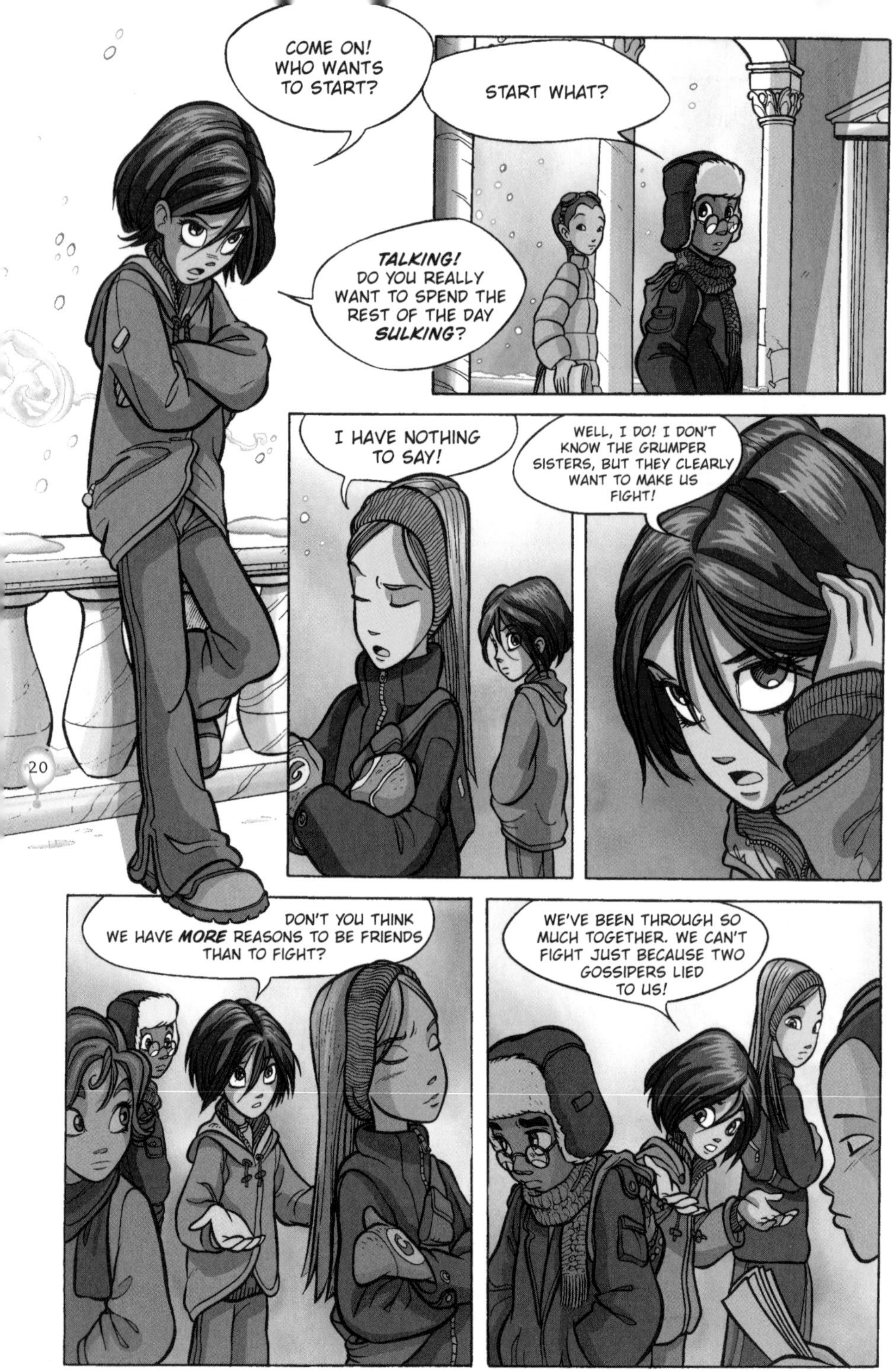
COME ON! WHO WANTS TO START?
START WHAT?
TALKING! DO YOU REALLY WANT TO SPEND THE REST OF THE DAY *SULKING*?
I HAVE NOTHING TO SAY!
WELL, I DO! I DON'T KNOW THE GRUMPER SISTERS, BUT THEY CLEARLY WANT TO MAKE US FIGHT!
DON'T YOU THINK WE HAVE *MORE* REASONS TO BE FRIENDS THAN TO FIGHT?
WE'VE BEEN THROUGH SO MUCH TOGETHER. WE CAN'T FIGHT JUST BECAUSE TWO GOSSIPERS LIED TO US!

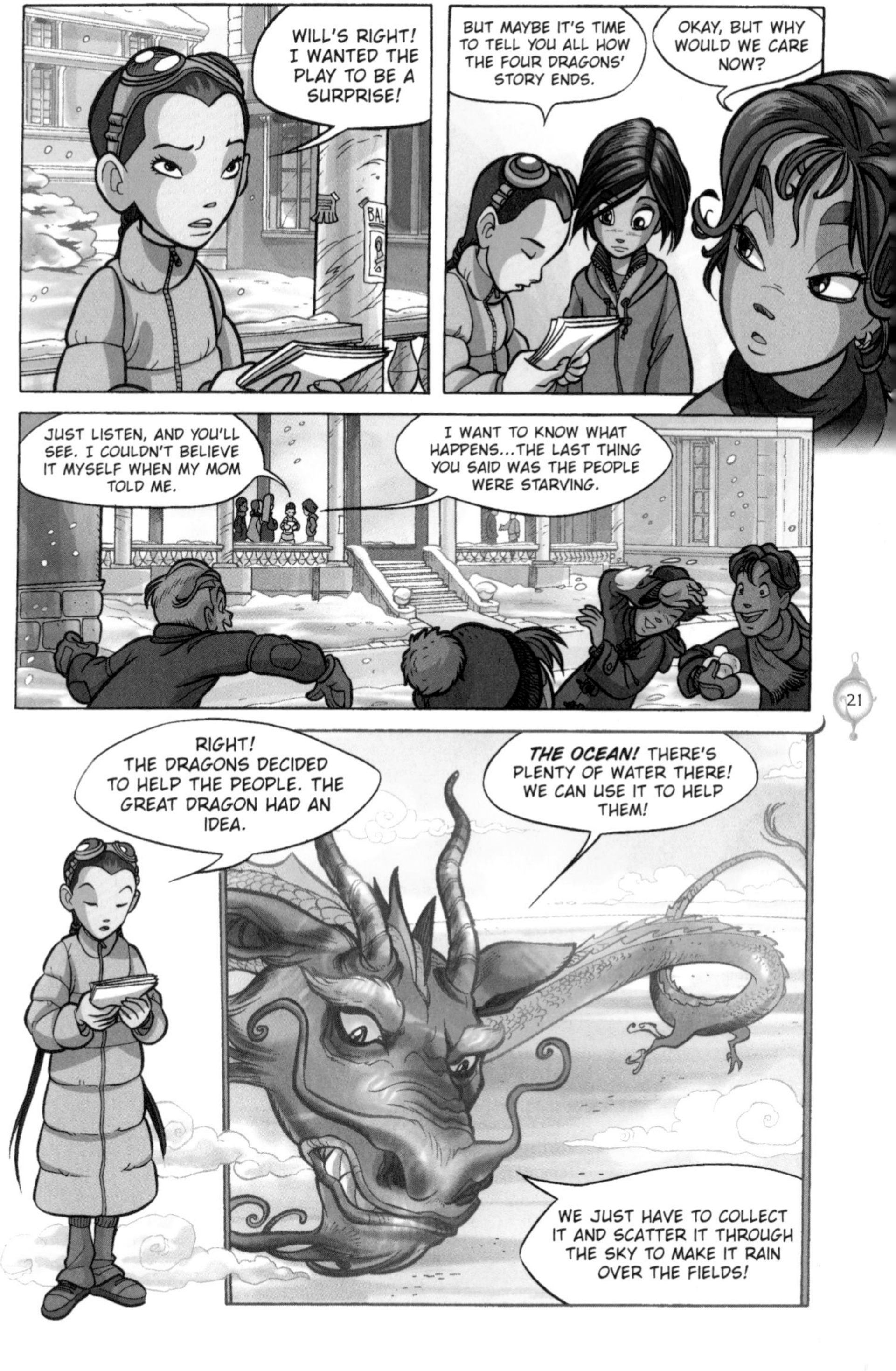
WILL'S RIGHT! I WANTED THE PLAY TO BE A SURPRISE!
BAL
BUT MAYBE IT'S TIME TO TELL YOU ALL HOW THE FOUR DRAGONS' STORY ENDS.
OKAY, BUT WHY WOULD WE CARE NOW?
JUST LISTEN, AND YOU'LL SEE. I COULDN'T BELIEVE IT MYSELF WHEN MY MOM TOLD ME.
I WANT TO KNOW WHAT HAPPENS...THE LAST THING YOU SAID WAS THE PEOPLE WERE STARVING.
RIGHT! THE DRAGONS DECIDED TO HELP THE PEOPLE. THE GREAT DRAGON HAD AN IDEA.
THE OCEAN! THERE'S PLENTY OF WATER THERE! WE CAN USE IT TO HELP THEM!
WE JUST HAVE TO COLLECT IT AND SCATTER IT THROUGH THE SKY TO MAKE IT RAIN OVER THE FIELDS!

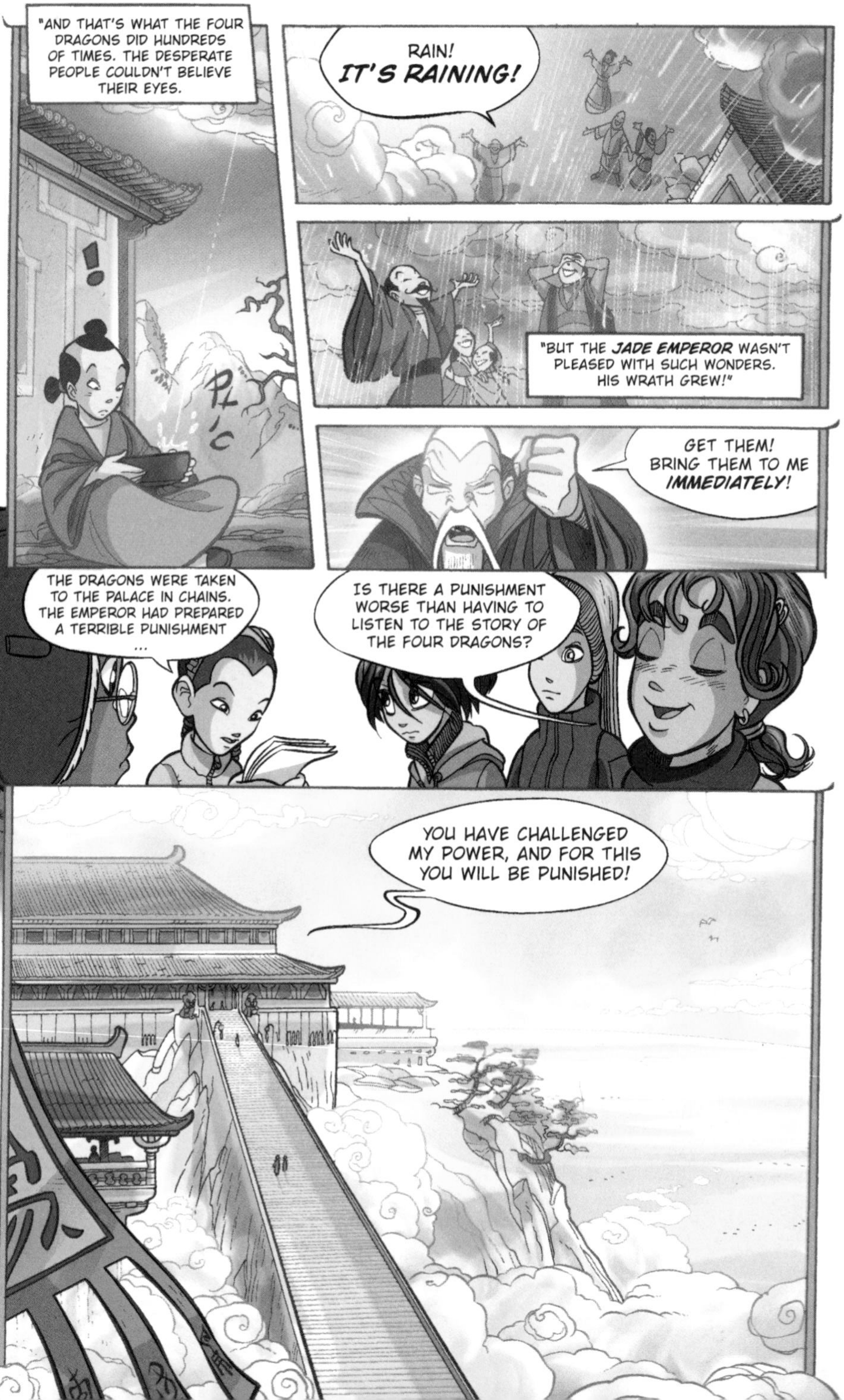
"AND THAT'S WHAT THE FOUR DRAGONS DID HUNDREDS OF TIMES. THE DESPERATE PEOPLE COULDN'T BELIEVE THEIR EYES.
RAIN! IT'S RAINING!
!
PLIC
"BUT THE JADE EMPEROR WASN'T PLEASED WITH SUCH WONDERS. HIS WRATH GREW!"
GET THEM! BRING THEM TO ME IMMEDIATELY!
THE DRAGONS WERE TAKEN TO THE PALACE IN CHAINS. THE EMPEROR HAD PREPARED A TERRIBLE PUNISHMENT ...
IS THERE A PUNISHMENT WORSE THAN HAVING TO LISTEN TO THE STORY OF THE FOUR DRAGONS?
YOU HAVE CHALLENGED MY POWER, AND FOR THIS YOU WILL BE PUNISHED!

I ORDER *THE KING OF THE PEAKS*...

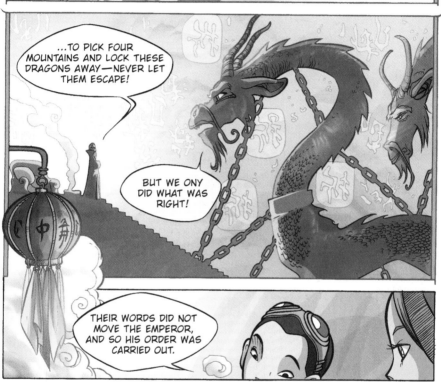

...TO PICK FOUR MOUNTAINS AND LOCK THESE DRAGONS AWAY—NEVER LET THEM ESCAPE!

BUT WE ONY DID WHAT WAS RIGHT!

THEIR WORDS DID NOT MOVE THE EMPEROR, AND SO HIS ORDER WAS CARRIED OUT.

AS YOU WISHED, YOUR MAJESTY!

THIS IS WHAT HAPPENS TO THOSE WHO ANGER ME!

NOW THEY WILL NEVER BE ABLE TO *DO GOOD* EVER AGAIN!

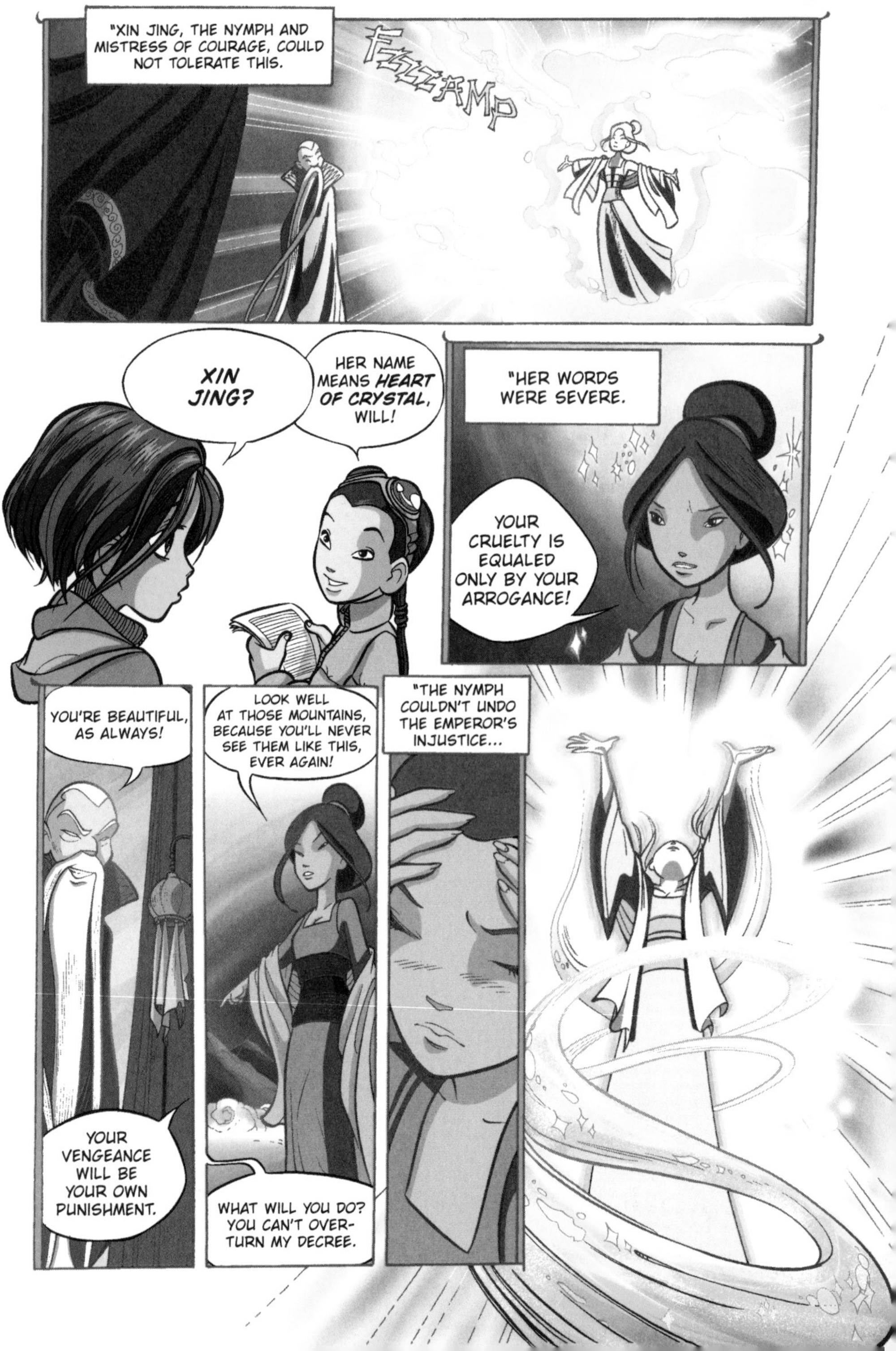
"XIN JING, THE NYMPH AND MISTRESS OF COURAGE, COULD NOT TOLERATE THIS.
FSSSAMP
XIN JING?
HER NAME MEANS HEART OF CRYSTAL, WILL!
"HER WORDS WERE SEVERE.
YOUR CRUELTY IS EQUALED ONLY BY YOUR ARROGANCE!
YOU'RE BEAUTIFUL, AS ALWAYS!
YOUR VENGEANCE WILL BE YOUR OWN PUNISHMENT.
LOOK WELL AT THOSE MOUNTAINS, BECAUSE YOU'LL NEVER SEE THEM LIKE THIS, EVER AGAIN!
WHAT WILL YOU DO? YOU CAN'T OVER-TURN MY DECREE.
"THE NYMPH COULDN'T UNDO THE EMPEROR'S INJUSTICE...

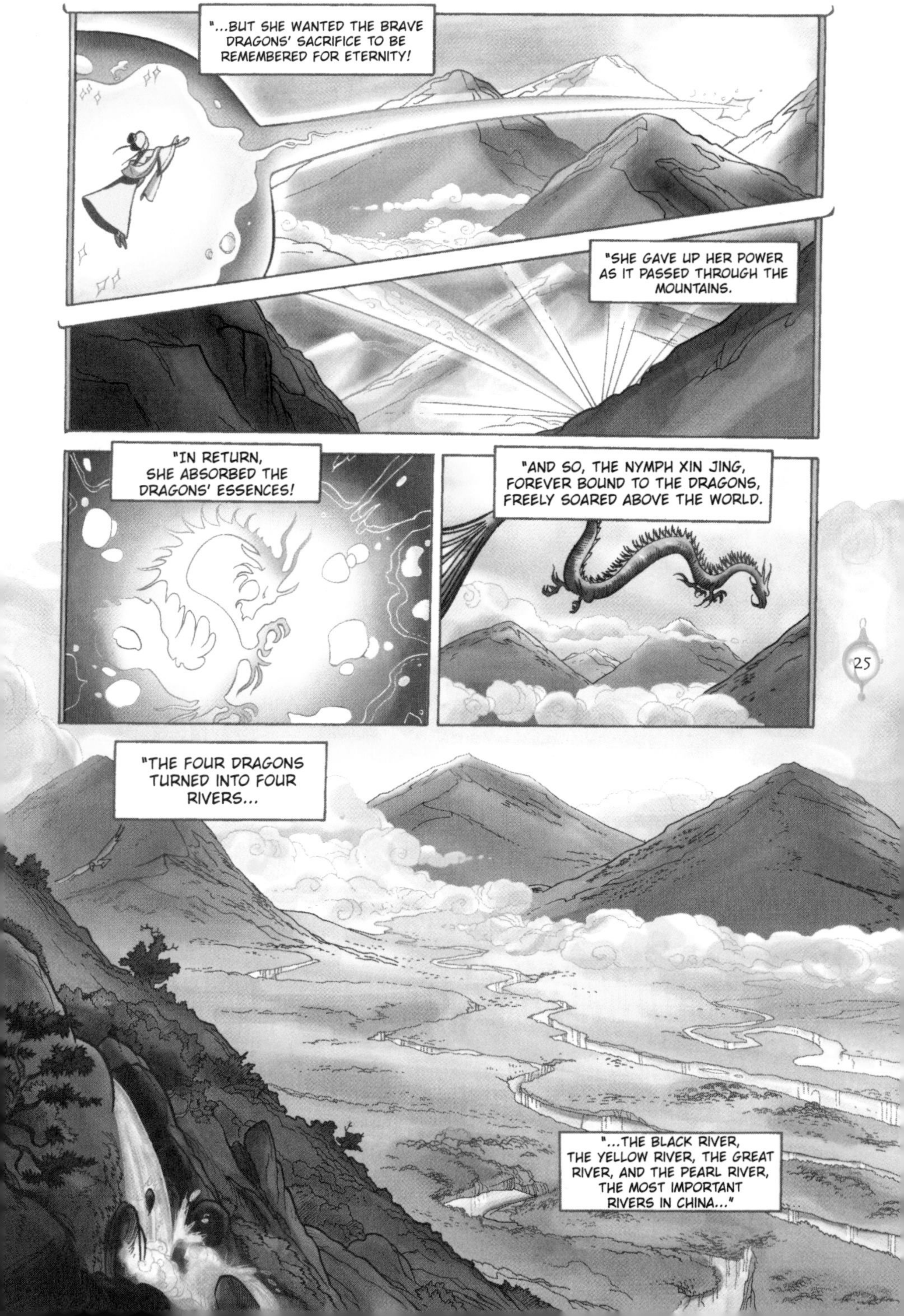
"...BUT SHE WANTED THE BRAVE DRAGONS' SACRIFICE TO BE REMEMBERED FOR ETERNITY!
"SHE GAVE UP HER POWER AS IT PASSED THROUGH THE MOUNTAINS.
"IN RETURN, SHE ABSORBED THE DRAGONS' ESSENCES!
"AND SO, THE NYMPH XIN JING, FOREVER BOUND TO THE DRAGONS, FREELY SOARED ABOVE THE WORLD.
"THE FOUR DRAGONS TURNED INTO FOUR RIVERS...
"...THE BLACK RIVER, THE YELLOW RIVER, THE GREAT RIVER, AND THE PEARL RIVER, THE MOST IMPORTANT RIVERS IN CHINA..."

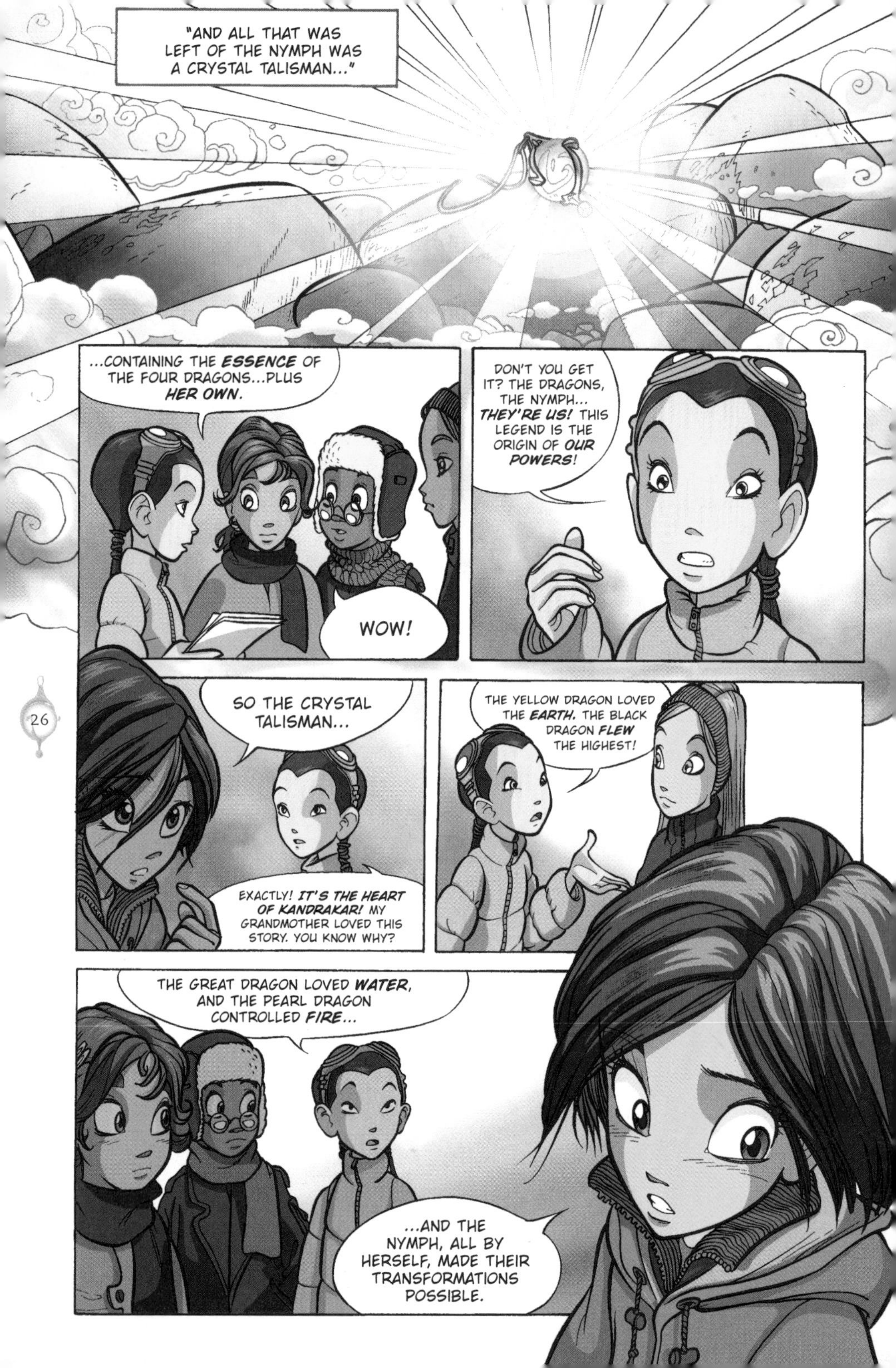
"AND ALL THAT WAS LEFT OF THE NYMPH WAS A CRYSTAL TALISMAN..."
...CONTAINING THE ESSENCE OF THE FOUR DRAGONS...PLUS HER OWN.
WOW!
DON'T YOU GET IT? THE DRAGONS, THE NYMPH... THEY'RE US! THIS LEGEND IS THE ORIGIN OF OUR POWERS!
SO THE CRYSTAL TALISMAN...
EXACTLY! IT'S THE HEART OF KANDRAKAR! MY GRANDMOTHER LOVED THIS STORY. YOU KNOW WHY?
THE YELLOW DRAGON LOVED THE EARTH. THE BLACK DRAGON FLEW THE HIGHEST!
THE GREAT DRAGON LOVED WATER, AND THE PEARL DRAGON CONTROLLED FIRE...
...AND THE NYMPH, ALL BY HERSELF, MADE THEIR TRANSFORMATIONS POSSIBLE.

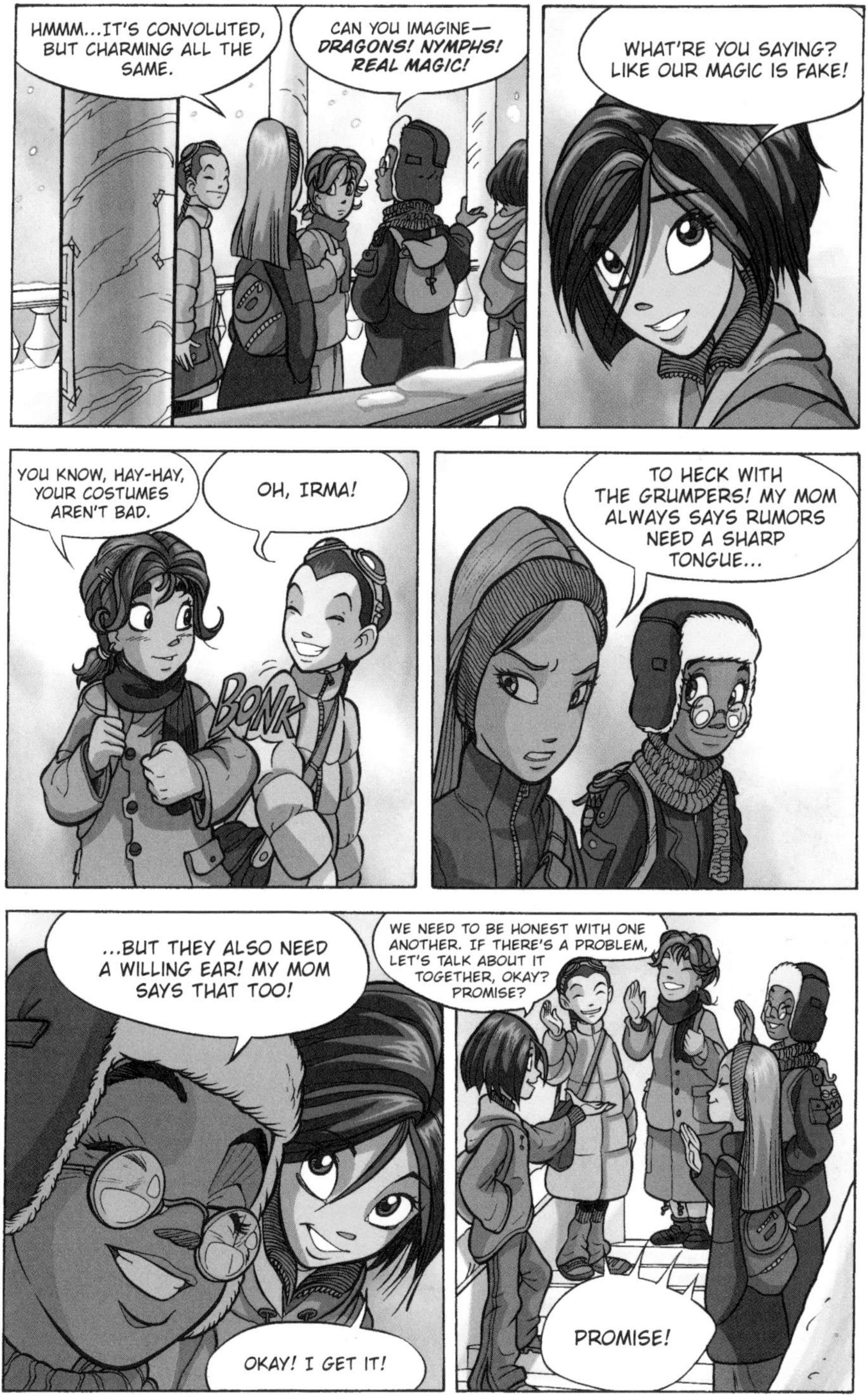
HMMM...IT'S CONVOLUTED, BUT CHARMING ALL THE SAME.
CAN YOU IMAGINE—DRAGONS! NYMPHS! REAL MAGIC!
WHAT'RE YOU SAYING? LIKE OUR MAGIC IS FAKE!
YOU KNOW, HAY-HAY, YOUR COSTUMES AREN'T BAD.
OH, IRMA!
BONK
TO HECK WITH THE GRUMPERS! MY MOM ALWAYS SAYS RUMORS NEED A SHARP TONGUE...
...BUT THEY ALSO NEED A WILLING EAR! MY MOM SAYS THAT TOO!
OKAY! I GET IT!
WE NEED TO BE HONEST WITH ONE ANOTHER. IF THERE'S A PROBLEM, LET'S TALK ABOUT IT TOGETHER, OKAY? PROMISE?
PROMISE!

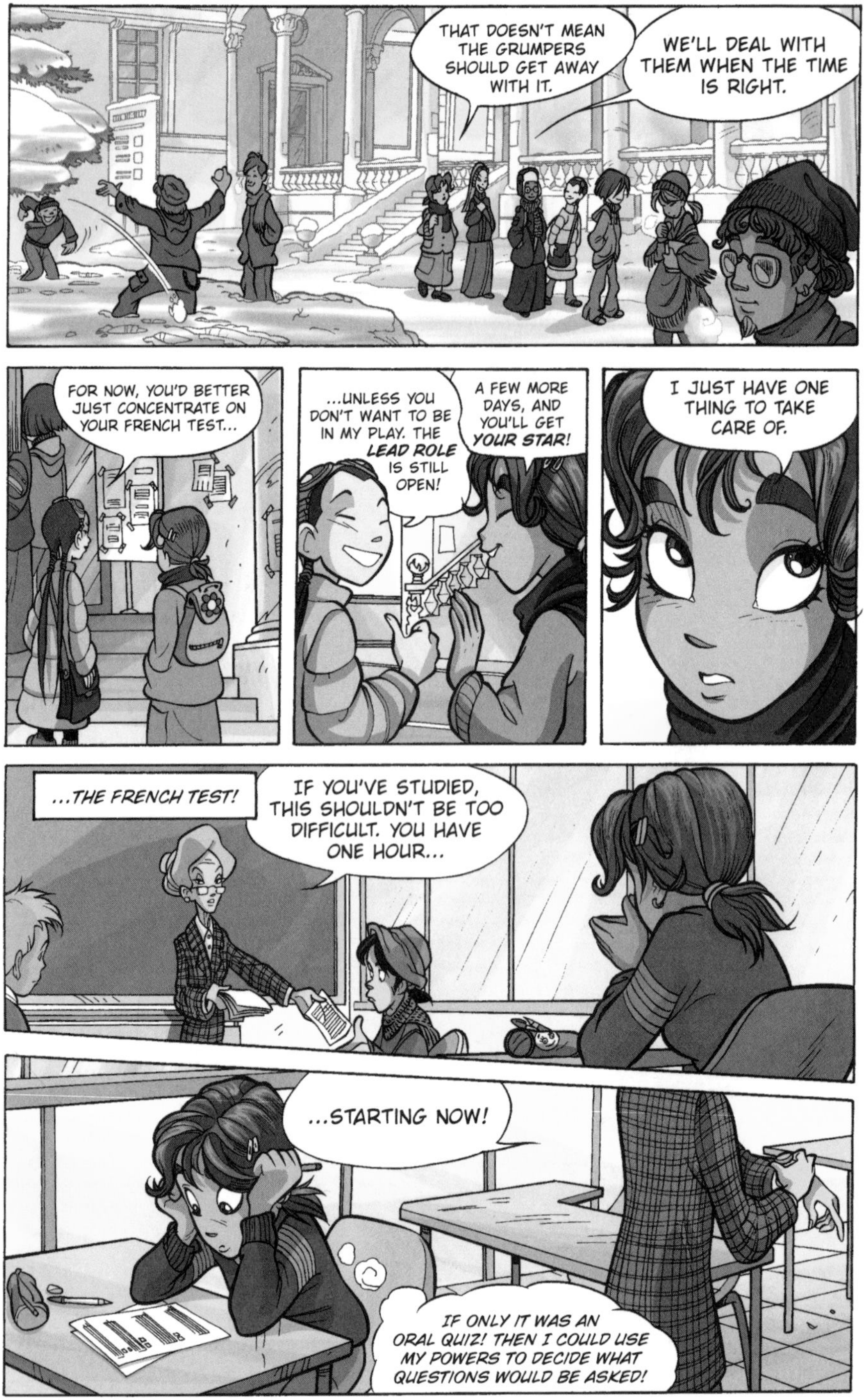
THAT DOESN'T MEAN THE GRUMPERS SHOULD GET AWAY WITH IT.
WE'LL DEAL WITH THEM WHEN THE TIME IS RIGHT.
FOR NOW, YOU'D BETTER JUST CONCENTRATE ON YOUR FRENCH TEST...
...UNLESS YOU DON'T WANT TO BE IN MY PLAY. THE LEAD ROLE IS STILL OPEN!
A FEW MORE DAYS, AND YOU'LL GET YOUR STAR!
I JUST HAVE ONE THING TO TAKE CARE OF.
...THE FRENCH TEST!
IF YOU'VE STUDIED, THIS SHOULDN'T BE TOO DIFFICULT. YOU HAVE ONE HOUR...
...STARTING NOW!
IF ONLY IT WAS AN ORAL QUIZ! THEN I COULD USE MY POWERS TO DECIDE WHAT QUESTIONS WOULD BE ASKED!

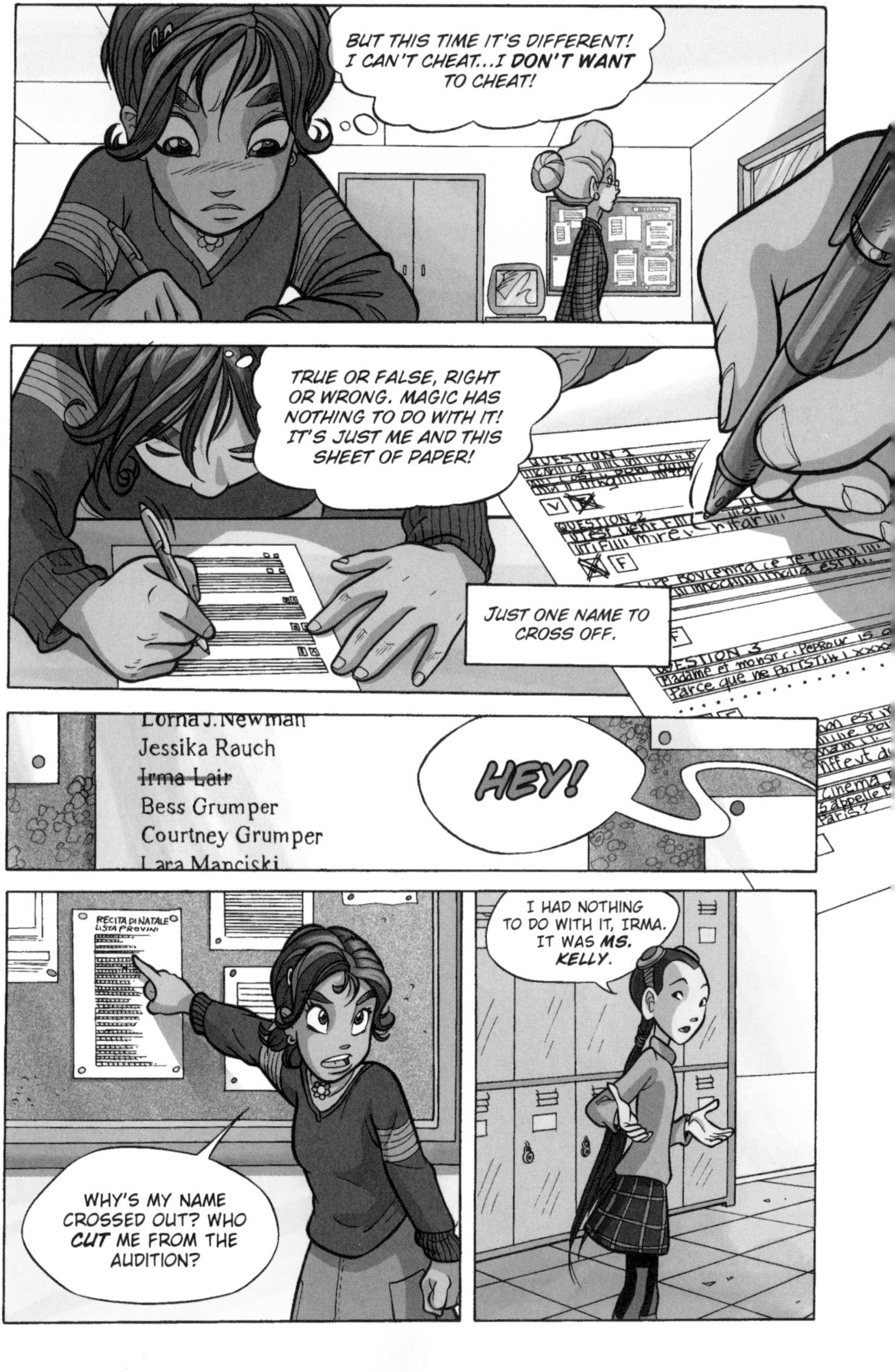

BUT THIS TIME IT'S DIFFERENT! I CAN'T CHEAT...I **DON'T WANT** TO CHEAT!
TRUE OR FALSE, RIGHT OR WRONG. MAGIC HAS NOTHING TO DO WITH IT! IT'S JUST ME AND THIS SHEET OF PAPER!
QUESTION 1
QUESTION 2
QUESTION 3
JUST ONE NAME TO CROSS OFF.
Jessika Rauch
~~Irma Lair~~
Bess Grumper
Courtney Grumper
HEY!
RECITA DI NATALE
LISTA PROVINI
WHY'S MY NAME CROSSED OUT? WHO ***CUT*** ME FROM THE AUDITION?
I HAD NOTHING TO DO WITH IT, IRMA. IT WAS **MS. KELLY**.

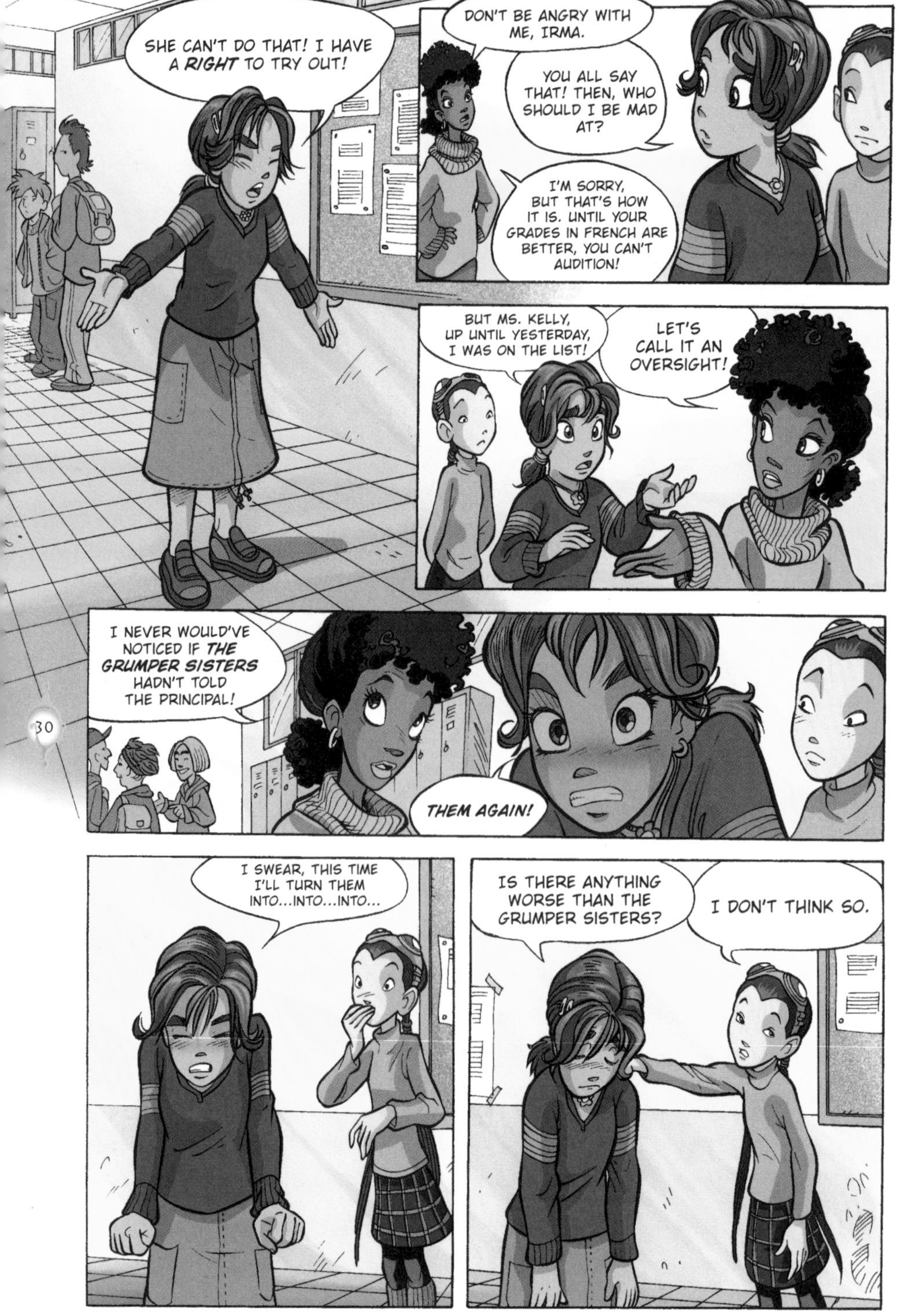
SHE CAN'T DO THAT! I HAVE A RIGHT TO TRY OUT!
DON'T BE ANGRY WITH ME, IRMA.
YOU ALL SAY THAT! THEN, WHO SHOULD I BE MAD AT?
I'M SORRY, BUT THAT'S HOW IT IS. UNTIL YOUR GRADES IN FRENCH ARE BETTER, YOU CAN'T AUDITION!
BUT MS. KELLY, UP UNTIL YESTERDAY, I WAS ON THE LIST!
LET'S CALL IT AN OVERSIGHT!
I NEVER WOULD'VE NOTICED IF THE GRUMPER SISTERS HADN'T TOLD THE PRINCIPAL!
THEM AGAIN!
I SWEAR, THIS TIME I'LL TURN THEM INTO...INTO...INTO...
IS THERE ANYTHING WORSE THAN THE GRUMPER SISTERS?
I DON'T THINK SO.

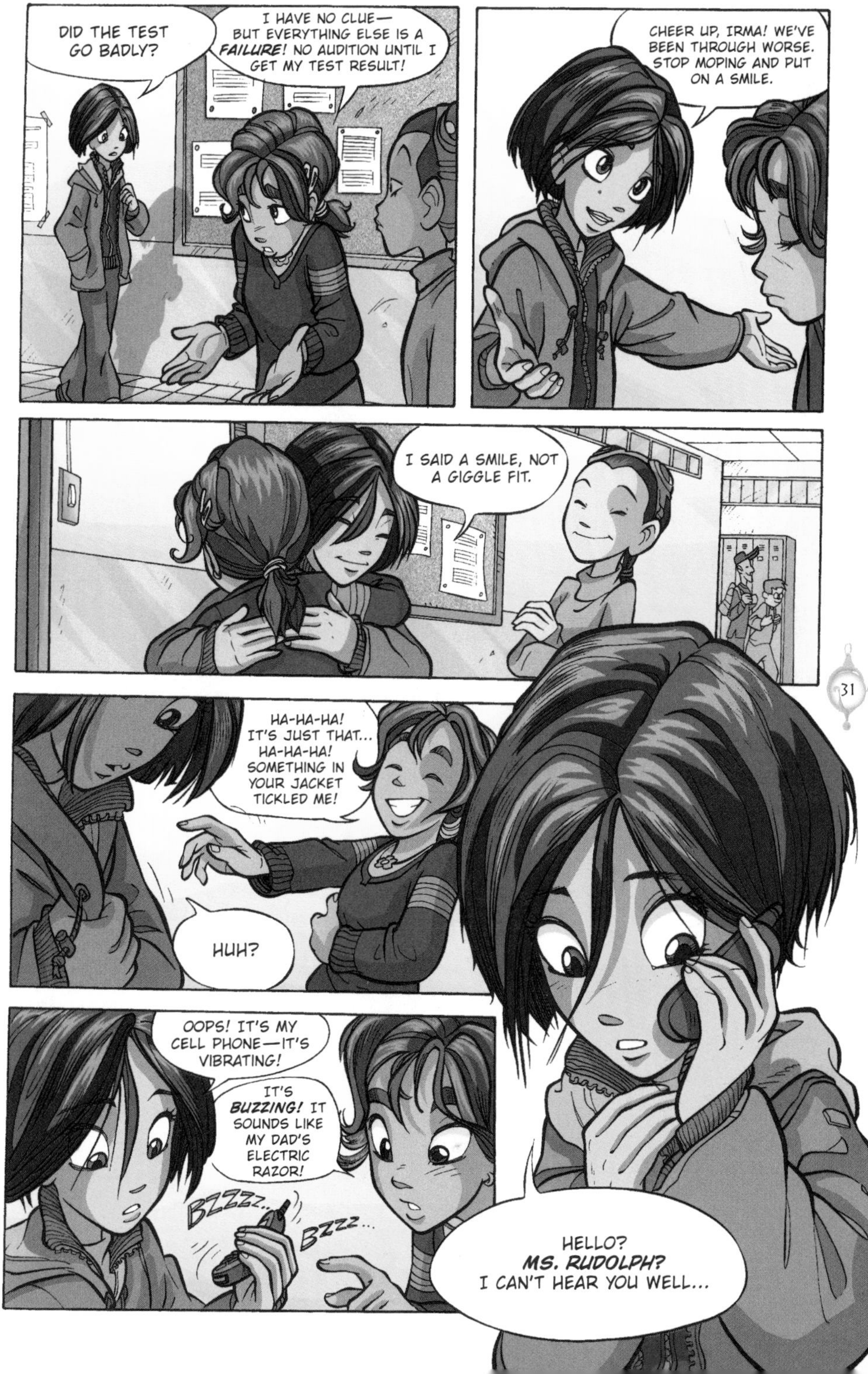
DID THE TEST GO BADLY?
I HAVE NO CLUE— BUT EVERYTHING ELSE IS A FAILURE! NO AUDITION UNTIL I GET MY TEST RESULT!
CHEER UP, IRMA! WE'VE BEEN THROUGH WORSE. STOP MOPING AND PUT ON A SMILE.
I SAID A SMILE, NOT A GIGGLE FIT.
HA-HA-HA! IT'S JUST THAT... HA-HA-HA! SOMETHING IN YOUR JACKET TICKLED ME!
HUH?
OOPS! IT'S MY CELL PHONE—IT'S VIBRATING!
IT'S BUZZING! IT SOUNDS LIKE MY DAD'S ELECTRIC RAZOR!
BZZZZ..
BZZZ...
HELLO? MS. RUDOLPH? I CAN'T HEAR YOU WELL...

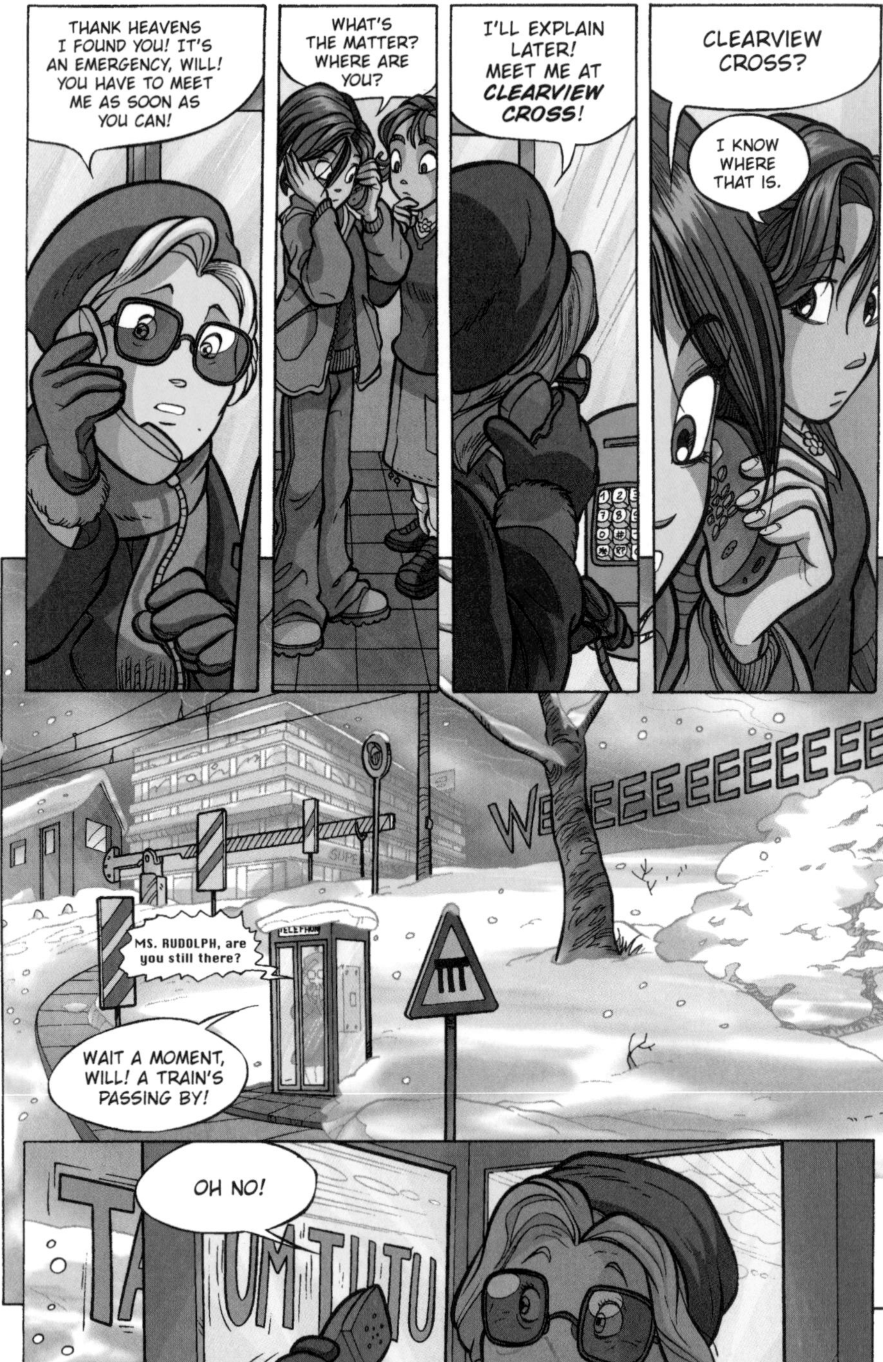
THANK HEAVENS I FOUND YOU! IT'S AN EMERGENCY, WILL! YOU HAVE TO MEET ME AS SOON AS YOU CAN!
WHAT'S THE MATTER? WHERE ARE YOU?
I'LL EXPLAIN LATER! MEET ME AT ***CLEARVIEW CROSS***!
CLEARVIEW CROSS?
I KNOW WHERE THAT IS.
WEEEEEEEEEEEE
MS. RUDOLPH, are you still there?
WAIT A MOMENT, WILL! A TRAIN'S PASSING BY!
OH NO!
TA UM TUTU

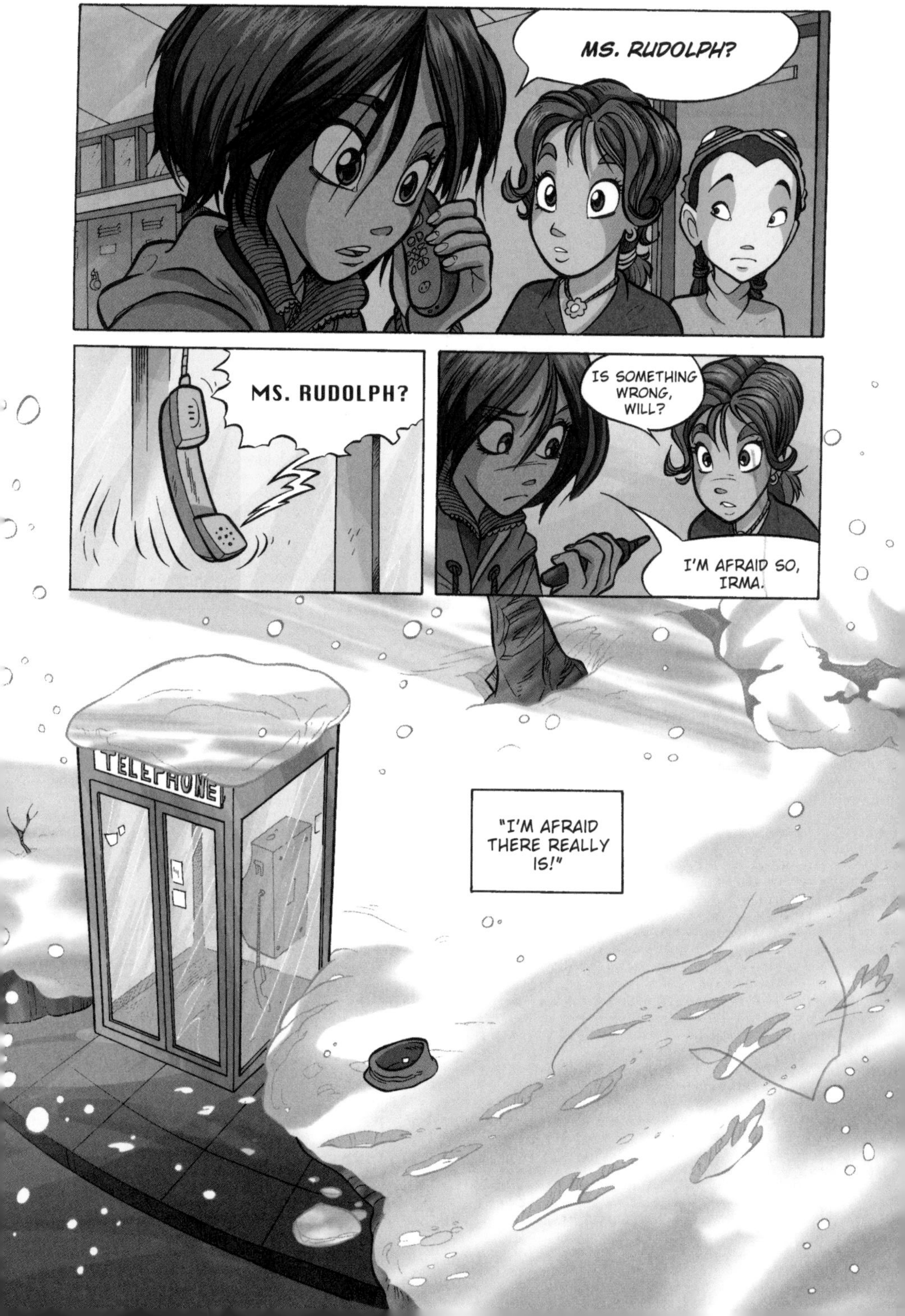

MS. RUDOLPH?
MS. RUDOLPH?
IS SOMETHING WRONG, WILL?
I'M AFRAID SO, IRMA.
TELEPHONE
"I'M AFRAID THERE REALLY IS!"

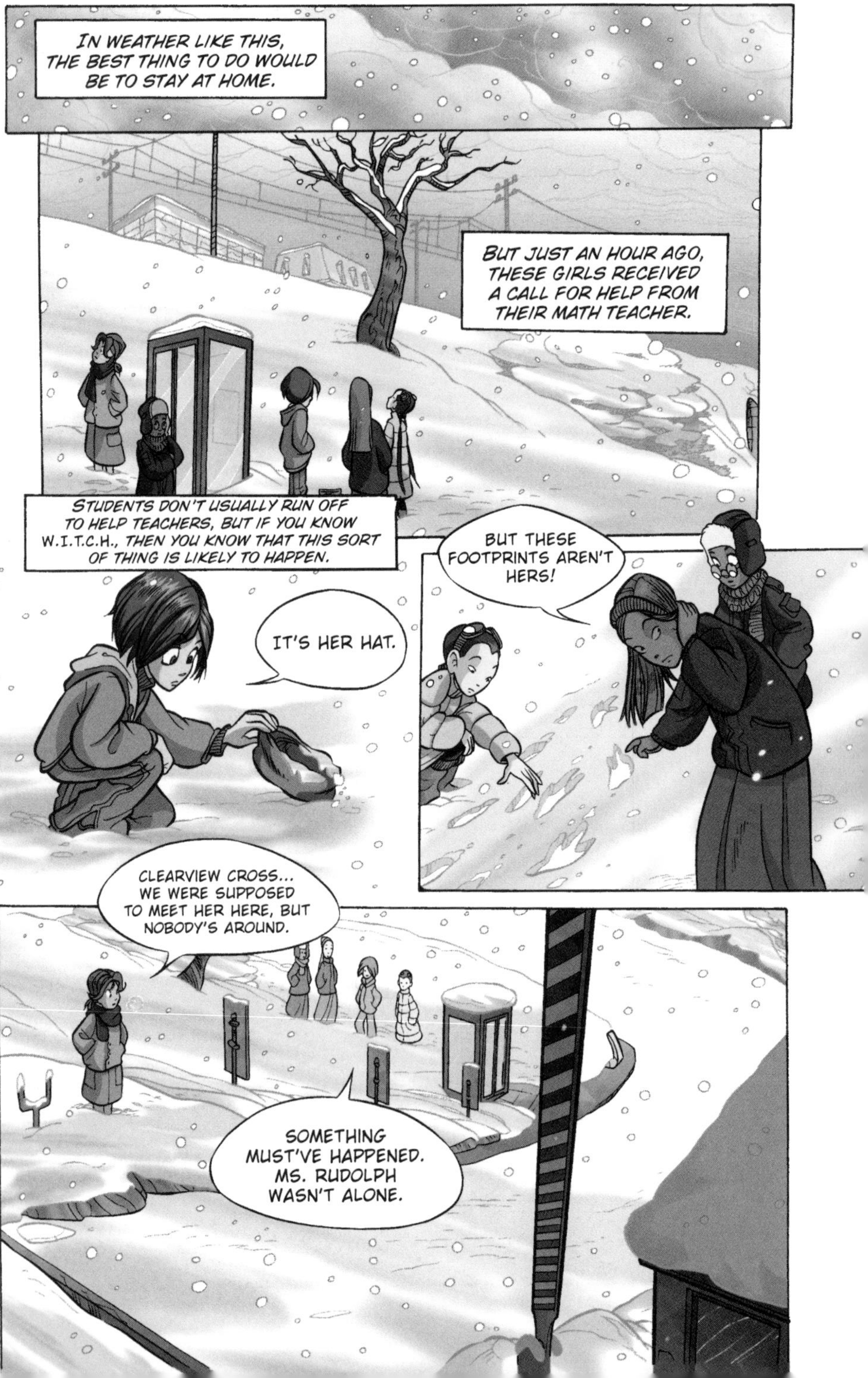
IN WEATHER LIKE THIS, THE BEST THING TO DO WOULD BE TO STAY AT HOME.
BUT JUST AN HOUR AGO, THESE GIRLS RECEIVED A CALL FOR HELP FROM THEIR MATH TEACHER.
STUDENTS DON'T USUALLY RUN OFF TO HELP TEACHERS, BUT IF YOU KNOW W.I.T.C.H., THEN YOU KNOW THAT THIS SORT OF THING IS LIKELY TO HAPPEN.
IT'S HER HAT.
BUT THESE FOOTPRINTS AREN'T HERS!
CLEARVIEW CROSS... WE WERE SUPPOSED TO MEET HER HERE, BUT NOBODY'S AROUND.
SOMETHING MUST'VE HAPPENED. MS. RUDOLPH WASN'T ALONE.

34

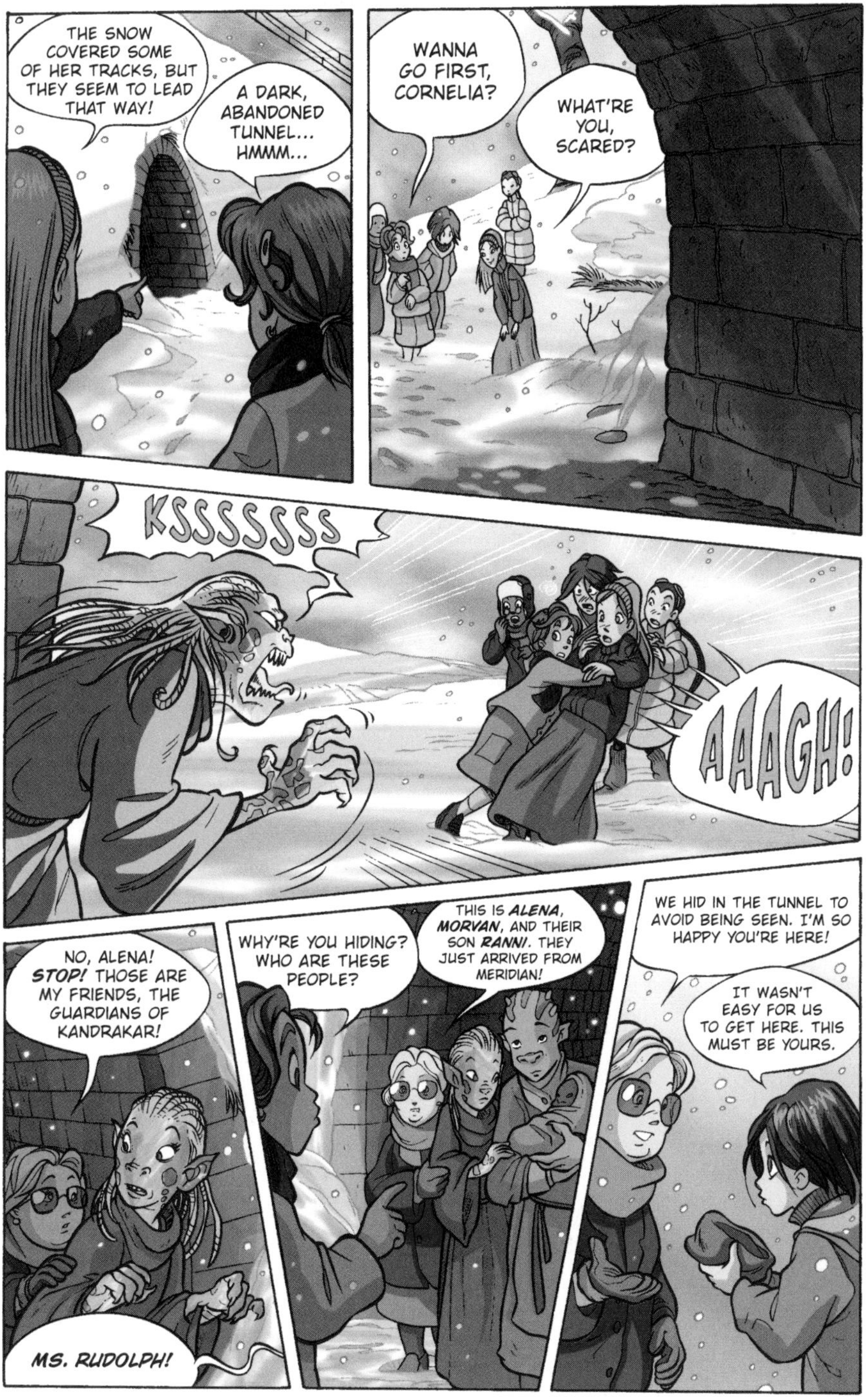
THE SNOW COVERED SOME OF HER TRACKS, BUT THEY SEEM TO LEAD THAT WAY!
A DARK, ABANDONED TUNNEL... HMMM...
WANNA GO FIRST, CORNELIA?
WHAT'RE YOU, SCARED?
KSSSSSSS
AAAGH!
NO, ALENA! STOP! THOSE ARE MY FRIENDS, THE GUARDIANS OF KANDRAKAR!
MS. RUDOLPH!
WHY'RE YOU HIDING? WHO ARE THESE PEOPLE?
THIS IS ALENA, MORVAN, AND THEIR SON RANNI. THEY JUST ARRIVED FROM MERIDIAN!
WE HID IN THE TUNNEL TO AVOID BEING SEEN. I'M SO HAPPY YOU'RE HERE!
IT WASN'T EASY FOR US TO GET HERE. THIS MUST BE YOURS.

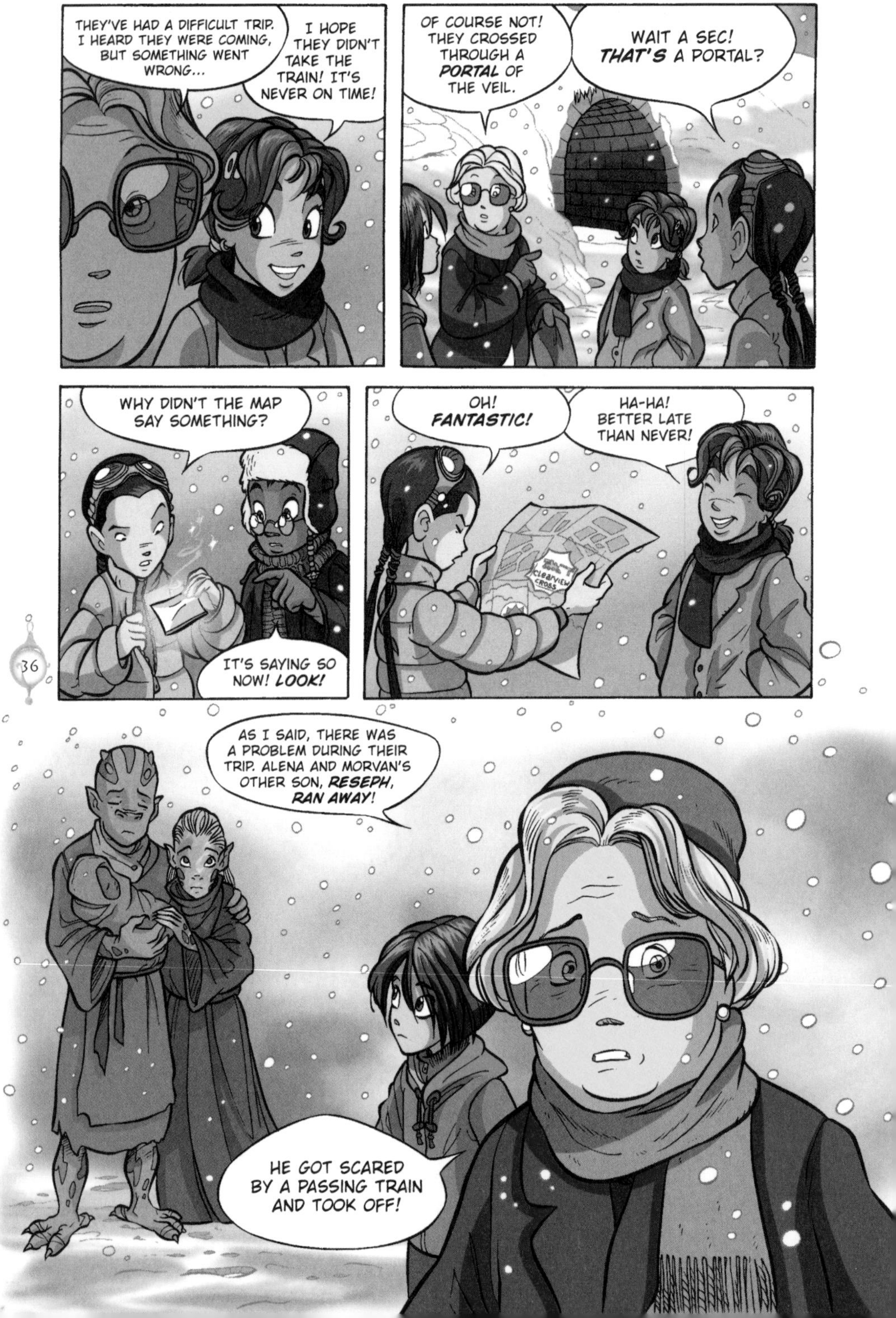
THEY'VE HAD A DIFFICULT TRIP. I HEARD THEY WERE COMING, BUT SOMETHING WENT WRONG...
I HOPE THEY DIDN'T TAKE THE TRAIN! IT'S NEVER ON TIME!
OF COURSE NOT! THEY CROSSED THROUGH A PORTAL OF THE VEIL.
WAIT A SEC! THAT'S A PORTAL?
WHY DIDN'T THE MAP SAY SOMETHING?
IT'S SAYING SO NOW! LOOK!
OH! FANTASTIC!
HA-HA! BETTER LATE THAN NEVER!
AS I SAID, THERE WAS A PROBLEM DURING THEIR TRIP. ALENA AND MORVAN'S OTHER SON, RESEPH, RAN AWAY!
HE GOT SCARED BY A PASSING TRAIN AND TOOK OFF!

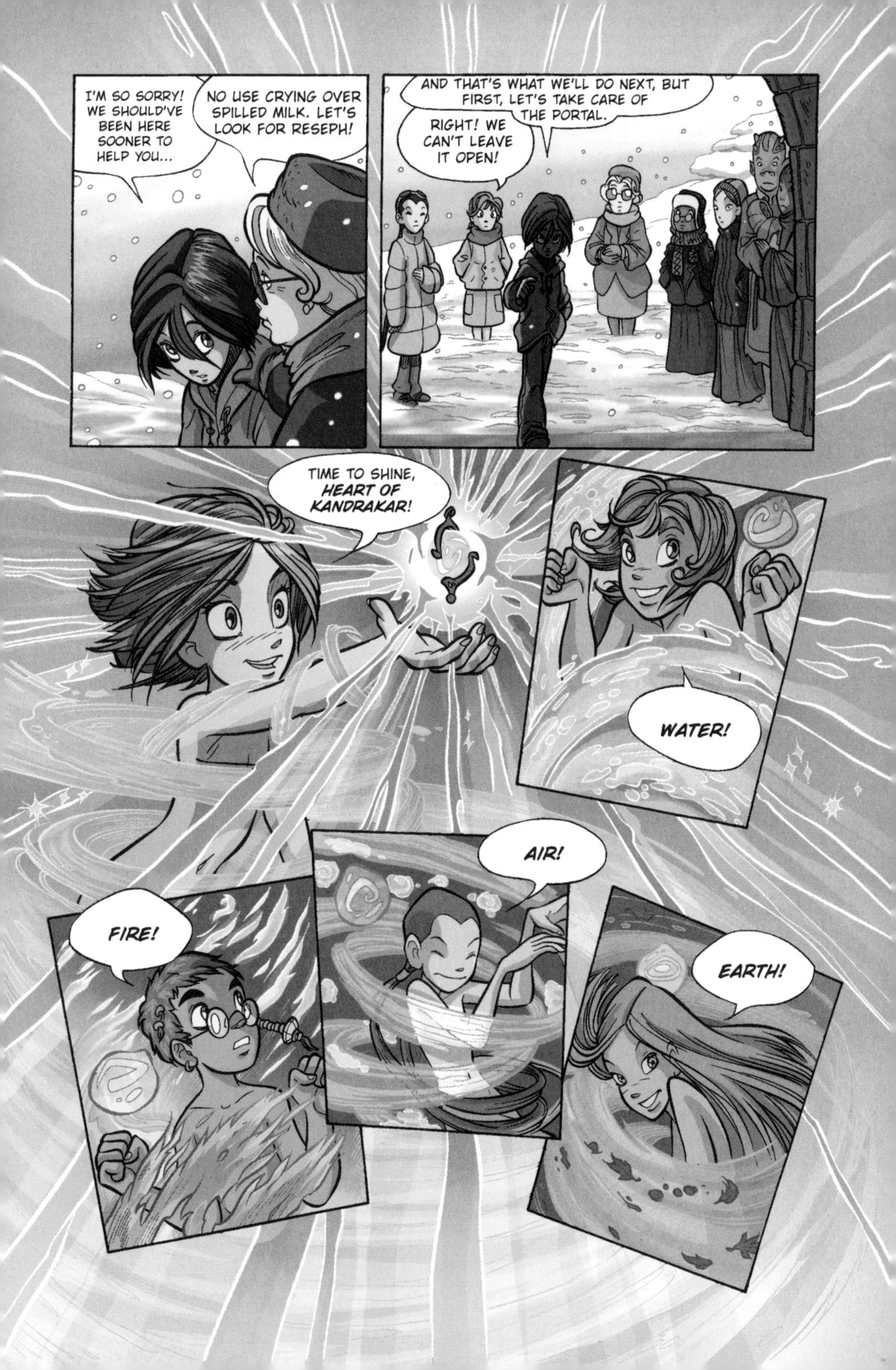
I'M SO SORRY! WE SHOULD'VE BEEN HERE SOONER TO HELP YOU...
NO USE CRYING OVER SPILLED MILK. LET'S LOOK FOR RESEPH!
AND THAT'S WHAT WE'LL DO NEXT, BUT FIRST, LET'S TAKE CARE OF THE PORTAL.
RIGHT! WE CAN'T LEAVE IT OPEN!
TIME TO SHINE, *HEART OF KANDRAKAR*!
WATER!
AIR!
FIRE!
EARTH!

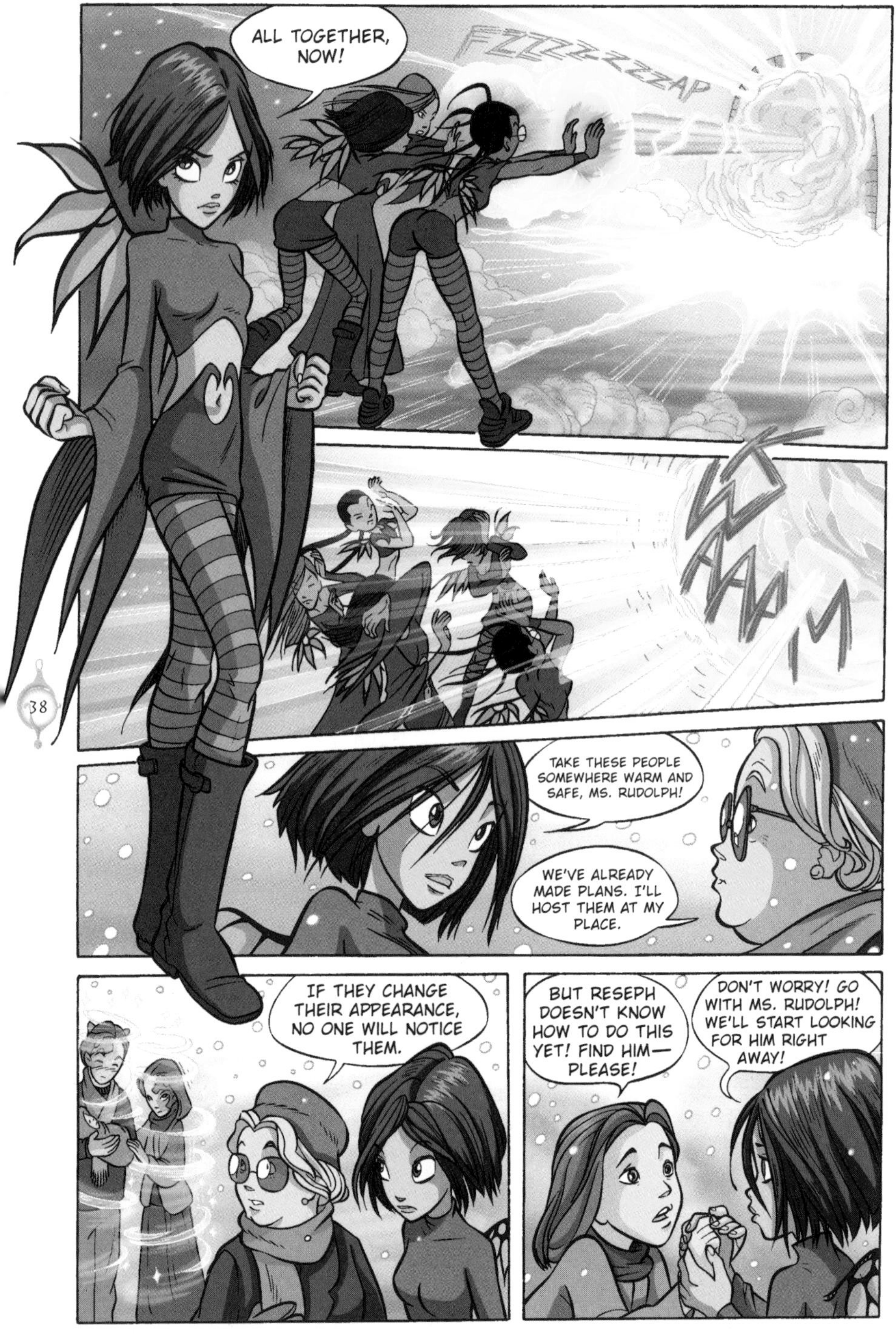

ALL TOGETHER, NOW!
FZZZZZZZZZAP
WAAAM
TAKE THESE PEOPLE SOMEWHERE WARM AND SAFE, MS. RUDOLPH!
WE'VE ALREADY MADE PLANS. I'LL HOST THEM AT MY PLACE.
IF THEY CHANGE THEIR APPEARANCE, NO ONE WILL NOTICE THEM.
BUT RESEPH DOESN'T KNOW HOW TO DO THIS YET! FIND HIM—PLEASE!
DON'T WORRY! GO WITH MS. RUDOLPH! WE'LL START LOOKING FOR HIM RIGHT AWAY!

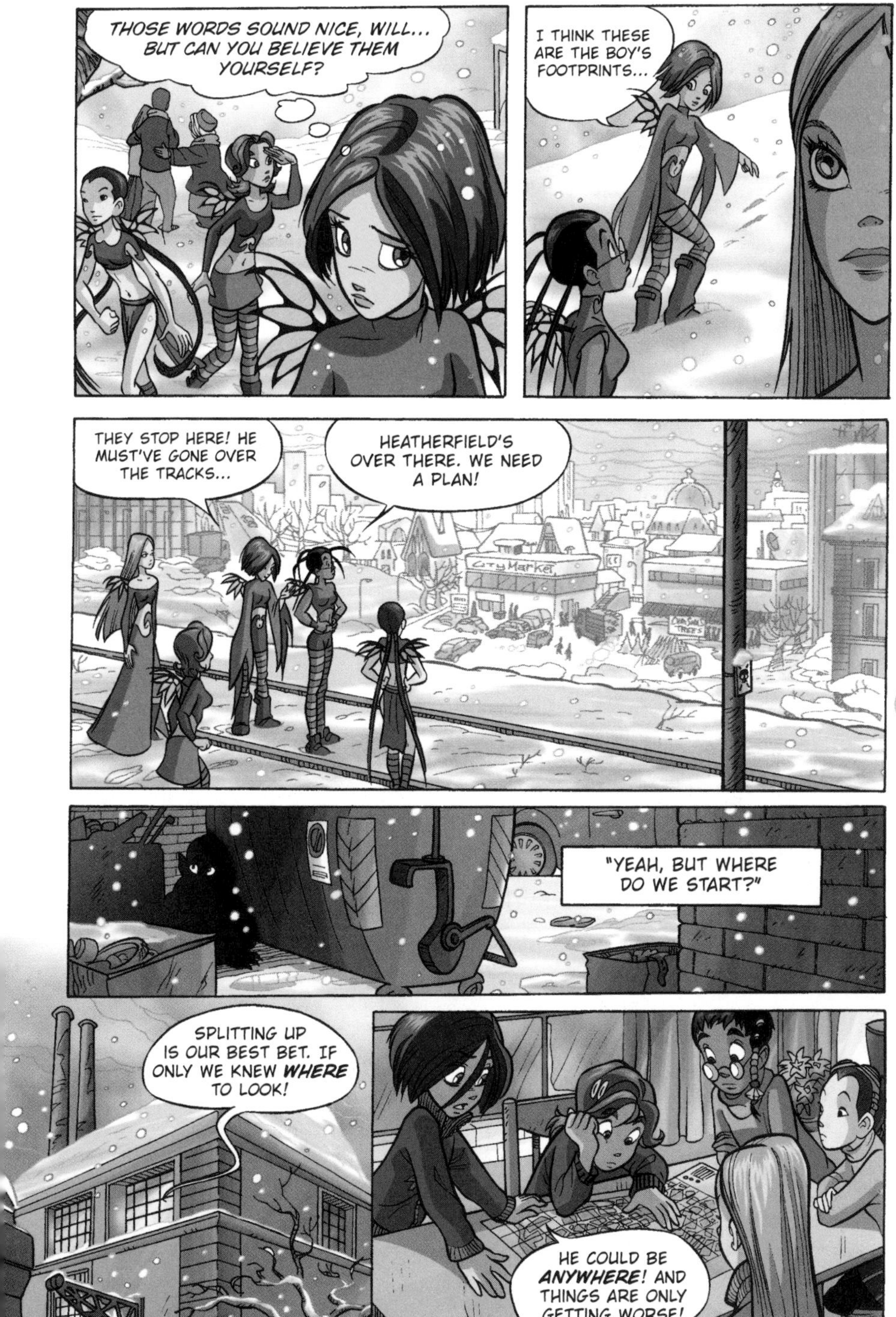
THOSE WORDS SOUND NICE, WILL... BUT CAN YOU BELIEVE THEM YOURSELF?
I THINK THESE ARE THE BOY'S FOOTPRINTS...
THEY STOP HERE! HE MUST'VE GONE OVER THE TRACKS...
HEATHERFIELD'S OVER THERE. WE NEED A PLAN!
City Market
"YEAH, BUT WHERE DO WE START?"
SPLITTING UP IS OUR BEST BET. IF ONLY WE KNEW *WHERE* TO LOOK!
HE COULD BE *ANYWHERE*! AND THINGS ARE ONLY GETTING WORSE!

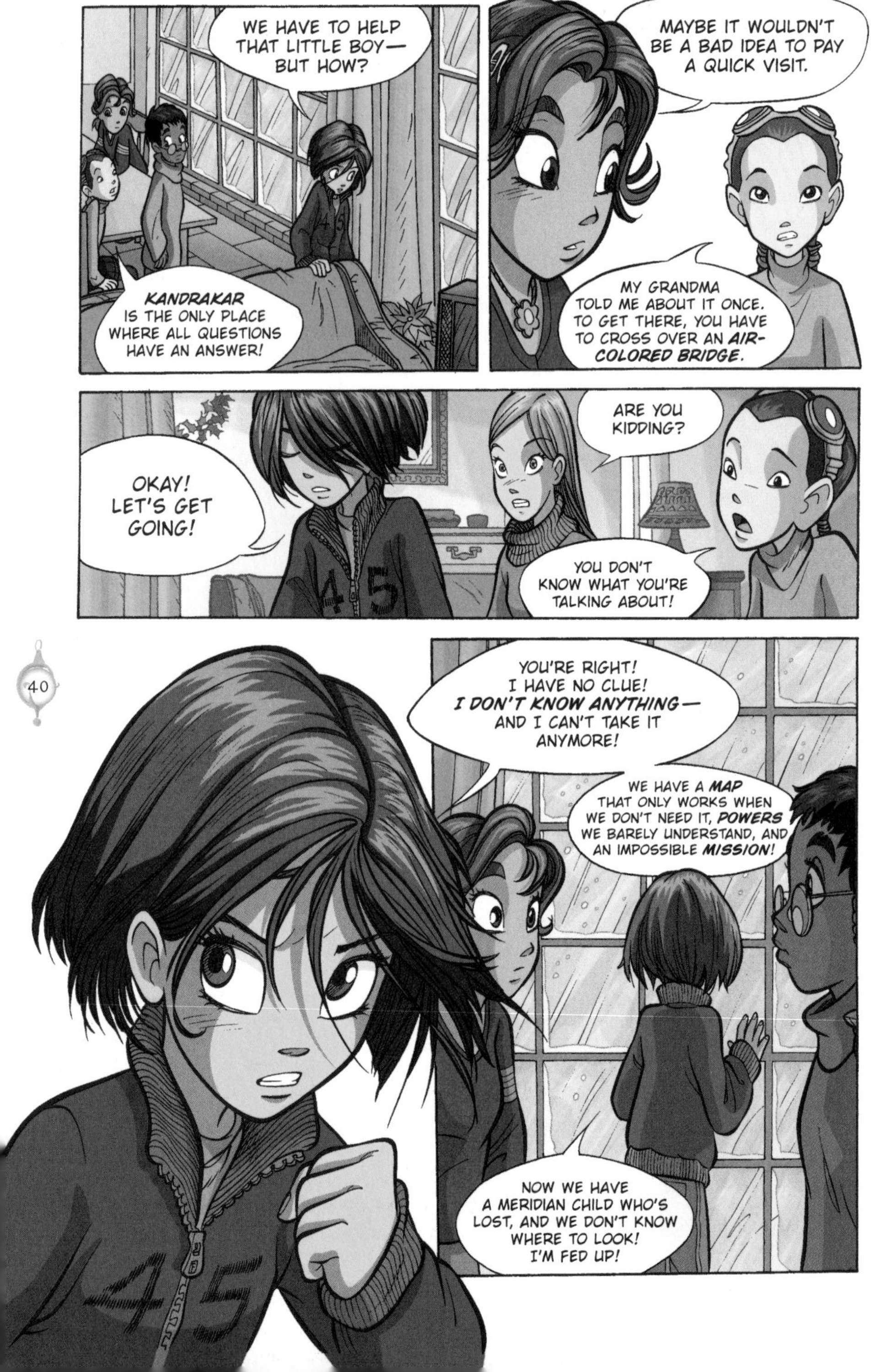

WE HAVE TO HELP THAT LITTLE BOY— BUT HOW?
KANDRAKAR IS THE ONLY PLACE WHERE ALL QUESTIONS HAVE AN ANSWER!
MAYBE IT WOULDN'T BE A BAD IDEA TO PAY A QUICK VISIT.
MY GRANDMA TOLD ME ABOUT IT ONCE. TO GET THERE, YOU HAVE TO CROSS OVER AN AIR-COLORED BRIDGE.
OKAY! LET'S GET GOING!
ARE YOU KIDDING?
YOU DON'T KNOW WHAT YOU'RE TALKING ABOUT!
YOU'RE RIGHT! I HAVE NO CLUE! I DON'T KNOW ANYTHING— AND I CAN'T TAKE IT ANYMORE!
WE HAVE A MAP THAT ONLY WORKS WHEN WE DON'T NEED IT, POWERS WE BARELY UNDERSTAND, AND AN IMPOSSIBLE MISSION!
NOW WE HAVE A MERIDIAN CHILD WHO'S LOST, AND WE DON'T KNOW WHERE TO LOOK! I'M FED UP!

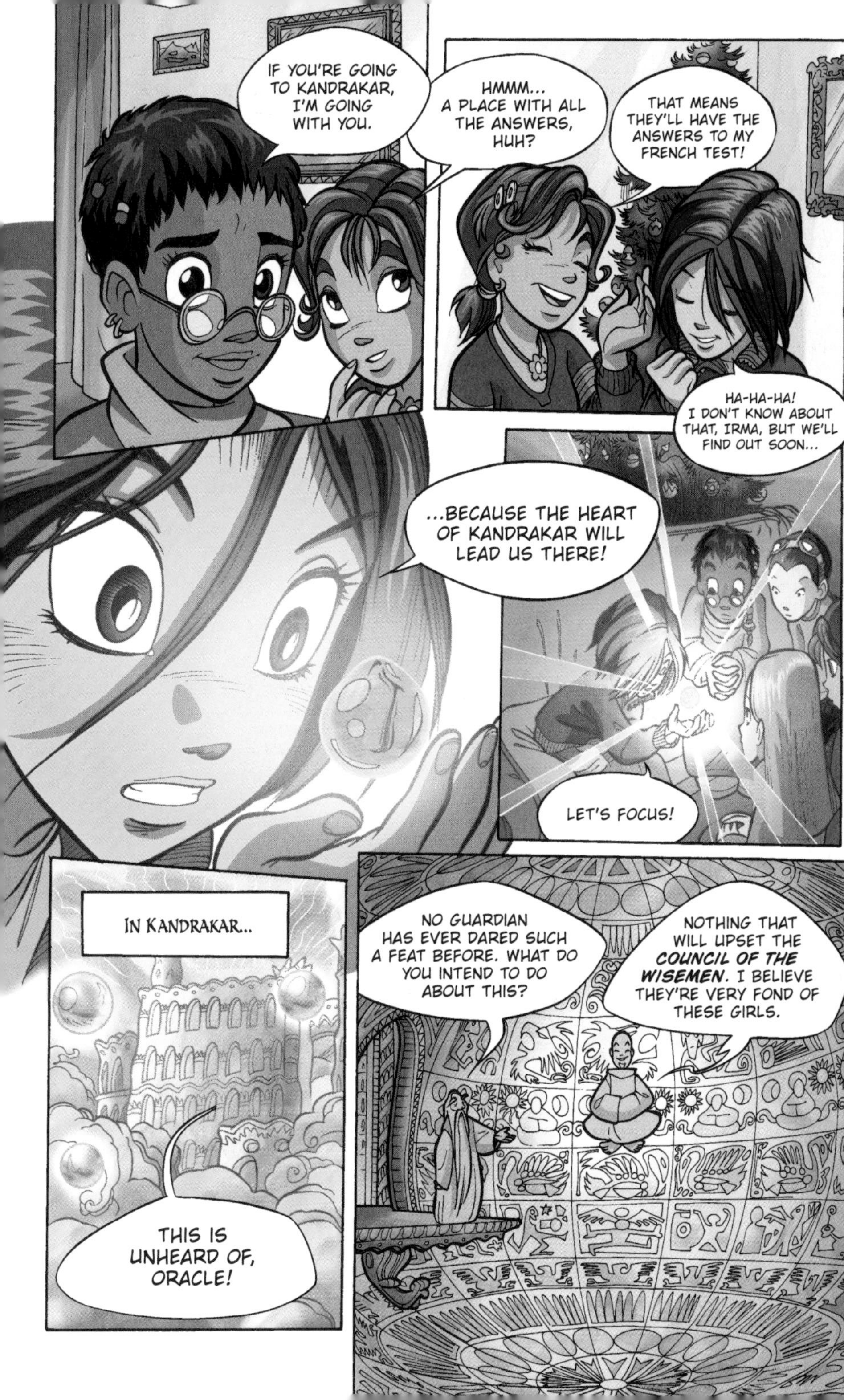
IF YOU'RE GOING TO KANDRAKAR, I'M GOING WITH YOU.
HMMM... A PLACE WITH ALL THE ANSWERS, HUH?
THAT MEANS THEY'LL HAVE THE ANSWERS TO MY FRENCH TEST!
HA-HA-HA! I DON'T KNOW ABOUT THAT, IRMA, BUT WE'LL FIND OUT SOON...
...BECAUSE THE HEART OF KANDRAKAR WILL LEAD US THERE!
LET'S FOCUS!
IN KANDRAKAR...
THIS IS UNHEARD OF, ORACLE!
NO GUARDIAN HAS EVER DARED SUCH A FEAT BEFORE. WHAT DO YOU INTEND TO DO ABOUT THIS?
NOTHING THAT WILL UPSET THE *COUNCIL OF THE WISEMEN*. I BELIEVE THEY'RE VERY FOND OF THESE GIRLS.

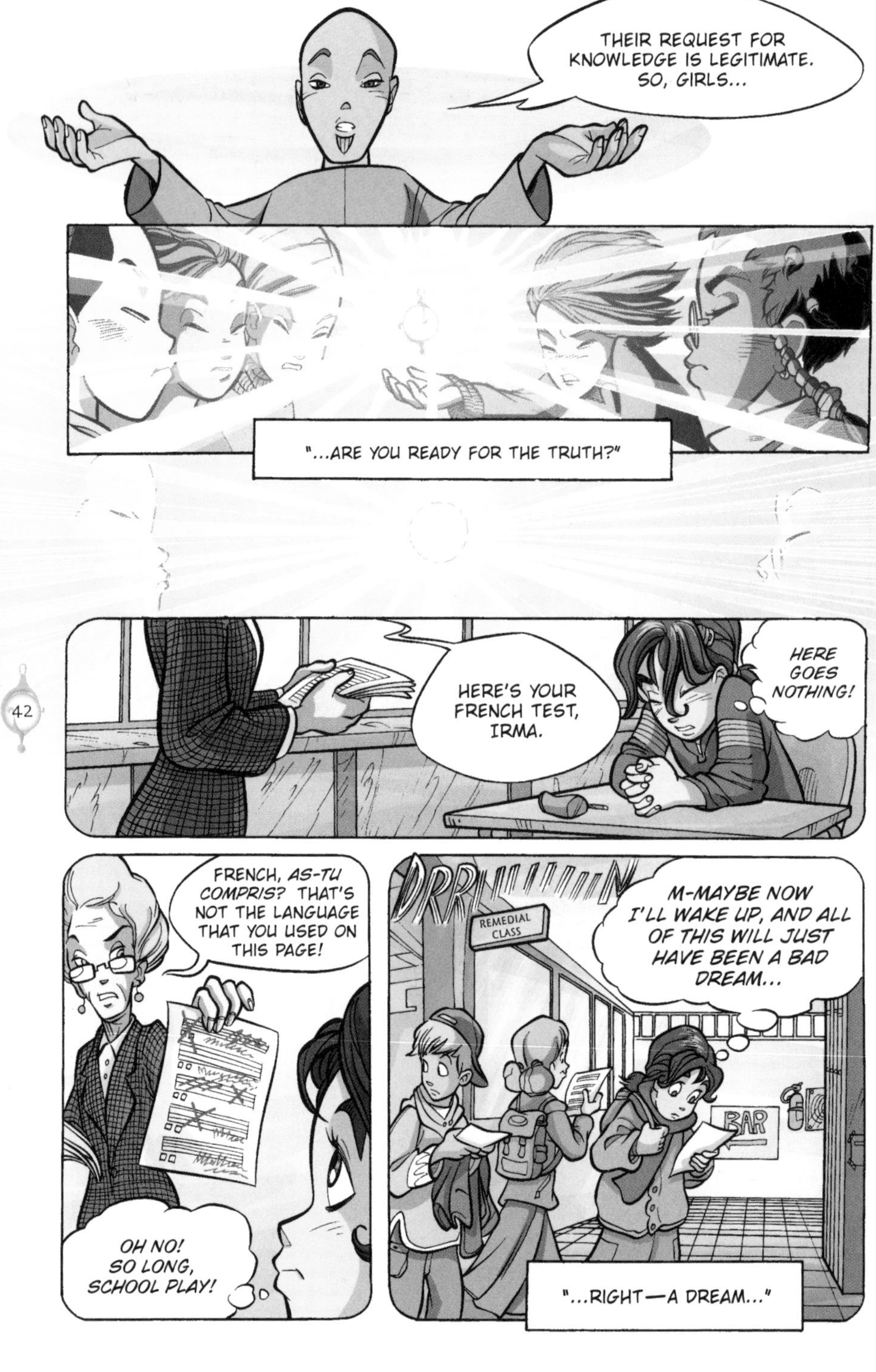
THEIR REQUEST FOR KNOWLEDGE IS LEGITIMATE. SO, GIRLS...
"...ARE YOU READY FOR THE TRUTH?"
HERE'S YOUR FRENCH TEST, IRMA.
HERE GOES NOTHING!
FRENCH, AS-TU COMPRIS? THAT'S NOT THE LANGUAGE THAT YOU USED ON THIS PAGE!
OH NO! SO LONG, SCHOOL PLAY!
DRRRNNNNNNNN
REMEDIAL CLASS
M-MAYBE NOW I'LL WAKE UP, AND ALL OF THIS WILL JUST HAVE BEEN A BAD DREAM...
BAR
"...RIGHT—A DREAM..."

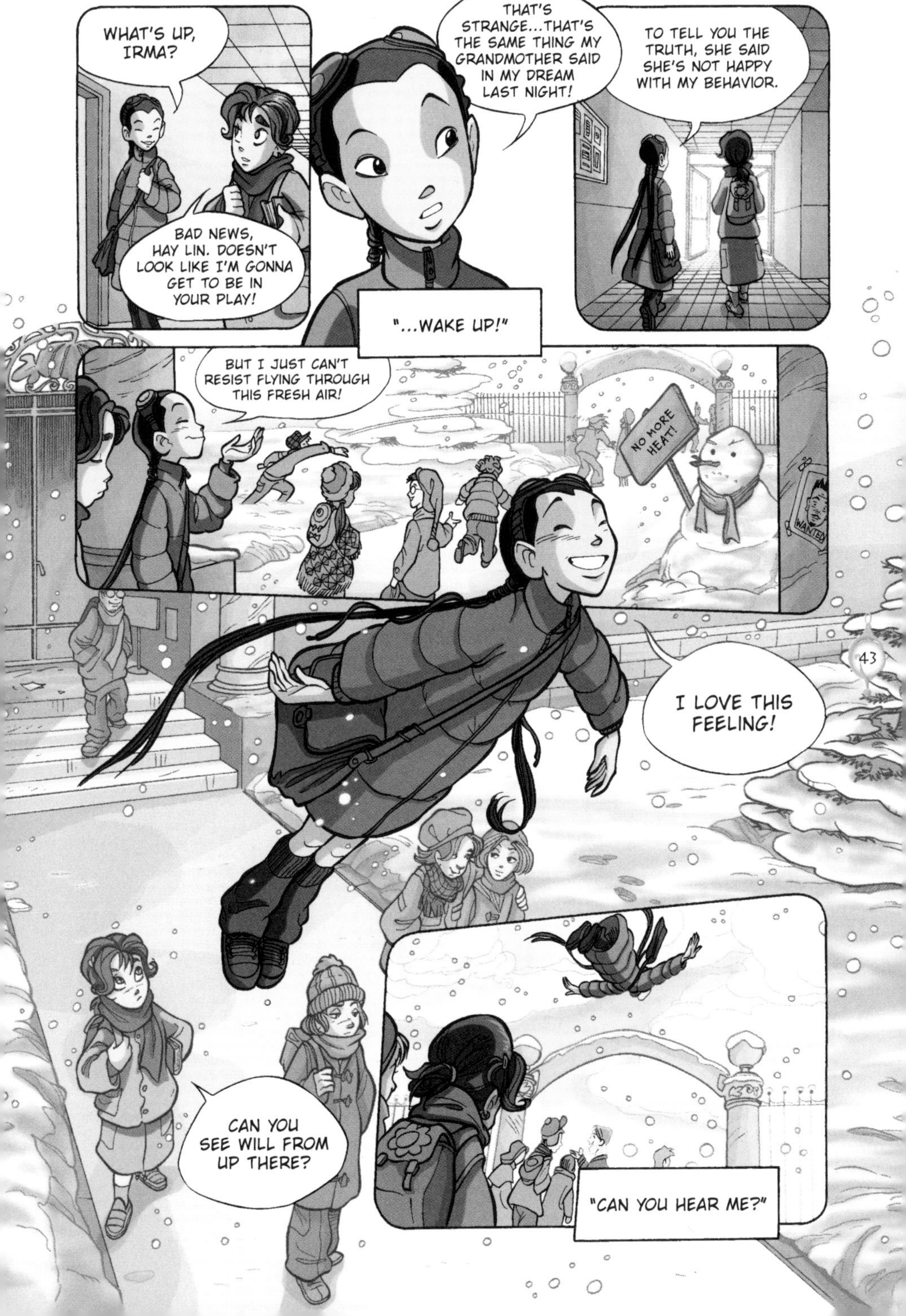
WHAT'S UP, IRMA?
BAD NEWS, HAY LIN. DOESN'T LOOK LIKE I'M GONNA GET TO BE IN YOUR PLAY!
THAT'S STRANGE...THAT'S THE SAME THING MY GRANDMOTHER SAID IN MY DREAM LAST NIGHT!
"...WAKE UP!"
TO TELL YOU THE TRUTH, SHE SAID SHE'S NOT HAPPY WITH MY BEHAVIOR.
BUT I JUST CAN'T RESIST FLYING THROUGH THIS FRESH AIR!
NO MORE HEAT!
WANTED
I LOVE THIS FEELING!
CAN YOU SEE WILL FROM UP THERE?
"CAN YOU HEAR ME?"

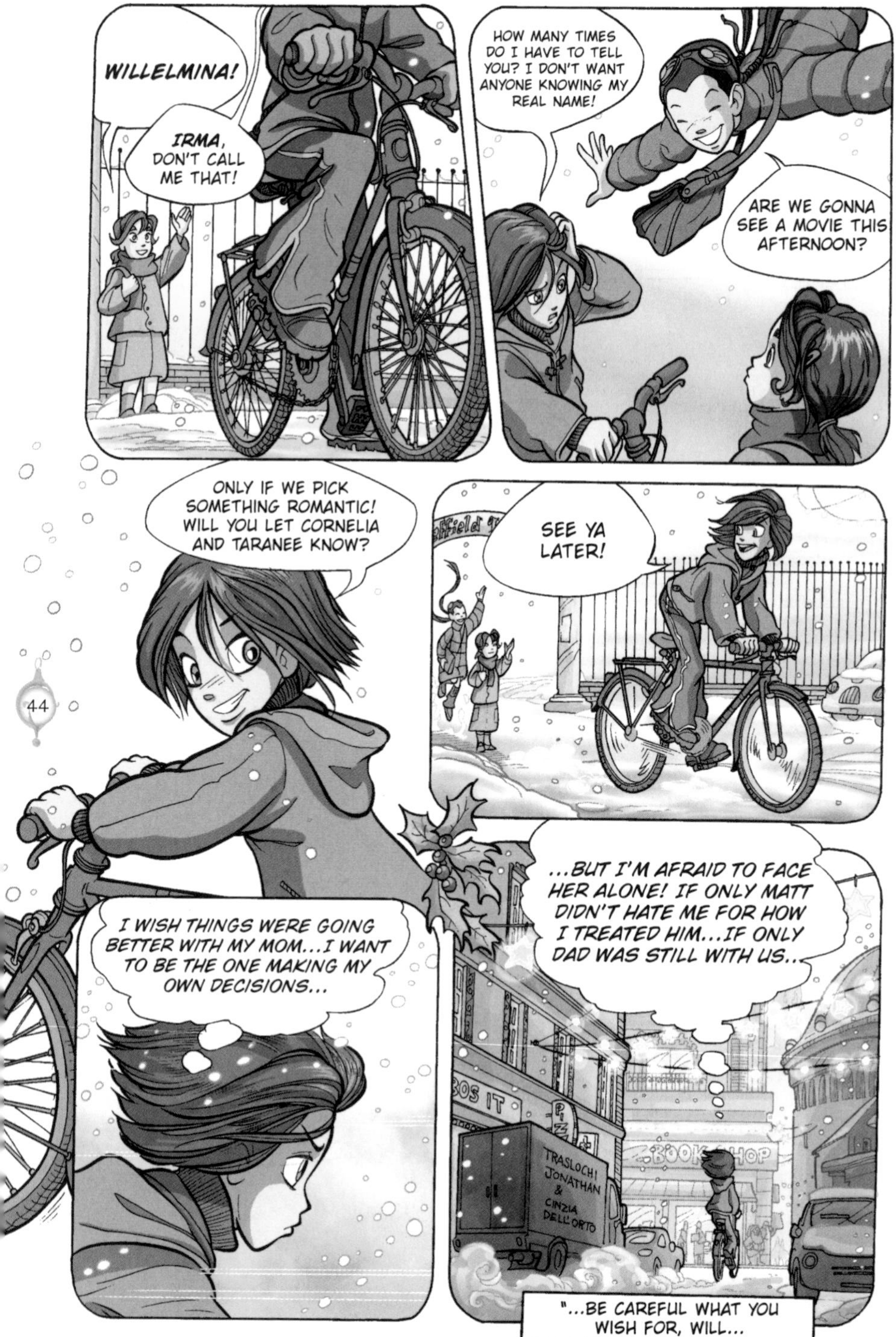
WILLELMINA!
IRMA, DON'T CALL ME THAT!
HOW MANY TIMES DO I HAVE TO TELL YOU? I DON'T WANT ANYONE KNOWING MY REAL NAME!
ARE WE GONNA SEE A MOVIE THIS AFTERNOON?
ONLY IF WE PICK SOMETHING ROMANTIC! WILL YOU LET CORNELIA AND TARANEE KNOW?
SEE YA LATER!
I WISH THINGS WERE GOING BETTER WITH MY MOM... I WANT TO BE THE ONE MAKING MY OWN DECISIONS...
...BUT I'M AFRAID TO FACE HER ALONE! IF ONLY MATT DIDN'T HATE ME FOR HOW I TREATED HIM... IF ONLY DAD WAS STILL WITH US...
"...BE CAREFUL WHAT YOU WISH FOR, WILL...
TRASLOCHI JONATHAN & CINZIA DELL'ORTO

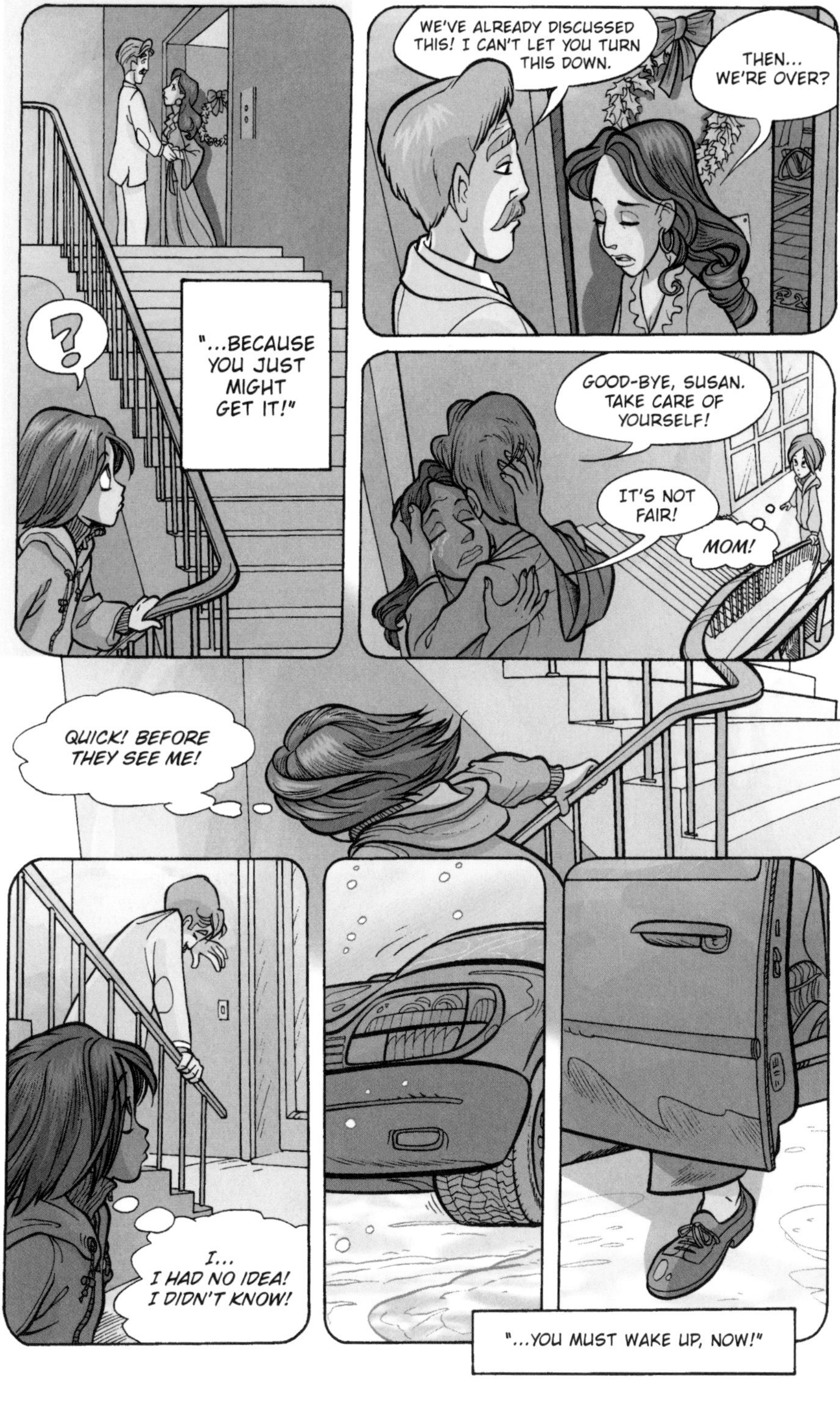

?
"...BECAUSE YOU JUST MIGHT GET IT!"
WE'VE ALREADY DISCUSSED THIS! I CAN'T LET YOU TURN THIS DOWN.
THEN... WE'RE OVER?
GOOD-BYE, SUSAN. TAKE CARE OF YOURSELF!
IT'S NOT FAIR!
MOM!
QUICK! BEFORE THEY SEE ME!
I... I HAD NO IDEA! I DIDN'T KNOW!
"...YOU MUST WAKE UP, NOW!"

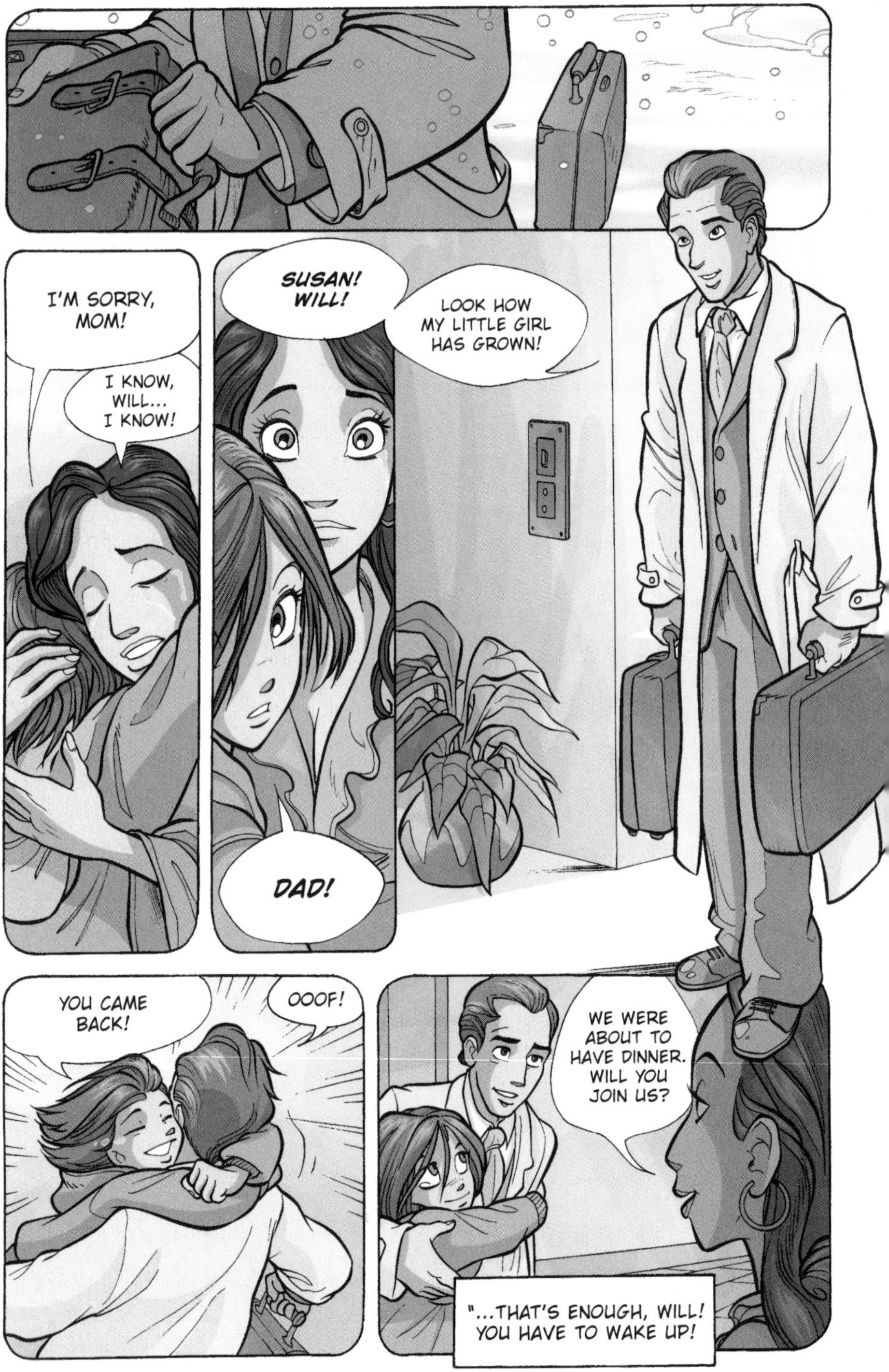
I'M SORRY, MOM!
I KNOW, WILL... I KNOW!
SUSAN! WILL!
LOOK HOW MY LITTLE GIRL HAS GROWN!
DAD!
YOU CAME BACK!
OOOF!
WE WERE ABOUT TO HAVE DINNER. WILL YOU JOIN US?
"...THAT'S ENOUGH, WILL! YOU HAVE TO WAKE UP!

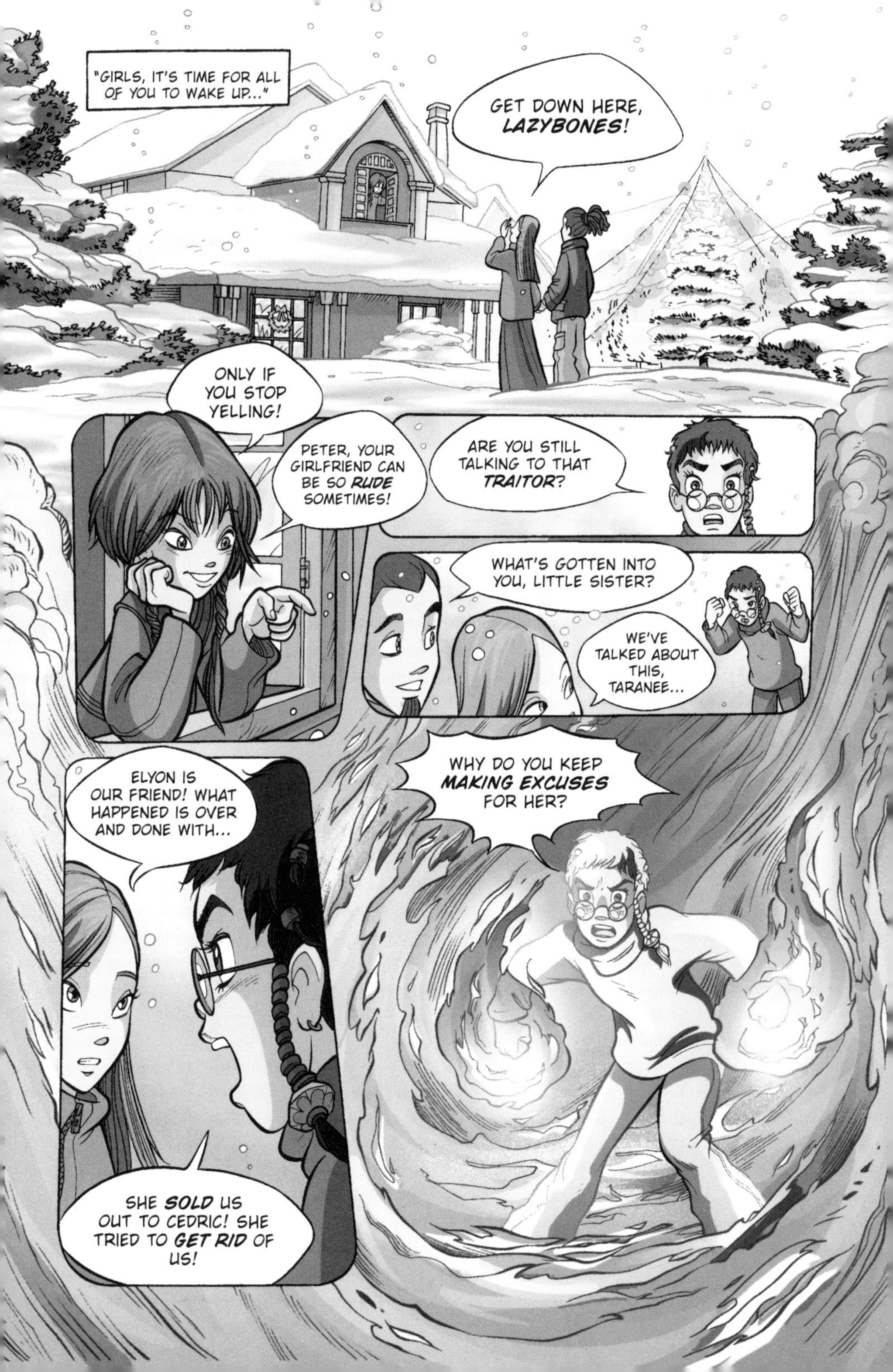
"GIRLS, IT'S TIME FOR ALL OF YOU TO WAKE UP..."
GET DOWN HERE, LAZYBONES!
ONLY IF YOU STOP YELLING!
PETER, YOUR GIRLFRIEND CAN BE SO RUDE SOMETIMES!
ARE YOU STILL TALKING TO THAT TRAITOR?
WHAT'S GOTTEN INTO YOU, LITTLE SISTER?
WE'VE TALKED ABOUT THIS, TARANEE...
ELYON IS OUR FRIEND! WHAT HAPPENED IS OVER AND DONE WITH...
SHE SOLD US OUT TO CEDRIC! SHE TRIED TO GET RID OF US!
WHY DO YOU KEEP MAKING EXCUSES FOR HER?

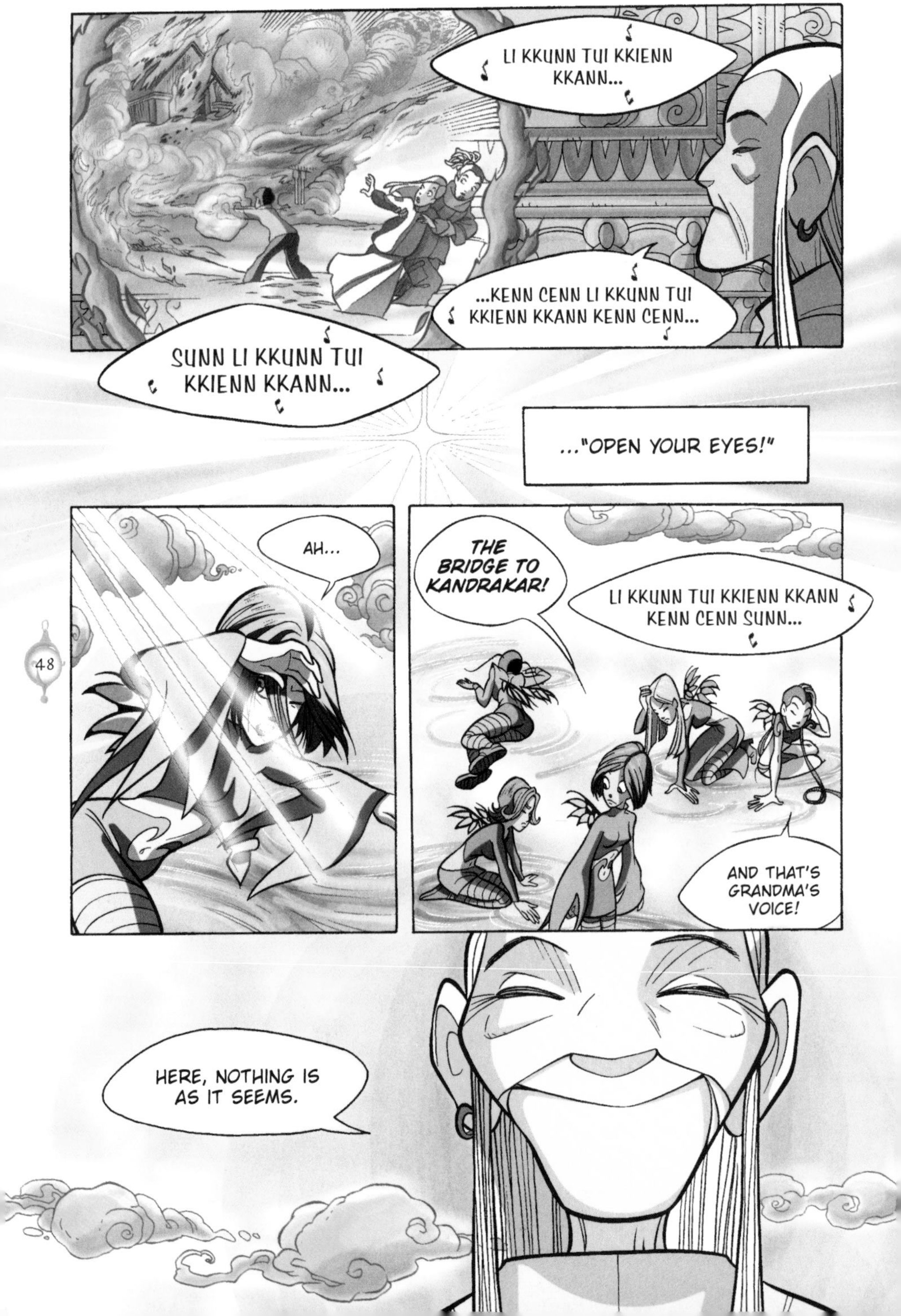
LI KKUNN TUI KKIENN KKANN...
...KENN CENN LI KKUNN TUI KKIENN KKANN KENN CENN...
SUNN LI KKUNN TUI KKIENN KKANN...
..."OPEN YOUR EYES!"
AH...
THE BRIDGE TO KANDRAKAR!
LI KKUNN TUI KKIENN KKANN KENN CENN SUNN...
AND THAT'S GRANDMA'S VOICE!
HERE, NOTHING IS AS IT SEEMS.

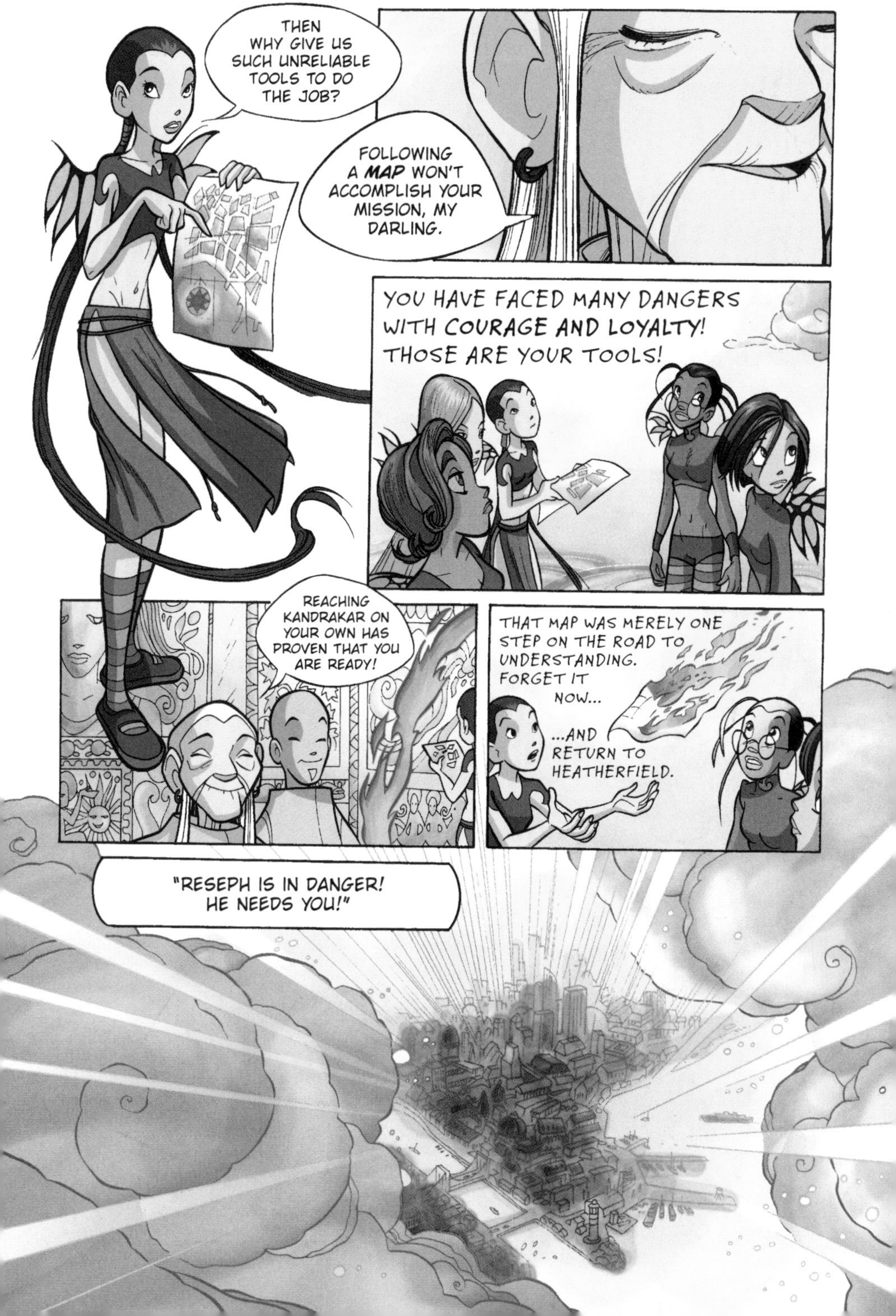
THEN WHY GIVE US SUCH UNRELIABLE TOOLS TO DO THE JOB?
FOLLOWING A MAP WON'T ACCOMPLISH YOUR MISSION, MY DARLING.
YOU HAVE FACED MANY DANGERS WITH COURAGE AND LOYALTY! THOSE ARE YOUR TOOLS!
REACHING KANDRAKAR ON YOUR OWN HAS PROVEN THAT YOU ARE READY!
THAT MAP WAS MERELY ONE STEP ON THE ROAD TO UNDERSTANDING. FORGET IT NOW...
...AND RETURN TO HEATHERFIELD.
"RESEPH IS IN DANGER! HE NEEDS YOU!"

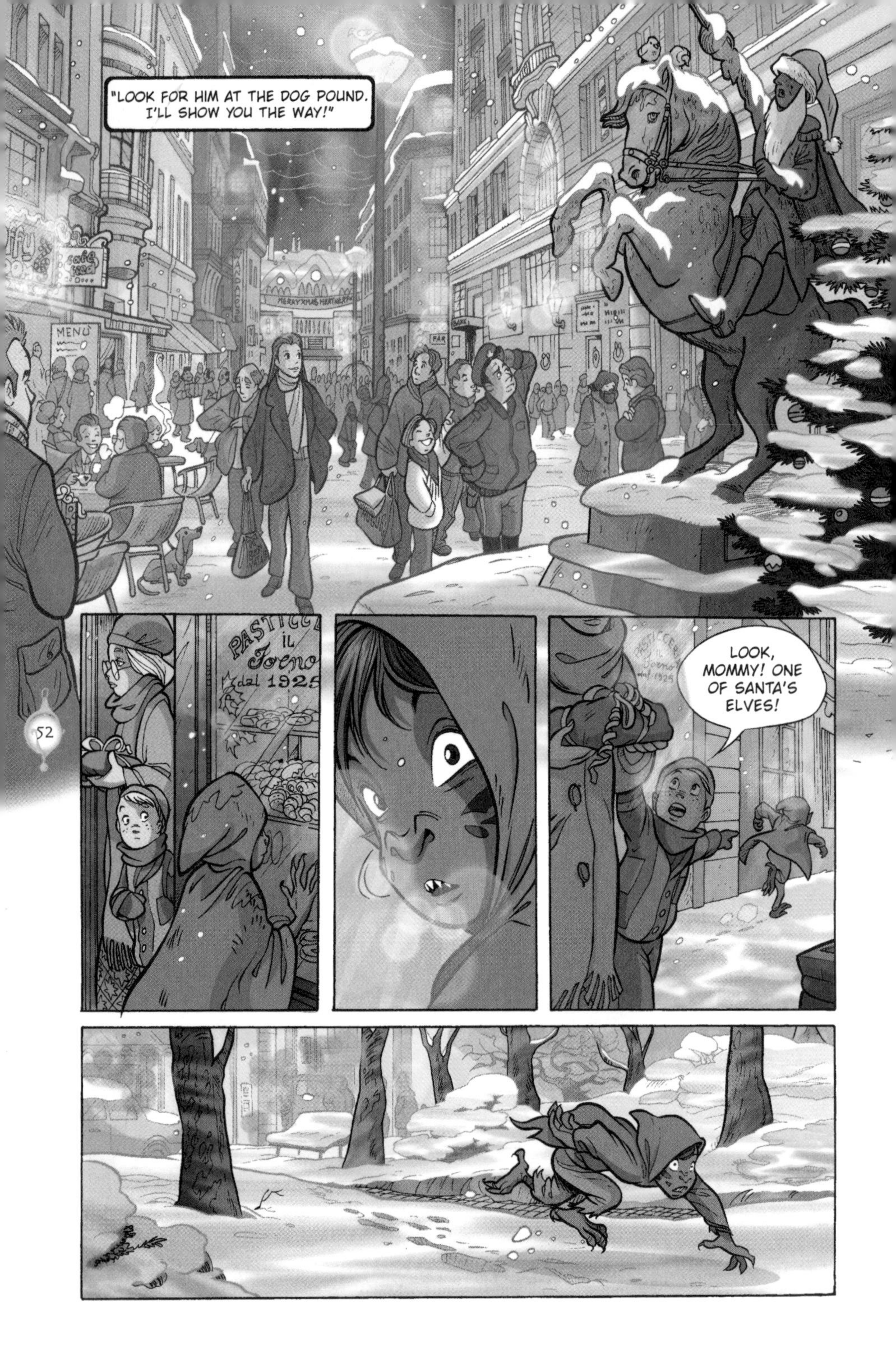
"LOOK FOR HIM AT THE DOG POUND. I'LL SHOW YOU THE WAY!"
MENU
BANK
LOOK, MOMMY! ONE OF SANTA'S ELVES!

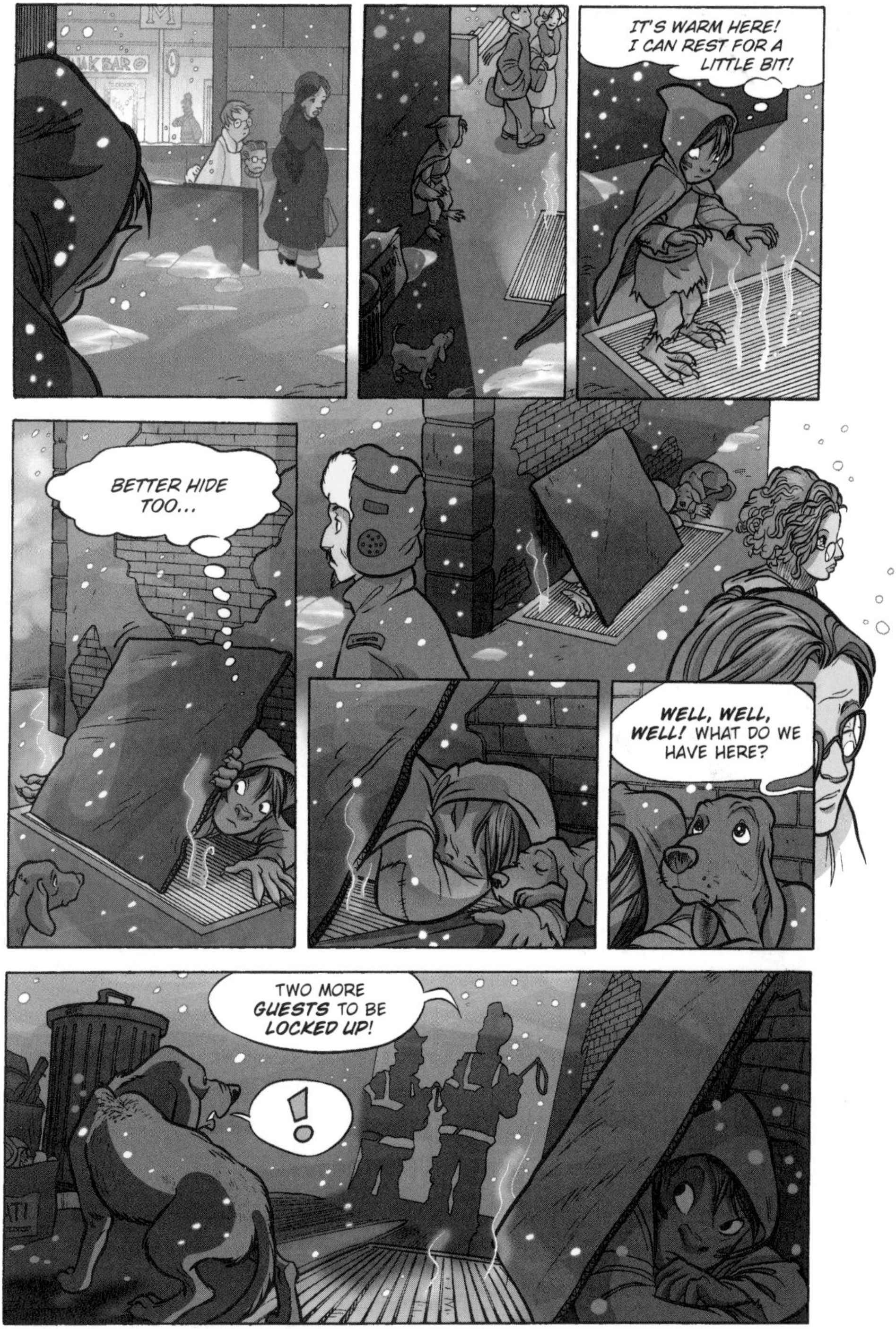

IT'S WARM HERE! I CAN REST FOR A LITTLE BIT!
BETTER HIDE TOO...
WELL, WELL, WELL! WHAT DO WE HAVE HERE?
TWO MORE GUESTS TO BE LOCKED UP!
!

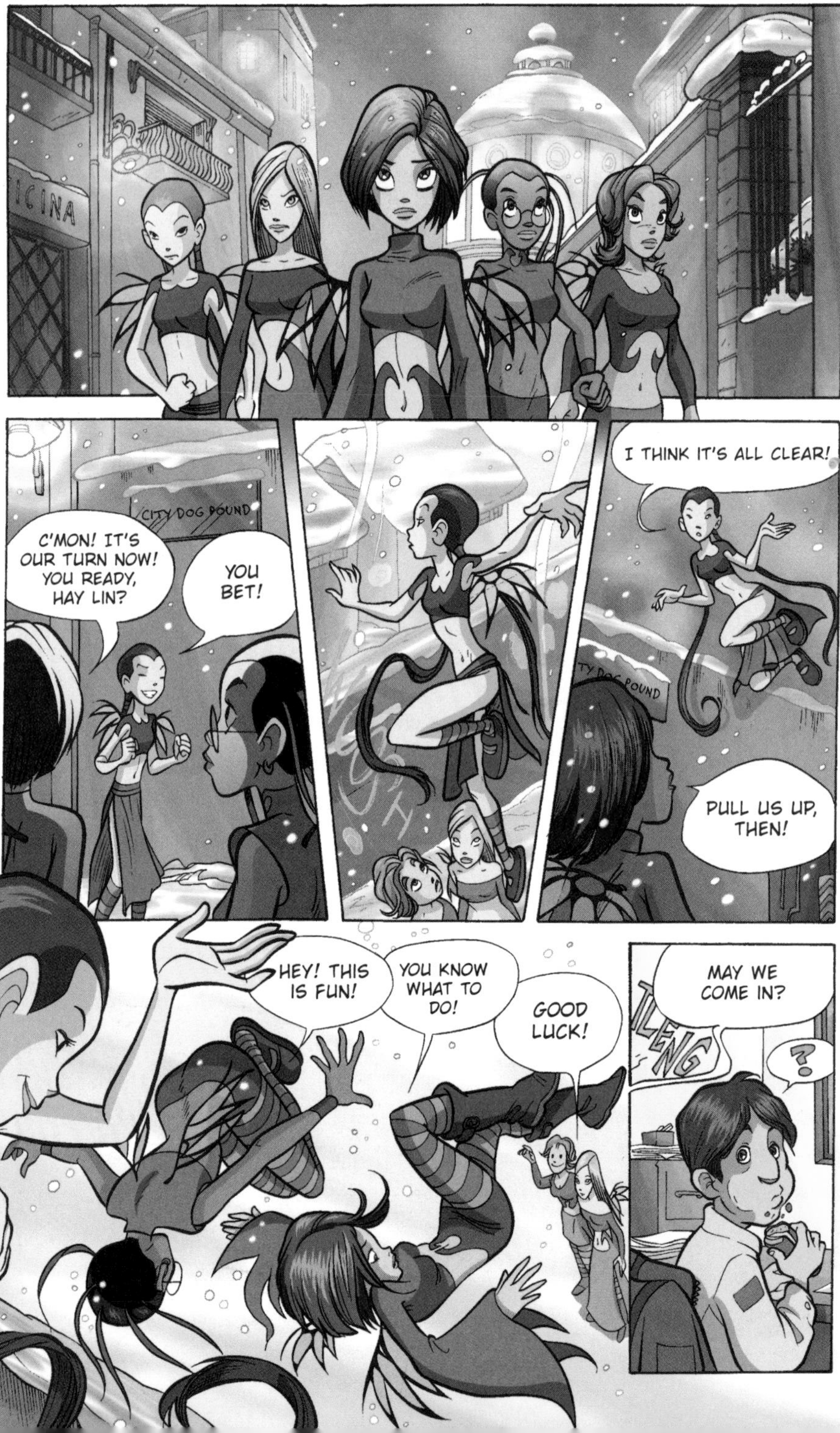

TICINA
CITY DOG POUND
C'MON! IT'S OUR TURN NOW! YOU READY, HAY LIN?
YOU BET!
I THINK IT'S ALL CLEAR!
PULL US UP, THEN!
HEY! THIS IS FUN!
YOU KNOW WHAT TO DO!
GOOD LUCK!
TLENG
MAY WE COME IN?
?

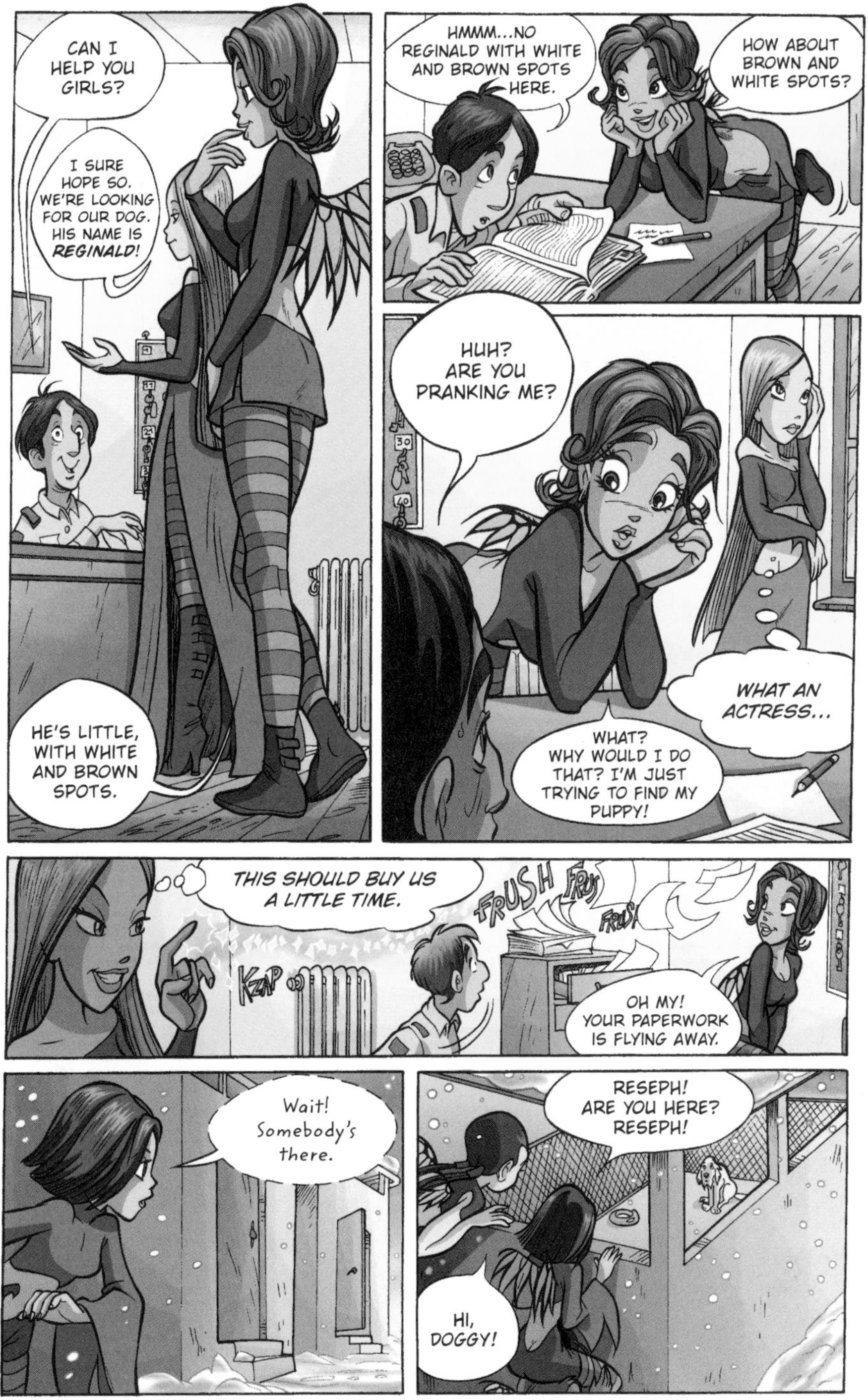
CAN I HELP YOU GIRLS?
I SURE HOPE SO. WE'RE LOOKING FOR OUR DOG. HIS NAME IS *REGINALD!*
HE'S LITTLE, WITH WHITE AND BROWN SPOTS.
HMMM...NO REGINALD WITH WHITE AND BROWN SPOTS HERE.
HOW ABOUT BROWN AND WHITE SPOTS?
HUH? ARE YOU PRANKING ME?
WHAT? WHY WOULD I DO THAT? I'M JUST TRYING TO FIND MY PUPPY!
WHAT AN ACTRESS...
THIS SHOULD BUY US A LITTLE TIME.
KZAP
FRUSH
FRUS
OH MY! YOUR PAPERWORK IS FLYING AWAY.
Wait! Somebody's there.
RESEPH! ARE YOU HERE? RESEPH!
HI, DOGGY!

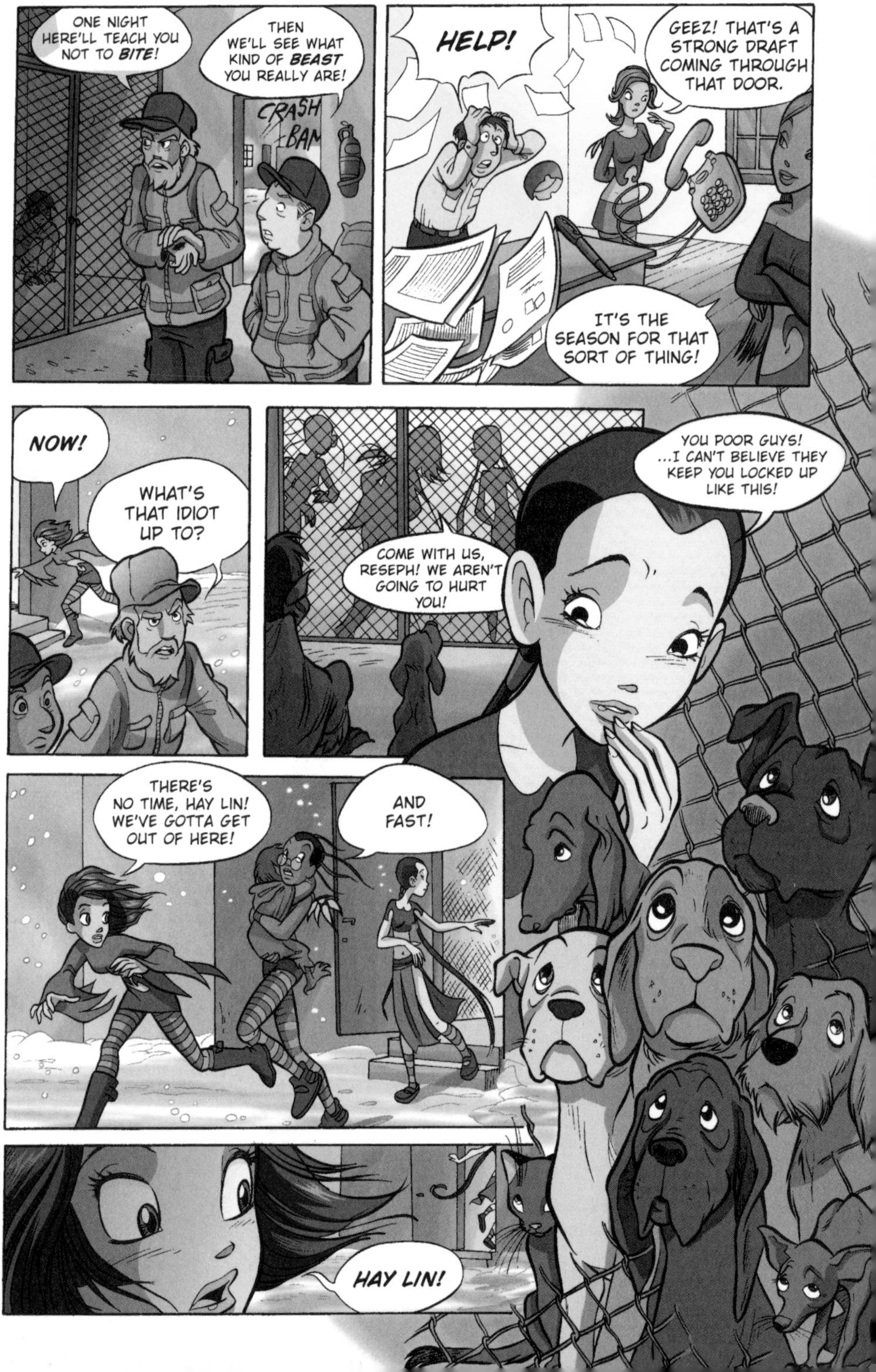
ONE NIGHT HERE'LL TEACH YOU NOT TO *BITE*!
THEN WE'LL SEE WHAT KIND OF *BEAST* YOU REALLY ARE!
CRASH
BAM
HELP!
GEEZ! THAT'S A STRONG DRAFT COMING THROUGH THAT DOOR.
IT'S THE SEASON FOR THAT SORT OF THING!
NOW!
WHAT'S THAT IDIOT UP TO?
COME WITH US, RESEPH! WE AREN'T GOING TO HURT YOU!
YOU POOR GUYS! ...I CAN'T BELIEVE THEY KEEP YOU LOCKED UP LIKE THIS!
THERE'S NO TIME, HAY LIN! WE'VE GOTTA GET OUT OF HERE!
AND FAST!
HAY LIN!

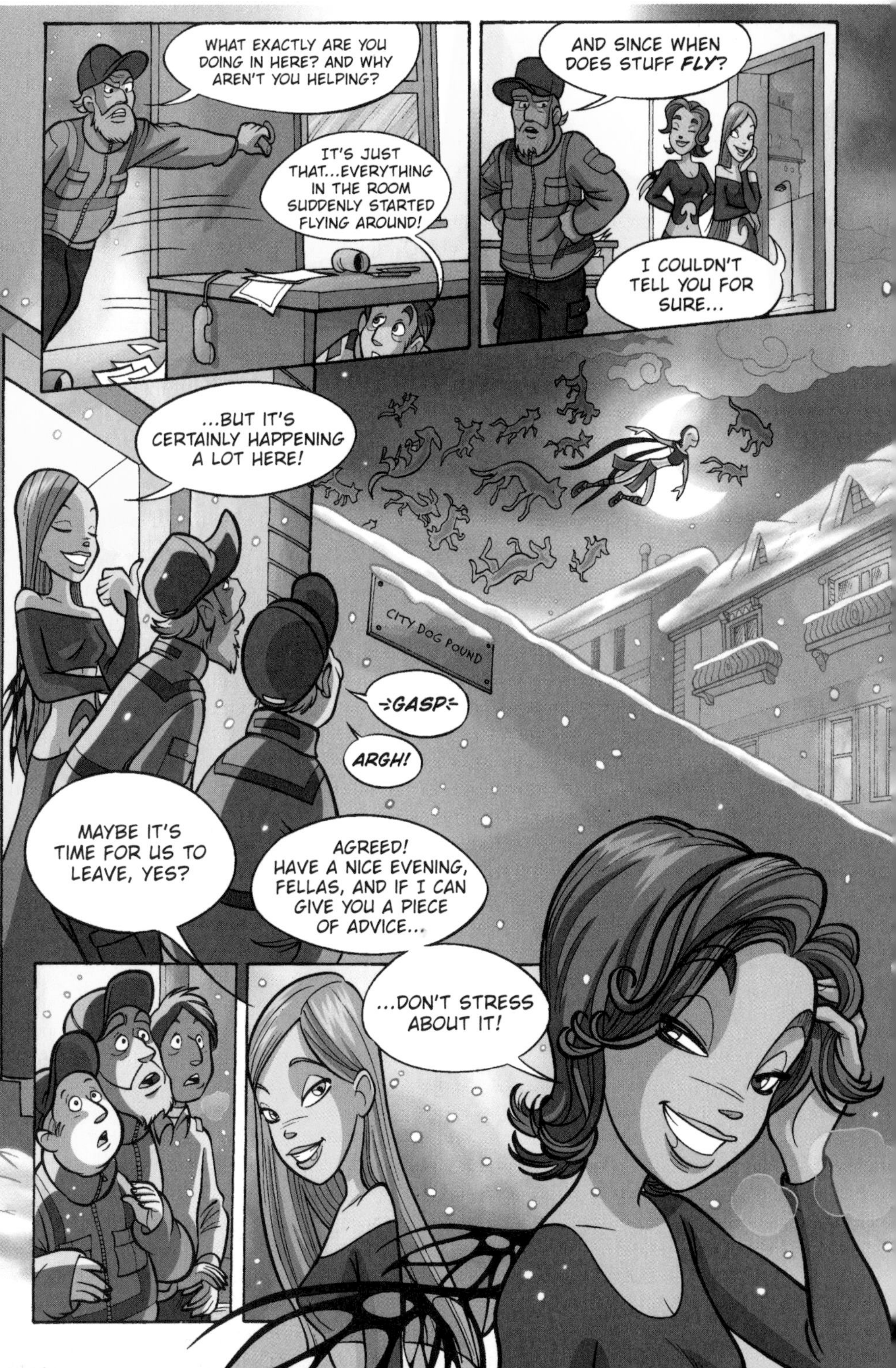
WHAT EXACTLY ARE YOU DOING IN HERE? AND WHY AREN'T YOU HELPING?
IT'S JUST THAT...EVERYTHING IN THE ROOM SUDDENLY STARTED FLYING AROUND!
AND SINCE WHEN DOES STUFF *FLY*?
I COULDN'T TELL YOU FOR SURE...
...BUT IT'S CERTAINLY HAPPENING A LOT HERE!
CITY DOG POUND
GASP
ARGH!
MAYBE IT'S TIME FOR US TO LEAVE, YES?
AGREED! HAVE A NICE EVENING, FELLAS, AND IF I CAN GIVE YOU A PIECE OF ADVICE...
...DON'T STRESS ABOUT IT!

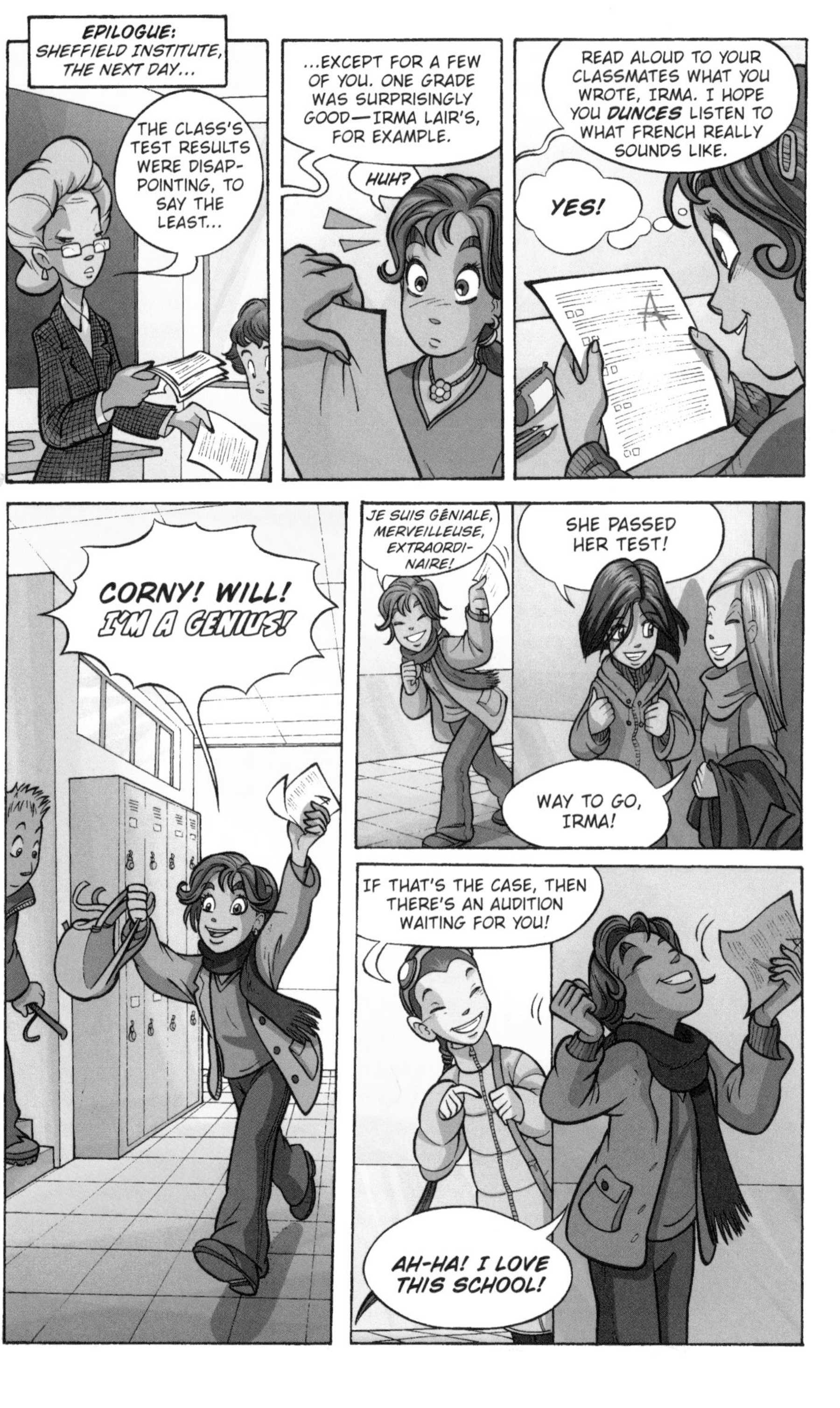
EPILOGUE: SHEFFIELD INSTITUTE, THE NEXT DAY...
THE CLASS'S TEST RESULTS WERE DISAPPOINTING, TO SAY THE LEAST...
...EXCEPT FOR A FEW OF YOU. ONE GRADE WAS SURPRISINGLY GOOD—IRMA LAIR'S, FOR EXAMPLE.
HUH?
READ ALOUD TO YOUR CLASSMATES WHAT YOU WROTE, IRMA. I HOPE YOU DUNCES LISTEN TO WHAT FRENCH REALLY SOUNDS LIKE.
YES!
A
CORNY! WILL! I'M A GENIUS!
JE SUIS GÊNIALE, MERVEILLEUSE, EXTRAORDINAIRE!
SHE PASSED HER TEST!
WAY TO GO, IRMA!
IF THAT'S THE CASE, THEN THERE'S AN AUDITION WAITING FOR YOU!
AH-HA! I LOVE THIS SCHOOL!

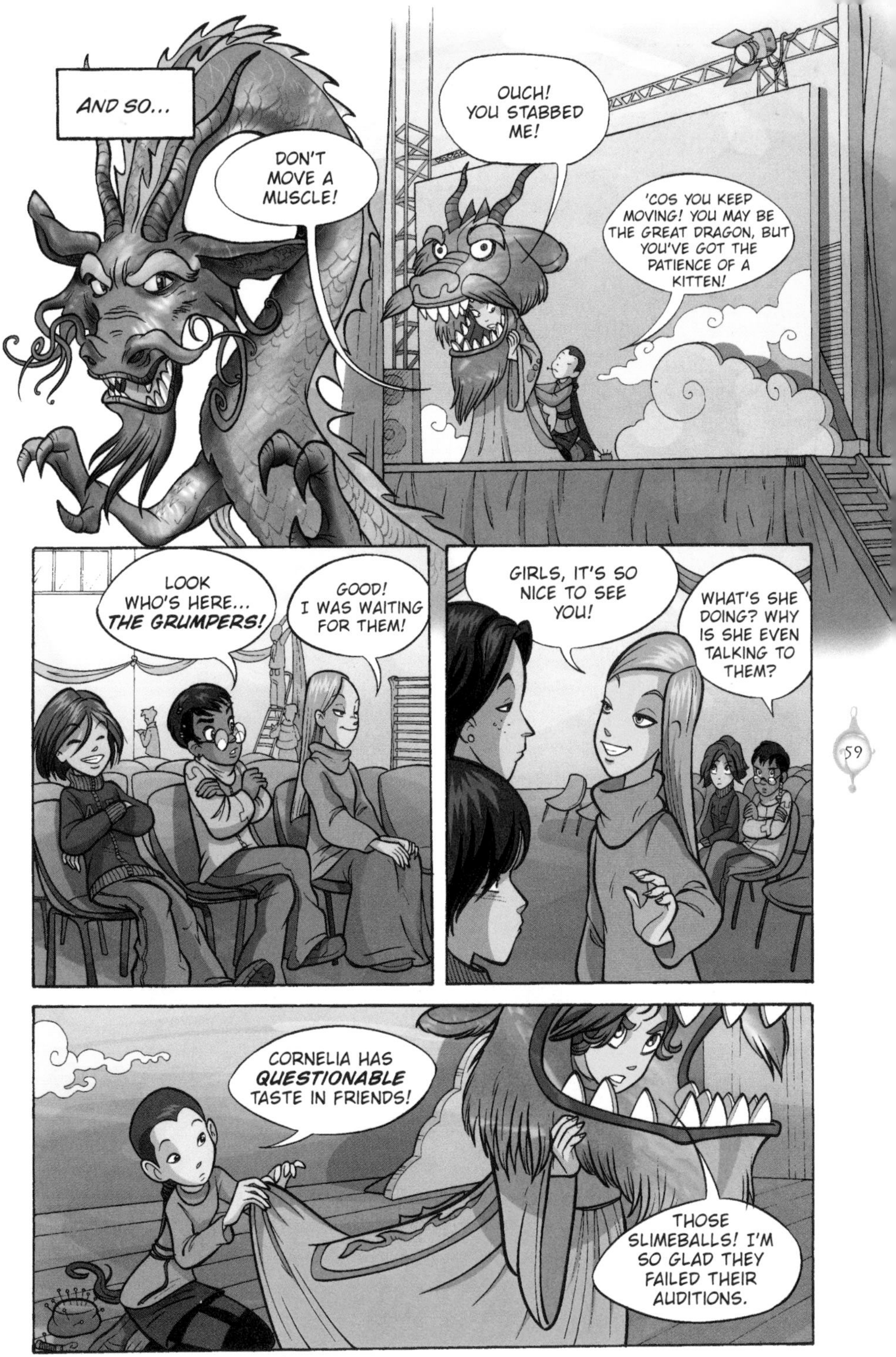
AND SO...
DON'T MOVE A MUSCLE!
OUCH! YOU STABBED ME!
'COS YOU KEEP MOVING! YOU MAY BE THE GREAT DRAGON, BUT YOU'VE GOT THE PATIENCE OF A KITTEN!
LOOK WHO'S HERE... *THE GRUMPERS!*
GOOD! I WAS WAITING FOR THEM!
GIRLS, IT'S SO NICE TO SEE YOU!
WHAT'S SHE DOING? WHY IS SHE EVEN TALKING TO THEM?
CORNELIA HAS ***QUESTIONABLE*** TASTE IN FRIENDS!
THOSE SLIMEBALLS! I'M SO GLAD THEY FAILED THEIR AUDITIONS.

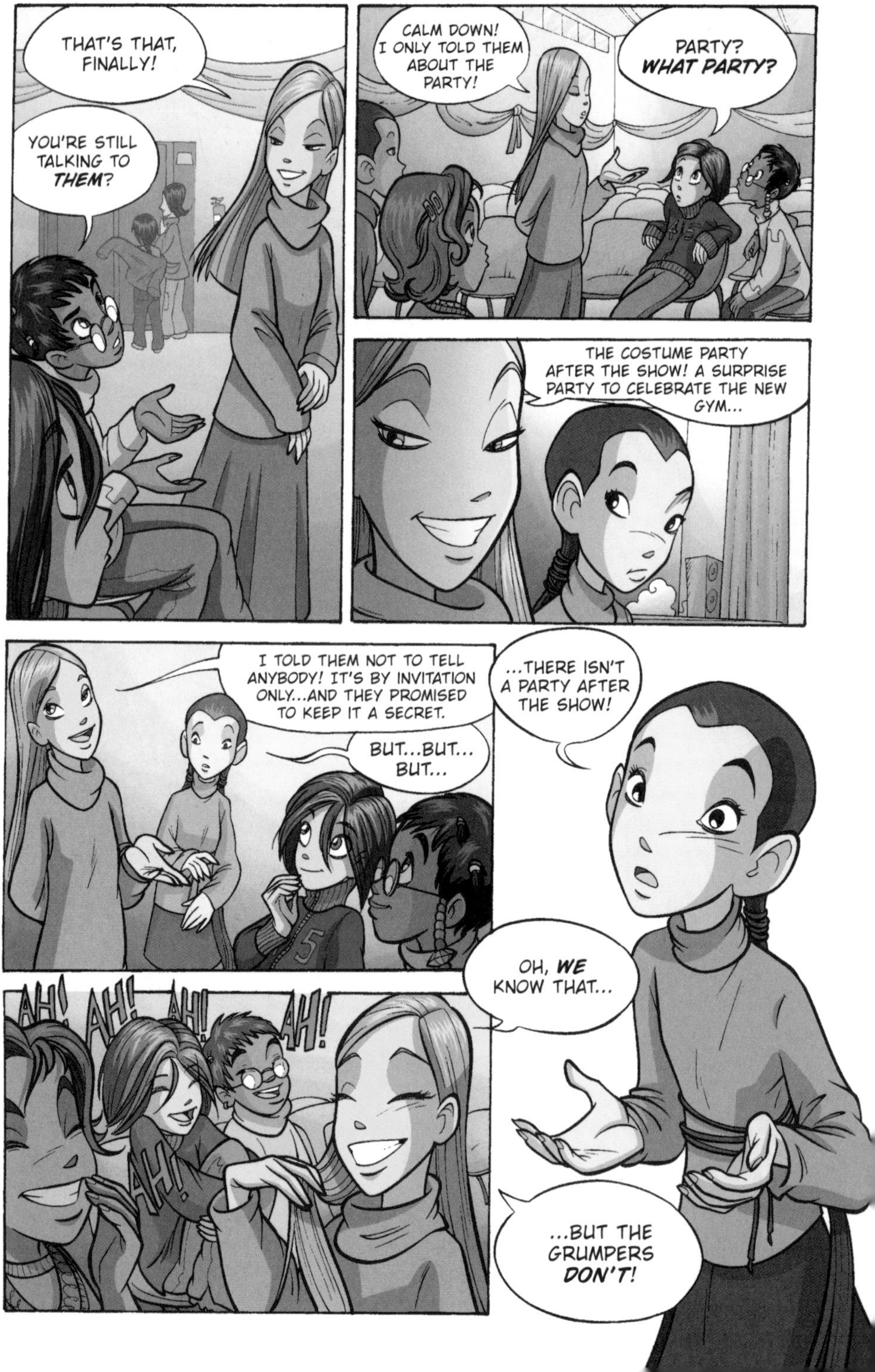
THAT'S THAT, FINALLY!
YOU'RE STILL TALKING TO *THEM*?
CALM DOWN! I ONLY TOLD THEM ABOUT THE PARTY!
PARTY? *WHAT PARTY?*
THE COSTUME PARTY AFTER THE SHOW! A SURPRISE PARTY TO CELEBRATE THE NEW GYM...
I TOLD THEM NOT TO TELL ANYBODY! IT'S BY INVITATION ONLY...AND THEY PROMISED TO KEEP IT A SECRET.
BUT...BUT... BUT...
...THERE ISN'T A PARTY AFTER THE SHOW!
OH, *WE* KNOW THAT...
AH! AH! AH! AH!
AH!
...BUT THE GRUMPERS *DON'T*!

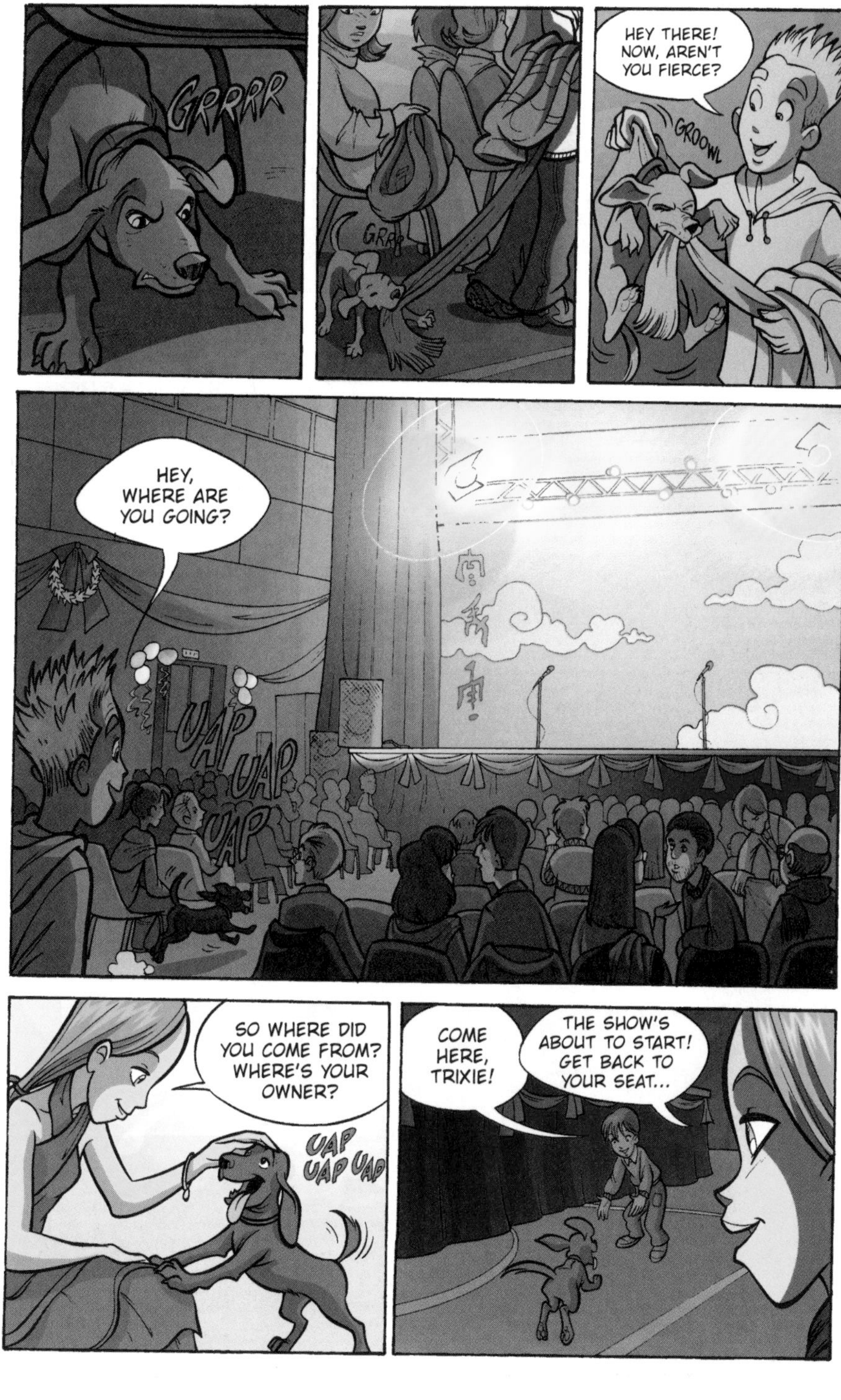
GRRRR
GRRR
HEY THERE! NOW, AREN'T YOU FIERCE?
GROOWL
HEY, WHERE ARE YOU GOING?
UAP UAP UAP
SO WHERE DID YOU COME FROM? WHERE'S YOUR OWNER?
UAP UAP UAP
COME HERE, TRIXIE!
THE SHOW'S ABOUT TO START! GET BACK TO YOUR SEAT...

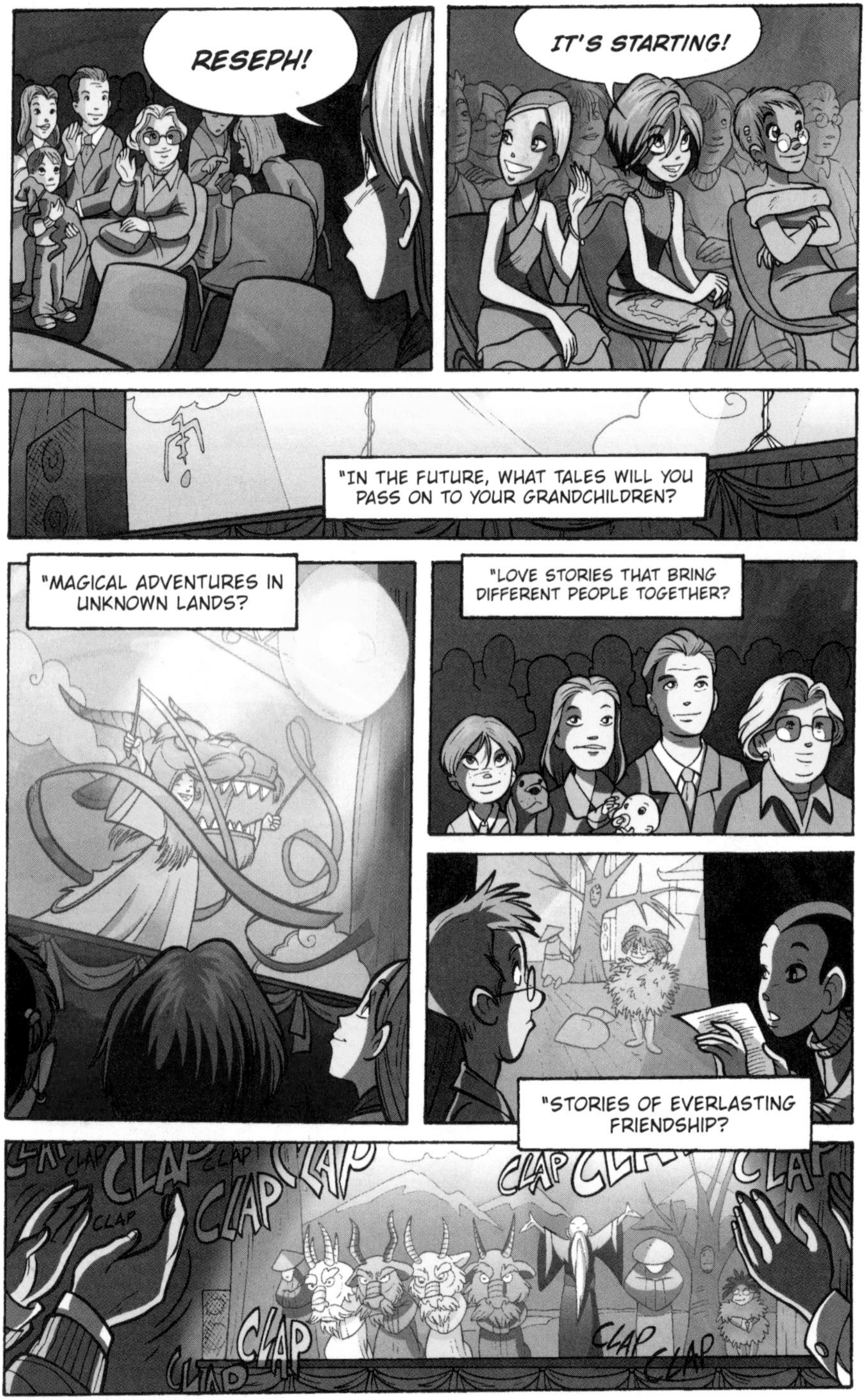
RESEPH!
IT'S STARTING!
"IN THE FUTURE, WHAT TALES WILL YOU PASS ON TO YOUR GRANDCHILDREN?
"MAGICAL ADVENTURES IN UNKNOWN LANDS?
"LOVE STORIES THAT BRING DIFFERENT PEOPLE TOGETHER?
"STORIES OF EVERLASTING FRIENDSHIP?
CLAP CLAP CLAP CLAP CLAP CLAP CLAP CLAP CLAP CLAP CLAP CLAP CLAP CLAP

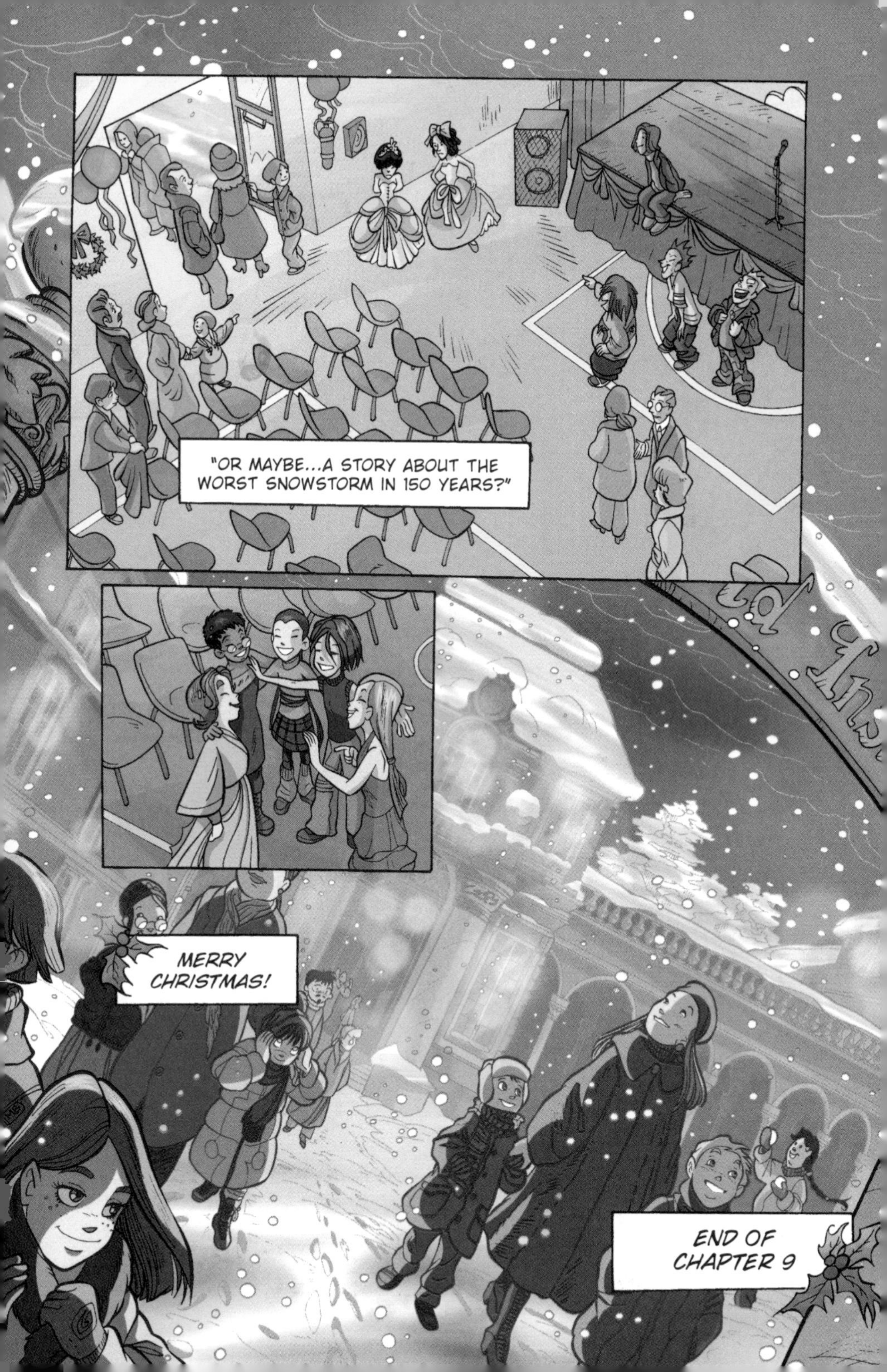
"OR MAYBE...A STORY ABOUT THE WORST SNOWSTORM IN 150 YEARS?"
MERRY CHRISTMAS!
END OF CHAPTER 9

W.i.t.c.h.

Will Irma Taranee Cornelia Hay Lin

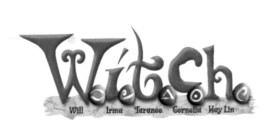

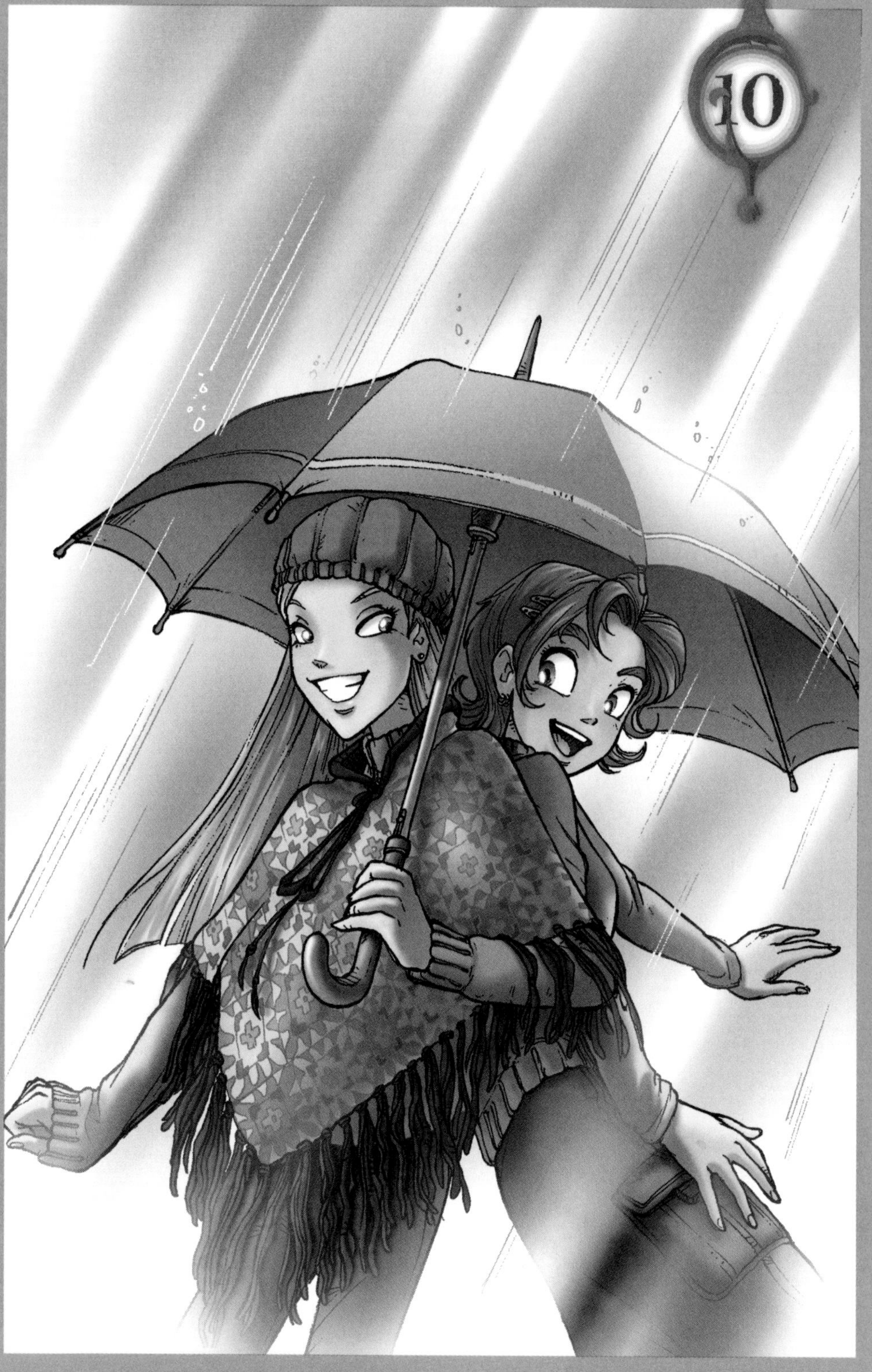
10

A BRIDGE BETWEEN TWO WORLDS

"Friendship is a dry passage in the pouring rain."

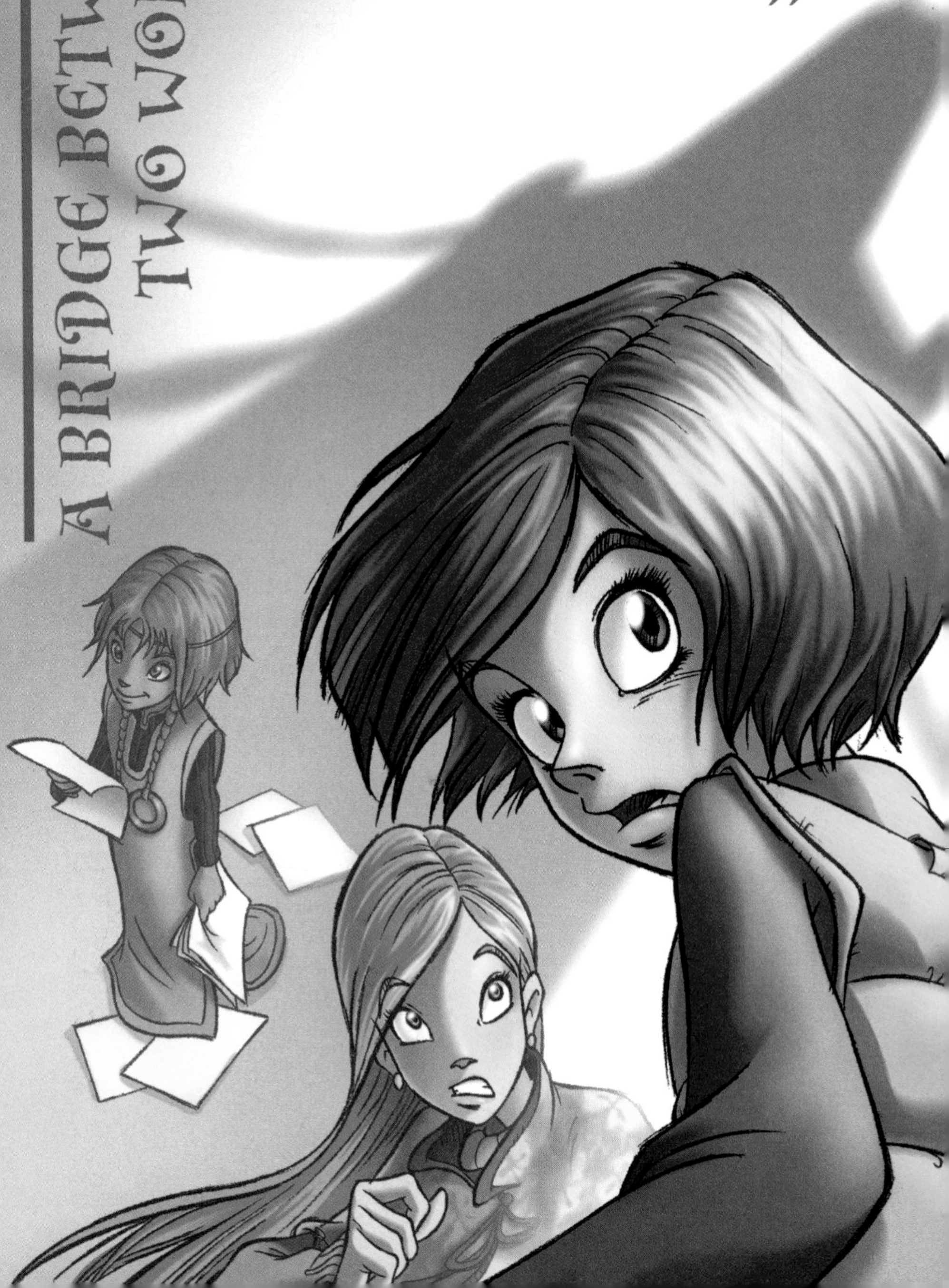

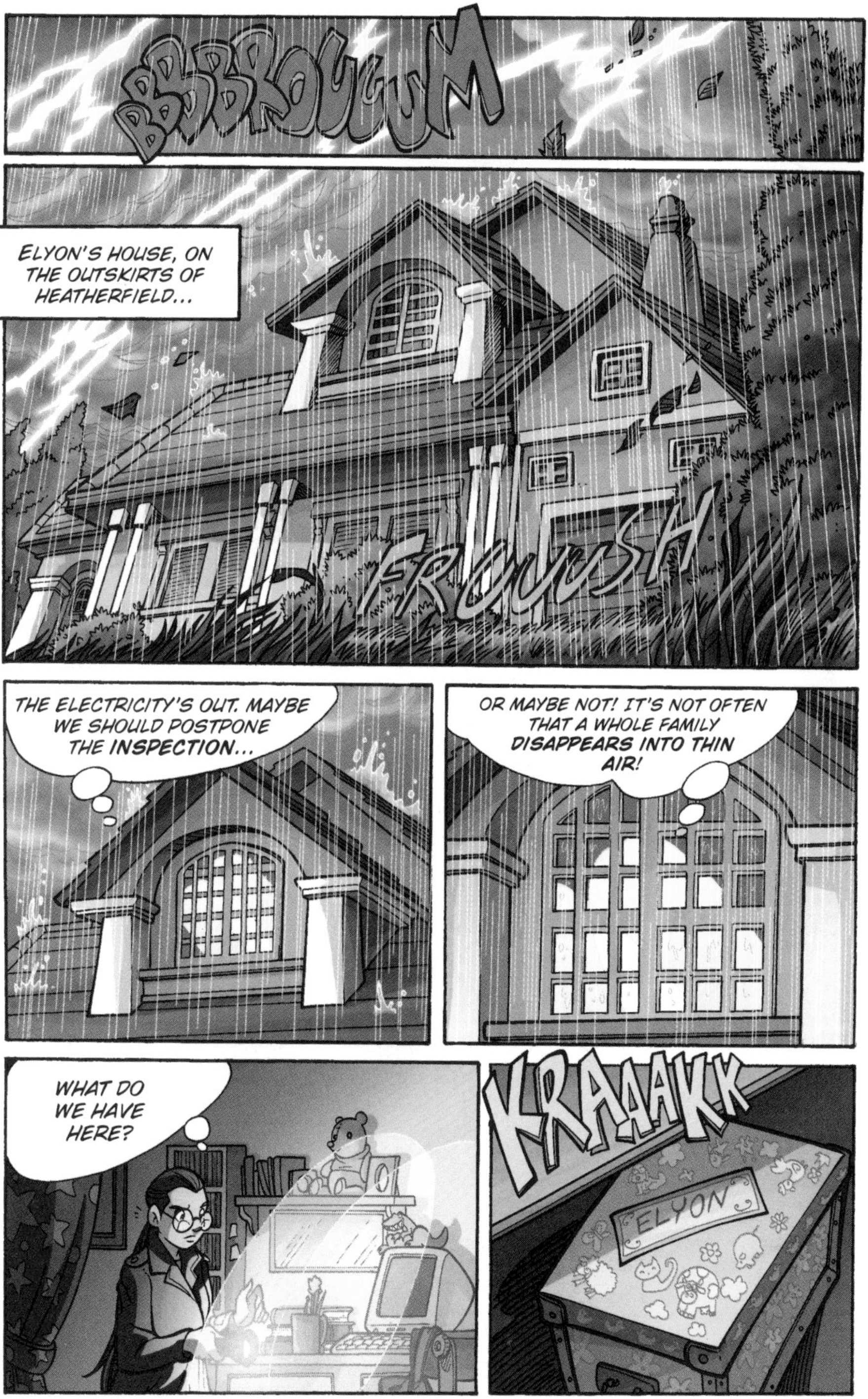
BBBBROUUUM
ELYON'S HOUSE, ON THE OUTSKIRTS OF HEATHERFIELD...
FROUUSH
THE ELECTRICITY'S OUT. MAYBE WE SHOULD POSTPONE THE INSPECTION...
OR MAYBE NOT! IT'S NOT OFTEN THAT A WHOLE FAMILY DISAPPEARS INTO THIN AIR!
WHAT DO WE HAVE HERE?
KRAAAKK
ELYON

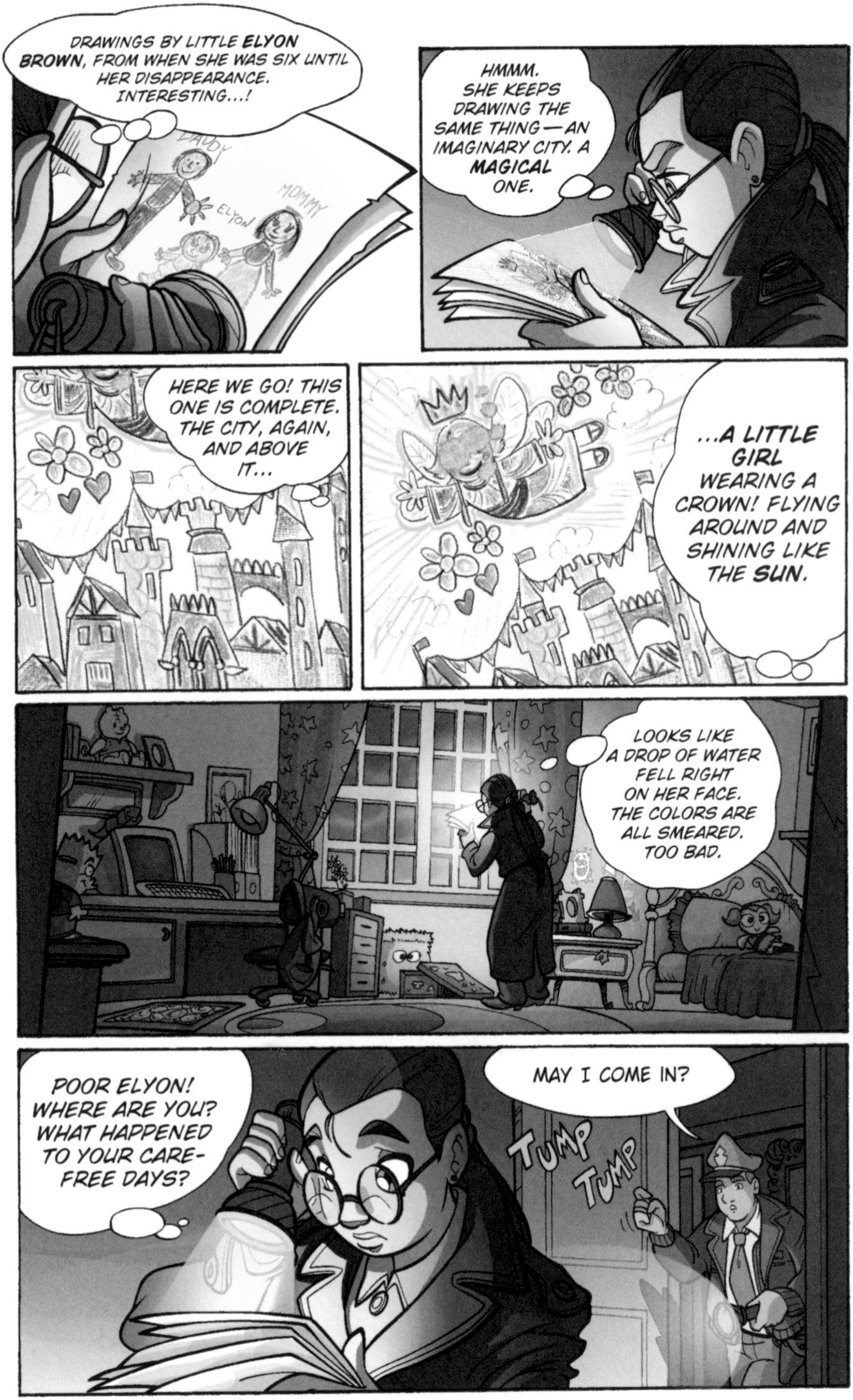
DRAWINGS BY LITTLE ELYON BROWN, FROM WHEN SHE WAS SIX UNTIL HER DISAPPEARANCE. INTERESTING...!
DADDY
MOMMY
ELYON
HMMM. SHE KEEPS DRAWING THE SAME THING—AN IMAGINARY CITY. A MAGICAL ONE.
HERE WE GO! THIS ONE IS COMPLETE. THE CITY, AGAIN, AND ABOVE IT...
...A LITTLE GIRL WEARING A CROWN! FLYING AROUND AND SHINING LIKE THE SUN.
LOOKS LIKE A DROP OF WATER FELL RIGHT ON HER FACE. THE COLORS ARE ALL SMEARED. TOO BAD.
POOR ELYON! WHERE ARE YOU? WHAT HAPPENED TO YOUR CARE-FREE DAYS?
MAY I COME IN?
TUMP TUMP

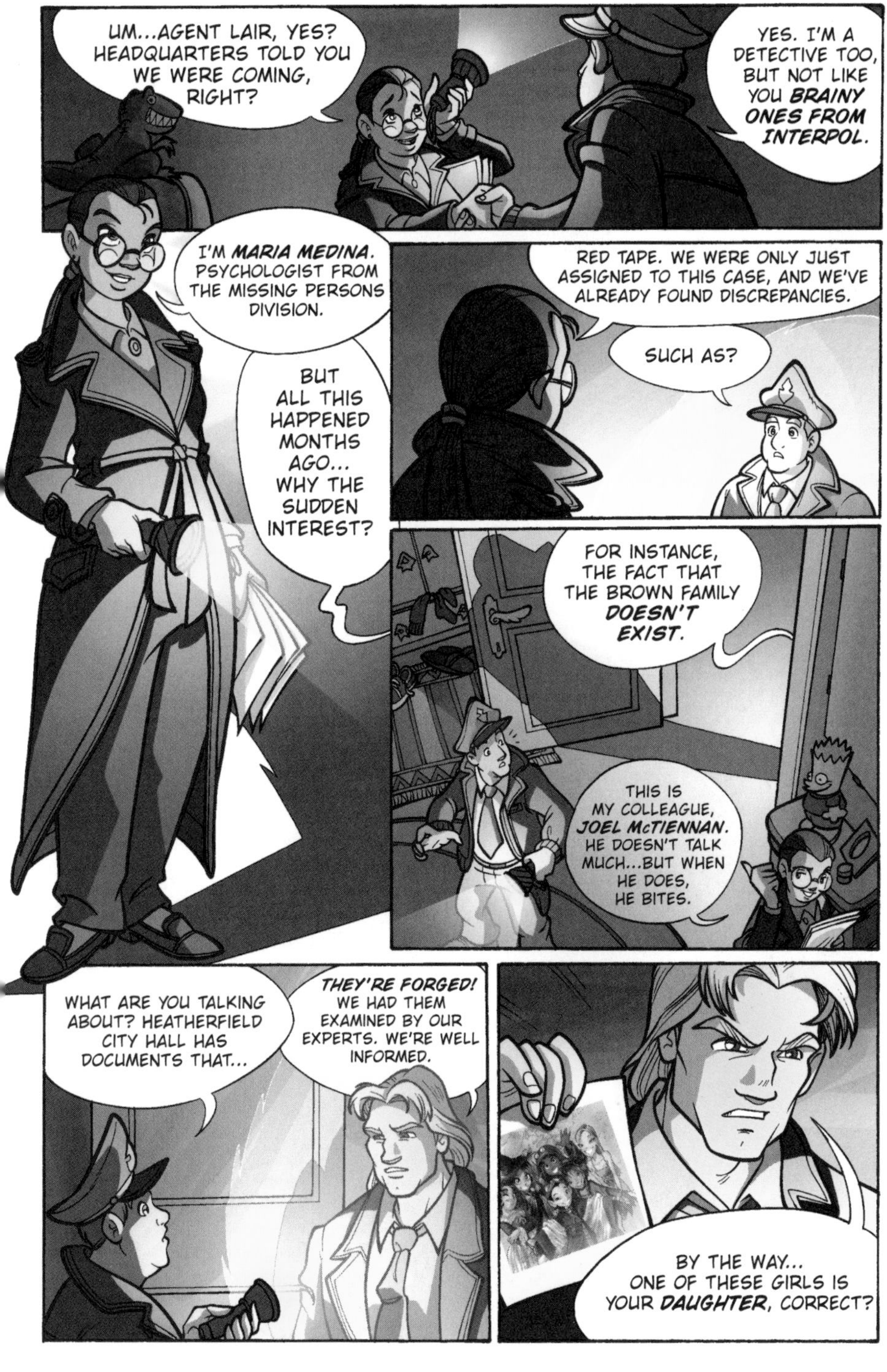
UM...AGENT LAIR, YES? HEADQUARTERS TOLD YOU WE WERE COMING, RIGHT?
YES. I'M A DETECTIVE TOO, BUT NOT LIKE YOU BRAINY ONES FROM INTERPOL.
I'M MARIA MEDINA. PSYCHOLOGIST FROM THE MISSING PERSONS DIVISION.
BUT ALL THIS HAPPENED MONTHS AGO... WHY THE SUDDEN INTEREST?
RED TAPE. WE WERE ONLY JUST ASSIGNED TO THIS CASE, AND WE'VE ALREADY FOUND DISCREPANCIES.
SUCH AS?
FOR INSTANCE, THE FACT THAT THE BROWN FAMILY DOESN'T EXIST.
THIS IS MY COLLEAGUE, JOEL McTIENNAN. HE DOESN'T TALK MUCH...BUT WHEN HE DOES, HE BITES.
WHAT ARE YOU TALKING ABOUT? HEATHERFIELD CITY HALL HAS DOCUMENTS THAT...
THEY'RE FORGED! WE HAD THEM EXAMINED BY OUR EXPERTS. WE'RE WELL INFORMED.
BY THE WAY... ONE OF THESE GIRLS IS YOUR DAUGHTER, CORRECT?

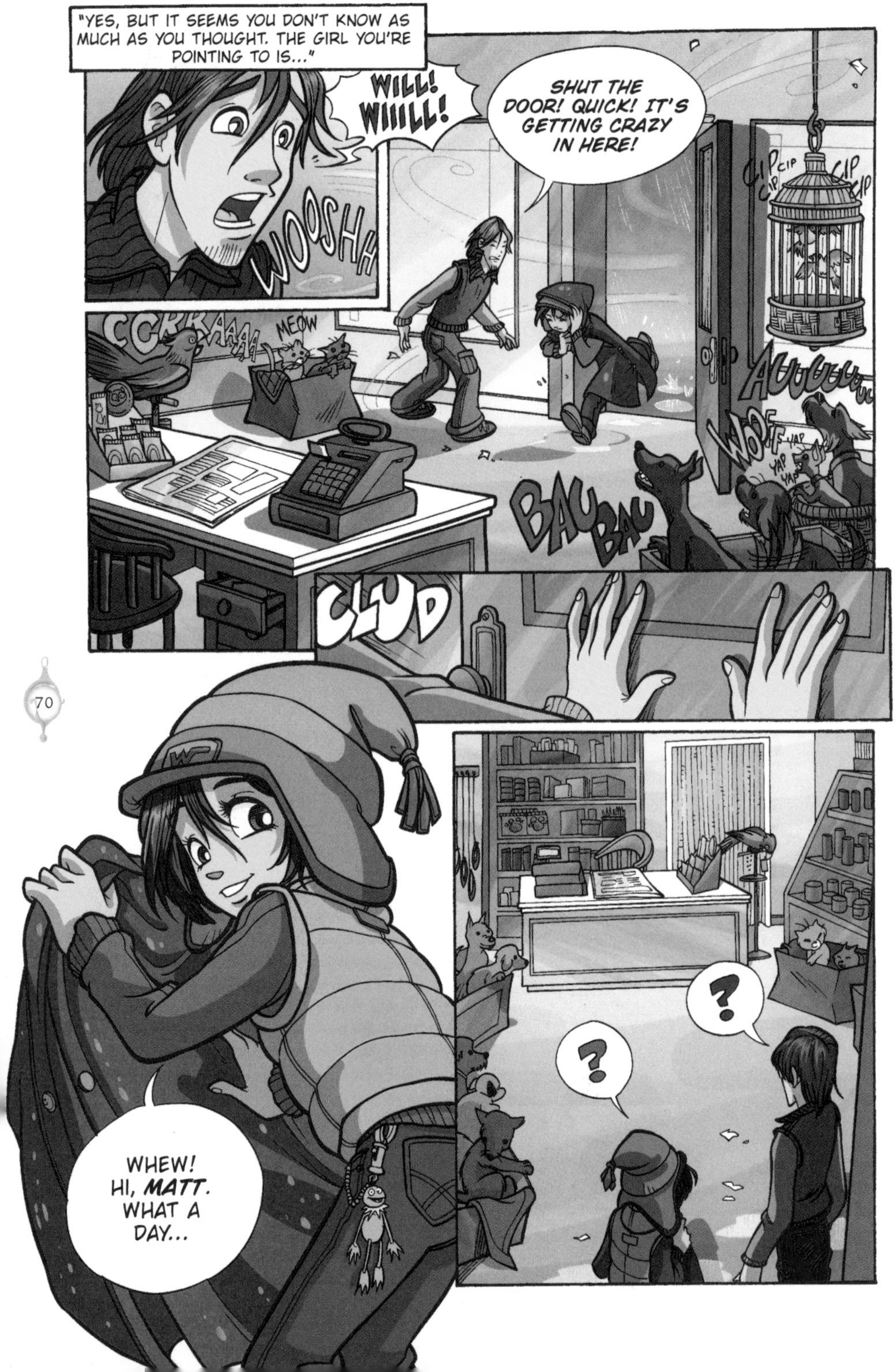
"YES, BUT IT SEEMS YOU DON'T KNOW AS MUCH AS YOU THOUGHT. THE GIRL YOU'RE POINTING TO IS..."
WILL! WIIIILL!
SHUT THE DOOR! QUICK! IT'S GETTING CRAZY IN HERE!
WOOSHH
CIP CIP CIP CIP
CCRRAAAA
MEOW
AUUUUU
WOOF
YAP YAP YAP
BAU BAU
CLUD
WHEW! HI, *MATT*. WHAT A DAY...
?
?

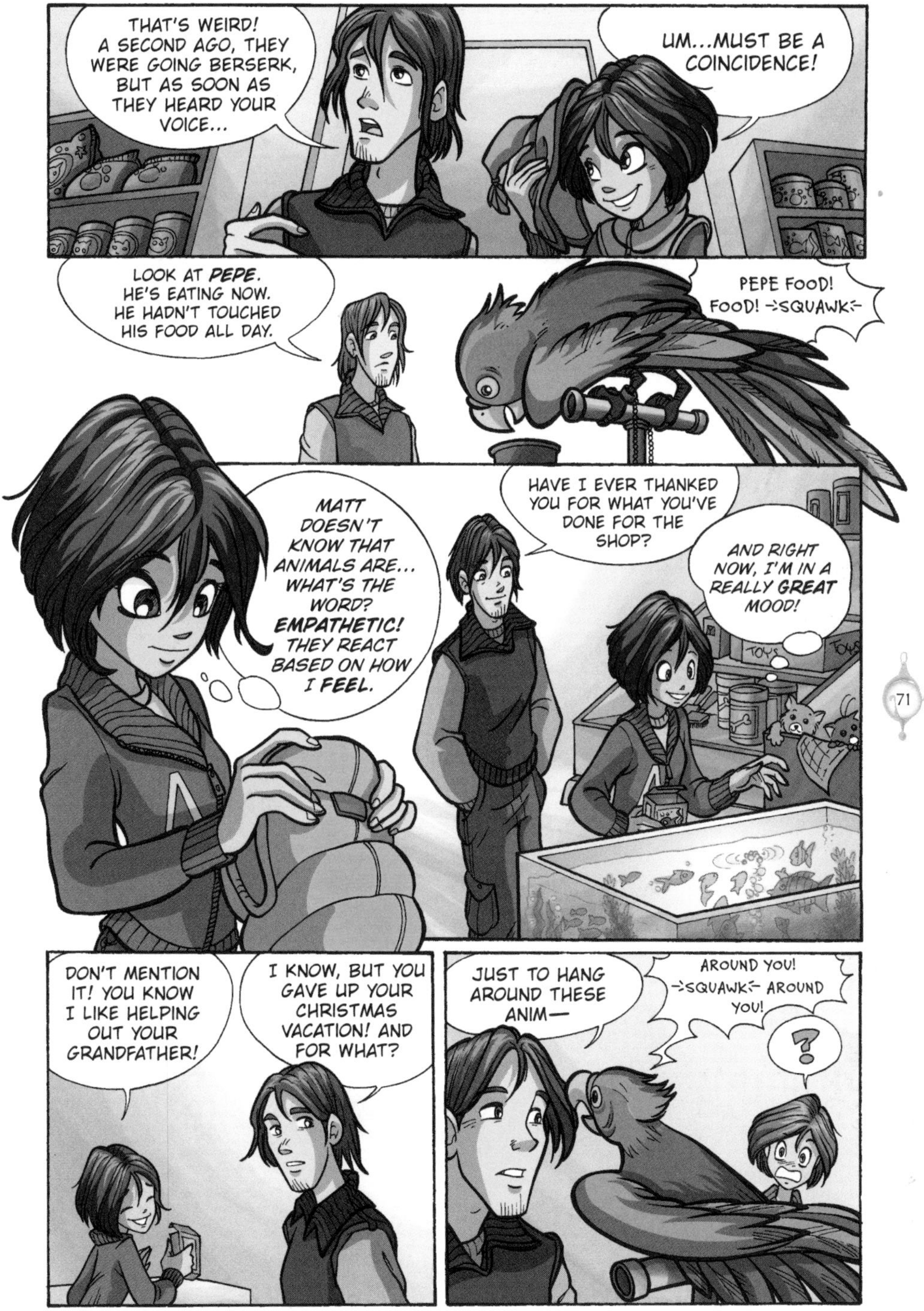
THAT'S WEIRD! A SECOND AGO, THEY WERE GOING BERSERK, BUT AS SOON AS THEY HEARD YOUR VOICE...
UM...MUST BE A COINCIDENCE!
LOOK AT PEPE. HE'S EATING NOW. HE HADN'T TOUCHED HIS FOOD ALL DAY.
PEPE FOOD! FOOD! SQUAWK
MATT DOESN'T KNOW THAT ANIMALS ARE... WHAT'S THE WORD? EMPATHETIC! THEY REACT BASED ON HOW I FEEL.
HAVE I EVER THANKED YOU FOR WHAT YOU'VE DONE FOR THE SHOP?
AND RIGHT NOW, I'M IN A REALLY GREAT MOOD!
DON'T MENTION IT! YOU KNOW I LIKE HELPING OUT YOUR GRANDFATHER!
I KNOW, BUT YOU GAVE UP YOUR CHRISTMAS VACATION! AND FOR WHAT?
JUST TO HANG AROUND THESE ANIM—
AROUND YOU! SQUAWK AROUND YOU!
?

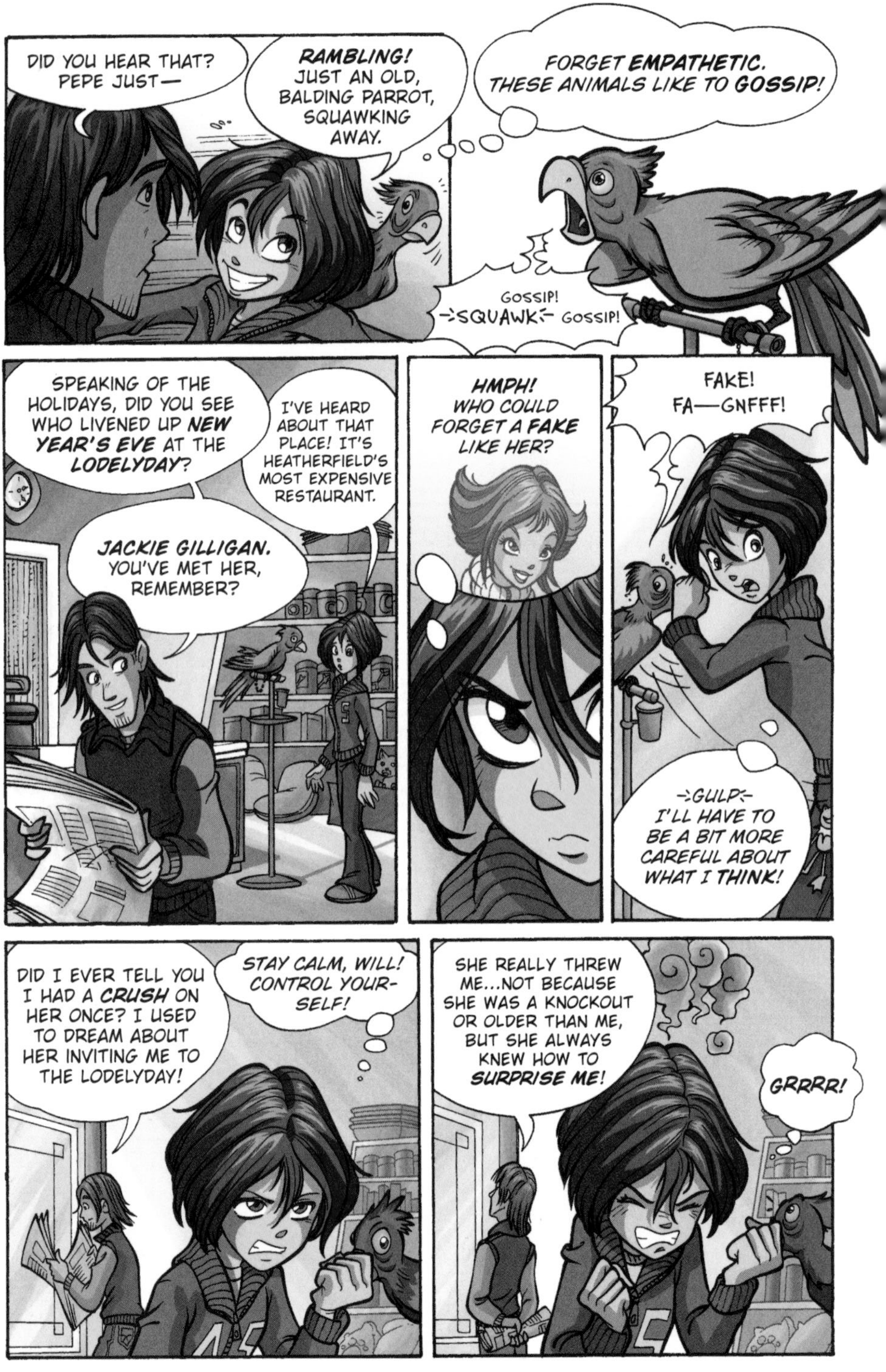
DID YOU HEAR THAT? PEPE JUST—
RAMBLING! JUST AN OLD, BALDING PARROT, SQUAWKING AWAY.
FORGET EMPATHETIC. THESE ANIMALS LIKE TO GOSSIP!
GOSSIP! -SQUAWK- GOSSIP!
SPEAKING OF THE HOLIDAYS, DID YOU SEE WHO LIVENED UP NEW YEAR'S EVE AT THE LODELYDAY?
I'VE HEARD ABOUT THAT PLACE! IT'S HEATHERFIELD'S MOST EXPENSIVE RESTAURANT.
JACKIE GILLIGAN. YOU'VE MET HER, REMEMBER?
HMPH! WHO COULD FORGET A FAKE LIKE HER?
FAKE! FA—GNFFF!
-GULP- I'LL HAVE TO BE A BIT MORE CAREFUL ABOUT WHAT I THINK!
DID I EVER TELL YOU I HAD A CRUSH ON HER ONCE? I USED TO DREAM ABOUT HER INVITING ME TO THE LODELYDAY!
STAY CALM, WILL! CONTROL YOURSELF!
SHE REALLY THREW ME...NOT BECAUSE SHE WAS A KNOCKOUT OR OLDER THAN ME, BUT SHE ALWAYS KNEW HOW TO SURPRISE ME!
GRRRR!

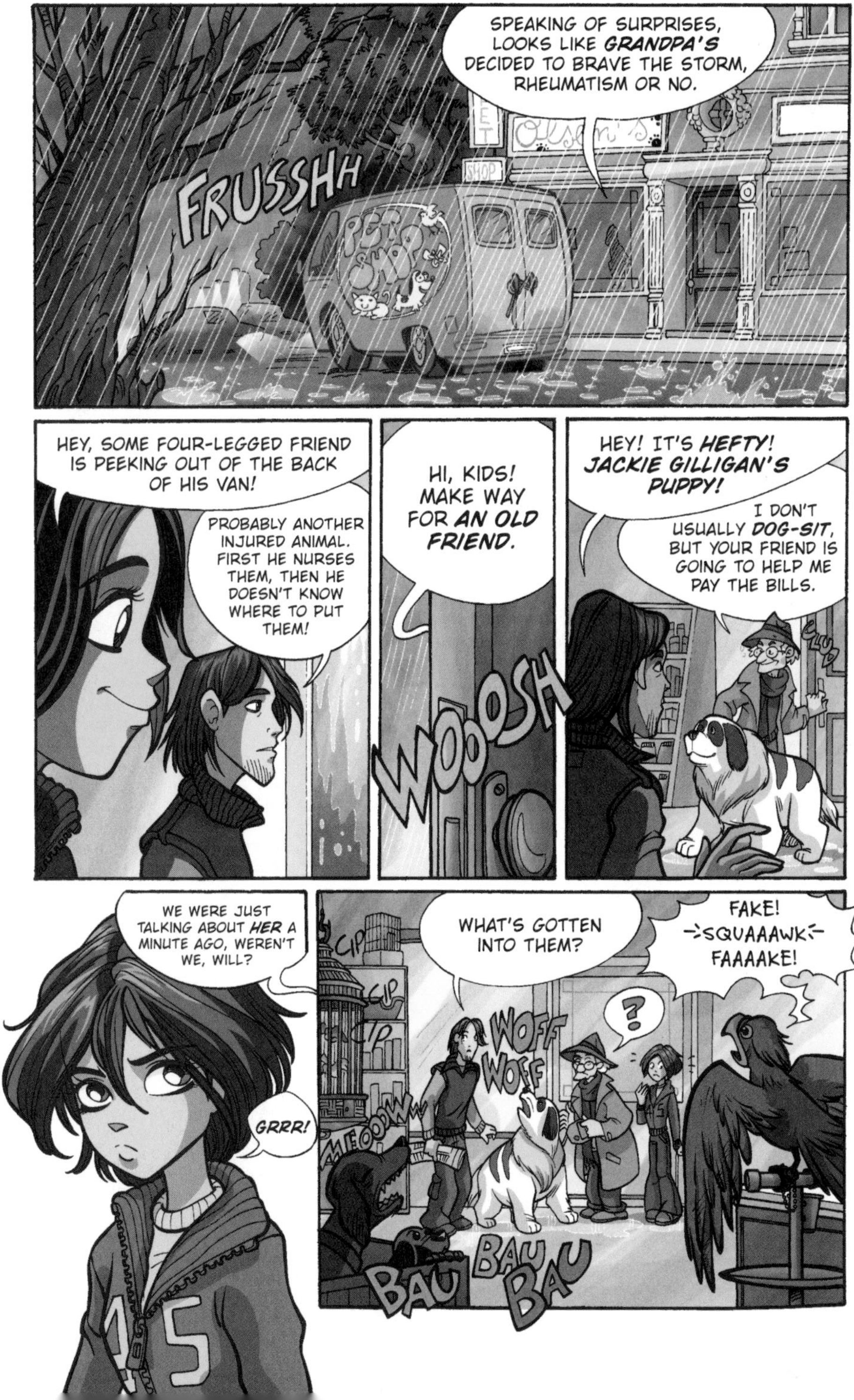
SPEAKING OF SURPRISES, LOOKS LIKE GRANDPA'S DECIDED TO BRAVE THE STORM, RHEUMATISM OR NO.
FRUSSHH
PET SHOP
SHOP
HEY, SOME FOUR-LEGGED FRIEND IS PEEKING OUT OF THE BACK OF HIS VAN!
PROBABLY ANOTHER INJURED ANIMAL. FIRST HE NURSES THEM, THEN HE DOESN'T KNOW WHERE TO PUT THEM!
HI, KIDS! MAKE WAY FOR AN OLD FRIEND.
WOOOSH
HEY! IT'S HEFTY! JACKIE GILLIGAN'S PUPPY!
I DON'T USUALLY DOG-SIT, BUT YOUR FRIEND IS GOING TO HELP ME PAY THE BILLS.
WE WERE JUST TALKING ABOUT HER A MINUTE AGO, WEREN'T WE, WILL?
GRRR!
WHAT'S GOTTEN INTO THEM?
FAKE! SQUAAAWK FAAAAKE!
?
WOFF WOFF
MEOOOWW
BAU BAU BAU BAU

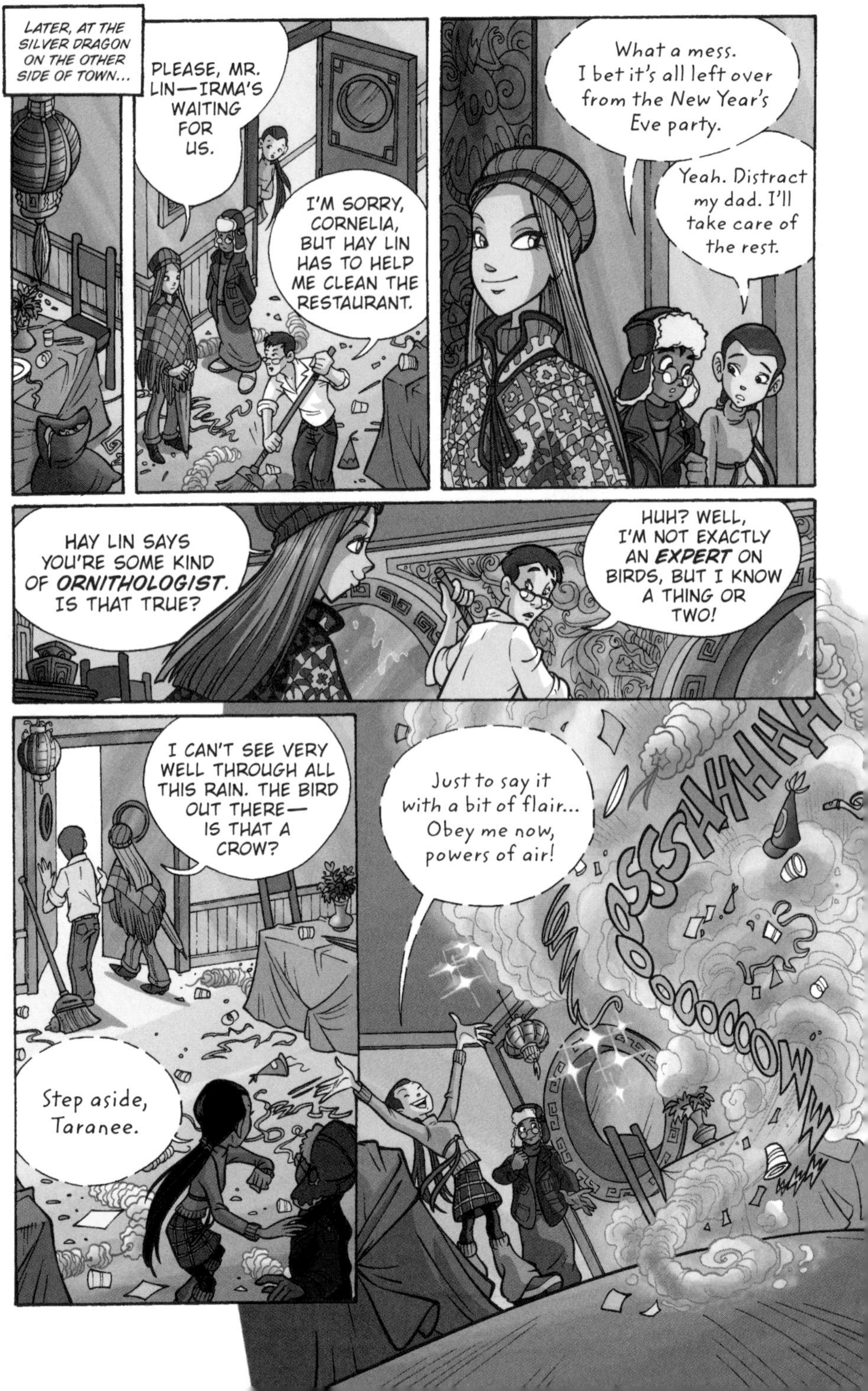

LATER, AT THE SILVER DRAGON ON THE OTHER SIDE OF TOWN...
PLEASE, MR. LIN—IRMA'S WAITING FOR US.
I'M SORRY, CORNELIA, BUT HAY LIN HAS TO HELP ME CLEAN THE RESTAURANT.
What a mess. I bet it's all left over from the New Year's Eve party.
Yeah. Distract my dad. I'll take care of the rest.
HAY LIN SAYS YOU'RE SOME KIND OF ORNITHOLOGIST. IS THAT TRUE?
HUH? WELL, I'M NOT EXACTLY AN EXPERT ON BIRDS, BUT I KNOW A THING OR TWO!
I CAN'T SEE VERY WELL THROUGH ALL THIS RAIN. THE BIRD OUT THERE— IS THAT A CROW?
Step aside, Taranee.
Just to say it with a bit of flair... Obey me now, powers of air!
WHOOOOOOOOOSSSSHHHHH

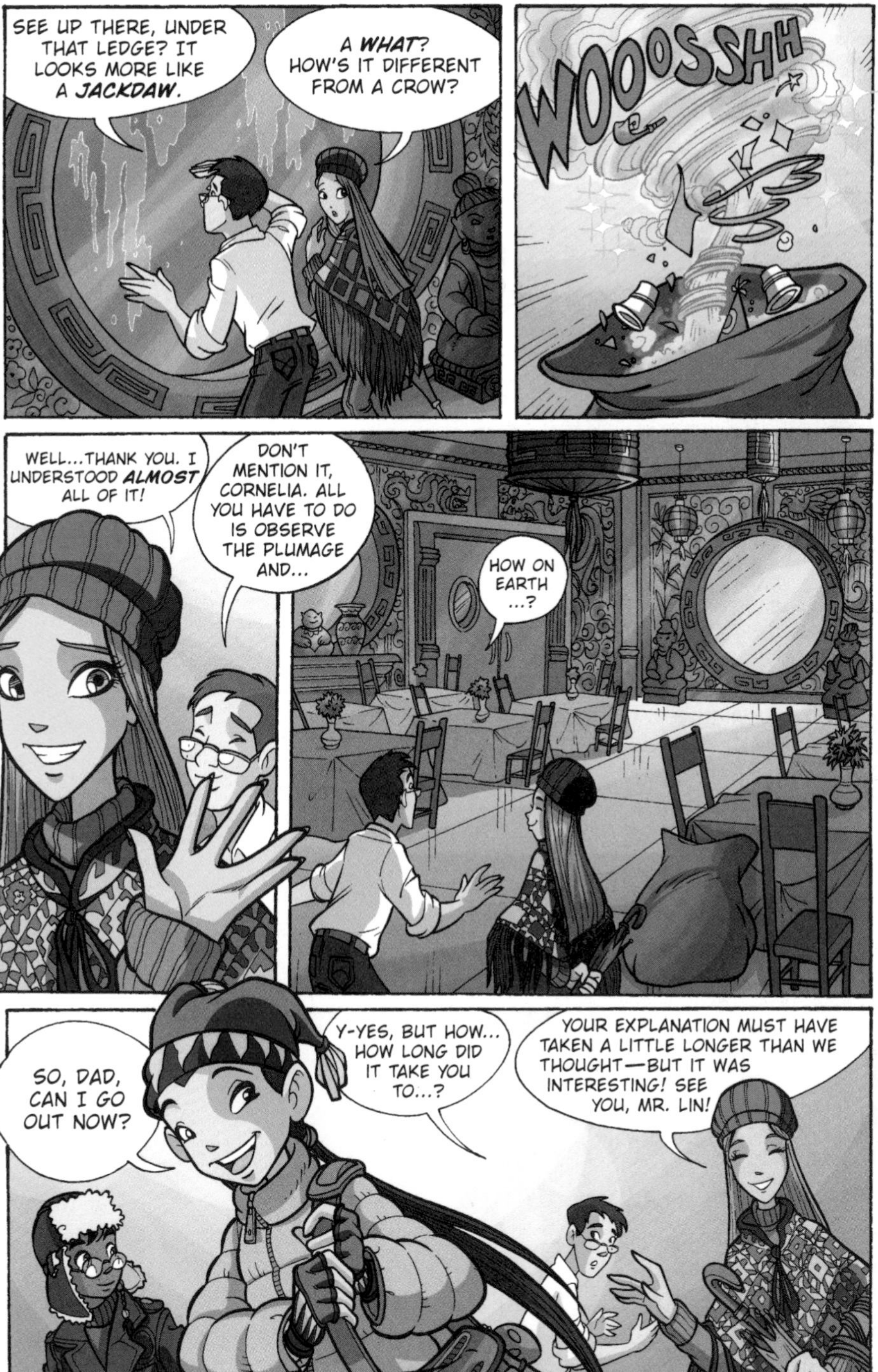

SEE UP THERE, UNDER THAT LEDGE? IT LOOKS MORE LIKE A JACKDAW.
A WHAT? HOW'S IT DIFFERENT FROM A CROW?
WOOOSSHH
WELL...THANK YOU. I UNDERSTOOD ALMOST ALL OF IT!
DON'T MENTION IT, CORNELIA. ALL YOU HAVE TO DO IS OBSERVE THE PLUMAGE AND...
HOW ON EARTH ...?
SO, DAD, CAN I GO OUT NOW?
Y-YES, BUT HOW... HOW LONG DID IT TAKE YOU TO...?
YOUR EXPLANATION MUST HAVE TAKEN A LITTLE LONGER THAN WE THOUGHT—BUT IT WAS INTERESTING! SEE YOU, MR. LIN!

FRUUUSSHH

THE SILVER DRACON

CHINESE RESTAURANT

THE WEATHER'S SO GROSS! I WISH IRMA WAS HERE TO USE HER WATER POWERS.

LET IT RAIN. NO NEED TO CRY! MY UMBRELLA WILL KEEP US DRY!

NO OFFENSE, CORNELIA, BUT IRMA'S BETTER WITH RHYMES AND RAIN!

SO, WHAT? ARE YOU NEW MEMBERS OF THE IRMA FAN CLUB OR SOMETHING?

PROBLEM SOLVED!

IT ONLY TOOK A PHONE CALL TO FIND A WAY TO **AVOID** ALL THIS RAIN.

HI! HOP IN IF YOU CAN MANAGE TO FIND SOME ROOM BETWEEN MY **SURFBOARDS**.

OH NO! IT'S TARANEE'S BROTHER, PETER!

SCREEEEKK

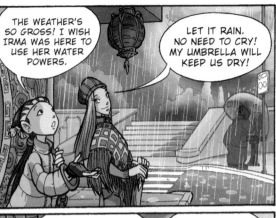

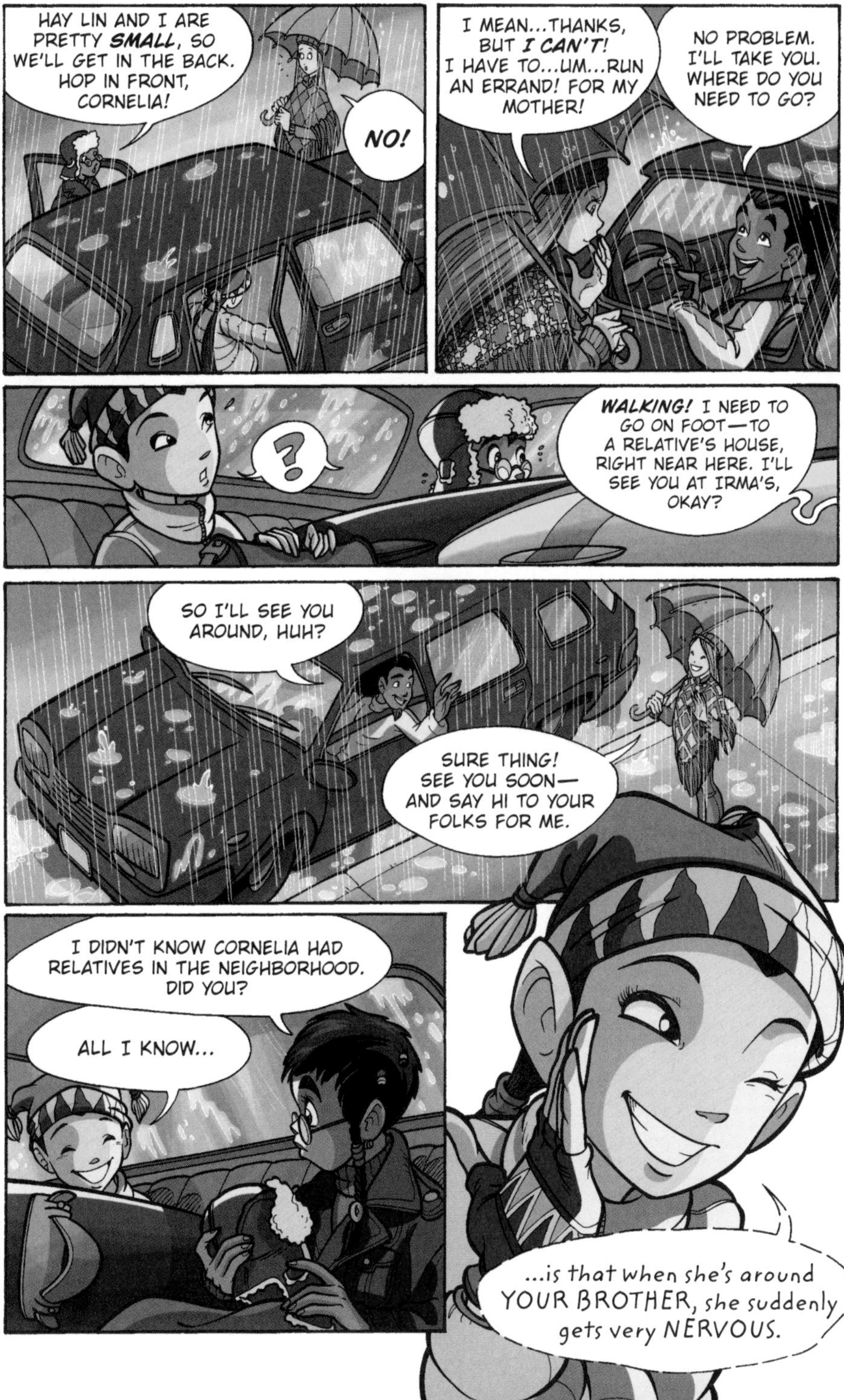
HAY LIN AND I ARE PRETTY SMALL, SO WE'LL GET IN THE BACK. HOP IN FRONT, CORNELIA!
NO!
I MEAN...THANKS, BUT I CAN'T! I HAVE TO...UM...RUN AN ERRAND! FOR MY MOTHER!
NO PROBLEM. I'LL TAKE YOU. WHERE DO YOU NEED TO GO?
?
WALKING! I NEED TO GO ON FOOT—TO A RELATIVE'S HOUSE, RIGHT NEAR HERE. I'LL SEE YOU AT IRMA'S, OKAY?
SO I'LL SEE YOU AROUND, HUH?
SURE THING! SEE YOU SOON—AND SAY HI TO YOUR FOLKS FOR ME.
I DIDN'T KNOW CORNELIA HAD RELATIVES IN THE NEIGHBORHOOD. DID YOU?
ALL I KNOW...
...is that when she's around YOUR BROTHER, she suddenly gets very NERVOUS.

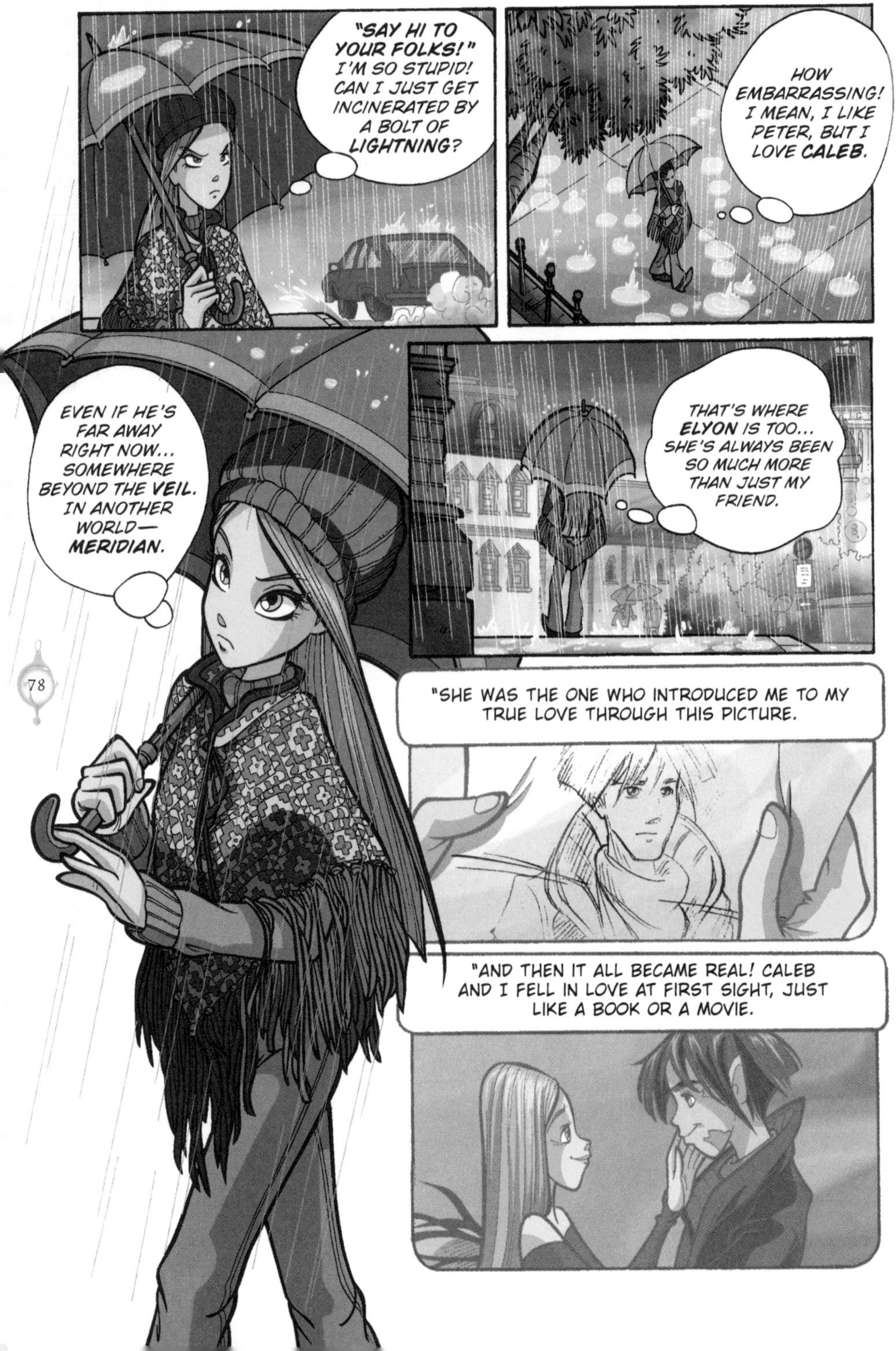
"SAY HI TO YOUR FOLKS!" I'M SO STUPID! CAN I JUST GET INCINERATED BY A BOLT OF LIGHTNING?
HOW EMBARRASSING! I MEAN, I LIKE PETER, BUT I LOVE CALEB.
EVEN IF HE'S FAR AWAY RIGHT NOW... SOMEWHERE BEYOND THE VEIL. IN ANOTHER WORLD— MERIDIAN.
THAT'S WHERE ELYON IS TOO... SHE'S ALWAYS BEEN SO MUCH MORE THAN JUST MY FRIEND.
"SHE WAS THE ONE WHO INTRODUCED ME TO MY TRUE LOVE THROUGH THIS PICTURE.
"AND THEN IT ALL BECAME REAL! CALEB AND I FELL IN LOVE AT FIRST SIGHT, JUST LIKE A BOOK OR A MOVIE.

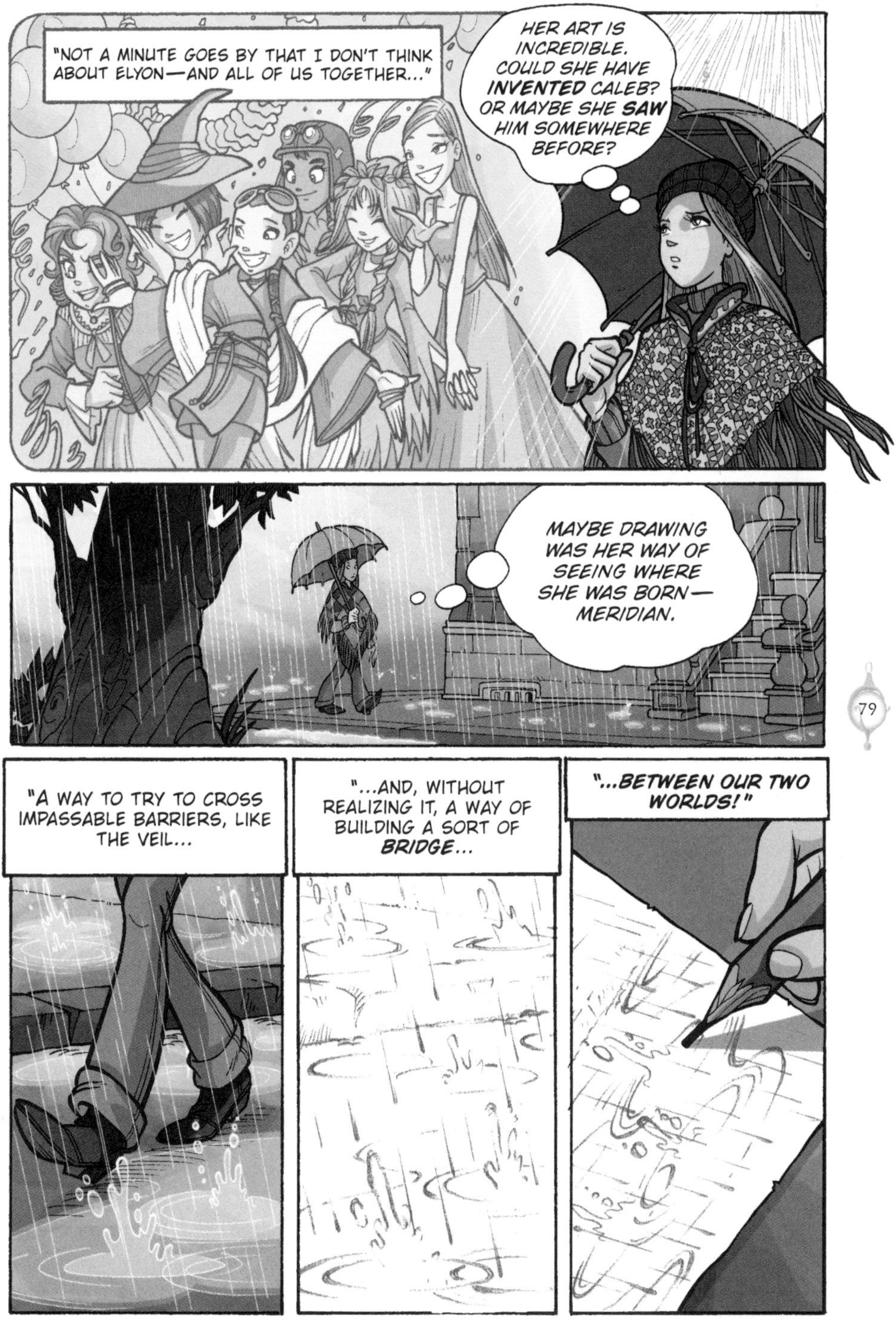
"NOT A MINUTE GOES BY THAT I DON'T THINK ABOUT ELYON—AND ALL OF US TOGETHER..."
HER ART IS INCREDIBLE. COULD SHE HAVE INVENTED CALEB? OR MAYBE SHE SAW HIM SOMEWHERE BEFORE?
MAYBE DRAWING WAS HER WAY OF SEEING WHERE SHE WAS BORN—MERIDIAN.
"A WAY TO TRY TO CROSS IMPASSABLE BARRIERS, LIKE THE VEIL...
"...AND, WITHOUT REALIZING IT, A WAY OF BUILDING A SORT OF BRIDGE...
"...BETWEEN OUR TWO WORLDS!"

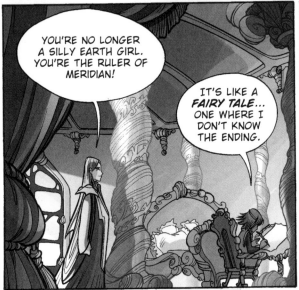

WHAT ARE YOU DRAWING, *ELYON*?

RAIN, *CEDRIC!* IT REMINDS ME OF AFTERNOONS IN HEATHERFIELD.

YOU'RE NO LONGER A SILLY EARTH GIRL. YOU'RE THE RULER OF MERIDIAN!

IT'S LIKE A *FAIRY TALE*... ONE WHERE I DON'T KNOW THE ENDING.

FAIRY TALES ARE USELESS INVENTIONS.

THINK SO? MY *PARENTS* TOLD ME LOTS, AND I LOVED DRAWING THEM!

ONCE UPON A TIME THERE WAS A LITTLE QUEEN, WHO REIGNED OVER A *SAD, DREARY* WORLD...

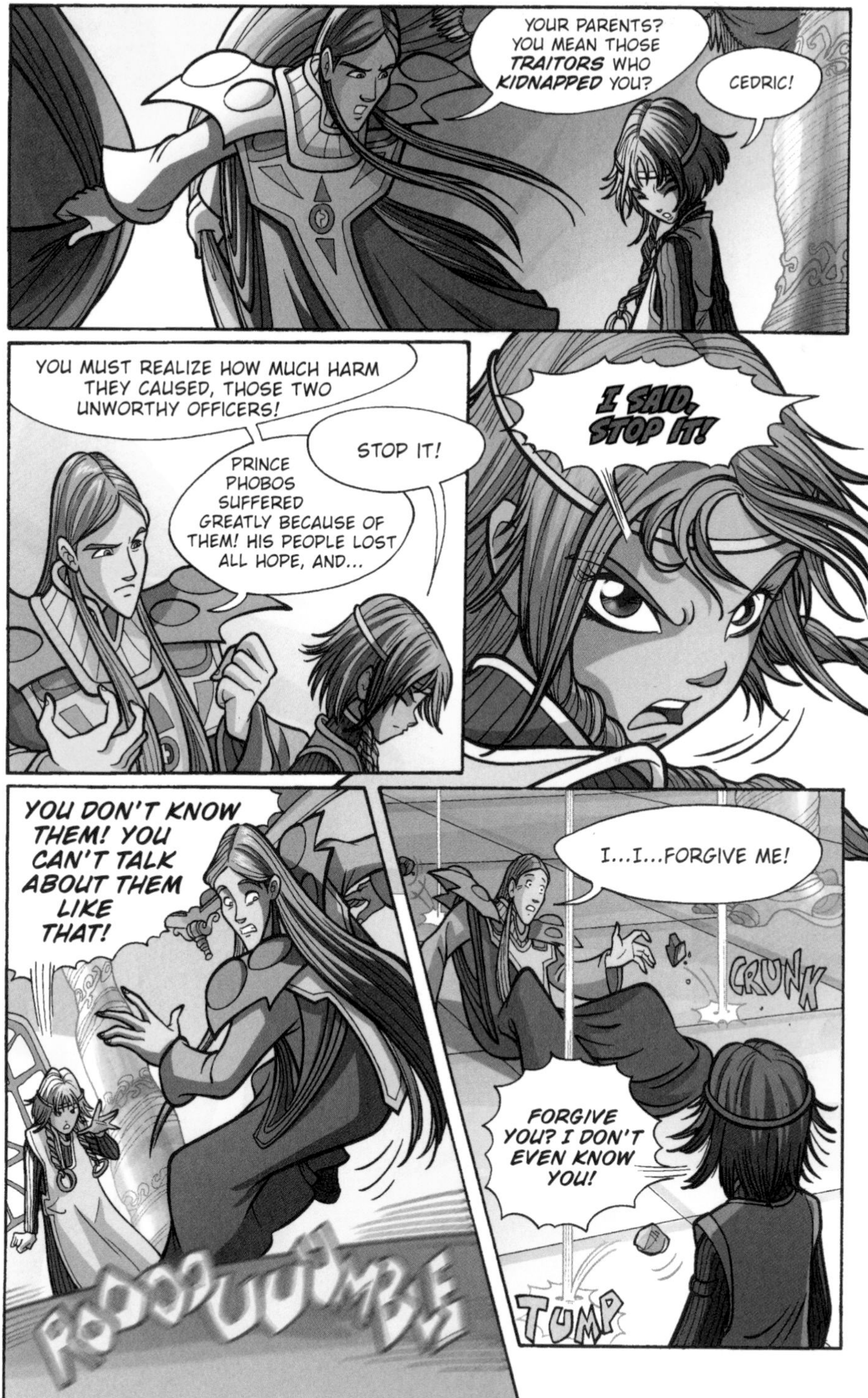
YOUR PARENTS? YOU MEAN THOSE TRAITORS WHO KIDNAPPED YOU?
CEDRIC!
YOU MUST REALIZE HOW MUCH HARM THEY CAUSED, THOSE TWO UNWORTHY OFFICERS!
PRINCE PHOBOS SUFFERED GREATLY BECAUSE OF THEM! HIS PEOPLE LOST ALL HOPE, AND...
STOP IT!
I SAID, STOP IT!
YOU DON'T KNOW THEM! YOU CAN'T TALK ABOUT THEM LIKE THAT!
I...I...FORGIVE ME!
CRUNK
FORGIVE YOU? I DON'T EVEN KNOW YOU!
TUMP

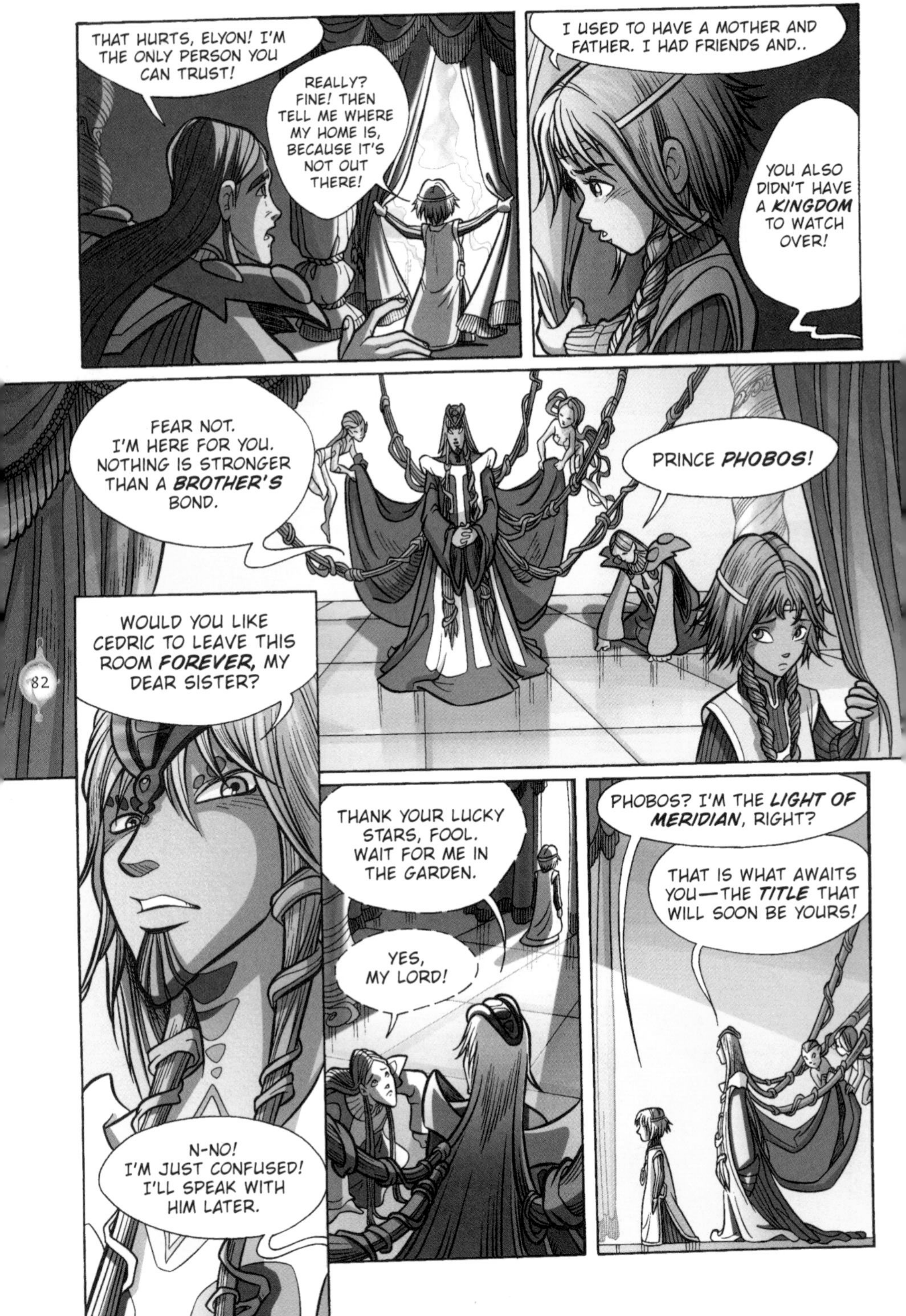

THAT HURTS, ELYON! I'M THE ONLY PERSON YOU CAN TRUST!
REALLY? FINE! THEN TELL ME WHERE MY HOME IS, BECAUSE IT'S NOT OUT THERE!
I USED TO HAVE A MOTHER AND FATHER. I HAD FRIENDS AND..
YOU ALSO DIDN'T HAVE A KINGDOM TO WATCH OVER!
FEAR NOT. I'M HERE FOR YOU. NOTHING IS STRONGER THAN A BROTHER'S BOND.
PRINCE PHOBOS!
WOULD YOU LIKE CEDRIC TO LEAVE THIS ROOM FOREVER, MY DEAR SISTER?
N-NO! I'M JUST CONFUSED! I'LL SPEAK WITH HIM LATER.
THANK YOUR LUCKY STARS, FOOL. WAIT FOR ME IN THE GARDEN.
YES, MY LORD!
PHOBOS? I'M THE LIGHT OF MERIDIAN, RIGHT?
THAT IS WHAT AWAITS YOU—THE TITLE THAT WILL SOON BE YOURS!

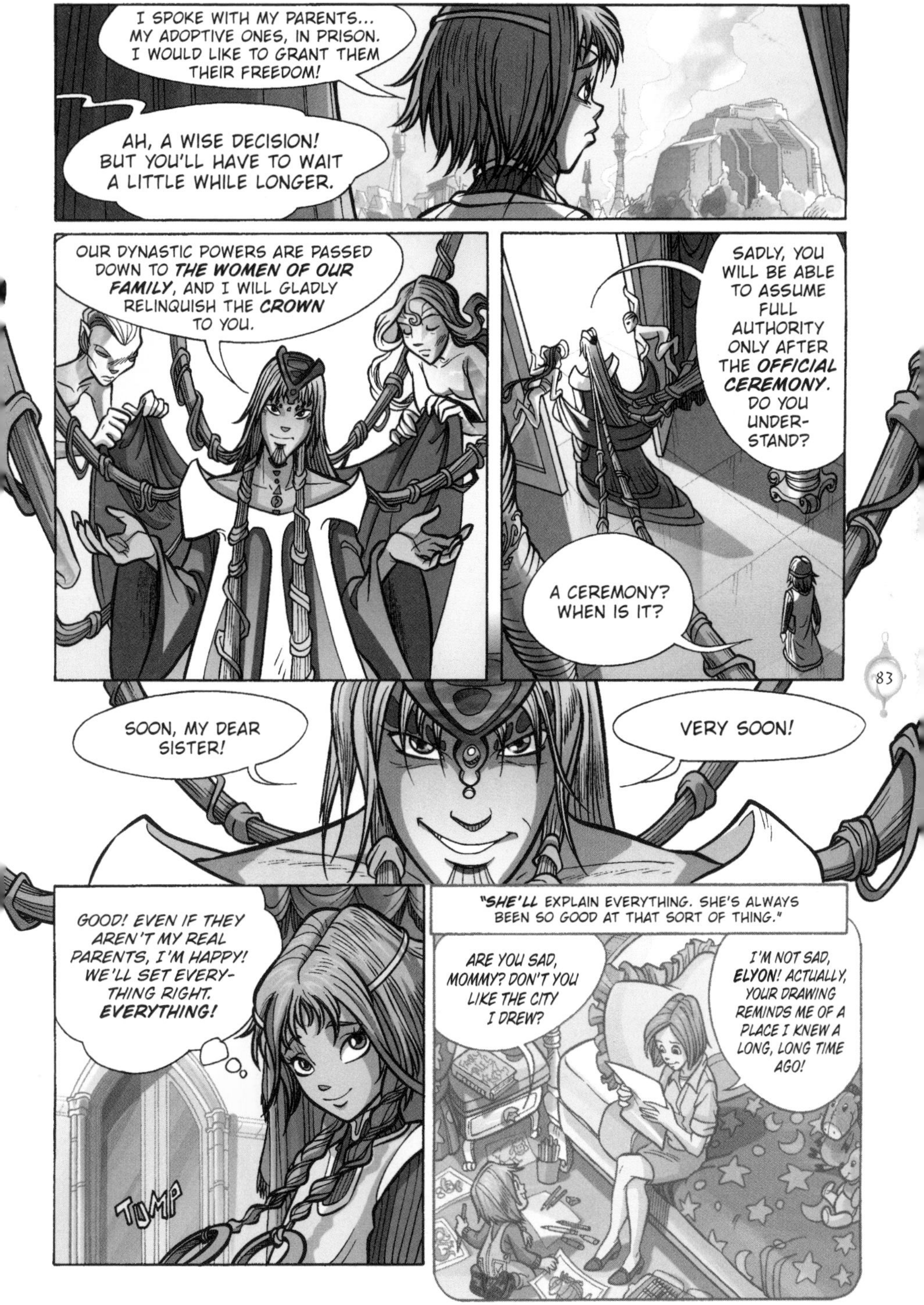
I SPOKE WITH MY PARENTS... MY ADOPTIVE ONES, IN PRISON. I WOULD LIKE TO GRANT THEM THEIR FREEDOM!
AH, A WISE DECISION! BUT YOU'LL HAVE TO WAIT A LITTLE WHILE LONGER.
OUR DYNASTIC POWERS ARE PASSED DOWN TO **THE WOMEN OF OUR FAMILY**, AND I WILL GLADLY RELINQUISH THE **CROWN** TO YOU.
SADLY, YOU WILL BE ABLE TO ASSUME FULL AUTHORITY ONLY AFTER THE **OFFICIAL CEREMONY**. DO YOU UNDER-STAND?
A CEREMONY? WHEN IS IT?
SOON, MY DEAR SISTER!
VERY SOON!
*GOOD! EVEN IF THEY AREN'T MY REAL PARENTS, I'M HAPPY! WE'LL SET EVERY-THING RIGHT. **EVERYTHING!***
TUMP
"**SHE'LL** EXPLAIN EVERYTHING. SHE'S ALWAYS BEEN SO GOOD AT THAT SORT OF THING."
ARE YOU SAD, MOMMY? DON'T YOU LIKE THE CITY I DREW?
*I'M NOT SAD, **ELYON**! ACTUALLY, YOUR DRAWING REMINDS ME OF A PLACE I KNEW A LONG, LONG TIME AGO!*

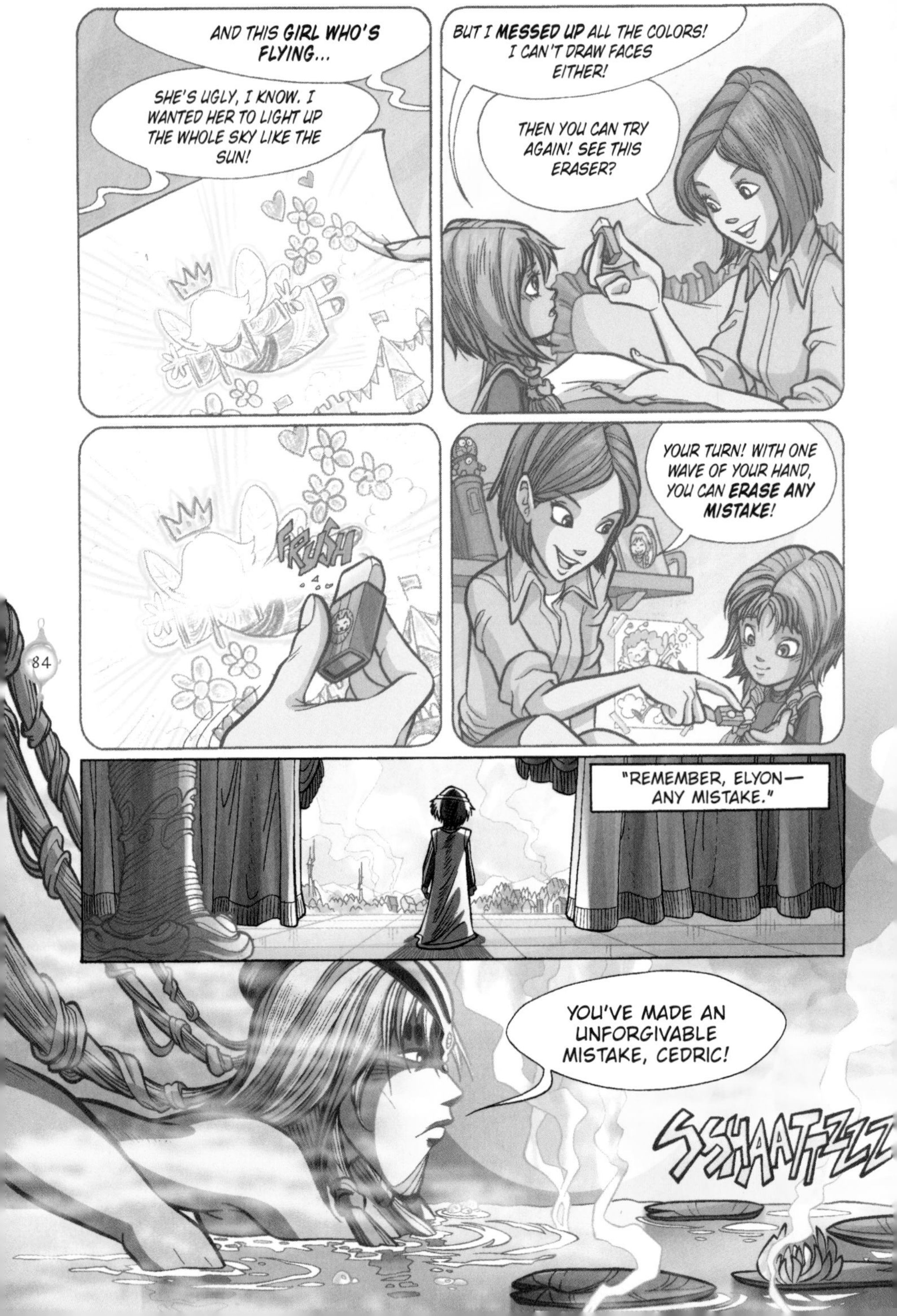
AND THIS **GIRL WHO'S FLYING**...
SHE'S UGLY, I KNOW. I WANTED HER TO LIGHT UP THE WHOLE SKY LIKE THE SUN!
BUT I **MESSED UP** ALL THE COLORS! I CAN'T DRAW FACES EITHER!
THEN YOU CAN TRY AGAIN! SEE THIS ERASER?
FRUSH
YOUR TURN! WITH ONE WAVE OF YOUR HAND, YOU CAN **ERASE ANY MISTAKE**!
"REMEMBER, ELYON— ANY MISTAKE."
YOU'VE MADE AN UNFORGIVABLE MISTAKE, CEDRIC!
SSHAATZZZ

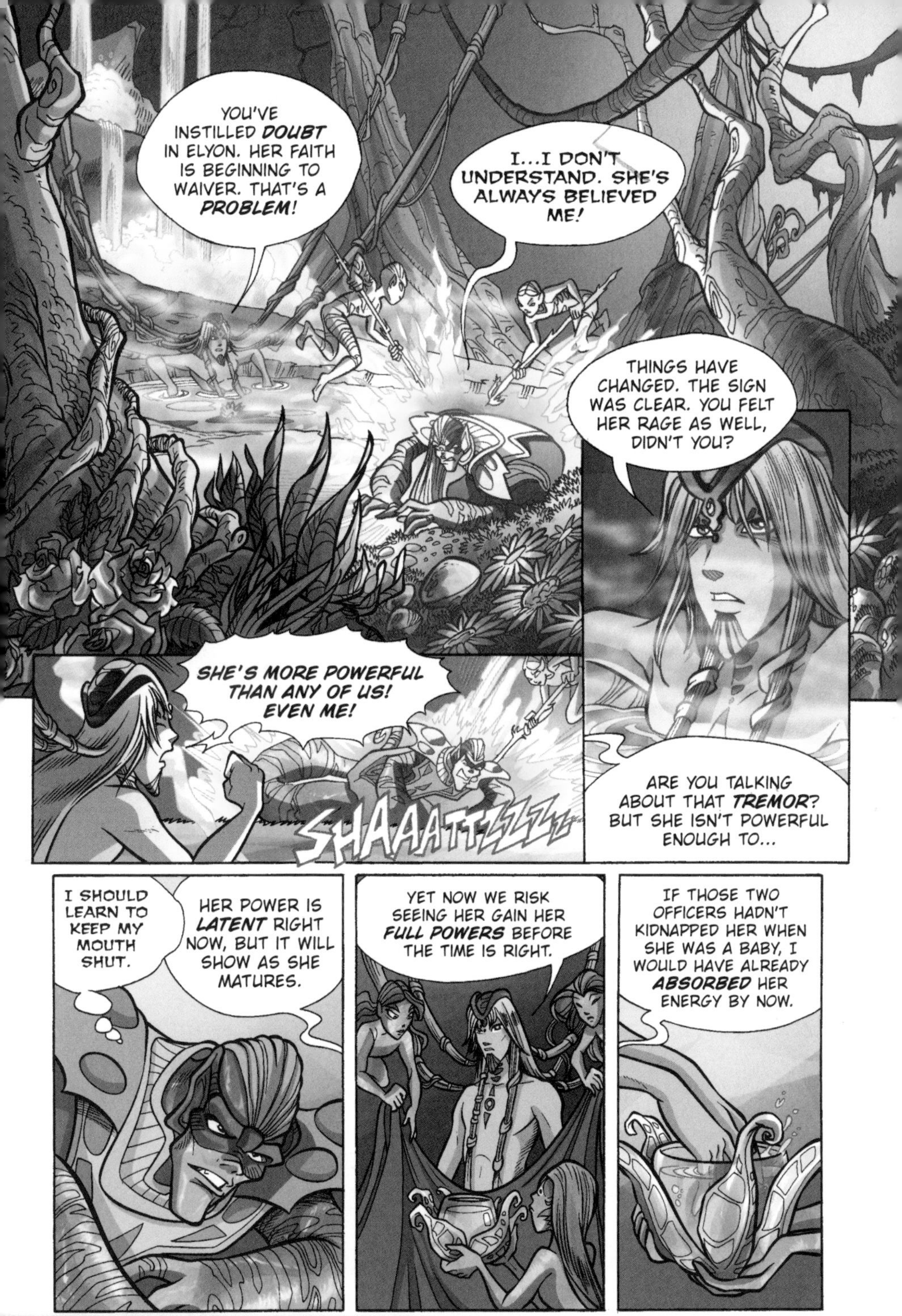
YOU'VE INSTILLED DOUBT IN ELYON. HER FAITH IS BEGINNING TO WAIVER. THAT'S A PROBLEM!
I...I DON'T UNDERSTAND. SHE'S ALWAYS BELIEVED ME!
THINGS HAVE CHANGED. THE SIGN WAS CLEAR. YOU FELT HER RAGE AS WELL, DIDN'T YOU?
SHE'S MORE POWERFUL THAN ANY OF US! EVEN ME!
SHAAATTZZZ
ARE YOU TALKING ABOUT THAT TREMOR? BUT SHE ISN'T POWERFUL ENOUGH TO...
I SHOULD LEARN TO KEEP MY MOUTH SHUT.
HER POWER IS LATENT RIGHT NOW, BUT IT WILL SHOW AS SHE MATURES.
YET NOW WE RISK SEEING HER GAIN HER FULL POWERS BEFORE THE TIME IS RIGHT.
IF THOSE TWO OFFICERS HADN'T KIDNAPPED HER WHEN SHE WAS A BABY, I WOULD HAVE ALREADY ABSORBED HER ENERGY BY NOW.

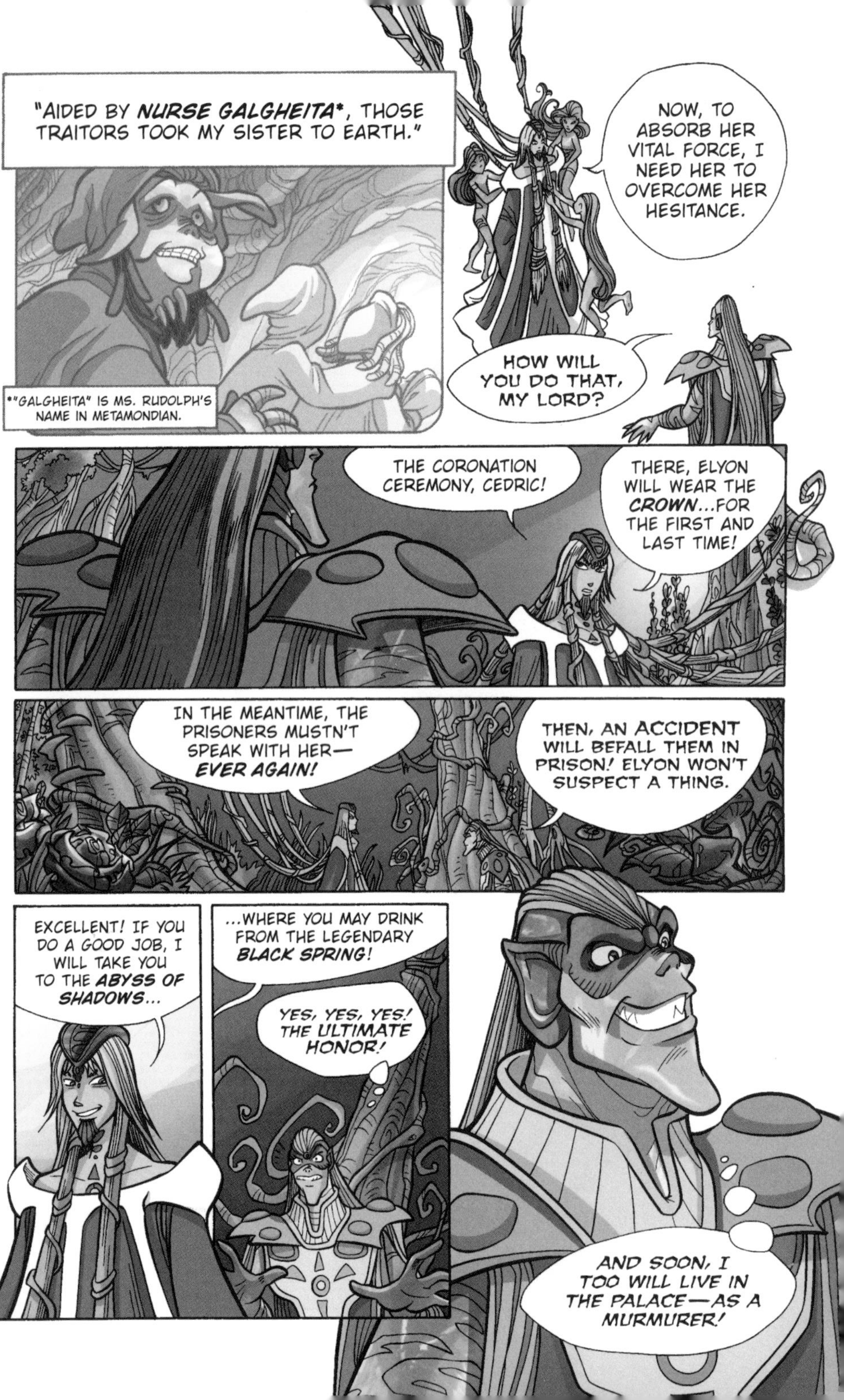
"AIDED BY NURSE GALGHEITA*, THOSE TRAITORS TOOK MY SISTER TO EARTH."
*"GALGHEITA" IS MS. RUDOLPH'S NAME IN METAMONDIAN.
NOW, TO ABSORB HER VITAL FORCE, I NEED HER TO OVERCOME HER HESITANCE.
HOW WILL YOU DO THAT, MY LORD?
THE CORONATION CEREMONY, CEDRIC!
THERE, ELYON WILL WEAR THE CROWN...FOR THE FIRST AND LAST TIME!
IN THE MEANTIME, THE PRISONERS MUSTN'T SPEAK WITH HER— EVER AGAIN!
THEN, AN ACCIDENT WILL BEFALL THEM IN PRISON! ELYON WON'T SUSPECT A THING.
EXCELLENT! IF YOU DO A GOOD JOB, I WILL TAKE YOU TO THE ABYSS OF SHADOWS...
...WHERE YOU MAY DRINK FROM THE LEGENDARY BLACK SPRING!
YES, YES, YES! THE ULTIMATE HONOR!
AND SOON, I TOO WILL LIVE IN THE PALACE—AS A MURMURER!

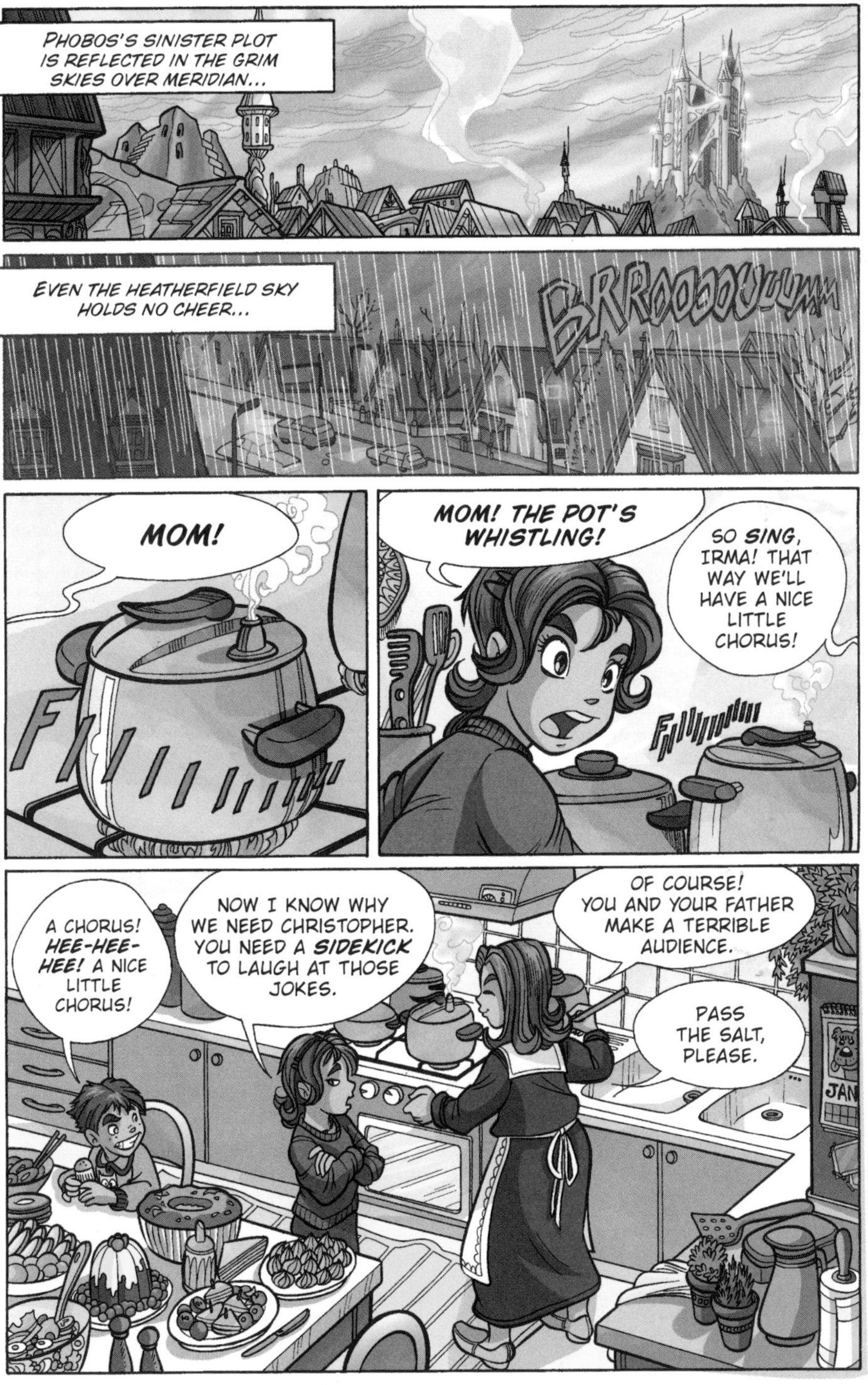
PHOBOS'S SINISTER PLOT IS REFLECTED IN THE GRIM SKIES OVER MERIDIAN...
EVEN THE HEATHERFIELD SKY HOLDS NO CHEER...
BRROOOOUUMM
MOM!
FIIIIIIII
MOM! THE POT'S WHISTLING!
SO SING, IRMA! THAT WAY WE'LL HAVE A NICE LITTLE CHORUS!
FIIIIIIII
A CHORUS! HEE-HEE-HEE! A NICE LITTLE CHORUS!
NOW I KNOW WHY WE NEED CHRISTOPHER. YOU NEED A SIDEKICK TO LAUGH AT THOSE JOKES.
OF COURSE! YOU AND YOUR FATHER MAKE A TERRIBLE AUDIENCE.
PASS THE SALT, PLEASE.

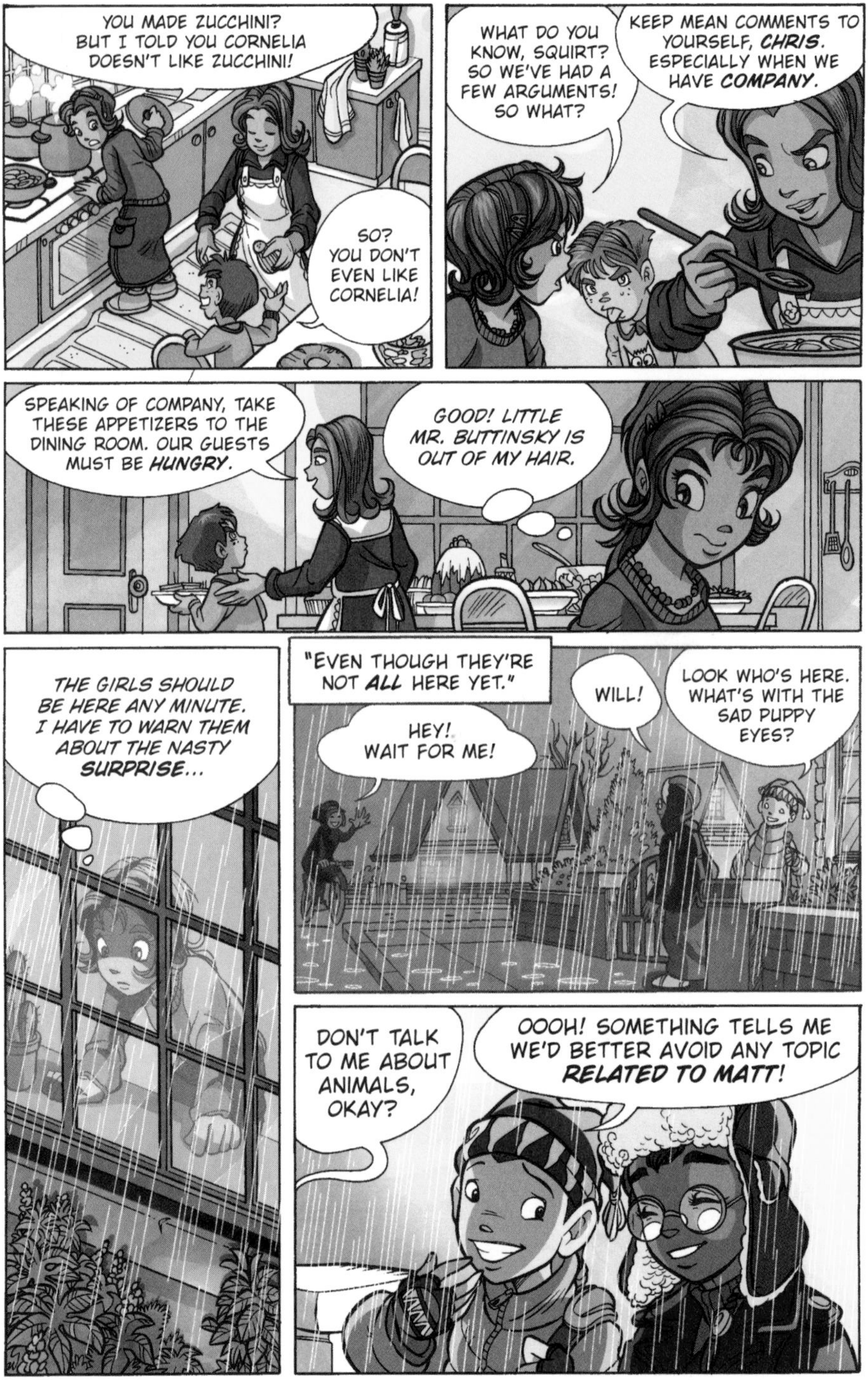
YOU MADE ZUCCHINI? BUT I TOLD YOU CORNELIA DOESN'T LIKE ZUCCHINI!
SO? YOU DON'T EVEN LIKE CORNELIA!
WHAT DO YOU KNOW, SQUIRT? SO WE'VE HAD A FEW ARGUMENTS! SO WHAT?
KEEP MEAN COMMENTS TO YOURSELF, **CHRIS**. ESPECIALLY WHEN WE HAVE **COMPANY**.
SPEAKING OF COMPANY, TAKE THESE APPETIZERS TO THE DINING ROOM. OUR GUESTS MUST BE **HUNGRY**.
GOOD! LITTLE MR. BUTTINSKY IS OUT OF MY HAIR.
THE GIRLS SHOULD BE HERE ANY MINUTE. I HAVE TO WARN THEM ABOUT THE NASTY ***SURPRISE***...
"EVEN THOUGH THEY'RE NOT ***ALL*** HERE YET."
HEY! WAIT FOR ME!
WILL!
LOOK WHO'S HERE. WHAT'S WITH THE SAD PUPPY EYES?
DON'T TALK TO ME ABOUT ANIMALS, OKAY?
OOOH! SOMETHING TELLS ME WE'D BETTER AVOID ANY TOPIC ***RELATED TO MATT***!

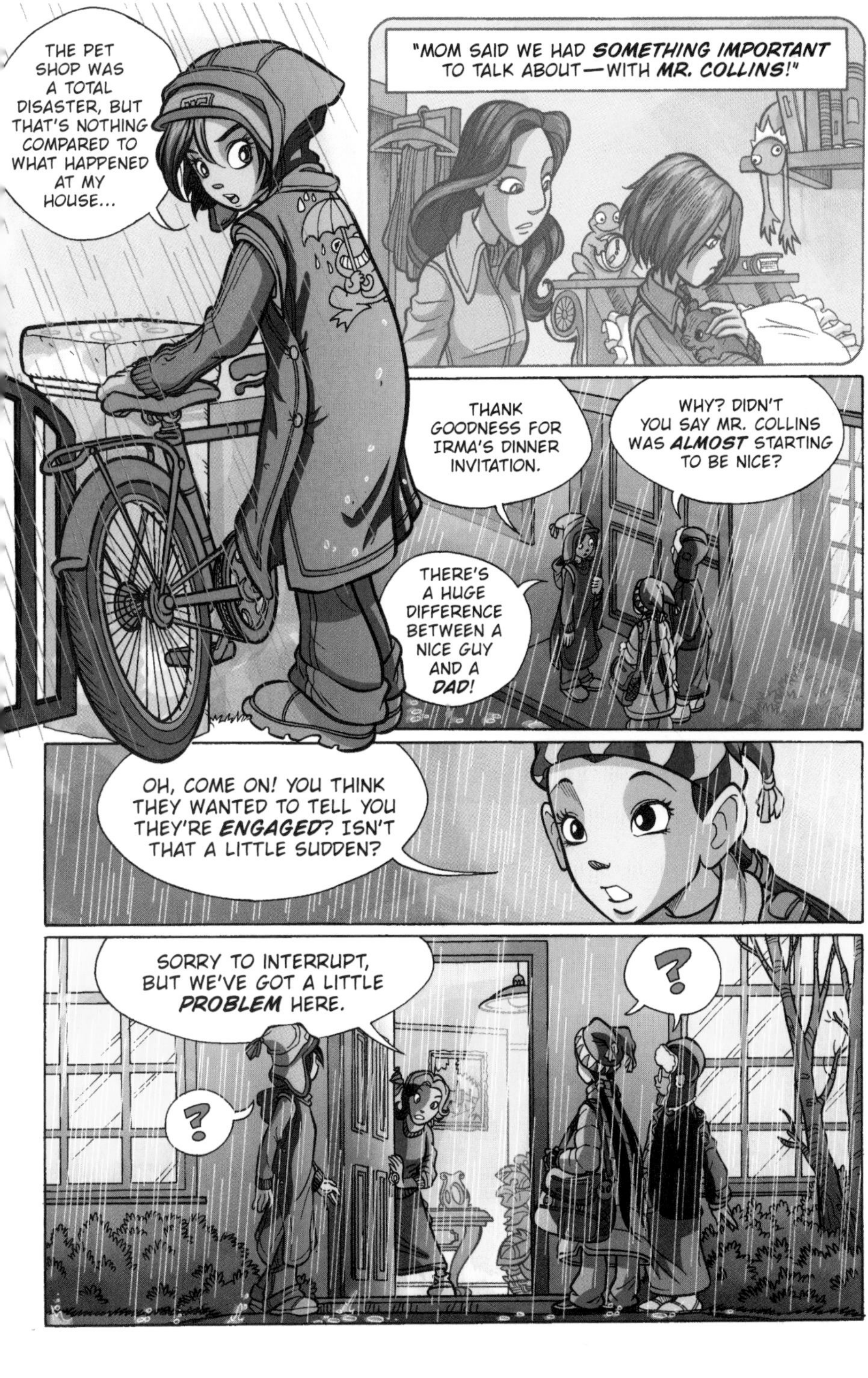
THE PET SHOP WAS A TOTAL DISASTER, BUT THAT'S NOTHING COMPARED TO WHAT HAPPENED AT MY HOUSE...
"MOM SAID WE HAD SOMETHING IMPORTANT TO TALK ABOUT—WITH MR. COLLINS!"
THANK GOODNESS FOR IRMA'S DINNER INVITATION.
WHY? DIDN'T YOU SAY MR. COLLINS WAS ALMOST STARTING TO BE NICE?
THERE'S A HUGE DIFFERENCE BETWEEN A NICE GUY AND A DAD!
OH, COME ON! YOU THINK THEY WANTED TO TELL YOU THEY'RE ENGAGED? ISN'T THAT A LITTLE SUDDEN?
SORRY TO INTERRUPT, BUT WE'VE GOT A LITTLE PROBLEM HERE.
?
?

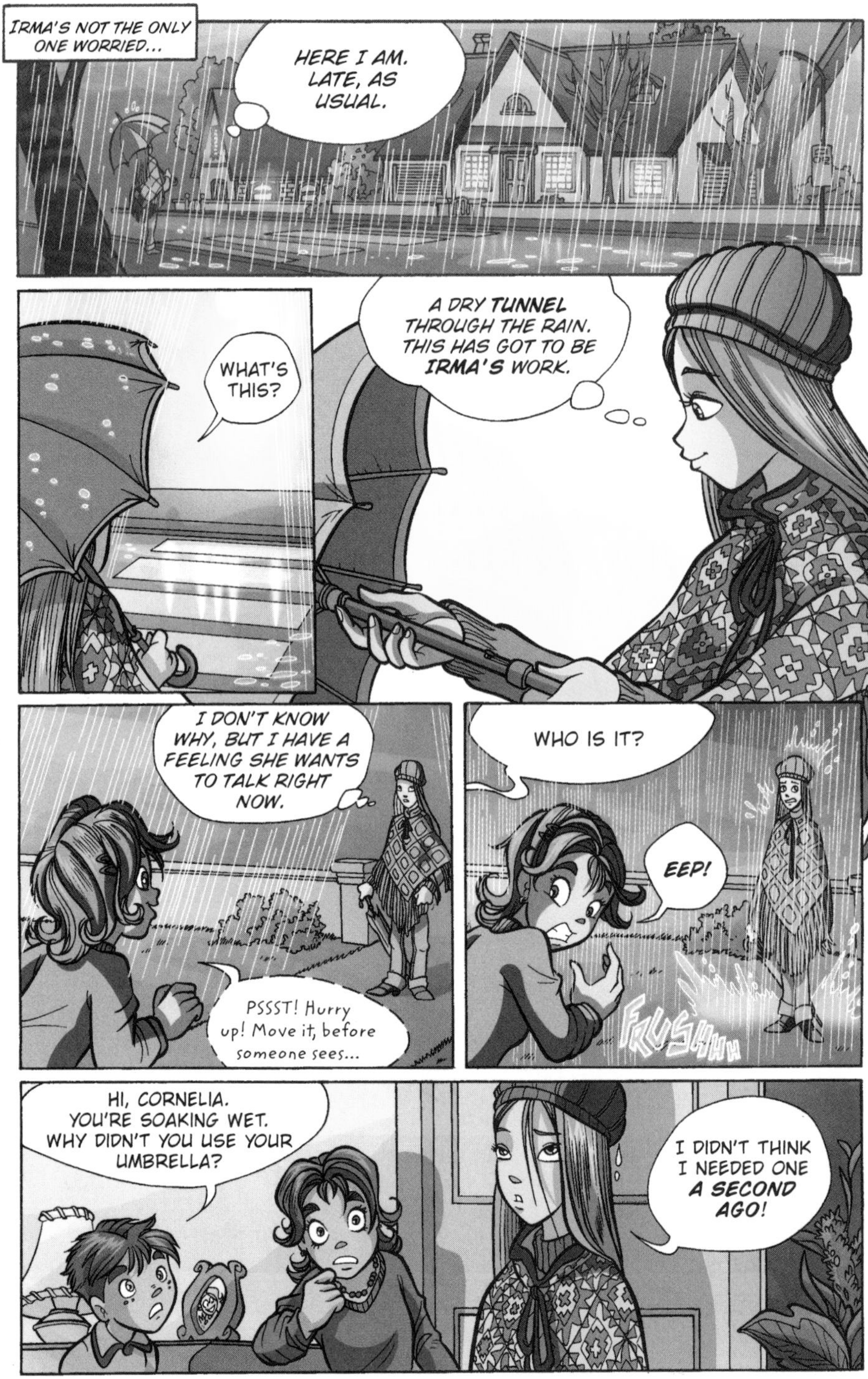
IRMA'S NOT THE ONLY ONE WORRIED...
HERE I AM. LATE, AS USUAL.
WHAT'S THIS?
A DRY TUNNEL THROUGH THE RAIN. THIS HAS GOT TO BE IRMA'S WORK.
I DON'T KNOW WHY, BUT I HAVE A FEELING SHE WANTS TO TALK RIGHT NOW.
PSSST! Hurry up! Move it, before someone sees...
WHO IS IT?
EEP!
FRUSHHH
HI, CORNELIA. YOU'RE SOAKING WET. WHY DIDN'T YOU USE YOUR UMBRELLA?
I DIDN'T THINK I NEEDED ONE A SECOND AGO!

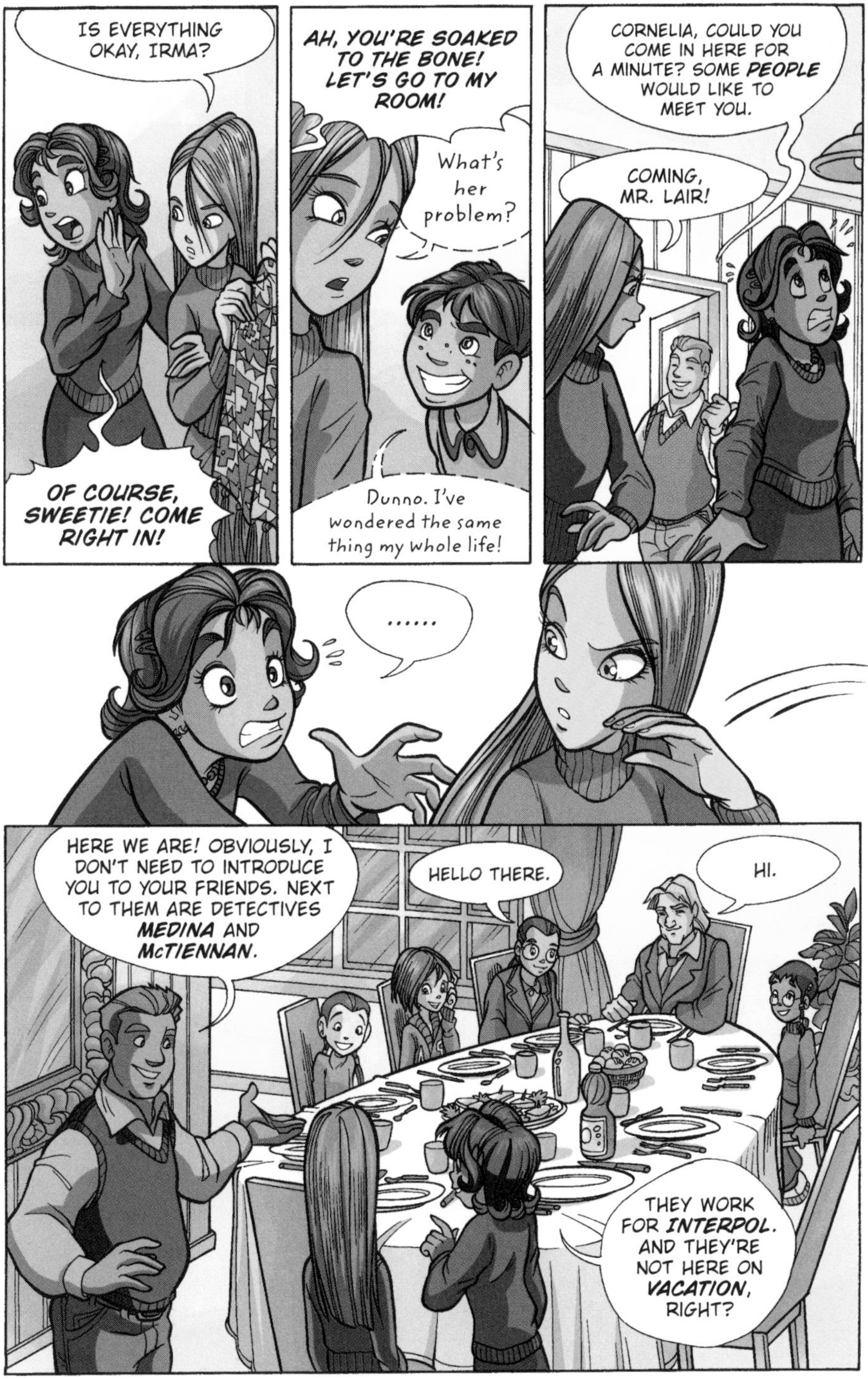
IS EVERYTHING OKAY, IRMA?
OF COURSE, SWEETIE! COME RIGHT IN!
AH, YOU'RE SOAKED TO THE BONE! LET'S GO TO MY ROOM!
What's her problem?
Dunno. I've wondered the same thing my whole life!
CORNELIA, COULD YOU COME IN HERE FOR A MINUTE? SOME PEOPLE WOULD LIKE TO MEET YOU.
COMING, MR. LAIR!
......
HERE WE ARE! OBVIOUSLY, I DON'T NEED TO INTRODUCE YOU TO YOUR FRIENDS. NEXT TO THEM ARE DETECTIVES MEDINA AND McTIENNAN.
HELLO THERE.
HI.
THEY WORK FOR INTERPOL. AND THEY'RE NOT HERE ON VACATION, RIGHT?

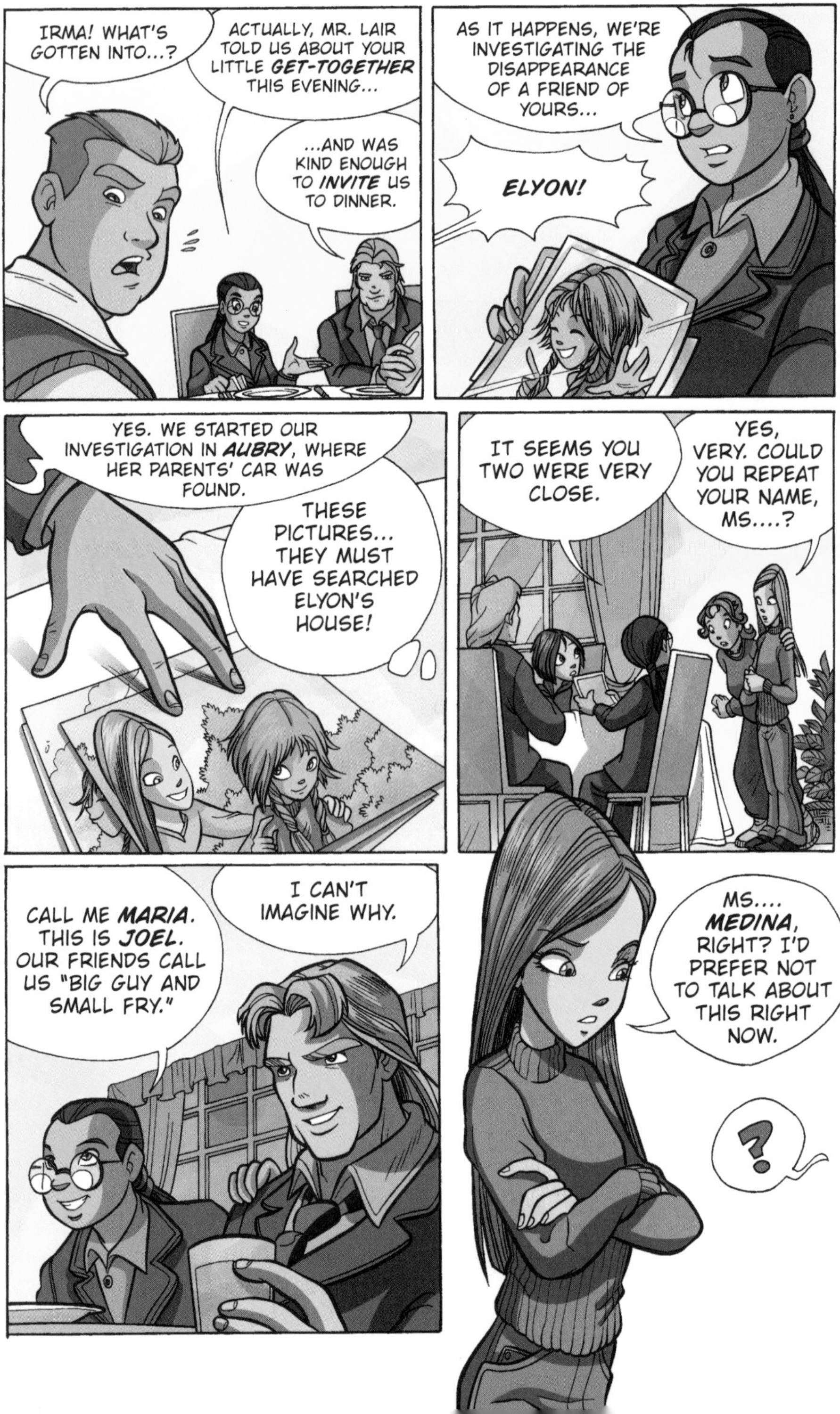
IRMA! WHAT'S GOTTEN INTO...?
ACTUALLY, MR. LAIR TOLD US ABOUT YOUR LITTLE GET-TOGETHER THIS EVENING...
...AND WAS KIND ENOUGH TO INVITE US TO DINNER.
AS IT HAPPENS, WE'RE INVESTIGATING THE DISAPPEARANCE OF A FRIEND OF YOURS...
ELYON!
YES. WE STARTED OUR INVESTIGATION IN AUBRY, WHERE HER PARENTS' CAR WAS FOUND.
THESE PICTURES... THEY MUST HAVE SEARCHED ELYON'S HOUSE!
IT SEEMS YOU TWO WERE VERY CLOSE.
YES, VERY. COULD YOU REPEAT YOUR NAME, MS....?
CALL ME MARIA. THIS IS JOEL. OUR FRIENDS CALL US "BIG GUY AND SMALL FRY."
I CAN'T IMAGINE WHY.
MS.... MEDINA, RIGHT? I'D PREFER NOT TO TALK ABOUT THIS RIGHT NOW.
?

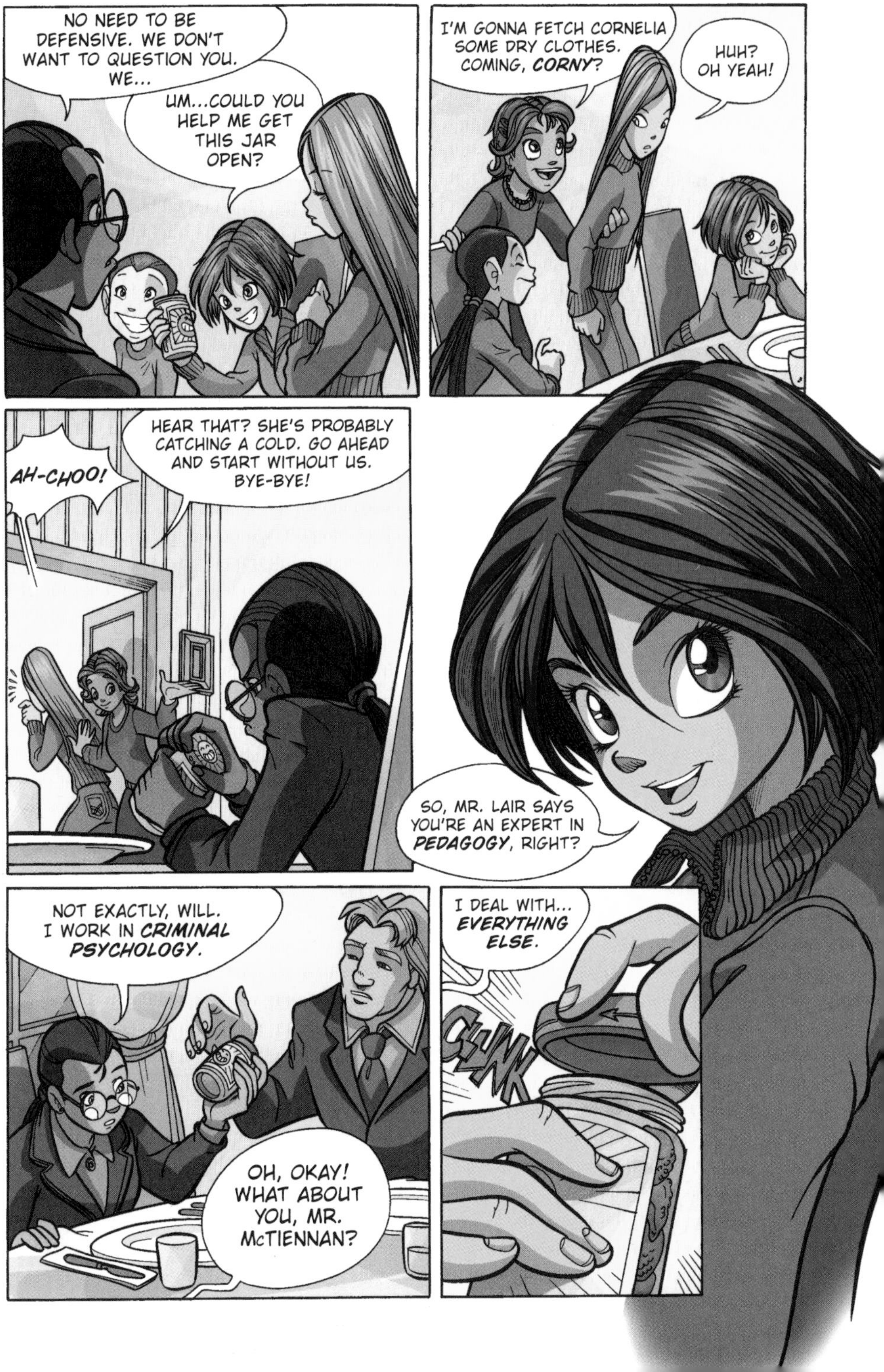
NO NEED TO BE DEFENSIVE. WE DON'T WANT TO QUESTION YOU. WE...
UM...COULD YOU HELP ME GET THIS JAR OPEN?
I'M GONNA FETCH CORNELIA SOME DRY CLOTHES. COMING, CORNY?
HUH? OH YEAH!
AH-CHOO!
HEAR THAT? SHE'S PROBABLY CATCHING A COLD. GO AHEAD AND START WITHOUT US. BYE-BYE!
SO, MR. LAIR SAYS YOU'RE AN EXPERT IN PEDAGOGY, RIGHT?
NOT EXACTLY, WILL. I WORK IN CRIMINAL PSYCHOLOGY.
OH, OKAY! WHAT ABOUT YOU, MR. McTIENNAN?
I DEAL WITH... EVERYTHING ELSE.
CLUNK

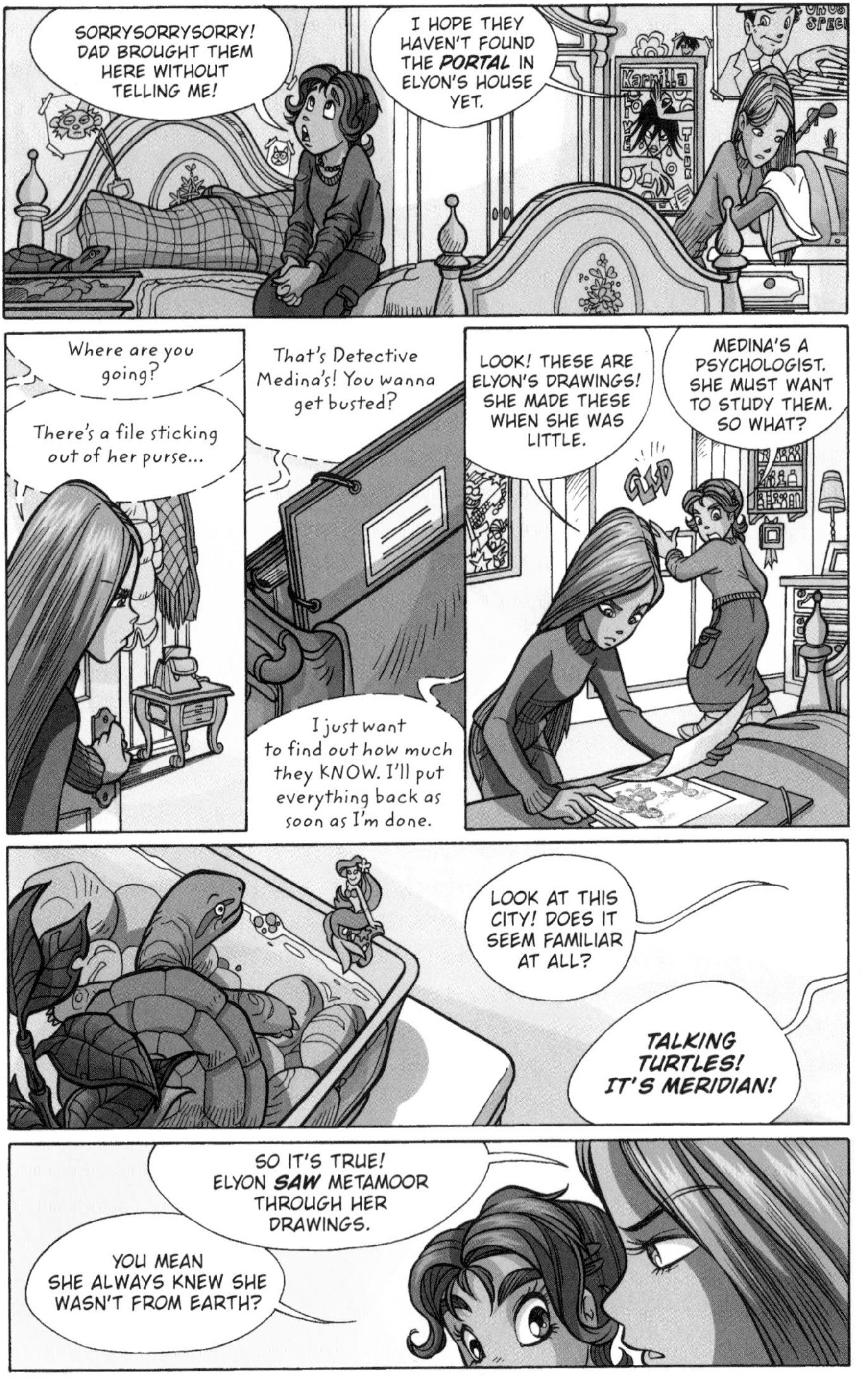
SORRYSORRYSORRY! DAD BROUGHT THEM HERE WITHOUT TELLING ME!
I HOPE THEY HAVEN'T FOUND THE ***PORTAL*** IN ELYON'S HOUSE YET.
Where are you going?
There's a file sticking out of her purse...
That's Detective Medina's! You wanna get busted?
I just want to find out how much they KNOW. I'll put everything back as soon as I'm done.
LOOK! THESE ARE ELYON'S DRAWINGS! SHE MADE THESE WHEN SHE WAS LITTLE.
MEDINA'S A PSYCHOLOGIST. SHE MUST WANT TO STUDY THEM. SO WHAT?
LOOK AT THIS CITY! DOES IT SEEM FAMILIAR AT ALL?
TALKING TURTLES! IT'S MERIDIAN!
SO IT'S TRUE! ELYON ***SAW*** METAMOOR THROUGH HER DRAWINGS.
YOU MEAN SHE ALWAYS KNEW SHE WASN'T FROM EARTH?

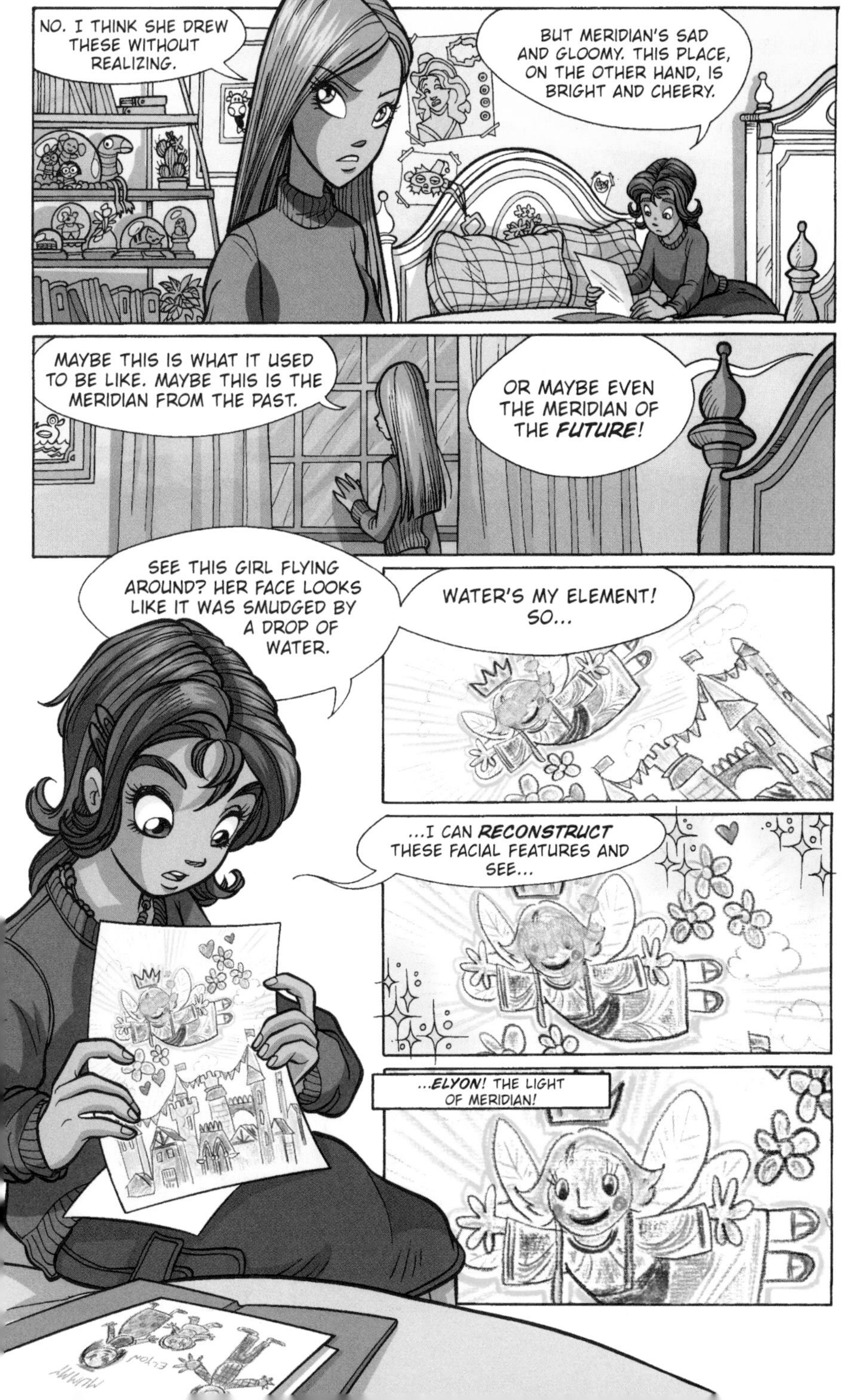
NO. I THINK SHE DREW THESE WITHOUT REALIZING.
BUT MERIDIAN'S SAD AND GLOOMY. THIS PLACE, ON THE OTHER HAND, IS BRIGHT AND CHEERY.
MAYBE THIS IS WHAT IT USED TO BE LIKE. MAYBE THIS IS THE MERIDIAN FROM THE PAST.
OR MAYBE EVEN THE MERIDIAN OF THE ***FUTURE***!
SEE THIS GIRL FLYING AROUND? HER FACE LOOKS LIKE IT WAS SMUDGED BY A DROP OF WATER.
WATER'S MY ELEMENT! SO...
...I CAN ***RECONSTRUCT*** THESE FACIAL FEATURES AND SEE...
...***ELYON***! THE LIGHT OF MERIDIAN!

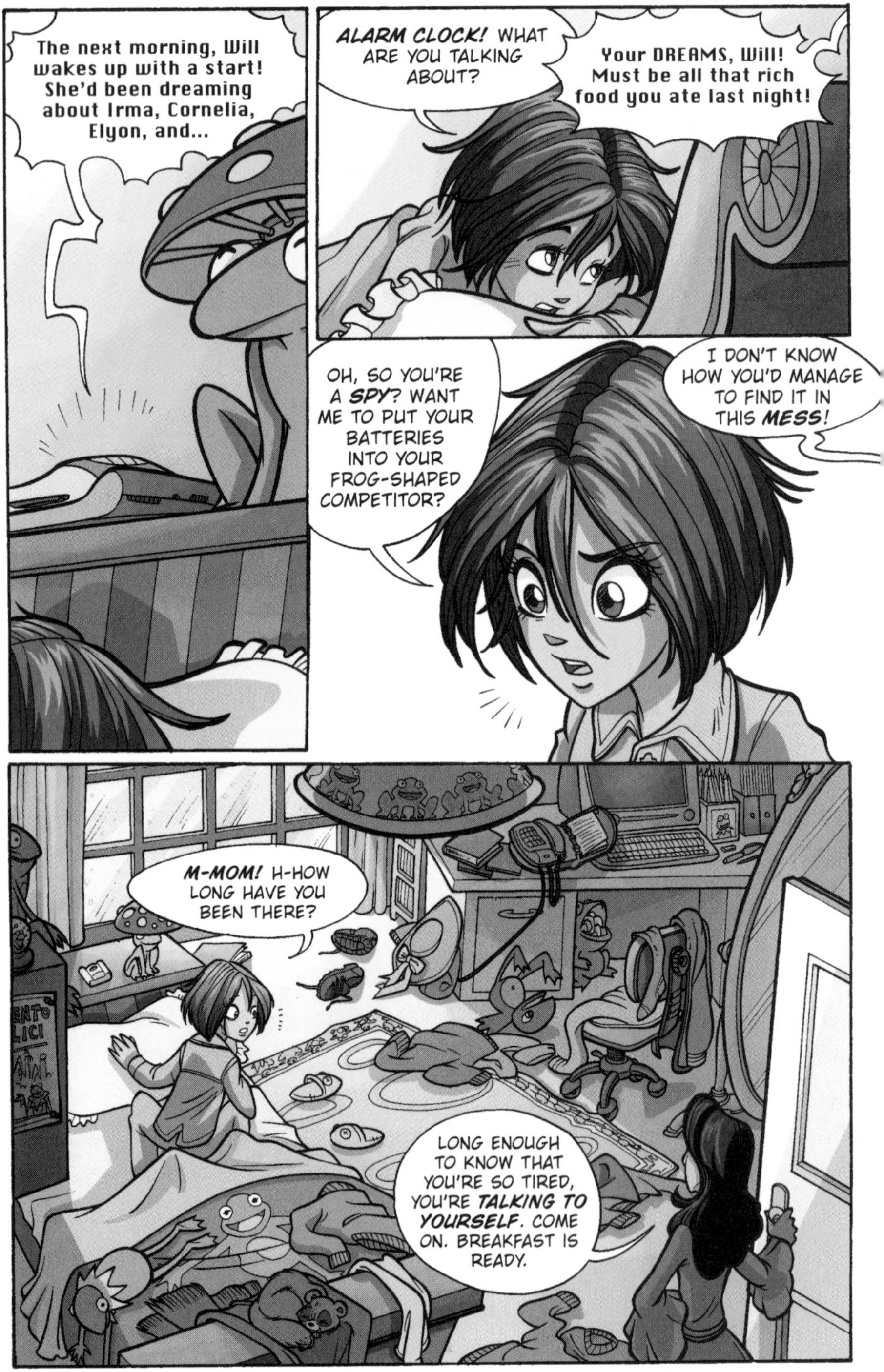

The next morning, Will wakes up with a start! She'd been dreaming about Irma, Cornelia, Elyon, and...
ALARM CLOCK! WHAT ARE YOU TALKING ABOUT?
Your DREAMS, Will! Must be all that rich food you ate last night!
OH, SO YOU'RE A SPY? WANT ME TO PUT YOUR BATTERIES INTO YOUR FROG-SHAPED COMPETITOR?
I DON'T KNOW HOW YOU'D MANAGE TO FIND IT IN THIS MESS!
M-MOM! H-HOW LONG HAVE YOU BEEN THERE?
LONG ENOUGH TO KNOW THAT YOU'RE SO TIRED, YOU'RE TALKING TO YOURSELF. COME ON. BREAKFAST IS READY.

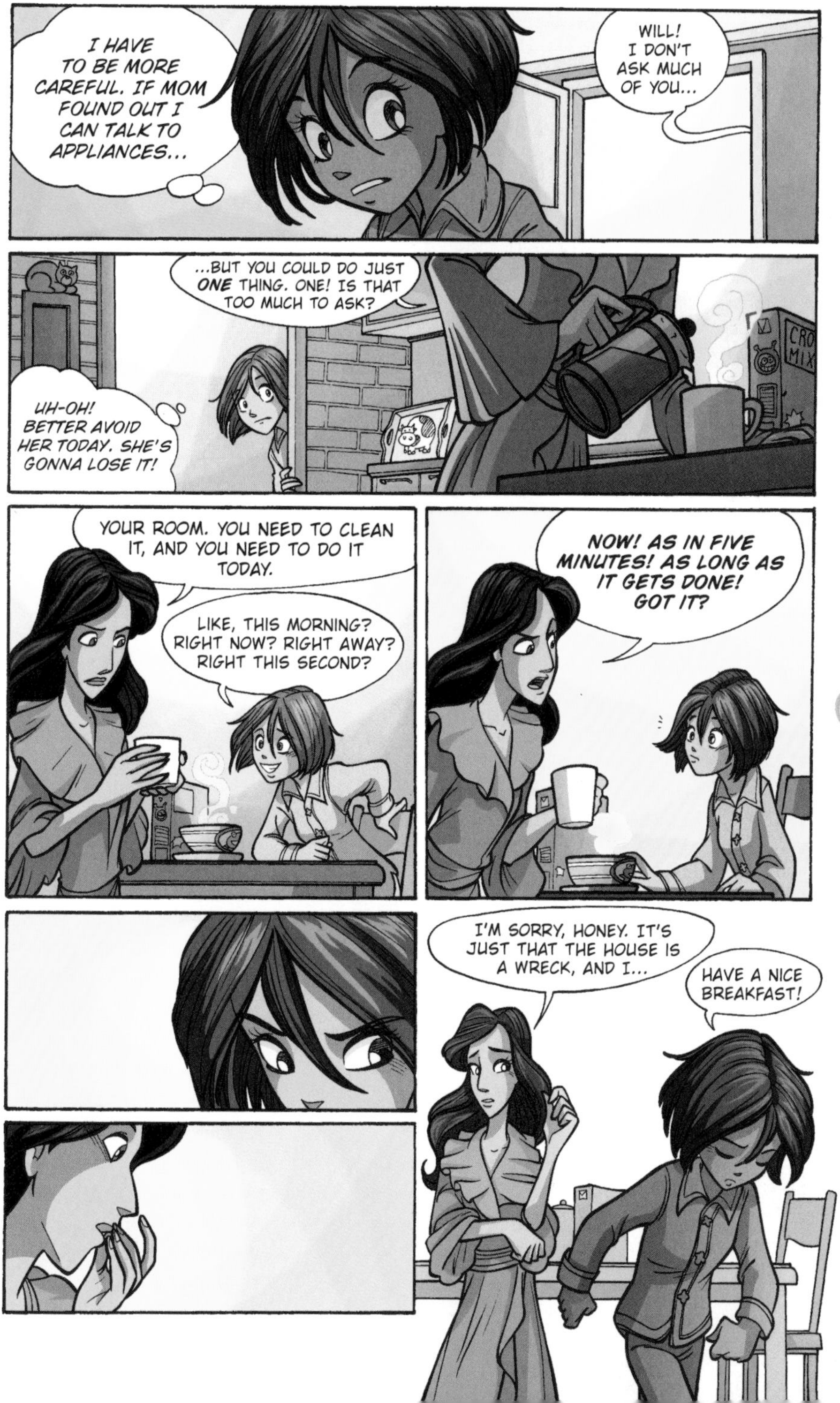
I HAVE TO BE MORE CAREFUL. IF MOM FOUND OUT I CAN TALK TO APPLIANCES...
WILL! I DON'T ASK MUCH OF YOU...
...BUT YOU COULD DO JUST ONE THING. ONE! IS THAT TOO MUCH TO ASK?
UH-OH! BETTER AVOID HER TODAY. SHE'S GONNA LOSE IT!
YOUR ROOM. YOU NEED TO CLEAN IT, AND YOU NEED TO DO IT TODAY.
LIKE, THIS MORNING? RIGHT NOW? RIGHT AWAY? RIGHT THIS SECOND?
NOW! AS IN FIVE MINUTES! AS LONG AS IT GETS DONE! GOT IT?
I'M SORRY, HONEY. IT'S JUST THAT THE HOUSE IS A WRECK, AND I...
HAVE A NICE BREAKFAST!

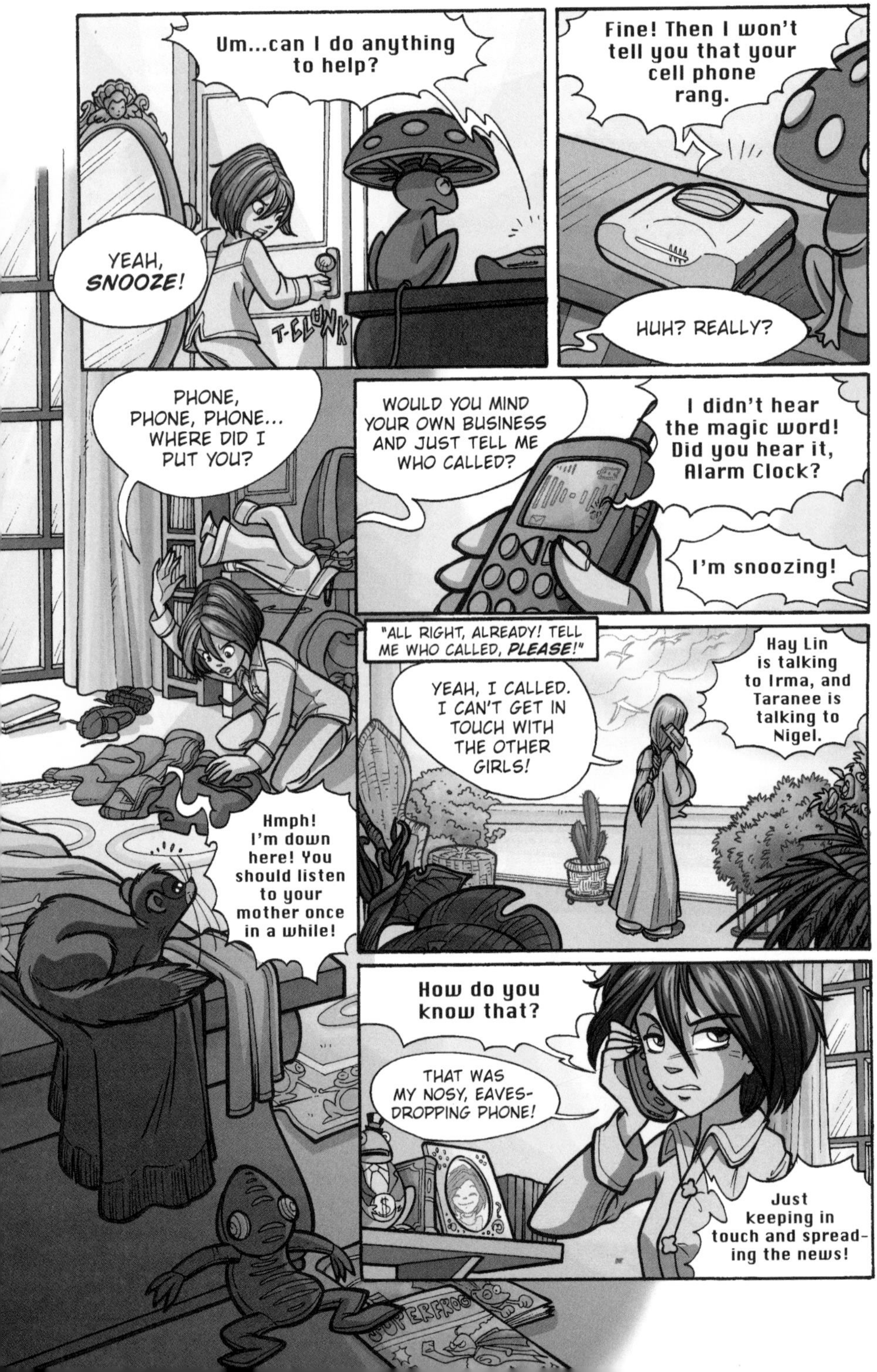
Um...can I do anything to help?
YEAH, SNOOZE!
T-BLUNK
Fine! Then I won't tell you that your cell phone rang.
HUH? REALLY?
PHONE, PHONE, PHONE... WHERE DID I PUT YOU?
WOULD YOU MIND YOUR OWN BUSINESS AND JUST TELL ME WHO CALLED?
I didn't hear the magic word! Did you hear it, Alarm Clock?
I'm snoozing!
Hmph! I'm down here! You should listen to your mother once in a while!
"ALL RIGHT, ALREADY! TELL ME WHO CALLED, PLEASE!"
YEAH, I CALLED. I CAN'T GET IN TOUCH WITH THE OTHER GIRLS!
Hay Lin is talking to Irma, and Taranee is talking to Nigel.
How do you know that?
THAT WAS MY NOSY, EAVES-DROPPING PHONE!
Just keeping in touch and spread-ing the news!
SUPERFROG

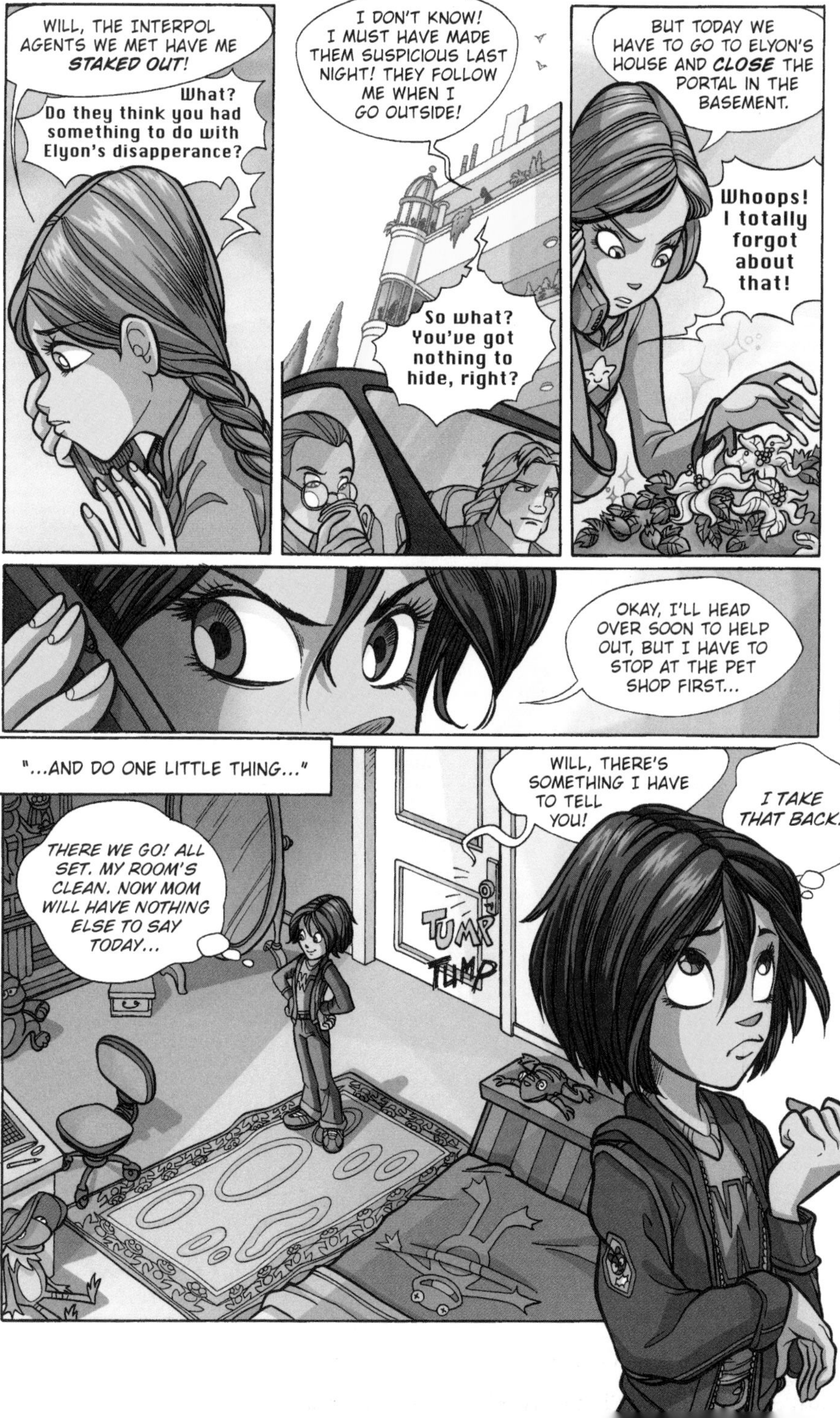
WILL, THE INTERPOL AGENTS WE MET HAVE ME *STAKED OUT*!
What? Do they think you had something to do with Elyon's disapperance?
I DON'T KNOW! I MUST HAVE MADE THEM SUSPICIOUS LAST NIGHT! THEY FOLLOW ME WHEN I GO OUTSIDE!
So what? You've got nothing to hide, right?
BUT TODAY WE HAVE TO GO TO ELYON'S HOUSE AND *CLOSE* THE PORTAL IN THE BASEMENT.
Whoops! I totally forgot about that!
OKAY, I'LL HEAD OVER SOON TO HELP OUT, BUT I HAVE TO STOP AT THE PET SHOP FIRST...
"...AND DO ONE LITTLE THING..."
THERE WE GO! ALL SET. MY ROOM'S CLEAN. NOW MOM WILL HAVE NOTHING ELSE TO SAY TODAY...
WILL, THERE'S SOMETHING I HAVE TO TELL YOU!
TUMP TUMP
I TAKE THAT BACK.

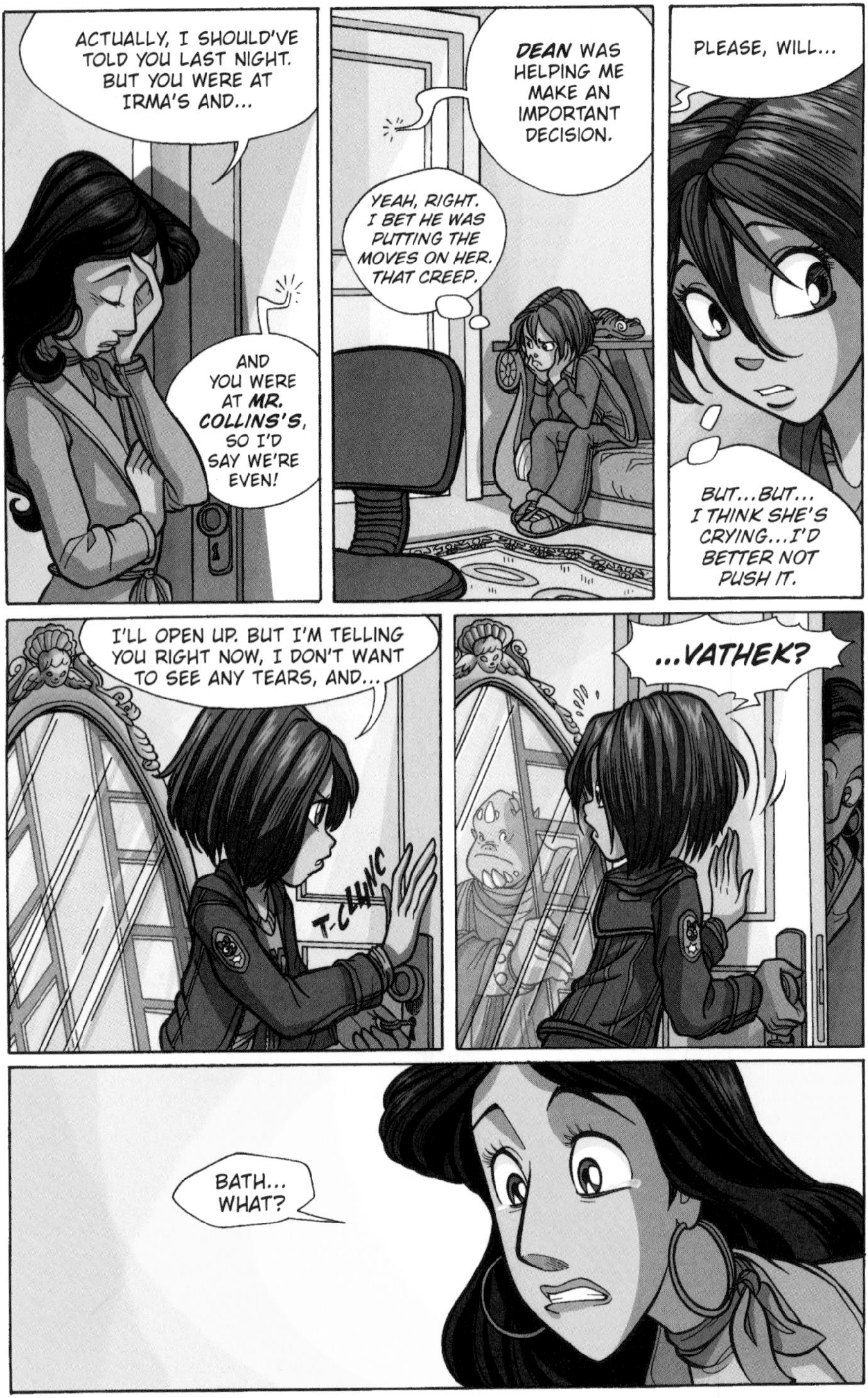
ACTUALLY, I SHOULD'VE TOLD YOU LAST NIGHT. BUT YOU WERE AT IRMA'S AND...
AND YOU WERE AT MR. COLLINS'S, SO I'D SAY WE'RE EVEN!
DEAN WAS HELPING ME MAKE AN IMPORTANT DECISION.
YEAH, RIGHT. I BET HE WAS PUTTING THE MOVES ON HER. THAT CREEP.
PLEASE, WILL...
BUT...BUT... I THINK SHE'S CRYING...I'D BETTER NOT PUSH IT.
I'LL OPEN UP. BUT I'M TELLING YOU RIGHT NOW, I DON'T WANT TO SEE ANY TEARS, AND...
T-CLUNC
...VATHEK?
BATH... WHAT?

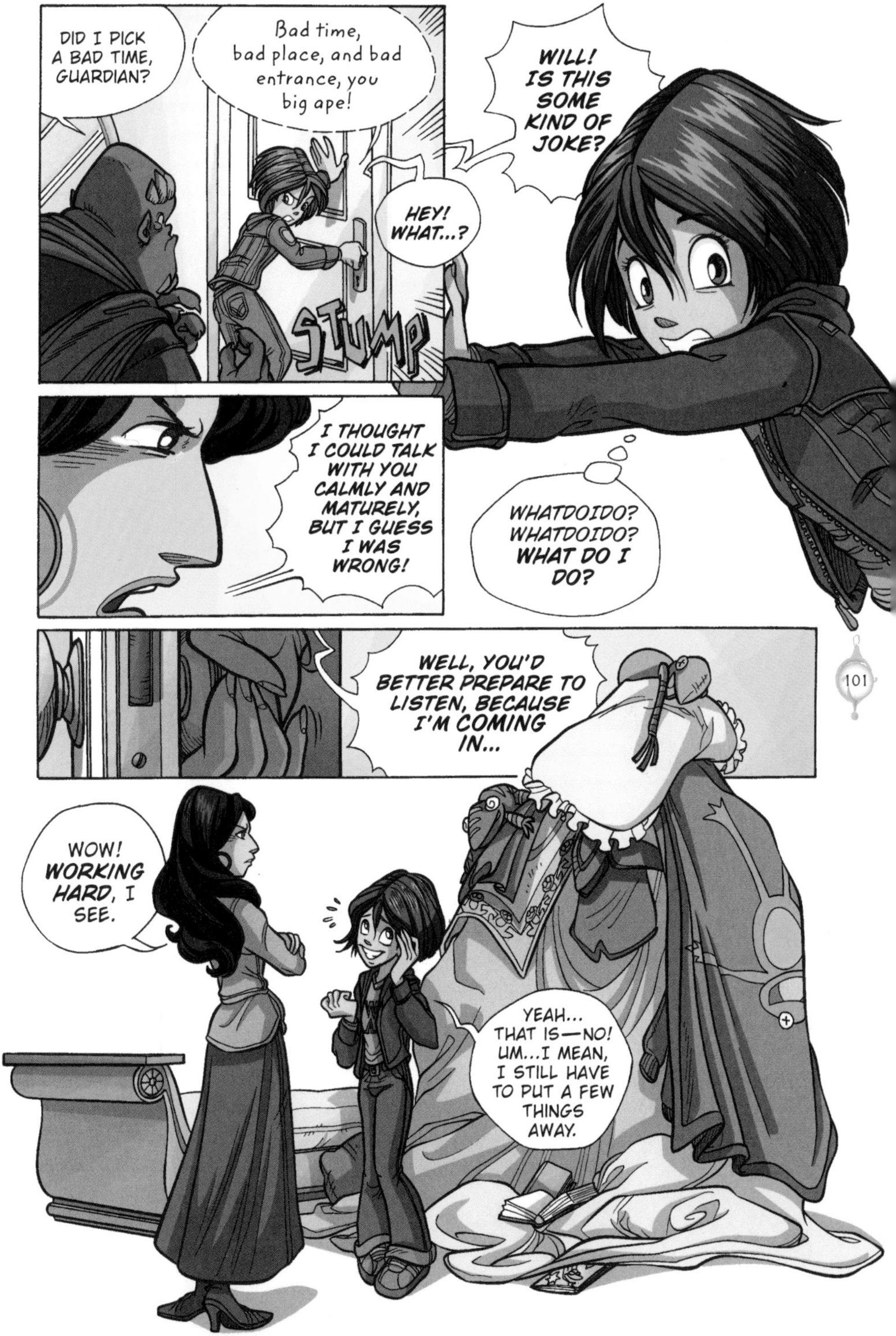
DID I PICK A BAD TIME, GUARDIAN?
Bad time, bad place, and bad entrance, you big ape!
WILL! IS THIS SOME KIND OF JOKE?
HEY! WHAT...?
STUMP
I THOUGHT I COULD TALK WITH YOU CALMLY AND MATURELY, BUT I GUESS I WAS WRONG!
WHATDOIDO? WHATDOIDO? WHAT DO I DO?
WELL, YOU'D BETTER PREPARE TO LISTEN, BECAUSE I'M COMING IN...
WOW! WORKING HARD, I SEE.
YEAH... THAT IS—NO! UM...I MEAN, I STILL HAVE TO PUT A FEW THINGS AWAY.

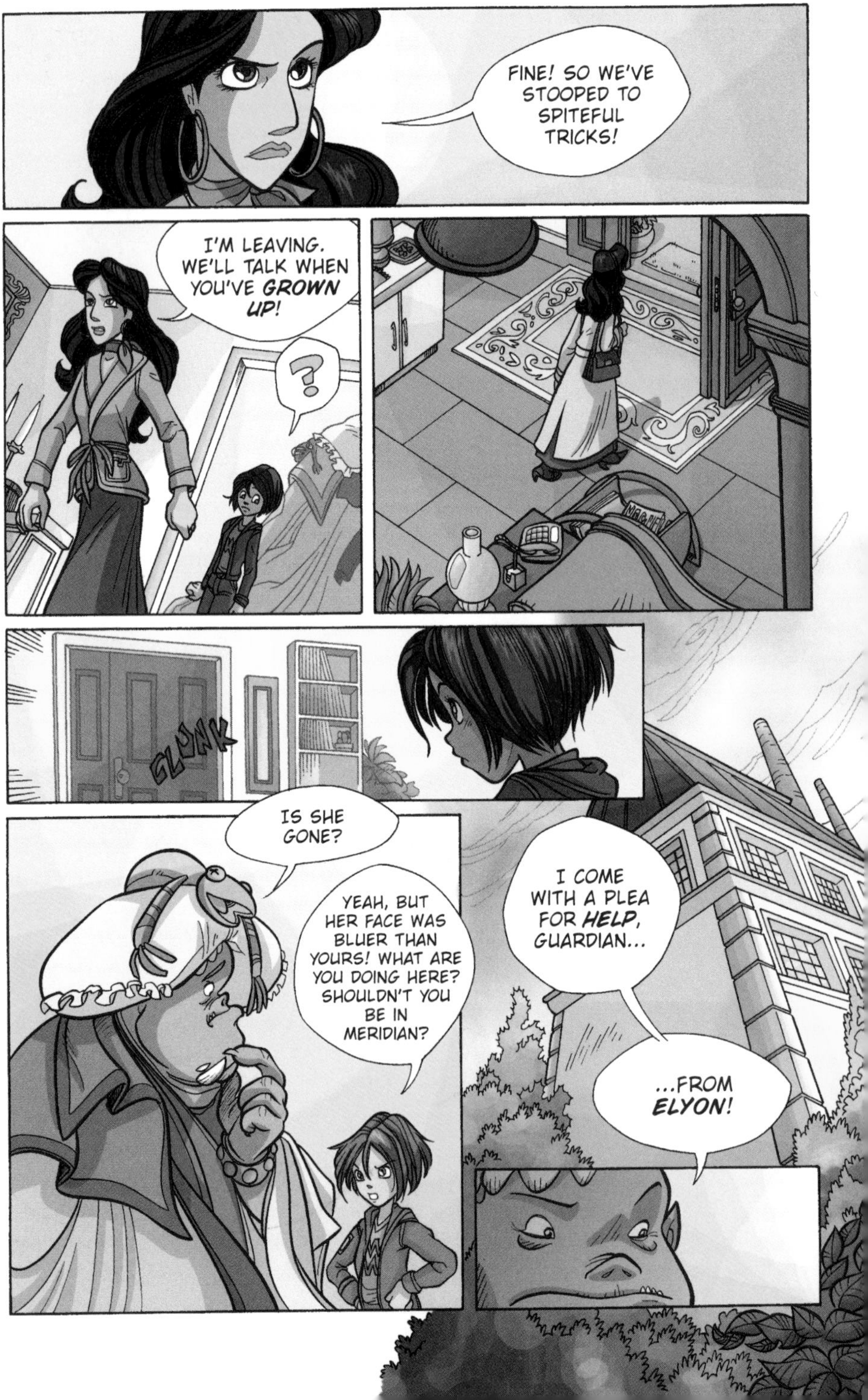
FINE! SO WE'VE STOOPED TO SPITEFUL TRICKS!
I'M LEAVING. WE'LL TALK WHEN YOU'VE GROWN UP!
?
GLUNK
IS SHE GONE?
YEAH, BUT HER FACE WAS BLUER THAN YOURS! WHAT ARE YOU DOING HERE? SHOULDN'T YOU BE IN MERIDIAN?
I COME WITH A PLEA FOR HELP, GUARDIAN...
...FROM ELYON!

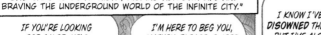
"**SHE** CAME TO US AT NIGHT, RISKING HER OWN LIFE AND BRAVING THE UNDERGROUND WORLD OF THE INFINITE CITY."

IF YOU'RE LOOKING FOR CALEB, HE'S RECRUITING REBELS IN YOUR NAME!

I'M HERE TO BEG YOU, VATHEK. PLEASE. I NEED YOU TO FREE MY ADOPTIVE PARENTS!

I KNOW I'VE **DISOWNED** THEM, BUT I'VE ALSO SEEN WHERE THEY'RE LOCKED UP. IT'S HORRIBLE!

THAT PRISON IS YOUR BROTHER'S DOING — HE CONFINES THOSE WHO OPPOSE HIM!

THEY'RE SUFFERING! I CAN **SENSE** IT! THEY'LL NEVER SURVIVE TO MY CORONATION.

NO ONE CAN BREAK INTO THE PRISON, NOT EVEN ME! YOU SHOULD ASK THE **GUARDIANS** FOR HELP.

EXCEPT FOR CORNELIA, THEY HATE ME. THEY'D NEVER HELP.

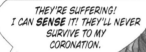

REALLY? I'M NOT EXACTLY A GENIUS...

...BUT IT'S EASY TO SEE THAT IF YOU'VE COME ALL THE WAY HERE, ELUDING PHOBOS'S CONTROL, YOU DON'T TRUST HIM EITHER.

PERHAPS THE MOMENT HAS COME TO BELIEVE IN SOMEONE ELSE, **LIGHT OF MERIDIAN!**

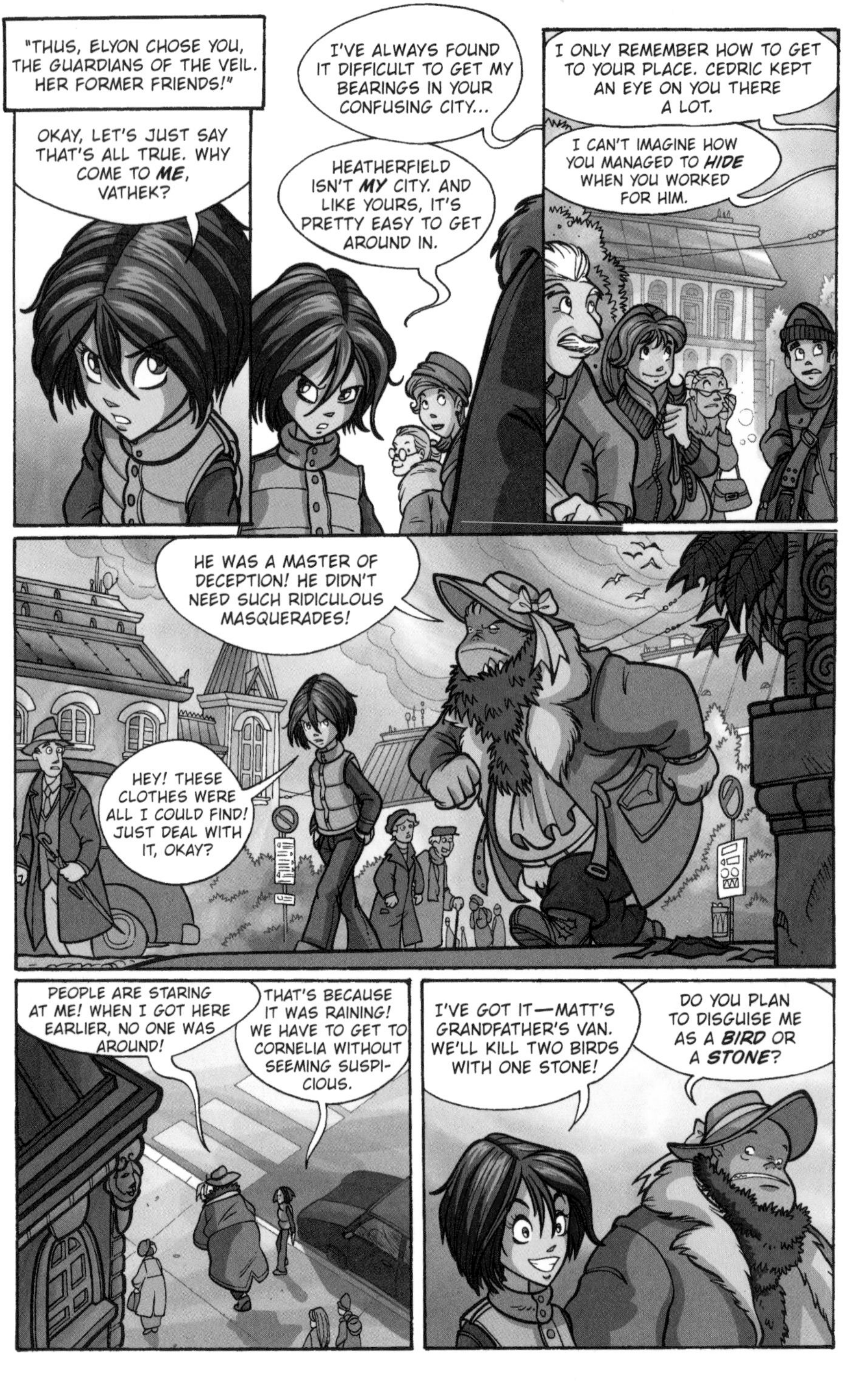
"THUS, ELYON CHOSE YOU, THE GUARDIANS OF THE VEIL. HER FORMER FRIENDS!"
OKAY, LET'S JUST SAY THAT'S ALL TRUE. WHY COME TO *ME*, VATHEK?
I'VE ALWAYS FOUND IT DIFFICULT TO GET MY BEARINGS IN YOUR CONFUSING CITY...
HEATHERFIELD ISN'T *MY* CITY. AND LIKE YOURS, IT'S PRETTY EASY TO GET AROUND IN.
I ONLY REMEMBER HOW TO GET TO YOUR PLACE. CEDRIC KEPT AN EYE ON YOU THERE A LOT.
I CAN'T IMAGINE HOW YOU MANAGED TO *HIDE* WHEN YOU WORKED FOR HIM.
HE WAS A MASTER OF DECEPTION! HE DIDN'T NEED SUCH RIDICULOUS MASQUERADES!
HEY! THESE CLOTHES WERE ALL I COULD FIND! JUST DEAL WITH IT, OKAY?
PEOPLE ARE STARING AT ME! WHEN I GOT HERE EARLIER, NO ONE WAS AROUND!
THAT'S BECAUSE IT WAS RAINING! WE HAVE TO GET TO CORNELIA WITHOUT SEEMING SUSPI-CIOUS.
I'VE GOT IT—MATT'S GRANDFATHER'S VAN. WE'LL KILL TWO BIRDS WITH ONE STONE!
DO YOU PLAN TO DISGUISE ME AS A *BIRD* OR A *STONE*?

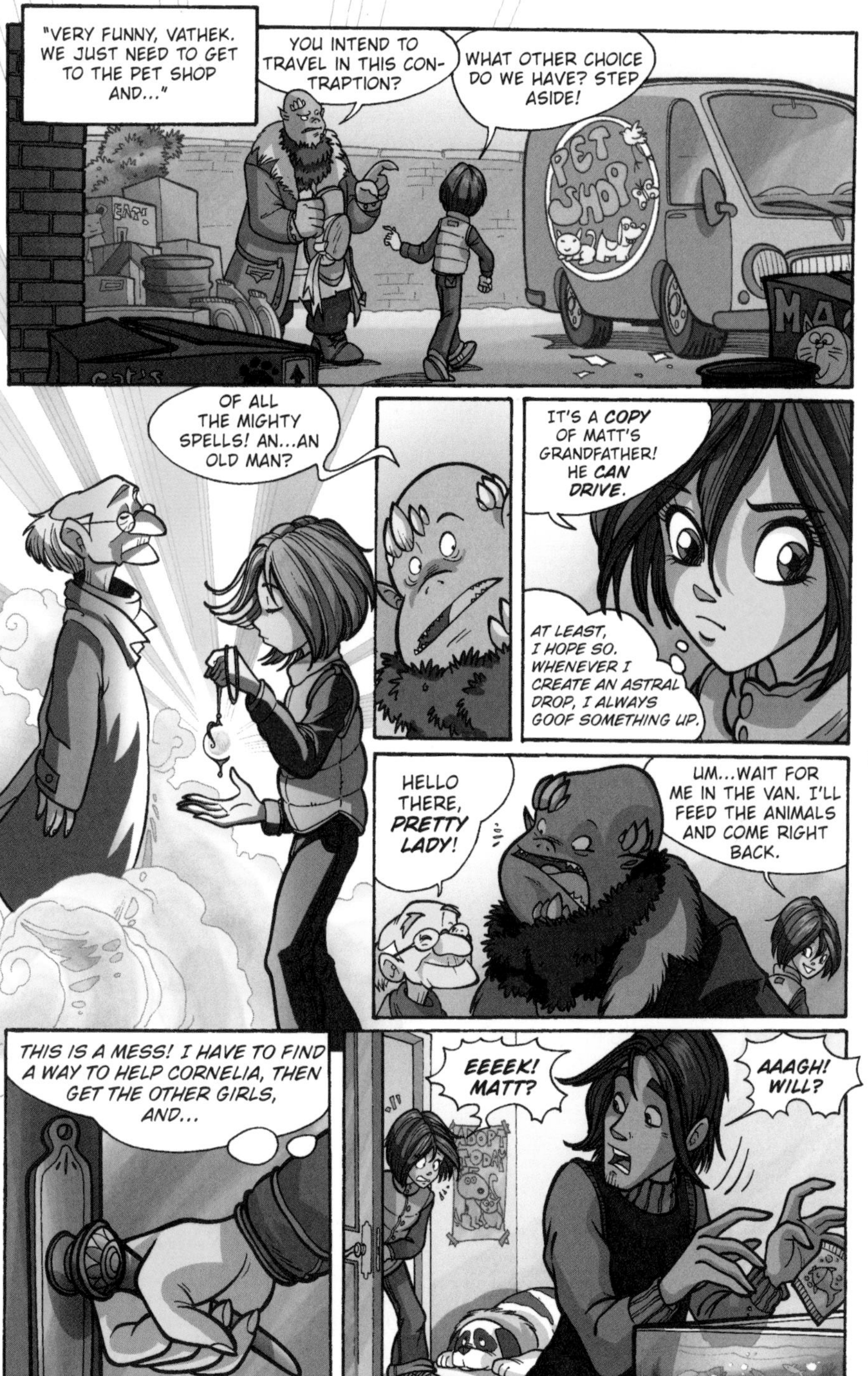
"VERY FUNNY, VATHEK. WE JUST NEED TO GET TO THE PET SHOP AND..."
YOU INTEND TO TRAVEL IN THIS CONTRAPTION?
WHAT OTHER CHOICE DO WE HAVE? STEP ASIDE!
PET SHOP
OF ALL THE MIGHTY SPELLS! AN...AN OLD MAN?
IT'S A *COPY* OF MATT'S GRANDFATHER! HE *CAN DRIVE*.
AT LEAST, I HOPE SO. WHENEVER I CREATE AN ASTRAL DROP, I ALWAYS GOOF SOMETHING UP.
HELLO THERE, ***PRETTY LADY!***
UM...WAIT FOR ME IN THE VAN. I'LL FEED THE ANIMALS AND COME RIGHT BACK.
THIS IS A MESS! I HAVE TO FIND A WAY TO HELP CORNELIA, THEN GET THE OTHER GIRLS, AND...
EEEEK! MATT?
AAAGH! WILL?

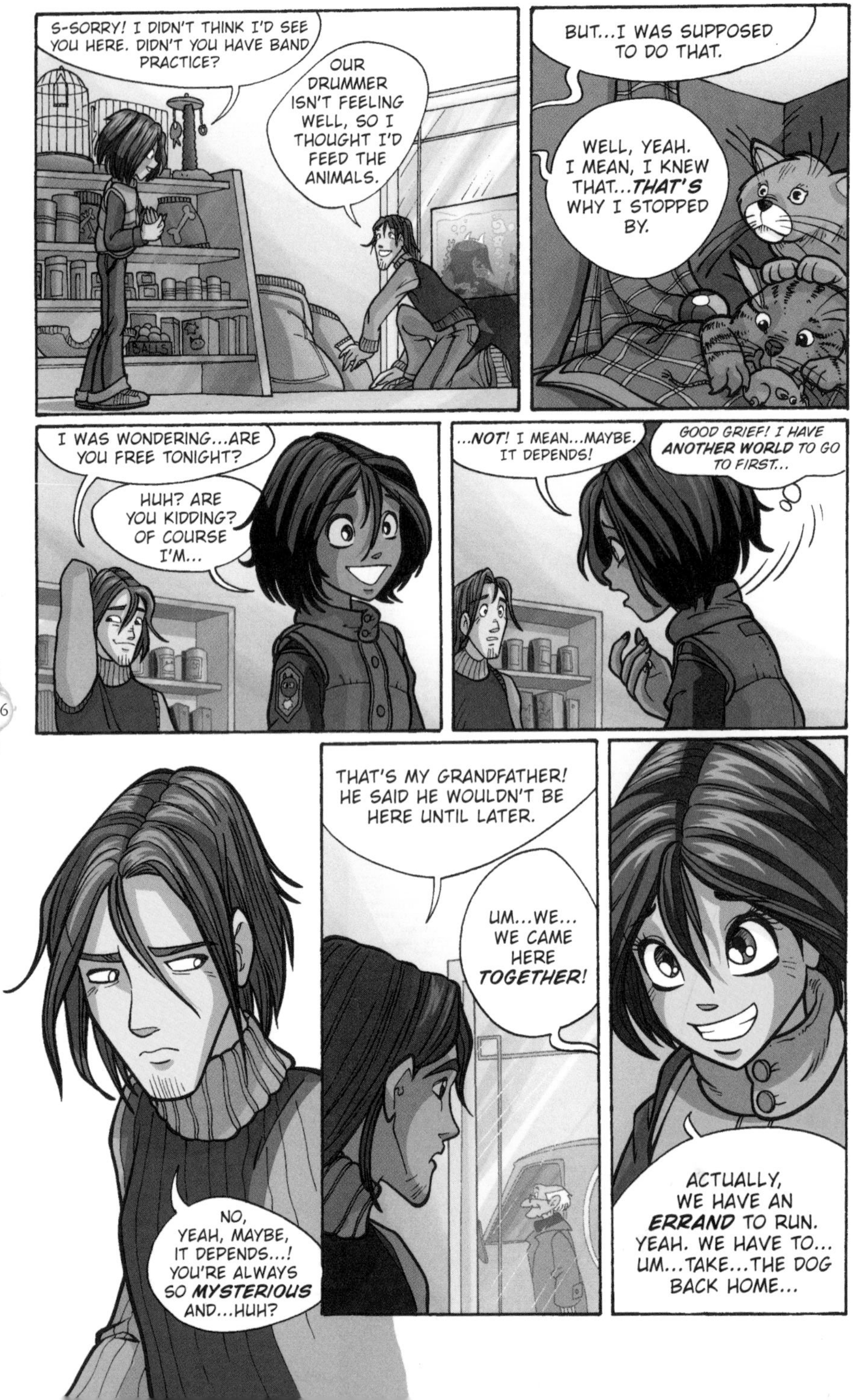
S-SORRY! I DIDN'T THINK I'D SEE YOU HERE. DIDN'T YOU HAVE BAND PRACTICE?
OUR DRUMMER ISN'T FEELING WELL, SO I THOUGHT I'D FEED THE ANIMALS.
BALLS
BUT...I WAS SUPPOSED TO DO THAT.
WELL, YEAH. I MEAN, I KNEW THAT...*THAT'S* WHY I STOPPED BY.
I WAS WONDERING...ARE YOU FREE TONIGHT?
HUH? ARE YOU KIDDING? OF COURSE I'M...
...*NOT*! I MEAN...MAYBE. IT DEPENDS!
GOOD GRIEF! I HAVE ***ANOTHER WORLD*** *TO GO TO FIRST...*
NO, YEAH, MAYBE, IT DEPENDS...! YOU'RE ALWAYS SO ***MYSTERIOUS*** AND...HUH?
THAT'S MY GRANDFATHER! HE SAID HE WOULDN'T BE HERE UNTIL LATER.
UM...WE... WE CAME HERE ***TOGETHER***!
ACTUALLY, WE HAVE AN ***ERRAND*** TO RUN. YEAH. WE HAVE TO... UM...TAKE...THE DOG BACK HOME...

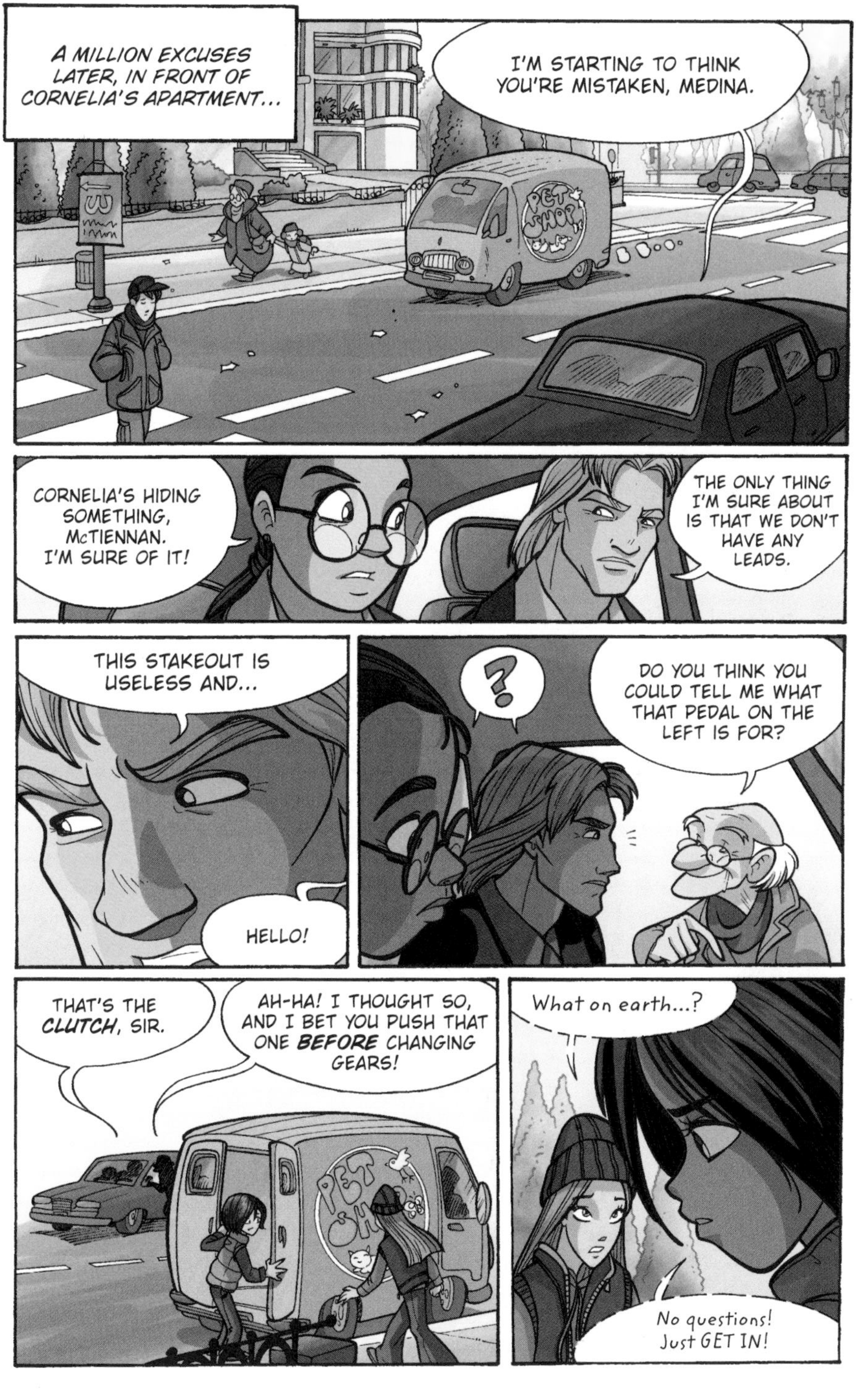
A MILLION EXCUSES LATER, IN FRONT OF CORNELIA'S APARTMENT...
I'M STARTING TO THINK YOU'RE MISTAKEN, MEDINA.
PET SHOP
CORNELIA'S HIDING SOMETHING, McTIENNAN. I'M SURE OF IT!
THE ONLY THING I'M SURE ABOUT IS THAT WE DON'T HAVE ANY LEADS.
THIS STAKEOUT IS USELESS AND...
HELLO!
?
DO YOU THINK YOU COULD TELL ME WHAT THAT PEDAL ON THE LEFT IS FOR?
THAT'S THE CLUTCH, SIR.
AH-HA! I THOUGHT SO, AND I BET YOU PUSH THAT ONE BEFORE CHANGING GEARS!
PET SHOP
What on earth...?
No questions! Just GET IN!

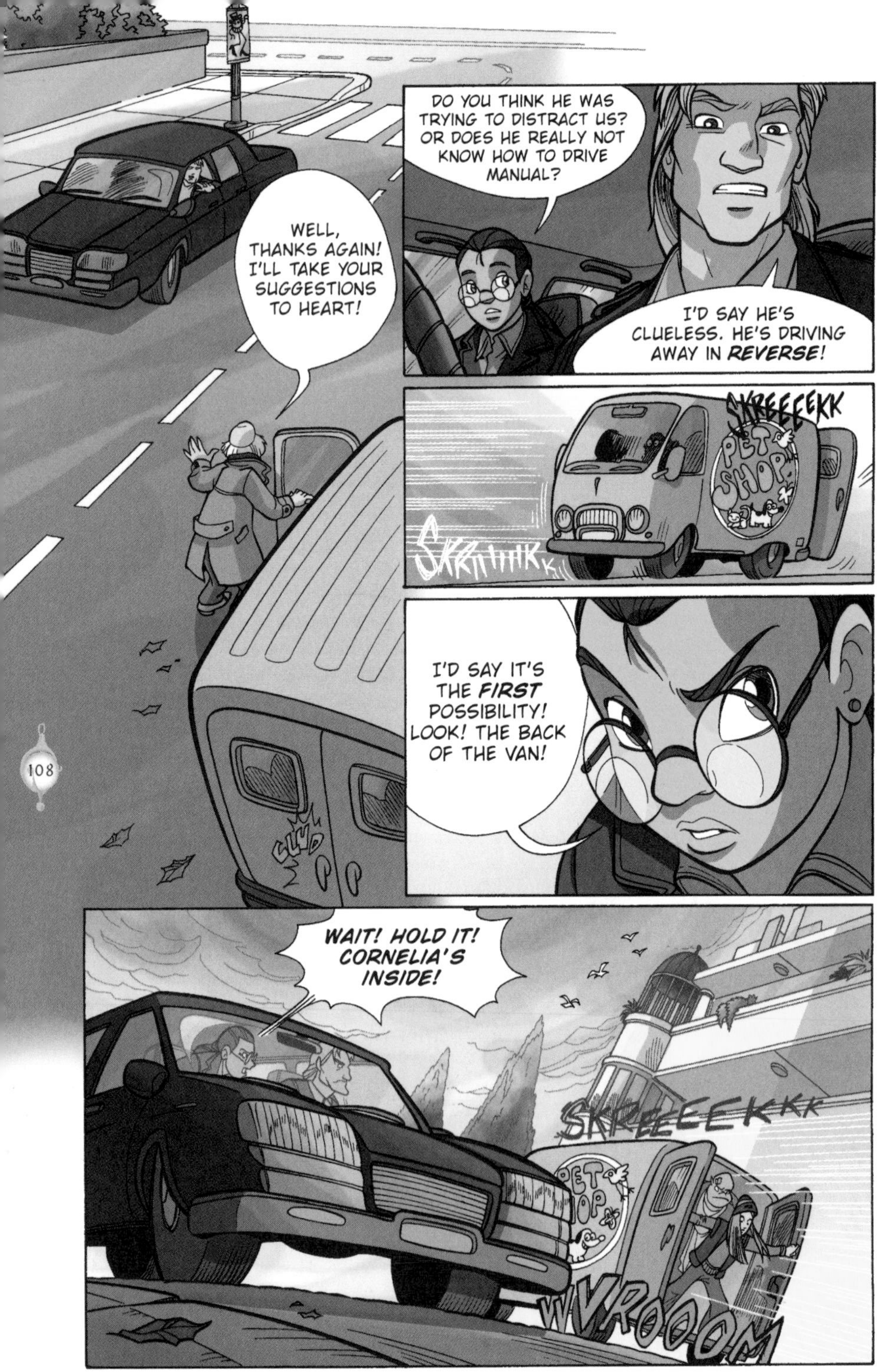

WELL, THANKS AGAIN! I'LL TAKE YOUR SUGGESTIONS TO HEART!
DO YOU THINK HE WAS TRYING TO DISTRACT US? OR DOES HE REALLY NOT KNOW HOW TO DRIVE MANUAL?
I'D SAY HE'S CLUELESS. HE'S DRIVING AWAY IN *REVERSE*!
PET SHOP
SKREEEEKK
SKRIIIIIIKK
CLUD
I'D SAY IT'S THE *FIRST* POSSIBILITY! LOOK! THE BACK OF THE VAN!
WAIT! HOLD IT! CORNELIA'S INSIDE!
SKREEEEEKKKK
PET SHOP
WVROOOM

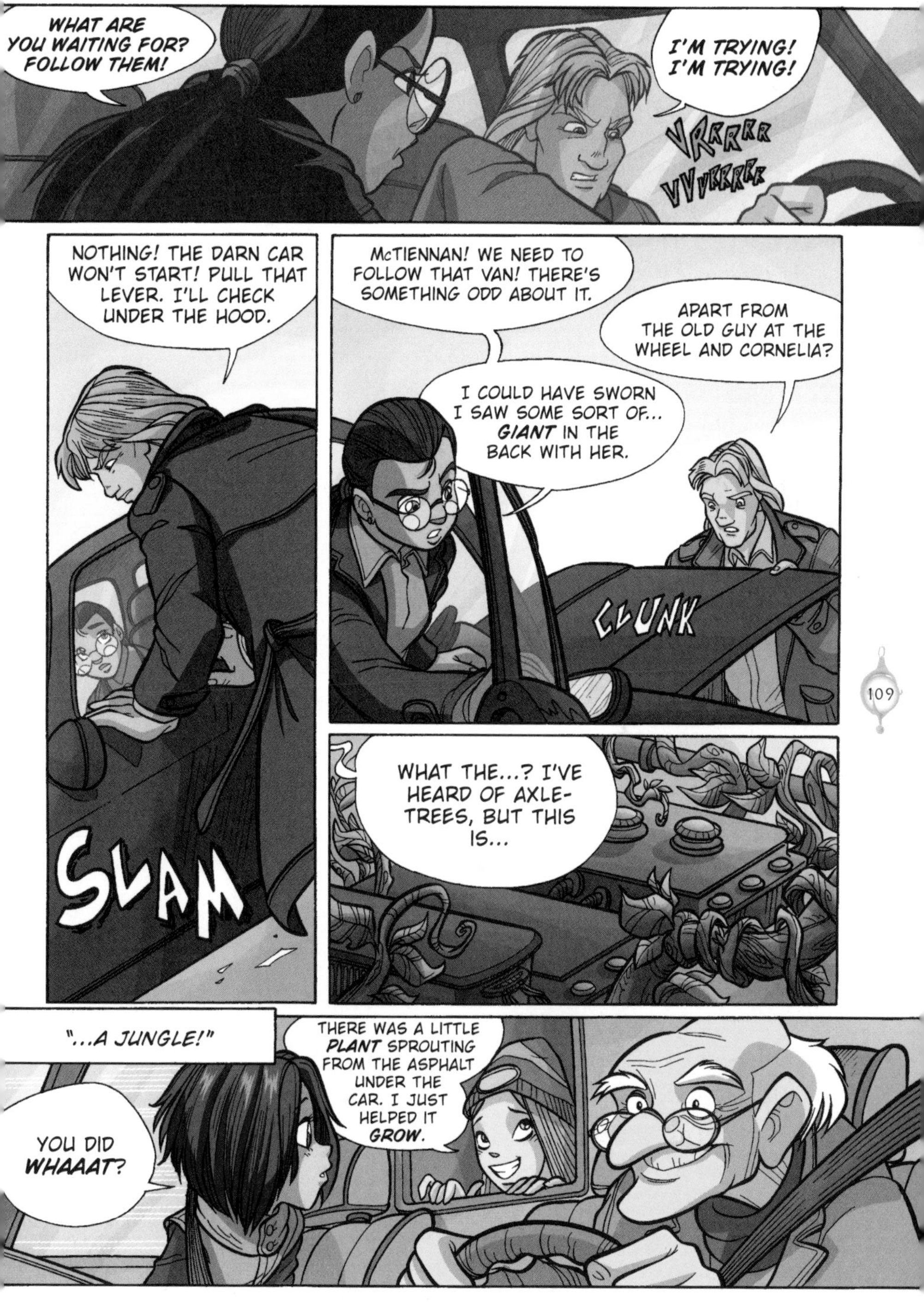

WHAT ARE YOU WAITING FOR? FOLLOW THEM!
I'M TRYING! I'M TRYING!
VRRRRR
VVVRRRRR
NOTHING! THE DARN CAR WON'T START! PULL THAT LEVER. I'LL CHECK UNDER THE HOOD.
SLAM
McTIENNAN! WE NEED TO FOLLOW THAT VAN! THERE'S SOMETHING ODD ABOUT IT.
APART FROM THE OLD GUY AT THE WHEEL AND CORNELIA?
I COULD HAVE SWORN I SAW SOME SORT OF... *GIANT* IN THE BACK WITH HER.
CLUNK
WHAT THE...? I'VE HEARD OF AXLE-TREES, BUT THIS IS...
"...A JUNGLE!"
THERE WAS A LITTLE *PLANT* SPROUTING FROM THE ASPHALT UNDER THE CAR. I JUST HELPED IT *GROW*.
YOU DID *WHAAAT*?

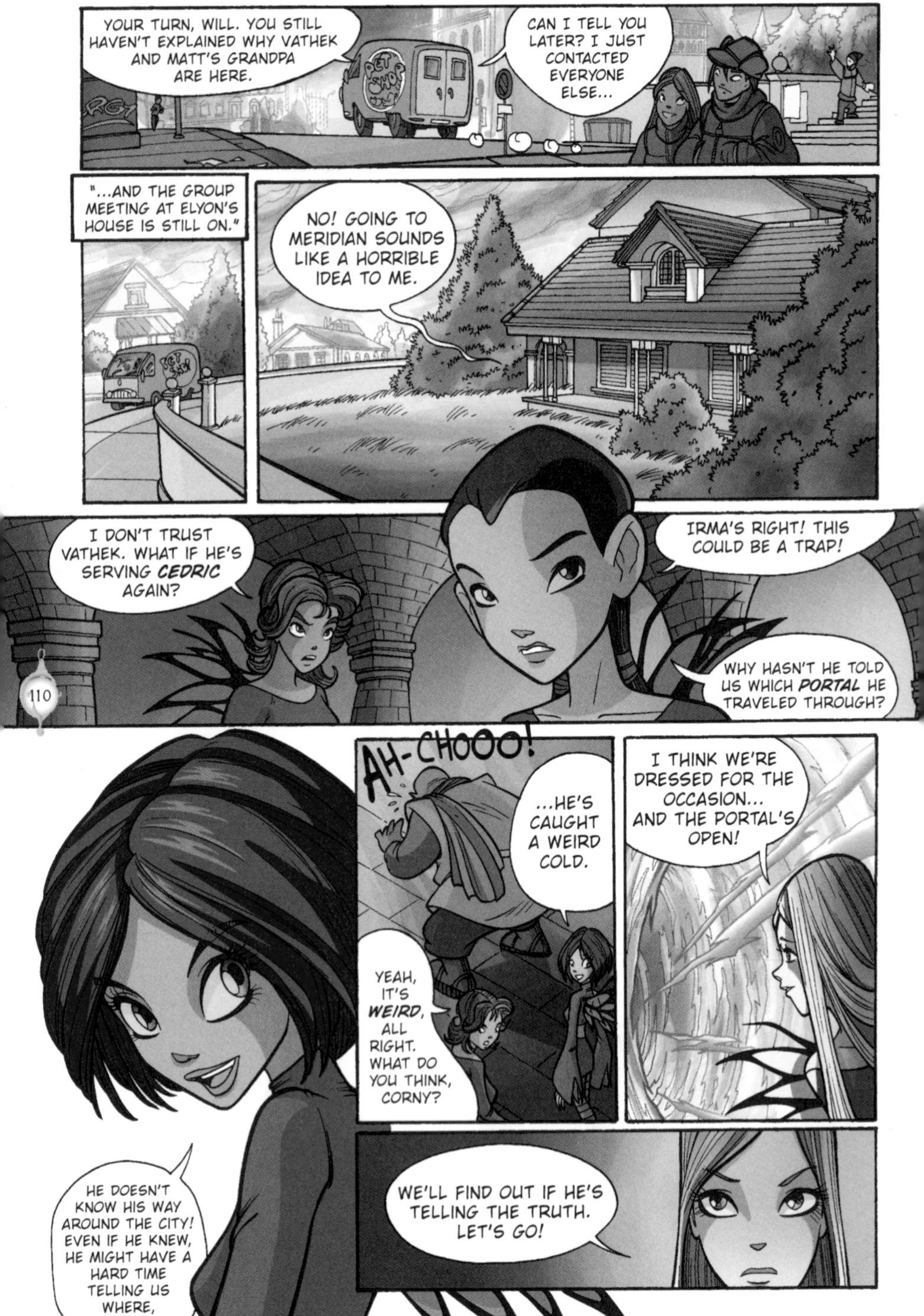

YOUR TURN, WILL. YOU STILL HAVEN'T EXPLAINED WHY VATHEK AND MATT'S GRANDPA ARE HERE.
CAN I TELL YOU LATER? I JUST CONTACTED EVERYONE ELSE...
"...AND THE GROUP MEETING AT ELYON'S HOUSE IS STILL ON."
NO! GOING TO MERIDIAN SOUNDS LIKE A HORRIBLE IDEA TO ME.
I DON'T TRUST VATHEK. WHAT IF HE'S SERVING **CEDRIC** AGAIN?
IRMA'S RIGHT! THIS COULD BE A TRAP!
WHY HASN'T HE TOLD US WHICH **PORTAL** HE TRAVELED THROUGH?
HE DOESN'T KNOW HIS WAY AROUND THE CITY! EVEN IF HE KNEW, HE MIGHT HAVE A HARD TIME TELLING US WHERE, BECAUSE...
AH-CHOOO!
...HE'S CAUGHT A WEIRD COLD.
YEAH, IT'S **WEIRD**, ALL RIGHT. WHAT DO YOU THINK, CORNY?
I THINK WE'RE DRESSED FOR THE OCCASION... AND THE PORTAL'S OPEN!
WE'LL FIND OUT IF HE'S TELLING THE TRUTH. LET'S GO!

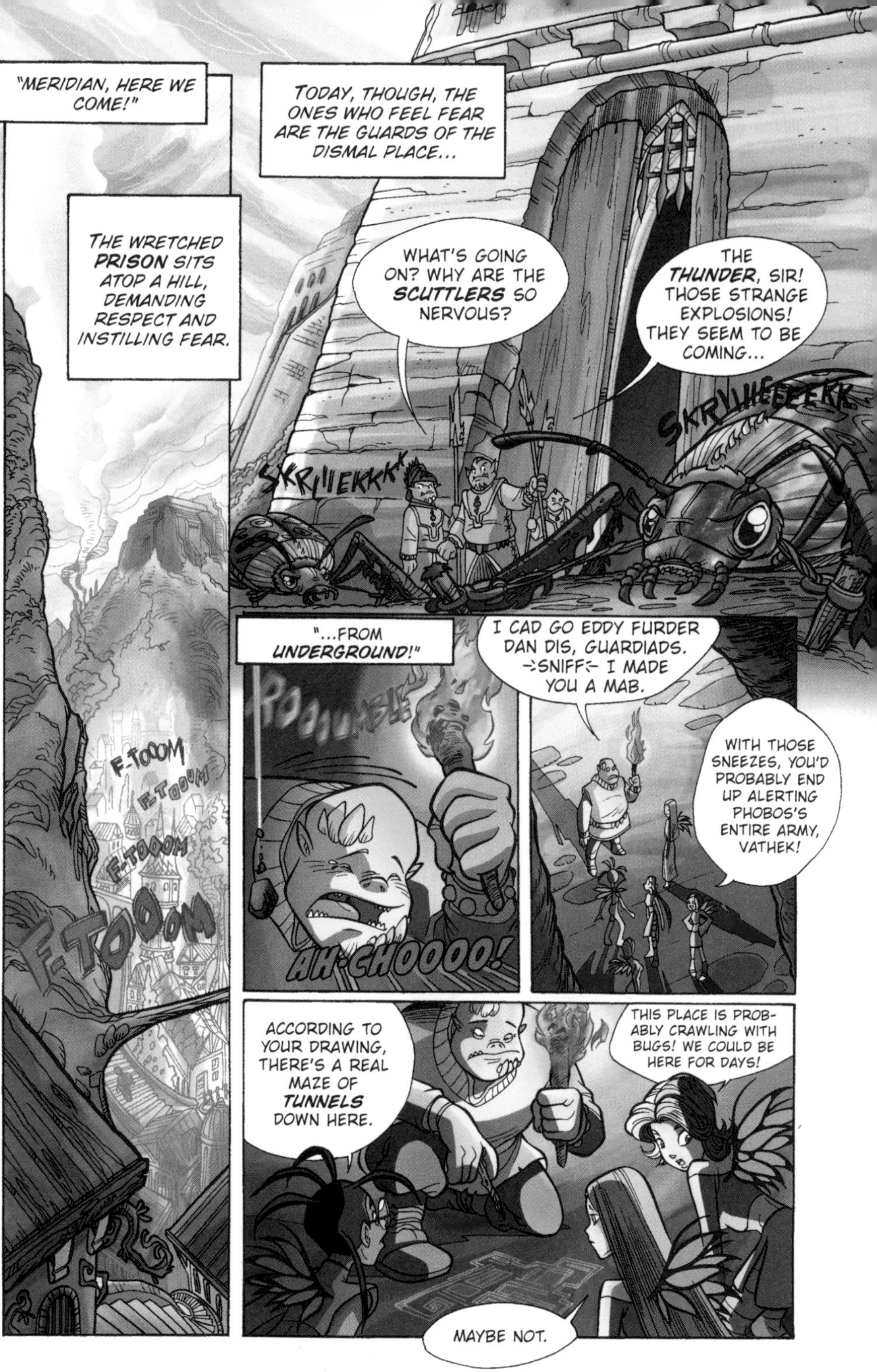
"MERIDIAN, HERE WE COME!"
THE WRETCHED PRISON SITS ATOP A HILL, DEMANDING RESPECT AND INSTILLING FEAR.
F-TOOOM
F-TOOOM
F-TOOOM
F-TOOOM
TODAY, THOUGH, THE ONES WHO FEEL FEAR ARE THE GUARDS OF THE DISMAL PLACE...
WHAT'S GOING ON? WHY ARE THE SCUTTLERS SO NERVOUS?
THE THUNDER, SIR! THOSE STRANGE EXPLOSIONS! THEY SEEM TO BE COMING...
SKRIIIEKKK
SKRIIIEEEEKK
"...FROM UNDERGROUND!"
AH-CHOOOOO!
I CAD GO EDDY FURDER DAN DIS, GUARDIADS. SNIFF I MADE YOU A MAB.
WITH THOSE SNEEZES, YOU'D PROBABLY END UP ALERTING PHOBOS'S ENTIRE ARMY, VATHEK!
ACCORDING TO YOUR DRAWING, THERE'S A REAL MAZE OF TUNNELS DOWN HERE.
THIS PLACE IS PROBABLY CRAWLING WITH BUGS! WE COULD BE HERE FOR DAYS!
MAYBE NOT.

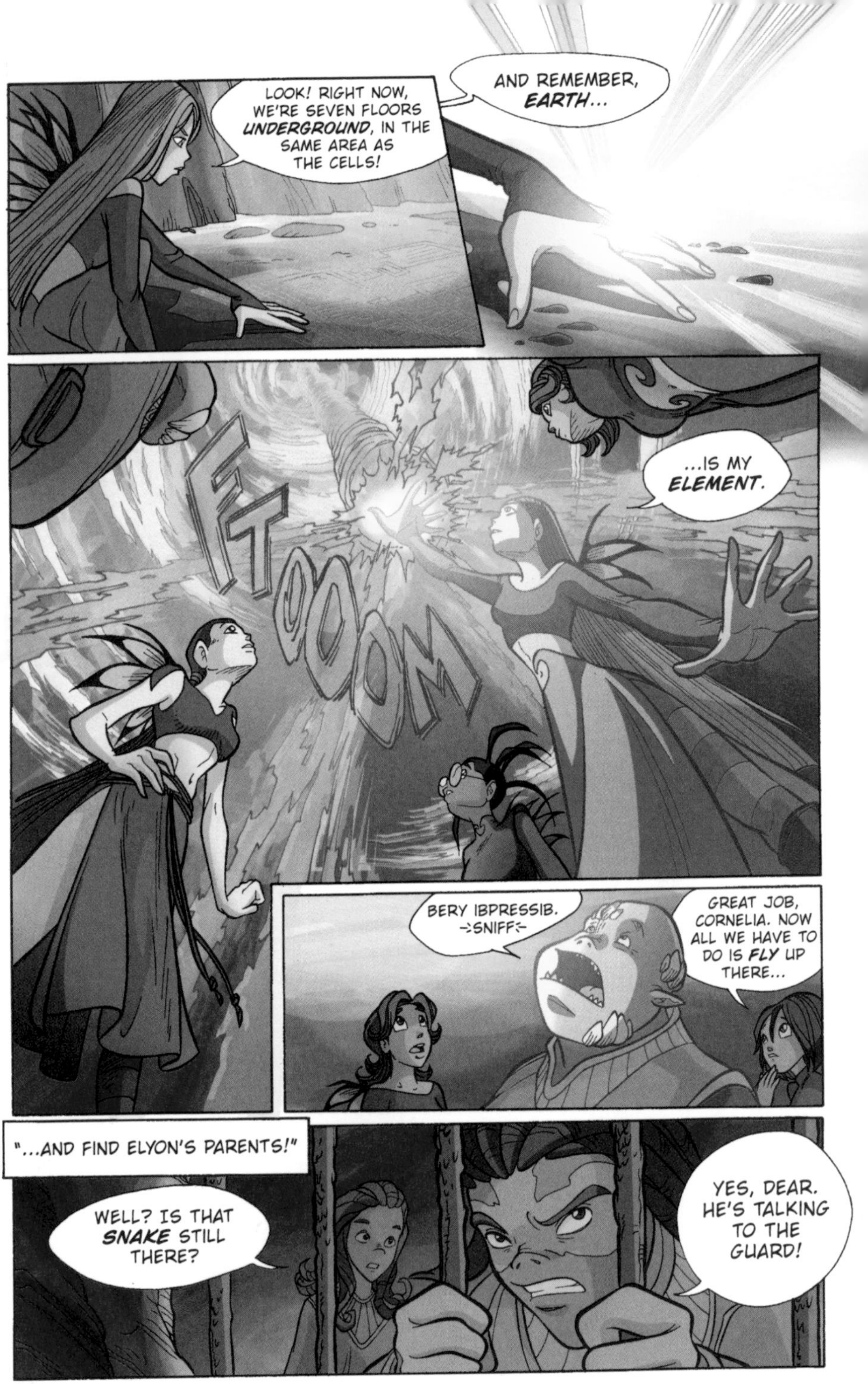
LOOK! RIGHT NOW, WE'RE SEVEN FLOORS UNDERGROUND, IN THE SAME AREA AS THE CELLS!
AND REMEMBER, EARTH...
...IS MY ELEMENT.
FTOOOM
BERY IBPRESSIB. -SNIFF-
GREAT JOB, CORNELIA. NOW ALL WE HAVE TO DO IS FLY UP THERE...
"...AND FIND ELYON'S PARENTS!"
WELL? IS THAT SNAKE STILL THERE?
YES, DEAR. HE'S TALKING TO THE GUARD!

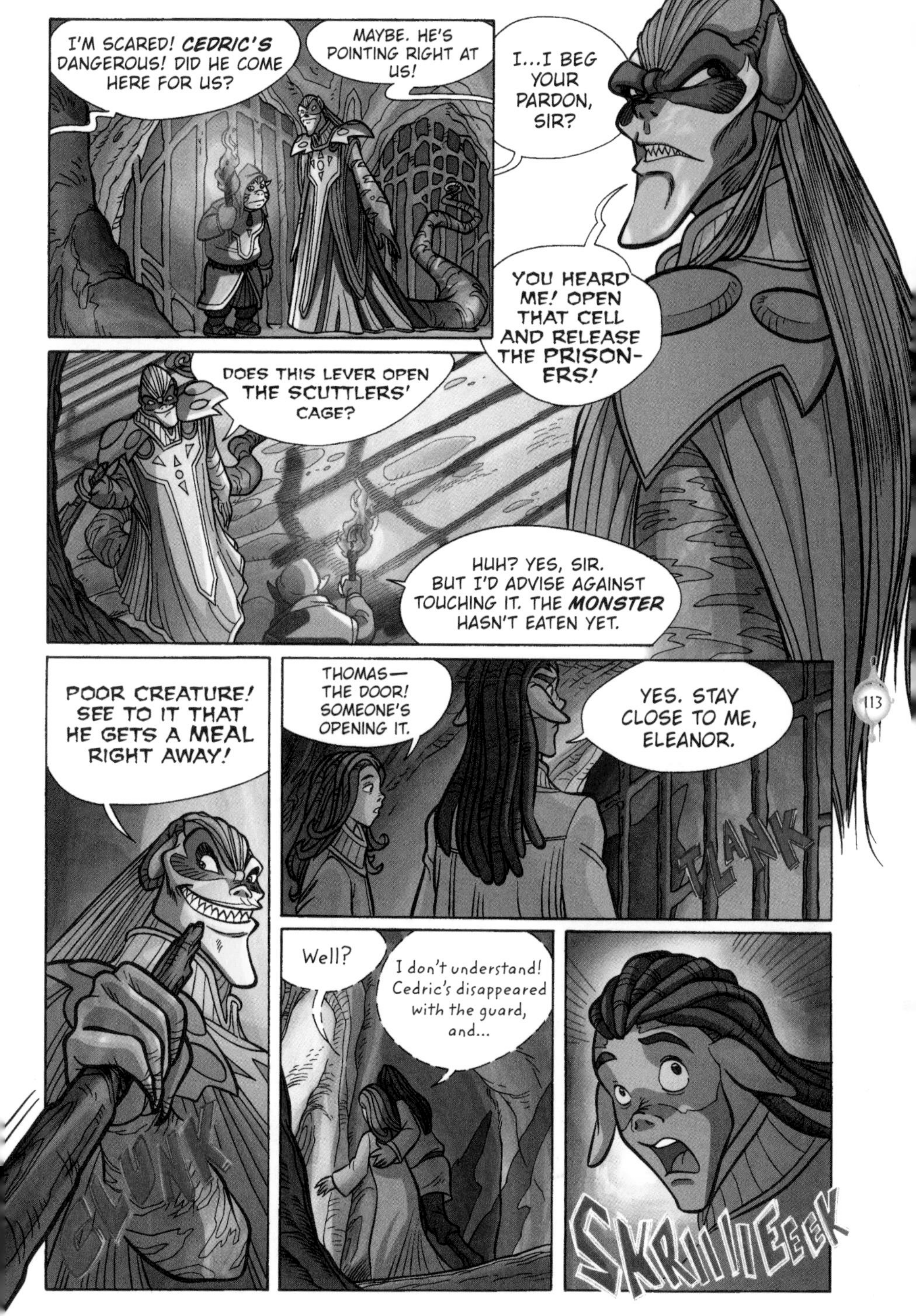
I'M SCARED! **CEDRIC'S** DANGEROUS! DID HE COME HERE FOR US?
MAYBE. HE'S POINTING RIGHT AT US!
I...I BEG YOUR PARDON, SIR?
YOU HEARD ME! OPEN THAT CELL AND RELEASE THE PRISON-ERS!
DOES THIS LEVER OPEN THE SCUTTLERS' CAGE?
HUH? YES, SIR. BUT I'D ADVISE AGAINST TOUCHING IT. THE **MONSTER** HASN'T EATEN YET.
POOR CREATURE! SEE TO IT THAT HE GETS A MEAL RIGHT AWAY!
CHUNK
THOMAS— THE DOOR! SOMEONE'S OPENING IT.
YES. STAY CLOSE TO ME, ELEANOR.
TLANK
Well?
I don't understand! Cedric's disappeared with the guard, and...
SKRIIIEEEK

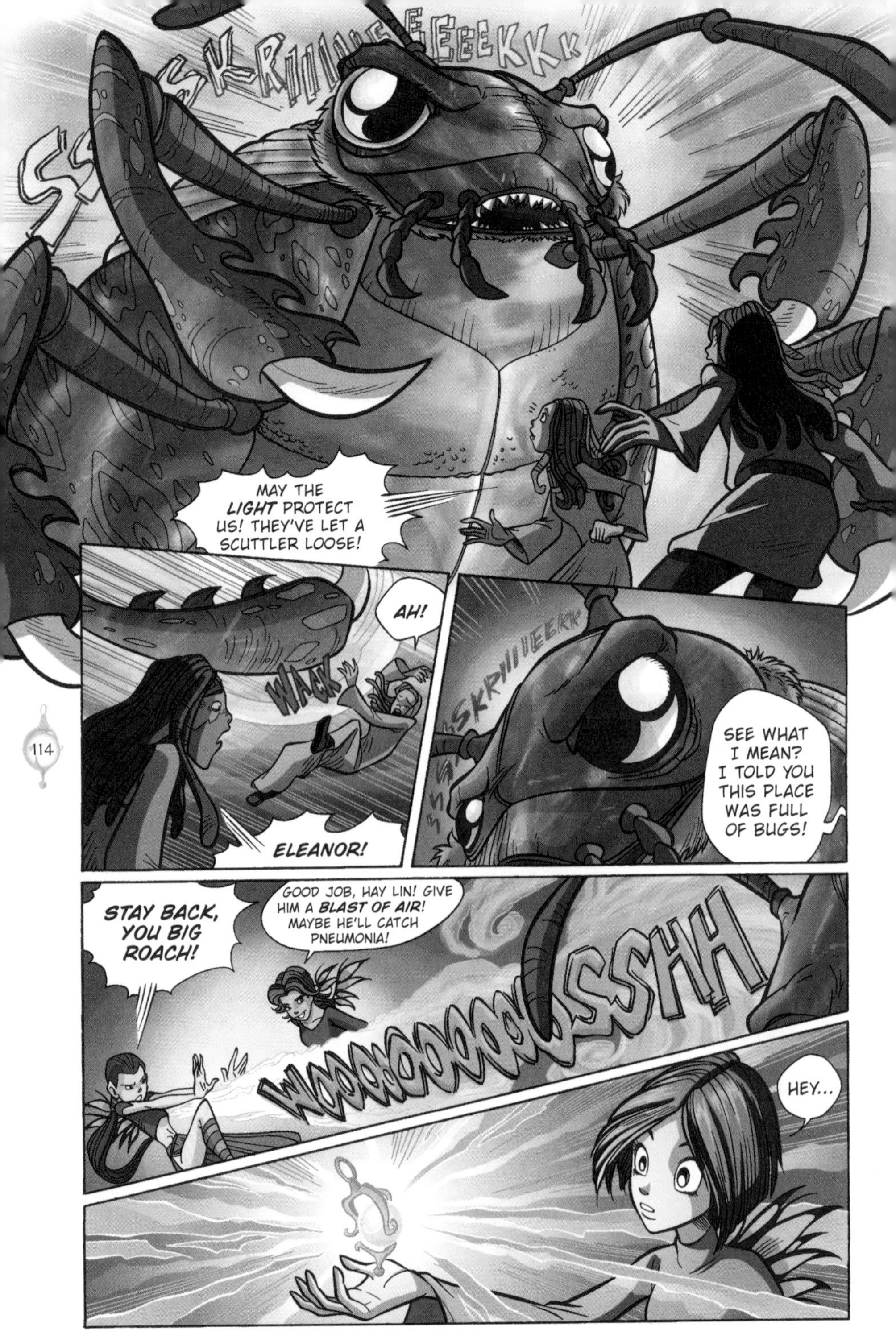
SSSKRIIIIEEEEKKk
MAY THE LIGHT PROTECT US! THEY'VE LET A SCUTTLER LOOSE!
AH!
WACK
ELEANOR!
SKRIIIEEKK
SEE WHAT I MEAN? I TOLD YOU THIS PLACE WAS FULL OF BUGS!
STAY BACK, YOU BIG ROACH!
GOOD JOB, HAY LIN! GIVE HIM A BLAST OF AIR! MAYBE HE'LL CATCH PNEUMONIA!
WOOOOOOOOSSHH
HEY...

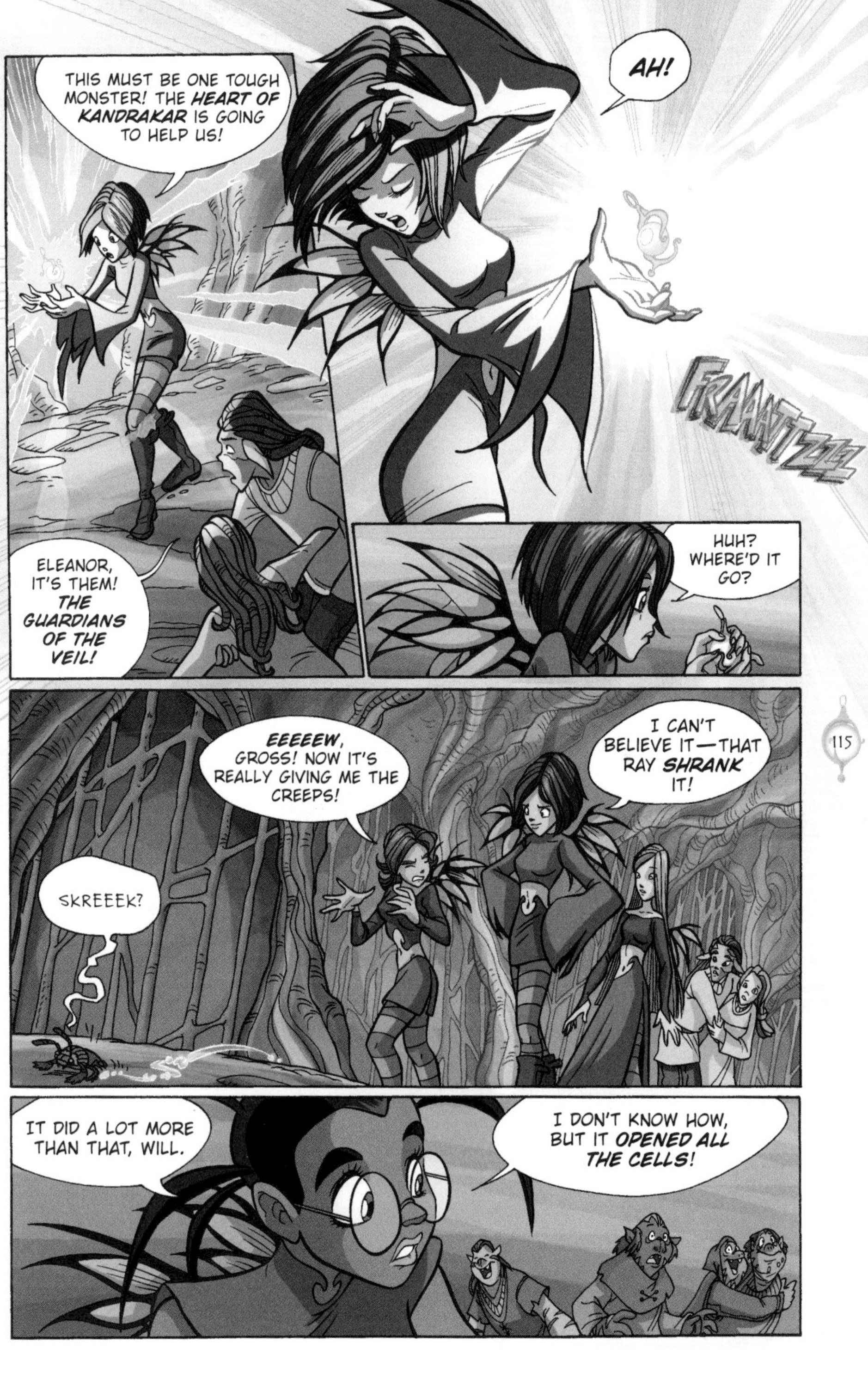
THIS MUST BE ONE TOUGH MONSTER! THE HEART OF KANDRAKAR IS GOING TO HELP US!
AH!
FRAAATZZZ
ELEANOR, IT'S THEM! THE GUARDIANS OF THE VEIL!
HUH? WHERE'D IT GO?
EEEEEW, GROSS! NOW IT'S REALLY GIVING ME THE CREEPS!
I CAN'T BELIEVE IT—THAT RAY SHRANK IT!
SKREEEK?
IT DID A LOT MORE THAN THAT, WILL.
I DON'T KNOW HOW, BUT IT OPENED ALL THE CELLS!

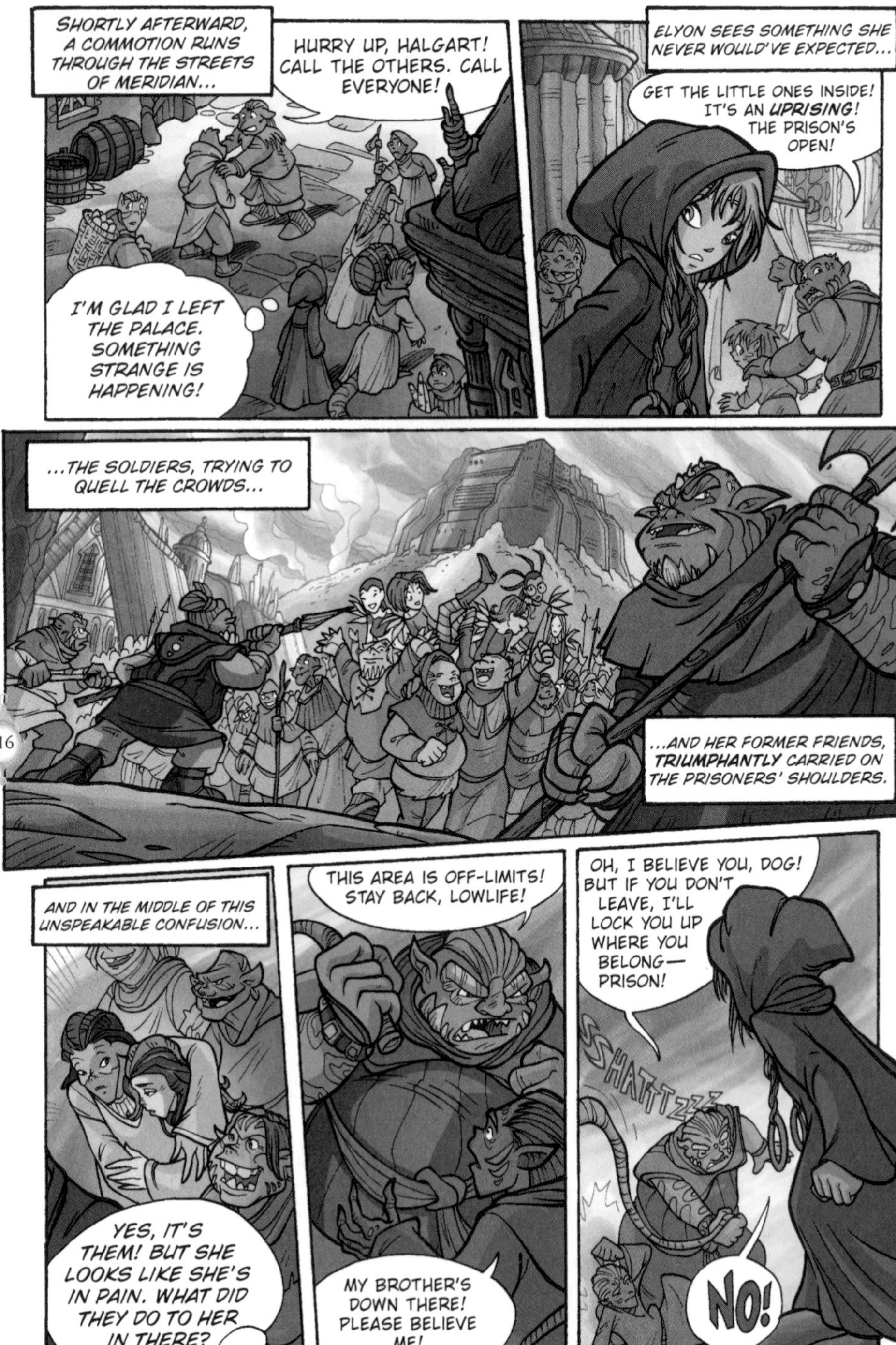
SHORTLY AFTERWARD, A COMMOTION RUNS THROUGH THE STREETS OF MERIDIAN...
HURRY UP, HALGART! CALL THE OTHERS. CALL EVERYONE!
I'M GLAD I LEFT THE PALACE. SOMETHING STRANGE IS HAPPENING!
ELYON SEES SOMETHING SHE NEVER WOULD'VE EXPECTED...
GET THE LITTLE ONES INSIDE! IT'S AN UPRISING! THE PRISON'S OPEN!
...THE SOLDIERS, TRYING TO QUELL THE CROWDS...
...AND HER FORMER FRIENDS, TRIUMPHANTLY CARRIED ON THE PRISONERS' SHOULDERS.
AND IN THE MIDDLE OF THIS UNSPEAKABLE CONFUSION...
YES, IT'S THEM! BUT SHE LOOKS LIKE SHE'S IN PAIN. WHAT DID THEY DO TO HER IN THERE?
THIS AREA IS OFF-LIMITS! STAY BACK, LOWLIFE!
MY BROTHER'S DOWN THERE! PLEASE BELIEVE ME!
OH, I BELIEVE YOU, DOG! BUT IF YOU DON'T LEAVE, I'LL LOCK YOU UP WHERE YOU BELONG—PRISON!
SSHATTTZZZ
NO!

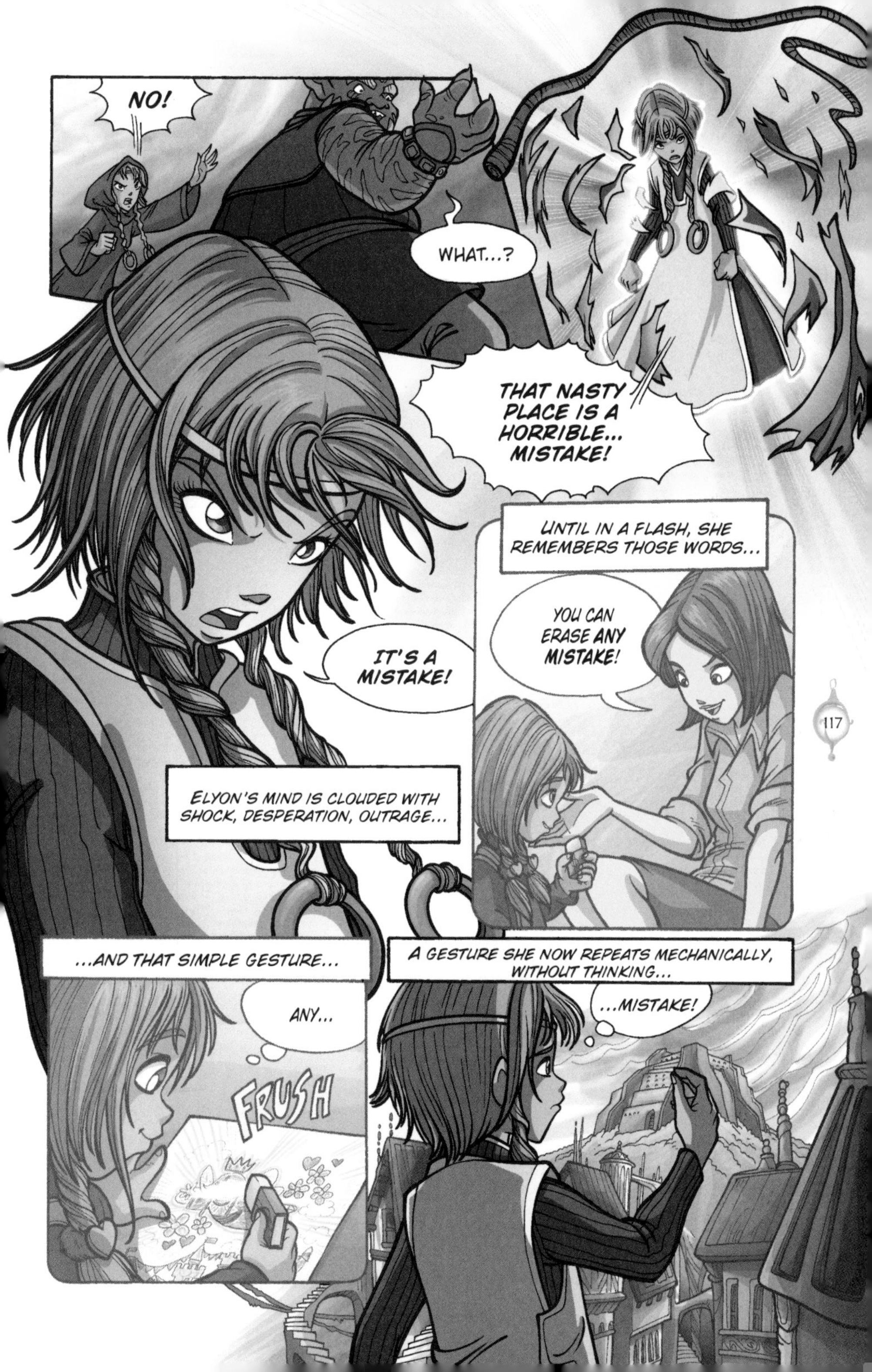
NO!
WHAT...?
THAT NASTY PLACE IS A HORRIBLE... MISTAKE!
IT'S A MISTAKE!
UNTIL IN A FLASH, SHE REMEMBERS THOSE WORDS...
YOU CAN ERASE ANY MISTAKE!
ELYON'S MIND IS CLOUDED WITH SHOCK, DESPERATION, OUTRAGE...
...AND THAT SIMPLE GESTURE...
ANY...
FRUSH
A GESTURE SHE NOW REPEATS MECHANICALLY, WITHOUT THINKING...
...MISTAKE!

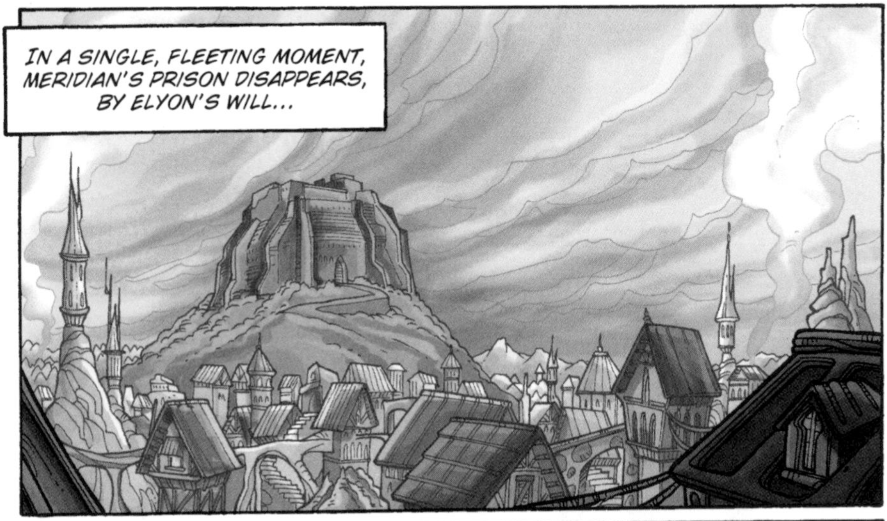
IN A SINGLE, FLEETING MOMENT, MERIDIAN'S PRISON DISAPPEARS, BY ELYON'S WILL...

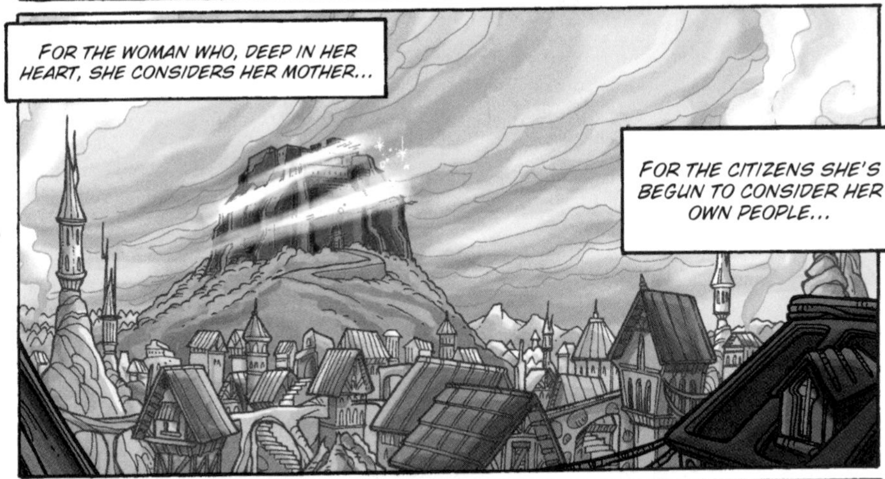
FOR THE WOMAN WHO, DEEP IN HER HEART, SHE CONSIDERS HER MOTHER...
FOR THE CITIZENS SHE'S BEGUN TO CONSIDER HER OWN PEOPLE...

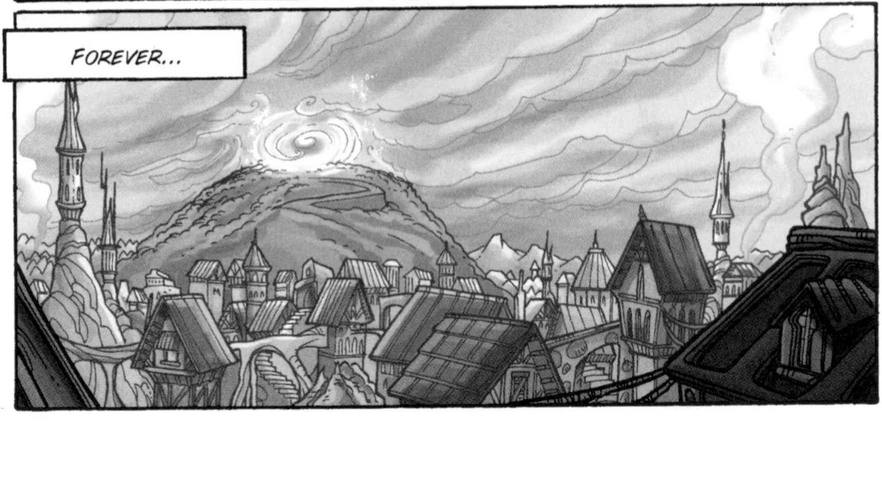
FOREVER...

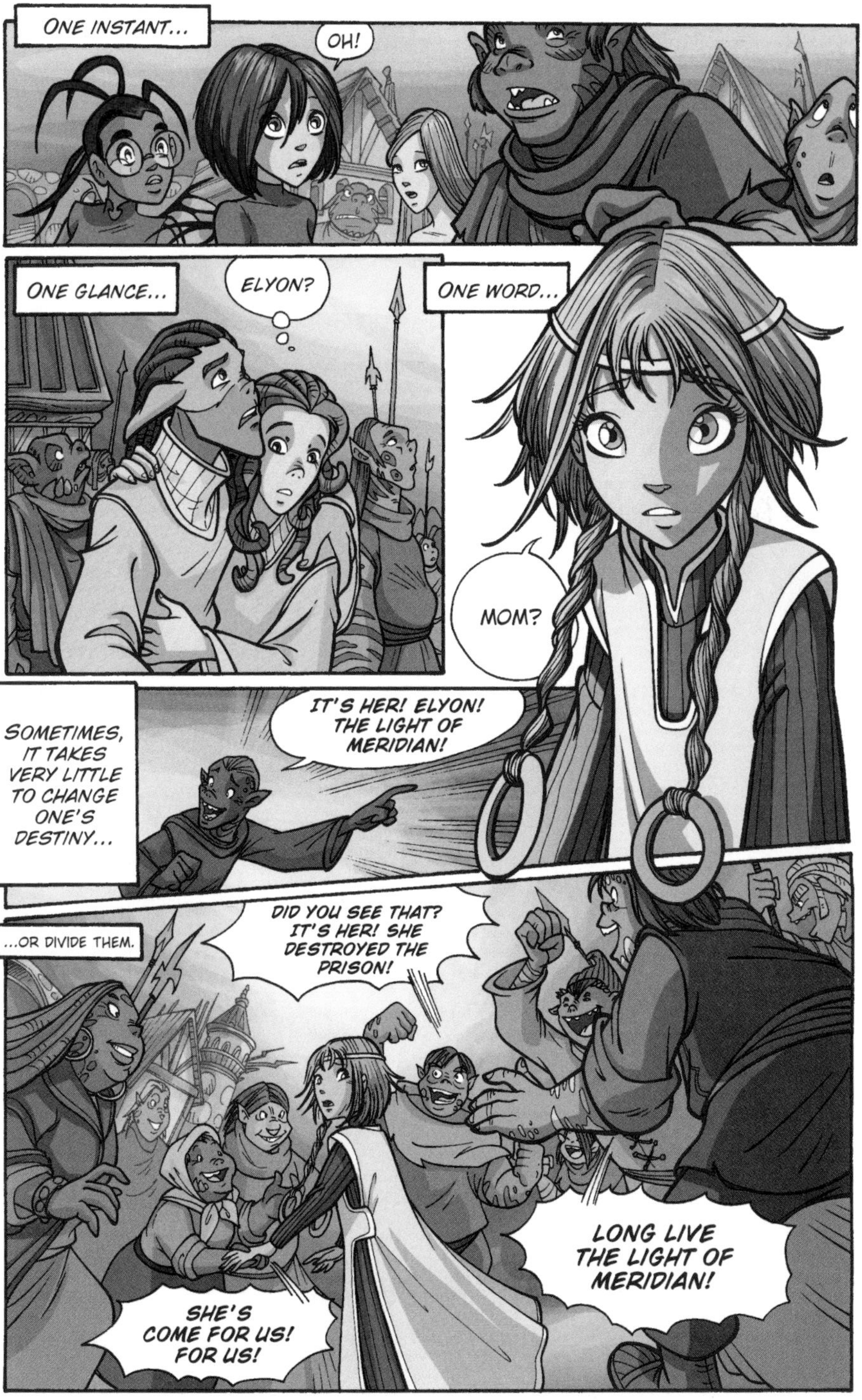
ONE INSTANT...
OH!
ONE GLANCE...
ELYON?
ONE WORD...
MOM?
SOMETIMES, IT TAKES VERY LITTLE TO CHANGE ONE'S DESTINY...
IT'S HER! ELYON! THE LIGHT OF MERIDIAN!
...OR DIVIDE THEM.
DID YOU SEE THAT? IT'S HER! SHE DESTROYED THE PRISON!
LONG LIVE THE LIGHT OF MERIDIAN!
SHE'S COME FOR US! FOR US!

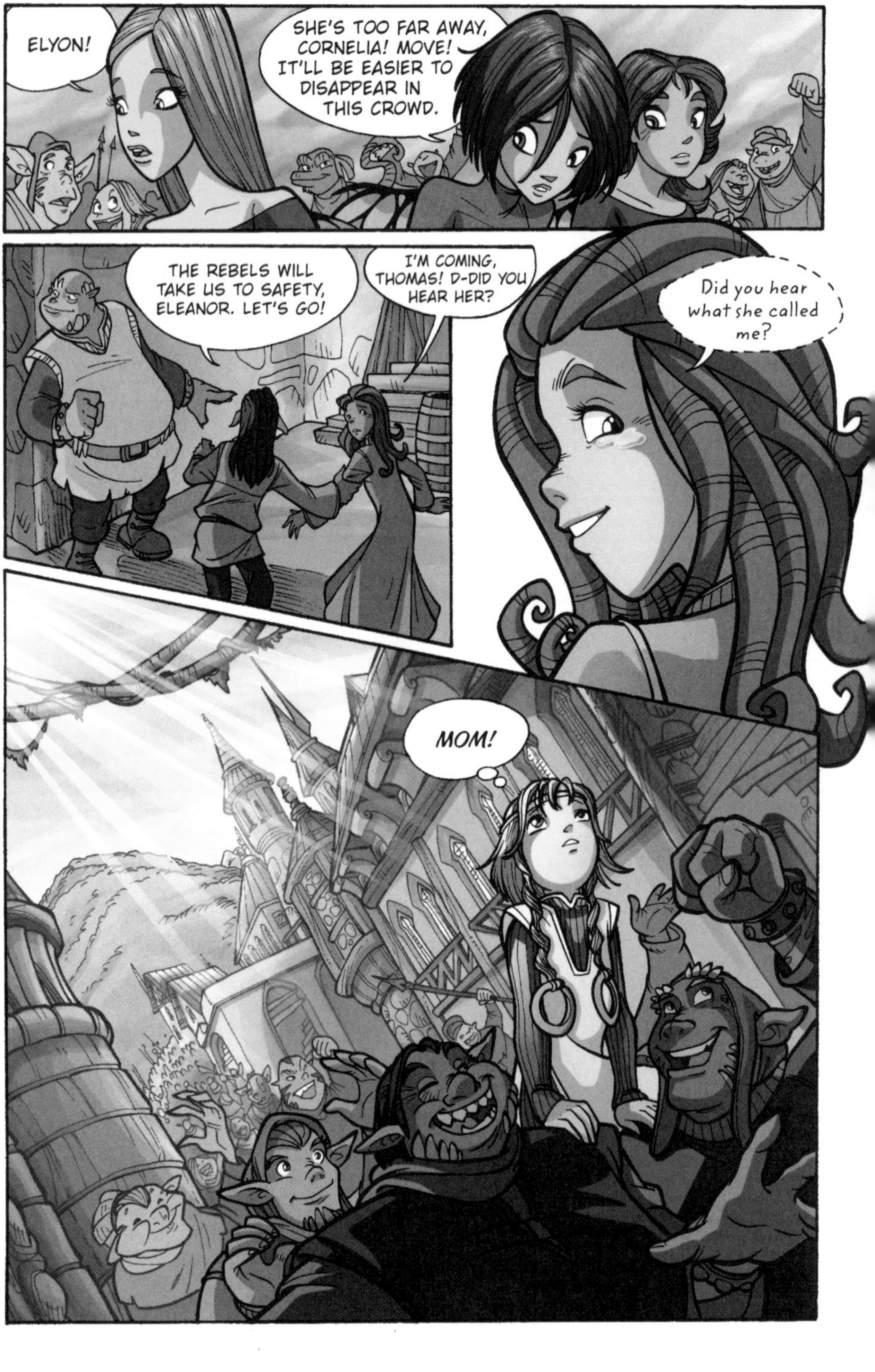
ELYON!
SHE'S TOO FAR AWAY, CORNELIA! MOVE! IT'LL BE EASIER TO DISAPPEAR IN THIS CROWD.
THE REBELS WILL TAKE US TO SAFETY, ELEANOR. LET'S GO!
I'M COMING, THOMAS! D-DID YOU HEAR HER?
Did you hear what she called me?
MOM!

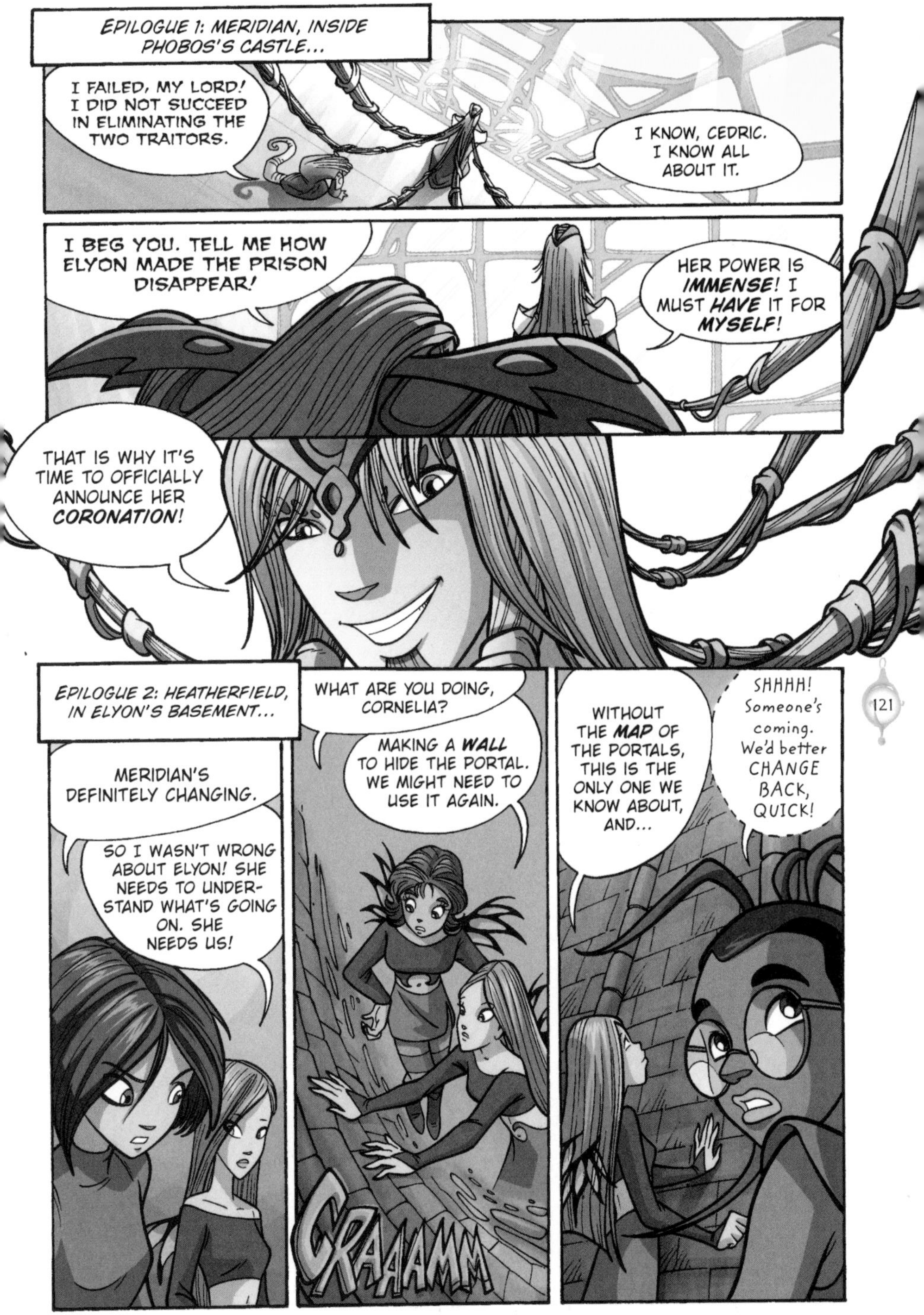
EPILOGUE 1: MERIDIAN, INSIDE PHOBOS'S CASTLE...
I FAILED, MY LORD! I DID NOT SUCCEED IN ELIMINATING THE TWO TRAITORS.
I KNOW, CEDRIC. I KNOW ALL ABOUT IT.
I BEG YOU. TELL ME HOW ELYON MADE THE PRISON DISAPPEAR!
HER POWER IS IMMENSE! I MUST HAVE IT FOR MYSELF!
THAT IS WHY IT'S TIME TO OFFICIALLY ANNOUNCE HER CORONATION!
EPILOGUE 2: HEATHERFIELD, IN ELYON'S BASEMENT...
MERIDIAN'S DEFINITELY CHANGING.
SO I WASN'T WRONG ABOUT ELYON! SHE NEEDS TO UNDER-STAND WHAT'S GOING ON. SHE NEEDS US!
WHAT ARE YOU DOING, CORNELIA?
MAKING A WALL TO HIDE THE PORTAL. WE MIGHT NEED TO USE IT AGAIN.
CRAAAMM
WITHOUT THE MAP OF THE PORTALS, THIS IS THE ONLY ONE WE KNOW ABOUT, AND...
SHHHH! Someone's coming. We'd better CHANGE BACK, QUICK!

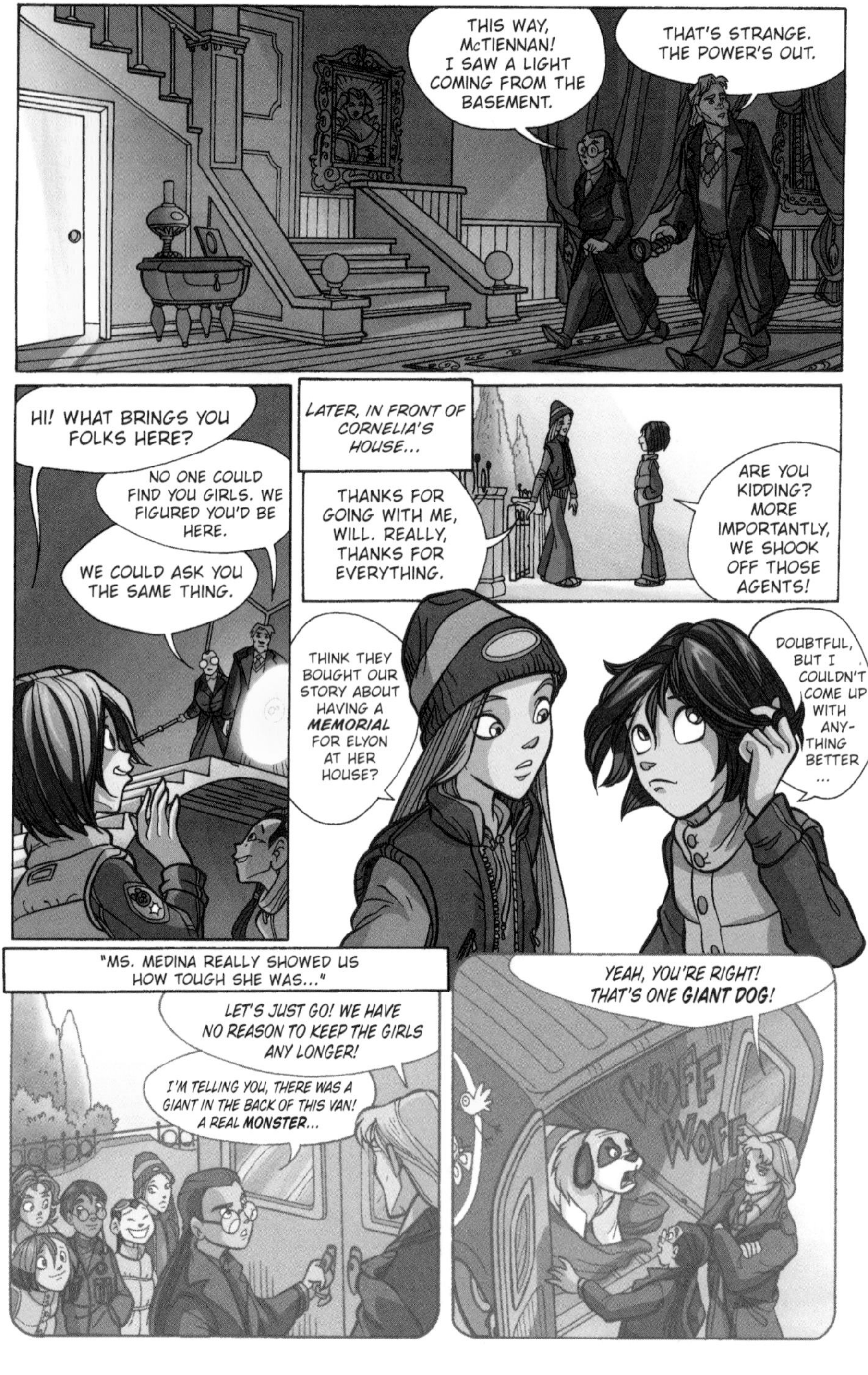

THIS WAY, McTIENNAN! I SAW A LIGHT COMING FROM THE BASEMENT.
THAT'S STRANGE. THE POWER'S OUT.
HI! WHAT BRINGS YOU FOLKS HERE?
NO ONE COULD FIND YOU GIRLS. WE FIGURED YOU'D BE HERE.
WE COULD ASK YOU THE SAME THING.
LATER, IN FRONT OF CORNELIA'S HOUSE...
THANKS FOR GOING WITH ME, WILL. REALLY, THANKS FOR EVERYTHING.
ARE YOU KIDDING? MORE IMPORTANTLY, WE SHOOK OFF THOSE AGENTS!
THINK THEY BOUGHT OUR STORY ABOUT HAVING A **MEMORIAL** FOR ELYON AT HER HOUSE?
DOUBTFUL, BUT I COULDN'T COME UP WITH ANYTHING BETTER...
"MS. MEDINA REALLY SHOWED US HOW TOUGH SHE WAS..."
LET'S JUST GO! WE HAVE NO REASON TO KEEP THE GIRLS ANY LONGER!
I'M TELLING YOU, THERE WAS A GIANT IN THE BACK OF THIS VAN! A REAL **MONSTER**...
YEAH, YOU'RE RIGHT! THAT'S ONE **GIANT DOG**!
WOFF WOFF

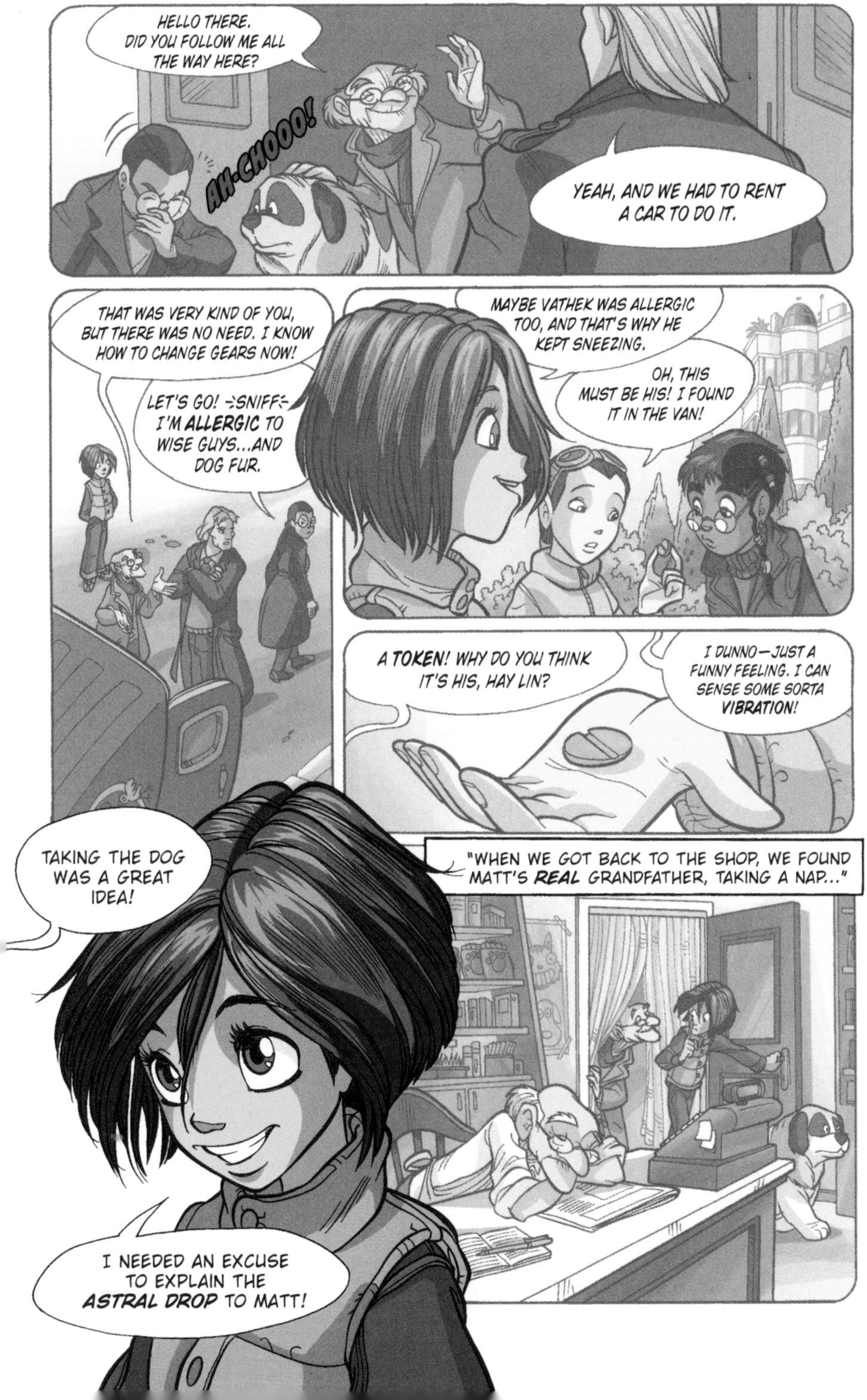
HELLO THERE. DID YOU FOLLOW ME ALL THE WAY HERE?
AH-CHOOO!
YEAH, AND WE HAD TO RENT A CAR TO DO IT.
THAT WAS VERY KIND OF YOU, BUT THERE WAS NO NEED. I KNOW HOW TO CHANGE GEARS NOW!
LET'S GO! SNIFF I'M ALLERGIC TO WISE GUYS...AND DOG FUR.
MAYBE VATHEK WAS ALLERGIC TOO, AND THAT'S WHY HE KEPT SNEEZING.
OH, THIS MUST BE HIS! I FOUND IT IN THE VAN!
A TOKEN! WHY DO YOU THINK IT'S HIS, HAY LIN?
I DUNNO—JUST A FUNNY FEELING. I CAN SENSE SOME SORTA VIBRATION!
TAKING THE DOG WAS A GREAT IDEA!
"WHEN WE GOT BACK TO THE SHOP, WE FOUND MATT'S REAL GRANDFATHER, TAKING A NAP..."
I NEEDED AN EXCUSE TO EXPLAIN THE ASTRAL DROP TO MATT!

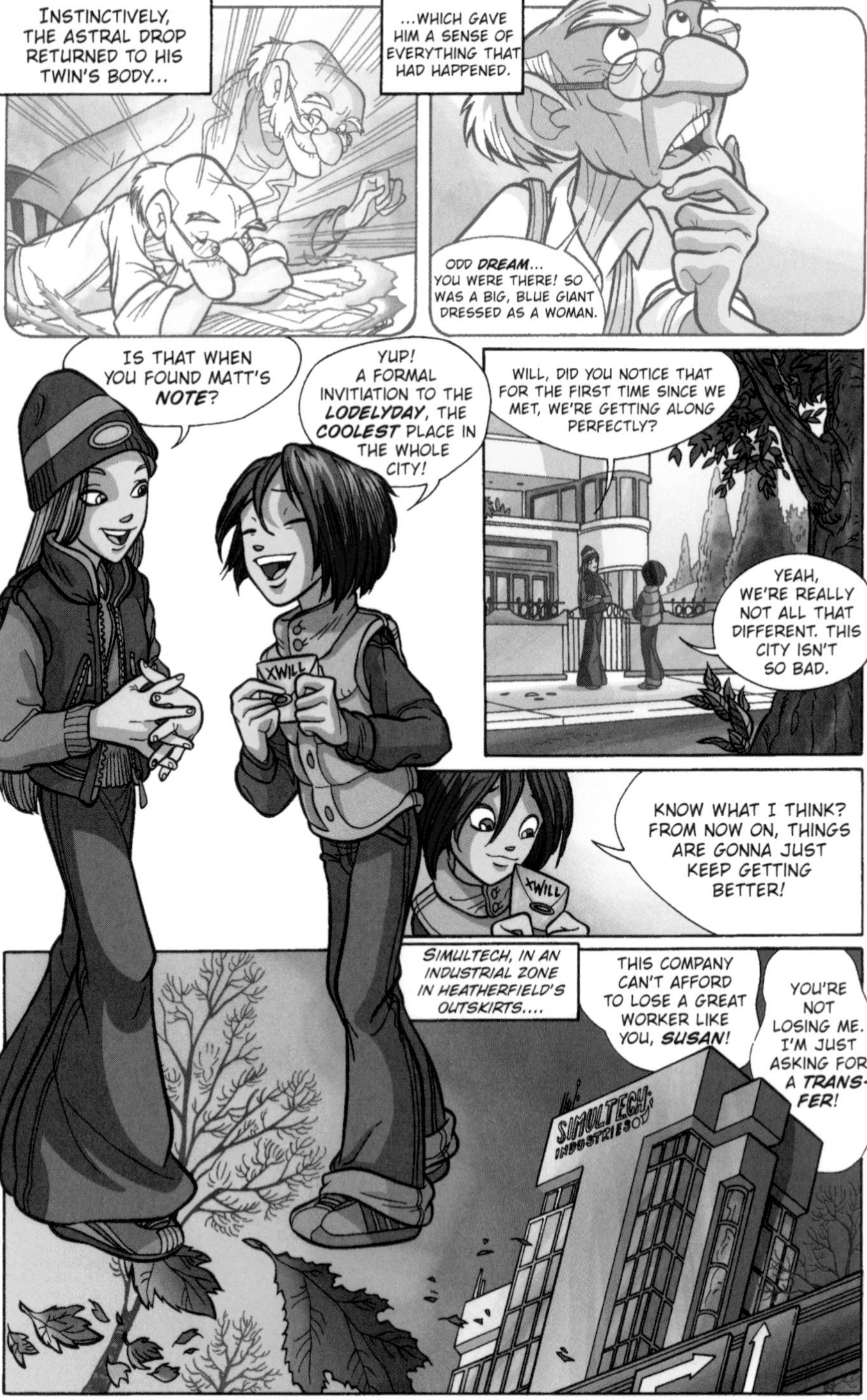
INSTINCTIVELY, THE ASTRAL DROP RETURNED TO HIS TWIN'S BODY...
...WHICH GAVE HIM A SENSE OF EVERYTHING THAT HAD HAPPENED.
ODD DREAM... YOU WERE THERE! SO WAS A BIG, BLUE GIANT DRESSED AS A WOMAN.
IS THAT WHEN YOU FOUND MATT'S NOTE?
YUP! A FORMAL INVITATION TO THE LODELYDAY, THE COOLEST PLACE IN THE WHOLE CITY!
XWILL
WILL, DID YOU NOTICE THAT FOR THE FIRST TIME SINCE WE MET, WE'RE GETTING ALONG PERFECTLY?
YEAH, WE'RE REALLY NOT ALL THAT DIFFERENT. THIS CITY ISN'T SO BAD.
KNOW WHAT I THINK? FROM NOW ON, THINGS ARE GONNA JUST KEEP GETTING BETTER!
XWILL
SIMULTECH, IN AN INDUSTRIAL ZONE IN HEATHERFIELD'S OUTSKIRTS....
THIS COMPANY CAN'T AFFORD TO LOSE A GREAT WORKER LIKE YOU, SUSAN!
YOU'RE NOT LOSING ME. I'M JUST ASKING FOR A TRANSFER!
SIMULTECH INDUSTRIES

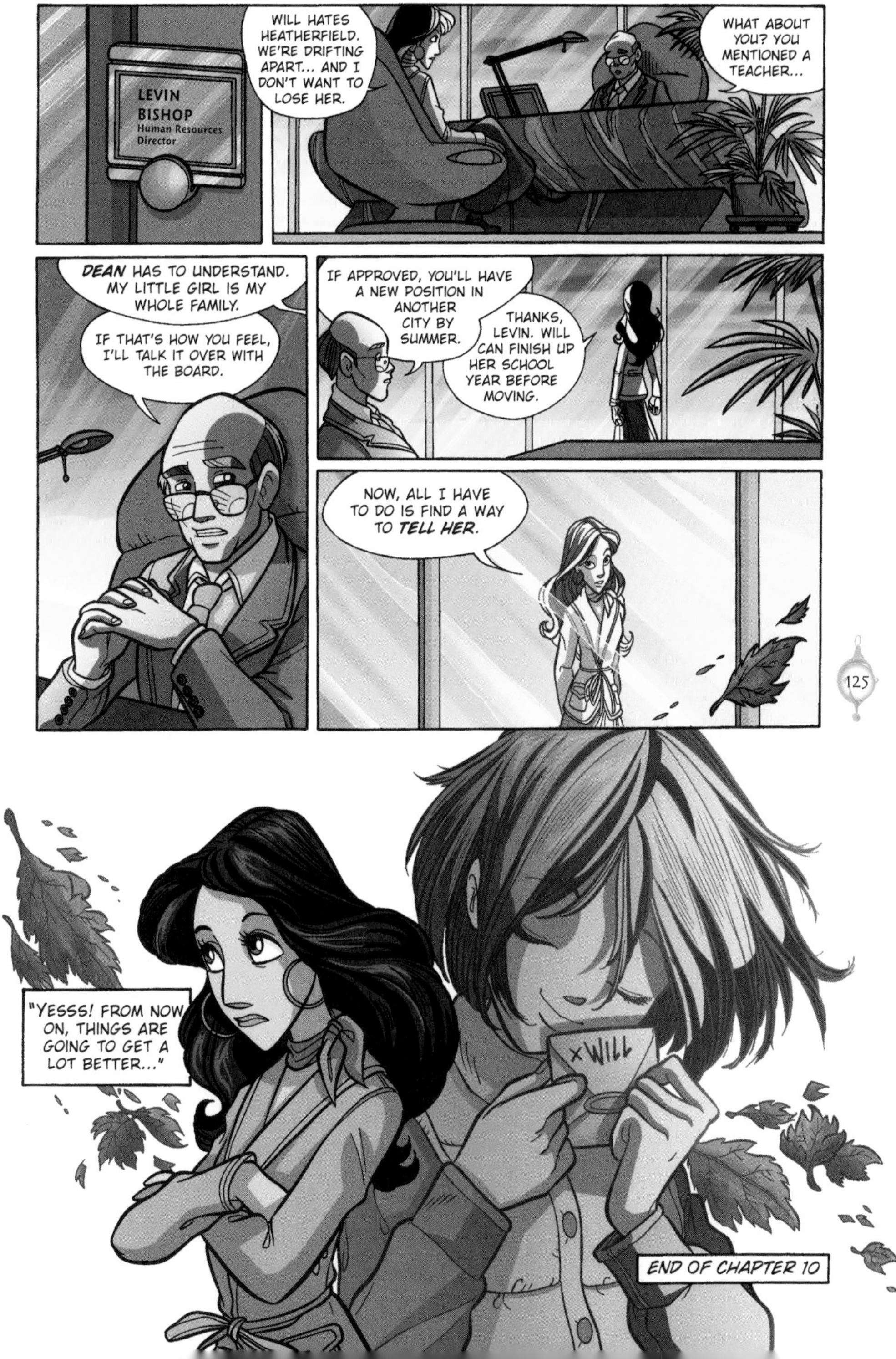
LEVIN
BISHOP
Human Resources
Director
WILL HATES HEATHERFIELD. WE'RE DRIFTING APART... AND I DON'T WANT TO LOSE HER.
WHAT ABOUT YOU? YOU MENTIONED A TEACHER...
DEAN HAS TO UNDERSTAND. MY LITTLE GIRL IS MY WHOLE FAMILY.
IF THAT'S HOW YOU FEEL, I'LL TALK IT OVER WITH THE BOARD.
IF APPROVED, YOU'LL HAVE A NEW POSITION IN ANOTHER CITY BY SUMMER.
THANKS, LEVIN. WILL CAN FINISH UP HER SCHOOL YEAR BEFORE MOVING.
NOW, ALL I HAVE TO DO IS FIND A WAY TO TELL HER.
"YESSS! FROM NOW ON, THINGS ARE GOING TO GET A LOT BETTER..."
x WILL
END OF CHAPTER 10

Will   Irma   Taranee   Cornelia   Hay Lin

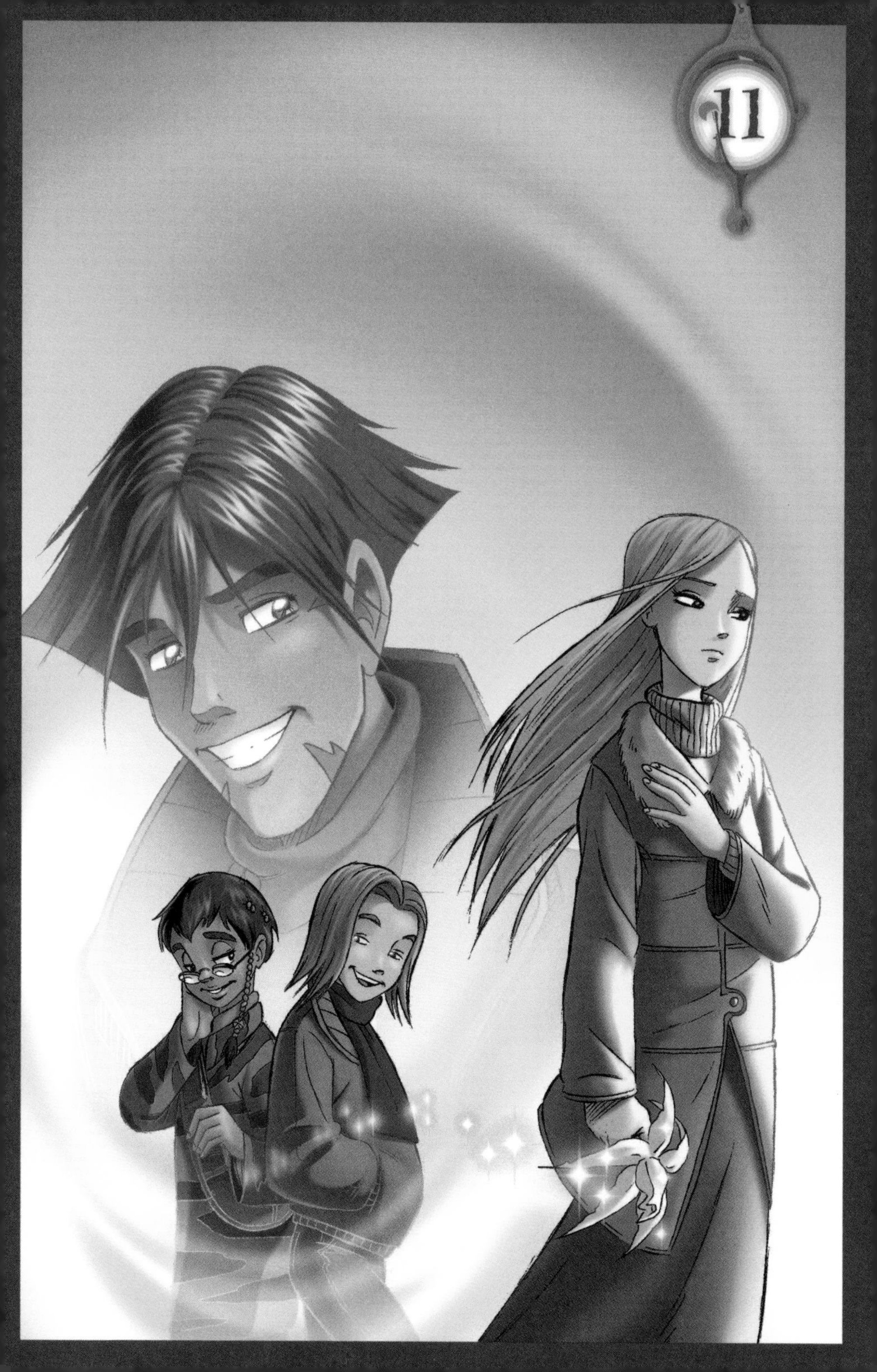
11

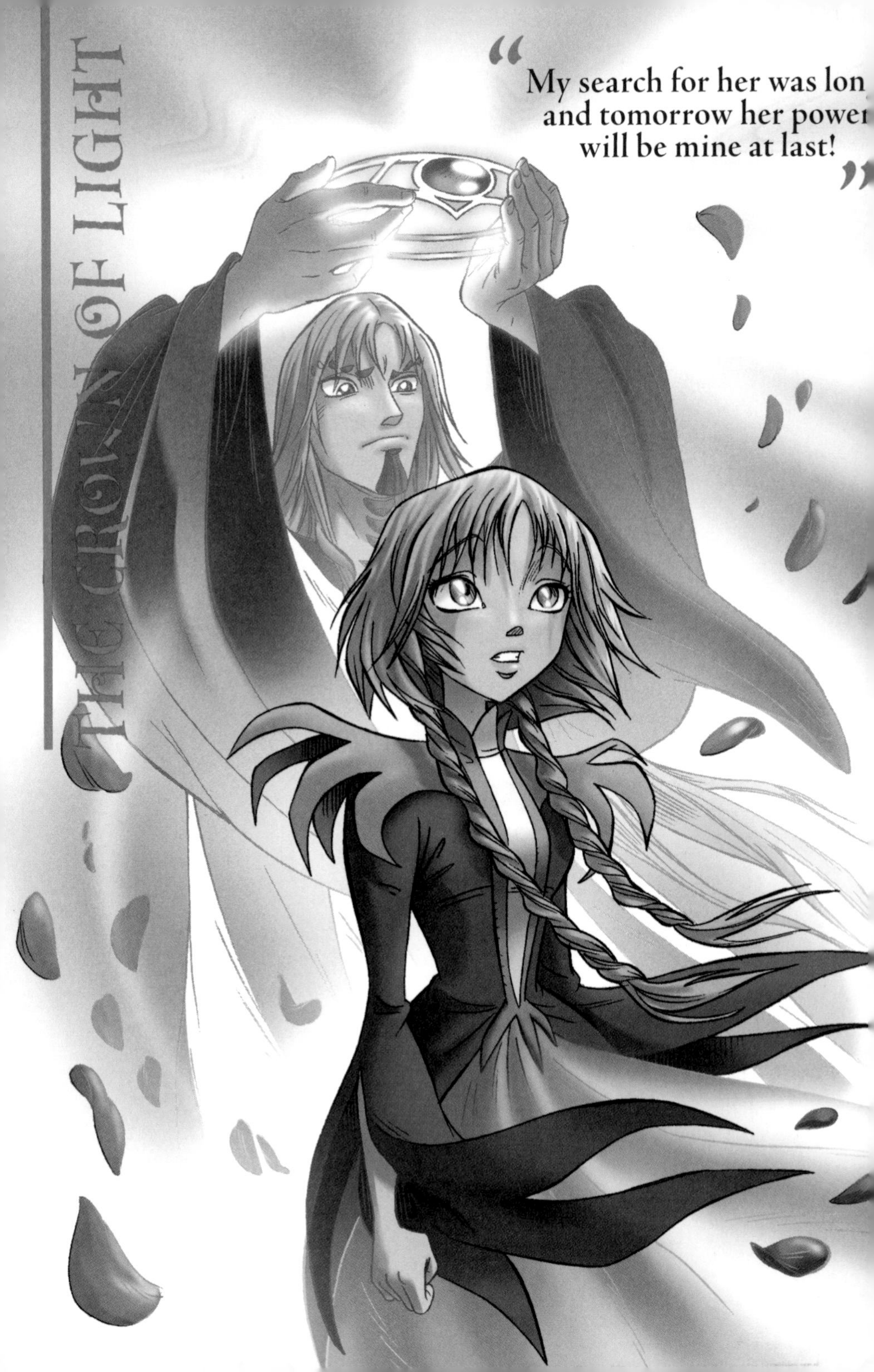
THE CROWN OF LIGHT
"My search for her was lon
and tomorrow her powe
will be mine at last!"

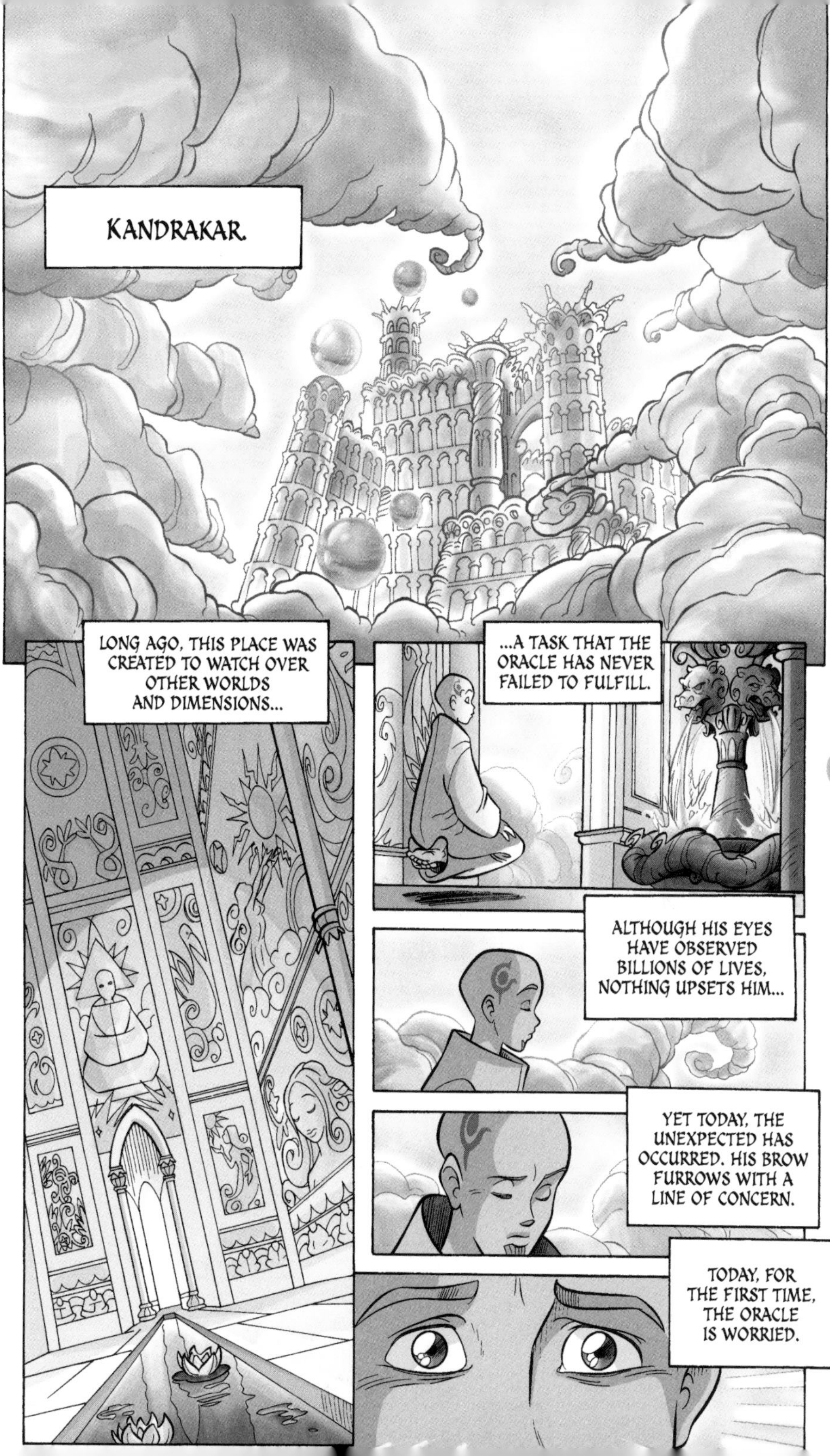
KANDRAKAR.
LONG AGO, THIS PLACE WAS CREATED TO WATCH OVER OTHER WORLDS AND DIMENSIONS...
...A TASK THAT THE ORACLE HAS NEVER FAILED TO FULFILL.
ALTHOUGH HIS EYES HAVE OBSERVED BILLIONS OF LIVES, NOTHING UPSETS HIM...
YET TODAY, THE UNEXPECTED HAS OCCURRED. HIS BROW FURROWS WITH A LINE OF CONCERN.
TODAY, FOR THE FIRST TIME, THE ORACLE IS WORRIED.

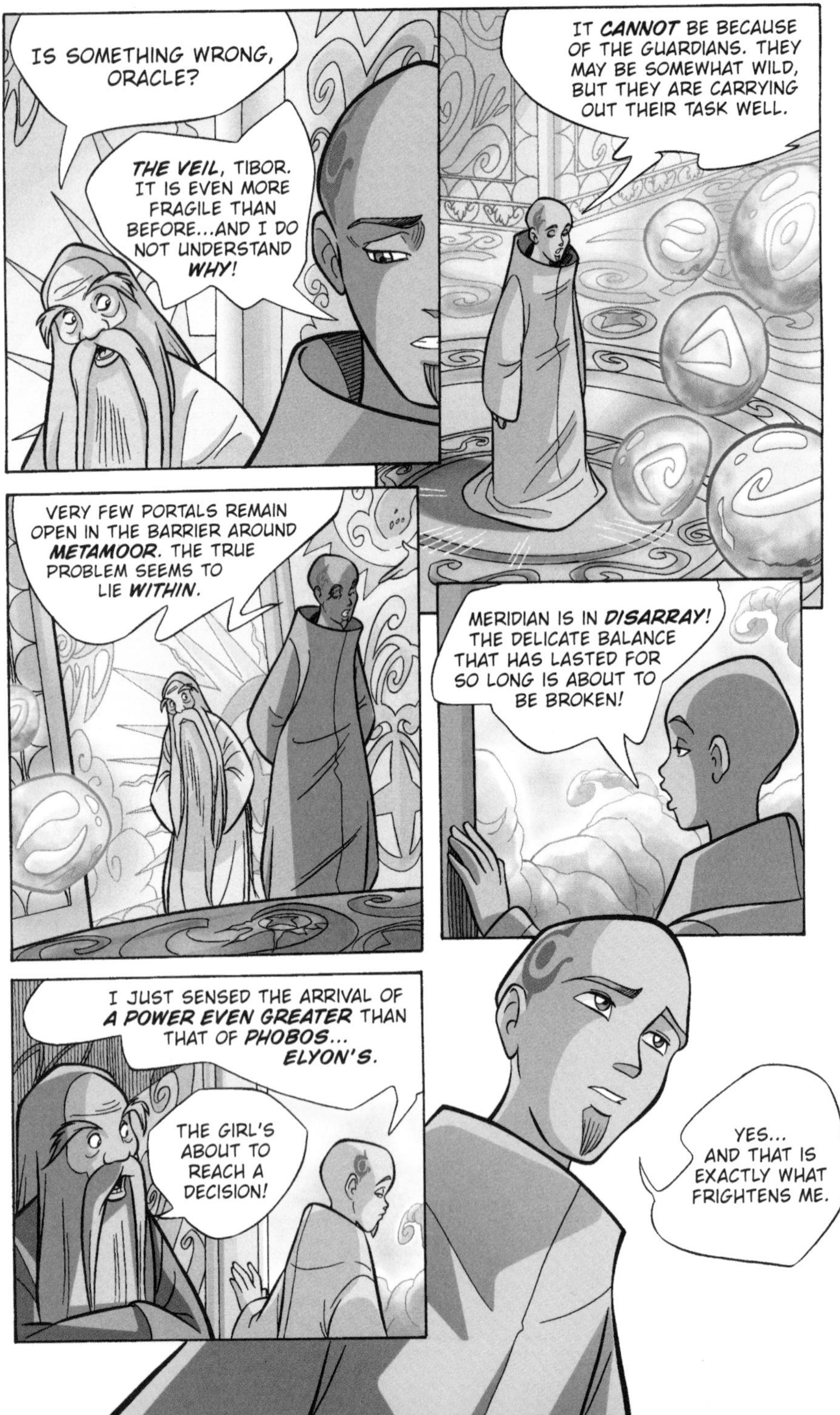
IS SOMETHING WRONG, ORACLE?
THE VEIL, TIBOR. IT IS EVEN MORE FRAGILE THAN BEFORE...AND I DO NOT UNDERSTAND WHY!
IT CANNOT BE BECAUSE OF THE GUARDIANS. THEY MAY BE SOMEWHAT WILD, BUT THEY ARE CARRYING OUT THEIR TASK WELL.
VERY FEW PORTALS REMAIN OPEN IN THE BARRIER AROUND METAMOOR. THE TRUE PROBLEM SEEMS TO LIE WITHIN.
MERIDIAN IS IN DISARRAY! THE DELICATE BALANCE THAT HAS LASTED FOR SO LONG IS ABOUT TO BE BROKEN!
I JUST SENSED THE ARRIVAL OF A POWER EVEN GREATER THAN THAT OF PHOBOS... ELYON'S.
THE GIRL'S ABOUT TO REACH A DECISION!
YES... AND THAT IS EXACTLY WHAT FRIGHTENS ME.

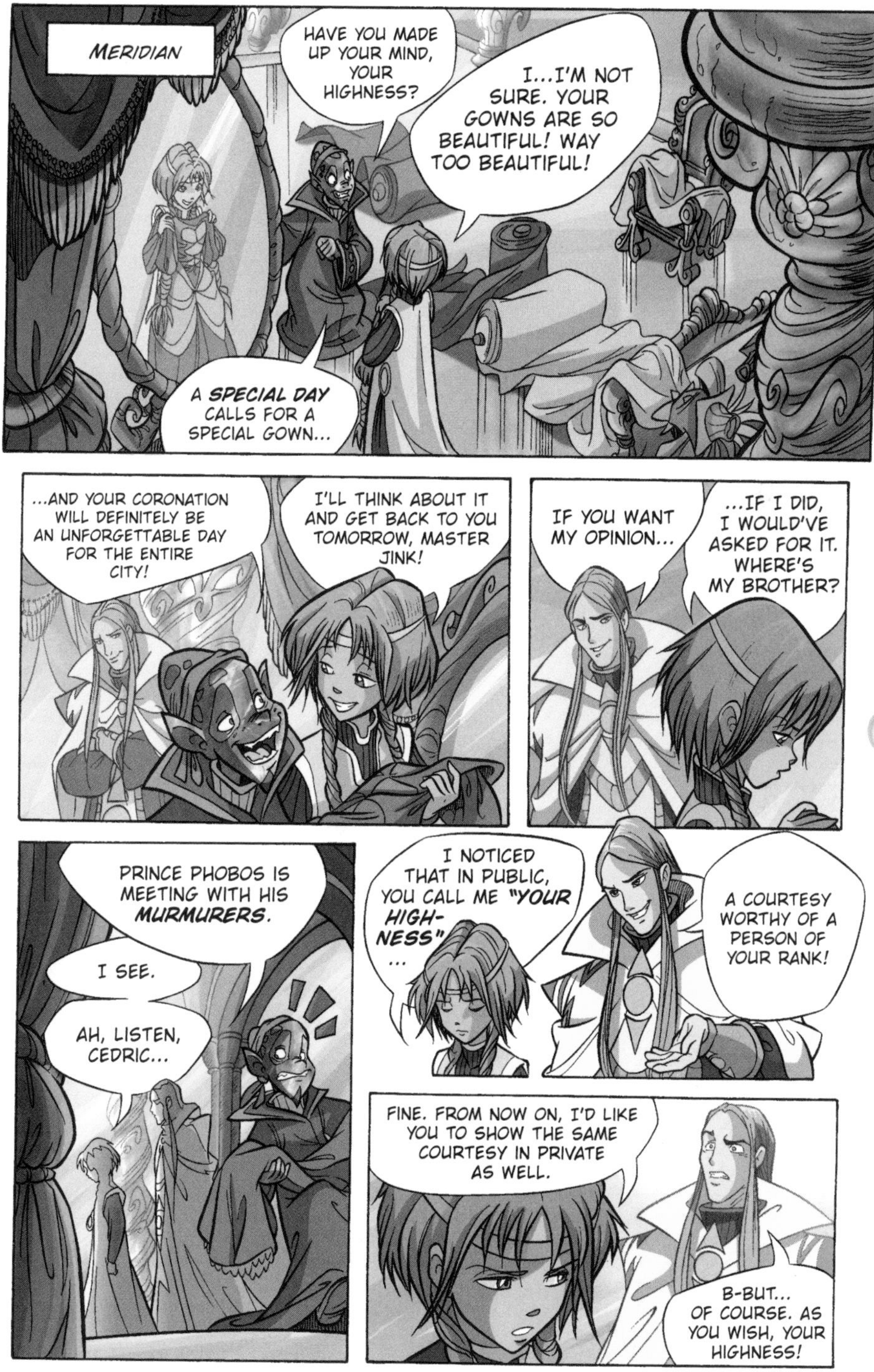
MERIDIAN
HAVE YOU MADE UP YOUR MIND, YOUR HIGHNESS?
I...I'M NOT SURE. YOUR GOWNS ARE SO BEAUTIFUL! WAY TOO BEAUTIFUL!
A SPECIAL DAY CALLS FOR A SPECIAL GOWN...
...AND YOUR CORONATION WILL DEFINITELY BE AN UNFORGETTABLE DAY FOR THE ENTIRE CITY!
I'LL THINK ABOUT IT AND GET BACK TO YOU TOMORROW, MASTER JINK!
IF YOU WANT MY OPINION...
...IF I DID, I WOULD'VE ASKED FOR IT. WHERE'S MY BROTHER?
PRINCE PHOBOS IS MEETING WITH HIS MURMURERS.
I SEE.
AH, LISTEN, CEDRIC...
I NOTICED THAT IN PUBLIC, YOU CALL ME "YOUR HIGH-NESS"...
A COURTESY WORTHY OF A PERSON OF YOUR RANK!
FINE. FROM NOW ON, I'D LIKE YOU TO SHOW THE SAME COURTESY IN PRIVATE AS WELL.
B-BUT... OF COURSE. AS YOU WISH, YOUR HIGHNESS!

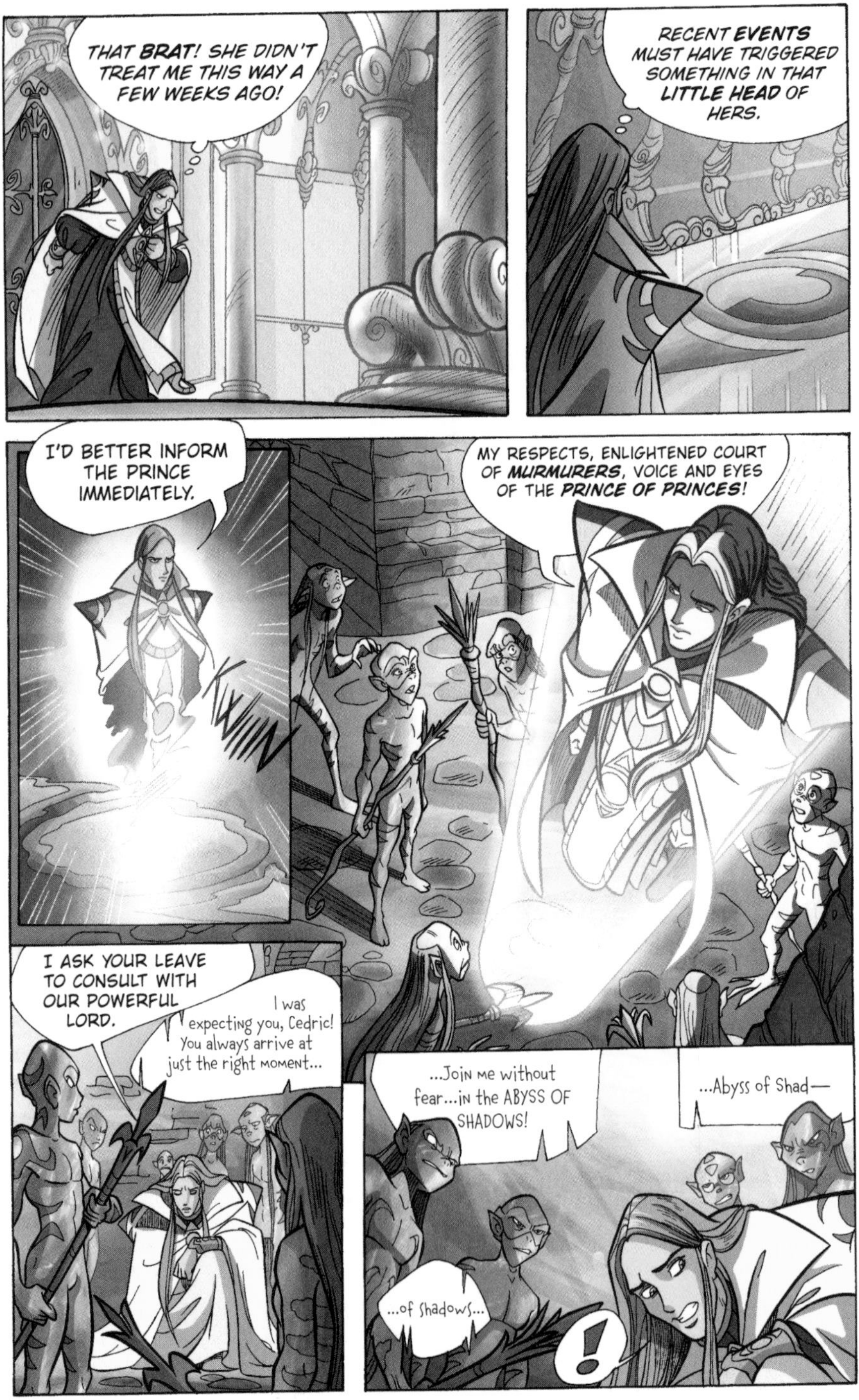

THAT **BRAT**! SHE DIDN'T TREAT ME THIS WAY A FEW WEEKS AGO!
RECENT **EVENTS** MUST HAVE TRIGGERED SOMETHING IN THAT **LITTLE HEAD** OF HERS.
I'D BETTER INFORM THE PRINCE IMMEDIATELY.
KXXIIN
MY RESPECTS, ENLIGHTENED COURT OF ***MURMURERS***, VOICE AND EYES OF THE ***PRINCE OF PRINCES***!
I ASK YOUR LEAVE TO CONSULT WITH OUR POWERFUL LORD.
I was expecting you, Cedric! You always arrive at just the right moment...
...Join me without fear...in the ABYSS OF SHADOWS!
...Abyss of Shad—
...of shadows...
!

132

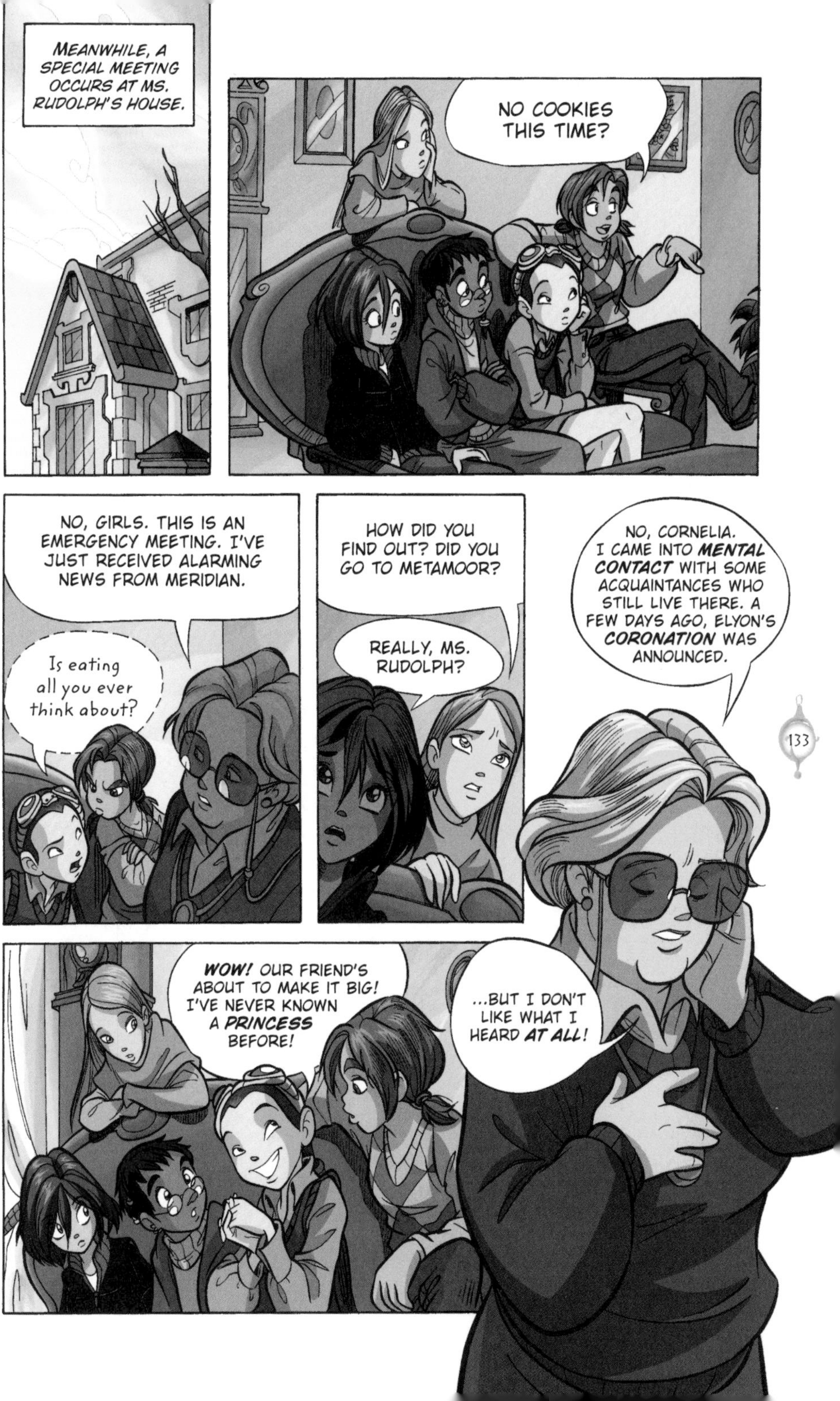
MEANWHILE, A SPECIAL MEETING OCCURS AT MS. RUDOLPH'S HOUSE.
NO COOKIES THIS TIME?
NO, GIRLS. THIS IS AN EMERGENCY MEETING. I'VE JUST RECEIVED ALARMING NEWS FROM MERIDIAN.
Is eating all you ever think about?
HOW DID YOU FIND OUT? DID YOU GO TO METAMOOR?
REALLY, MS. RUDOLPH?
NO, CORNELIA. I CAME INTO MENTAL CONTACT WITH SOME ACQUAINTANCES WHO STILL LIVE THERE. A FEW DAYS AGO, ELYON'S CORONATION WAS ANNOUNCED.
WOW! OUR FRIEND'S ABOUT TO MAKE IT BIG! I'VE NEVER KNOWN A PRINCESS BEFORE!
...BUT I DON'T LIKE WHAT I HEARD AT ALL!

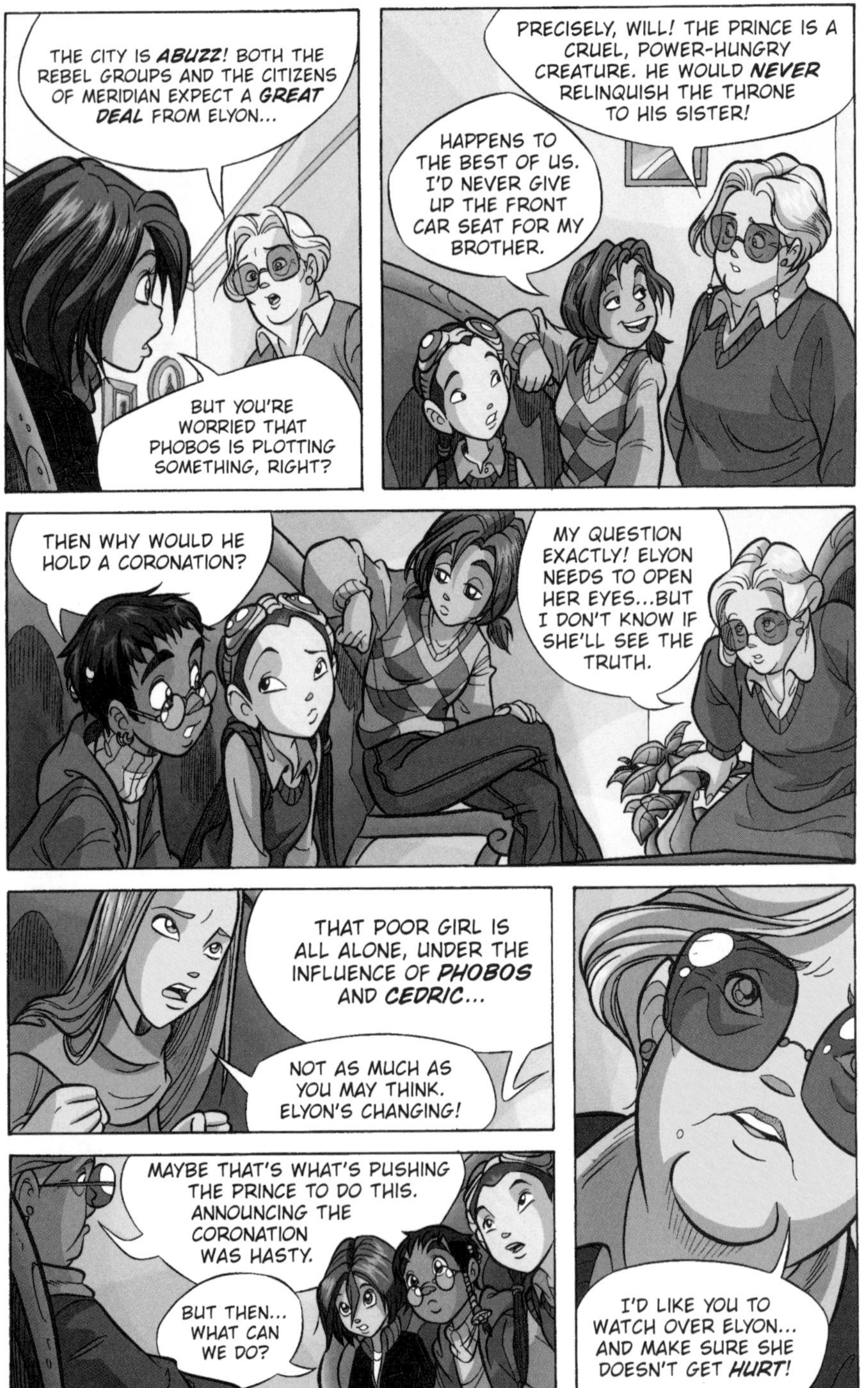
THE CITY IS ABUZZ! BOTH THE REBEL GROUPS AND THE CITIZENS OF MERIDIAN EXPECT A GREAT DEAL FROM ELYON...
BUT YOU'RE WORRIED THAT PHOBOS IS PLOTTING SOMETHING, RIGHT?
PRECISELY, WILL! THE PRINCE IS A CRUEL, POWER-HUNGRY CREATURE. HE WOULD NEVER RELINQUISH THE THRONE TO HIS SISTER!
HAPPENS TO THE BEST OF US. I'D NEVER GIVE UP THE FRONT CAR SEAT FOR MY BROTHER.
THEN WHY WOULD HE HOLD A CORONATION?
MY QUESTION EXACTLY! ELYON NEEDS TO OPEN HER EYES...BUT I DON'T KNOW IF SHE'LL SEE THE TRUTH.
THAT POOR GIRL IS ALL ALONE, UNDER THE INFLUENCE OF PHOBOS AND CEDRIC...
NOT AS MUCH AS YOU MAY THINK. ELYON'S CHANGING!
MAYBE THAT'S WHAT'S PUSHING THE PRINCE TO DO THIS. ANNOUNCING THE CORONATION WAS HASTY.
BUT THEN... WHAT CAN WE DO?
I'D LIKE YOU TO WATCH OVER ELYON... AND MAKE SURE SHE DOESN'T GET HURT!

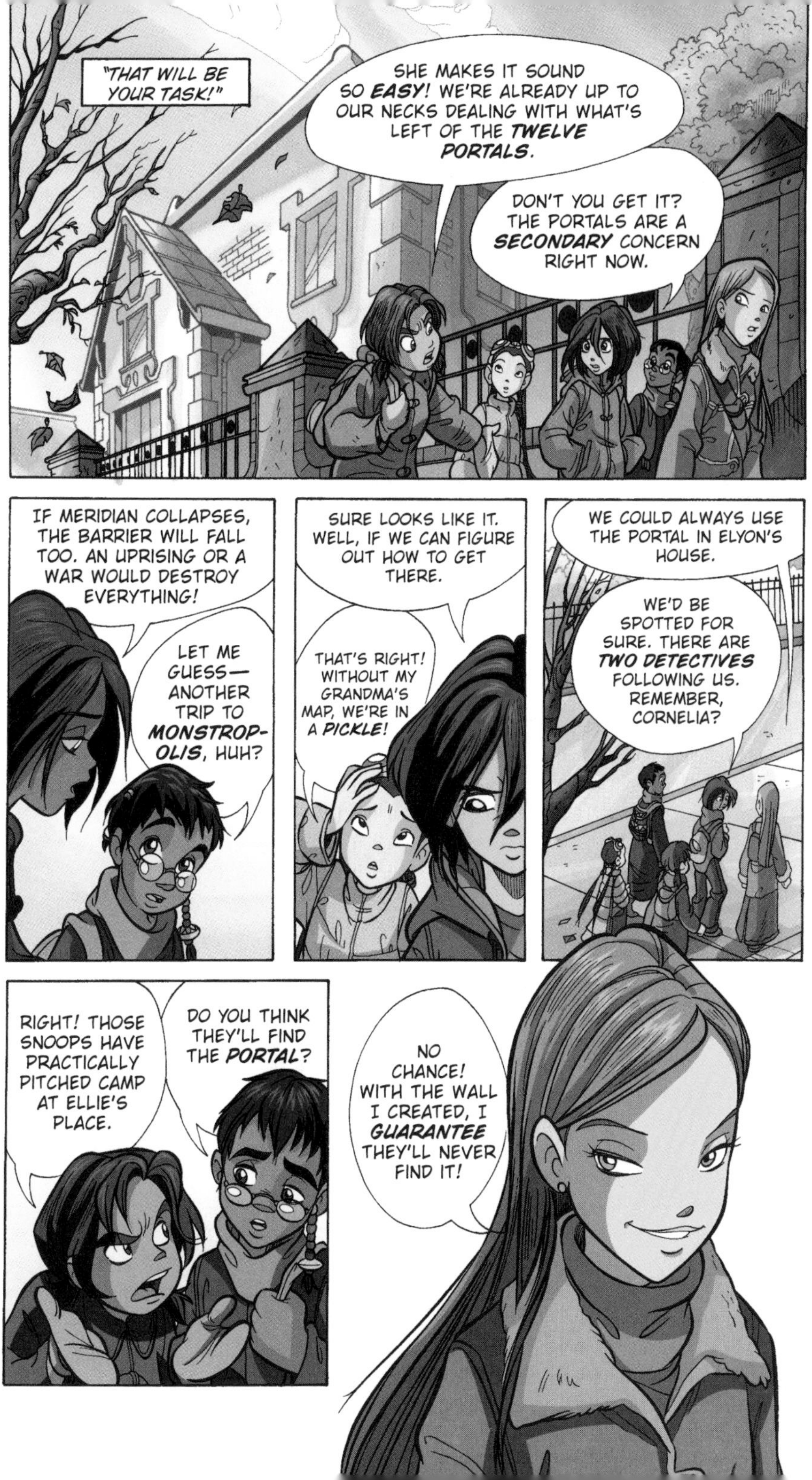
"THAT WILL BE YOUR TASK!"
SHE MAKES IT SOUND SO EASY! WE'RE ALREADY UP TO OUR NECKS DEALING WITH WHAT'S LEFT OF THE TWELVE PORTALS.
DON'T YOU GET IT? THE PORTALS ARE A SECONDARY CONCERN RIGHT NOW.
IF MERIDIAN COLLAPSES, THE BARRIER WILL FALL TOO. AN UPRISING OR A WAR WOULD DESTROY EVERYTHING!
LET ME GUESS— ANOTHER TRIP TO MONSTROP-OLIS, HUH?
SURE LOOKS LIKE IT. WELL, IF WE CAN FIGURE OUT HOW TO GET THERE.
THAT'S RIGHT! WITHOUT MY GRANDMA'S MAP, WE'RE IN A PICKLE!
WE COULD ALWAYS USE THE PORTAL IN ELYON'S HOUSE.
WE'D BE SPOTTED FOR SURE. THERE ARE TWO DETECTIVES FOLLOWING US. REMEMBER, CORNELIA?
RIGHT! THOSE SNOOPS HAVE PRACTICALLY PITCHED CAMP AT ELLIE'S PLACE.
DO YOU THINK THEY'LL FIND THE PORTAL?
NO CHANCE! WITH THE WALL I CREATED, I GUARANTEE THEY'LL NEVER FIND IT!

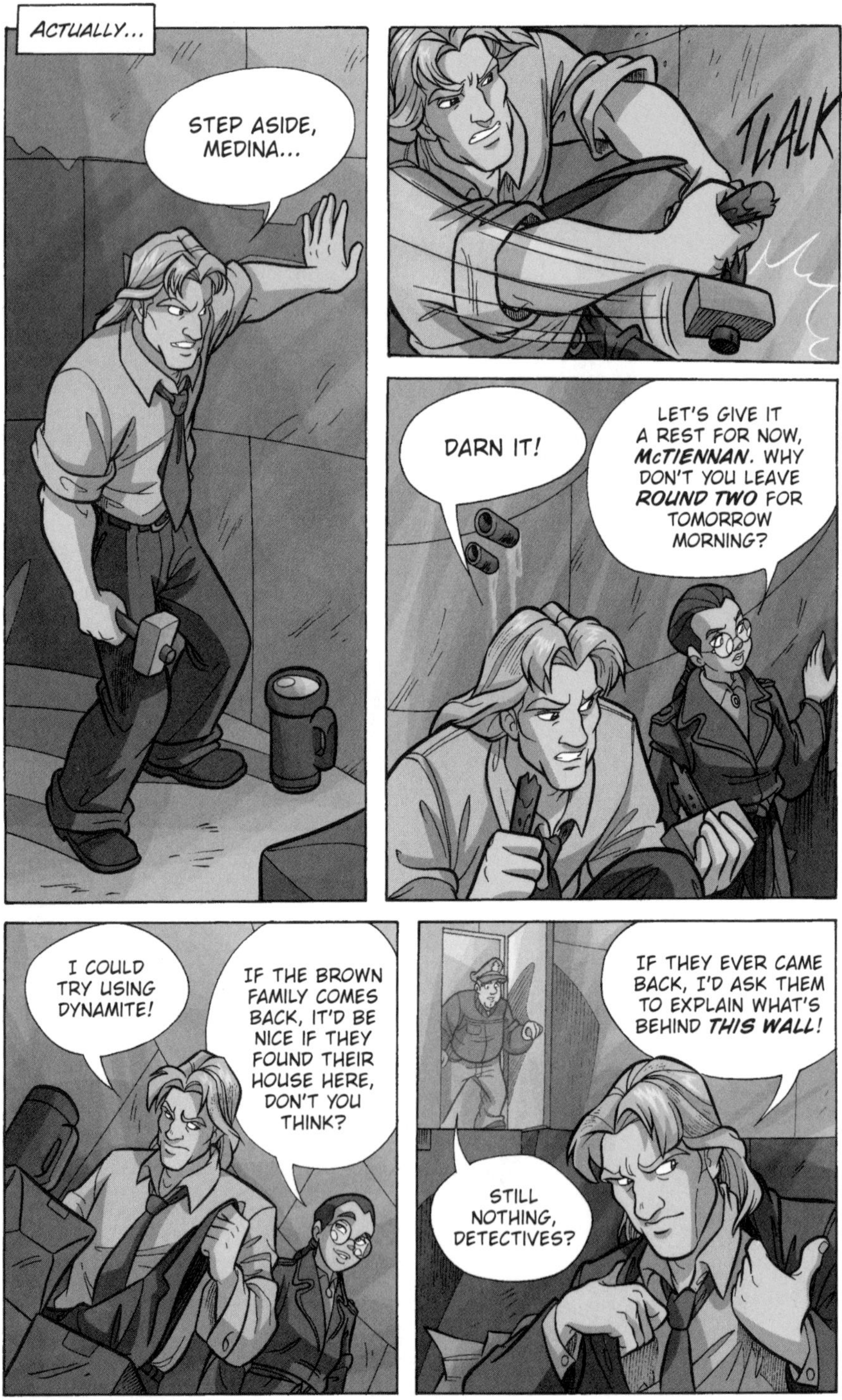
ACTUALLY...
STEP ASIDE, MEDINA...
TLALK
DARN IT!
LET'S GIVE IT A REST FOR NOW, McTIENNAN. WHY DON'T YOU LEAVE ROUND TWO FOR TOMORROW MORNING?
I COULD TRY USING DYNAMITE!
IF THE BROWN FAMILY COMES BACK, IT'D BE NICE IF THEY FOUND THEIR HOUSE HERE, DON'T YOU THINK?
IF THEY EVER CAME BACK, I'D ASK THEM TO EXPLAIN WHAT'S BEHIND THIS WALL!
STILL NOTHING, DETECTIVES?

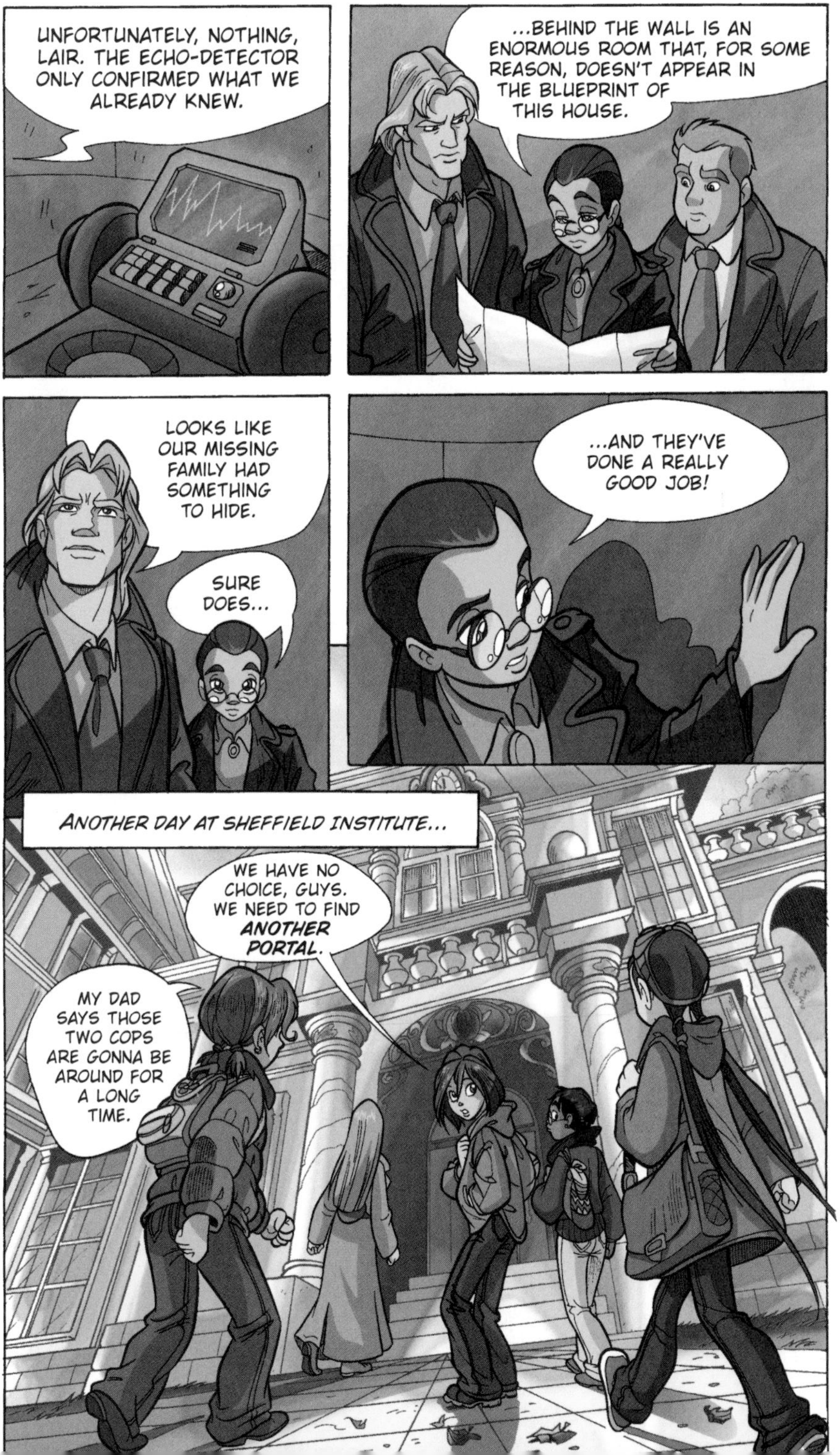
UNFORTUNATELY, NOTHING, LAIR. THE ECHO-DETECTOR ONLY CONFIRMED WHAT WE ALREADY KNEW.
...BEHIND THE WALL IS AN ENORMOUS ROOM THAT, FOR SOME REASON, DOESN'T APPEAR IN THE BLUEPRINT OF THIS HOUSE.
LOOKS LIKE OUR MISSING FAMILY HAD SOMETHING TO HIDE.
SURE DOES...
...AND THEY'VE DONE A REALLY GOOD JOB!
ANOTHER DAY AT SHEFFIELD INSTITUTE...
WE HAVE NO CHOICE, GUYS. WE NEED TO FIND **ANOTHER PORTAL**.
MY DAD SAYS THOSE TWO COPS ARE GONNA BE AROUND FOR A LONG TIME.

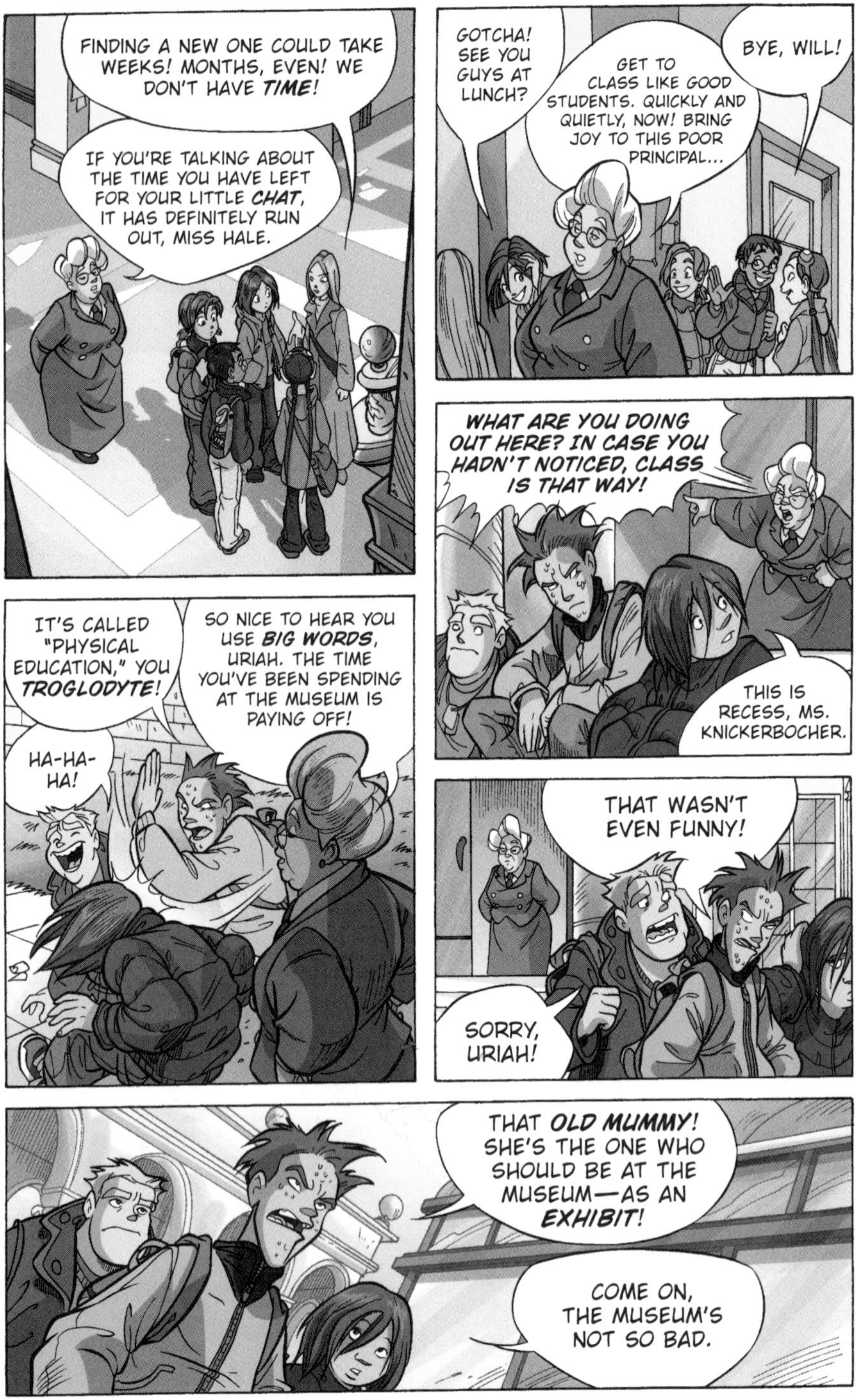
FINDING A NEW ONE COULD TAKE WEEKS! MONTHS, EVEN! WE DON'T HAVE TIME!
IF YOU'RE TALKING ABOUT THE TIME YOU HAVE LEFT FOR YOUR LITTLE CHAT, IT HAS DEFINITELY RUN OUT, MISS HALE.
GOTCHA! SEE YOU GUYS AT LUNCH?
GET TO CLASS LIKE GOOD STUDENTS. QUICKLY AND QUIETLY, NOW! BRING JOY TO THIS POOR PRINCIPAL...
BYE, WILL!
WHAT ARE YOU DOING OUT HERE? IN CASE YOU HADN'T NOTICED, CLASS IS THAT WAY!
THIS IS RECESS, MS. KNICKERBOCHER.
IT'S CALLED "PHYSICAL EDUCATION," YOU TROGLODYTE!
SO NICE TO HEAR YOU USE BIG WORDS, URIAH. THE TIME YOU'VE BEEN SPENDING AT THE MUSEUM IS PAYING OFF!
HA-HA-HA!
THAT WASN'T EVEN FUNNY!
SORRY, URIAH!
THAT OLD MUMMY! SHE'S THE ONE WHO SHOULD BE AT THE MUSEUM—AS AN EXHIBIT!
COME ON, THE MUSEUM'S NOT SO BAD.

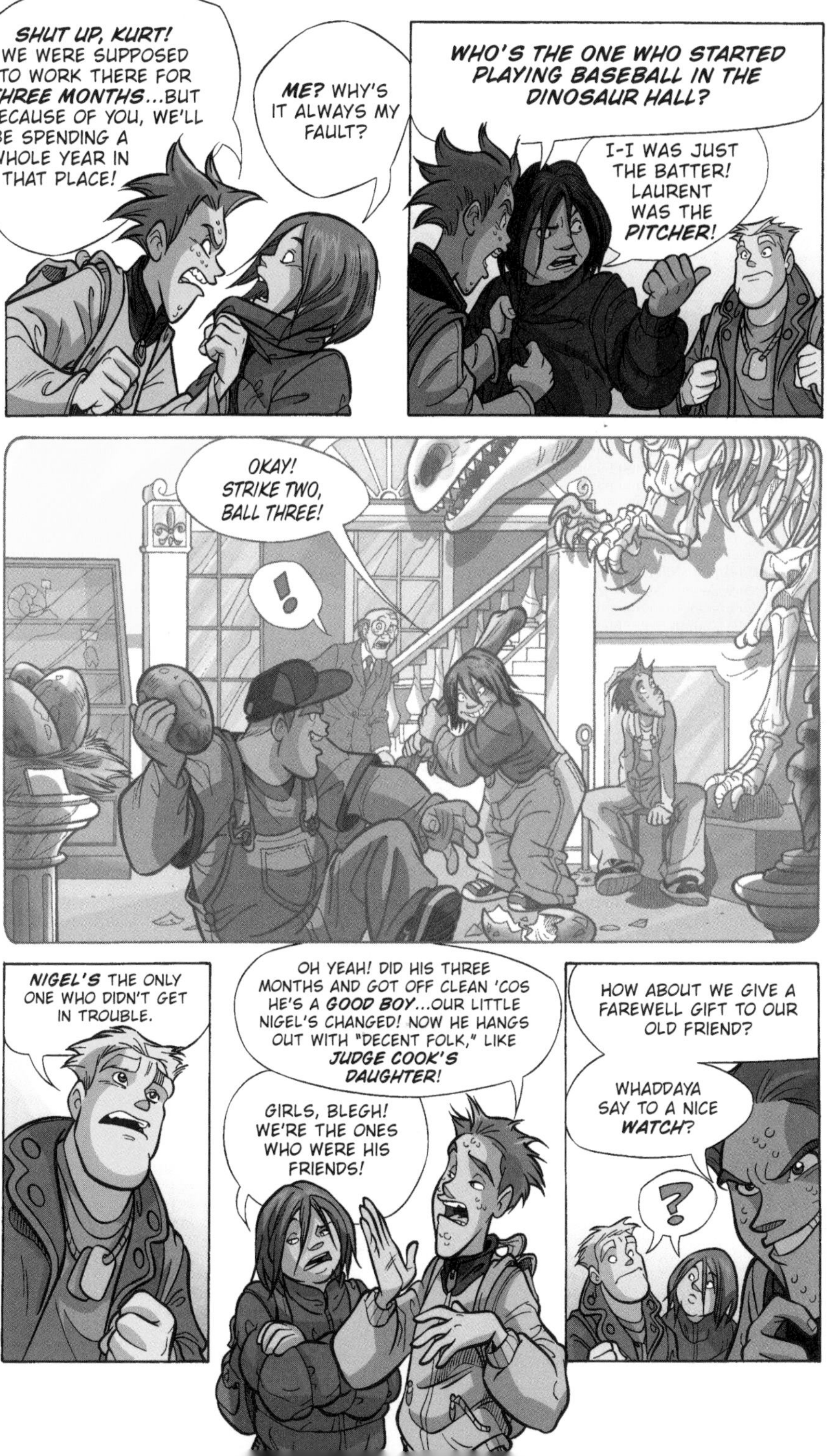
SHUT UP, KURT! WE WERE SUPPOSED TO WORK THERE FOR THREE MONTHS...BUT BECAUSE OF YOU, WE'LL BE SPENDING A WHOLE YEAR IN THAT PLACE!
ME? WHY'S IT ALWAYS MY FAULT?
WHO'S THE ONE WHO STARTED PLAYING BASEBALL IN THE DINOSAUR HALL?
I-I WAS JUST THE BATTER! LAURENT WAS THE PITCHER!
OKAY! STRIKE TWO, BALL THREE!
!
NIGEL'S THE ONLY ONE WHO DIDN'T GET IN TROUBLE.
OH YEAH! DID HIS THREE MONTHS AND GOT OFF CLEAN 'COS HE'S A GOOD BOY...OUR LITTLE NIGEL'S CHANGED! NOW HE HANGS OUT WITH "DECENT FOLK," LIKE JUDGE COOK'S DAUGHTER!
GIRLS, BLEGH! WE'RE THE ONES WHO WERE HIS FRIENDS!
HOW ABOUT WE GIVE A FAREWELL GIFT TO OUR OLD FRIEND?
WHADDAYA SAY TO A NICE WATCH?
?

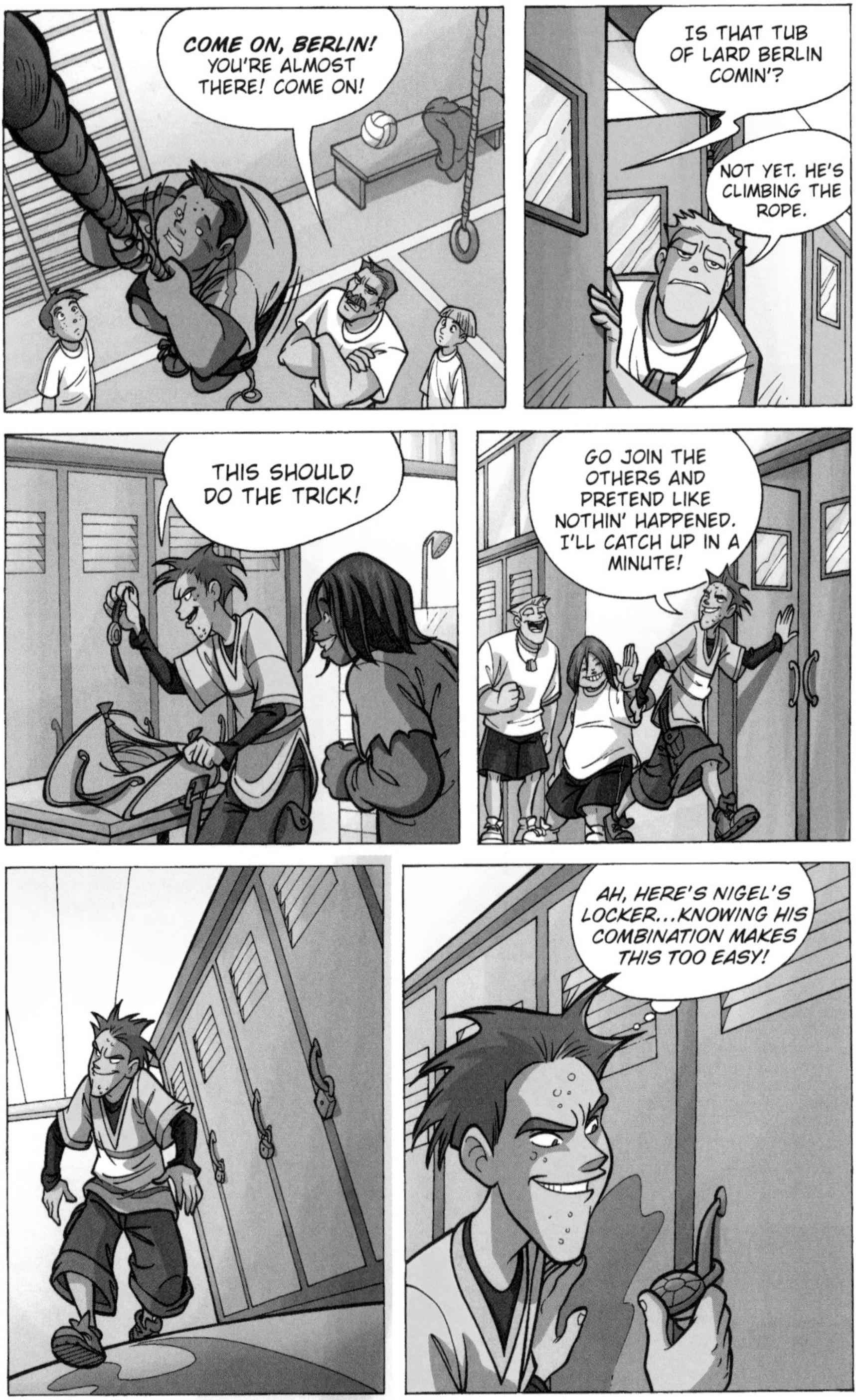
COME ON, BERLIN! YOU'RE ALMOST THERE! COME ON!
IS THAT TUB OF LARD BERLIN COMIN'?
NOT YET. HE'S CLIMBING THE ROPE.
THIS SHOULD DO THE TRICK!
GO JOIN THE OTHERS AND PRETEND LIKE NOTHIN' HAPPENED. I'LL CATCH UP IN A MINUTE!
AH, HERE'S NIGEL'S LOCKER...KNOWING HIS COMBINATION MAKES THIS TOO EASY!

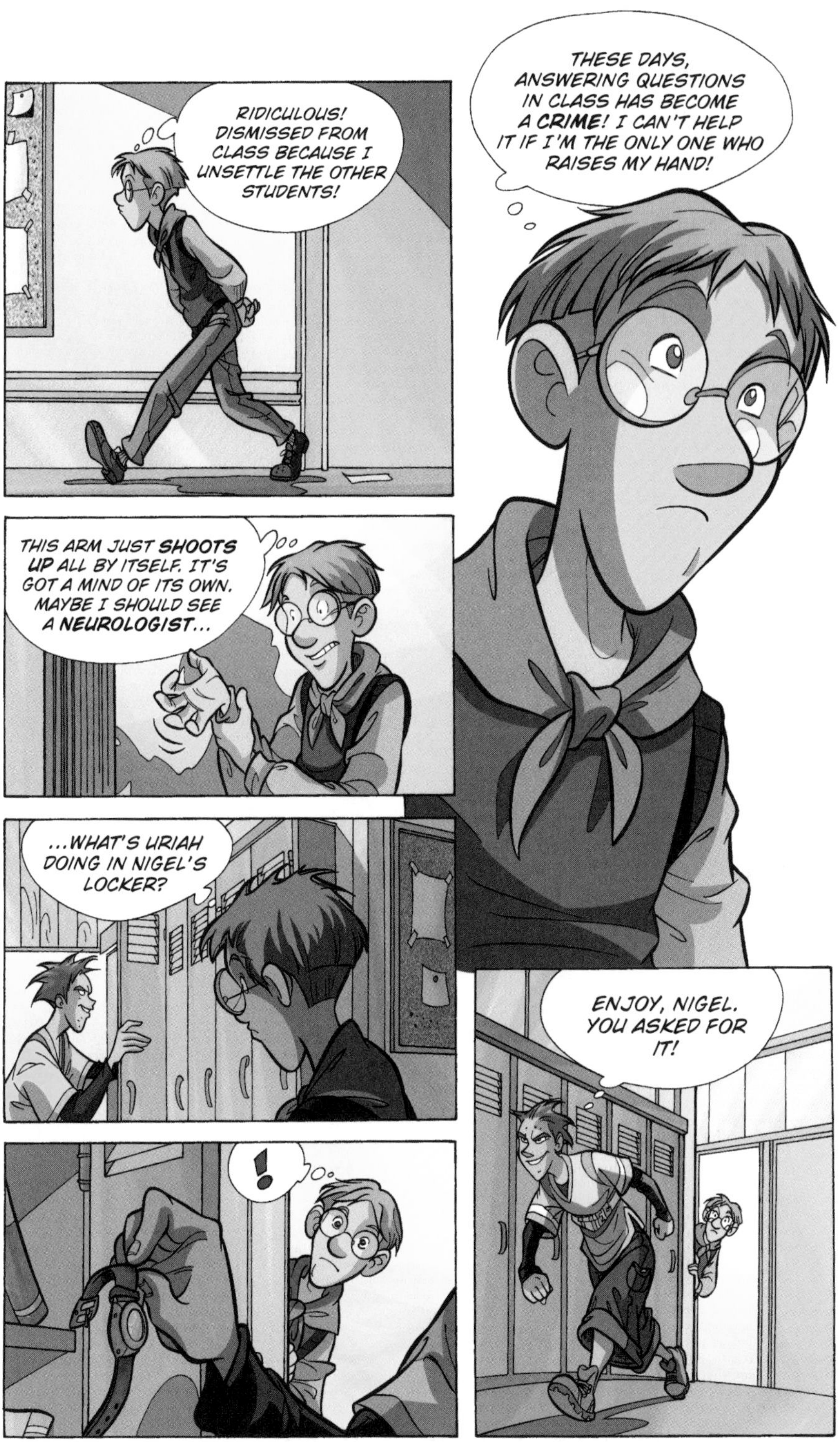
RIDICULOUS! DISMISSED FROM CLASS BECAUSE I UNSETTLE THE OTHER STUDENTS!
THESE DAYS, ANSWERING QUESTIONS IN CLASS HAS BECOME A **CRIME**! I CAN'T HELP IT IF I'M THE ONLY ONE WHO RAISES MY HAND!
THIS ARM JUST **SHOOTS UP** ALL BY ITSELF. IT'S GOT A MIND OF ITS OWN. MAYBE I SHOULD SEE A **NEUROLOGIST**...
...WHAT'S URIAH DOING IN NIGEL'S LOCKER?
!
ENJOY, NIGEL. YOU ASKED FOR IT!

I'VE BEEN THINKING IT OVER AND MIGHT HAVE THE *SOLUTION* TO OUR PROBLEM.

YOU FOUND A WAY TO GET TO *MERIDIAN*?

I THINK SO. THE PORTAL VATHEK USED TO GET TO HEATHERFIELD A FEW DAYS AGO.*

WHEN WE WENT BACK TO METAMOOR WITH HIM, WE USED THE PORTAL IN ELYON'S HOUSE.

*SEE THE PREVIOUS CHAPTER!

142

...WHICH MEANS THERE'S STILL AN OPEN PORTAL!

RIGHT! BUT *WHERE*?

THAT'S THE THING! *I DON'T KNOW*...BUT WE SHOULD BE ABLE TO FIGURE IT OUT WITH OUR *POWERS*!

WANT TO MEET UP AT MY PLACE AFTER SCHOOL?

COUNT ME IN!

OKAY! MAP OR NO MAP, WE MIGHT STILL—

RIIIING

HUH? THE BELL'S EARLY. WE STILL HAVE *TEN MINUTES* LEFT FOR LUNCH...

TO THE COURT-YARD, EVERYONE! KNICKERBOCHER'S MAKING AN ANNOUNCE-MENT.

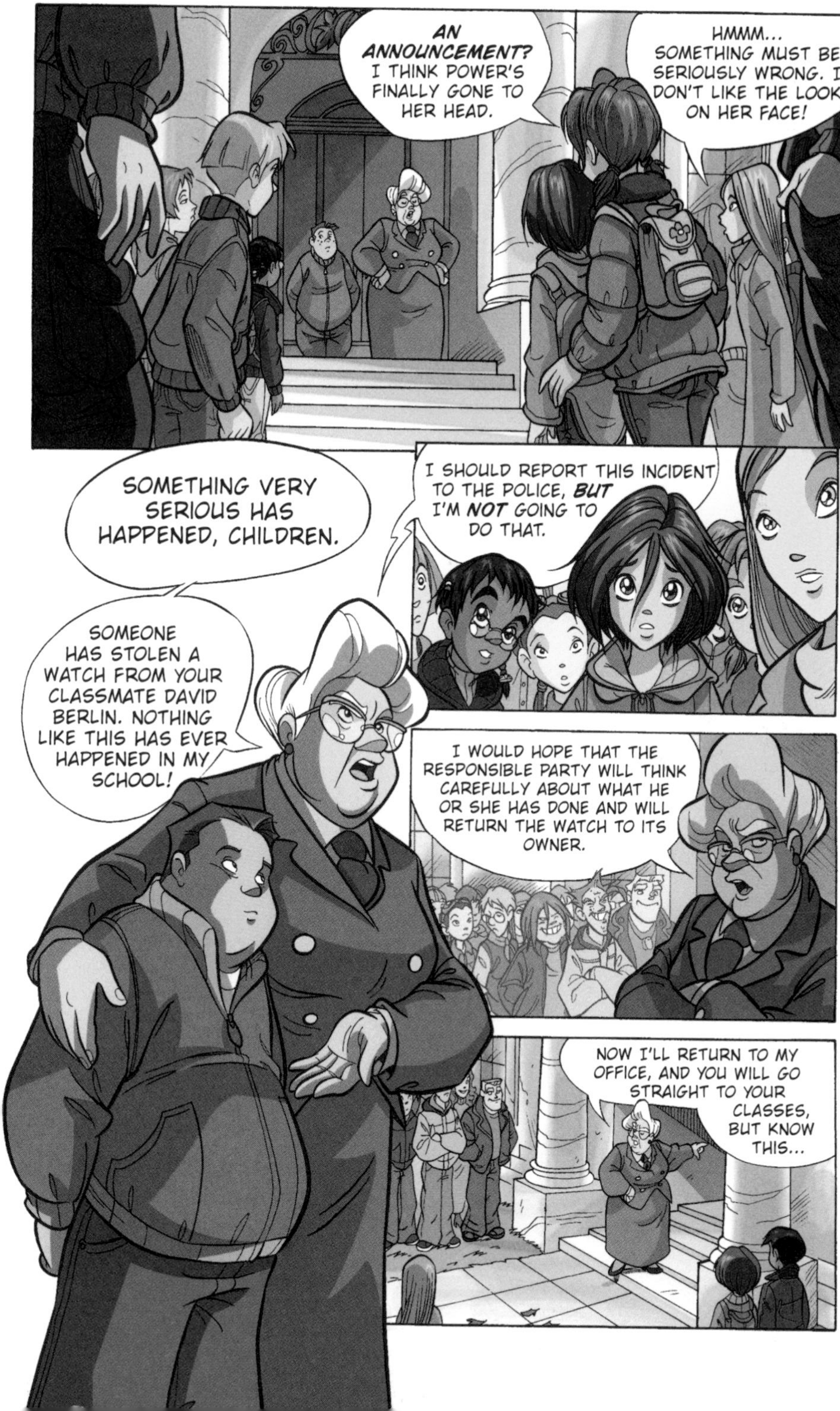

AN ANNOUNCEMENT? I THINK POWER'S FINALLY GONE TO HER HEAD.
HMMM... SOMETHING MUST BE SERIOUSLY WRONG. I DON'T LIKE THE LOOK ON HER FACE!
SOMETHING VERY SERIOUS HAS HAPPENED, CHILDREN.
SOMEONE HAS STOLEN A WATCH FROM YOUR CLASSMATE DAVID BERLIN. NOTHING LIKE THIS HAS EVER HAPPENED IN MY SCHOOL!
I SHOULD REPORT THIS INCIDENT TO THE POLICE, ***BUT*** I'M ***NOT*** GOING TO DO THAT.
I WOULD HOPE THAT THE RESPONSIBLE PARTY WILL THINK CAREFULLY ABOUT WHAT HE OR SHE HAS DONE AND WILL RETURN THE WATCH TO ITS OWNER.
NOW I'LL RETURN TO MY OFFICE, AND YOU WILL GO STRAIGHT TO YOUR CLASSES, BUT KNOW THIS...

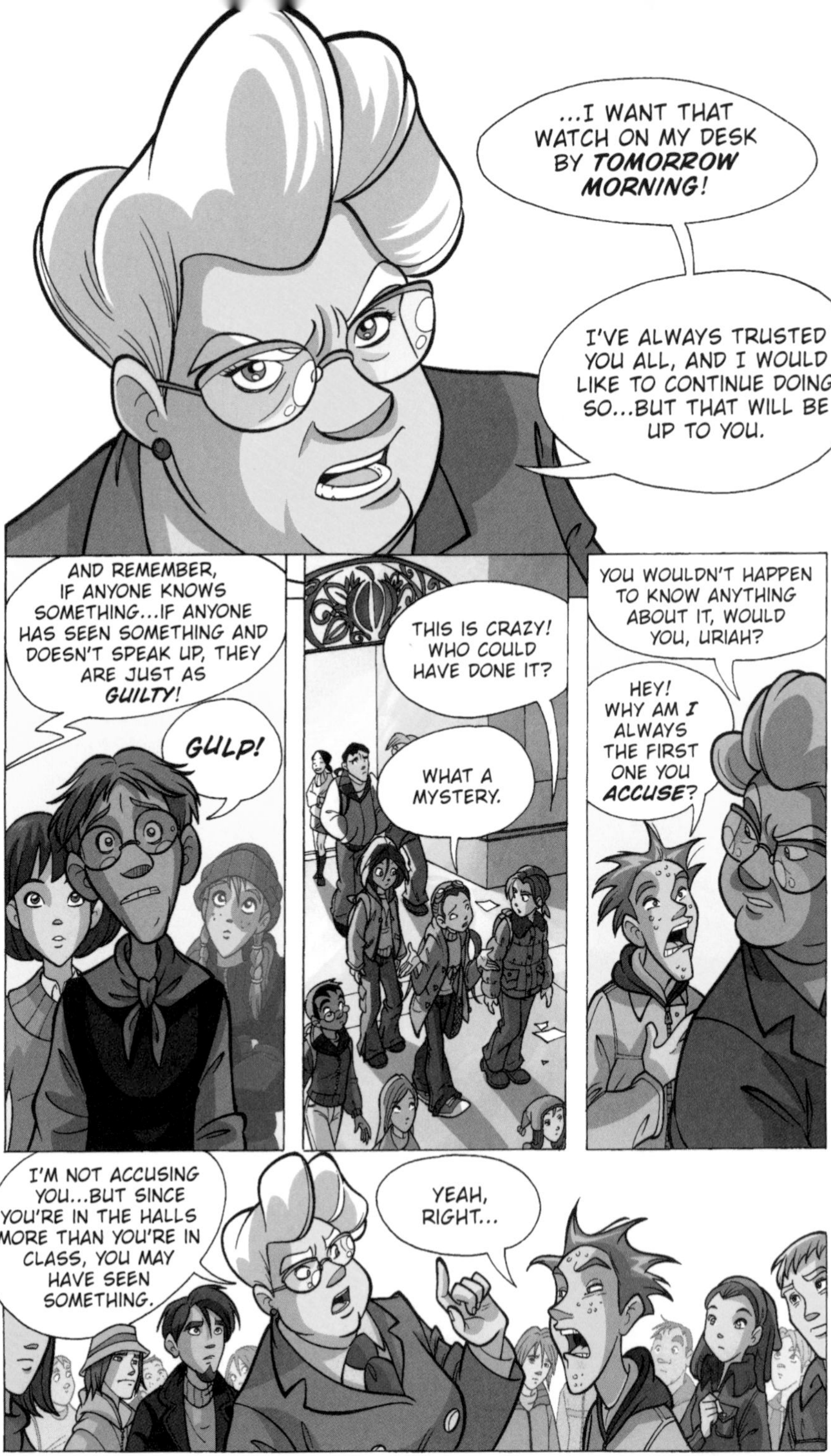
...I WANT THAT WATCH ON MY DESK BY TOMORROW MORNING!
I'VE ALWAYS TRUSTED YOU ALL, AND I WOULD LIKE TO CONTINUE DOING SO...BUT THAT WILL BE UP TO YOU.
AND REMEMBER, IF ANYONE KNOWS SOMETHING...IF ANYONE HAS SEEN SOMETHING AND DOESN'T SPEAK UP, THEY ARE JUST AS GUILTY!
GULP!
THIS IS CRAZY! WHO COULD HAVE DONE IT?
WHAT A MYSTERY.
YOU WOULDN'T HAPPEN TO KNOW ANYTHING ABOUT IT, WOULD YOU, URIAH?
HEY! WHY AM I ALWAYS THE FIRST ONE YOU ACCUSE?
I'M NOT ACCUSING YOU...BUT SINCE YOU'RE IN THE HALLS MORE THAN YOU'RE IN CLASS, YOU MAY HAVE SEEN SOMETHING.
YEAH, RIGHT...

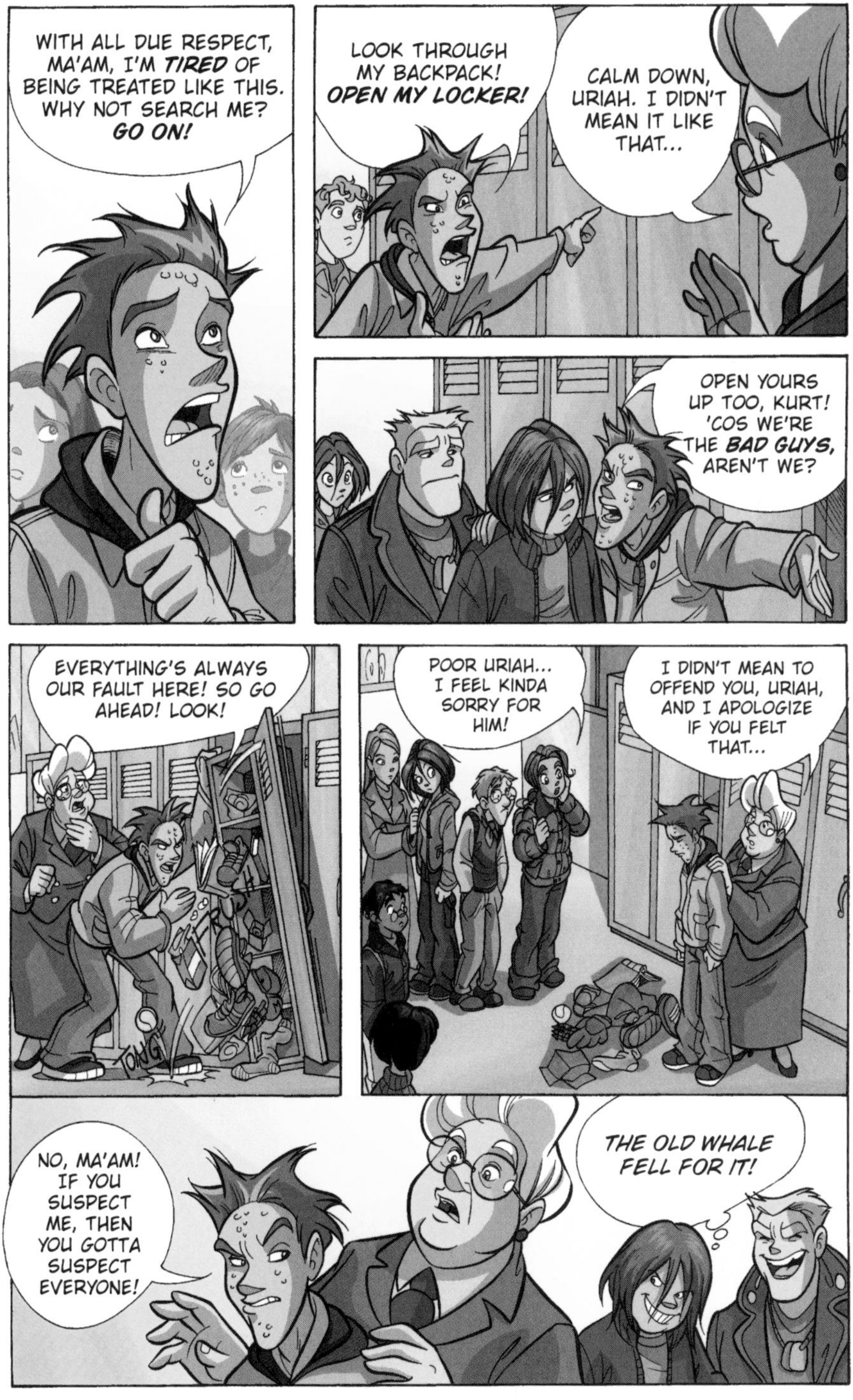
WITH ALL DUE RESPECT, MA'AM, I'M *TIRED* OF BEING TREATED LIKE THIS. WHY NOT SEARCH ME? ***GO ON!***
LOOK THROUGH MY BACKPACK! ***OPEN MY LOCKER!***
CALM DOWN, URIAH. I DIDN'T MEAN IT LIKE THAT...
OPEN YOURS UP TOO, KURT! 'COS WE'RE THE ***BAD GUYS,*** AREN'T WE?
EVERYTHING'S ALWAYS OUR FAULT HERE! SO GO AHEAD! LOOK!
TONG
POOR URIAH... I FEEL KINDA SORRY FOR HIM!
I DIDN'T MEAN TO OFFEND YOU, URIAH, AND I APOLOGIZE IF YOU FELT THAT...
NO, MA'AM! IF YOU SUSPECT ME, THEN YOU GOTTA SUSPECT EVERYONE!
THE OLD WHALE FELL FOR IT!

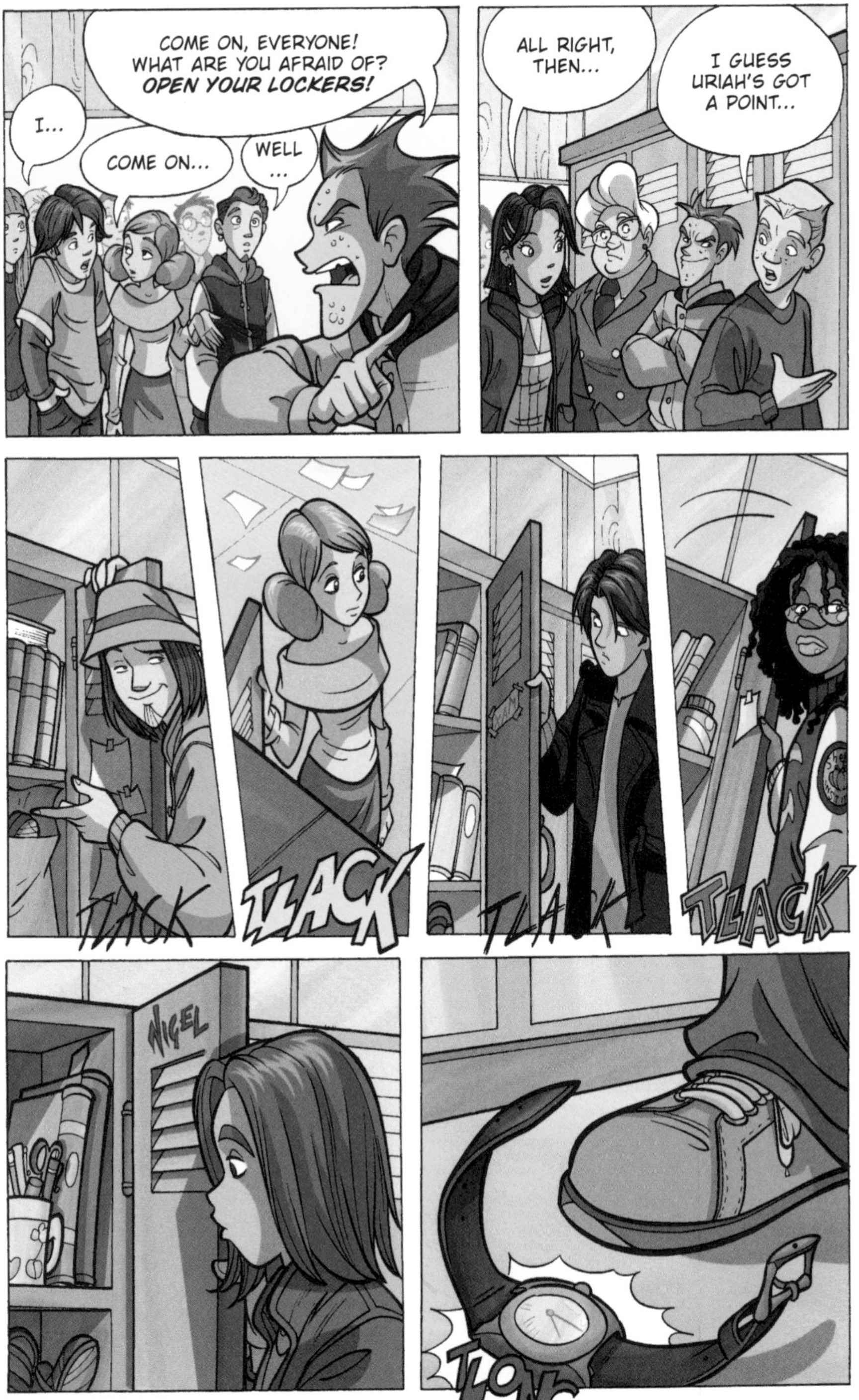
COME ON, EVERYONE! WHAT ARE YOU AFRAID OF? OPEN YOUR LOCKERS!
I...
COME ON...
WELL ...
ALL RIGHT, THEN...
I GUESS URIAH'S GOT A POINT...
TLACK
TLACK
TLACK
TLACK
NIGEL
TLONC

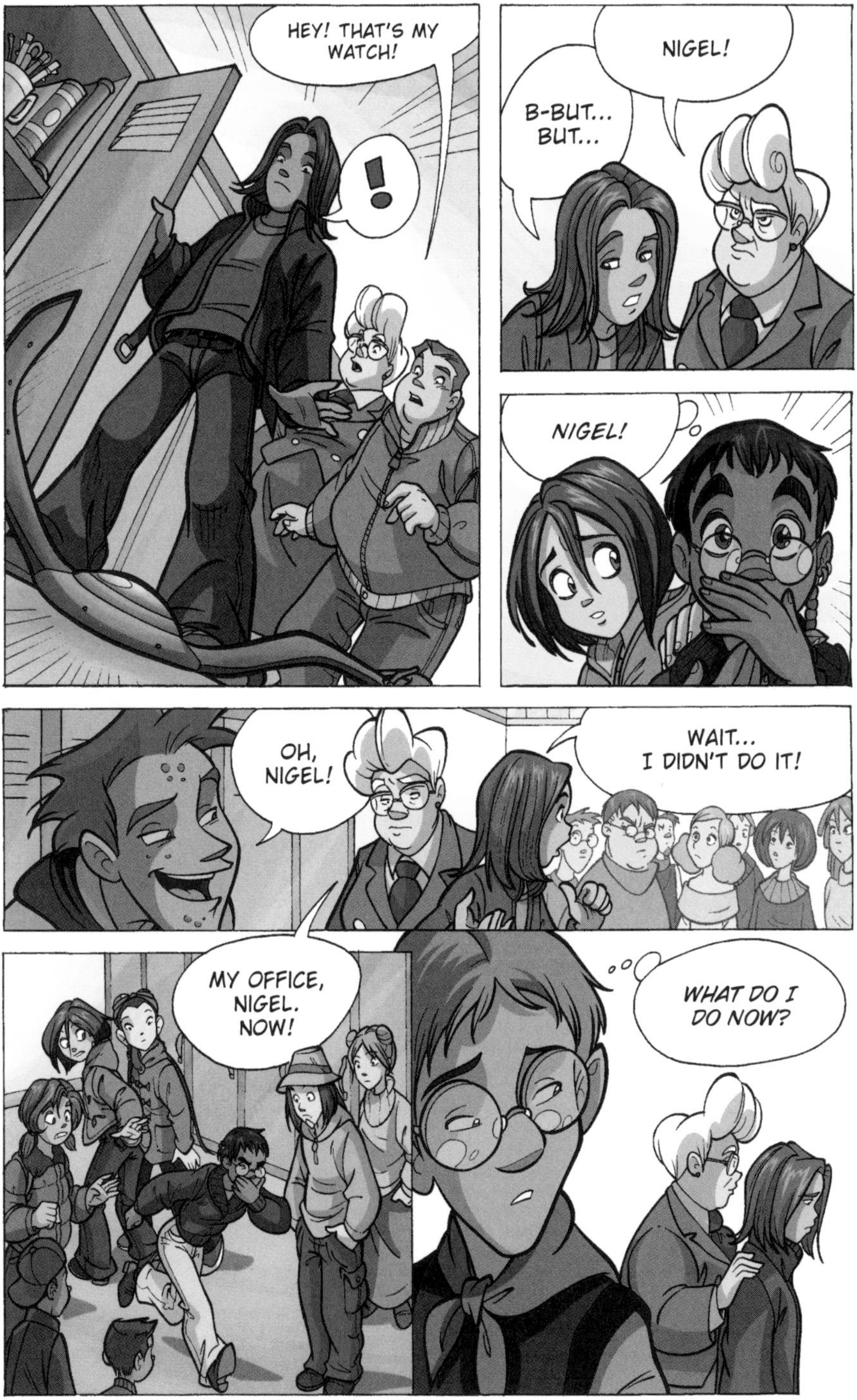
HEY! THAT'S MY WATCH!
!
B-BUT... BUT...
NIGEL!
NIGEL!
OH, NIGEL!
WAIT... I DIDN'T DO IT!
MY OFFICE, NIGEL. NOW!
WHAT DO I DO NOW?

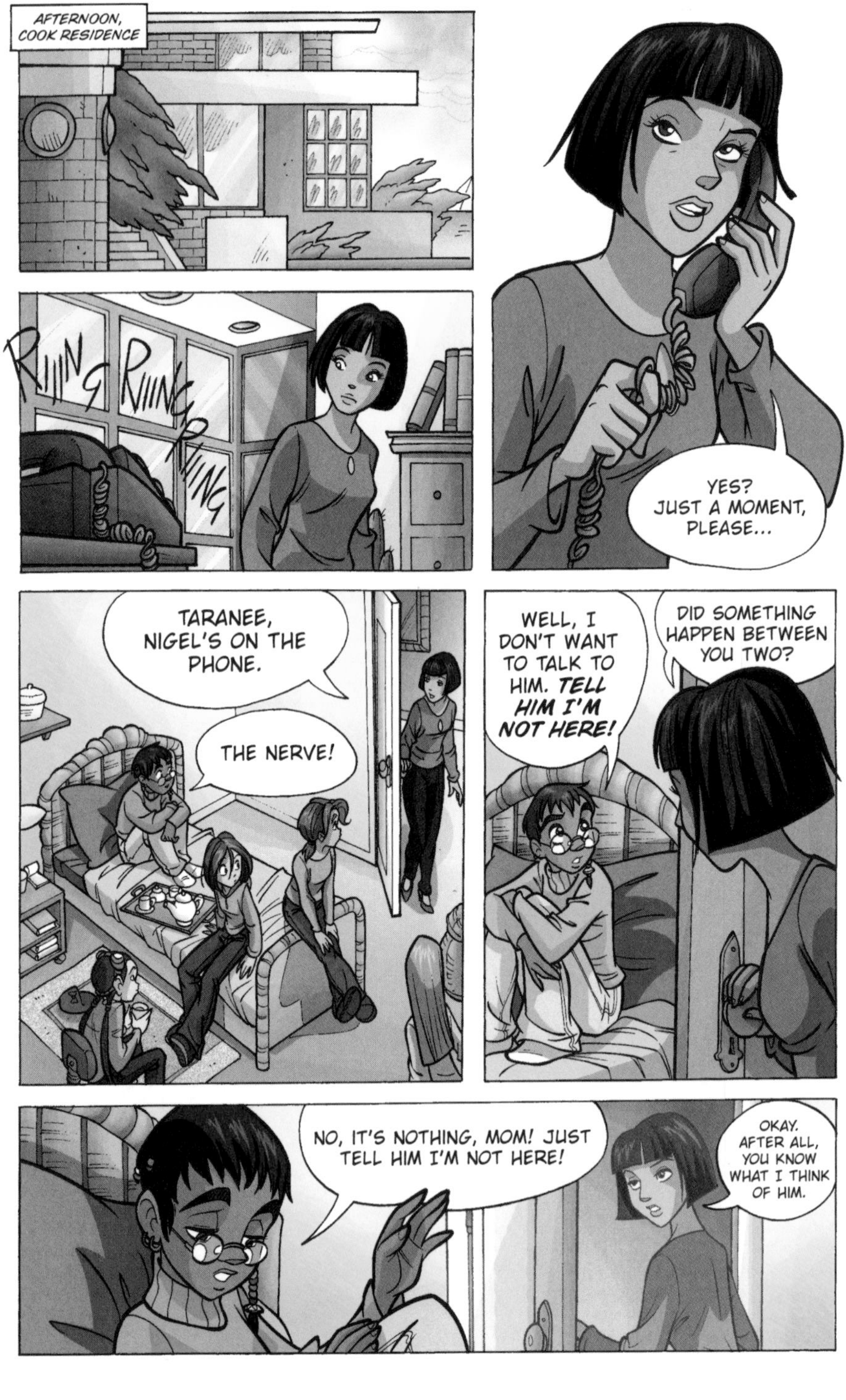
AFTERNOON, COOK RESIDENCE
RIIING RIIING RIIING
YES? JUST A MOMENT, PLEASE...
TARANEE, NIGEL'S ON THE PHONE.
THE NERVE!
WELL, I DON'T WANT TO TALK TO HIM. TELL HIM I'M NOT HERE!
DID SOMETHING HAPPEN BETWEEN YOU TWO?
NO, IT'S NOTHING, MOM! JUST TELL HIM I'M NOT HERE!
OKAY. AFTER ALL, YOU KNOW WHAT I THINK OF HIM.

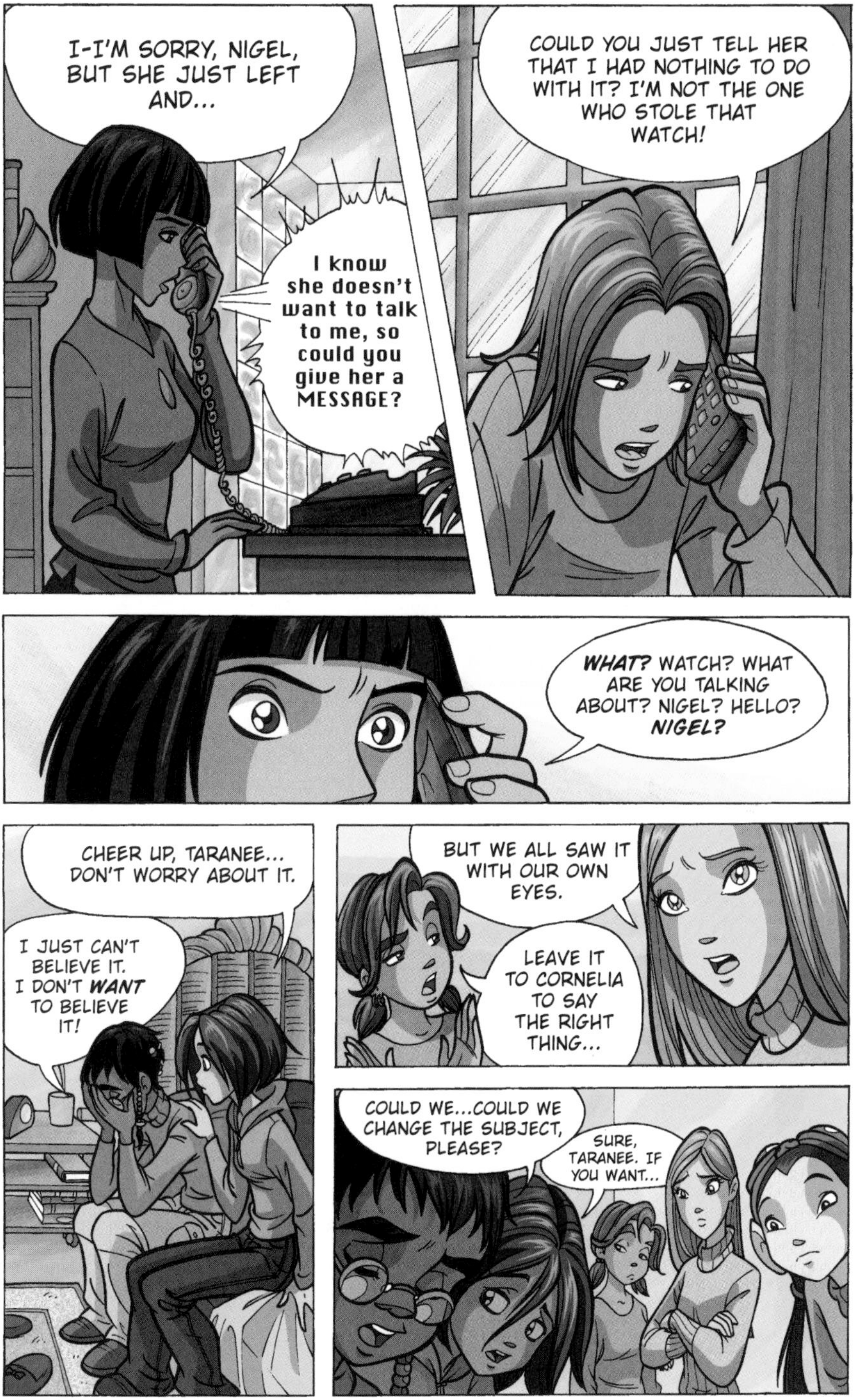
I-I'M SORRY, NIGEL, BUT SHE JUST LEFT AND...
I know she doesn't want to talk to me, so could you give her a MESSAGE?
COULD YOU JUST TELL HER THAT I HAD NOTHING TO DO WITH IT? I'M NOT THE ONE WHO STOLE THAT WATCH!
WHAT? WATCH? WHAT ARE YOU TALKING ABOUT? NIGEL? HELLO? ***NIGEL?***
CHEER UP, TARANEE... DON'T WORRY ABOUT IT.
I JUST CAN'T BELIEVE IT. I DON'T ***WANT*** TO BELIEVE IT!
BUT WE ALL SAW IT WITH OUR OWN EYES.
LEAVE IT TO CORNELIA TO SAY THE RIGHT THING...
COULD WE...COULD WE CHANGE THE SUBJECT, PLEASE?
SURE, TARANEE. IF YOU WANT...

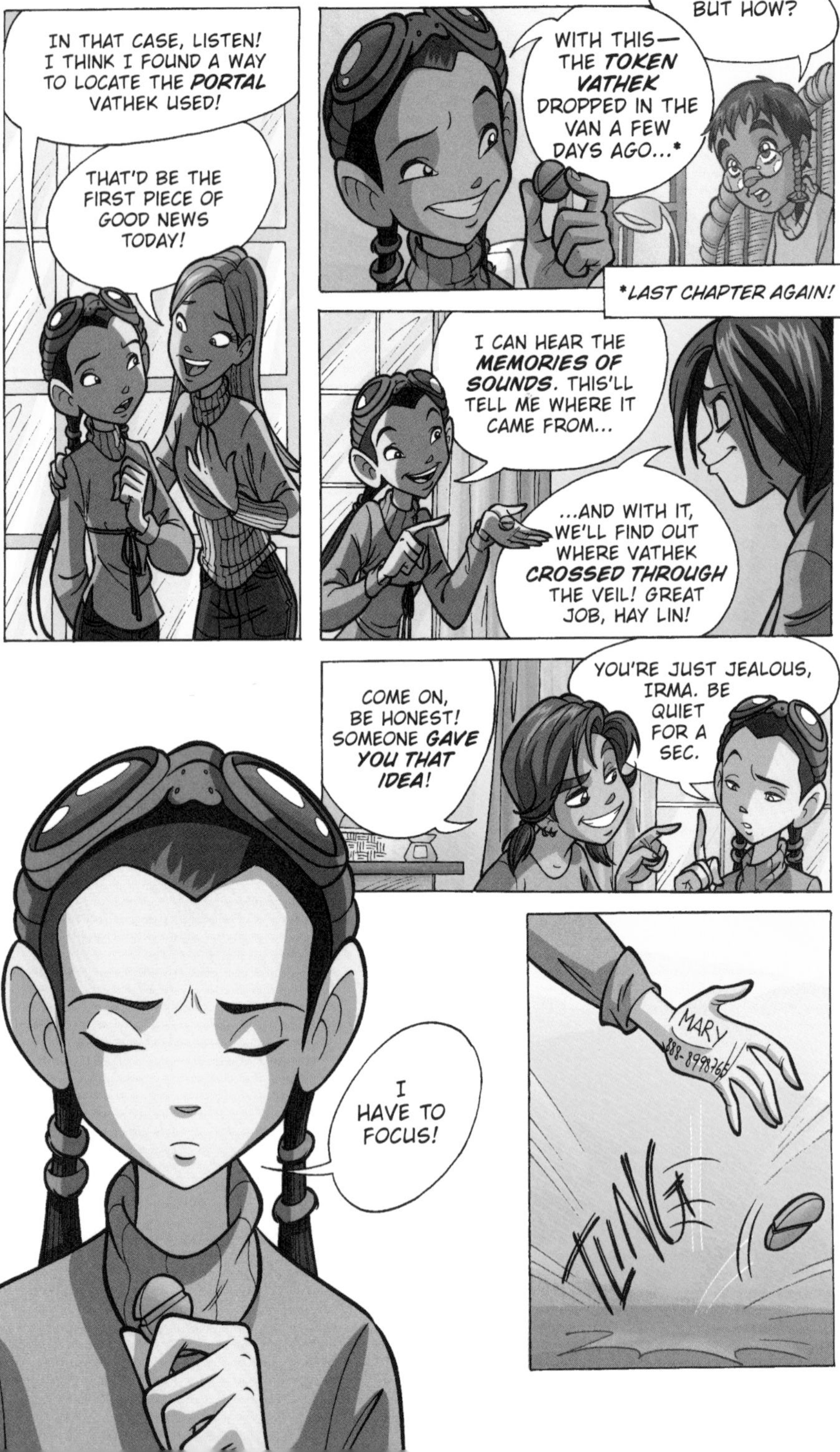

IN THAT CASE, LISTEN! I THINK I FOUND A WAY TO LOCATE THE PORTAL VATHEK USED!
THAT'D BE THE FIRST PIECE OF GOOD NEWS TODAY!
WITH THIS— THE TOKEN VATHEK DROPPED IN THE VAN A FEW DAYS AGO...*
BUT HOW?
*LAST CHAPTER AGAIN!
I CAN HEAR THE MEMORIES OF SOUNDS. THIS'LL TELL ME WHERE IT CAME FROM...
...AND WITH IT, WE'LL FIND OUT WHERE VATHEK CROSSED THROUGH THE VEIL! GREAT JOB, HAY LIN!
COME ON, BE HONEST! SOMEONE GAVE YOU THAT IDEA!
YOU'RE JUST JEALOUS, IRMA. BE QUIET FOR A SEC.
I HAVE TO FOCUS!
MARY
888-8998765
TLING

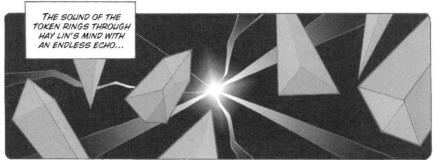

THE SOUND OF THE TOKEN RINGS THROUGH HAY LIN'S MIND WITH AN ENDLESS ECHO...

...AND BEFORE THE GIRL'S EYES PASS BLURRED AND JUMBLED IMAGES...

...THAT SOON SHARPEN.

OF COURSE. NOW I GET IT!

IT'S AN AMUSEMENT PARK! THE OLD ABANDONED *CARNIVAL* JUST OUTSIDE OF HEATHERFIELD.

YOU'RE SURE?

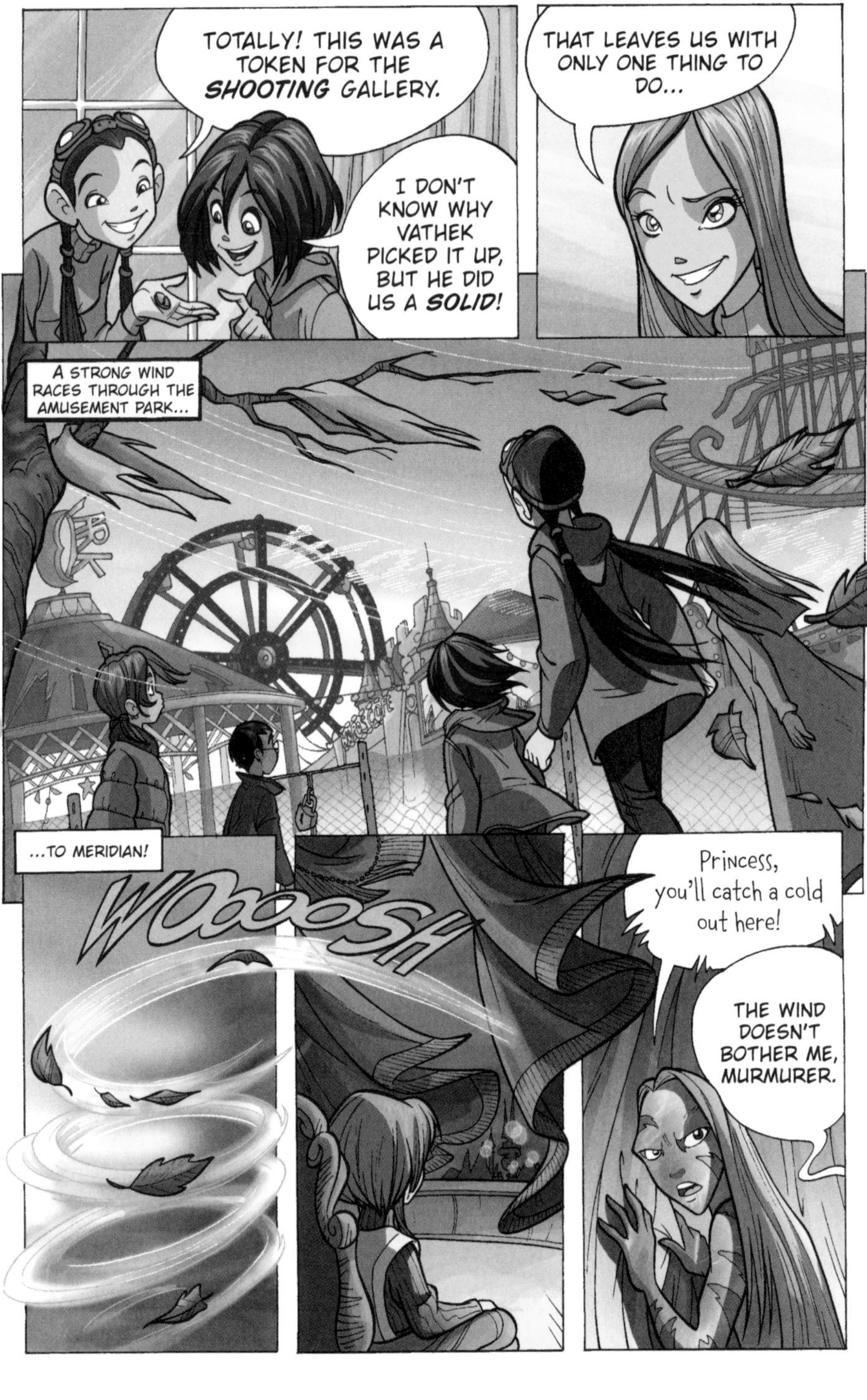
TOTALLY! THIS WAS A TOKEN FOR THE *SHOOTING* GALLERY.
I DON'T KNOW WHY VATHEK PICKED IT UP, BUT HE DID US A *SOLID*!
THAT LEAVES US WITH ONLY ONE THING TO DO...
A STRONG WIND RACES THROUGH THE AMUSEMENT PARK...
...TO MERIDIAN!
WOOOOSH
Princess, you'll catch a cold out here!
THE WIND DOESN'T BOTHER ME, MURMURER.

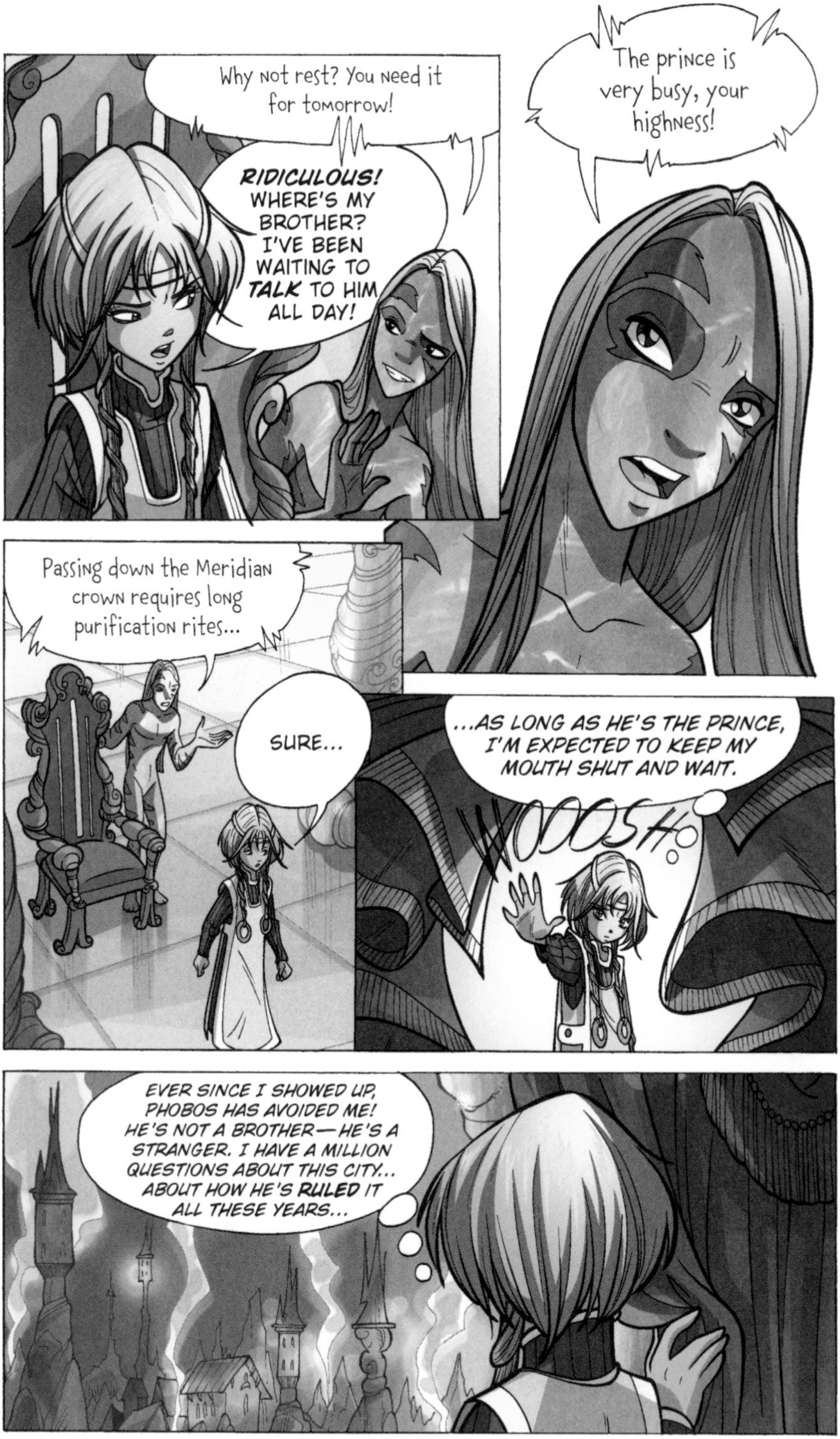
Why not rest? You need it for tomorrow!
RIDICULOUS! WHERE'S MY BROTHER? I'VE BEEN WAITING TO TALK TO HIM ALL DAY!
The prince is very busy, your highness!
Passing down the Meridian crown requires long purification rites...
SURE...
...AS LONG AS HE'S THE PRINCE, I'M EXPECTED TO KEEP MY MOUTH SHUT AND WAIT.
WOOOSH
EVER SINCE I SHOWED UP, PHOBOS HAS AVOIDED ME! HE'S NOT A BROTHER—HE'S A STRANGER. I HAVE A MILLION QUESTIONS ABOUT THIS CITY... ABOUT HOW HE'S RULED IT ALL THESE YEARS...

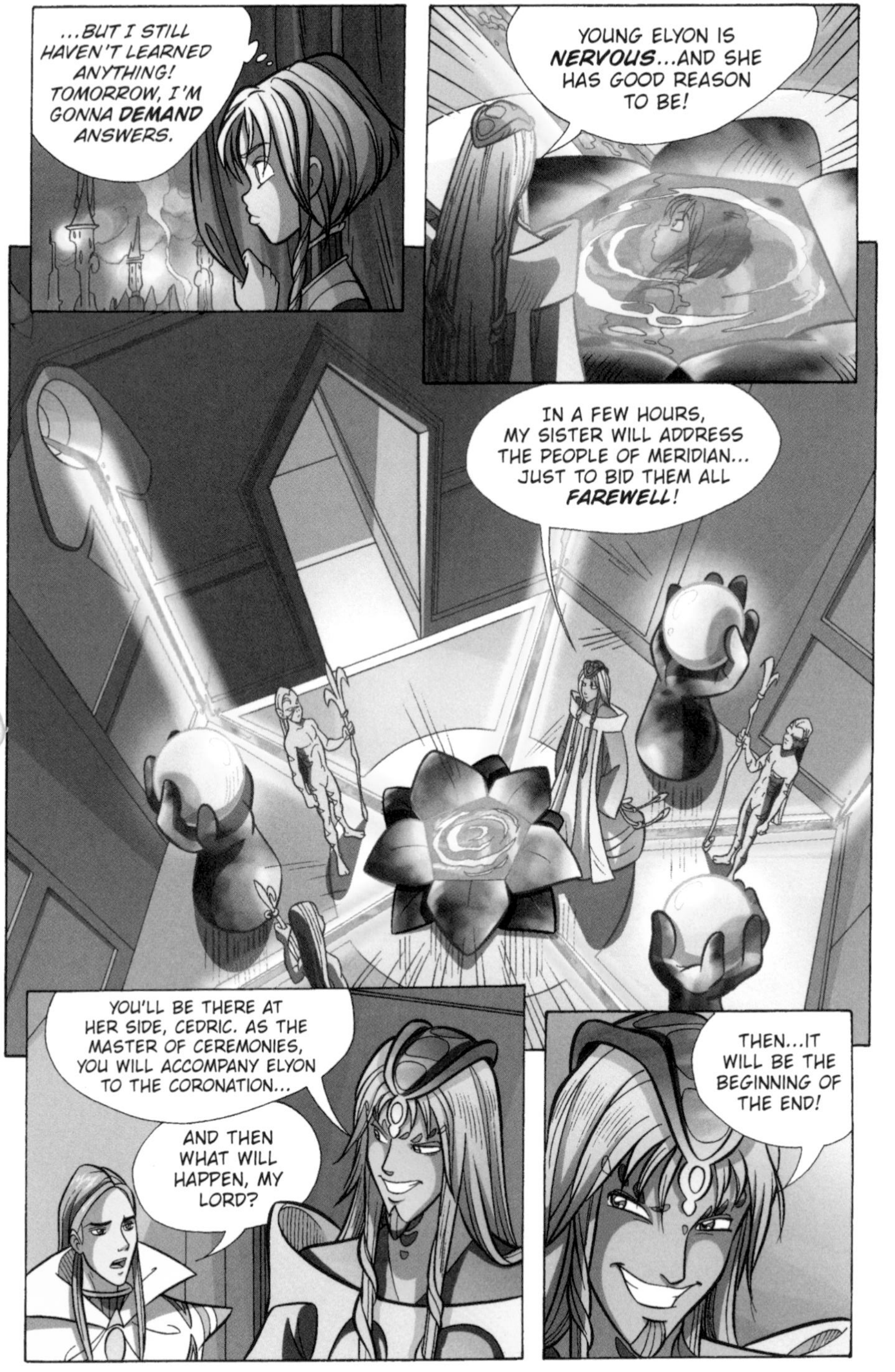
...BUT I STILL HAVEN'T LEARNED ANYTHING! TOMORROW, I'M GONNA DEMAND ANSWERS.
YOUNG ELYON IS NERVOUS...AND SHE HAS GOOD REASON TO BE!
IN A FEW HOURS, MY SISTER WILL ADDRESS THE PEOPLE OF MERIDIAN... JUST TO BID THEM ALL FAREWELL!
YOU'LL BE THERE AT HER SIDE, CEDRIC. AS THE MASTER OF CEREMONIES, YOU WILL ACCOMPANY ELYON TO THE CORONATION...
AND THEN WHAT WILL HAPPEN, MY LORD?
THEN...IT WILL BE THE BEGINNING OF THE END!

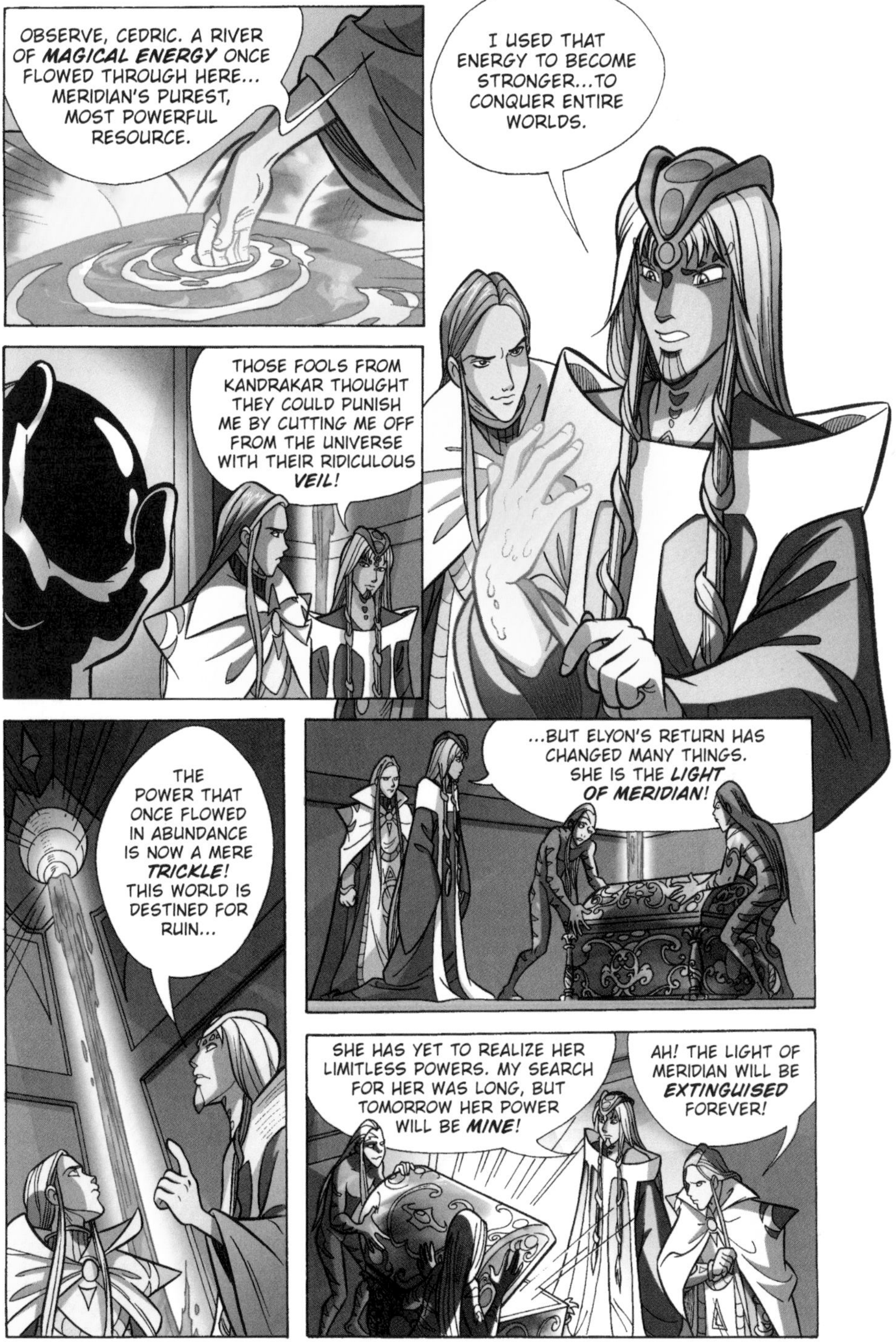
OBSERVE, CEDRIC. A RIVER OF MAGICAL ENERGY ONCE FLOWED THROUGH HERE... MERIDIAN'S PUREST, MOST POWERFUL RESOURCE.
I USED THAT ENERGY TO BECOME STRONGER...TO CONQUER ENTIRE WORLDS.
THOSE FOOLS FROM KANDRAKAR THOUGHT THEY COULD PUNISH ME BY CUTTING ME OFF FROM THE UNIVERSE WITH THEIR RIDICULOUS VEIL!
THE POWER THAT ONCE FLOWED IN ABUNDANCE IS NOW A MERE TRICKLE! THIS WORLD IS DESTINED FOR RUIN...
...BUT ELYON'S RETURN HAS CHANGED MANY THINGS. SHE IS THE LIGHT OF MERIDIAN!
SHE HAS YET TO REALIZE HER LIMITLESS POWERS. MY SEARCH FOR HER WAS LONG, BUT TOMORROW HER POWER WILL BE MINE!
AH! THE LIGHT OF MERIDIAN WILL BE EXTINGUISED FOREVER!

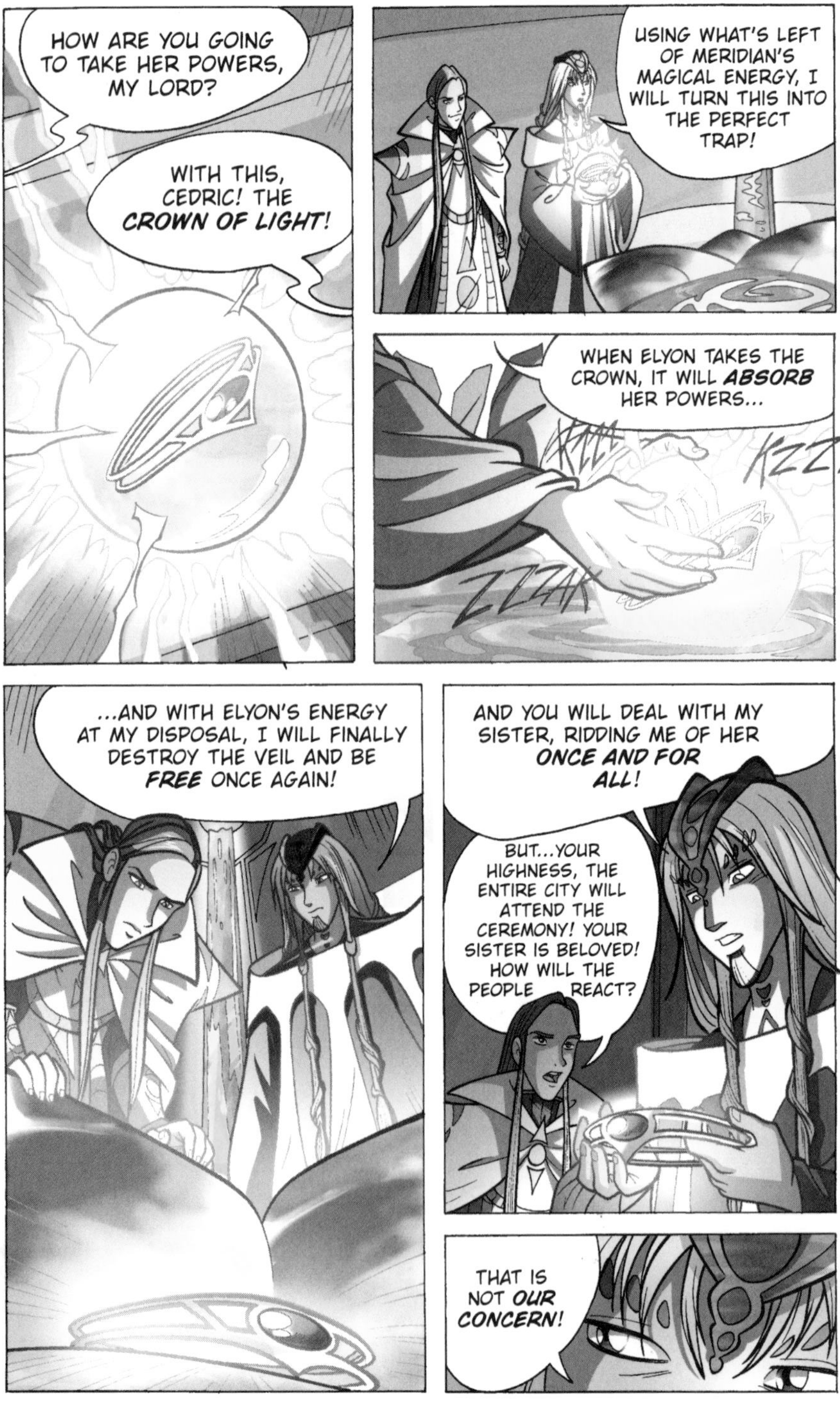
HOW ARE YOU GOING TO TAKE HER POWERS, MY LORD?
WITH THIS, CEDRIC! THE CROWN OF LIGHT!
USING WHAT'S LEFT OF MERIDIAN'S MAGICAL ENERGY, I WILL TURN THIS INTO THE PERFECT TRAP!
WHEN ELYON TAKES THE CROWN, IT WILL ABSORB HER POWERS...
KZZZ
ZZZAK
...AND WITH ELYON'S ENERGY AT MY DISPOSAL, I WILL FINALLY DESTROY THE VEIL AND BE FREE ONCE AGAIN!
AND YOU WILL DEAL WITH MY SISTER, RIDDING ME OF HER ONCE AND FOR ALL!
BUT...YOUR HIGHNESS, THE ENTIRE CITY WILL ATTEND THE CEREMONY! YOUR SISTER IS BELOVED! HOW WILL THE PEOPLE REACT?
THAT IS NOT OUR CONCERN!

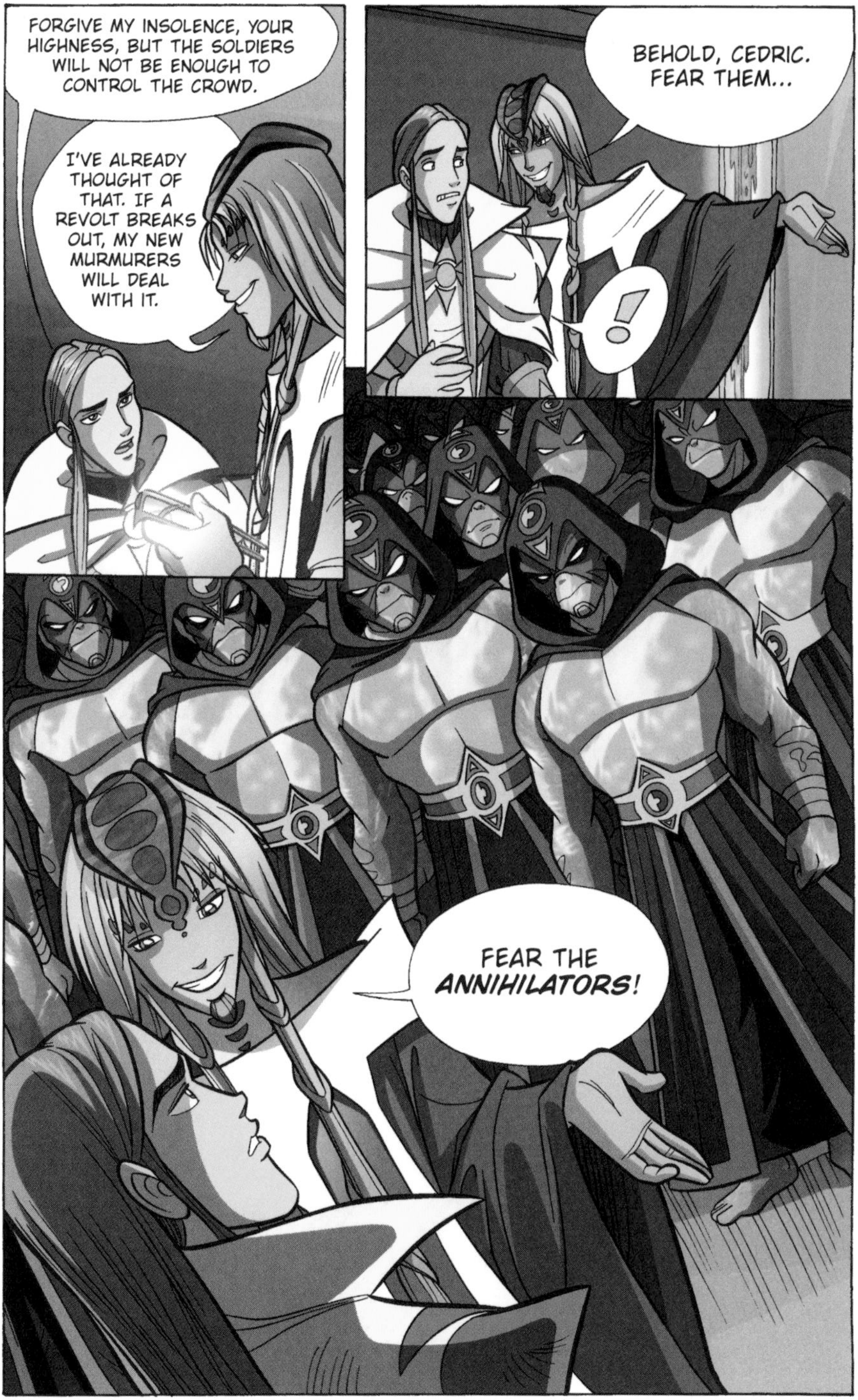
FORGIVE MY INSOLENCE, YOUR HIGHNESS, BUT THE SOLDIERS WILL NOT BE ENOUGH TO CONTROL THE CROWD.
I'VE ALREADY THOUGHT OF THAT. IF A REVOLT BREAKS OUT, MY NEW MURMURERS WILL DEAL WITH IT.
BEHOLD, CEDRIC. FEAR THEM...
!
FEAR THE *ANNIHILATORS*!

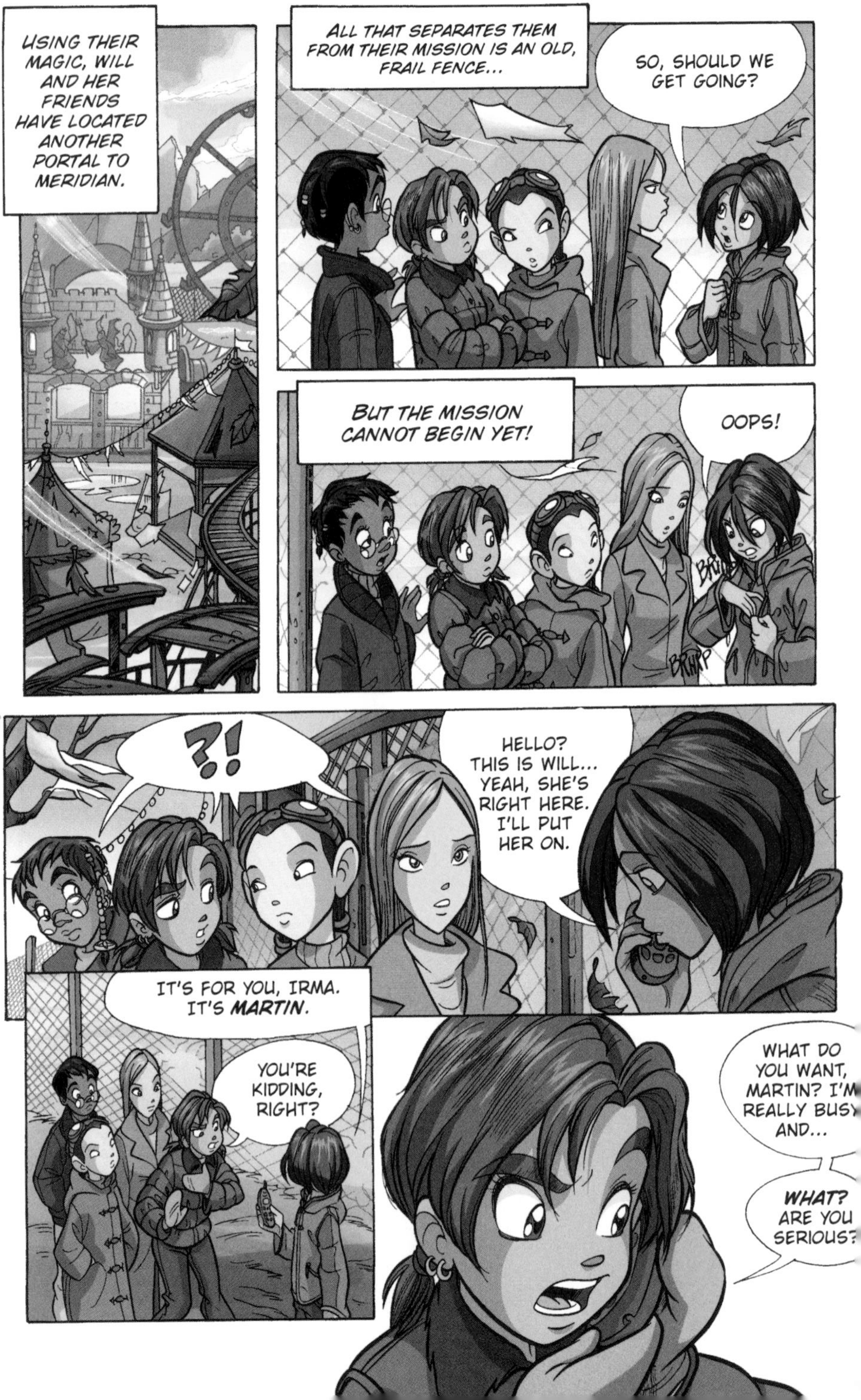
USING THEIR MAGIC, WILL AND HER FRIENDS HAVE LOCATED ANOTHER PORTAL TO MERIDIAN.
ALL THAT SEPARATES THEM FROM THEIR MISSION IS AN OLD, FRAIL FENCE...
SO, SHOULD WE GET GOING?
BUT THE MISSION CANNOT BEGIN YET!
OOPS!
BRHPP
?!
HELLO? THIS IS WILL... YEAH, SHE'S RIGHT HERE. I'LL PUT HER ON.
IT'S FOR YOU, IRMA. IT'S MARTIN.
YOU'RE KIDDING, RIGHT?
WHAT DO YOU WANT, MARTIN? I'M REALLY BUSY AND...
WHAT? ARE YOU SERIOUS?

"*OKAY!* WE'LL MEET YOU OVER AT THE GOLDEN IN HALF AN HOUR!"

I'M SORRY TO BOTHER YOU GUYS... BUT THIS IS REALLY SERIOUS!

YOUR FOLKS SAID YOU WERE OUT WITH WILL. SO I CALLED HER PLACE, AND HER MOM GAVE ME HER—

SPARE US THE DETAILS, MR. *METICULOUS!* GET TO THE POINT!

I REALLY WANTED TO TELL YOU EVERYTHING AT SCHOOL TODAY, BUT... WELL, I WAS *SCARED!*

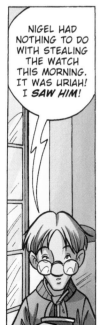

NIGEL HAD NOTHING TO DO WITH STEALING THE WATCH THIS MORNING. IT WAS URIAH! I *SAW HIM!*

WHY DIDN'T YOU TELL THE PRINCIPAL *RIGHT AWAY*?

I WAS AFRAID THOSE GUYS WOULD DO SOMETHING TO ME...BUT I CAN'T LET AN INNOCENT PERSON TAKE THE BLAME! WHAT SHOULD I DO, IRMA?

GIVE THE PRINCIPAL YOUR TELL-ALL ACCOUNT TOMORROW MORNING!

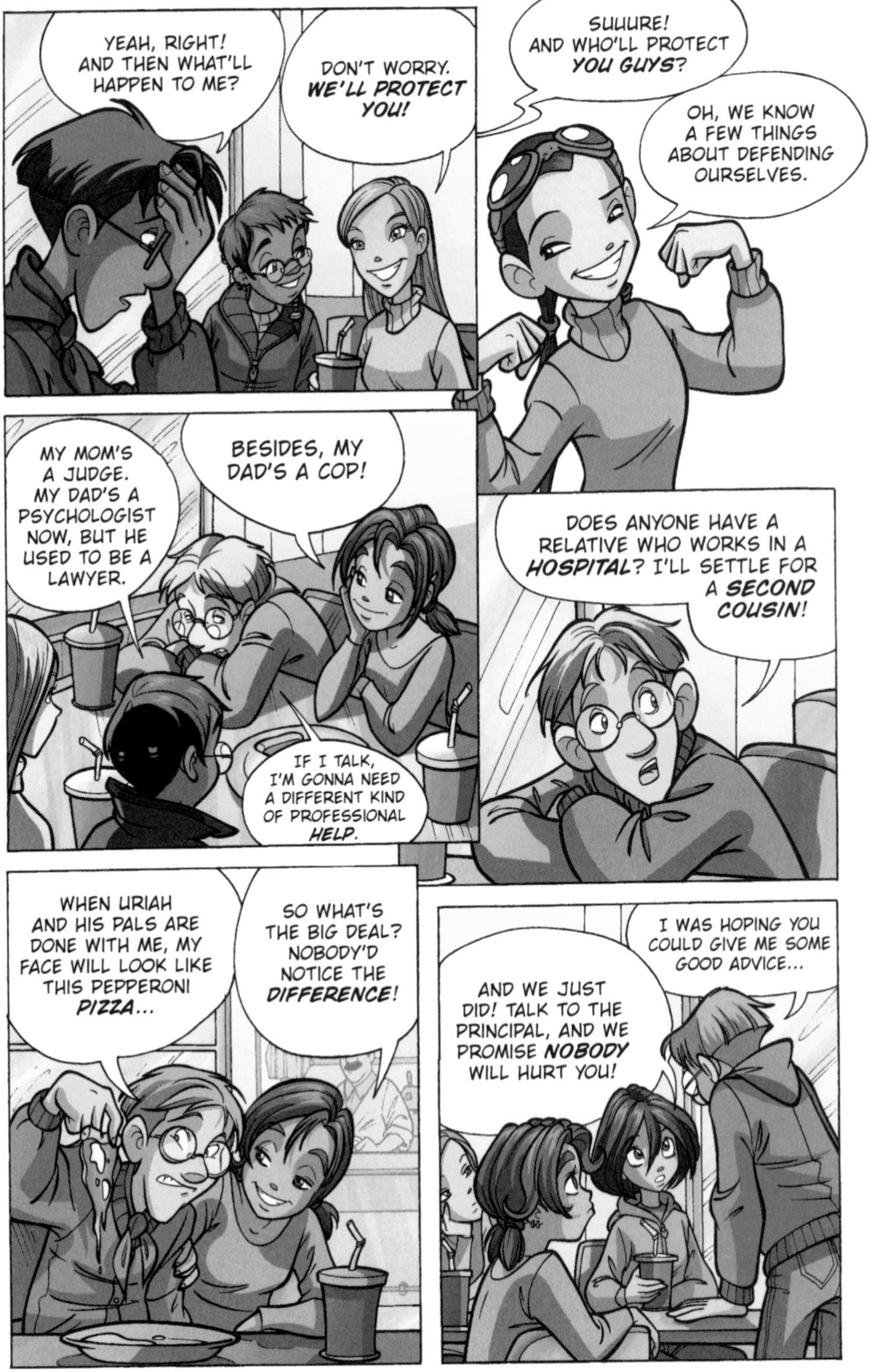
YEAH, RIGHT! AND THEN WHAT'LL HAPPEN TO ME?
DON'T WORRY. WE'LL PROTECT YOU!
SUUURE! AND WHO'LL PROTECT YOU GUYS?
OH, WE KNOW A FEW THINGS ABOUT DEFENDING OURSELVES.
MY MOM'S A JUDGE. MY DAD'S A PSYCHOLOGIST NOW, BUT HE USED TO BE A LAWYER.
BESIDES, MY DAD'S A COP!
IF I TALK, I'M GONNA NEED A DIFFERENT KIND OF PROFESSIONAL HELP.
DOES ANYONE HAVE A RELATIVE WHO WORKS IN A HOSPITAL? I'LL SETTLE FOR A SECOND COUSIN!
WHEN URIAH AND HIS PALS ARE DONE WITH ME, MY FACE WILL LOOK LIKE THIS PEPPERONI PIZZA...
SO WHAT'S THE BIG DEAL? NOBODY'D NOTICE THE DIFFERENCE!
I WAS HOPING YOU COULD GIVE ME SOME GOOD ADVICE...
AND WE JUST DID! TALK TO THE PRINCIPAL, AND WE PROMISE NOBODY WILL HURT YOU!

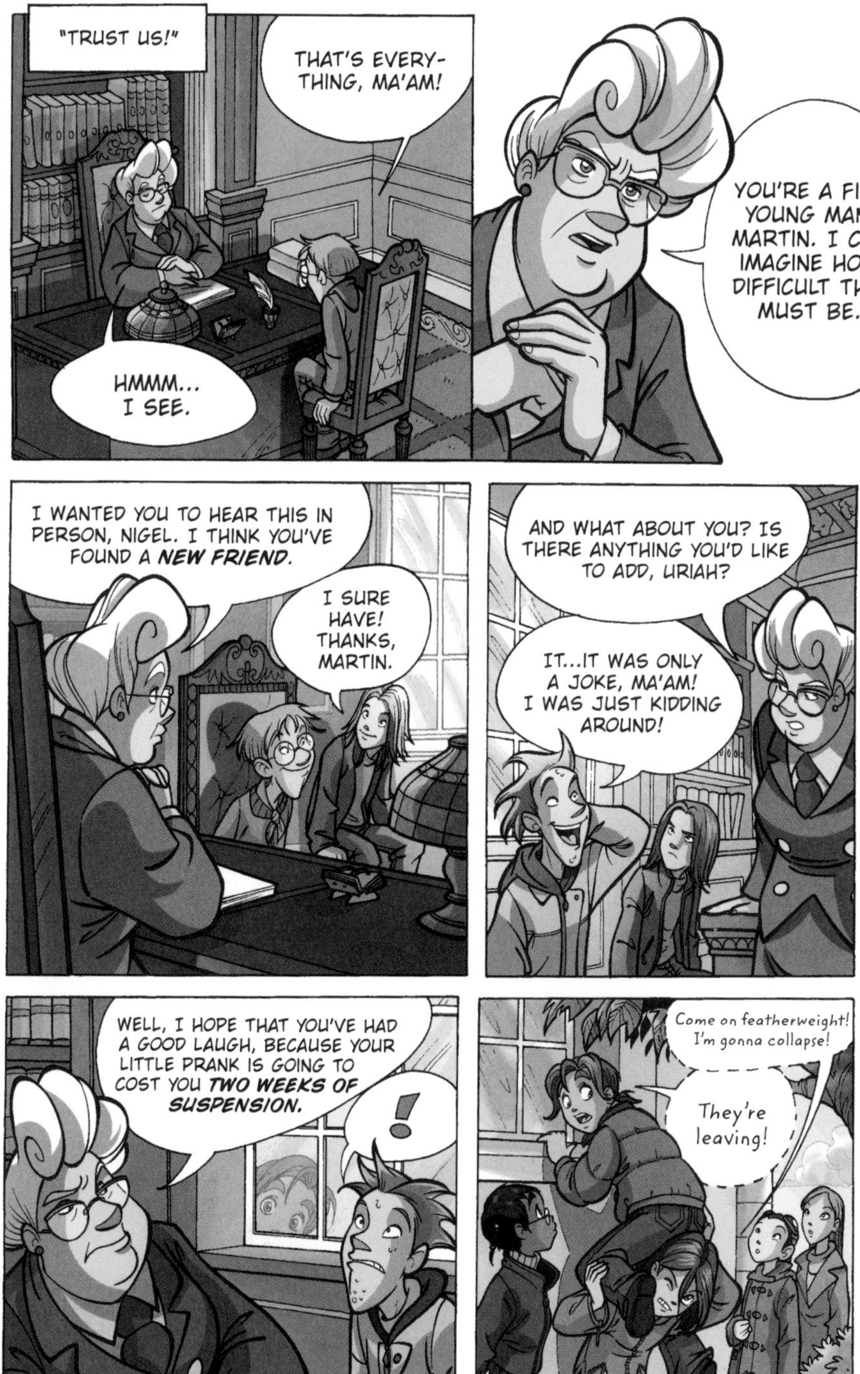
"TRUST US!"
THAT'S EVERY-THING, MA'AM!
HMMM... I SEE.
YOU'RE A FINE YOUNG MAN, MARTIN. I CAN IMAGINE HOW DIFFICULT THIS MUST BE.
I WANTED YOU TO HEAR THIS IN PERSON, NIGEL. I THINK YOU'VE FOUND A ***NEW FRIEND***.
I SURE HAVE! THANKS, MARTIN.
AND WHAT ABOUT YOU? IS THERE ANYTHING YOU'D LIKE TO ADD, URIAH?
IT...IT WAS ONLY A JOKE, MA'AM! I WAS JUST KIDDING AROUND!
WELL, I HOPE THAT YOU'VE HAD A GOOD LAUGH, BECAUSE YOUR LITTLE PRANK IS GOING TO COST YOU ***TWO WEEKS OF SUSPENSION.***
!
They're leaving!
Come on featherweight! I'm gonna collapse!

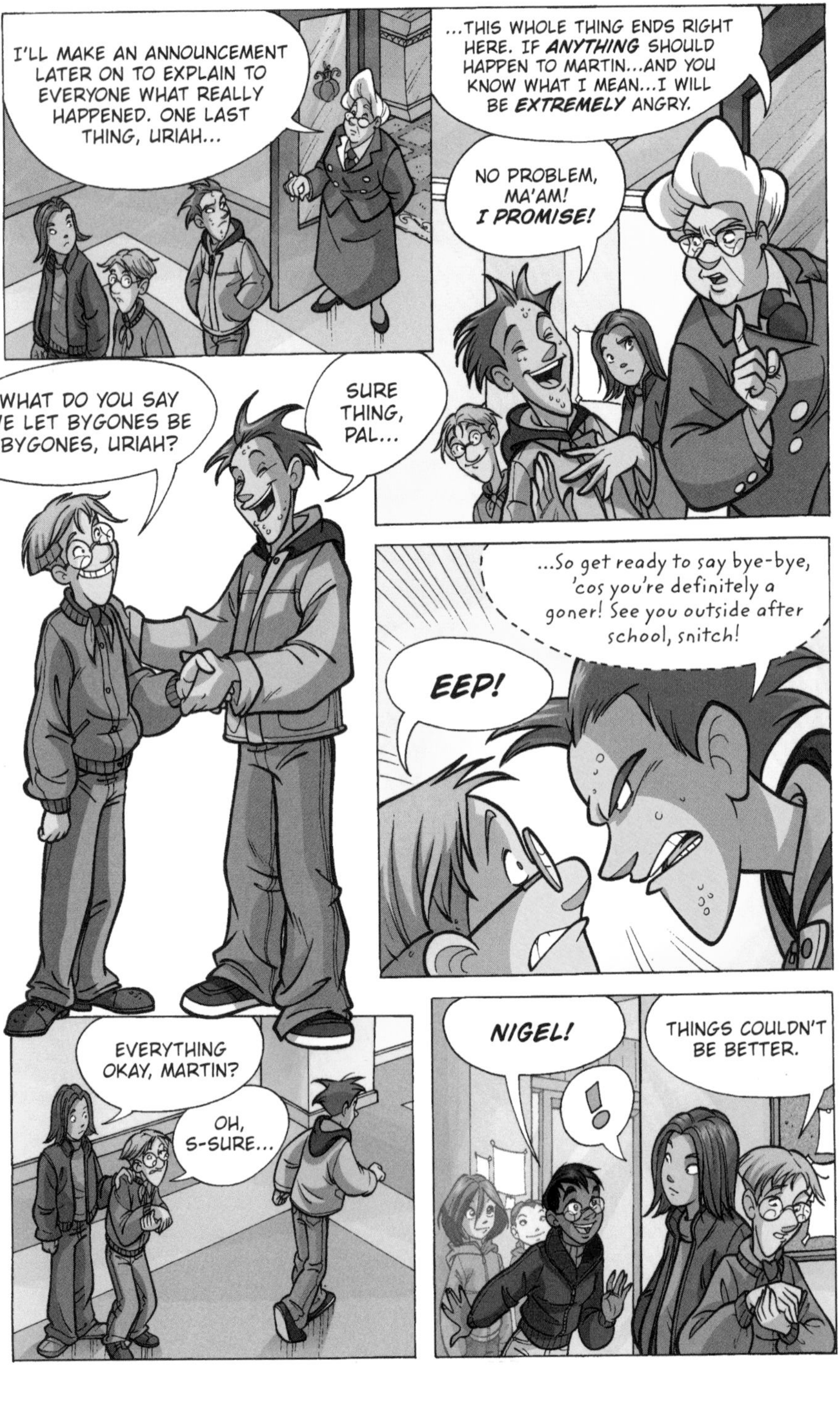
I'LL MAKE AN ANNOUNCEMENT LATER ON TO EXPLAIN TO EVERYONE WHAT REALLY HAPPENED. ONE LAST THING, URIAH...
...THIS WHOLE THING ENDS RIGHT HERE. IF ANYTHING SHOULD HAPPEN TO MARTIN...AND YOU KNOW WHAT I MEAN...I WILL BE EXTREMELY ANGRY.
NO PROBLEM, MA'AM! I PROMISE!
WHAT DO YOU SAY WE LET BYGONES BE BYGONES, URIAH?
SURE THING, PAL...
...So get ready to say bye-bye, 'cos you're definitely a goner! See you outside after school, snitch!
EEP!
EVERYTHING OKAY, MARTIN?
OH, S-SURE...
NIGEL!
!
THINGS COULDN'T BE BETTER.

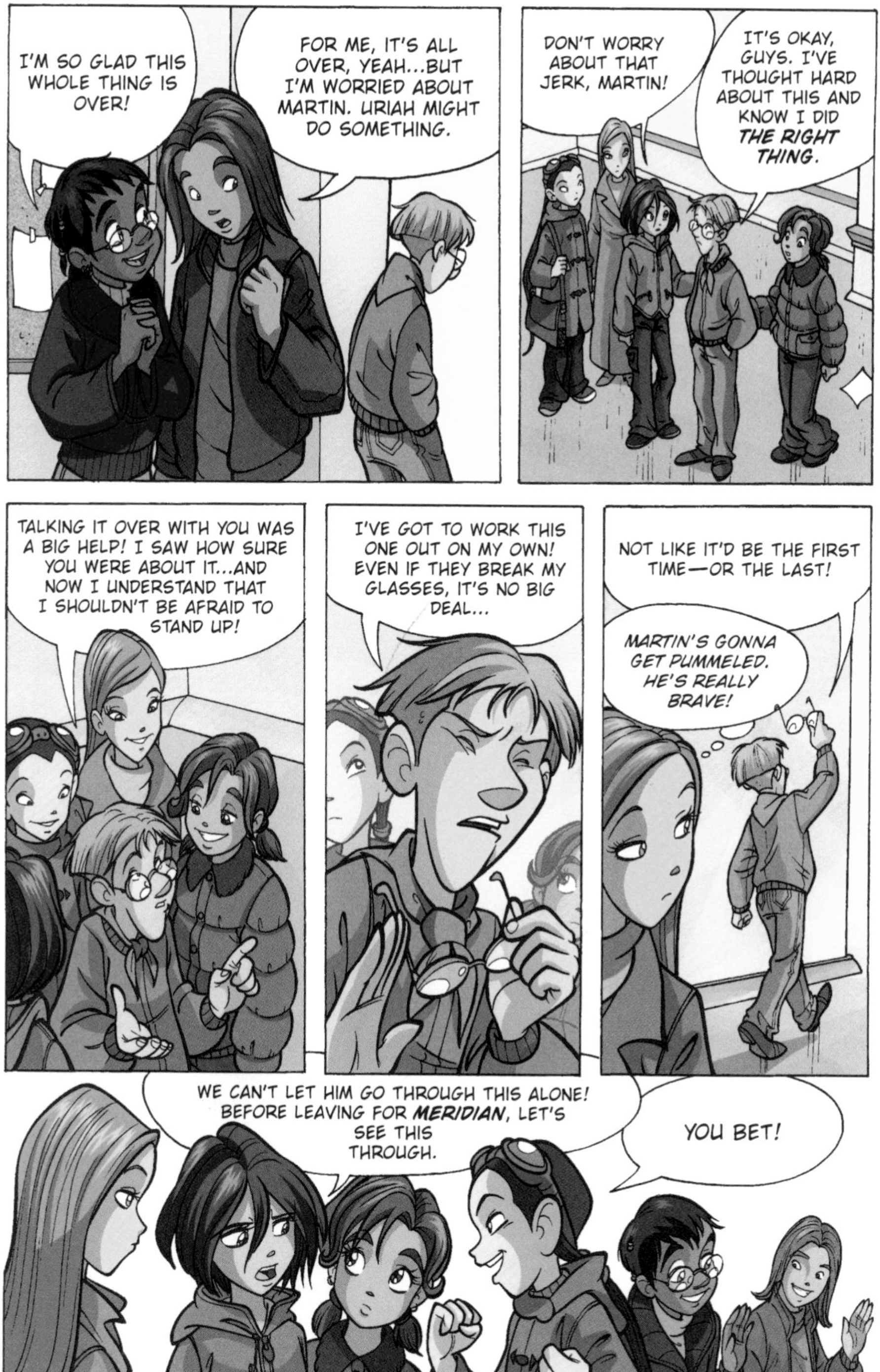
I'M SO GLAD THIS WHOLE THING IS OVER!
FOR ME, IT'S ALL OVER, YEAH...BUT I'M WORRIED ABOUT MARTIN. URIAH MIGHT DO SOMETHING.
DON'T WORRY ABOUT THAT JERK, MARTIN!
IT'S OKAY, GUYS. I'VE THOUGHT HARD ABOUT THIS AND KNOW I DID THE RIGHT THING.
TALKING IT OVER WITH YOU WAS A BIG HELP! I SAW HOW SURE YOU WERE ABOUT IT...AND NOW I UNDERSTAND THAT I SHOULDN'T BE AFRAID TO STAND UP!
I'VE GOT TO WORK THIS ONE OUT ON MY OWN! EVEN IF THEY BREAK MY GLASSES, IT'S NO BIG DEAL...
NOT LIKE IT'D BE THE FIRST TIME—OR THE LAST!
MARTIN'S GONNA GET PUMMELED. HE'S REALLY BRAVE!
WE CAN'T LET HIM GO THROUGH THIS ALONE! BEFORE LEAVING FOR MERIDIAN, LET'S SEE THIS THROUGH.
YOU BET!

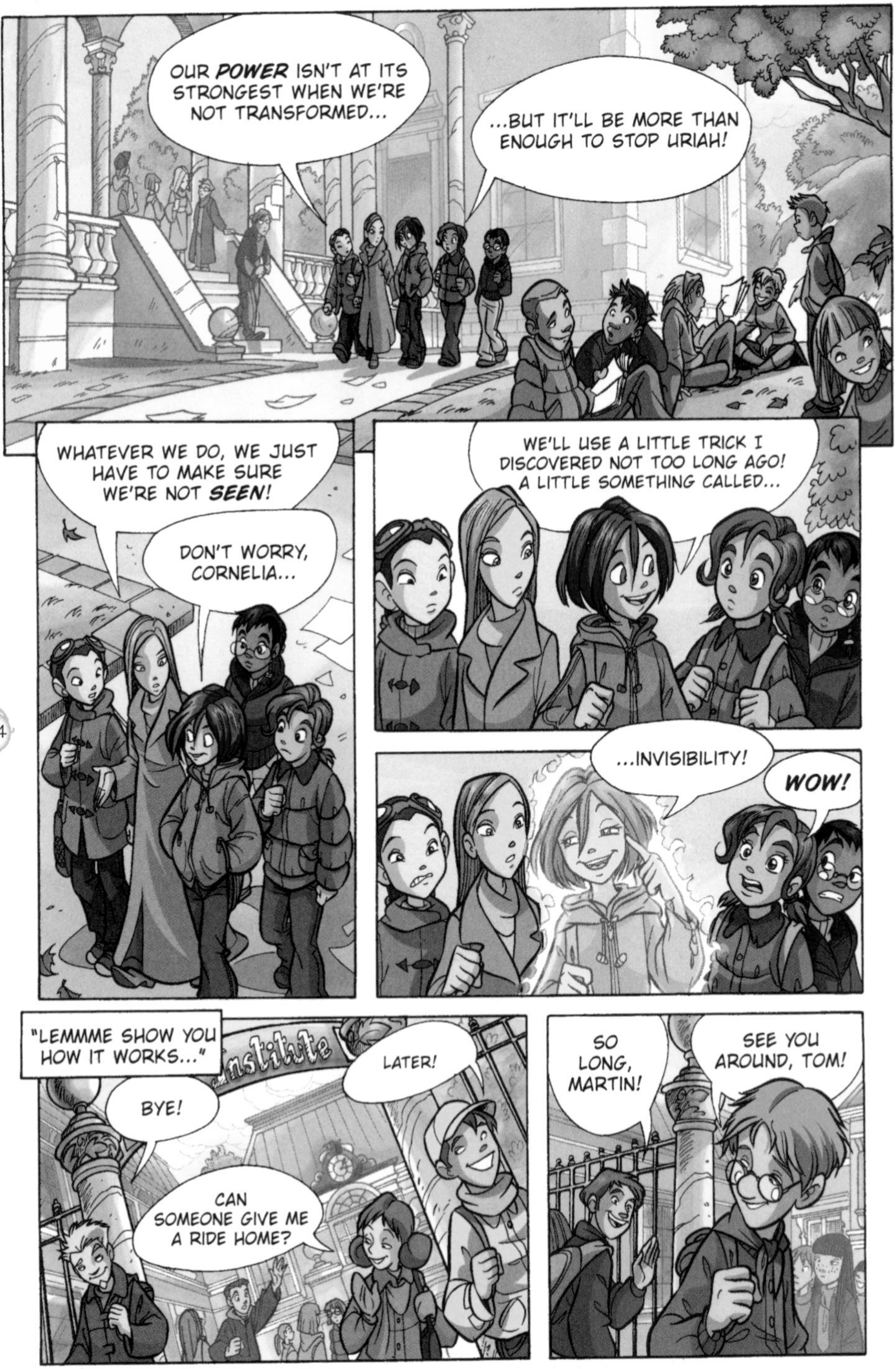
OUR POWER ISN'T AT ITS STRONGEST WHEN WE'RE NOT TRANSFORMED...
...BUT IT'LL BE MORE THAN ENOUGH TO STOP URIAH!
WHATEVER WE DO, WE JUST HAVE TO MAKE SURE WE'RE NOT SEEN!
DON'T WORRY, CORNELIA...
WE'LL USE A LITTLE TRICK I DISCOVERED NOT TOO LONG AGO! A LITTLE SOMETHING CALLED...
...INVISIBILITY!
WOW!
"LEMMME SHOW YOU HOW IT WORKS..."
BYE!
LATER!
CAN SOMEONE GIVE ME A RIDE HOME?
SO LONG, MARTIN!
SEE YOU AROUND, TOM!

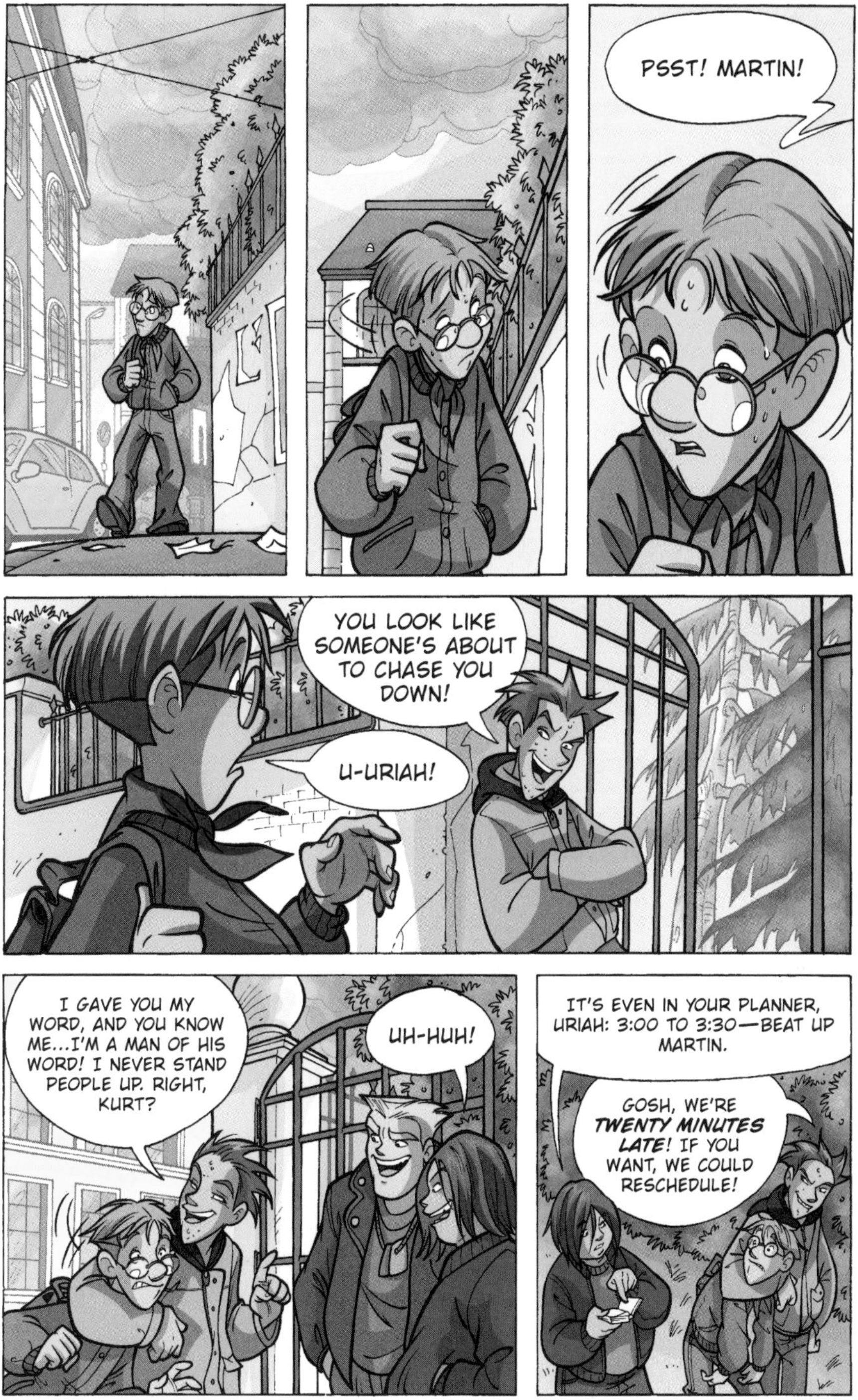
PSST! MARTIN!
YOU LOOK LIKE SOMEONE'S ABOUT TO CHASE YOU DOWN!
U-URIAH!
I GAVE YOU MY WORD, AND YOU KNOW ME...I'M A MAN OF HIS WORD! I NEVER STAND PEOPLE UP. RIGHT, KURT?
UH-HUH!
IT'S EVEN IN YOUR PLANNER, URIAH: 3:00 TO 3:30—BEAT UP MARTIN.
GOSH, WE'RE ***TWENTY MINUTES LATE***! IF YOU WANT, WE COULD RESCHEDULE!

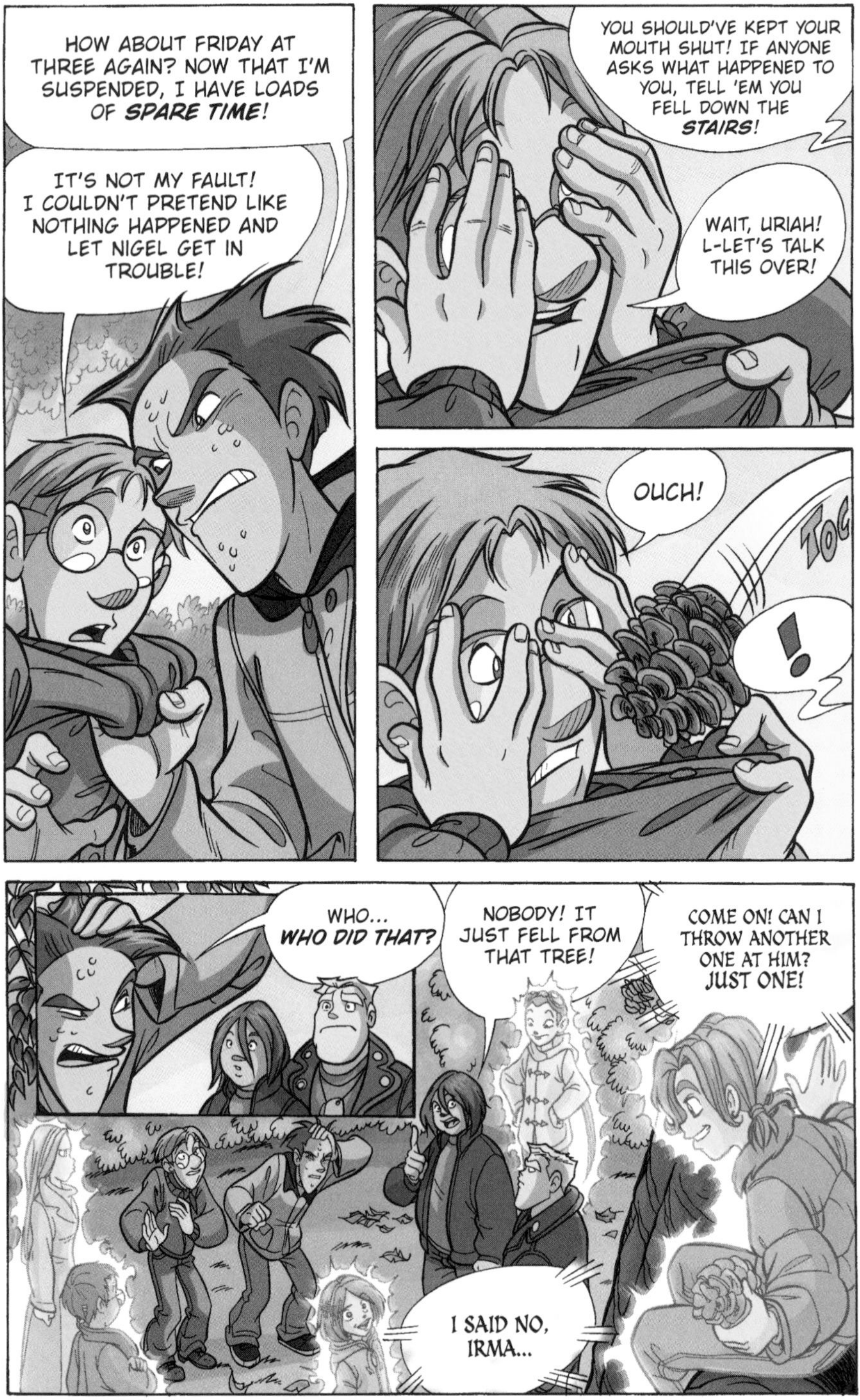
HOW ABOUT FRIDAY AT THREE AGAIN? NOW THAT I'M SUSPENDED, I HAVE LOADS OF SPARE TIME!
IT'S NOT MY FAULT! I COULDN'T PRETEND LIKE NOTHING HAPPENED AND LET NIGEL GET IN TROUBLE!
YOU SHOULD'VE KEPT YOUR MOUTH SHUT! IF ANYONE ASKS WHAT HAPPENED TO YOU, TELL 'EM YOU FELL DOWN THE STAIRS!
WAIT, URIAH! L-LET'S TALK THIS OVER!
OUCH!
!
WHO... WHO DID THAT?
NOBODY! IT JUST FELL FROM THAT TREE!
COME ON! CAN I THROW ANOTHER ONE AT HIM? JUST ONE!
I SAID NO, IRMA...

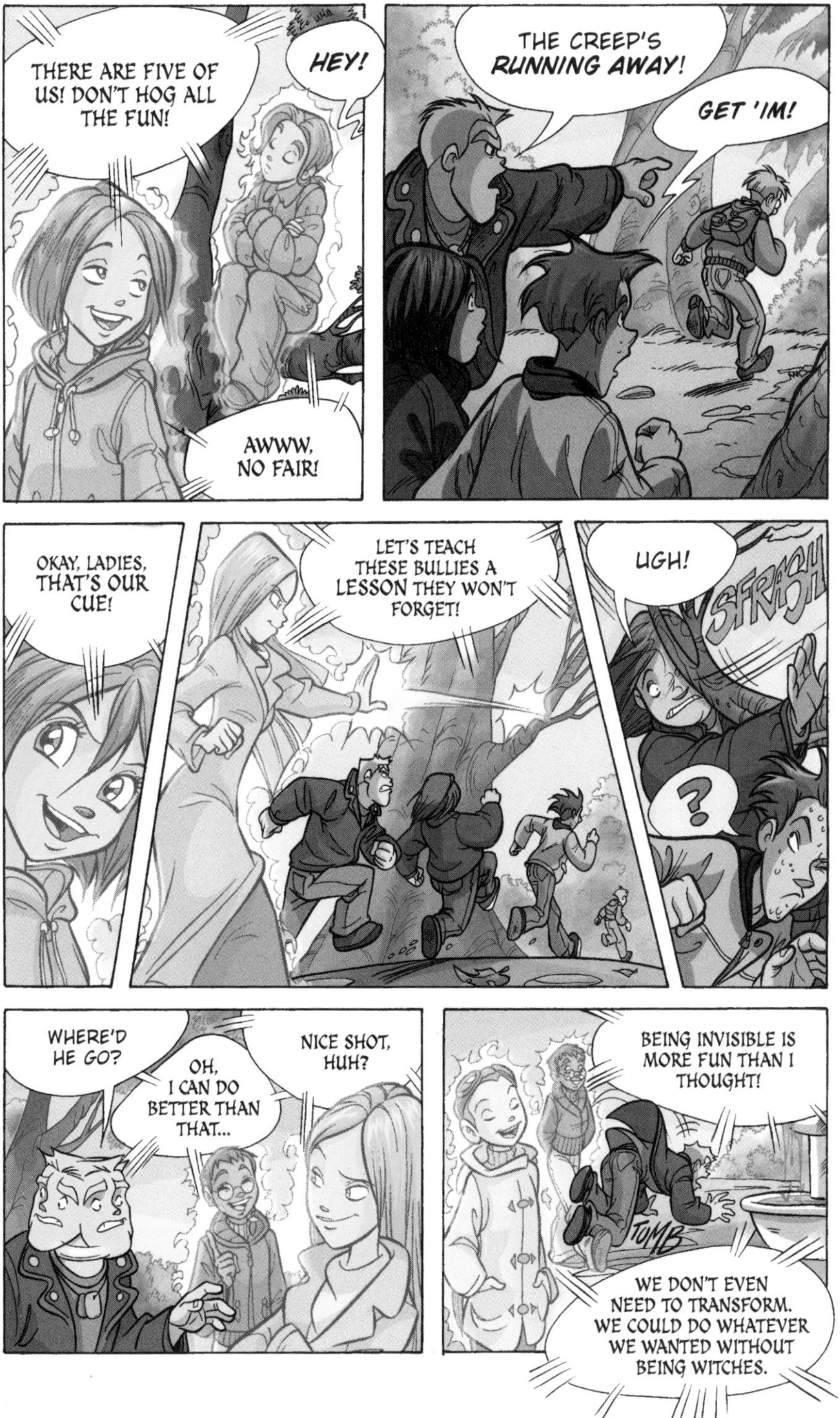
THERE ARE FIVE OF US! DON'T HOG ALL THE FUN!
HEY!
AWWW, NO FAIR!
THE CREEP'S RUNNING AWAY!
GET 'IM!
OKAY, LADIES, THAT'S OUR CUE!
LET'S TEACH THESE BULLIES A LESSON THEY WON'T FORGET!
UGH!
SFRASH
?
WHERE'D HE GO?
OH, I CAN DO BETTER THAN THAT...
NICE SHOT, HUH?
BEING INVISIBLE IS MORE FUN THAN I THOUGHT!
TUMB
WE DON'T EVEN NEED TO TRANSFORM. WE COULD DO WHATEVER WE WANTED WITHOUT BEING WITCHES.

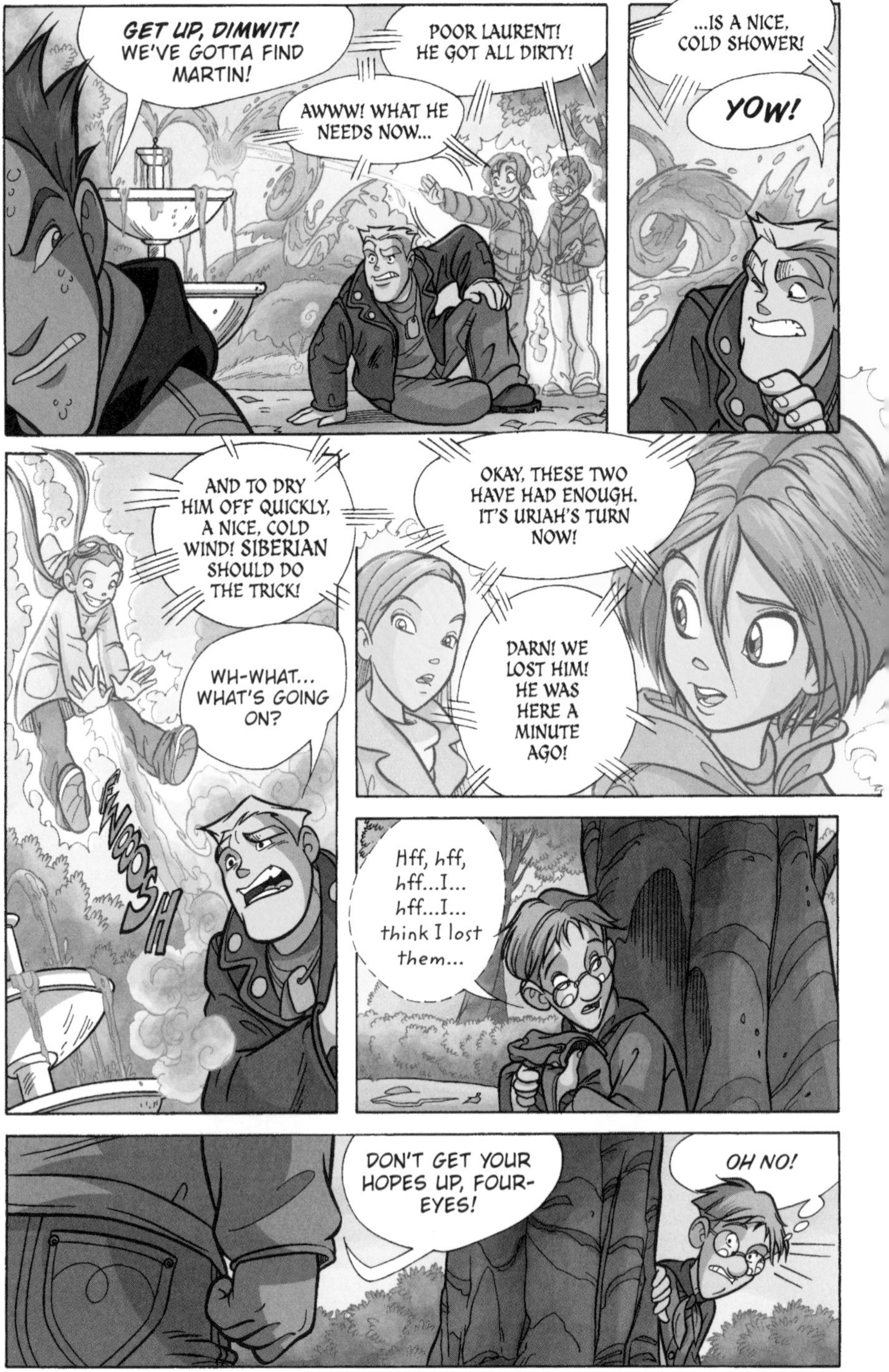
GET UP, DIMWIT! WE'VE GOTTA FIND MARTIN!
POOR LAURENT! HE GOT ALL DIRTY!
AWWW! WHAT HE NEEDS NOW...
...IS A NICE, COLD SHOWER!
YOW!
AND TO DRY HIM OFF QUICKLY, A NICE, COLD WIND! SIBERIAN SHOULD DO THE TRICK!
WH-WHAT... WHAT'S GOING ON?
FWOOOSH
OKAY, THESE TWO HAVE HAD ENOUGH. IT'S URIAH'S TURN NOW!
DARN! WE LOST HIM! HE WAS HERE A MINUTE AGO!
Hff, hff, hff...I... hff...I... think I lost them...
DON'T GET YOUR HOPES UP, FOUR-EYES!
OH NO!

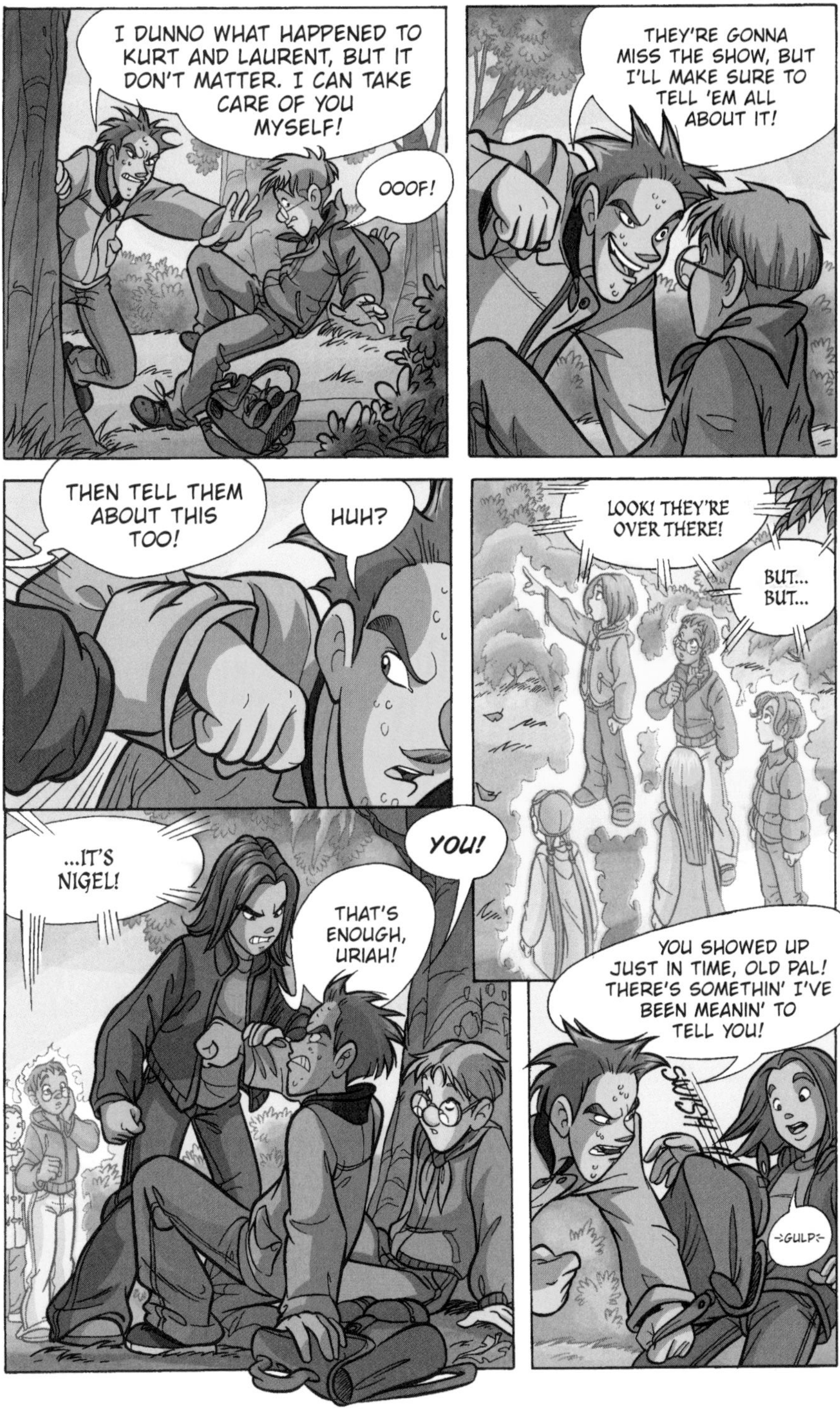
I DUNNO WHAT HAPPENED TO KURT AND LAURENT, BUT IT DON'T MATTER. I CAN TAKE CARE OF YOU MYSELF!
OOOF!
THEY'RE GONNA MISS THE SHOW, BUT I'LL MAKE SURE TO TELL 'EM ALL ABOUT IT!
THEN TELL THEM ABOUT THIS TOO!
HUH?
LOOK! THEY'RE OVER THERE!
BUT... BUT...
...IT'S NIGEL!
THAT'S ENOUGH, URIAH!
YOU!
YOU SHOWED UP JUST IN TIME, OLD PAL! THERE'S SOMETHIN' I'VE BEEN MEANIN' TO TELL YOU!
GULP

YOU MAY HAVE FORGOTTEN ABOUT YOUR FRIENDS...

STUMP

OOOF!

...BUT WE HAVEN'T FORGOTTEN ABOUT YOU!

EXCUSE ME...

TIP TAP

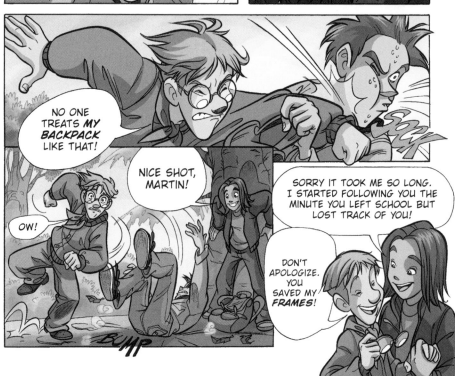

NO ONE TREATS *MY BACKPACK* LIKE THAT!

SOCK

NICE SHOT, MARTIN!

OW!

SORRY IT TOOK ME SO LONG. I STARTED FOLLOWING YOU THE MINUTE YOU LEFT SCHOOL BUT LOST TRACK OF YOU!

DON'T APOLOGIZE. YOU SAVED MY *FRAMES!*

BUMP

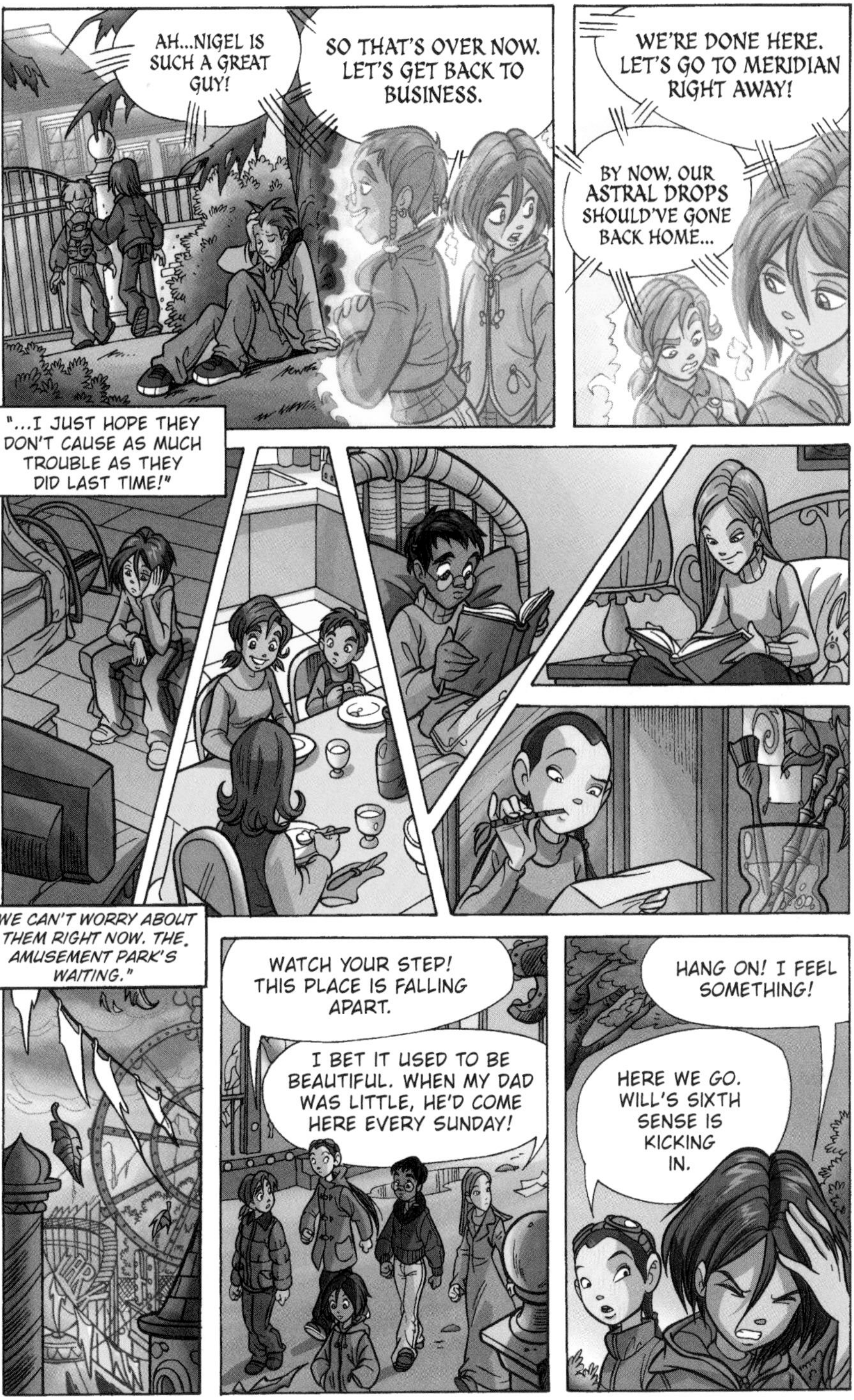
AH...NIGEL IS SUCH A GREAT GUY!
SO THAT'S OVER NOW. LET'S GET BACK TO BUSINESS.
WE'RE DONE HERE. LET'S GO TO MERIDIAN RIGHT AWAY!
BY NOW, OUR ASTRAL DROPS SHOULD'VE GONE BACK HOME...
"...I JUST HOPE THEY DON'T CAUSE AS MUCH TROUBLE AS THEY DID LAST TIME!"
"WE CAN'T WORRY ABOUT THEM RIGHT NOW. THE AMUSEMENT PARK'S WAITING."
WATCH YOUR STEP! THIS PLACE IS FALLING APART.
I BET IT USED TO BE BEAUTIFUL. WHEN MY DAD WAS LITTLE, HE'D COME HERE EVERY SUNDAY!
HANG ON! I FEEL SOMETHING!
HERE WE GO. WILL'S SIXTH SENSE IS KICKING IN.

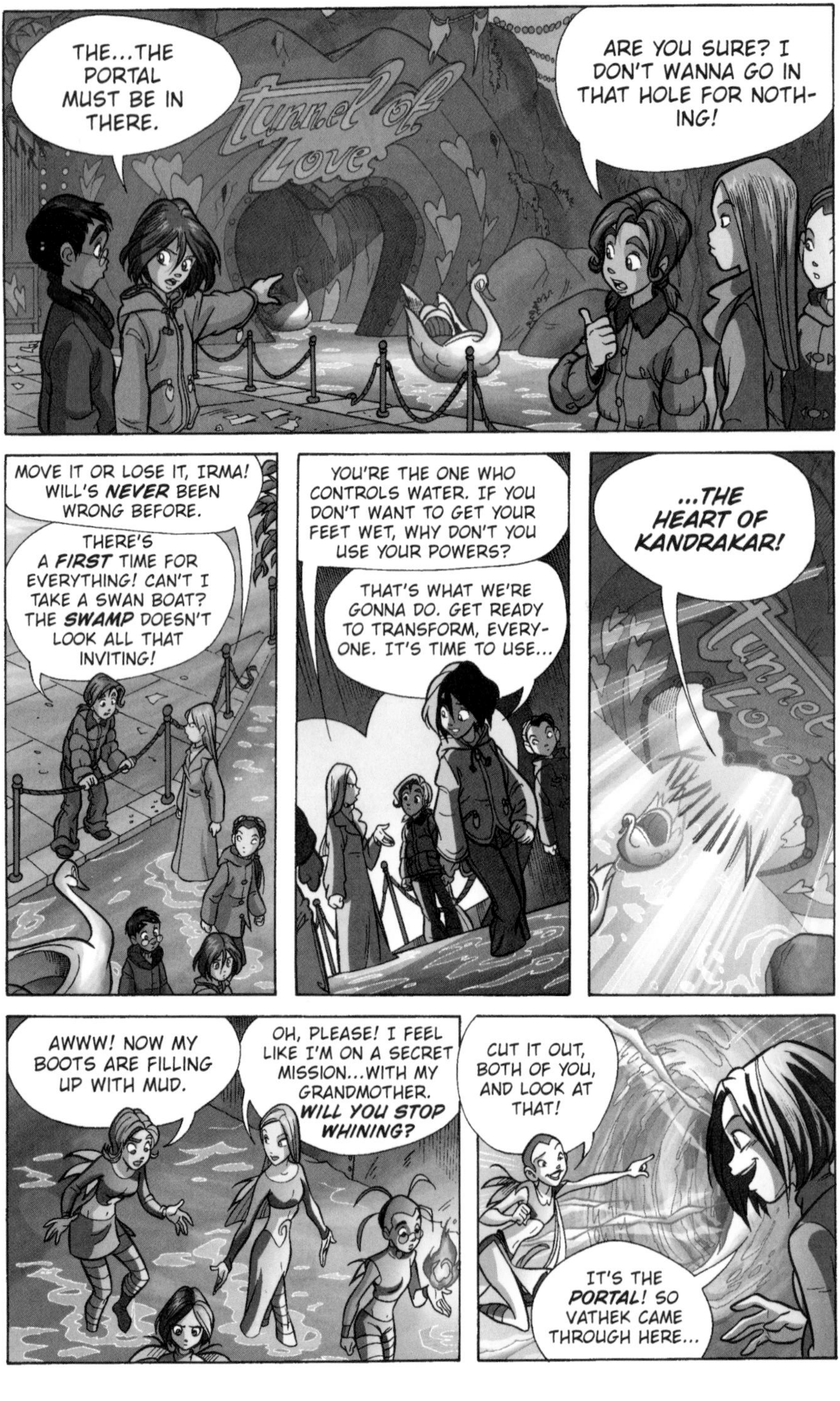
THE...THE PORTAL MUST BE IN THERE.
Tunnel of Love
ARE YOU SURE? I DON'T WANNA GO IN THAT HOLE FOR NOTHING!
MOVE IT OR LOSE IT, IRMA! WILL'S ***NEVER*** BEEN WRONG BEFORE.
THERE'S A ***FIRST*** TIME FOR EVERYTHING! CAN'T I TAKE A SWAN BOAT? THE ***SWAMP*** DOESN'T LOOK ALL THAT INVITING!
YOU'RE THE ONE WHO CONTROLS WATER. IF YOU DON'T WANT TO GET YOUR FEET WET, WHY DON'T YOU USE YOUR POWERS?
THAT'S WHAT WE'RE GONNA DO. GET READY TO TRANSFORM, EVERYONE. IT'S TIME TO USE...
...THE HEART OF KANDRAKAR!
AWWW! NOW MY BOOTS ARE FILLING UP WITH MUD.
OH, PLEASE! I FEEL LIKE I'M ON A SECRET MISSION...WITH MY GRANDMOTHER. ***WILL YOU STOP WHINING?***
CUT IT OUT, BOTH OF YOU, AND LOOK AT THAT!
IT'S THE ***PORTAL***! SO VATHEK CAME THROUGH HERE...

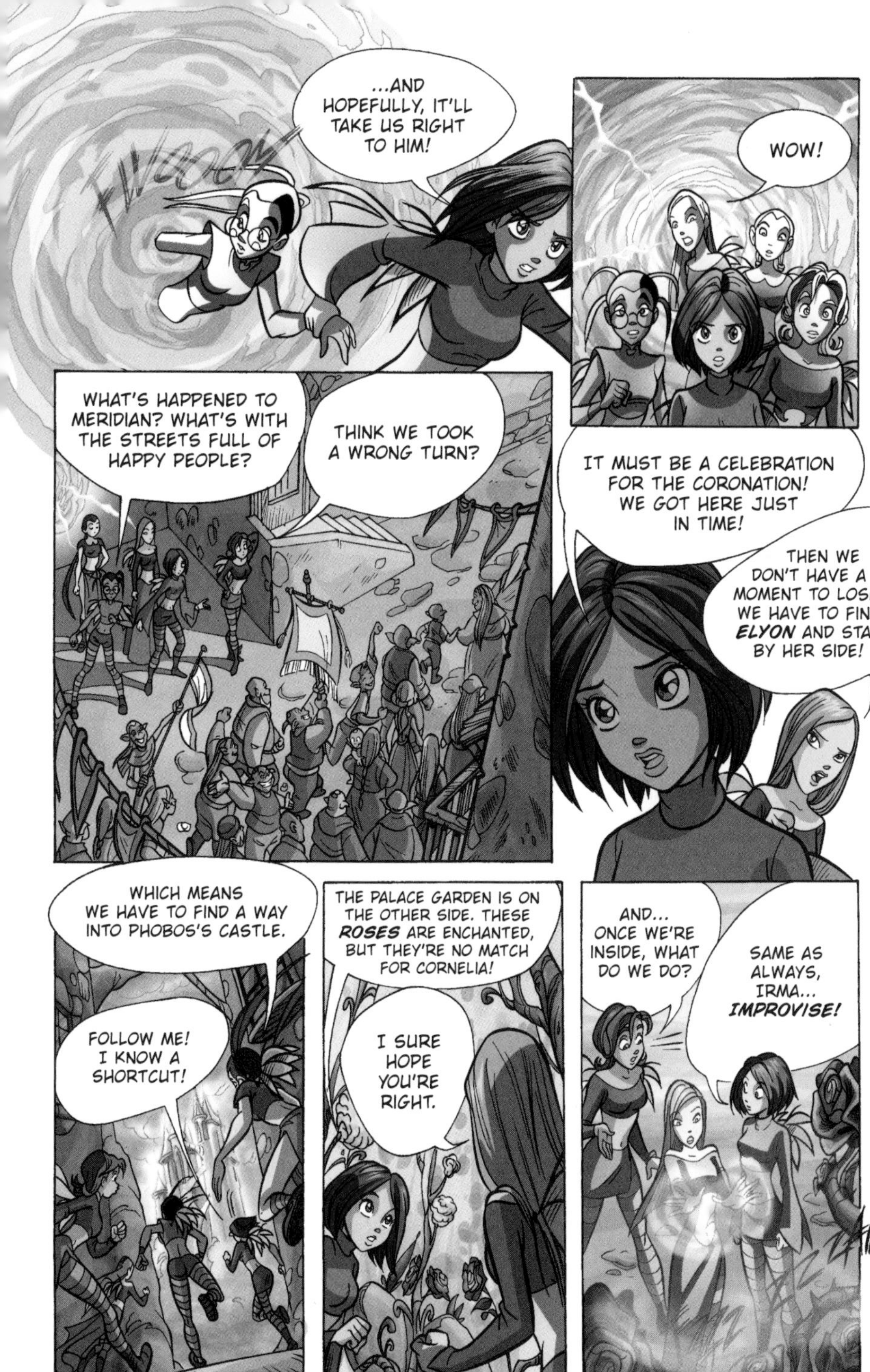
FWOOOM
...AND HOPEFULLY, IT'LL TAKE US RIGHT TO HIM!
WOW!
WHAT'S HAPPENED TO MERIDIAN? WHAT'S WITH THE STREETS FULL OF HAPPY PEOPLE?
THINK WE TOOK A WRONG TURN?
IT MUST BE A CELEBRATION FOR THE CORONATION! WE GOT HERE JUST IN TIME!
THEN WE DON'T HAVE A MOMENT TO LOSE. WE HAVE TO FIND **ELYON** AND STAY BY HER SIDE!
WHICH MEANS WE HAVE TO FIND A WAY INTO PHOBOS'S CASTLE.
FOLLOW ME! I KNOW A SHORTCUT!
THE PALACE GARDEN IS ON THE OTHER SIDE. THESE **ROSES** ARE ENCHANTED, BUT THEY'RE NO MATCH FOR CORNELIA!
I SURE HOPE YOU'RE RIGHT.
AND... ONCE WE'RE INSIDE, WHAT DO WE DO?
SAME AS ALWAYS, IRMA... **IMPROVISE!**

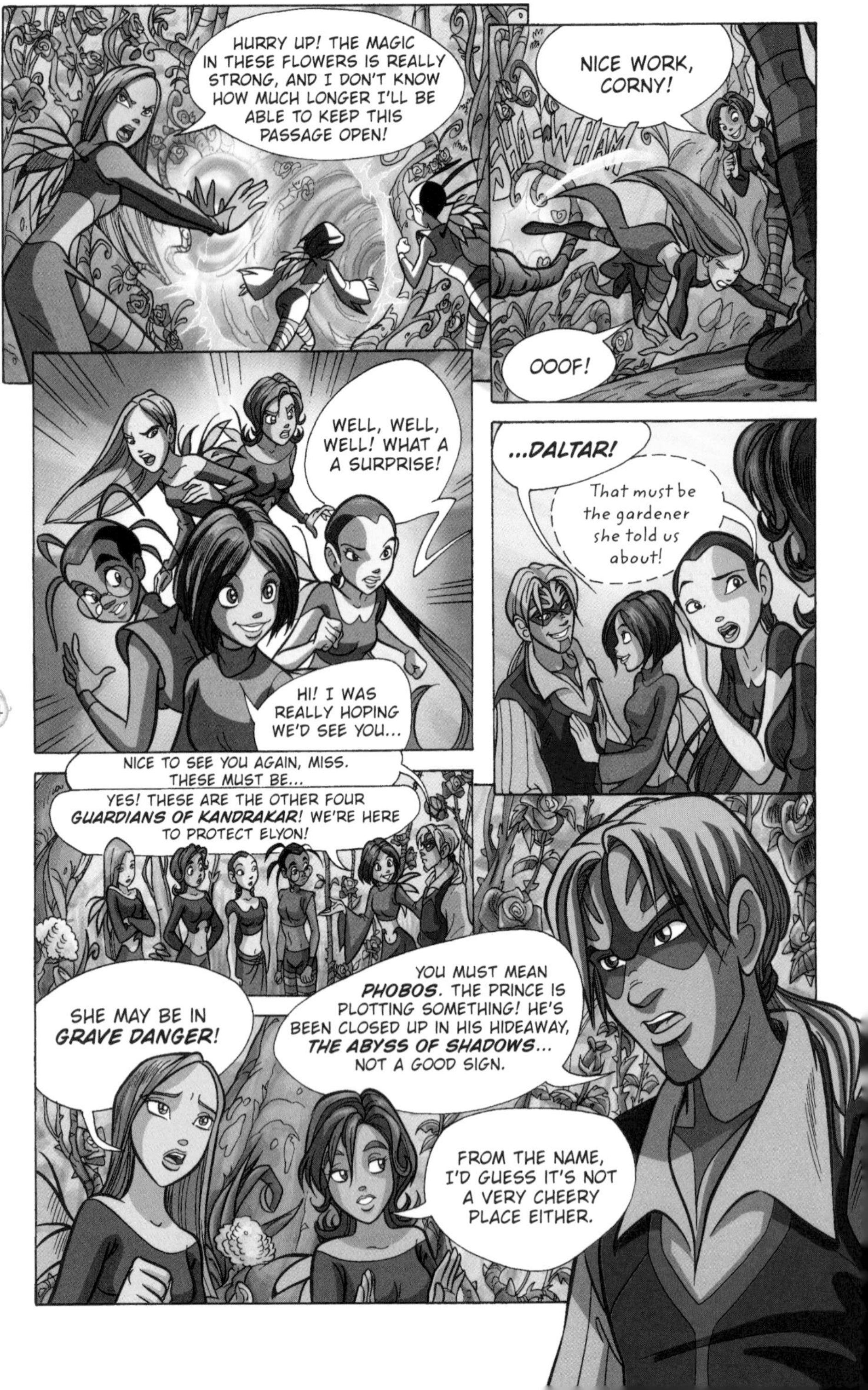
HURRY UP! THE MAGIC IN THESE FLOWERS IS REALLY STRONG, AND I DON'T KNOW HOW MUCH LONGER I'LL BE ABLE TO KEEP THIS PASSAGE OPEN!
NICE WORK, CORNY!
SHA-WHAM!
OOOF!
WELL, WELL, WELL! WHAT A A SURPRISE!
HI! I WAS REALLY HOPING WE'D SEE YOU...
...DALTAR!
That must be the gardener she told us about!
NICE TO SEE YOU AGAIN, MISS. THESE MUST BE...
YES! THESE ARE THE OTHER FOUR GUARDIANS OF KANDRAKAR! WE'RE HERE TO PROTECT ELYON!
SHE MAY BE IN GRAVE DANGER!
YOU MUST MEAN PHOBOS. THE PRINCE IS PLOTTING SOMETHING! HE'S BEEN CLOSED UP IN HIS HIDEAWAY, THE ABYSS OF SHADOWS... NOT A GOOD SIGN.
FROM THE NAME, I'D GUESS IT'S NOT A VERY CHEERY PLACE EITHER.

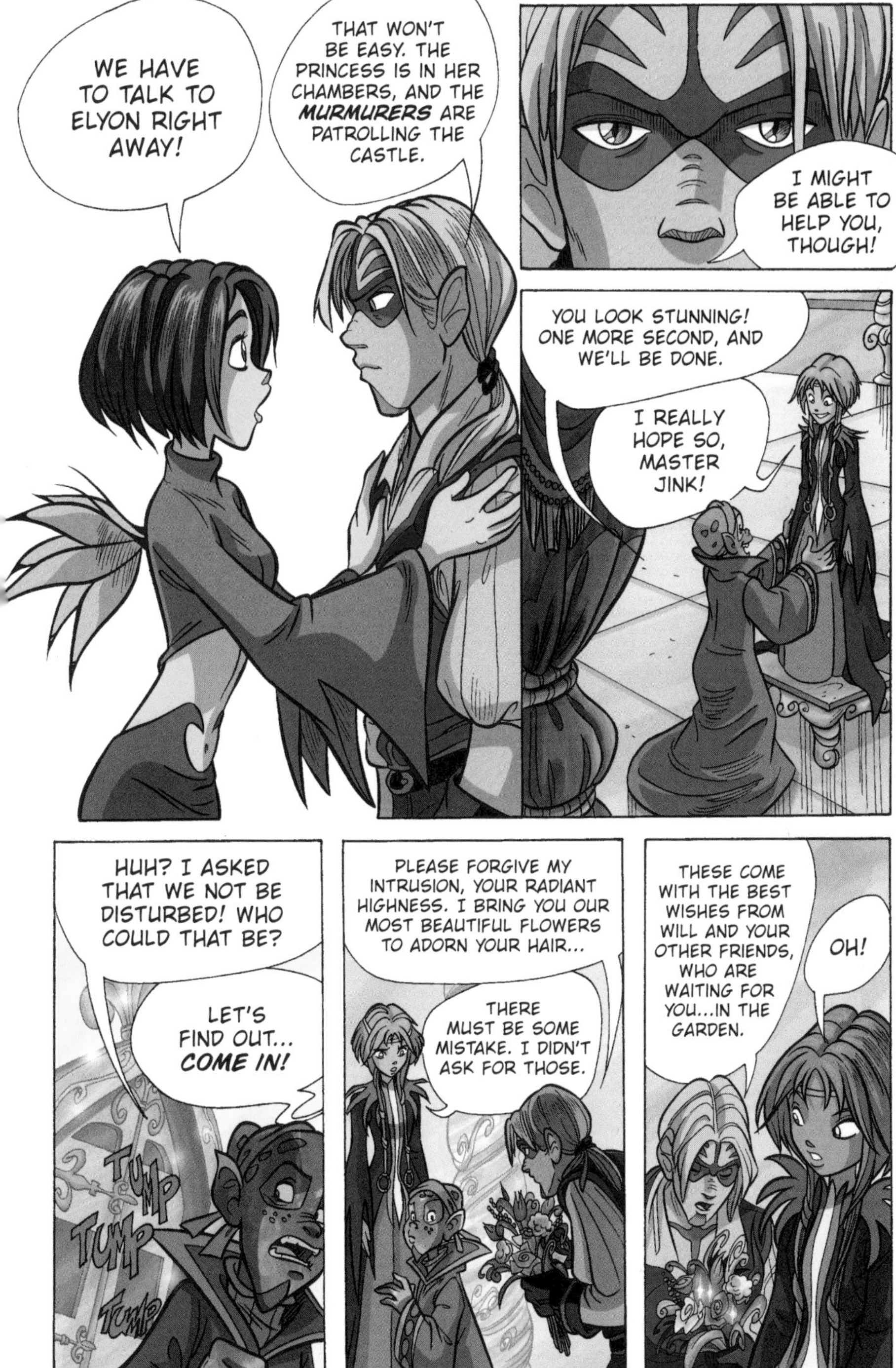
WE HAVE TO TALK TO ELYON RIGHT AWAY!
THAT WON'T BE EASY. THE PRINCESS IS IN HER CHAMBERS, AND THE MURMURERS ARE PATROLLING THE CASTLE.
I MIGHT BE ABLE TO HELP YOU, THOUGH!
YOU LOOK STUNNING! ONE MORE SECOND, AND WE'LL BE DONE.
I REALLY HOPE SO, MASTER JINK!
HUH? I ASKED THAT WE NOT BE DISTURBED! WHO COULD THAT BE?
LET'S FIND OUT... COME IN!
TUMP
TUMP
TUMP
PLEASE FORGIVE MY INTRUSION, YOUR RADIANT HIGHNESS. I BRING YOU OUR MOST BEAUTIFUL FLOWERS TO ADORN YOUR HAIR...
THERE MUST BE SOME MISTAKE. I DIDN'T ASK FOR THOSE.
THESE COME WITH THE BEST WISHES FROM WILL AND YOUR OTHER FRIENDS, WHO ARE WAITING FOR YOU...IN THE GARDEN.
OH!

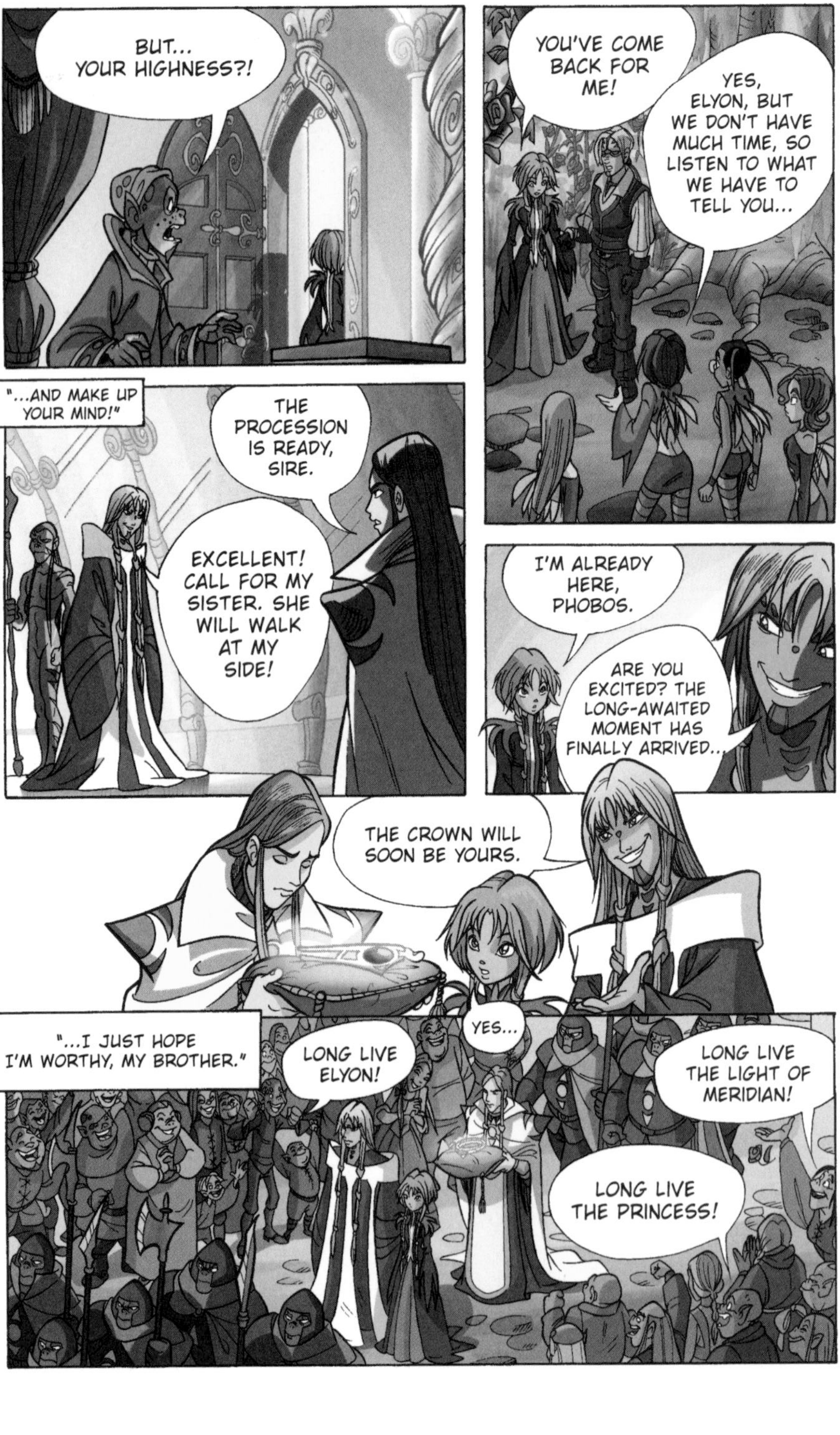
BUT... YOUR HIGHNESS?!
YOU'VE COME BACK FOR ME!
YES, ELYON, BUT WE DON'T HAVE MUCH TIME, SO LISTEN TO WHAT WE HAVE TO TELL YOU...
"...AND MAKE UP YOUR MIND!"
THE PROCESSION IS READY, SIRE.
EXCELLENT! CALL FOR MY SISTER. SHE WILL WALK AT MY SIDE!
I'M ALREADY HERE, PHOBOS.
ARE YOU EXCITED? THE LONG-AWAITED MOMENT HAS FINALLY ARRIVED...
THE CROWN WILL SOON BE YOURS.
"...I JUST HOPE I'M WORTHY, MY BROTHER."
YES...
LONG LIVE ELYON!
LONG LIVE THE LIGHT OF MERIDIAN!
LONG LIVE THE PRINCESS!

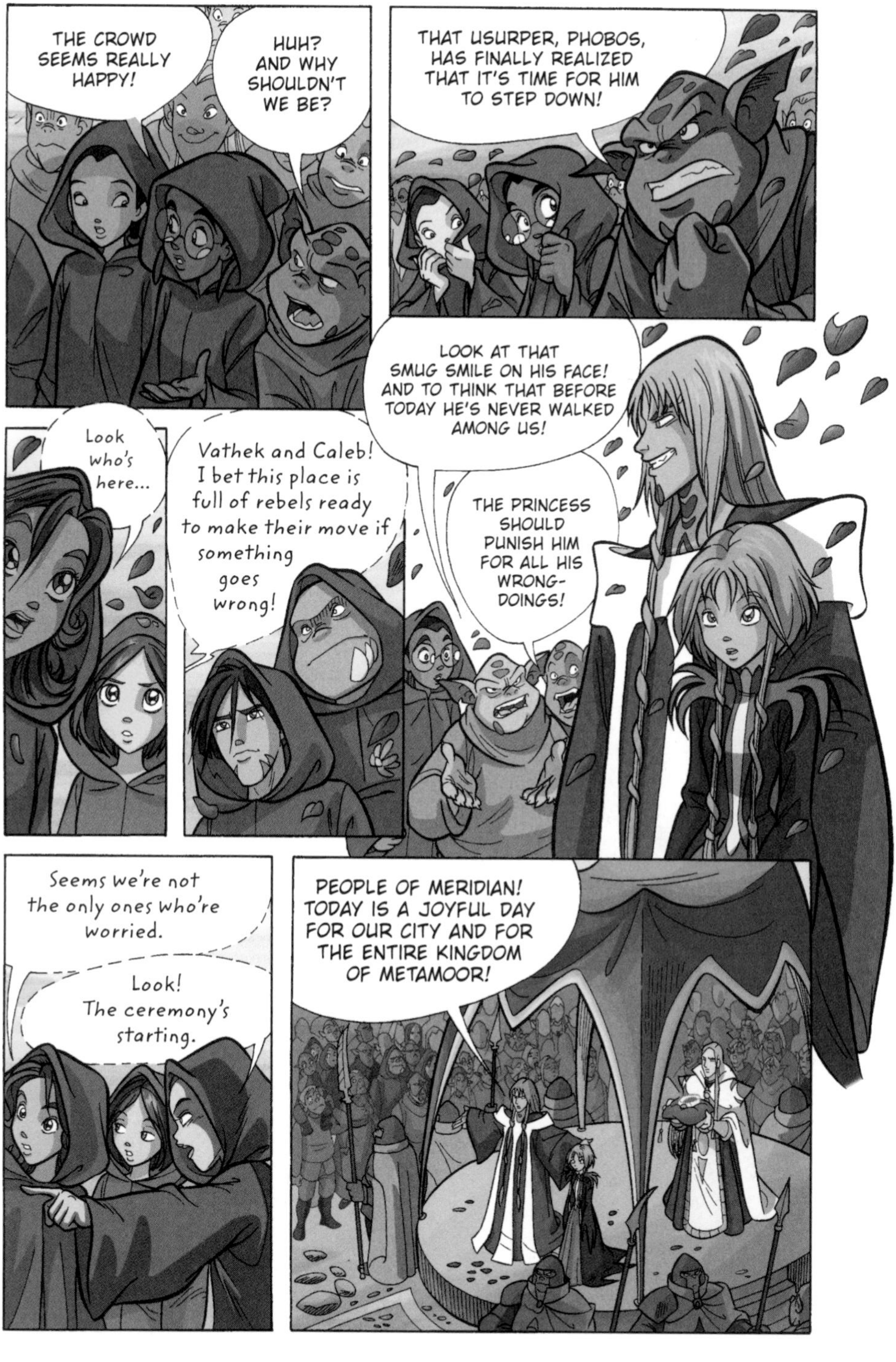
THE CROWD SEEMS REALLY HAPPY!
HUH? AND WHY SHOULDN'T WE BE?
THAT USURPER, PHOBOS, HAS FINALLY REALIZED THAT IT'S TIME FOR HIM TO STEP DOWN!
Look who's here...
Vathek and Caleb! I bet this place is full of rebels ready to make their move if something goes wrong!
LOOK AT THAT SMUG SMILE ON HIS FACE! AND TO THINK THAT BEFORE TODAY HE'S NEVER WALKED AMONG US!
THE PRINCESS SHOULD PUNISH HIM FOR ALL HIS WRONG-DOINGS!
Seems we're not the only ones who're worried.
Look! The ceremony's starting.
PEOPLE OF MERIDIAN! TODAY IS A JOYFUL DAY FOR OUR CITY AND FOR THE ENTIRE KINGDOM OF METAMOOR!

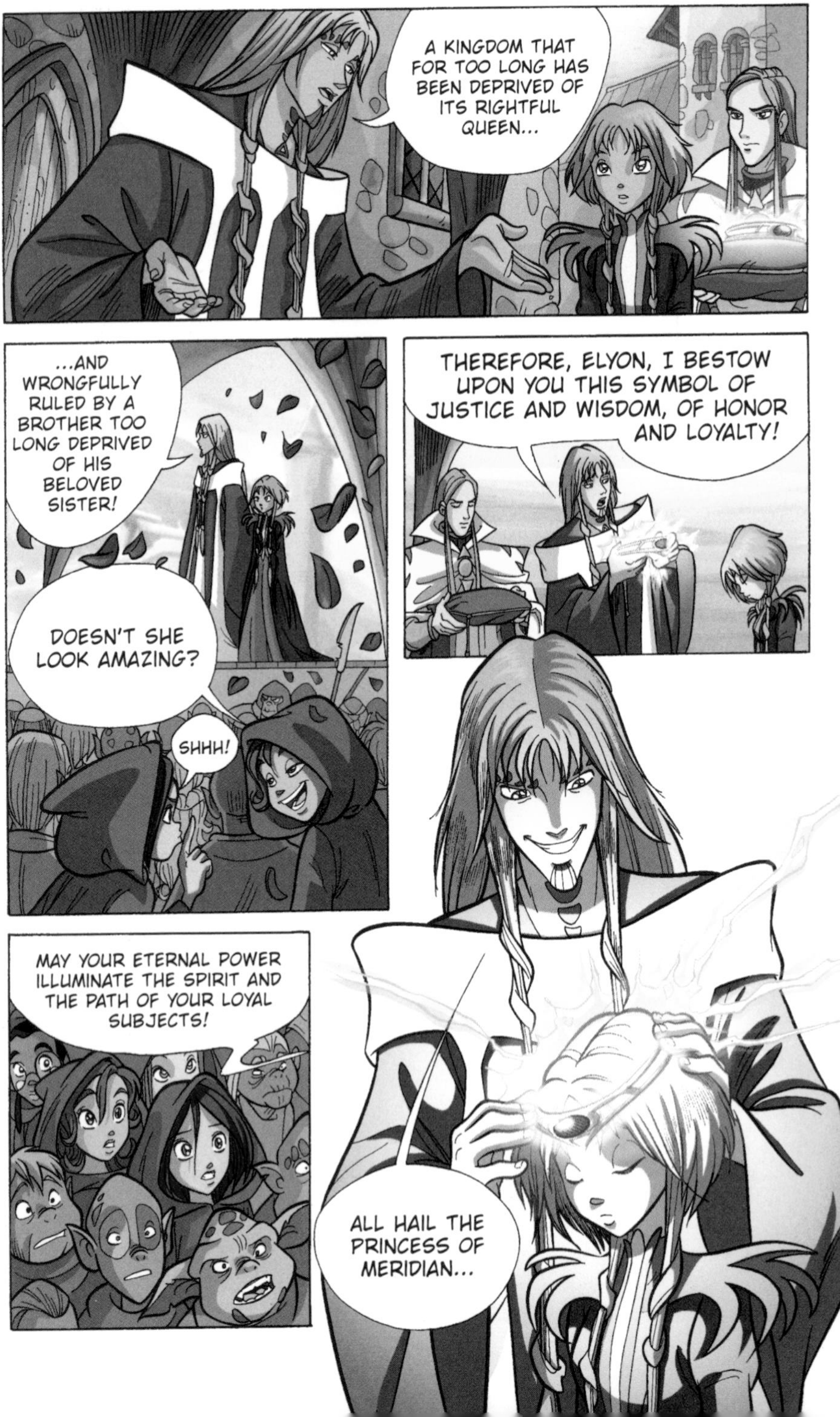
A KINGDOM THAT FOR TOO LONG HAS BEEN DEPRIVED OF ITS RIGHTFUL QUEEN...
...AND WRONGFULLY RULED BY A BROTHER TOO LONG DEPRIVED OF HIS BELOVED SISTER!
DOESN'T SHE LOOK AMAZING?
SHHH!
THEREFORE, ELYON, I BESTOW UPON YOU THIS SYMBOL OF JUSTICE AND WISDOM, OF HONOR AND LOYALTY!
MAY YOUR ETERNAL POWER ILLUMINATE THE SPIRIT AND THE PATH OF YOUR LOYAL SUBJECTS!
ALL HAIL THE PRINCESS OF MERIDIAN...

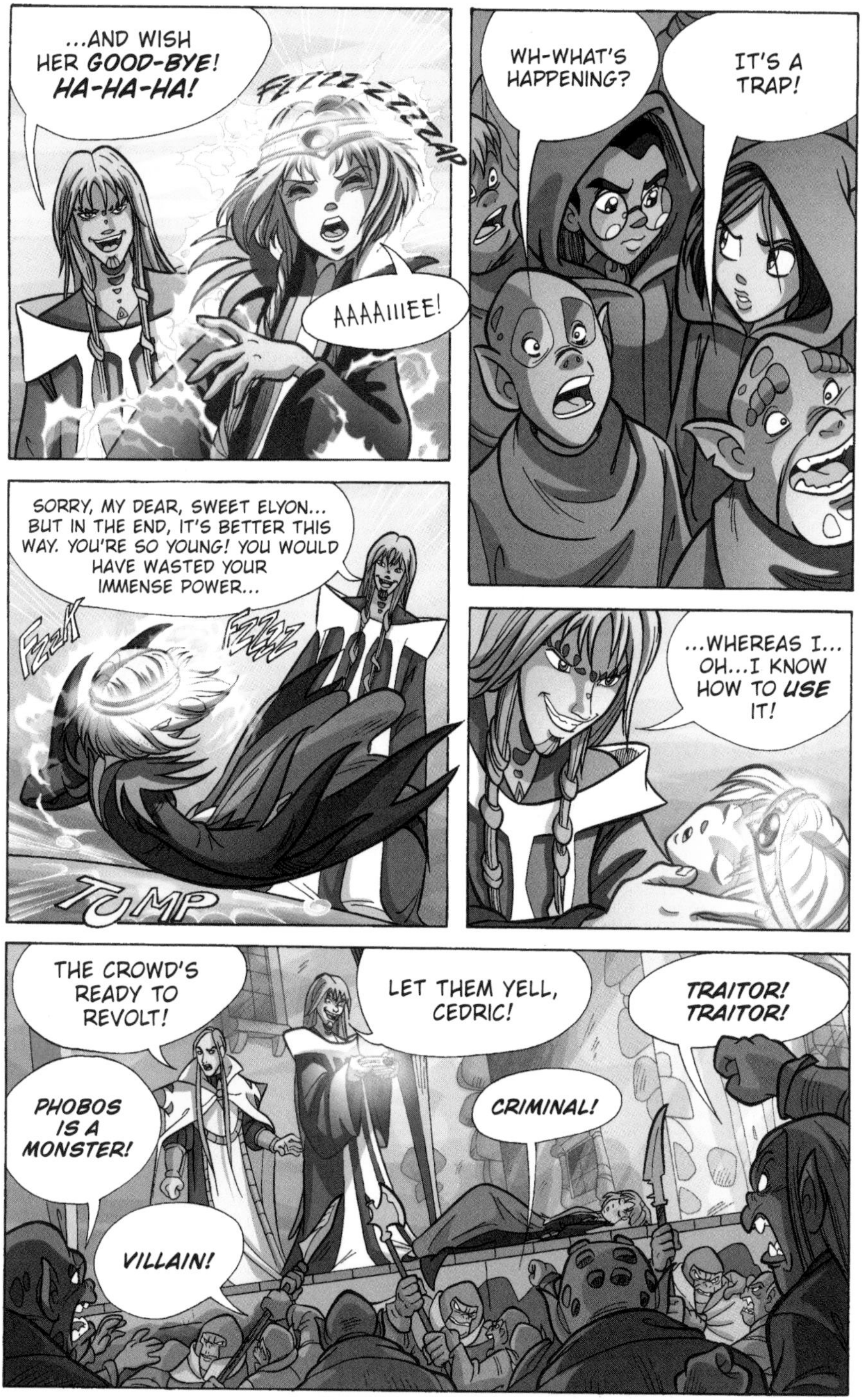
...AND WISH HER GOOD-BYE! HA-HA-HA!
AAAAIIIEE!
WH-WHAT'S HAPPENING?
IT'S A TRAP!
SORRY, MY DEAR, SWEET ELYON... BUT IN THE END, IT'S BETTER THIS WAY. YOU'RE SO YOUNG! YOU WOULD HAVE WASTED YOUR IMMENSE POWER...
TUMP
...WHEREAS I... OH...I KNOW HOW TO USE IT!
THE CROWD'S READY TO REVOLT!
LET THEM YELL, CEDRIC!
TRAITOR! TRAITOR!
PHOBOS IS A MONSTER!
CRIMINAL!
VILLAIN!

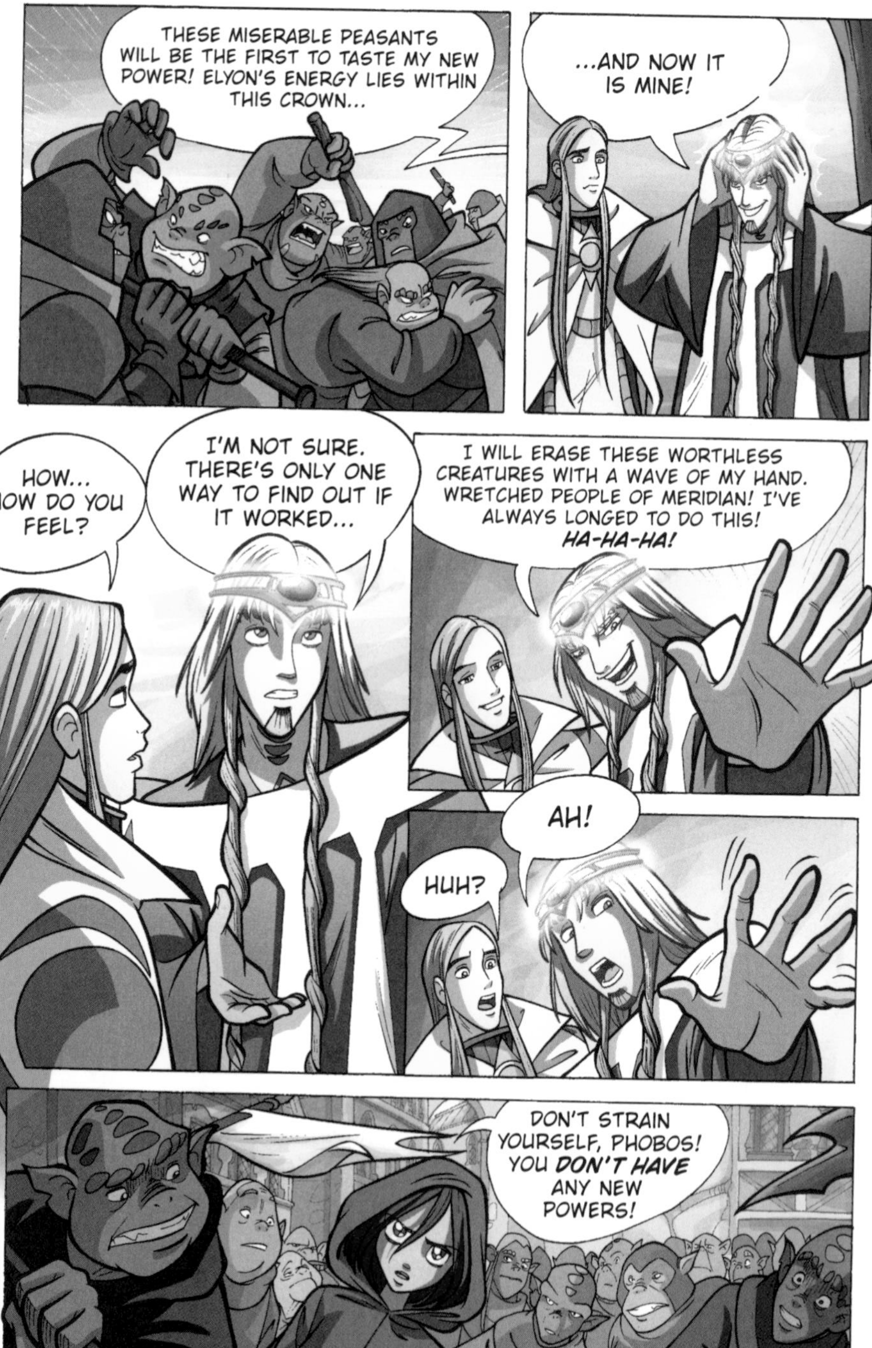
THESE MISERABLE PEASANTS WILL BE THE FIRST TO TASTE MY NEW POWER! ELYON'S ENERGY LIES WITHIN THIS CROWN...
...AND NOW IT IS MINE!
HOW... HOW DO YOU FEEL?
I'M NOT SURE. THERE'S ONLY ONE WAY TO FIND OUT IF IT WORKED...
I WILL ERASE THESE WORTHLESS CREATURES WITH A WAVE OF MY HAND. WRETCHED PEOPLE OF MERIDIAN! I'VE ALWAYS LONGED TO DO THIS! ***HA-HA-HA!***
AH!
HUH?
DON'T STRAIN YOURSELF, PHOBOS! YOU ***DON'T HAVE*** ANY NEW POWERS!

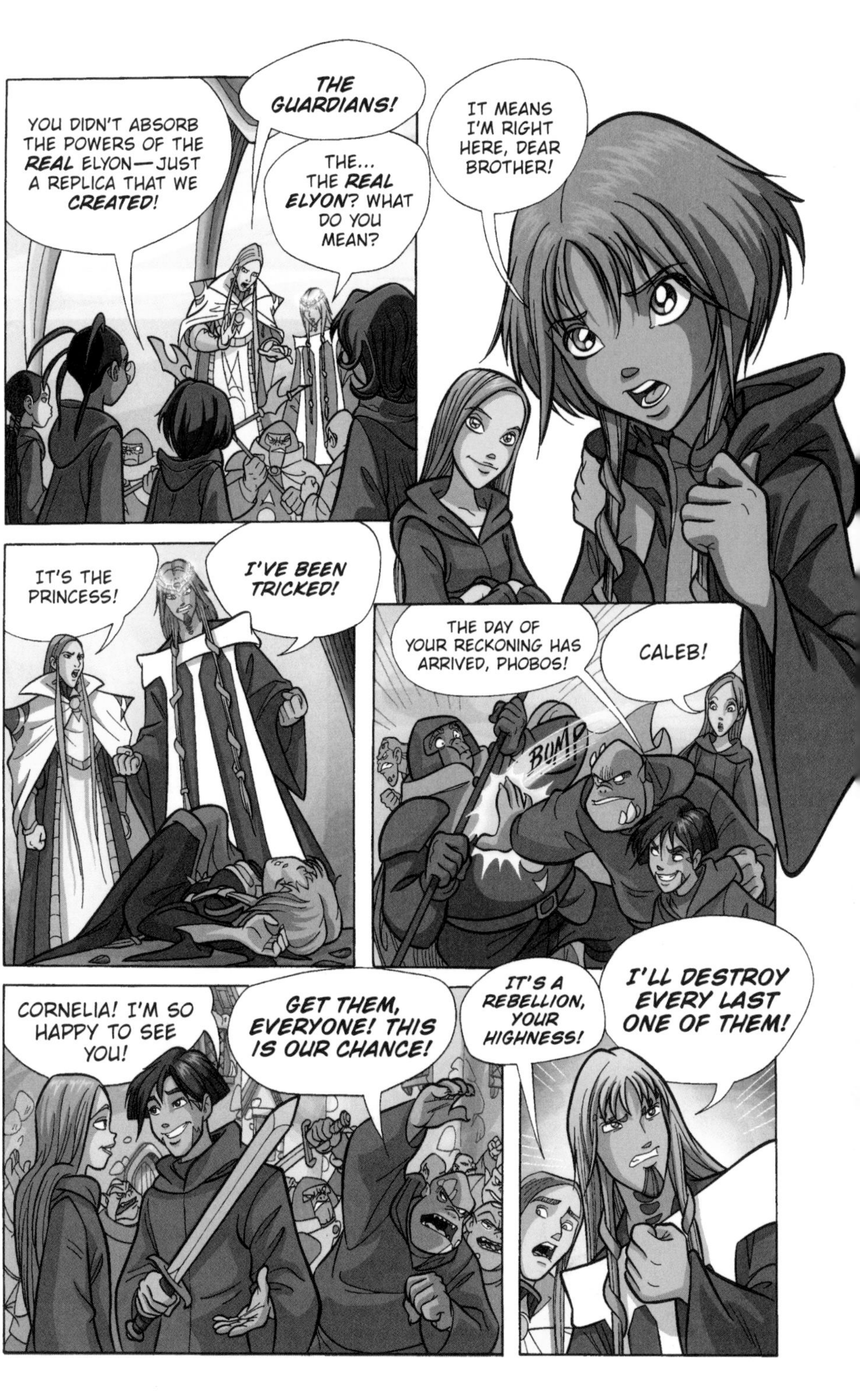
YOU DIDN'T ABSORB THE POWERS OF THE *REAL* ELYON—JUST A REPLICA THAT WE *CREATED*!
THE GUARDIANS!
THE... THE ***REAL ELYON***? WHAT DO YOU MEAN?
IT MEANS I'M RIGHT HERE, DEAR BROTHER!
IT'S THE PRINCESS!
I'VE BEEN TRICKED!
THE DAY OF YOUR RECKONING HAS ARRIVED, PHOBOS!
CALEB!
BOMP
CORNELIA! I'M SO HAPPY TO SEE YOU!
GET THEM, EVERYONE! THIS IS OUR CHANCE!
IT'S A REBELLION, YOUR HIGHNESS!
I'LL DESTROY EVERY LAST ONE OF THEM!

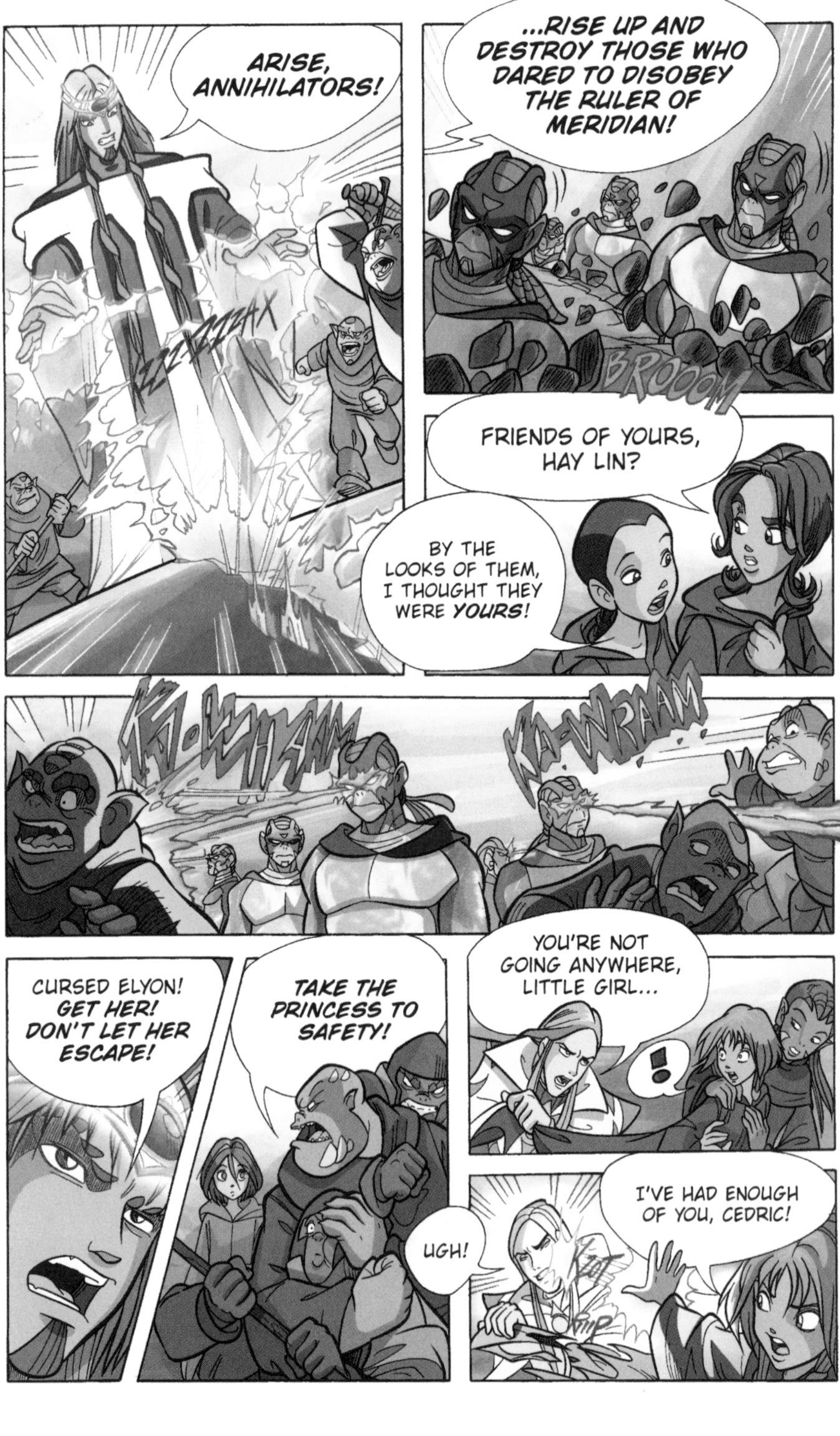
ARISE, ANNIHILATORS!
...RISE UP AND DESTROY THOSE WHO DARED TO DISOBEY THE RULER OF MERIDIAN!
BROOOM
FRIENDS OF YOURS, HAY LIN?
BY THE LOOKS OF THEM, I THOUGHT THEY WERE *YOURS*!
KA-WRAAM
CURSED ELYON! **GET HER! DON'T LET HER ESCAPE!**
TAKE THE PRINCESS TO SAFETY!
YOU'RE NOT GOING ANYWHERE, LITTLE GIRL...
!
UGH!
I'VE HAD ENOUGH OF YOU, CEDRIC!

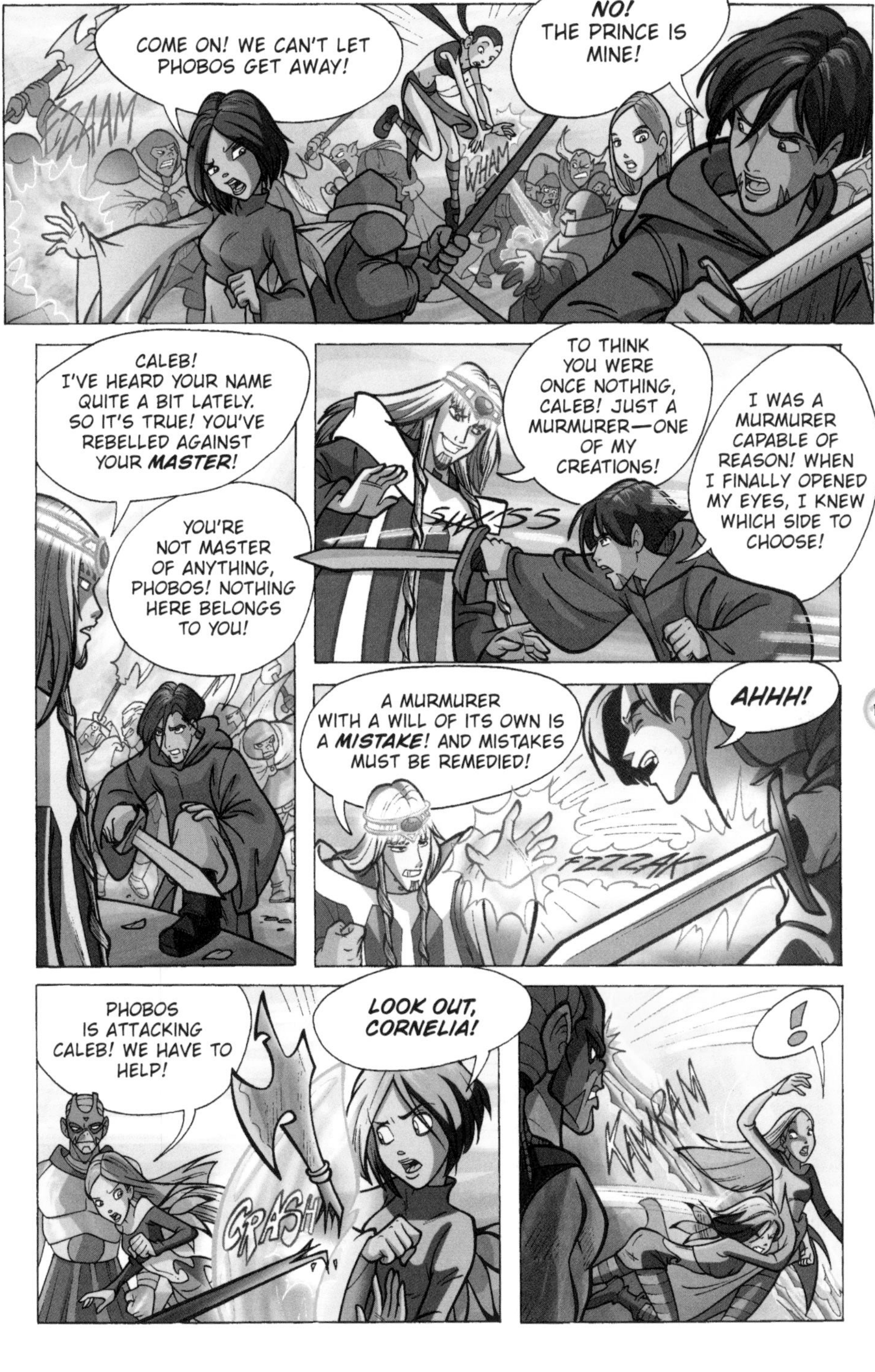
COME ON! WE CAN'T LET PHOBOS GET AWAY!
ZAAM
NO! THE PRINCE IS MINE!
WHAM
CALEB! I'VE HEARD YOUR NAME QUITE A BIT LATELY. SO IT'S TRUE! YOU'VE REBELLED AGAINST YOUR **MASTER**!
YOU'RE NOT MASTER OF ANYTHING, PHOBOS! NOTHING HERE BELONGS TO YOU!
TO THINK YOU WERE ONCE NOTHING, CALEB! JUST A MURMURER—ONE OF MY CREATIONS!
SHASS
I WAS A MURMURER CAPABLE OF REASON! WHEN I FINALLY OPENED MY EYES, I KNEW WHICH SIDE TO CHOOSE!
A MURMURER WITH A WILL OF ITS OWN IS A **MISTAKE**! AND MISTAKES MUST BE REMEDIED!
AHHH!
FZZZZAK
PHOBOS IS ATTACKING CALEB! WE HAVE TO HELP!
LOOK OUT, CORNELIA!
CRASH
!
KAWRAM

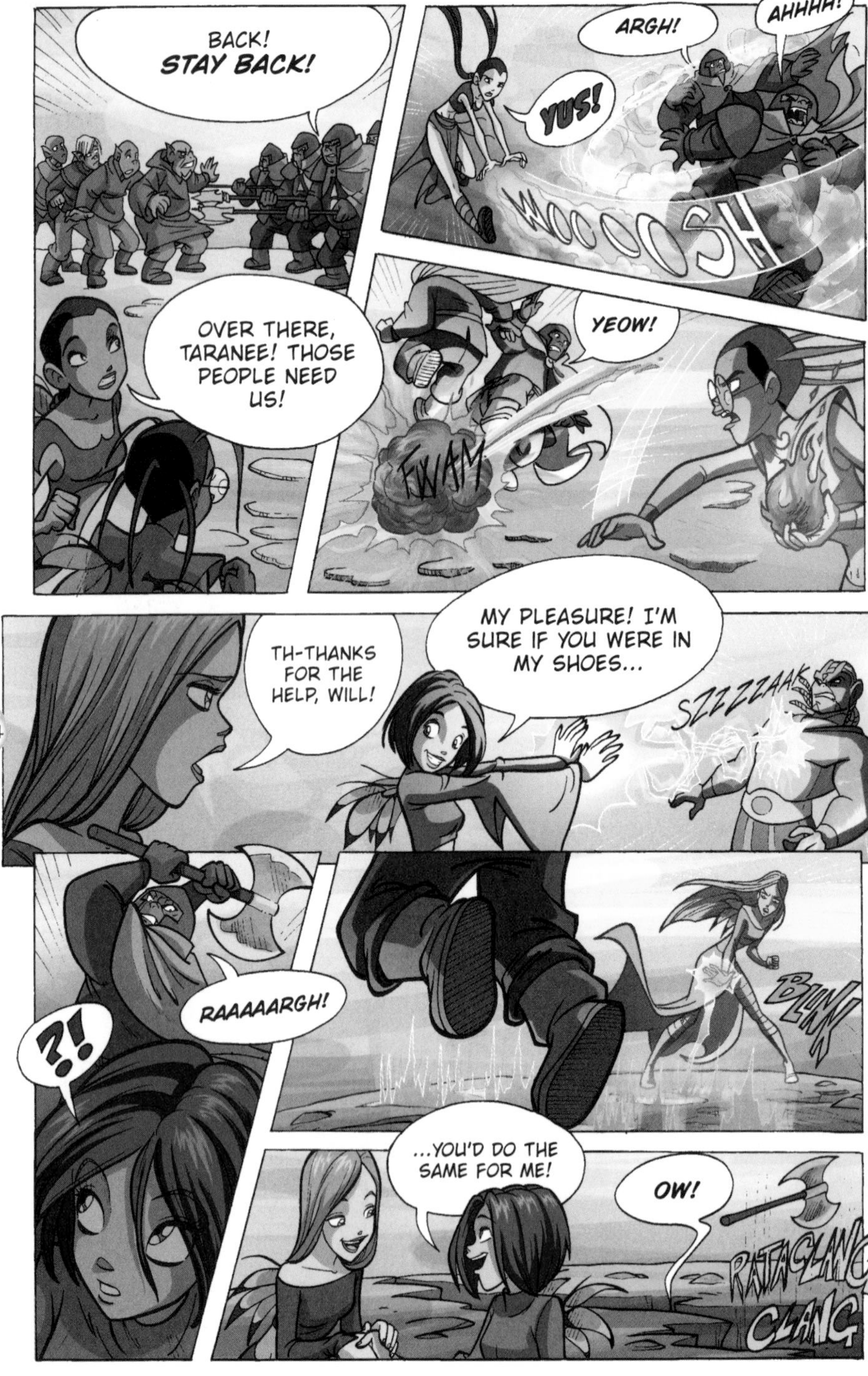
BACK!
STAY BACK!
ARGH!
AHHHH!
YUS!
WOOOOSH
OVER THERE, TARANEE! THOSE PEOPLE NEED US!
YEOW!
FWAM
TH-THANKS FOR THE HELP, WILL!
MY PLEASURE! I'M SURE IF YOU WERE IN MY SHOES...
SZZZZAAK
RAAAAARGH!
?!
BLINK
...YOU'D DO THE SAME FOR ME!
OW!
RATACLANG
CLANG

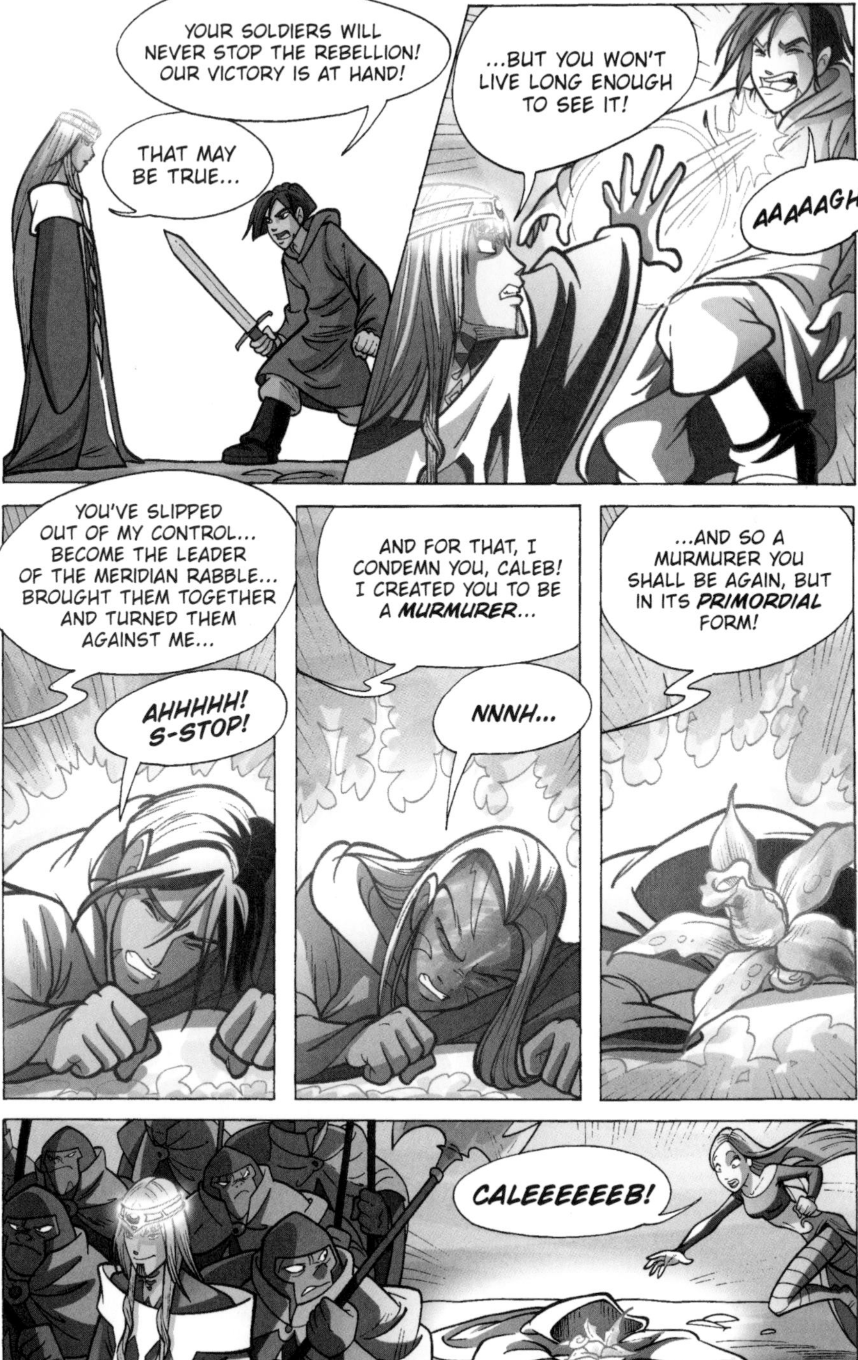
YOUR SOLDIERS WILL NEVER STOP THE REBELLION! OUR VICTORY IS AT HAND!
THAT MAY BE TRUE...
...BUT YOU WON'T LIVE LONG ENOUGH TO SEE IT!
AAAAAGH!
YOU'VE SLIPPED OUT OF MY CONTROL... BECOME THE LEADER OF THE MERIDIAN RABBLE... BROUGHT THEM TOGETHER AND TURNED THEM AGAINST ME...
AHHHHH! S-STOP!
AND FOR THAT, I CONDEMN YOU, CALEB! I CREATED YOU TO BE A MURMURER...
NNNH...
...AND SO A MURMURER YOU SHALL BE AGAIN, BUT IN ITS PRIMORDIAL FORM!
CALEEEEEEB!

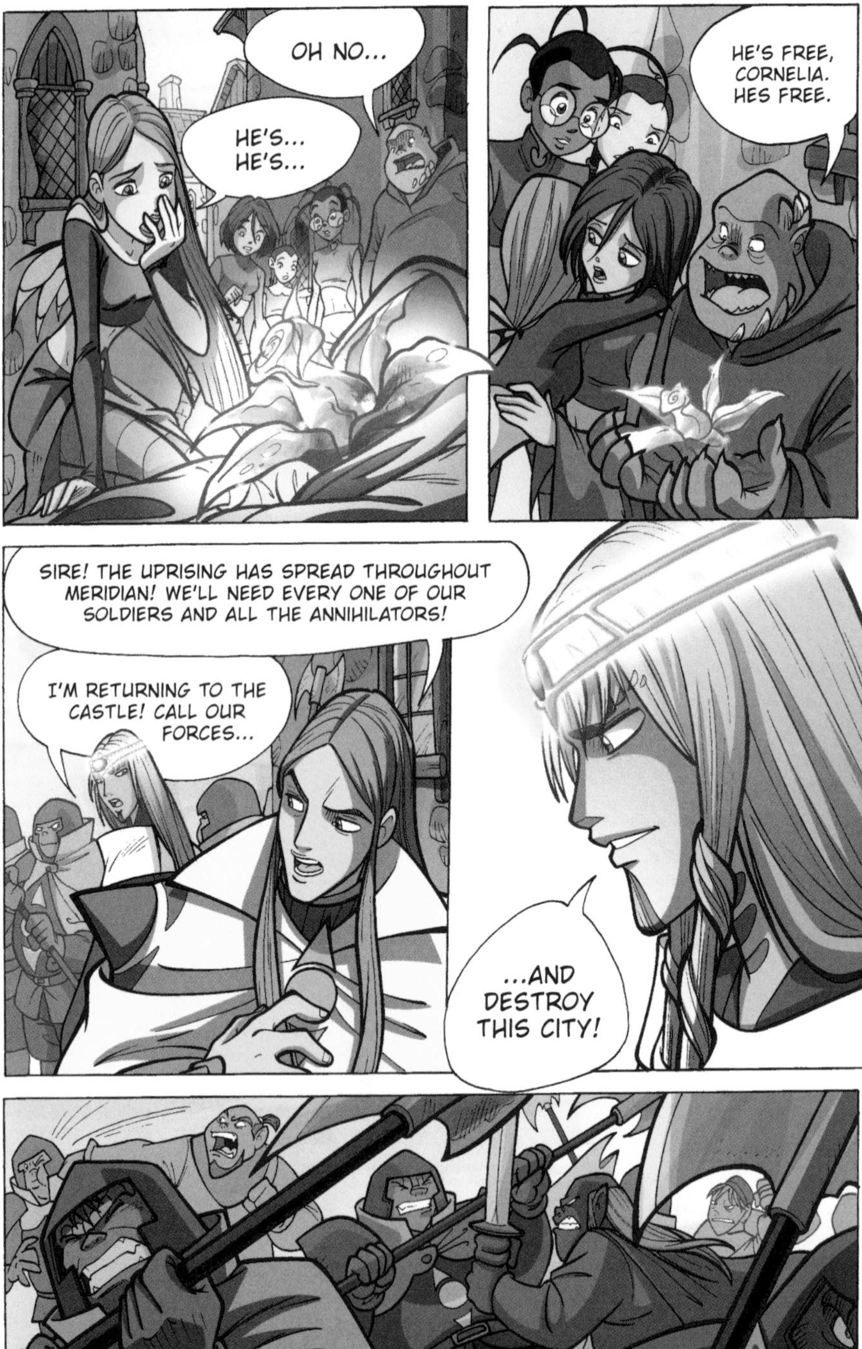
OH NO...
HE'S... HE'S...
HE'S FREE, CORNELIA. HES FREE.
SIRE! THE UPRISING HAS SPREAD THROUGHOUT MERIDIAN! WE'LL NEED EVERY ONE OF OUR SOLDIERS AND ALL THE ANNIHILATORS!
I'M RETURNING TO THE CASTLE! CALL OUR FORCES...
...AND DESTROY THIS CITY!

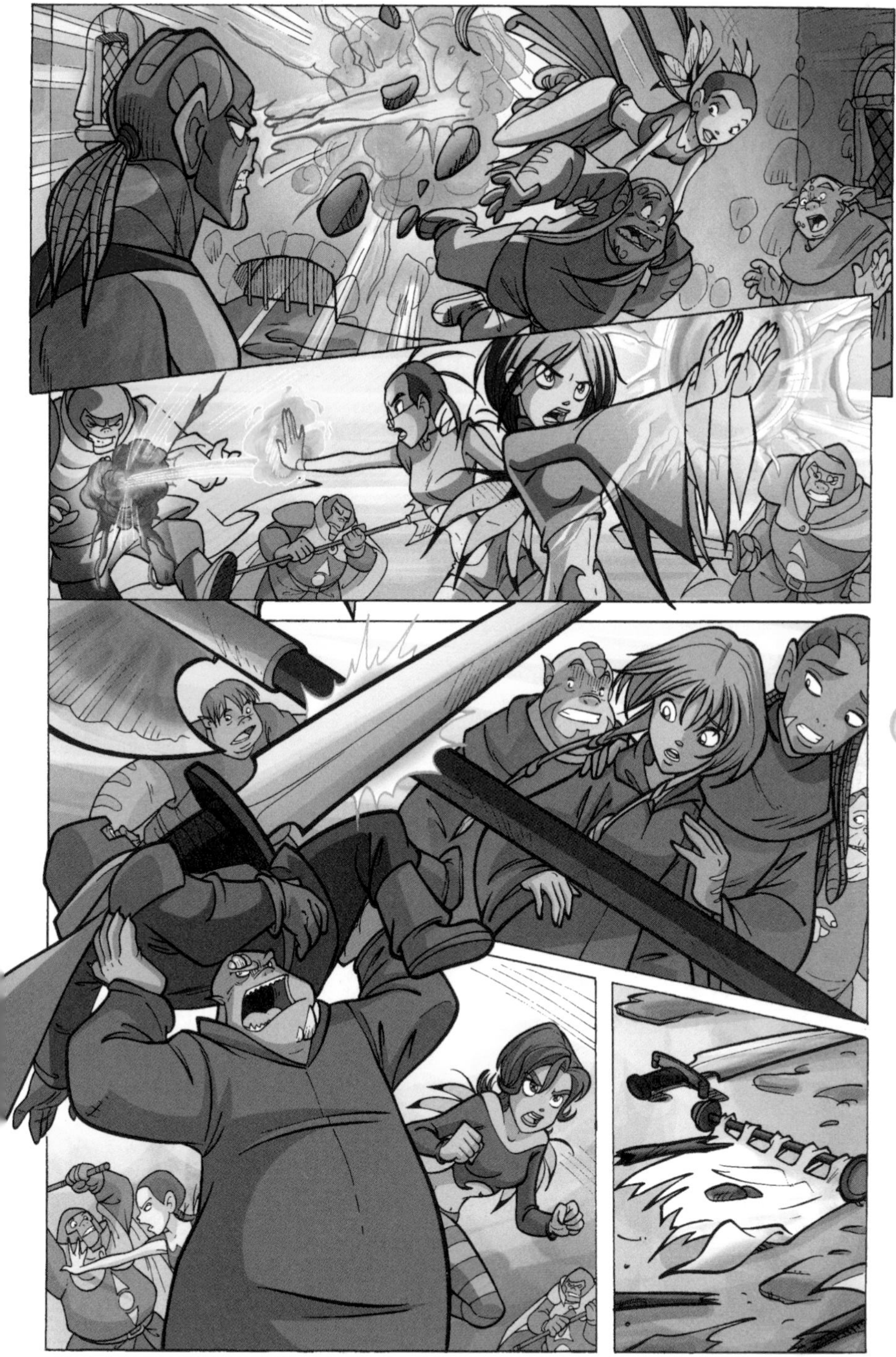

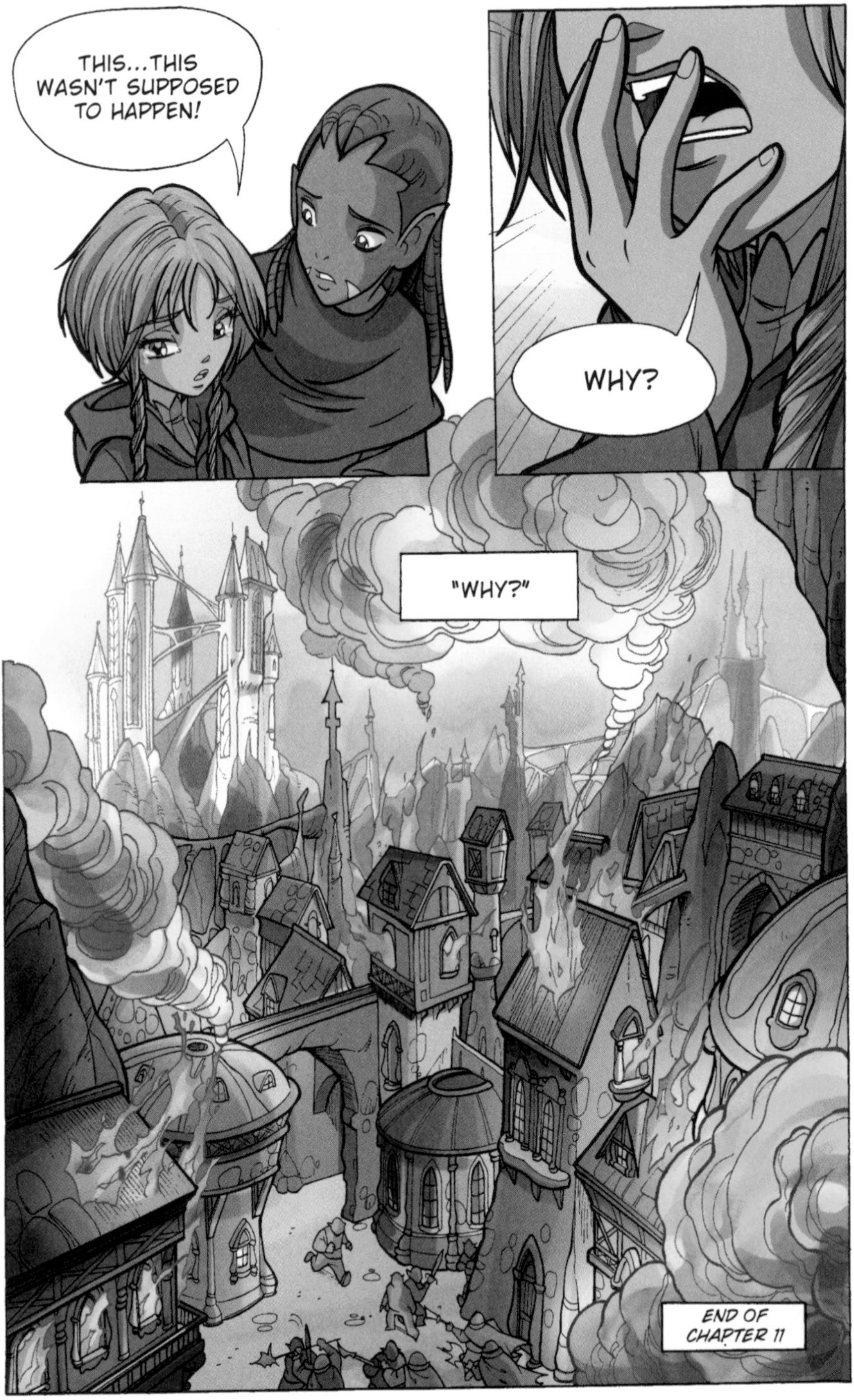
THIS...THIS WASN'T SUPPOSED TO HAPPEN!
WHY?
"WHY?"
END OF CHAPTER 11

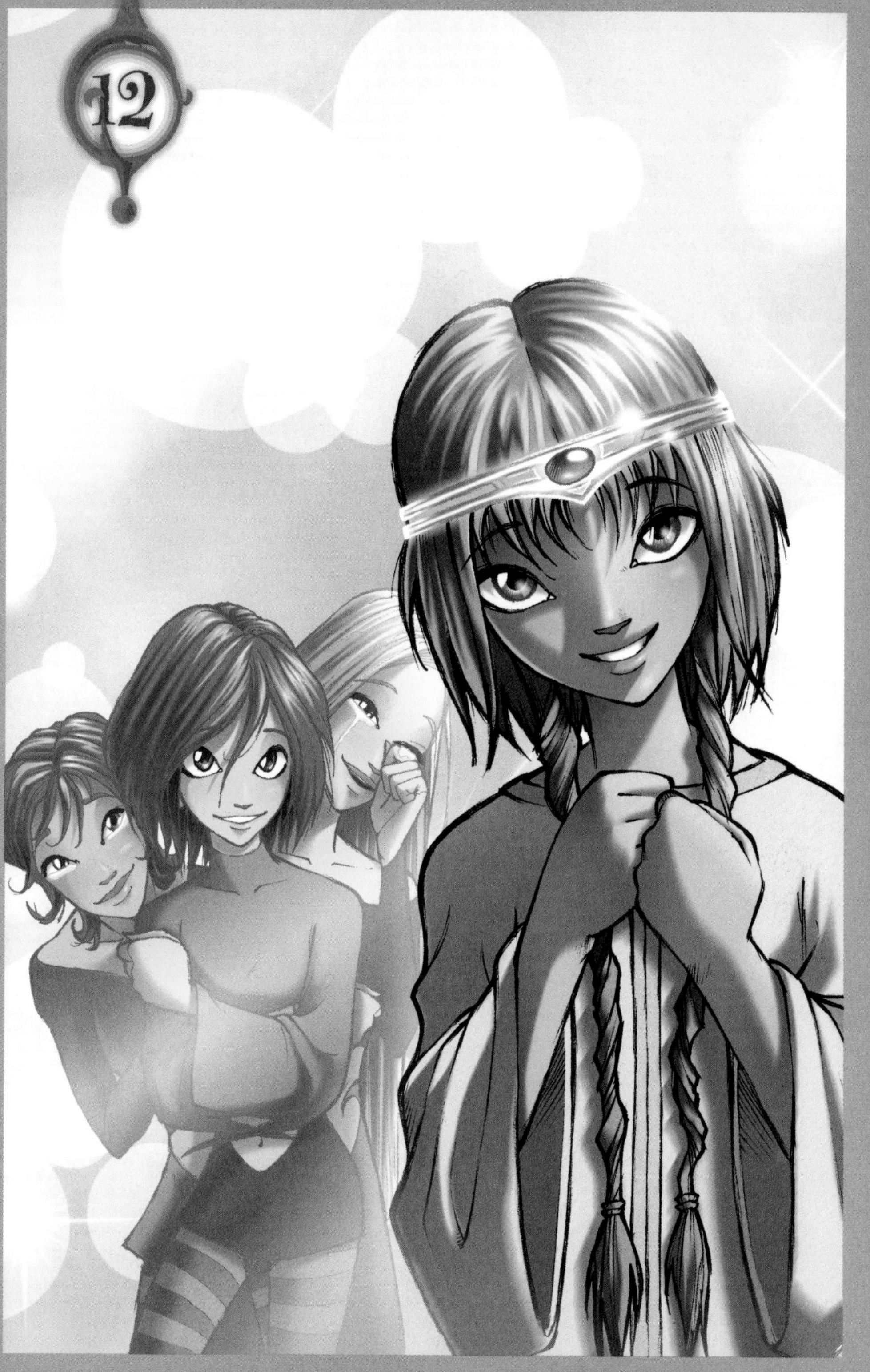
12

SO BE IT FOREVER

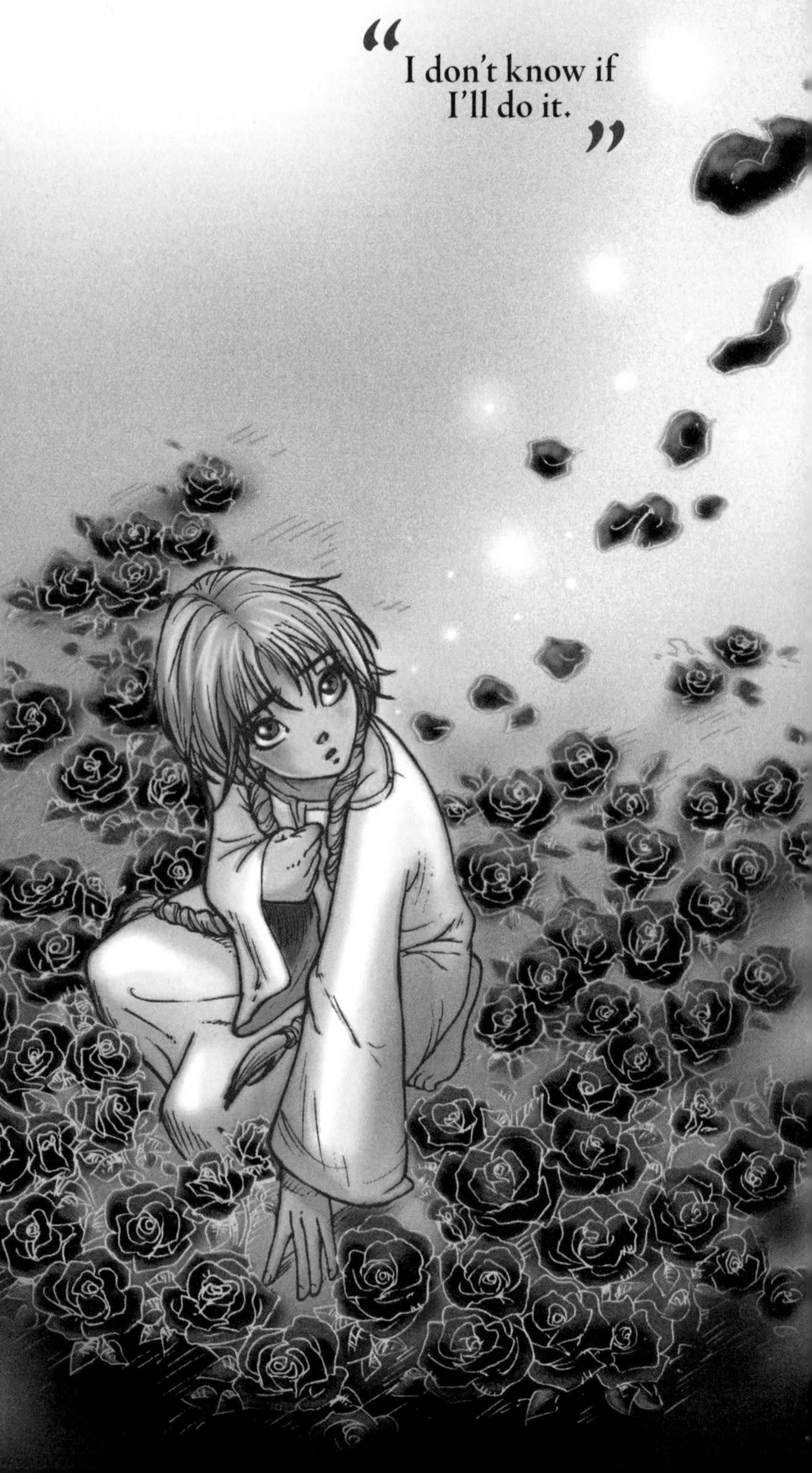
"I don't know if I'll do it."

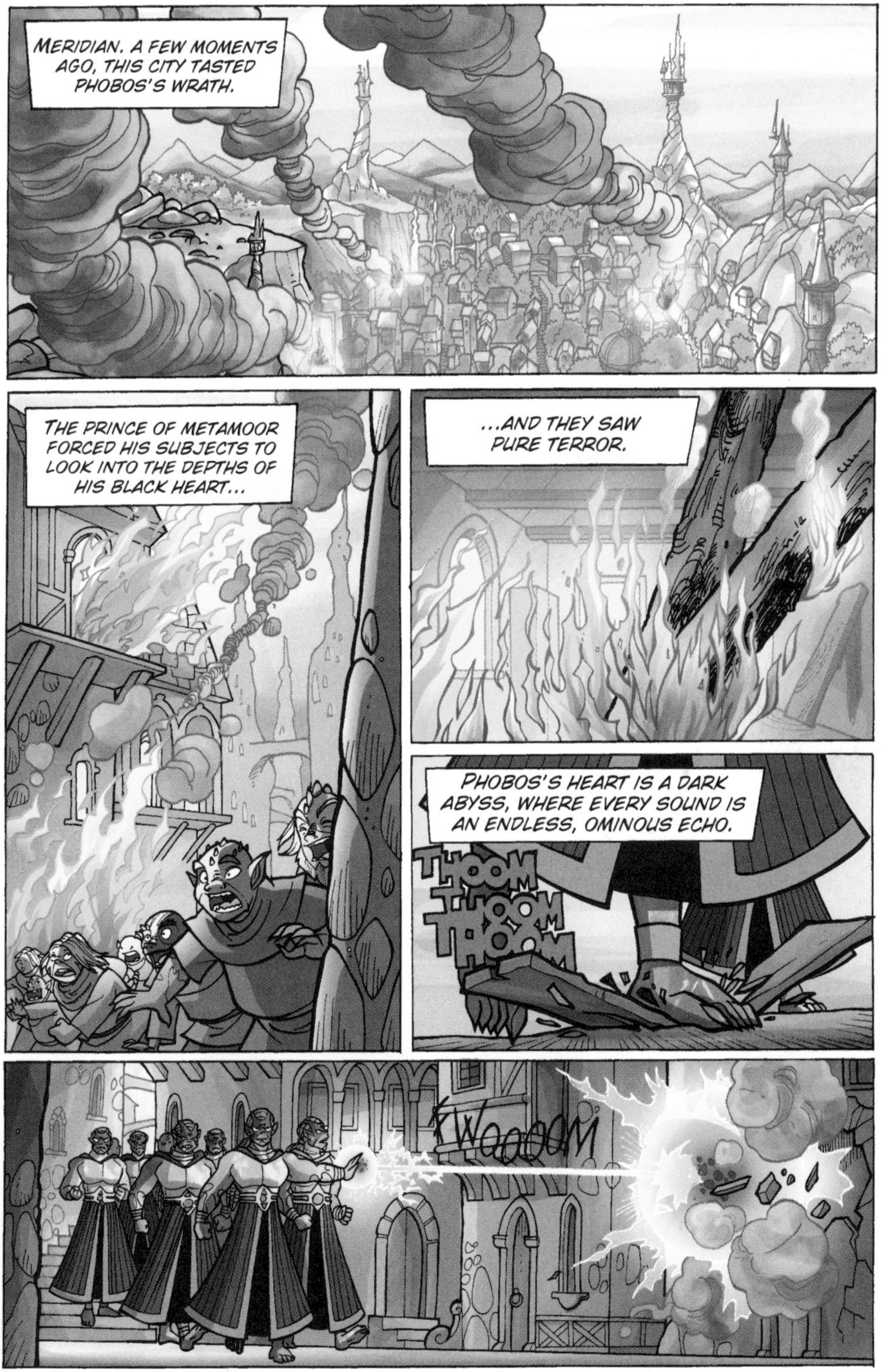
MERIDIAN. A FEW MOMENTS AGO, THIS CITY TASTED PHOBOS'S WRATH.
THE PRINCE OF METAMOOR FORCED HIS SUBJECTS TO LOOK INTO THE DEPTHS OF HIS BLACK HEART...
...AND THEY SAW PURE TERROR.
PHOBOS'S HEART IS A DARK ABYSS, WHERE EVERY SOUND IS AN ENDLESS, OMINOUS ECHO.
THOOM
THOOM
THOOM
KWOOOOOM

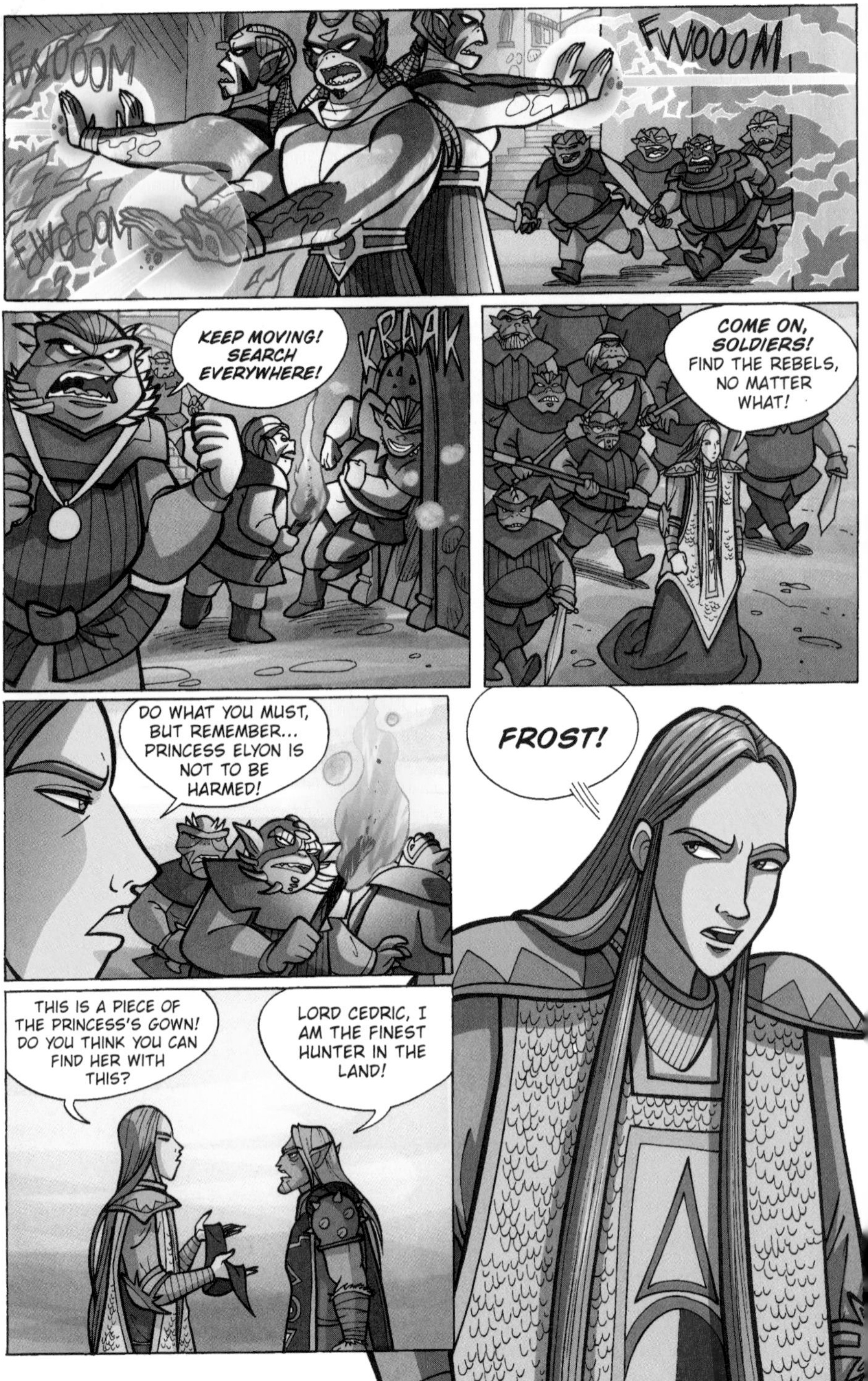
FWOOOM
FWOOOM
FWOOOM
KEEP MOVING! SEARCH EVERYWHERE!
KRAAK
COME ON, SOLDIERS! FIND THE REBELS, NO MATTER WHAT!
DO WHAT YOU MUST, BUT REMEMBER... PRINCESS ELYON IS NOT TO BE HARMED!
FROST!
THIS IS A PIECE OF THE PRINCESS'S GOWN! DO YOU THINK YOU CAN FIND HER WITH THIS?
LORD CEDRIC, I AM THE FINEST HUNTER IN THE LAND!

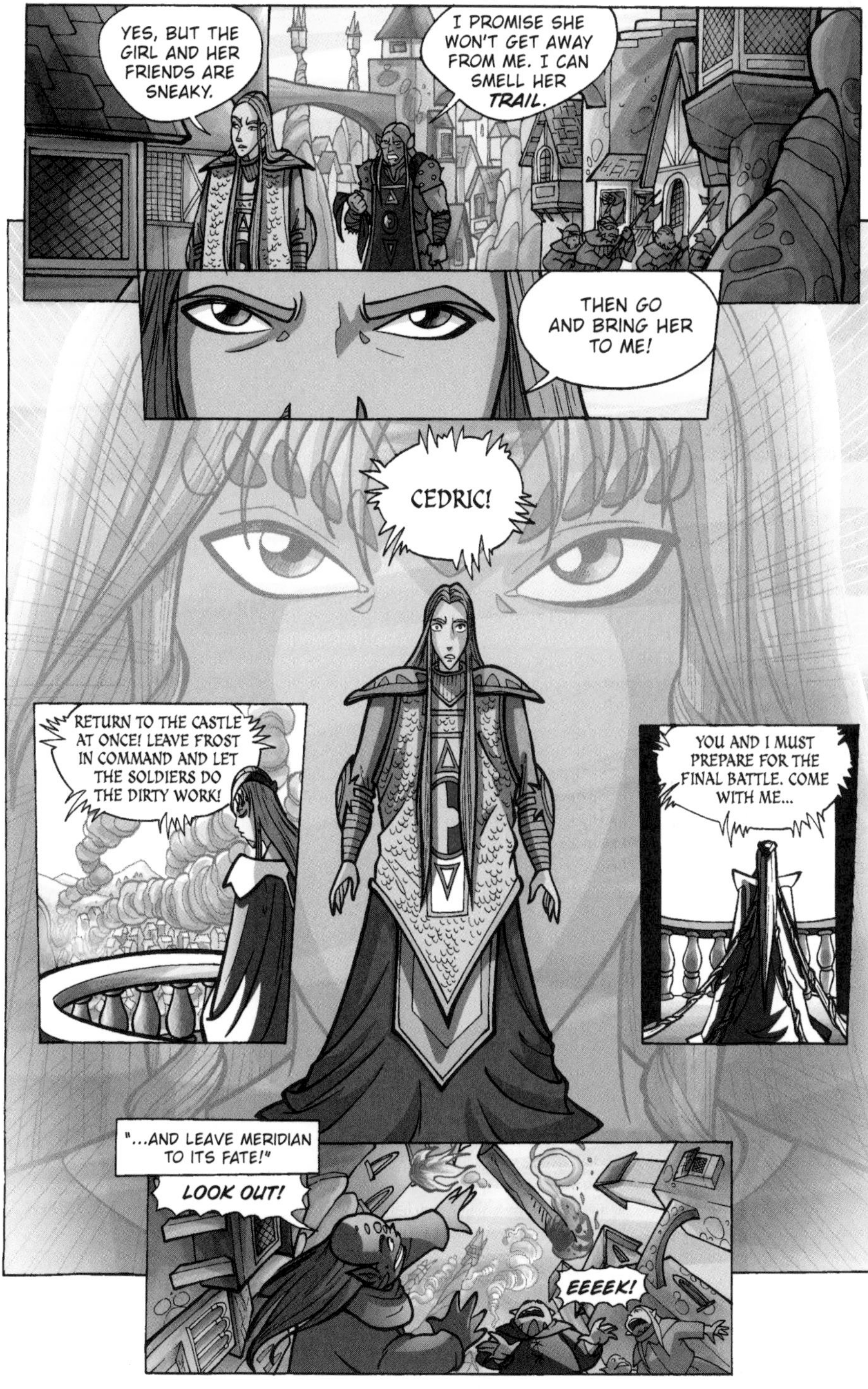
YES, BUT THE GIRL AND HER FRIENDS ARE SNEAKY.
I PROMISE SHE WON'T GET AWAY FROM ME. I CAN SMELL HER TRAIL.
THEN GO AND BRING HER TO ME!
CEDRIC!
RETURN TO THE CASTLE AT ONCE! LEAVE FROST IN COMMAND AND LET THE SOLDIERS DO THE DIRTY WORK!
YOU AND I MUST PREPARE FOR THE FINAL BATTLE. COME WITH ME...
"...AND LEAVE MERIDIAN TO ITS FATE!"
LOOK OUT!
EEEEK!

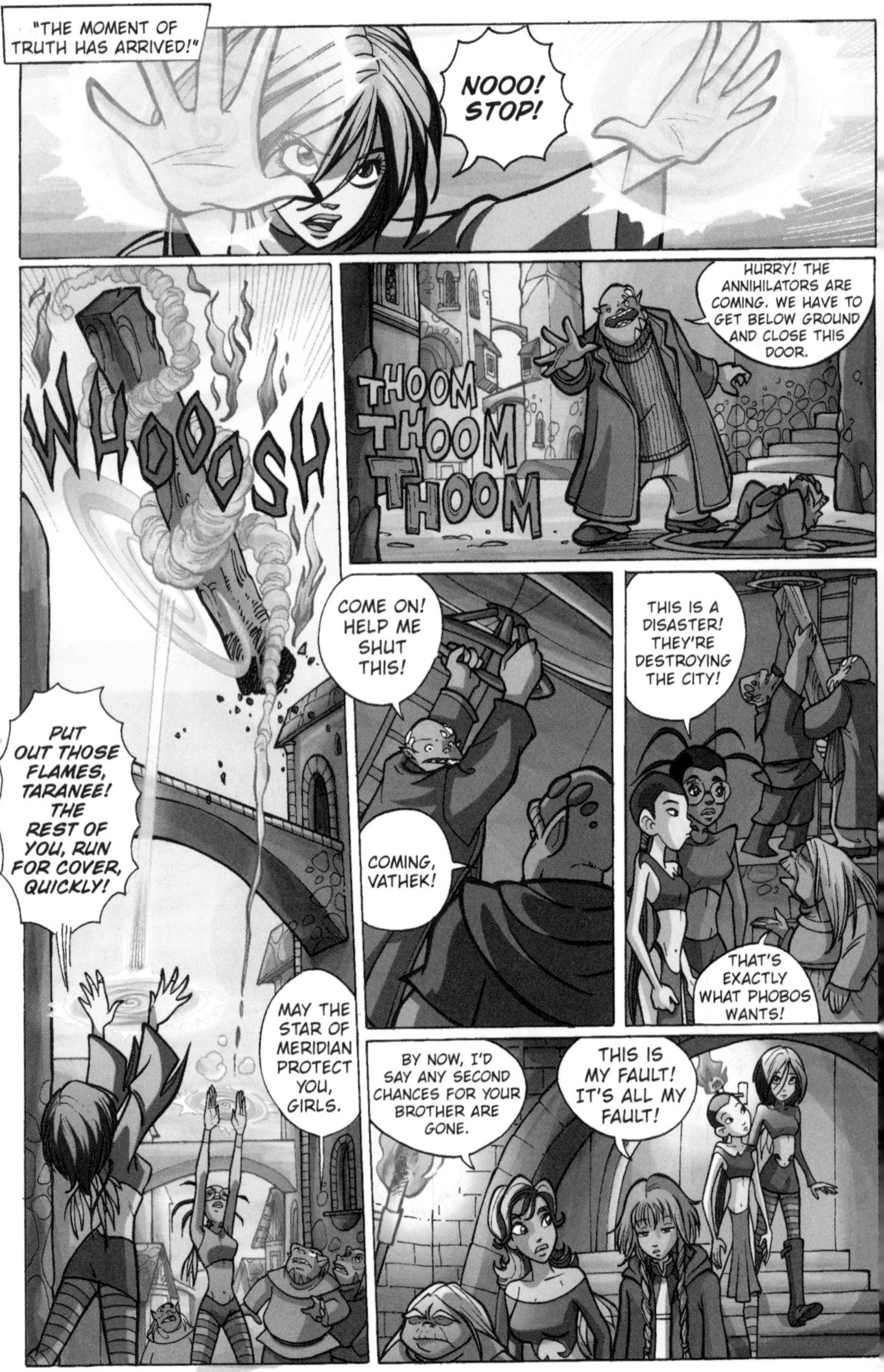
"THE MOMENT OF TRUTH HAS ARRIVED!"
NOOO! STOP!
WHOOOSH
PUT OUT THOSE FLAMES, TARANEE! THE REST OF YOU, RUN FOR COVER, QUICKLY!
MAY THE STAR OF MERIDIAN PROTECT YOU, GIRLS.
HURRY! THE ANNIHILATORS ARE COMING. WE HAVE TO GET BELOW GROUND AND CLOSE THIS DOOR.
THOOM THOOM THOOM
COME ON! HELP ME SHUT THIS!
COMING, VATHEK!
THIS IS A DISASTER! THEY'RE DESTROYING THE CITY!
THAT'S EXACTLY WHAT PHOBOS WANTS!
BY NOW, I'D SAY ANY SECOND CHANCES FOR YOUR BROTHER ARE GONE.
THIS IS MY FAULT! IT'S ALL MY FAULT!

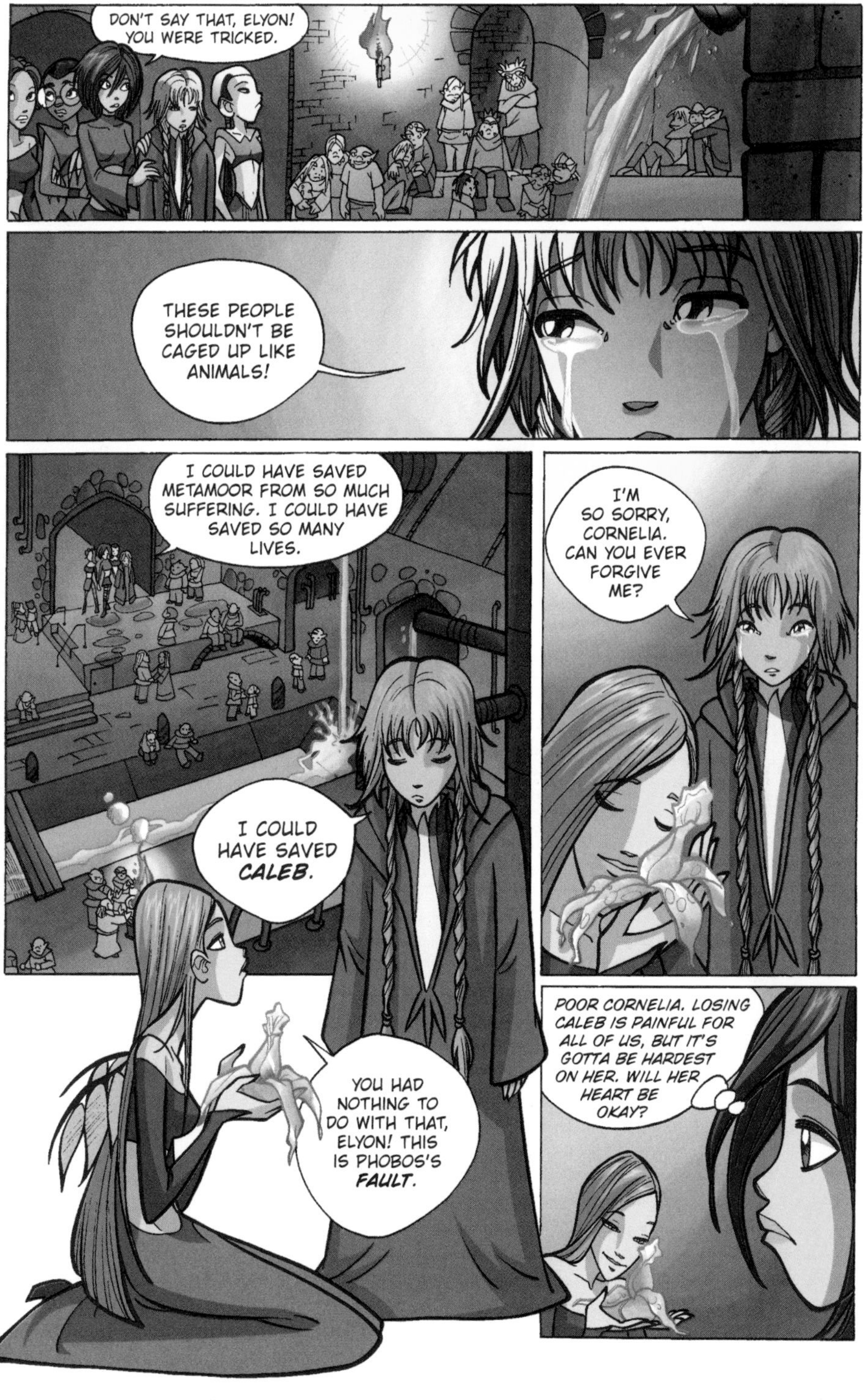
DON'T SAY THAT, ELYON! YOU WERE TRICKED.
THESE PEOPLE SHOULDN'T BE CAGED UP LIKE ANIMALS!
I COULD HAVE SAVED METAMOOR FROM SO MUCH SUFFERING. I COULD HAVE SAVED SO MANY LIVES.
I COULD HAVE SAVED ***CALEB***.
YOU HAD NOTHING TO DO WITH THAT, ELYON! THIS IS PHOBOS'S ***FAULT***.
I'M SO SORRY, CORNELIA. CAN YOU EVER FORGIVE ME?
POOR CORNELIA. LOSING CALEB IS PAINFUL FOR ALL OF US, BUT IT'S GOTTA BE HARDEST ON HER. WILL HER HEART BE OKAY?

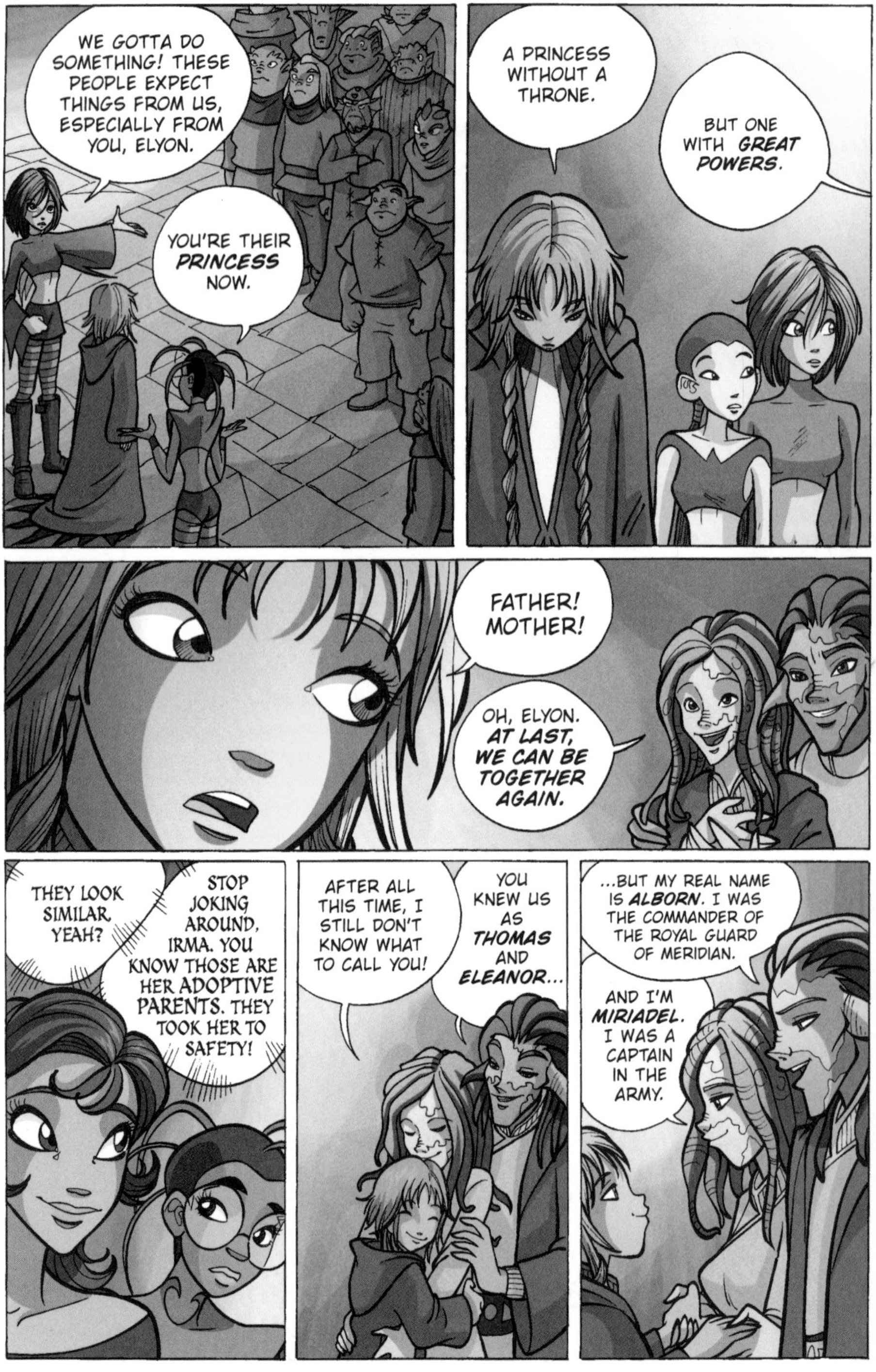
WE GOTTA DO SOMETHING! THESE PEOPLE EXPECT THINGS FROM US, ESPECIALLY FROM YOU, ELYON.
YOU'RE THEIR *PRINCESS* NOW.
A PRINCESS WITHOUT A THRONE.
BUT ONE WITH *GREAT POWERS*.
FATHER! MOTHER!
OH, ELYON. *AT LAST, WE CAN BE TOGETHER AGAIN.*
THEY LOOK SIMILAR, YEAH?
STOP JOKING AROUND, IRMA. YOU KNOW THOSE ARE HER ADOPTIVE PARENTS. THEY TOOK HER TO SAFETY!
AFTER ALL THIS TIME, I STILL DON'T KNOW WHAT TO CALL YOU!
YOU KNEW US AS *THOMAS* AND *ELEANOR*...
...BUT MY REAL NAME IS *ALBORN*. I WAS THE COMMANDER OF THE ROYAL GUARD OF MERIDIAN.
AND I'M *MIRIADEL*. I WAS A CAPTAIN IN THE ARMY.

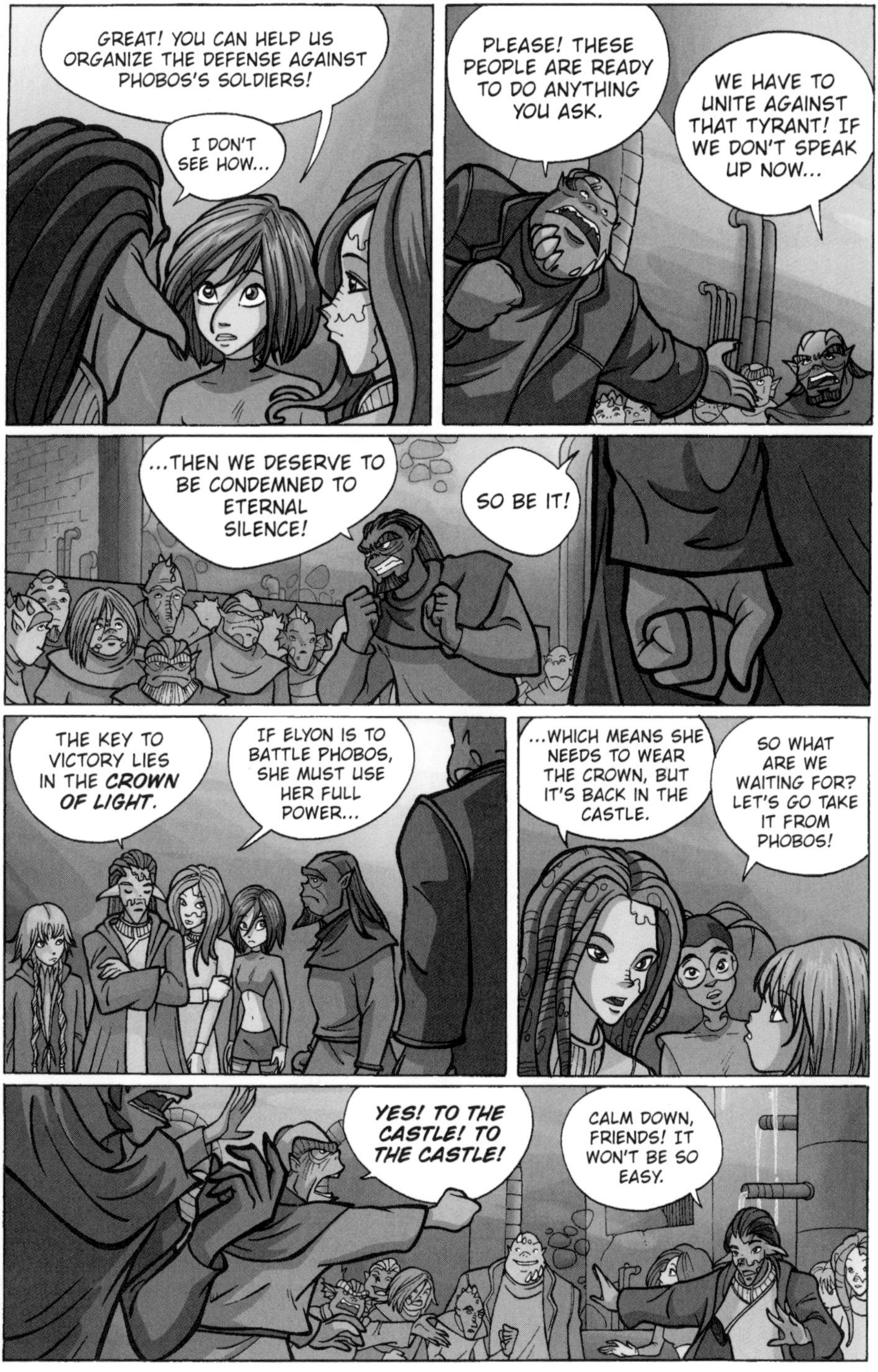
GREAT! YOU CAN HELP US ORGANIZE THE DEFENSE AGAINST PHOBOS'S SOLDIERS!
I DON'T SEE HOW...
PLEASE! THESE PEOPLE ARE READY TO DO ANYTHING YOU ASK.
WE HAVE TO UNITE AGAINST THAT TYRANT! IF WE DON'T SPEAK UP NOW...
...THEN WE DESERVE TO BE CONDEMNED TO ETERNAL SILENCE!
SO BE IT!
THE KEY TO VICTORY LIES IN THE ***CROWN OF LIGHT***.
IF ELYON IS TO BATTLE PHOBOS, SHE MUST USE HER FULL POWER...
...WHICH MEANS SHE NEEDS TO WEAR THE CROWN, BUT IT'S BACK IN THE CASTLE.
SO WHAT ARE WE WAITING FOR? LET'S GO TAKE IT FROM PHOBOS!
YES! TO THE CASTLE! TO THE CASTLE!
CALM DOWN, FRIENDS! IT WON'T BE SO EASY.

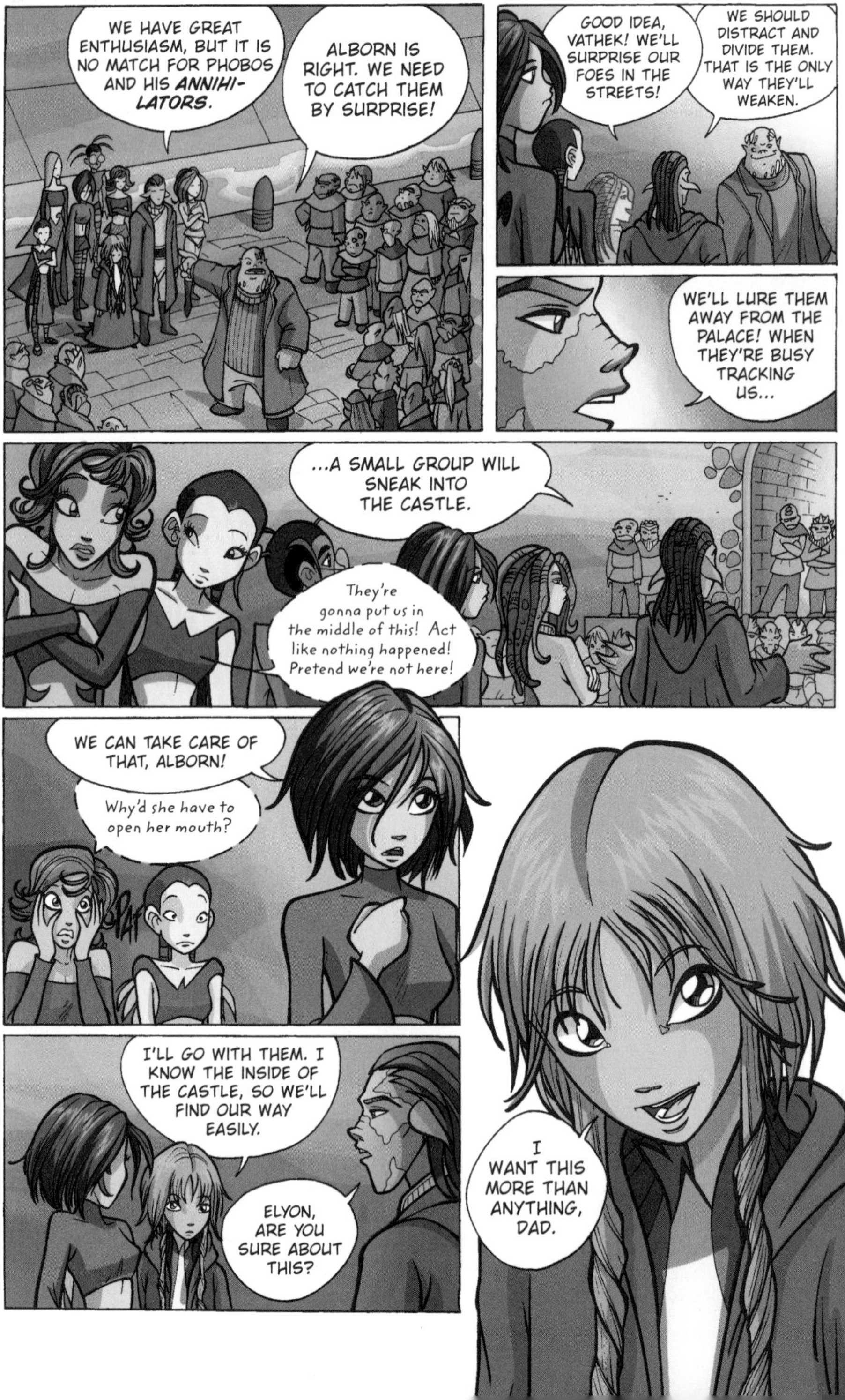
WE HAVE GREAT ENTHUSIASM, BUT IT IS NO MATCH FOR PHOBOS AND HIS ANNIHILATORS.
ALBORN IS RIGHT. WE NEED TO CATCH THEM BY SURPRISE!
GOOD IDEA, VATHEK! WE'LL SURPRISE OUR FOES IN THE STREETS!
WE SHOULD DISTRACT AND DIVIDE THEM. THAT IS THE ONLY WAY THEY'LL WEAKEN.
WE'LL LURE THEM AWAY FROM THE PALACE! WHEN THEY'RE BUSY TRACKING US...
...A SMALL GROUP WILL SNEAK INTO THE CASTLE.
They're gonna put us in the middle of this! Act like nothing happened! Pretend we're not here!
WE CAN TAKE CARE OF THAT, ALBORN!
Why'd she have to open her mouth?
I'LL GO WITH THEM. I KNOW THE INSIDE OF THE CASTLE, SO WE'LL FIND OUR WAY EASILY.
ELYON, ARE YOU SURE ABOUT THIS?
I WANT THIS MORE THAN ANYTHING, DAD.

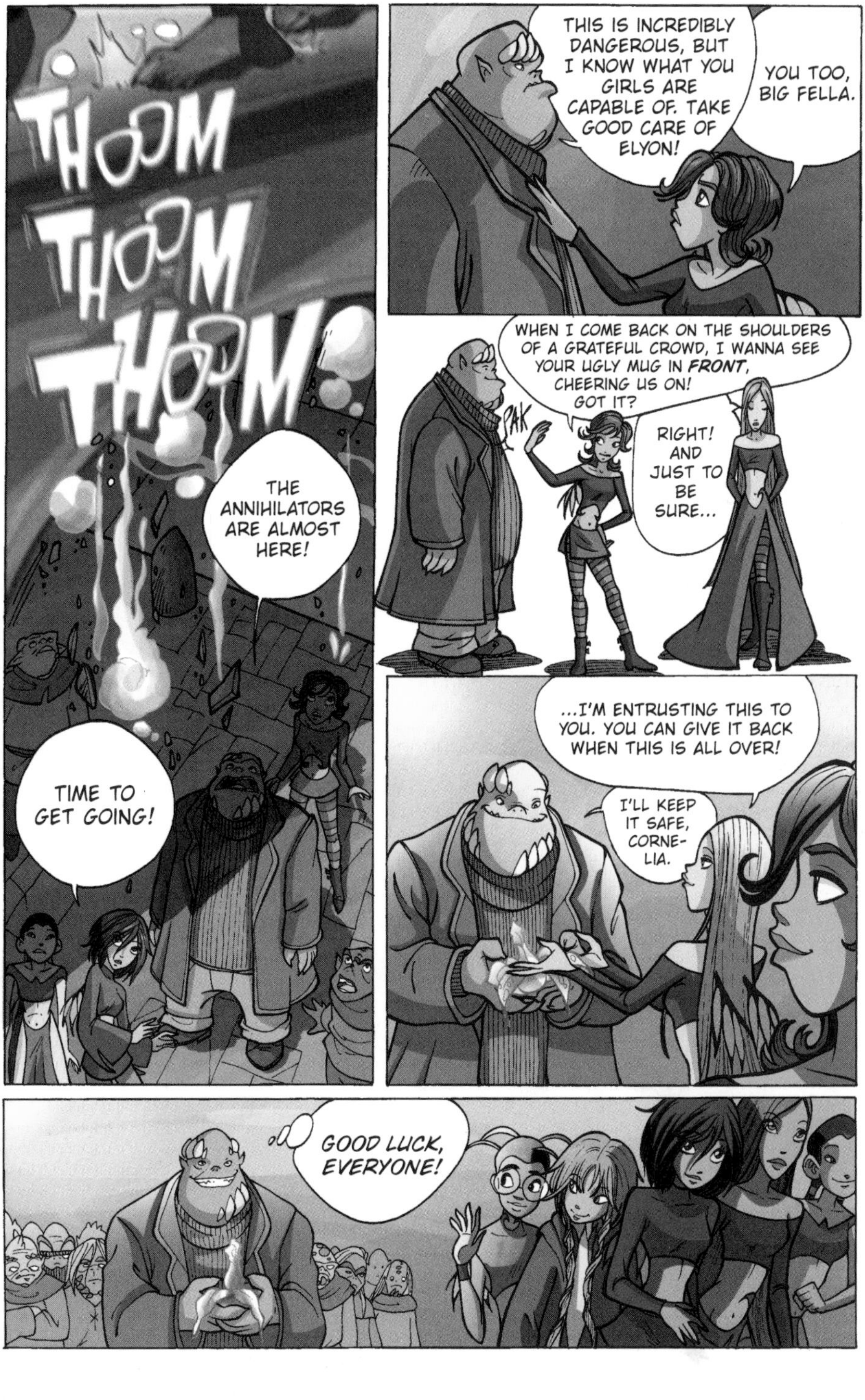
THOOM
THOOM
THOOM!
THE ANNIHILATORS ARE ALMOST HERE!
TIME TO GET GOING!
THIS IS INCREDIBLY DANGEROUS, BUT I KNOW WHAT YOU GIRLS ARE CAPABLE OF. TAKE GOOD CARE OF ELYON!
YOU TOO, BIG FELLA.
WHEN I COME BACK ON THE SHOULDERS OF A GRATEFUL CROWD, I WANNA SEE YOUR UGLY MUG IN FRONT, CHEERING US ON! GOT IT?
PAK
RIGHT! AND JUST TO BE SURE...
...I'M ENTRUSTING THIS TO YOU. YOU CAN GIVE IT BACK WHEN THIS IS ALL OVER!
I'LL KEEP IT SAFE, CORNELIA.
GOOD LUCK, EVERYONE!

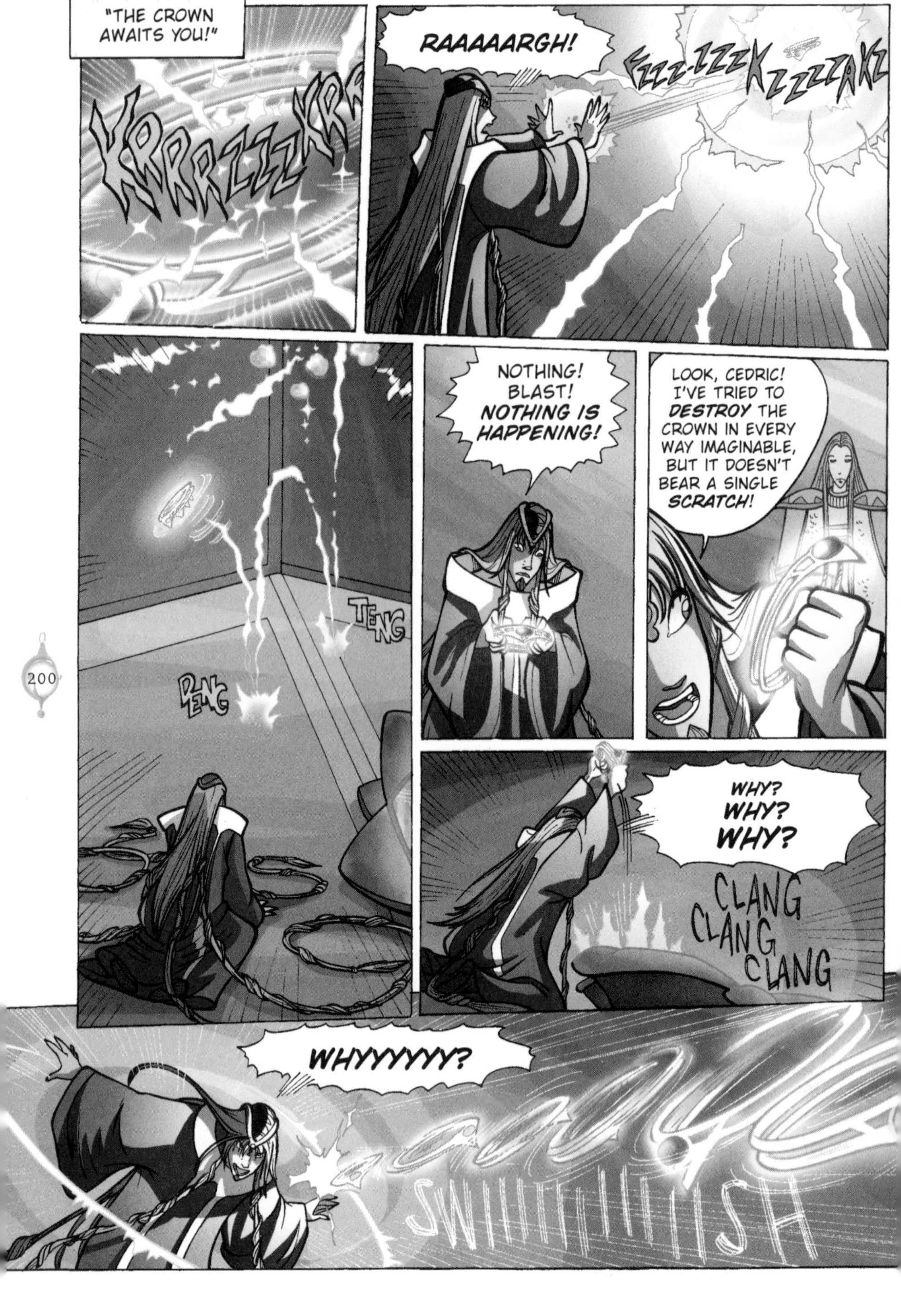
"THE CROWN AWAITS YOU!"
KRRZZZKRR
RAAAAARGH!
FZZZ-ZZZKZZZZZAKZ
TENG
DENG
NOTHING! BLAST! NOTHING IS HAPPENING!
LOOK, CEDRIC! I'VE TRIED TO DESTROY THE CROWN IN EVERY WAY IMAGINABLE, BUT IT DOESN'T BEAR A SINGLE SCRATCH!
WHY? WHY? WHY?
CLANG CLANG CLANG
WHYYYYYY?
SWIIIIIIIIISH

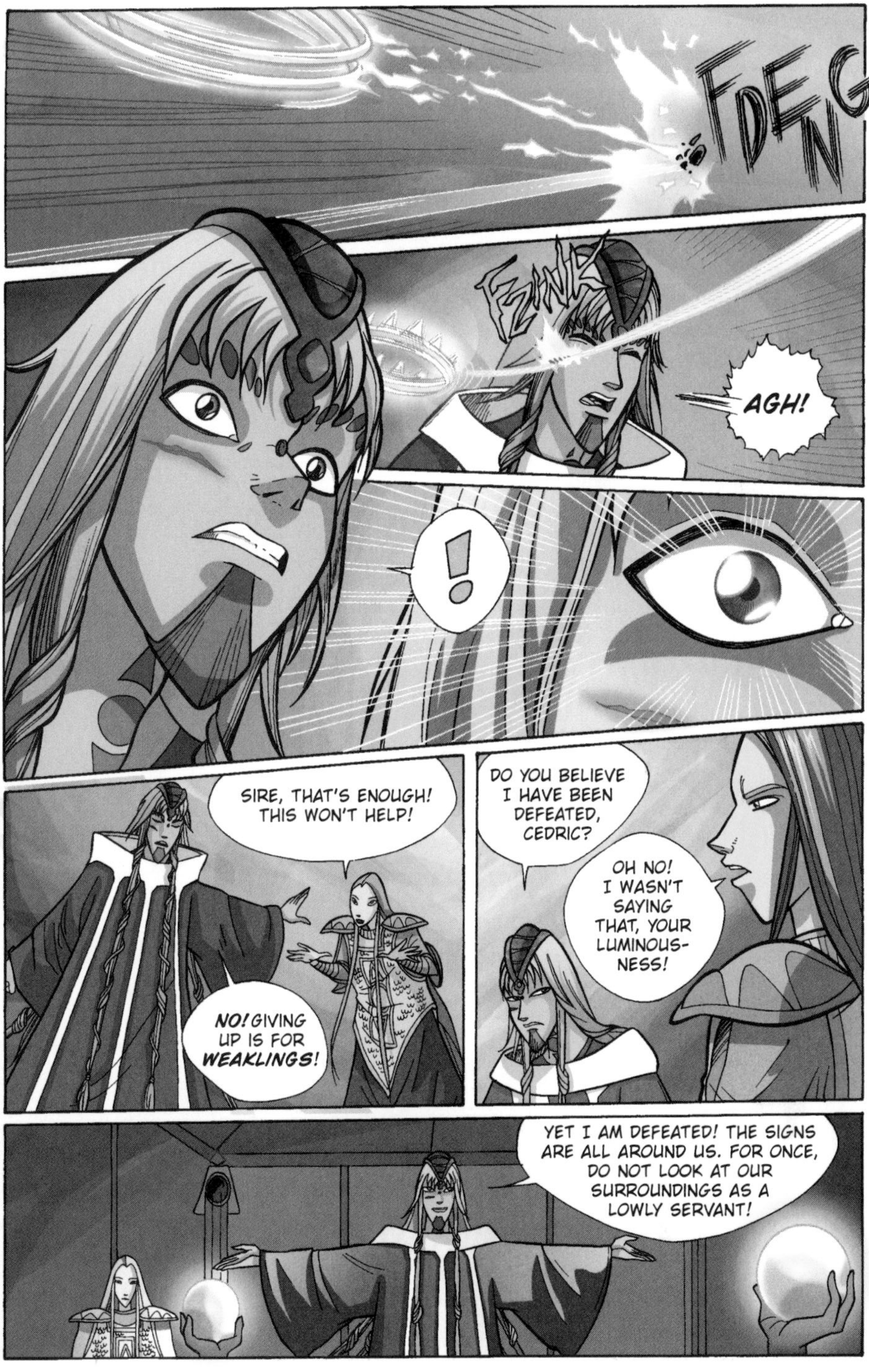
FDENG
FZINK
AGH!
!
SIRE, THAT'S ENOUGH! THIS WON'T HELP!
NO! GIVING UP IS FOR WEAKLINGS!
DO YOU BELIEVE I HAVE BEEN DEFEATED, CEDRIC?
OH NO! I WASN'T SAYING THAT, YOUR LUMINOUS-NESS!
YET I AM DEFEATED! THE SIGNS ARE ALL AROUND US. FOR ONCE, DO NOT LOOK AT OUR SURROUNDINGS AS A LOWLY SERVANT!

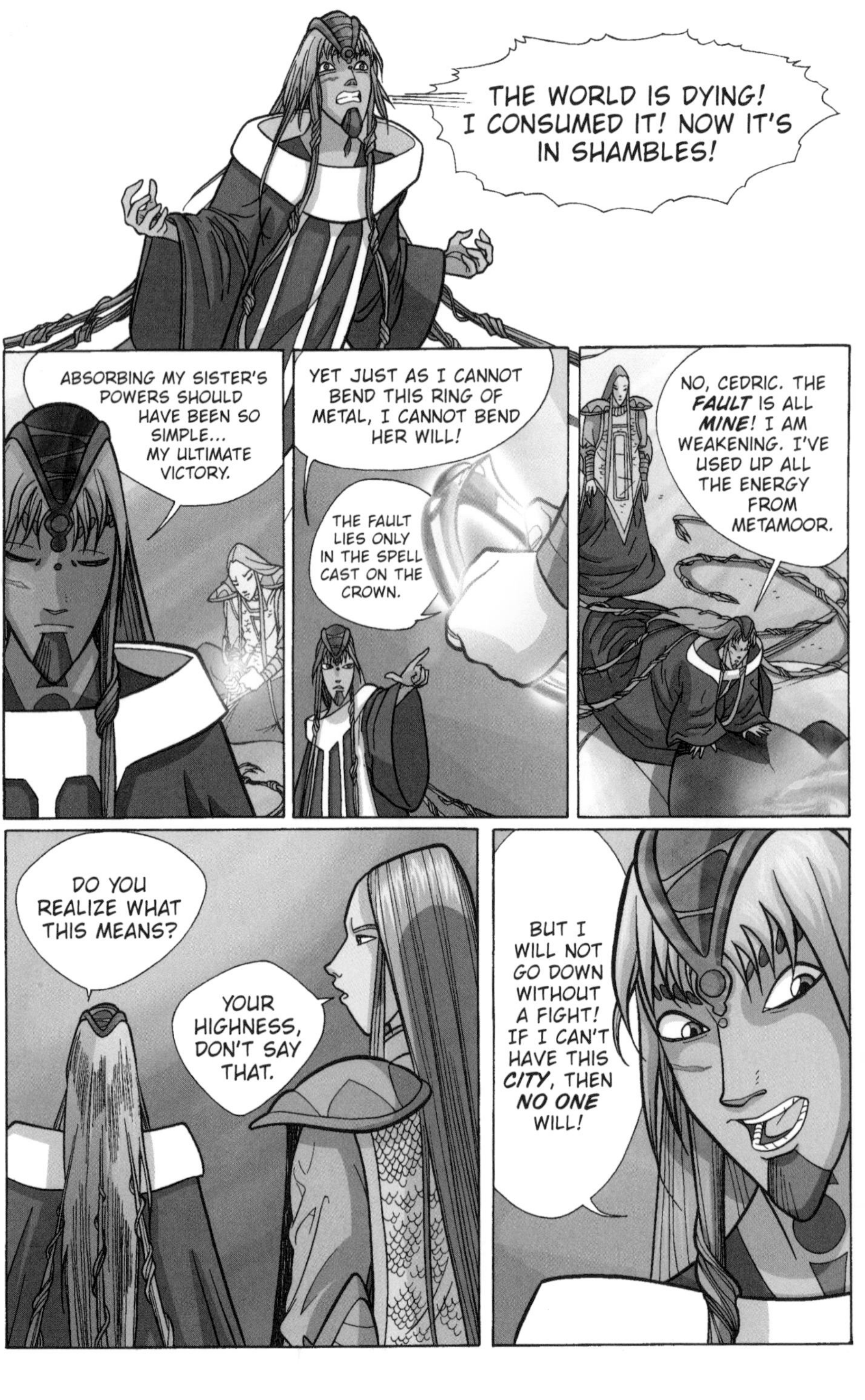
THE WORLD IS DYING! I CONSUMED IT! NOW IT'S IN SHAMBLES!
ABSORBING MY SISTER'S POWERS SHOULD HAVE BEEN SO SIMPLE... MY ULTIMATE VICTORY.
YET JUST AS I CANNOT BEND THIS RING OF METAL, I CANNOT BEND HER WILL!
THE FAULT LIES ONLY IN THE SPELL CAST ON THE CROWN.
NO, CEDRIC. THE ***FAULT*** IS ALL ***MINE***! I AM WEAKENING. I'VE USED UP ALL THE ENERGY FROM METAMOOR.
DO YOU REALIZE WHAT THIS MEANS?
YOUR HIGHNESS, DON'T SAY THAT.
BUT I WILL NOT GO DOWN WITHOUT A FIGHT! IF I CAN'T HAVE THIS ***CITY***, THEN ***NO ONE*** WILL!

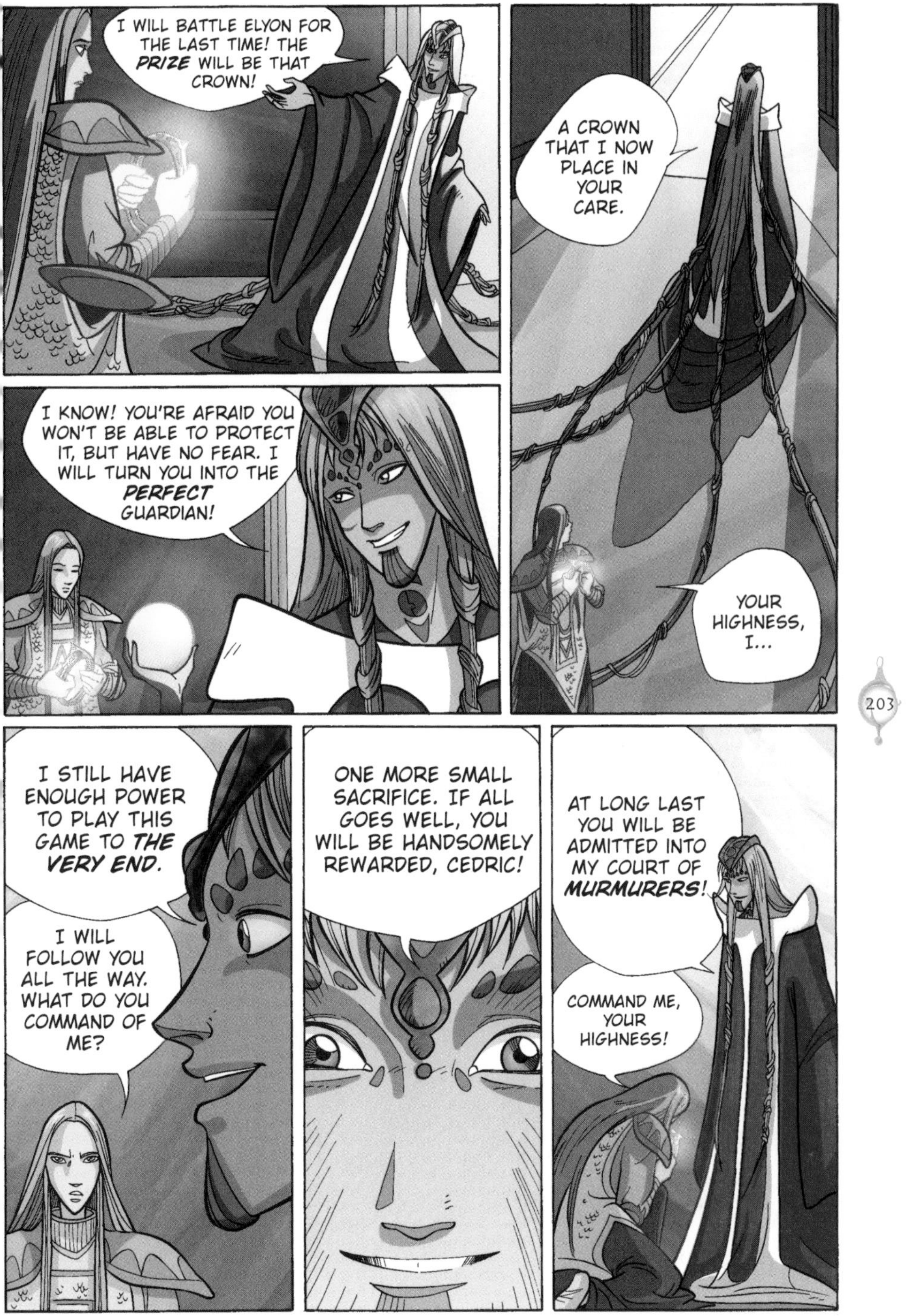

I WILL BATTLE ELYON FOR THE LAST TIME! THE PRIZE WILL BE THAT CROWN!
A CROWN THAT I NOW PLACE IN YOUR CARE.
I KNOW! YOU'RE AFRAID YOU WON'T BE ABLE TO PROTECT IT, BUT HAVE NO FEAR. I WILL TURN YOU INTO THE PERFECT GUARDIAN!
YOUR HIGHNESS, I...
I STILL HAVE ENOUGH POWER TO PLAY THIS GAME TO THE VERY END.
I WILL FOLLOW YOU ALL THE WAY. WHAT DO YOU COMMAND OF ME?
ONE MORE SMALL SACRIFICE. IF ALL GOES WELL, YOU WILL BE HANDSOMELY REWARDED, CEDRIC!
AT LONG LAST YOU WILL BE ADMITTED INTO MY COURT OF MURMURERS!
COMMAND ME, YOUR HIGHNESS!

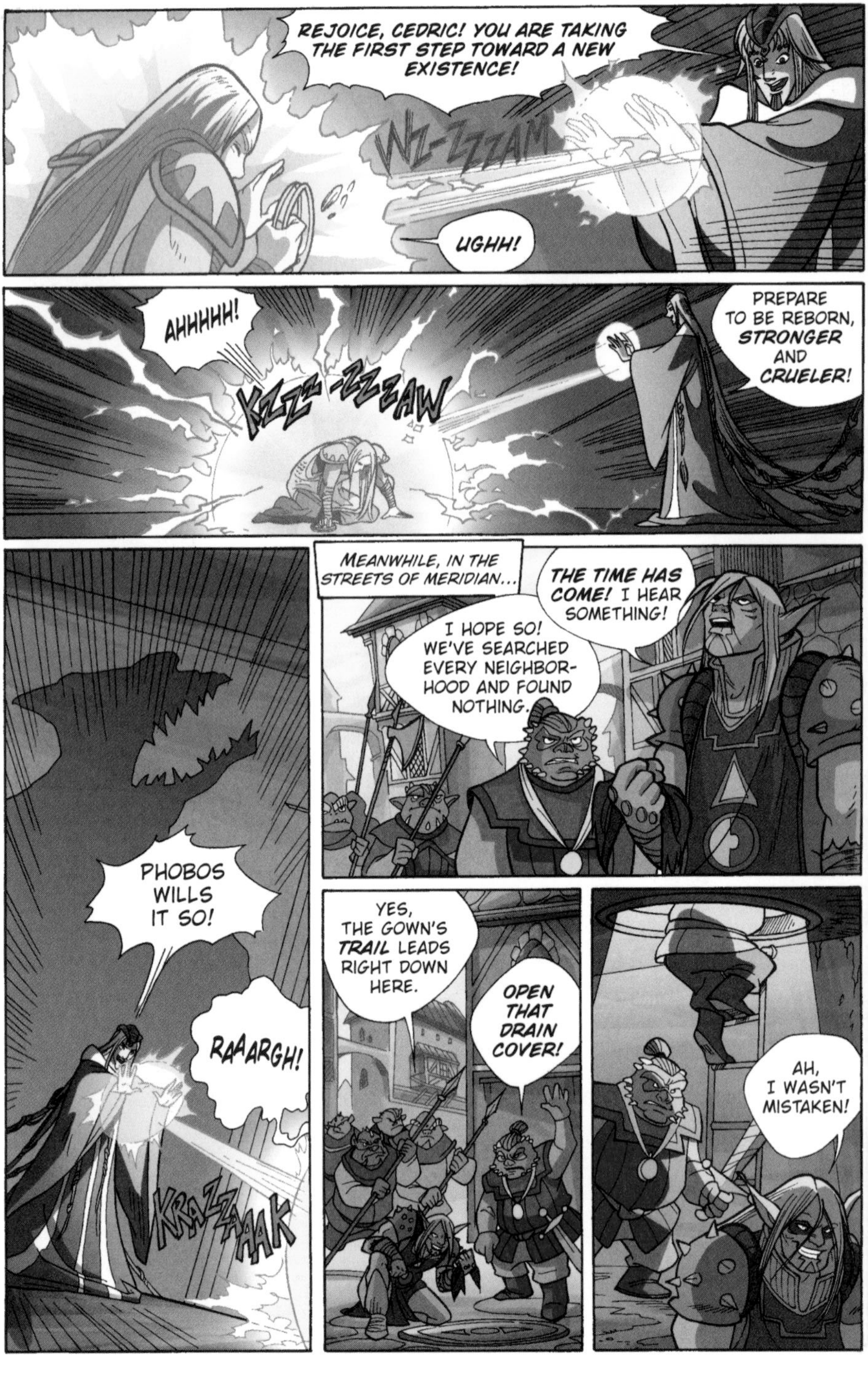
REJOICE, CEDRIC! YOU ARE TAKING THE FIRST STEP TOWARD A NEW EXISTENCE!
WZ-ZZZAM
UGHH!
AHHHHH!
KZZZ-ZZZAW
PREPARE TO BE REBORN, STRONGER AND CRUELER!
PHOBOS WILLS IT SO!
RAAARGH!
KRAZZZAAK
MEANWHILE, IN THE STREETS OF MERIDIAN...
THE TIME HAS COME! I HEAR SOMETHING!
I HOPE SO! WE'VE SEARCHED EVERY NEIGHBOR-HOOD AND FOUND NOTHING.
YES, THE GOWN'S TRAIL LEADS RIGHT DOWN HERE.
OPEN THAT DRAIN COVER!
AH, I WASN'T MISTAKEN!

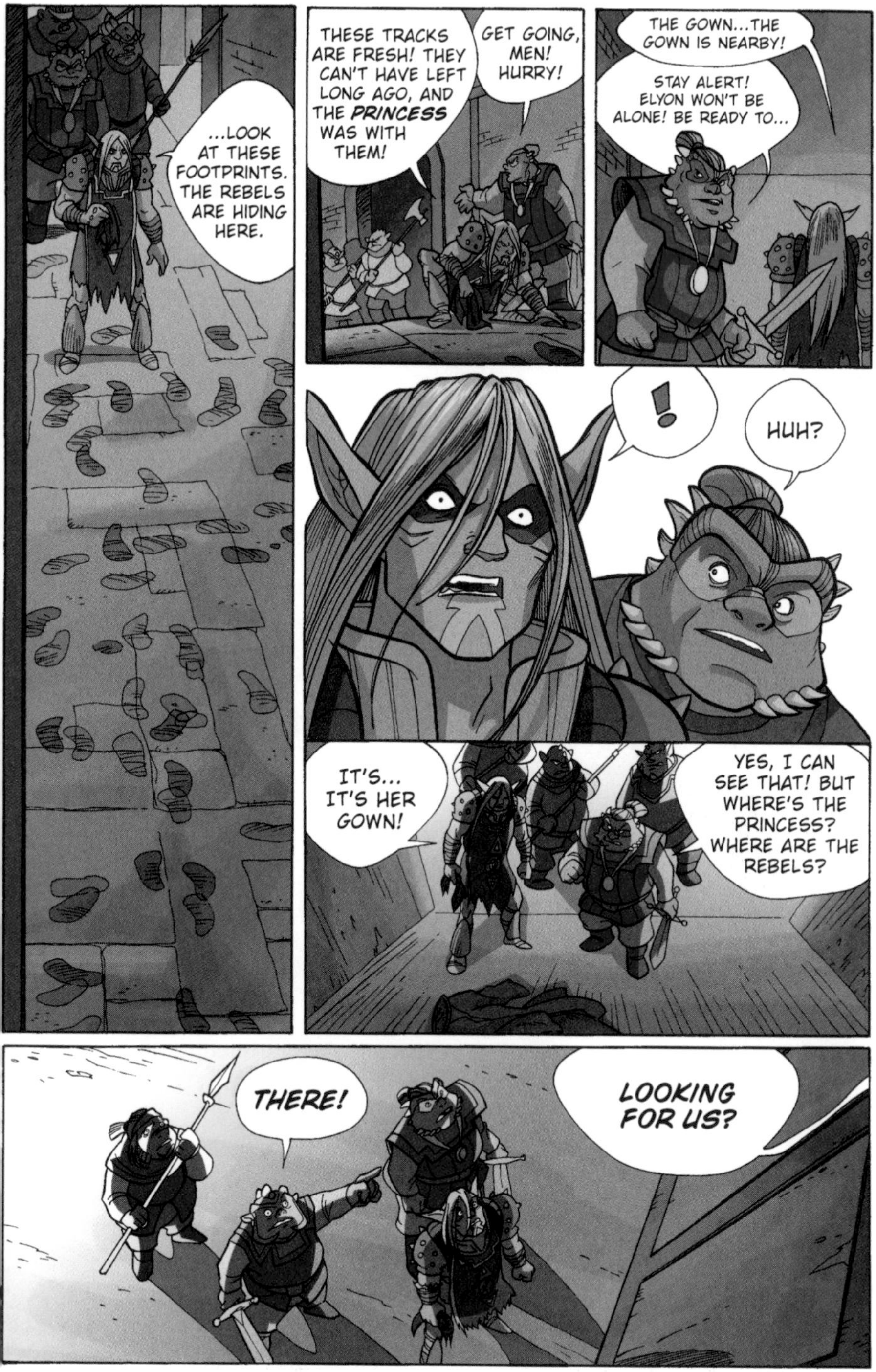
...LOOK AT THESE FOOTPRINTS. THE REBELS ARE HIDING HERE.
THESE TRACKS ARE FRESH! THEY CAN'T HAVE LEFT LONG AGO, AND THE PRINCESS WAS WITH THEM!
GET GOING, MEN! HURRY!
THE GOWN...THE GOWN IS NEARBY!
STAY ALERT! ELYON WON'T BE ALONE! BE READY TO...
!
HUH?
IT'S... IT'S HER GOWN!
YES, I CAN SEE THAT! BUT WHERE'S THE PRINCESS? WHERE ARE THE REBELS?
THERE!
LOOKING FOR US?

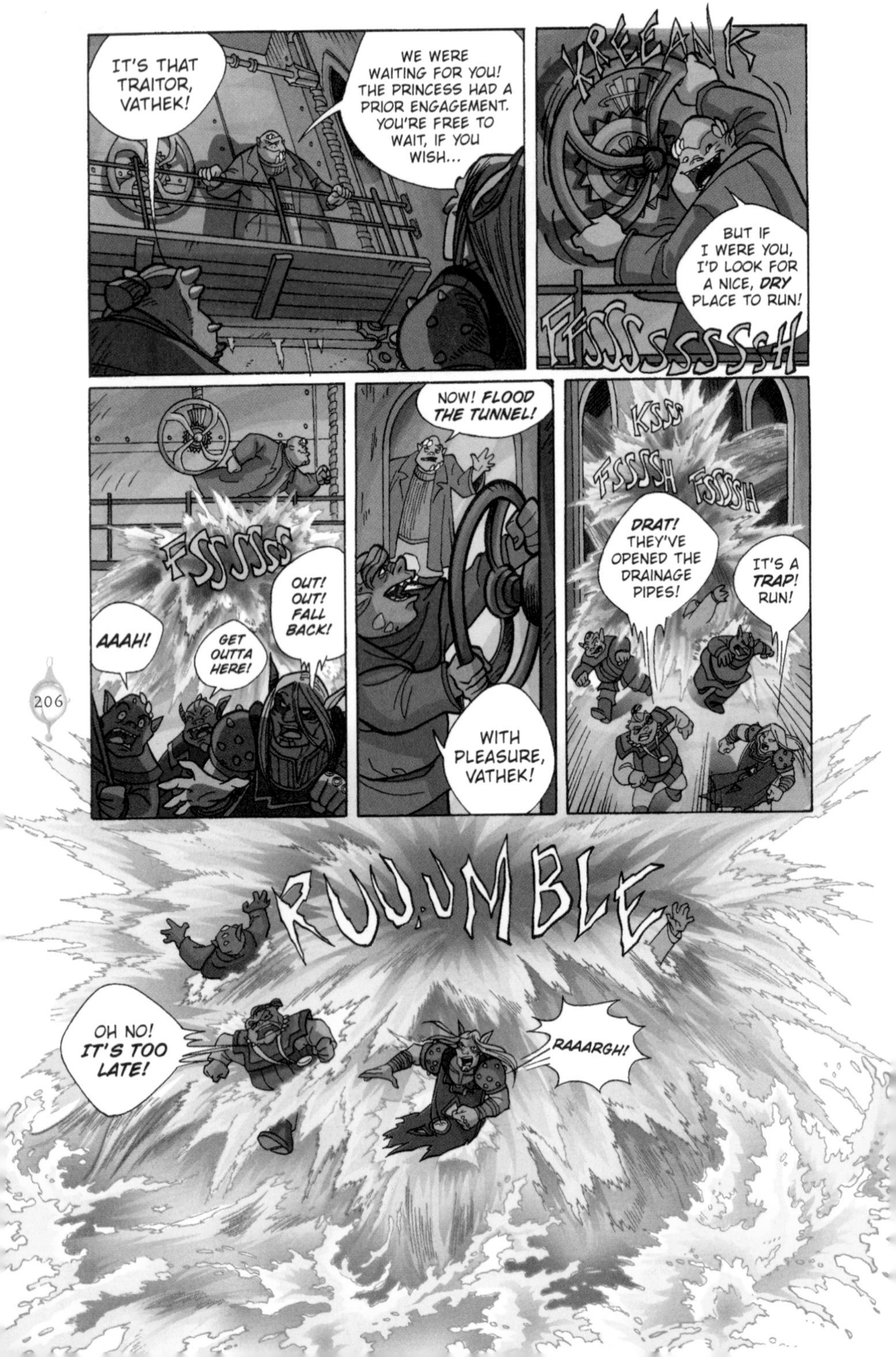
IT'S THAT TRAITOR, VATHEK!
WE WERE WAITING FOR YOU! THE PRINCESS HAD A PRIOR ENGAGEMENT. YOU'RE FREE TO WAIT, IF YOU WISH...
KREEANK
BUT IF I WERE YOU, I'D LOOK FOR A NICE, DRY PLACE TO RUN!
FFSSSSSSSSH
FSSSSSS
OUT! OUT! FALL BACK!
AAAH!
GET OUTTA HERE!
NOW! FLOOD THE TUNNEL!
WITH PLEASURE, VATHEK!
KSSS
FSSSSH
FSSSSH
DRAT! THEY'VE OPENED THE DRAINAGE PIPES!
IT'S A TRAP! RUN!
RUUUMBLE
OH NO! IT'S TOO LATE!
RAAARGH!

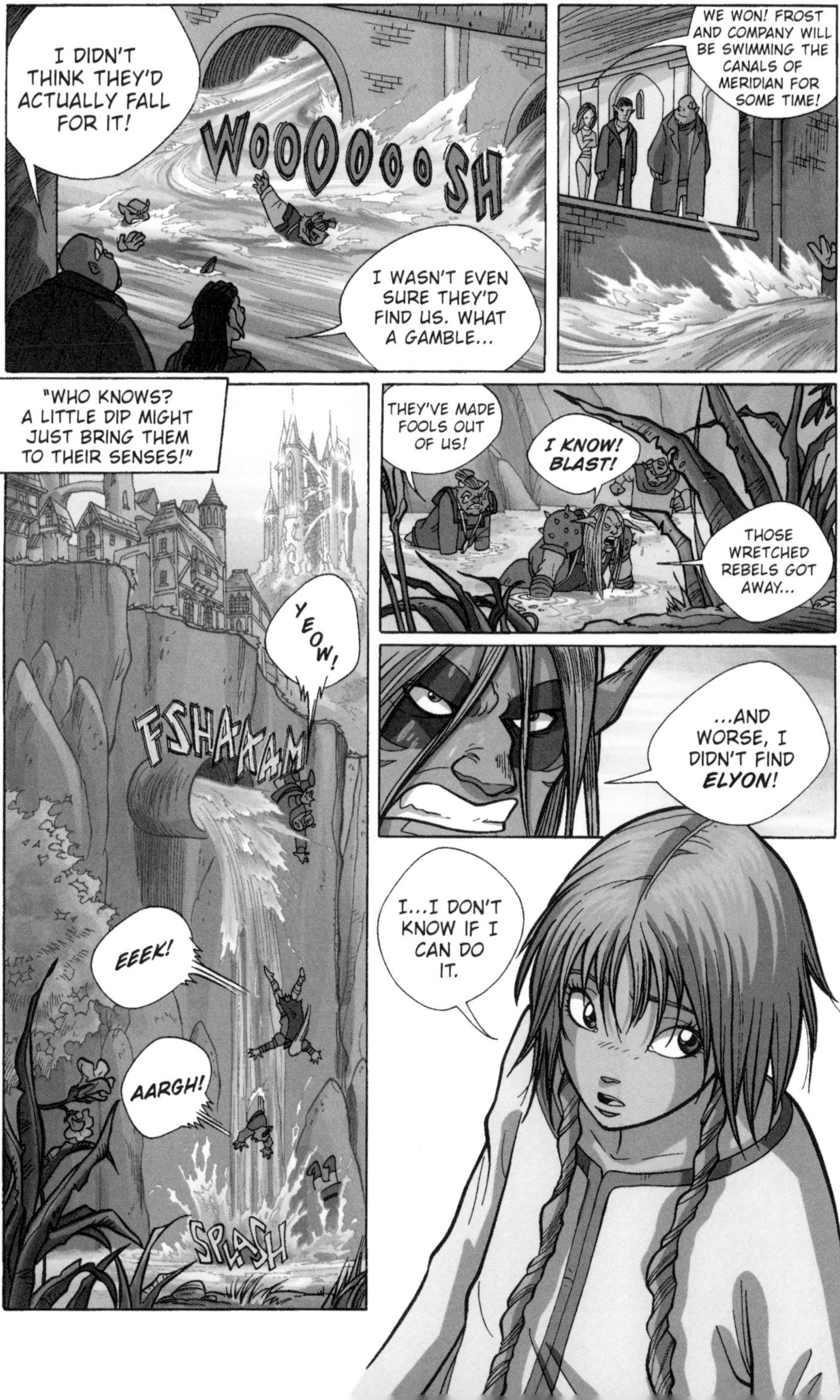

I DIDN'T THINK THEY'D ACTUALLY FALL FOR IT!
WOOOOOOSH
I WASN'T EVEN SURE THEY'D FIND US. WHAT A GAMBLE...
WE WON! FROST AND COMPANY WILL BE SWIMMING THE CANALS OF MERIDIAN FOR SOME TIME!
"WHO KNOWS? A LITTLE DIP MIGHT JUST BRING THEM TO THEIR SENSES!"
YEOW!
FSHAAAM
EEEK!
AARGH!
SPLASH
THEY'VE MADE FOOLS OUT OF US!
I KNOW! BLAST!
THOSE WRETCHED REBELS GOT AWAY...
...AND WORSE, I DIDN'T FIND ELYON!
I...I DON'T KNOW IF I CAN DO IT.

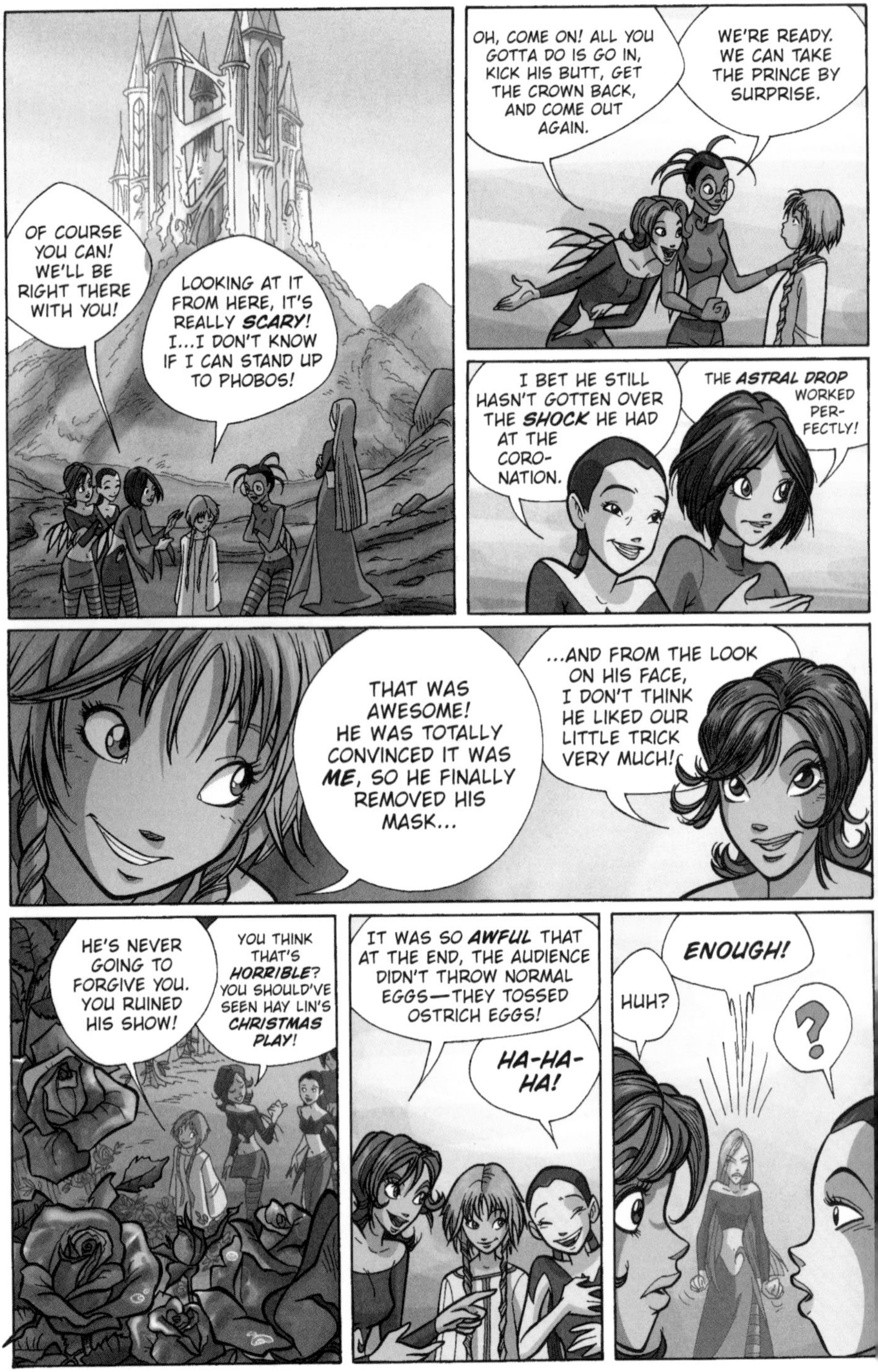
OF COURSE YOU CAN! WE'LL BE RIGHT THERE WITH YOU!
LOOKING AT IT FROM HERE, IT'S REALLY SCARY! I...I DON'T KNOW IF I CAN STAND UP TO PHOBOS!
OH, COME ON! ALL YOU GOTTA DO IS GO IN, KICK HIS BUTT, GET THE CROWN BACK, AND COME OUT AGAIN.
WE'RE READY. WE CAN TAKE THE PRINCE BY SURPRISE.
I BET HE STILL HASN'T GOTTEN OVER THE SHOCK HE HAD AT THE CORO-NATION.
THE ASTRAL DROP WORKED PER-FECTLY!
THAT WAS AWESOME! HE WAS TOTALLY CONVINCED IT WAS ME, SO HE FINALLY REMOVED HIS MASK...
...AND FROM THE LOOK ON HIS FACE, I DON'T THINK HE LIKED OUR LITTLE TRICK VERY MUCH!
HE'S NEVER GOING TO FORGIVE YOU. YOU RUINED HIS SHOW!
YOU THINK THAT'S HORRIBLE? YOU SHOULD'VE SEEN HAY LIN'S CHRISTMAS PLAY!
IT WAS SO AWFUL THAT AT THE END, THE AUDIENCE DIDN'T THROW NORMAL EGGS—THEY TOSSED OSTRICH EGGS!
HA-HA-HA!
HUH?
ENOUGH!
?

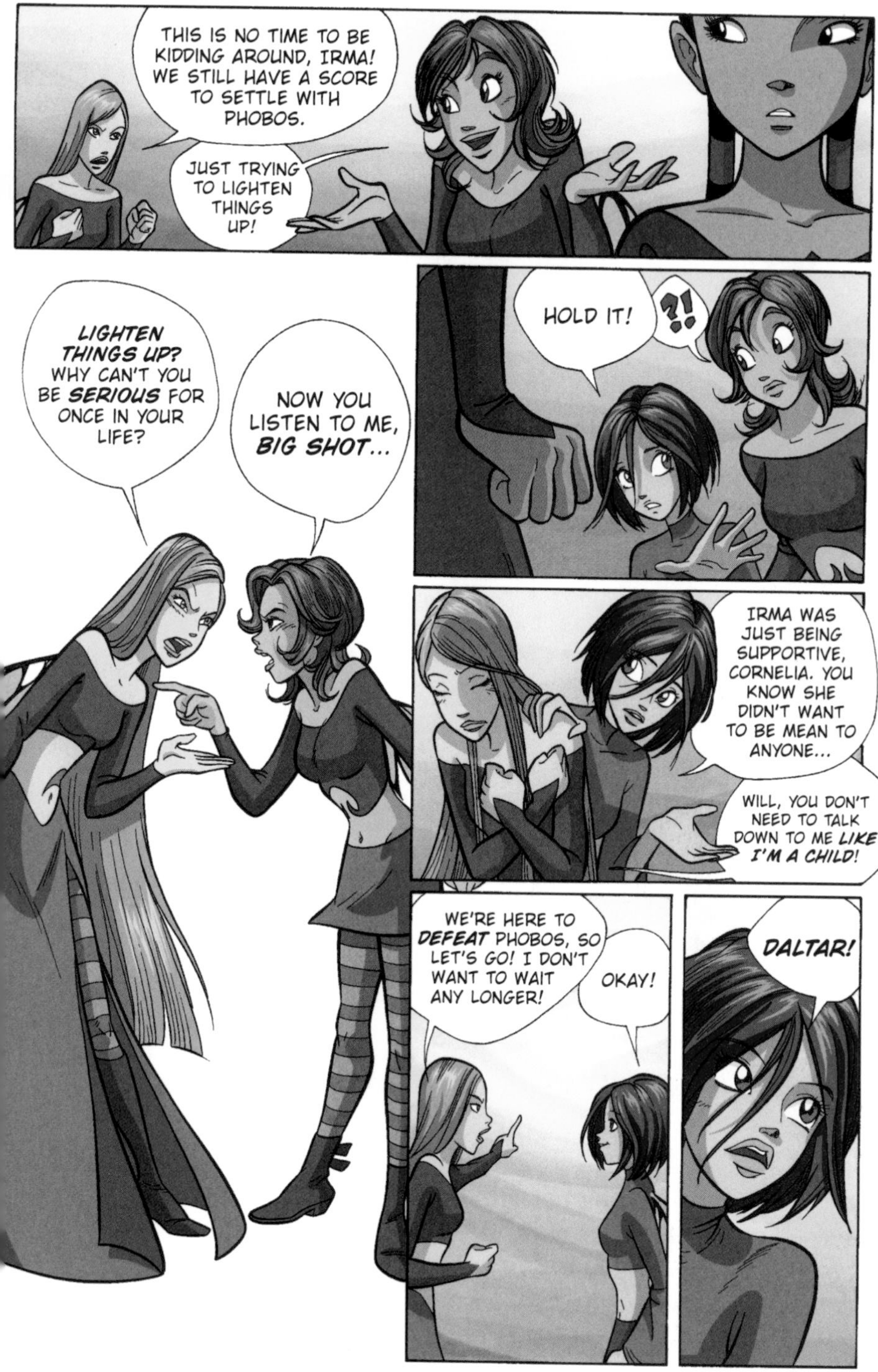
THIS IS NO TIME TO BE KIDDING AROUND, IRMA! WE STILL HAVE A SCORE TO SETTLE WITH PHOBOS.
JUST TRYING TO LIGHTEN THINGS UP!
LIGHTEN THINGS UP? WHY CAN'T YOU BE SERIOUS FOR ONCE IN YOUR LIFE?
NOW YOU LISTEN TO ME, BIG SHOT...
HOLD IT!
?!
IRMA WAS JUST BEING SUPPORTIVE, CORNELIA. YOU KNOW SHE DIDN'T WANT TO BE MEAN TO ANYONE...
WILL, YOU DON'T NEED TO TALK DOWN TO ME LIKE I'M A CHILD!
WE'RE HERE TO DEFEAT PHOBOS, SO LET'S GO! I DON'T WANT TO WAIT ANY LONGER!
OKAY!
DALTAR!

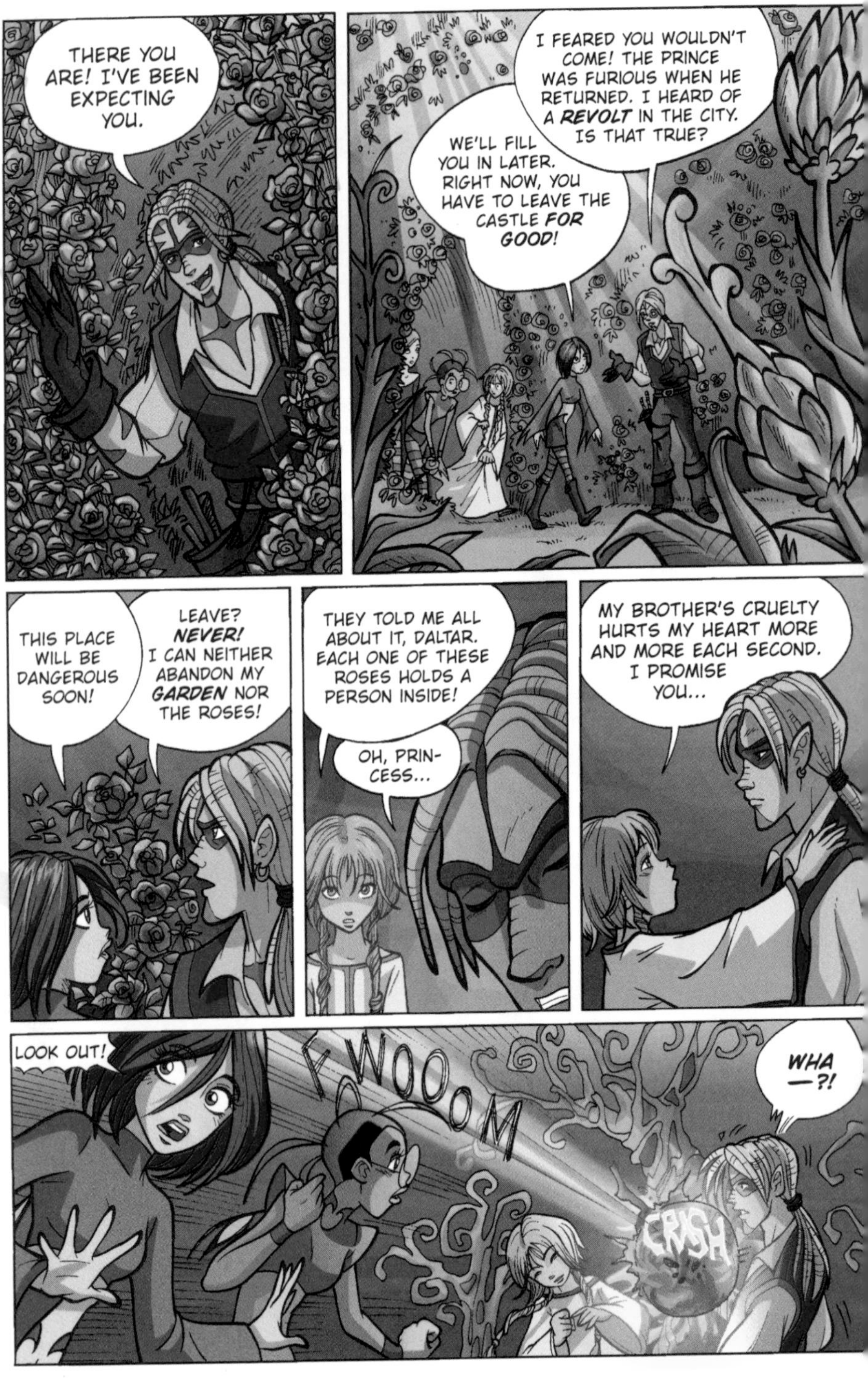
THERE YOU ARE! I'VE BEEN EXPECTING YOU.
I FEARED YOU WOULDN'T COME! THE PRINCE WAS FURIOUS WHEN HE RETURNED. I HEARD OF A REVOLT IN THE CITY. IS THAT TRUE?
WE'LL FILL YOU IN LATER. RIGHT NOW, YOU HAVE TO LEAVE THE CASTLE FOR GOOD!
THIS PLACE WILL BE DANGEROUS SOON!
LEAVE? NEVER! I CAN NEITHER ABANDON MY GARDEN NOR THE ROSES!
THEY TOLD ME ALL ABOUT IT, DALTAR. EACH ONE OF THESE ROSES HOLDS A PERSON INSIDE!
OH, PRIN-CESS...
MY BROTHER'S CRUELTY HURTS MY HEART MORE AND MORE EACH SECOND. I PROMISE YOU...
LOOK OUT!
FWOOOM
WHA—?!
CRASH

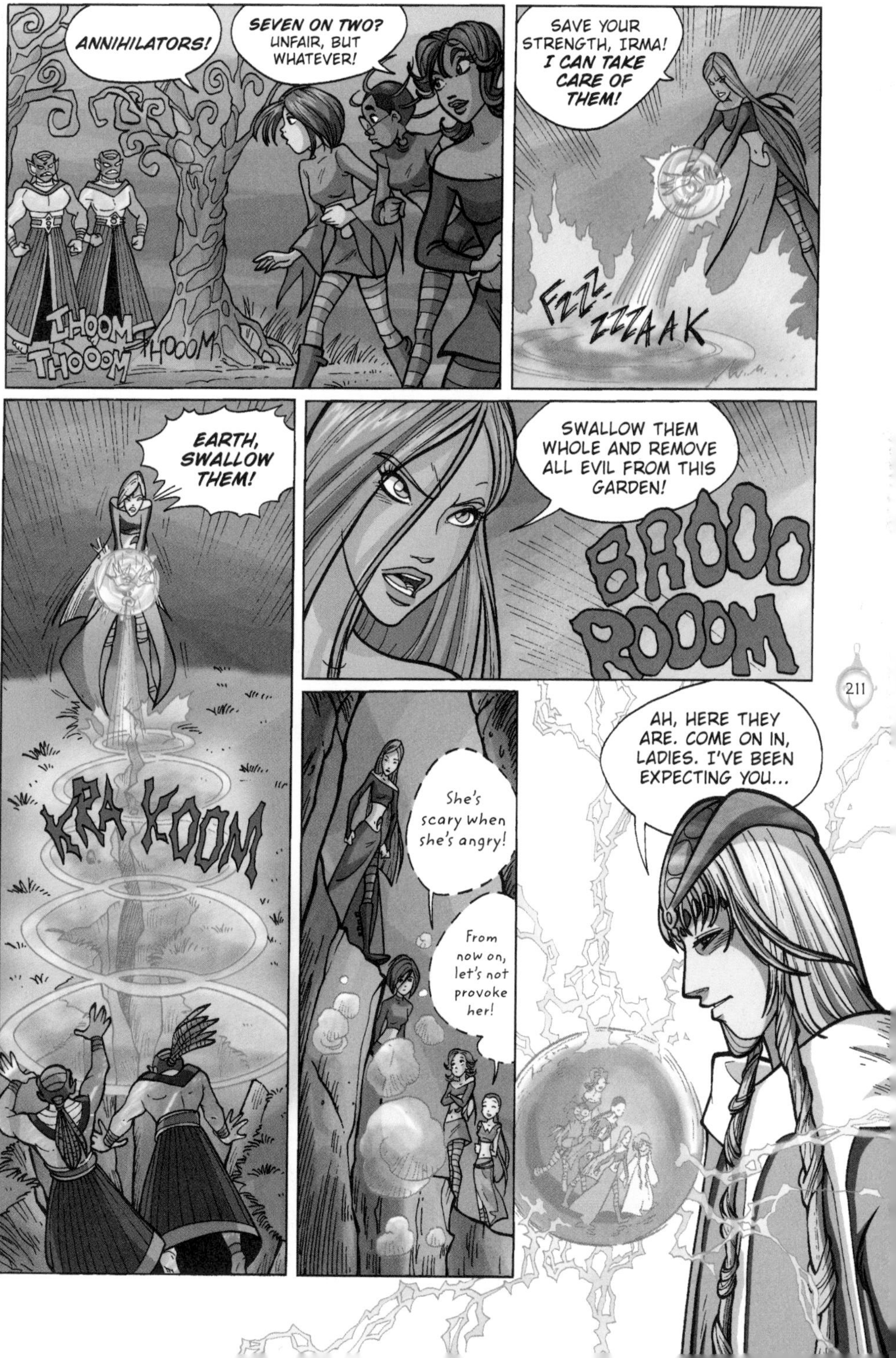
ANNIHILATORS!
SEVEN ON TWO? UNFAIR, BUT WHATEVER!
THOOM THOOOM THOOOM
SAVE YOUR STRENGTH, IRMA! I CAN TAKE CARE OF THEM!
FZZZ-ZZZAAK
EARTH, SWALLOW THEM!
KRA KOOM
SWALLOW THEM WHOLE AND REMOVE ALL EVIL FROM THIS GARDEN!
BROOO ROOOM
She's scary when she's angry!
From now on, let's not provoke her!
AH, HERE THEY ARE. COME ON IN, LADIES. I'VE BEEN EXPECTING YOU...

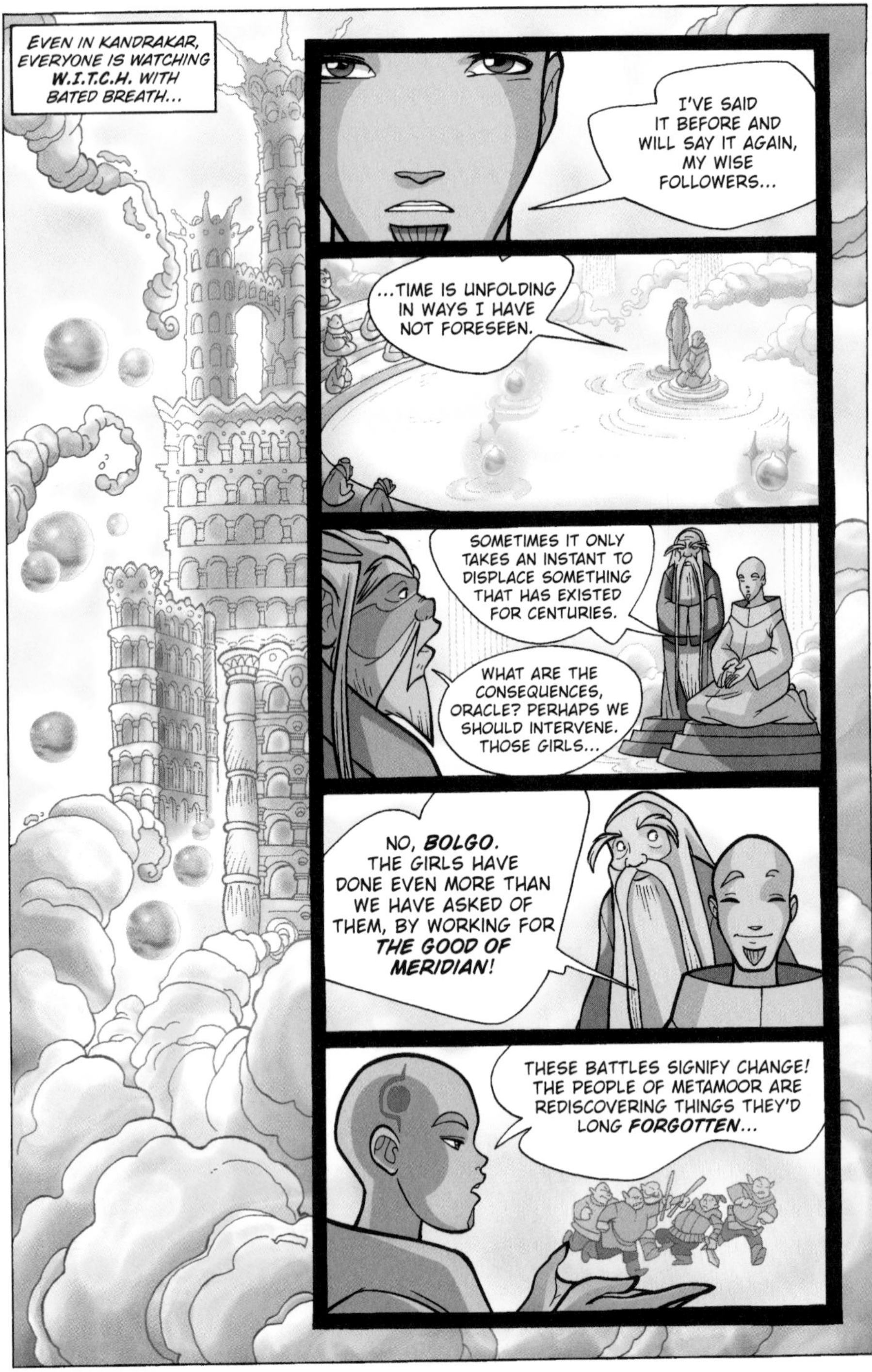
EVEN IN KANDRAKAR, EVERYONE IS WATCHING W.I.T.C.H. WITH BATED BREATH...
I'VE SAID IT BEFORE AND WILL SAY IT AGAIN, MY WISE FOLLOWERS...
...TIME IS UNFOLDING IN WAYS I HAVE NOT FORESEEN.
SOMETIMES IT ONLY TAKES AN INSTANT TO DISPLACE SOMETHING THAT HAS EXISTED FOR CENTURIES.
WHAT ARE THE CONSEQUENCES, ORACLE? PERHAPS WE SHOULD INTERVENE. THOSE GIRLS...
NO, BOLGO. THE GIRLS HAVE DONE EVEN MORE THAN WE HAVE ASKED OF THEM, BY WORKING FOR THE GOOD OF MERIDIAN!
THESE BATTLES SIGNIFY CHANGE! THE PEOPLE OF METAMOOR ARE REDISCOVERING THINGS THEY'D LONG FORGOTTEN...

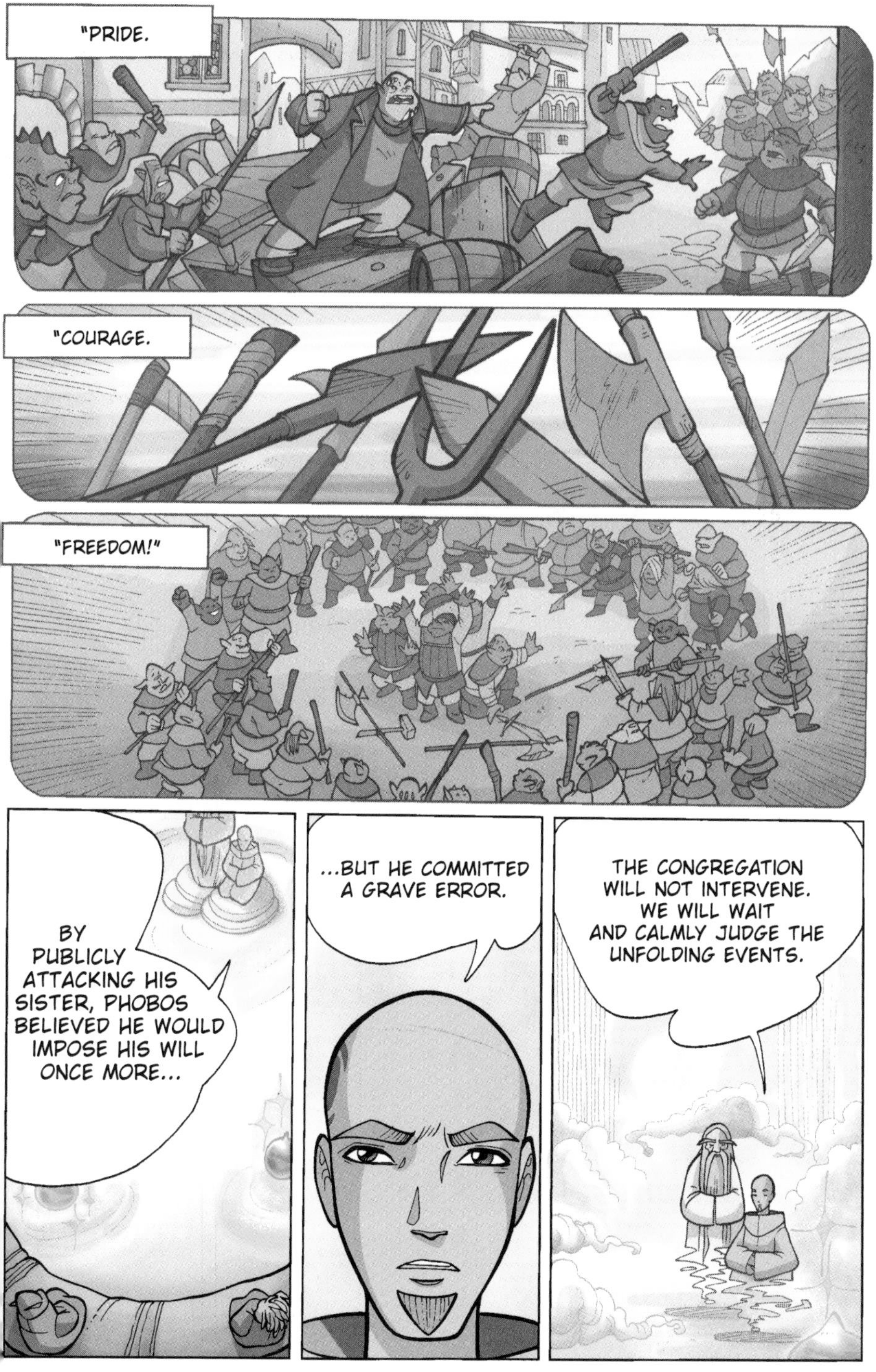
"PRIDE.
"COURAGE.
"FREEDOM!"
BY PUBLICLY ATTACKING HIS SISTER, PHOBOS BELIEVED HE WOULD IMPOSE HIS WILL ONCE MORE...
...BUT HE COMMITTED A GRAVE ERROR.
THE CONGREGATION WILL NOT INTERVENE. WE WILL WAIT AND CALMLY JUDGE THE UNFOLDING EVENTS.

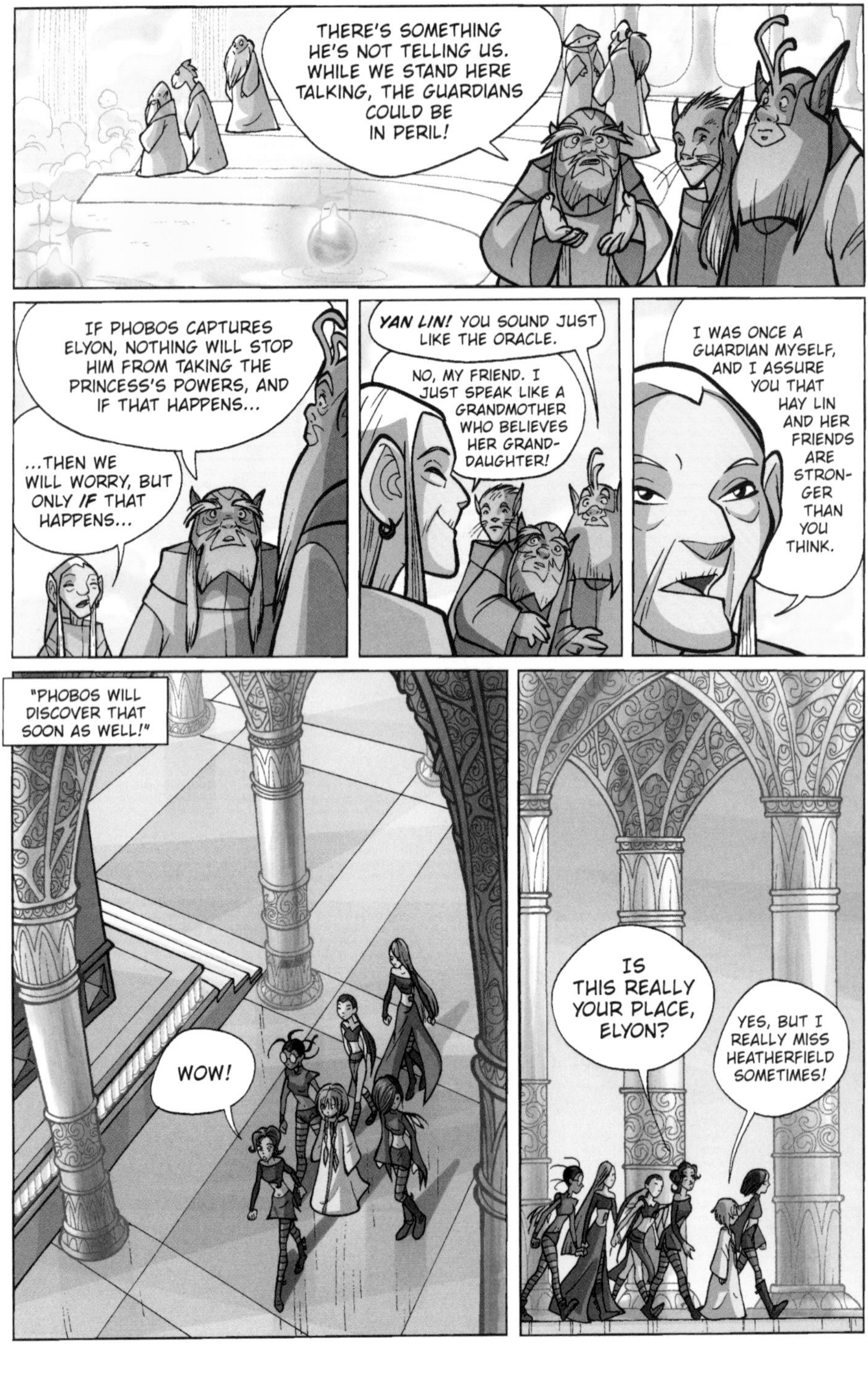
THERE'S SOMETHING HE'S NOT TELLING US. WHILE WE STAND HERE TALKING, THE GUARDIANS COULD BE IN PERIL!
IF PHOBOS CAPTURES ELYON, NOTHING WILL STOP HIM FROM TAKING THE PRINCESS'S POWERS, AND IF THAT HAPPENS...
...THEN WE WILL WORRY, BUT ONLY *IF* THAT HAPPENS...
YAN LIN! YOU SOUND JUST LIKE THE ORACLE.
NO, MY FRIEND. I JUST SPEAK LIKE A GRANDMOTHER WHO BELIEVES HER GRAND-DAUGHTER!
I WAS ONCE A GUARDIAN MYSELF, AND I ASSURE YOU THAT HAY LIN AND HER FRIENDS ARE STRONGER THAN YOU THINK.
"PHOBOS WILL DISCOVER THAT SOON AS WELL!"
WOW!
IS THIS REALLY YOUR PLACE, ELYON?
YES, BUT I REALLY MISS HEATHERFIELD SOMETIMES!

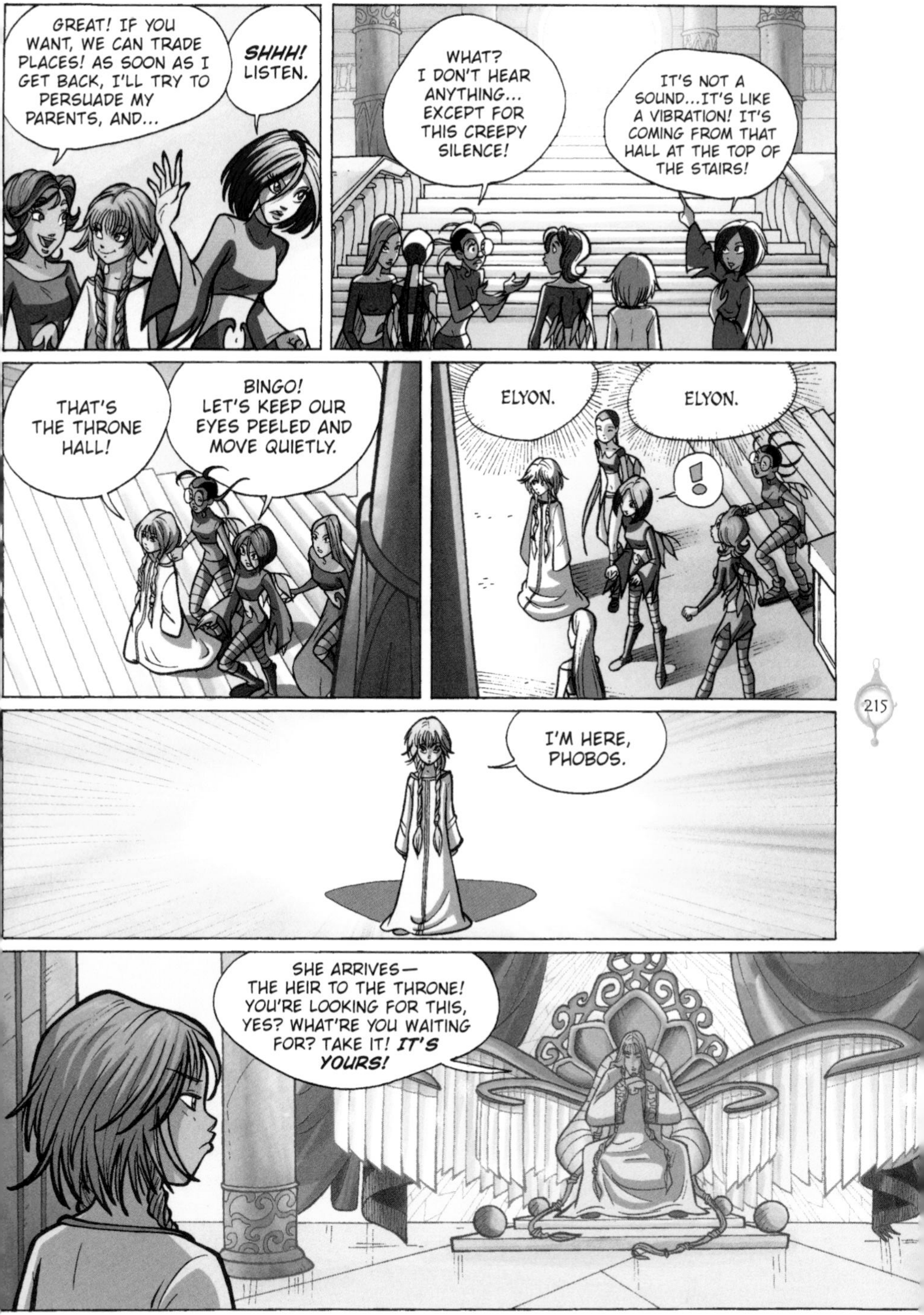
GREAT! IF YOU WANT, WE CAN TRADE PLACES! AS SOON AS I GET BACK, I'LL TRY TO PERSUADE MY PARENTS, AND...
SHHH! LISTEN.
WHAT? I DON'T HEAR ANYTHING... EXCEPT FOR THIS CREEPY SILENCE!
IT'S NOT A SOUND...IT'S LIKE A VIBRATION! IT'S COMING FROM THAT HALL AT THE TOP OF THE STAIRS!
THAT'S THE THRONE HALL!
BINGO! LET'S KEEP OUR EYES PEELED AND MOVE QUIETLY.
ELYON.
ELYON.
!
I'M HERE, PHOBOS.
SHE ARRIVES— THE HEIR TO THE THRONE! YOU'RE LOOKING FOR THIS, YES? WHAT'RE YOU WAITING FOR? TAKE IT! IT'S YOURS!

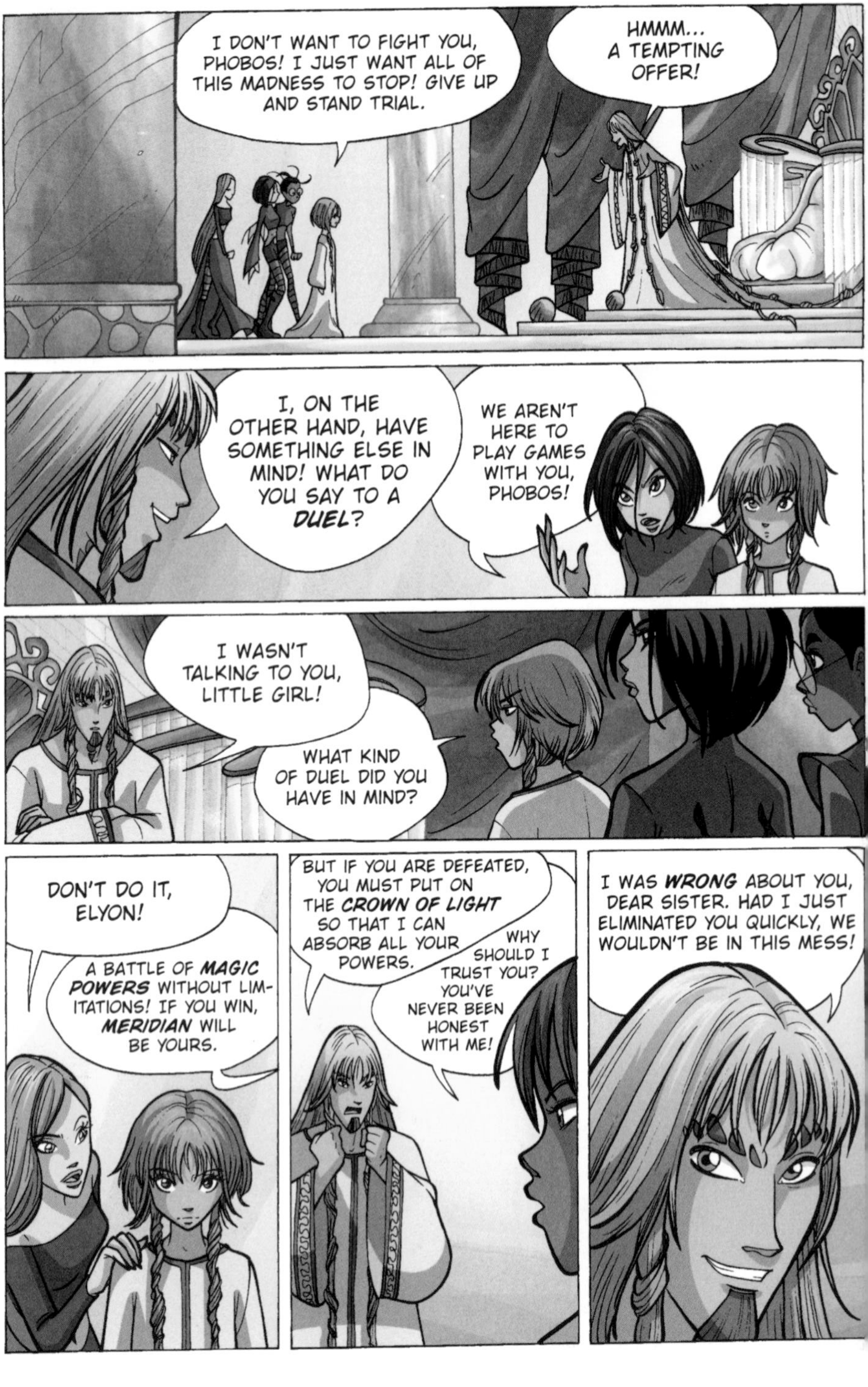

I DON'T WANT TO FIGHT YOU, PHOBOS! I JUST WANT ALL OF THIS MADNESS TO STOP! GIVE UP AND STAND TRIAL.
HMMM... A TEMPTING OFFER!
I, ON THE OTHER HAND, HAVE SOMETHING ELSE IN MIND! WHAT DO YOU SAY TO A DUEL?
WE AREN'T HERE TO PLAY GAMES WITH YOU, PHOBOS!
I WASN'T TALKING TO YOU, LITTLE GIRL!
WHAT KIND OF DUEL DID YOU HAVE IN MIND?
DON'T DO IT, ELYON!
A BATTLE OF MAGIC POWERS WITHOUT LIMITATIONS! IF YOU WIN, MERIDIAN WILL BE YOURS.
BUT IF YOU ARE DEFEATED, YOU MUST PUT ON THE CROWN OF LIGHT SO THAT I CAN ABSORB ALL YOUR POWERS.
WHY SHOULD I TRUST YOU? YOU'VE NEVER BEEN HONEST WITH ME!
I WAS WRONG ABOUT YOU, DEAR SISTER. HAD I JUST ELIMINATED YOU QUICKLY, WE WOULDN'T BE IN THIS MESS!

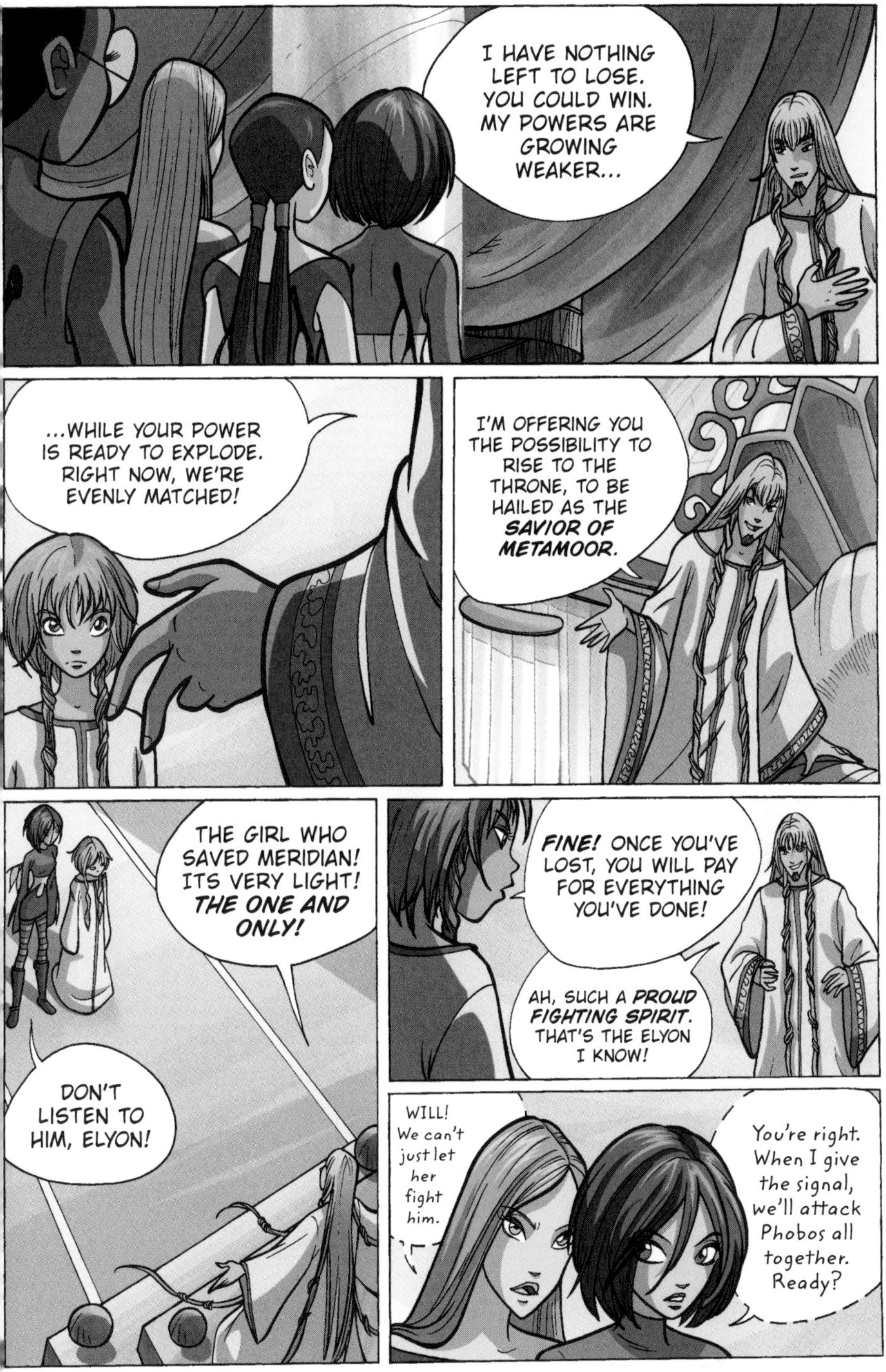
I HAVE NOTHING LEFT TO LOSE. YOU COULD WIN. MY POWERS ARE GROWING WEAKER...
...WHILE YOUR POWER IS READY TO EXPLODE. RIGHT NOW, WE'RE EVENLY MATCHED!
I'M OFFERING YOU THE POSSIBILITY TO RISE TO THE THRONE, TO BE HAILED AS THE ***SAVIOR OF METAMOOR.***
THE GIRL WHO SAVED MERIDIAN! ITS VERY LIGHT! ***THE ONE AND ONLY!***
DON'T LISTEN TO HIM, ELYON!
FINE! ONCE YOU'VE LOST, YOU WILL PAY FOR EVERYTHING YOU'VE DONE!
AH, SUCH A ***PROUD FIGHTING SPIRIT.*** THAT'S THE ELYON I KNOW!
WILL! We can't just let her fight him.
You're right. When I give the signal, we'll attack Phobos all together. Ready?

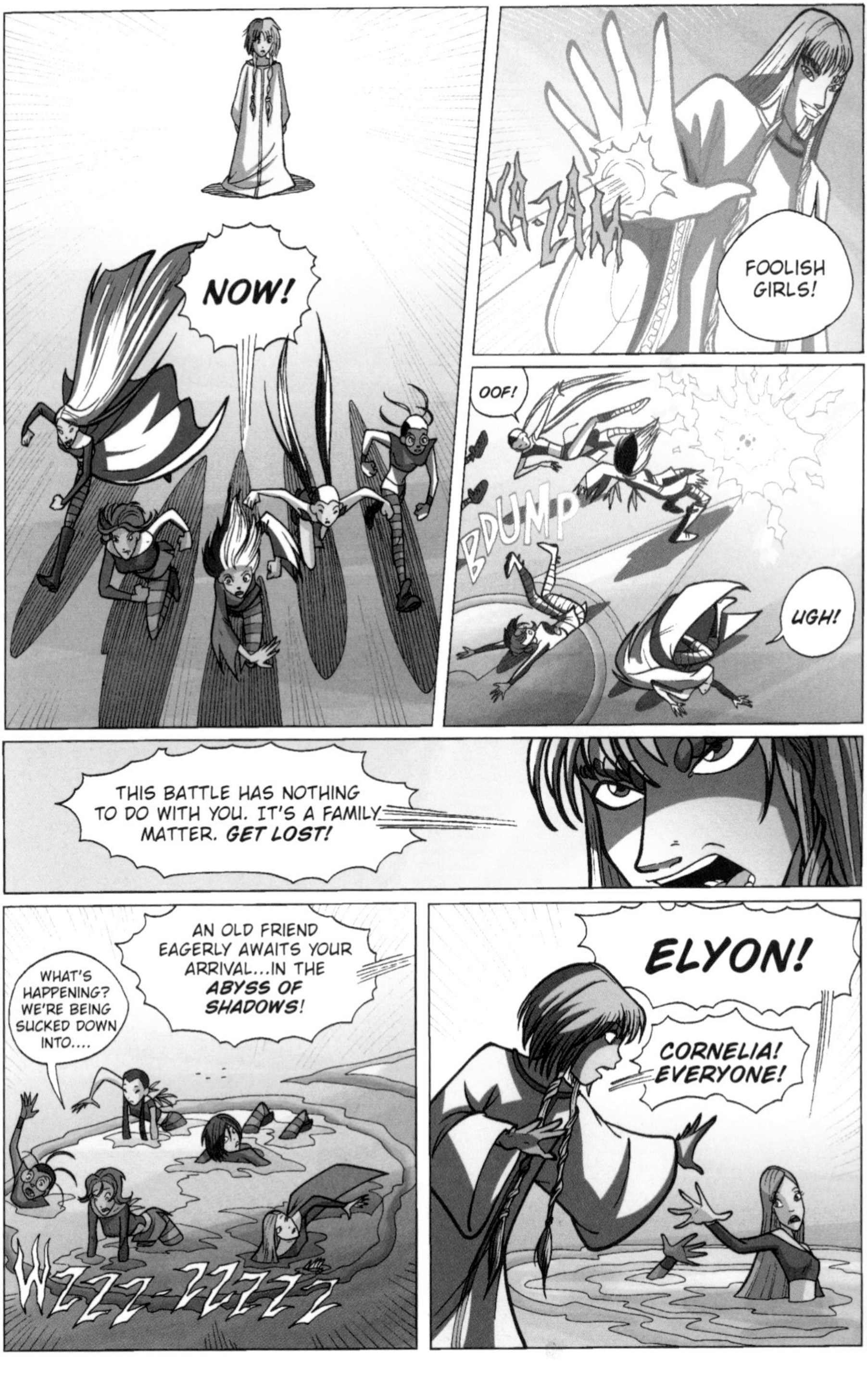
NOW!
KA-ZAM
FOOLISH GIRLS!
OOF!
BDUMP
UGH!
THIS BATTLE HAS NOTHING TO DO WITH YOU. IT'S A FAMILY MATTER. GET LOST!
AN OLD FRIEND EAGERLY AWAITS YOUR ARRIVAL...IN THE ABYSS OF SHADOWS!
WHAT'S HAPPENING? WE'RE BEING SUCKED DOWN INTO....
WZZZ-ZZZZZ
ELYON!
CORNELIA! EVERYONE!

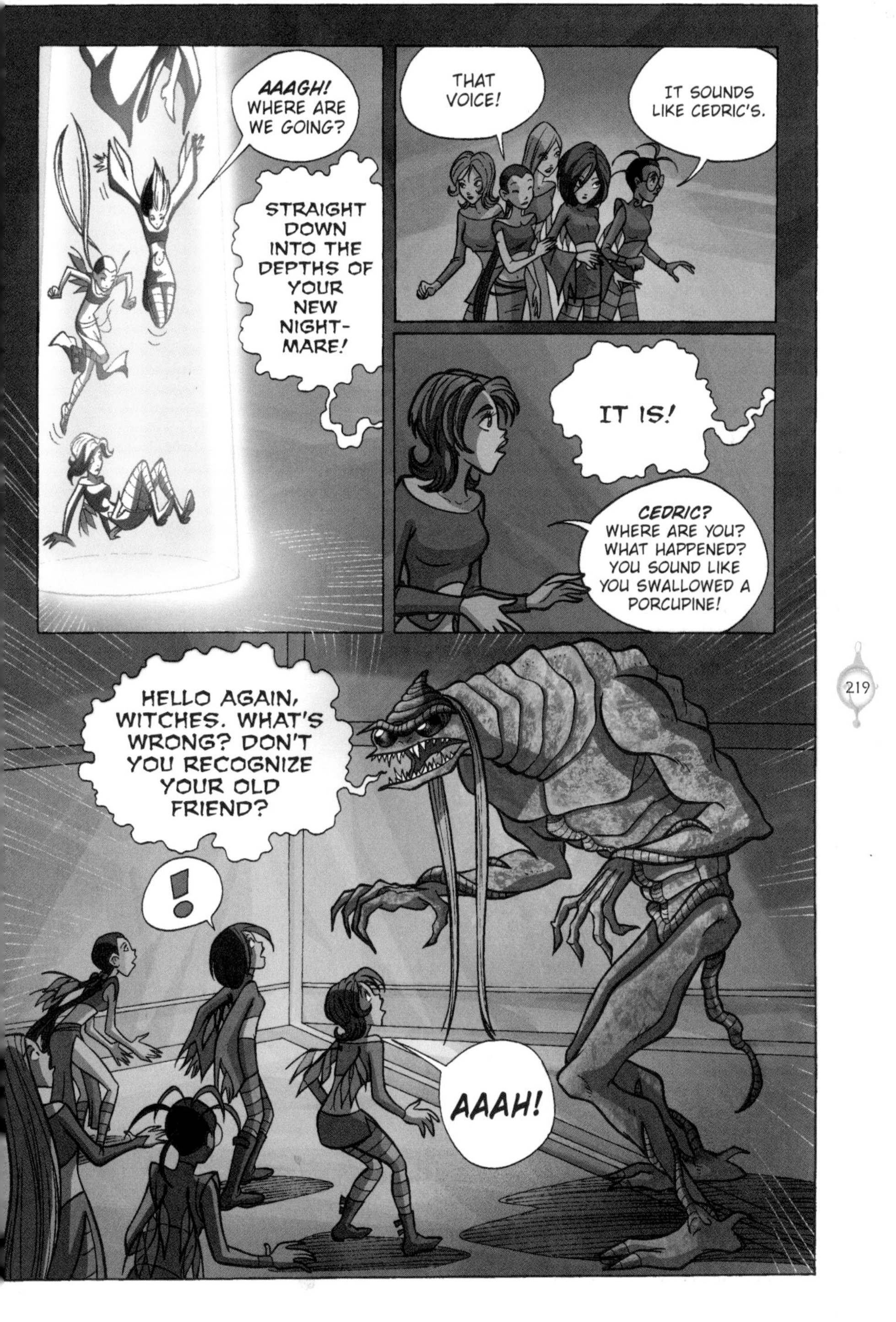
AAAGH! WHERE ARE WE GOING?
STRAIGHT DOWN INTO THE DEPTHS OF YOUR NEW NIGHT-MARE!
THAT VOICE!
IT SOUNDS LIKE CEDRIC'S.
IT IS!
CEDRIC? WHERE ARE YOU? WHAT HAPPENED? YOU SOUND LIKE YOU SWALLOWED A PORCUPINE!
HELLO AGAIN, WITCHES. WHAT'S WRONG? DON'T YOU RECOGNIZE YOUR OLD FRIEND?
!
AAAH!

"That which was born united, return to being part of the whole!"

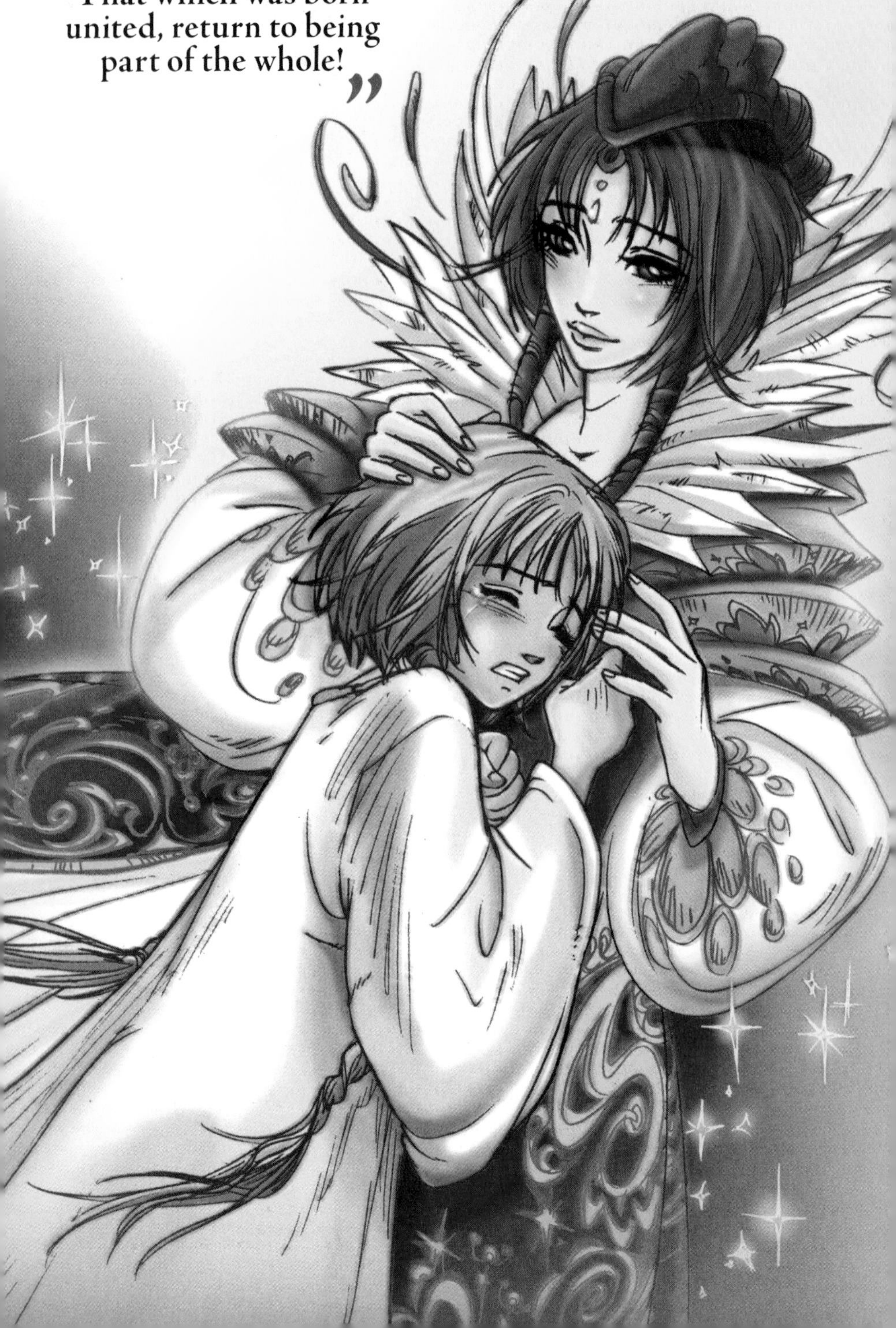

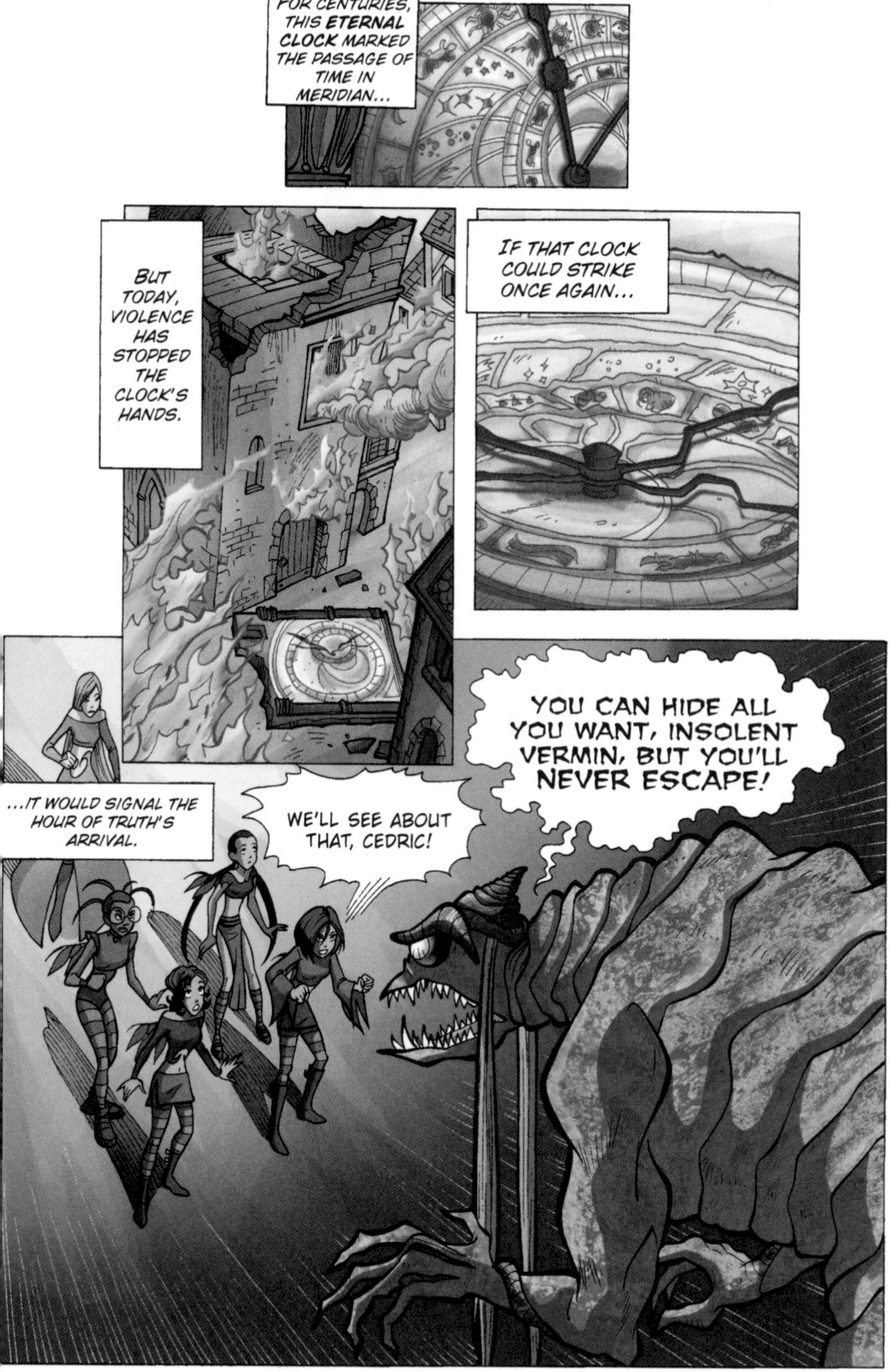

FOR CENTURIES, THIS **ETERNAL CLOCK** MARKED THE PASSAGE OF TIME IN MERIDIAN...
BUT TODAY, VIOLENCE HAS STOPPED THE CLOCK'S HANDS.
IF THAT CLOCK COULD STRIKE ONCE AGAIN...
...IT WOULD SIGNAL THE HOUR OF TRUTH'S ARRIVAL.
YOU CAN HIDE ALL YOU WANT, INSOLENT VERMIN, BUT YOU'LL **NEVER ESCAPE!**
WE'LL SEE ABOUT THAT, CEDRIC!

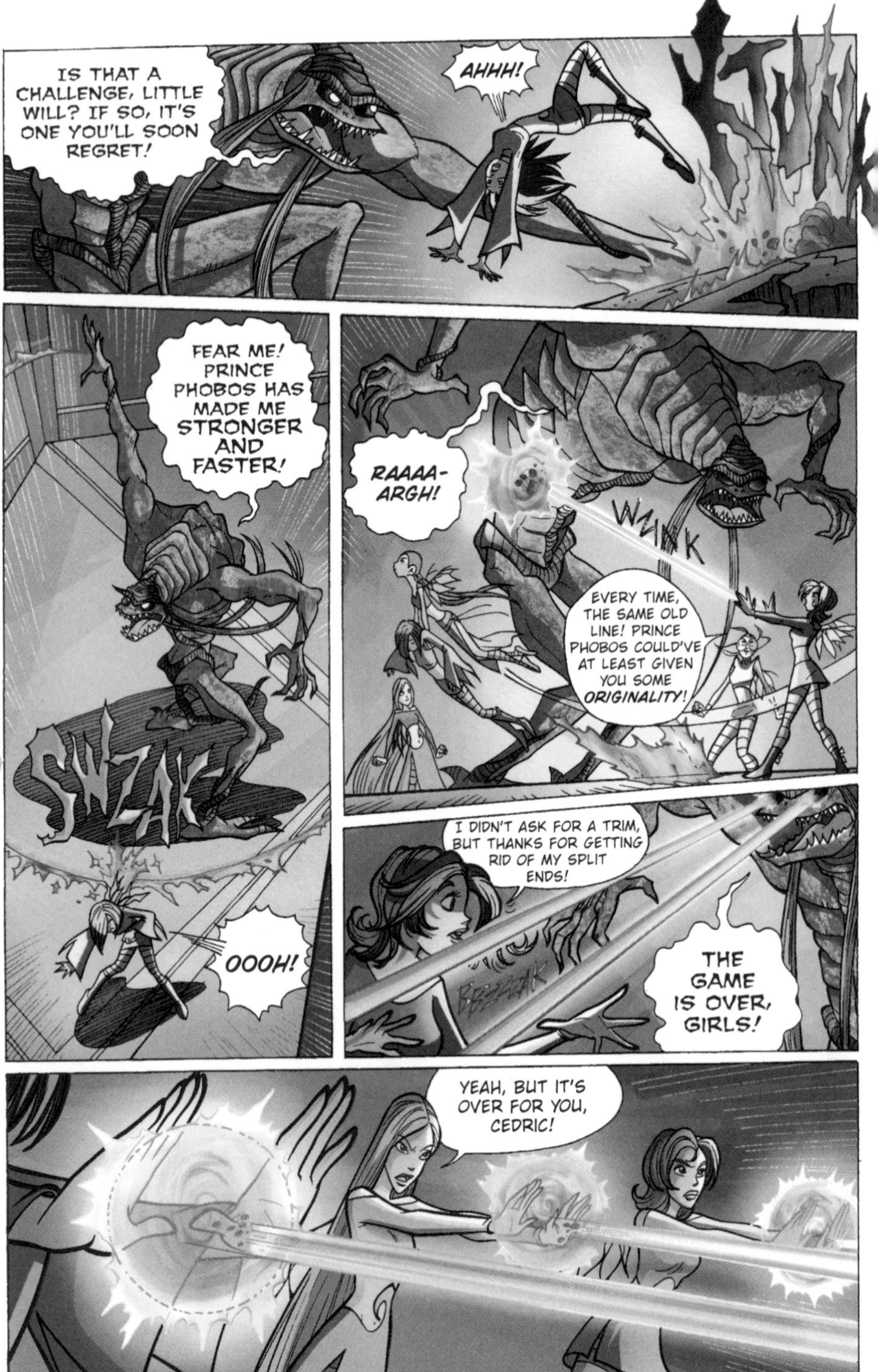
IS THAT A CHALLENGE, LITTLE WILL? IF SO, IT'S ONE YOU'LL SOON REGRET!
AHHH!
FEAR ME! PRINCE PHOBOS HAS MADE ME STRONGER AND FASTER!
SWZAK
OOOH!
RAAAA-ARGH!
WUNK
EVERY TIME, THE SAME OLD LINE! PRINCE PHOBOS COULD'VE AT LEAST GIVEN YOU SOME ORIGINALITY!
I DIDN'T ASK FOR A TRIM, BUT THANKS FOR GETTING RID OF MY SPLIT ENDS!
THE GAME IS OVER, GIRLS!
YEAH, BUT IT'S OVER FOR YOU, CEDRIC!

222

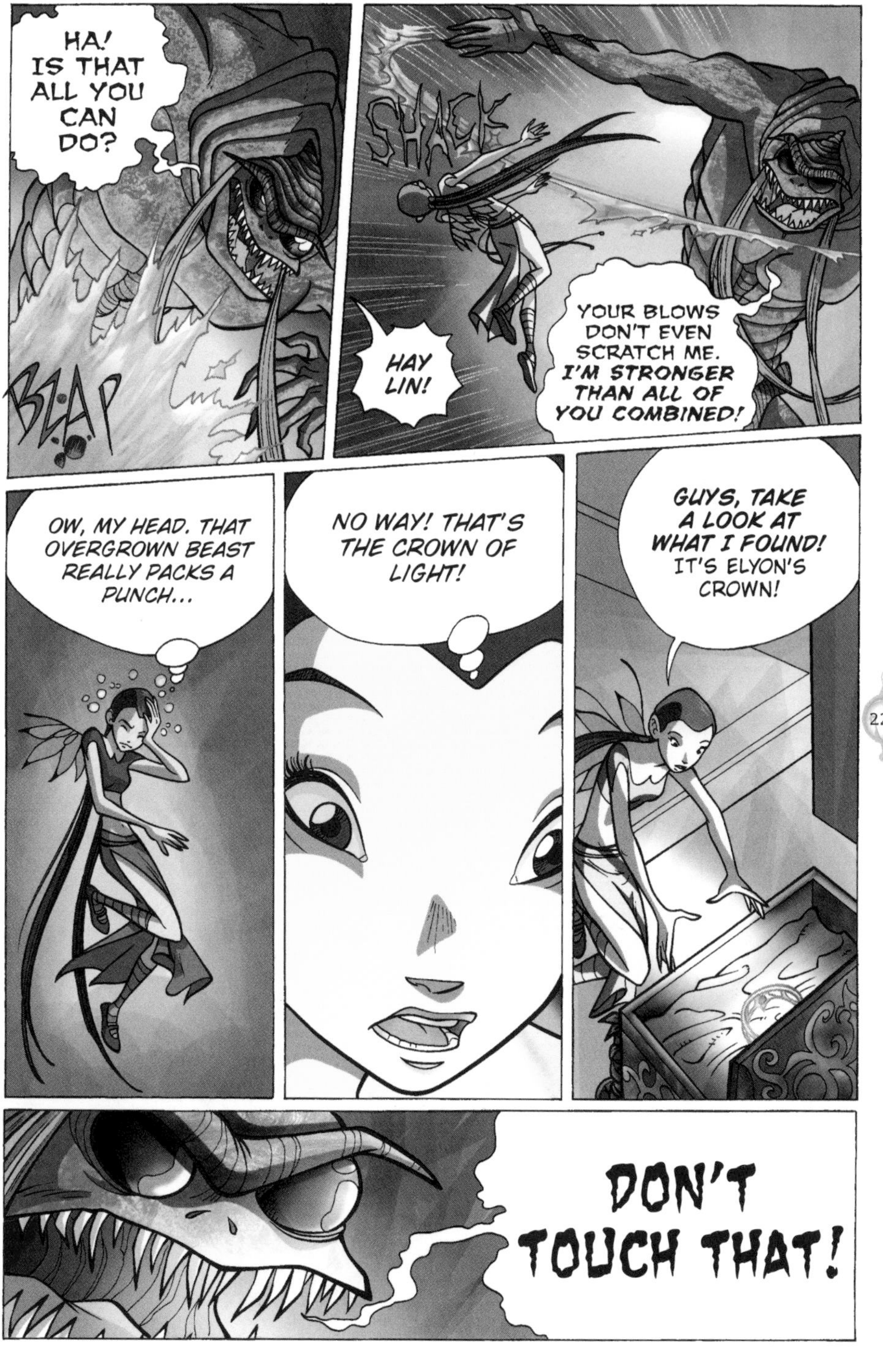
HA! IS THAT ALL YOU CAN DO?
BZZAP
SHACK
HAY LIN!
YOUR BLOWS DON'T EVEN SCRATCH ME. I'M STRONGER THAN ALL OF YOU COMBINED!
OW, MY HEAD. THAT OVERGROWN BEAST REALLY PACKS A PUNCH...
NO WAY! THAT'S THE CROWN OF LIGHT!
GUYS, TAKE A LOOK AT WHAT I FOUND! IT'S ELYON'S CROWN!
DON'T TOUCH THAT!

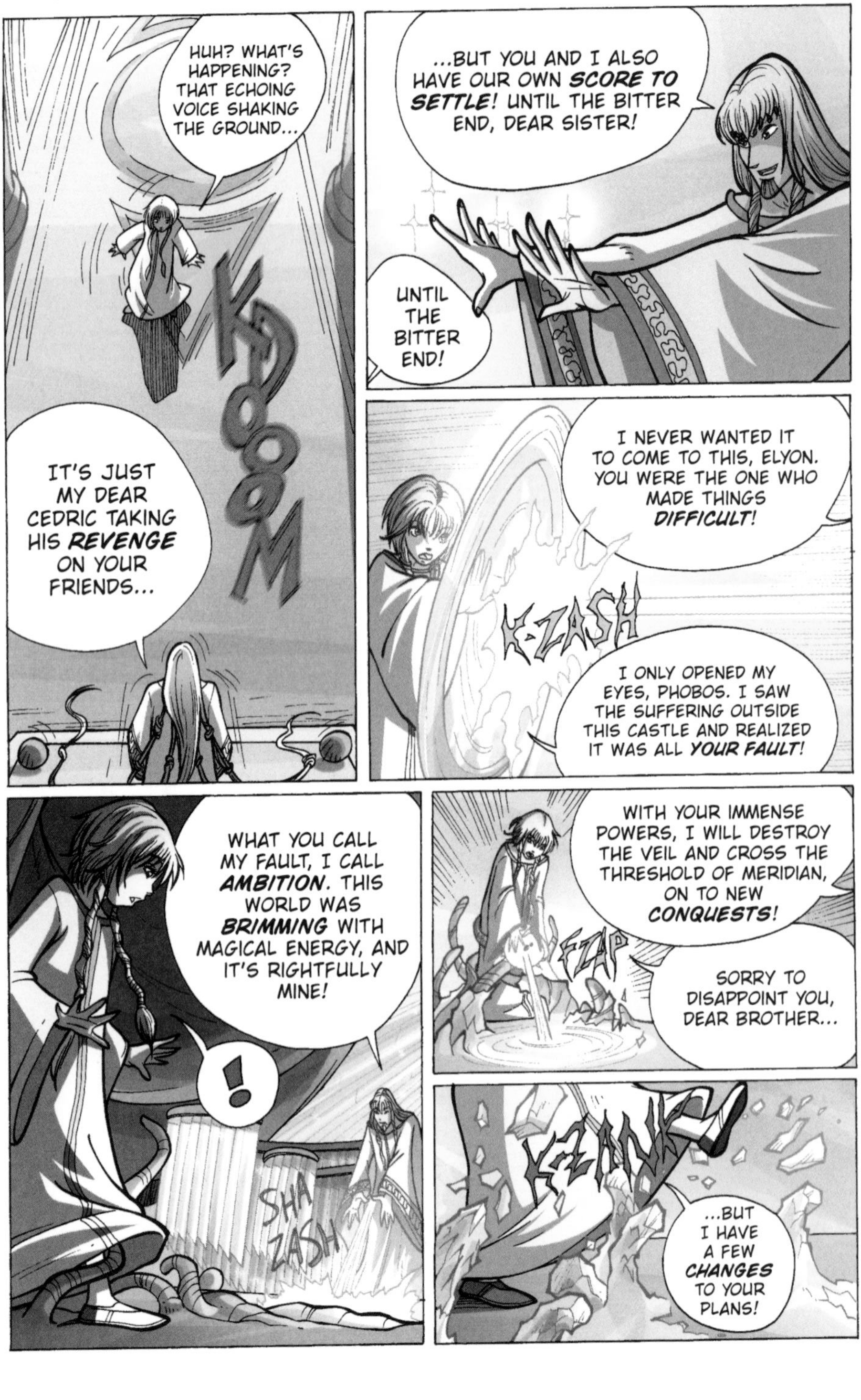
HUH? WHAT'S HAPPENING? THAT ECHOING VOICE SHAKING THE GROUND...
KADOOOOM
IT'S JUST MY DEAR CEDRIC TAKING HIS REVENGE ON YOUR FRIENDS...
...BUT YOU AND I ALSO HAVE OUR OWN SCORE TO SETTLE! UNTIL THE BITTER END, DEAR SISTER!
UNTIL THE BITTER END!
I NEVER WANTED IT TO COME TO THIS, ELYON. YOU WERE THE ONE WHO MADE THINGS DIFFICULT!
K-ZASH
I ONLY OPENED MY EYES, PHOBOS. I SAW THE SUFFERING OUTSIDE THIS CASTLE AND REALIZED IT WAS ALL YOUR FAULT!
WHAT YOU CALL MY FAULT, I CALL AMBITION. THIS WORLD WAS BRIMMING WITH MAGICAL ENERGY, AND IT'S RIGHTFULLY MINE!
!
SHA ZASH
WITH YOUR IMMENSE POWERS, I WILL DESTROY THE VEIL AND CROSS THE THRESHOLD OF MERIDIAN, ON TO NEW CONQUESTS!
FZAP
SORRY TO DISAPPOINT YOU, DEAR BROTHER...
K-ZANK
...BUT I HAVE A FEW CHANGES TO YOUR PLANS!

IT'S USELESS TO TRY TO RESIST ME, ELYON! YOU CAN'T ESCAPE YOUR DESTINY!

MY DESTINY IS TO RISE TO THE THRONE OF MERIDIAN. *IT'S MY RIGHT, BUT YOU TRIED TO DEFY ME!*

WRZZASH

VERY FUNNY! SINCE WHEN DO OLDER BROTHERS HAVE TO TAKE ORDERS FROM LITTLE SISTERS?

SINCE NOW!

KAWHRRR

BADOOM

MY GOOD-NESS!

ALBORN! THEY'RE BATTLING IN THE CASTLE!

I CAN HEAR THAT, MY FRIEND! RIGHT NOW, THERE'S *NOTHING* MORE WE CAN DO.

OUR BATTLE WAS TO DEFEAT PHOBOS'S ARMY— AND WE *WON!*

MERIDIAN'S *FUTURE* LIES IN THOSE GIRLS' HANDS!

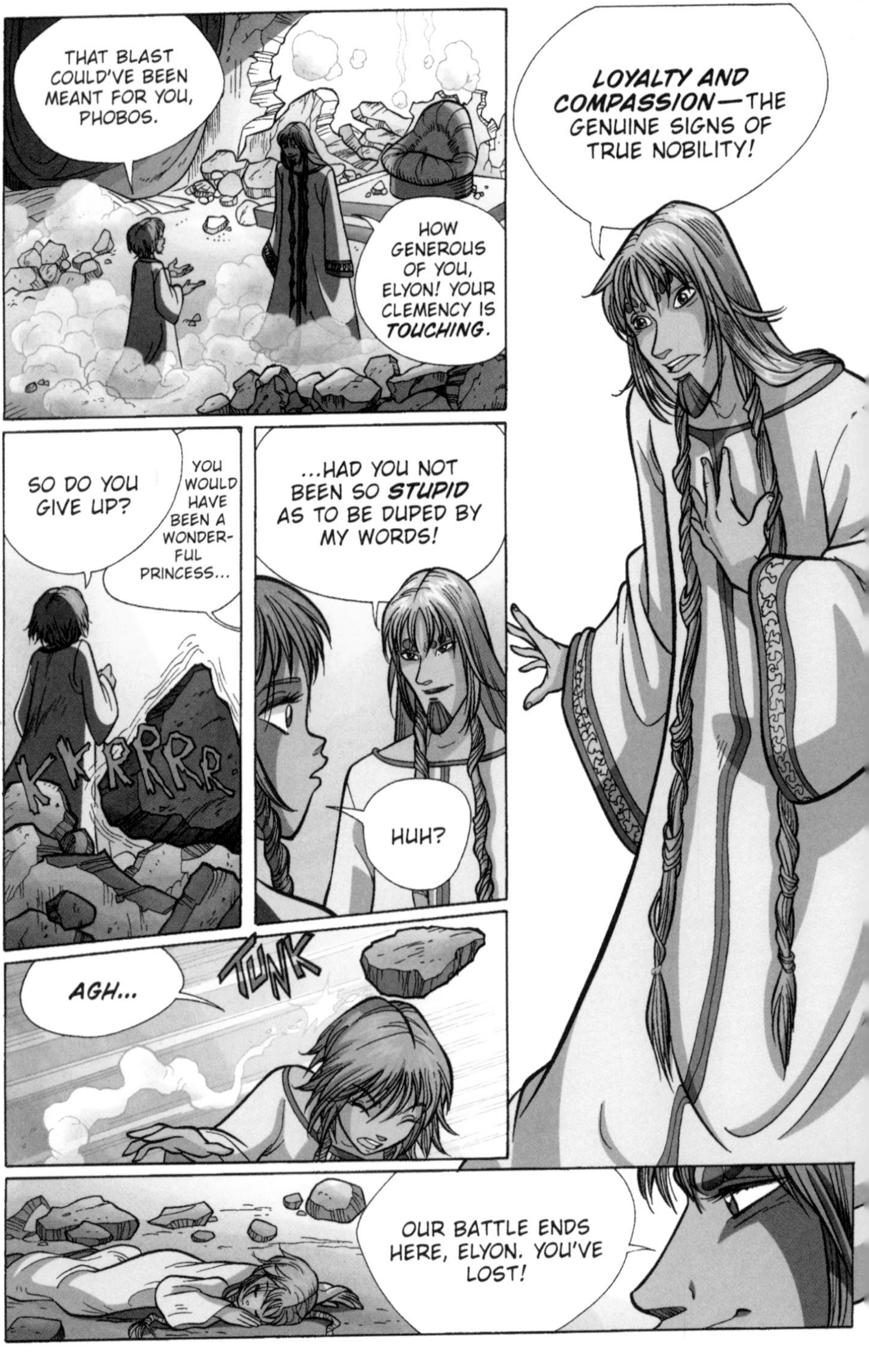
THAT BLAST COULD'VE BEEN MEANT FOR YOU, PHOBOS.
HOW GENEROUS OF YOU, ELYON! YOUR CLEMENCY IS TOUCHING.
LOYALTY AND COMPASSION—THE GENUINE SIGNS OF TRUE NOBILITY!
SO DO YOU GIVE UP?
YOU WOULD HAVE BEEN A WONDERFUL PRINCESS...
KKRRRR
...HAD YOU NOT BEEN SO STUPID AS TO BE DUPED BY MY WORDS!
HUH?
AGH...
TUNK
OUR BATTLE ENDS HERE, ELYON. YOU'VE LOST!

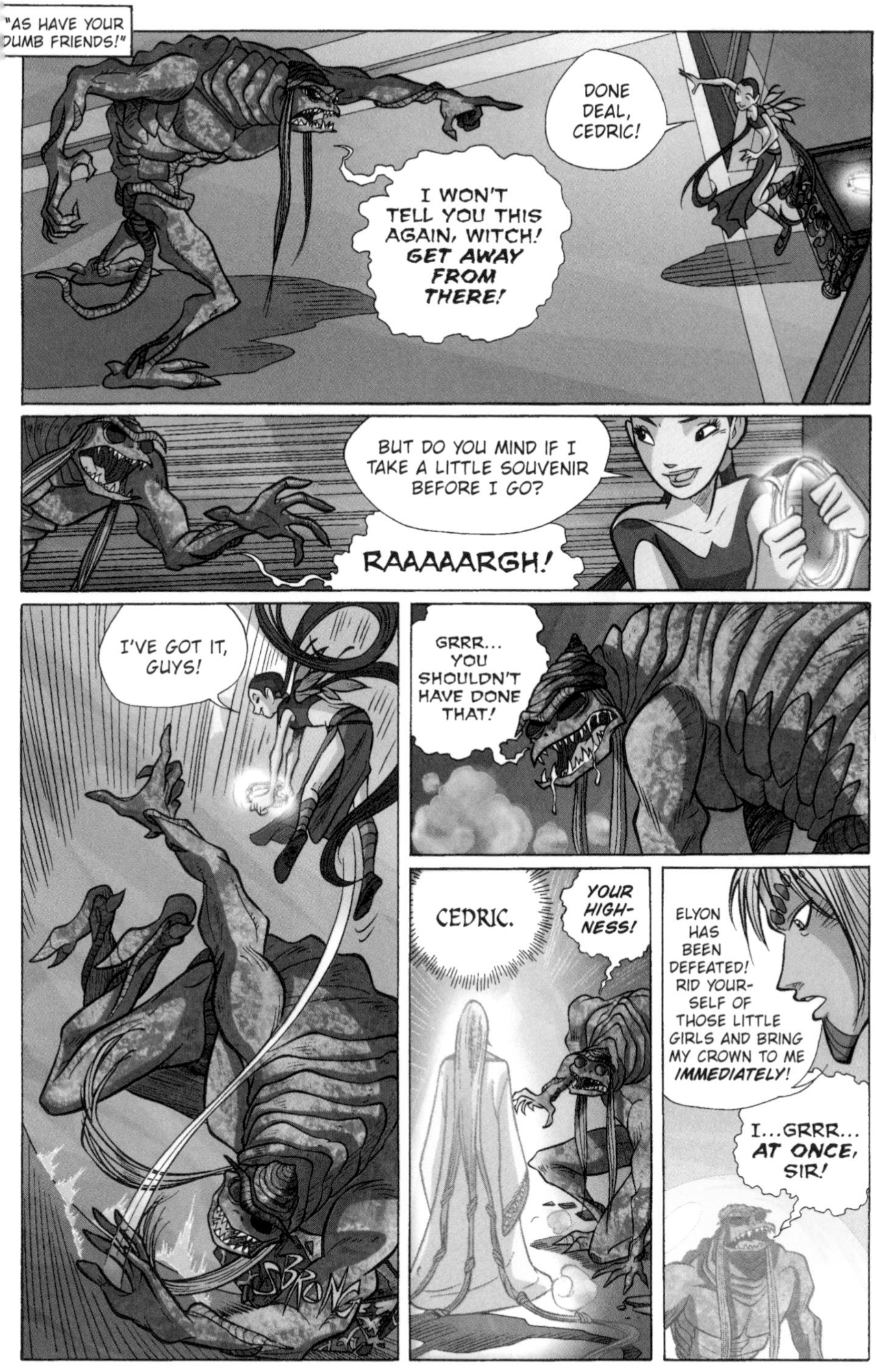
"AS HAVE YOUR DUMB FRIENDS!"
DONE DEAL, CEDRIC!
I WON'T TELL YOU THIS AGAIN, WITCH! GET AWAY FROM THERE!
BUT DO YOU MIND IF I TAKE A LITTLE SOUVENIR BEFORE I GO?
RAAAAARGH!
I'VE GOT IT, GUYS!
SBRONG
GRRR... YOU SHOULDN'T HAVE DONE THAT!
CEDRIC.
YOUR HIGHNESS!
ELYON HAS BEEN DEFEATED! RID YOURSELF OF THOSE LITTLE GIRLS AND BRING MY CROWN TO ME IMMEDIATELY!
I...GRRR... AT ONCE, SIR!

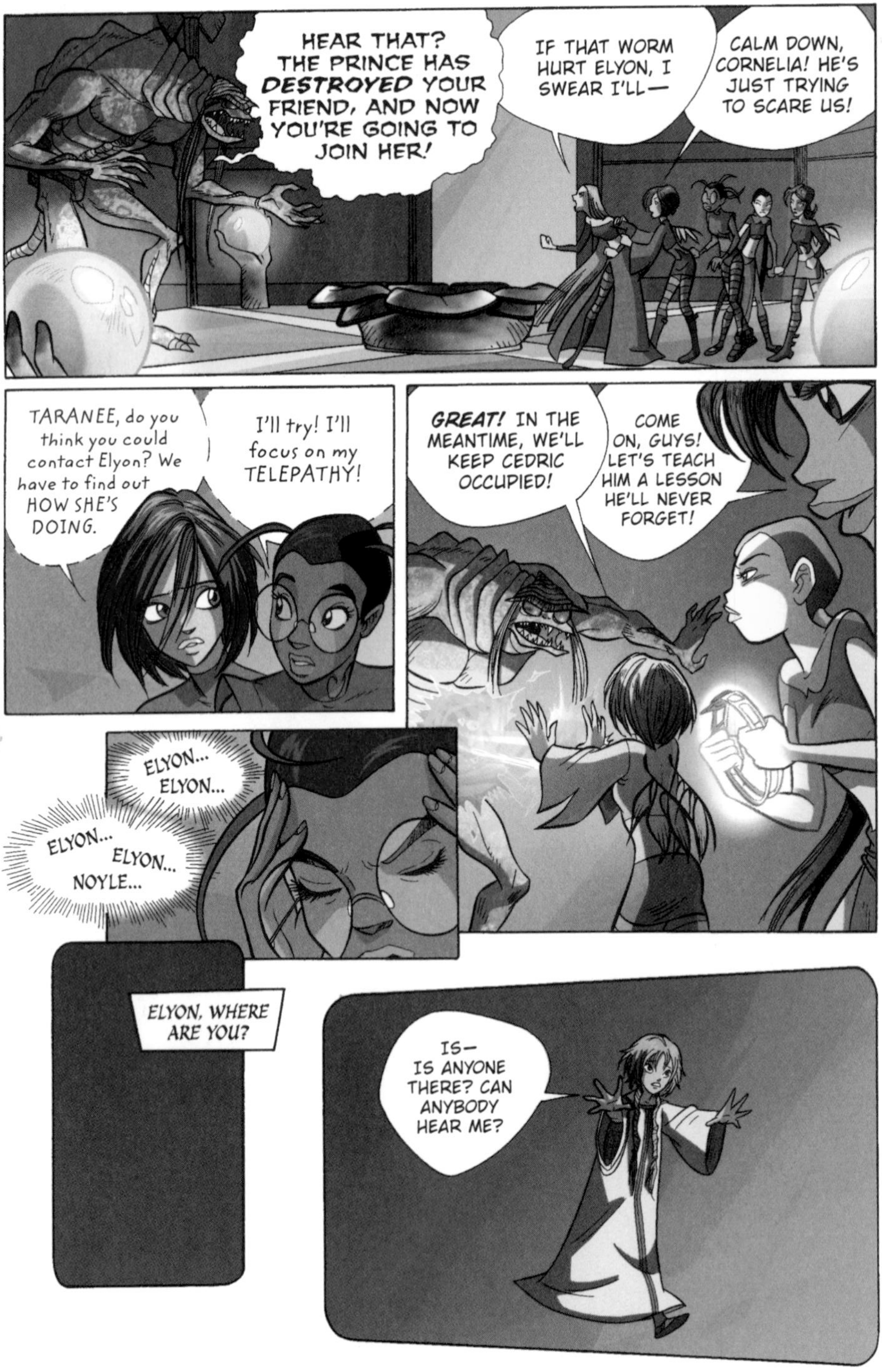
HEAR THAT? THE PRINCE HAS *DESTROYED* YOUR FRIEND, AND NOW YOU'RE GOING TO JOIN HER!
IF THAT WORM HURT ELYON, I SWEAR I'LL—
CALM DOWN, CORNELIA! HE'S JUST TRYING TO SCARE US!
TARANEE, do you think you could contact Elyon? We have to find out HOW SHE'S DOING.
I'll try! I'll focus on my TELEPATHY!
GREAT! IN THE MEANTIME, WE'LL KEEP CEDRIC OCCUPIED!
COME ON, GUYS! LET'S TEACH HIM A LESSON HE'LL NEVER FORGET!
ELYON... ELYON...
ELYON... ELYON... NOYLE...
ELYON, WHERE ARE YOU?
IS— IS ANYONE THERE? CAN ANYBODY HEAR ME?

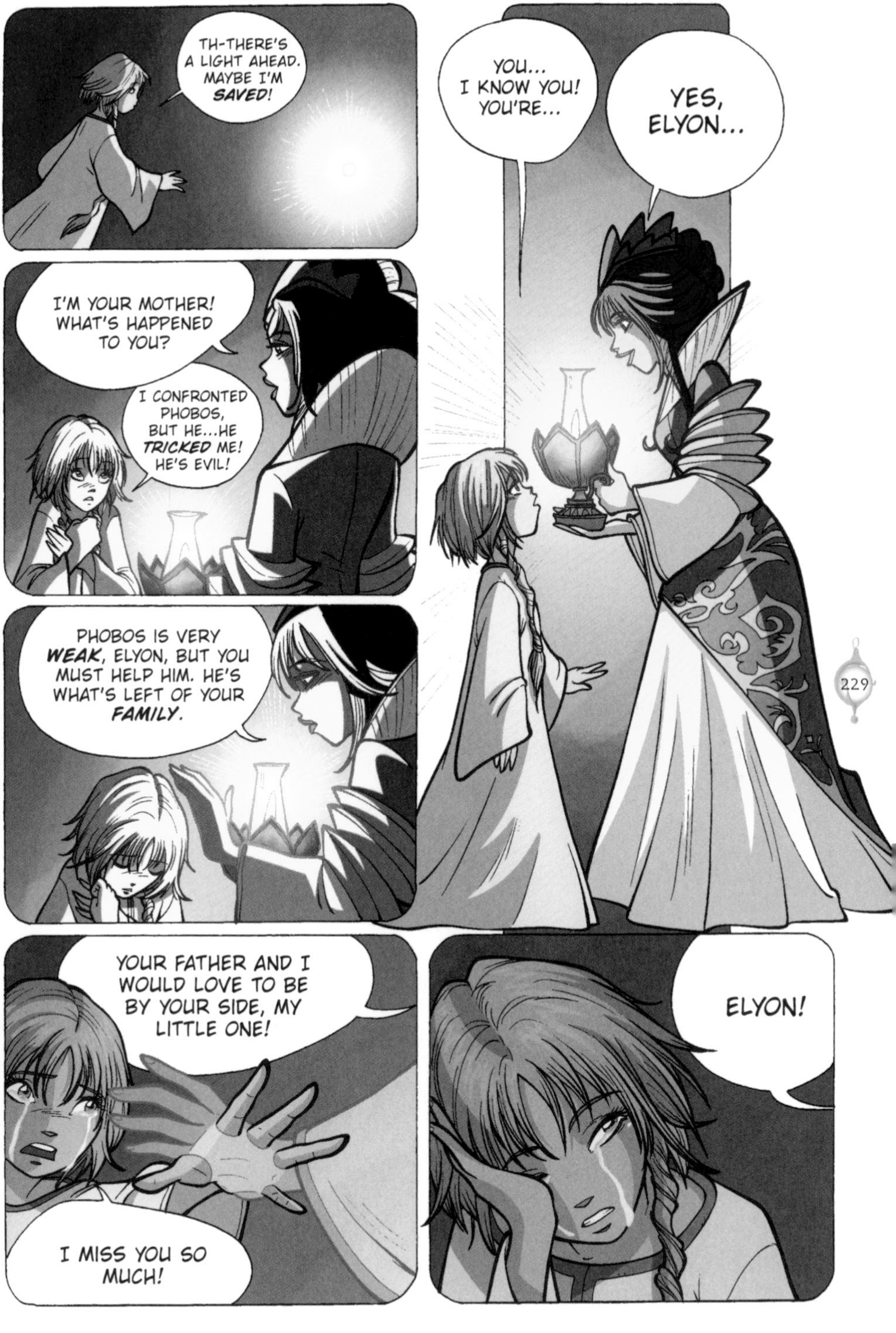
TH-THERE'S A LIGHT AHEAD. MAYBE I'M SAVED!
YOU... I KNOW YOU! YOU'RE...
YES, ELYON...
I'M YOUR MOTHER! WHAT'S HAPPENED TO YOU?
I CONFRONTED PHOBOS, BUT HE...HE TRICKED ME! HE'S EVIL!
PHOBOS IS VERY WEAK, ELYON, BUT YOU MUST HELP HIM. HE'S WHAT'S LEFT OF YOUR FAMILY.
YOUR FATHER AND I WOULD LOVE TO BE BY YOUR SIDE, MY LITTLE ONE!
I MISS YOU SO MUCH!
ELYON!

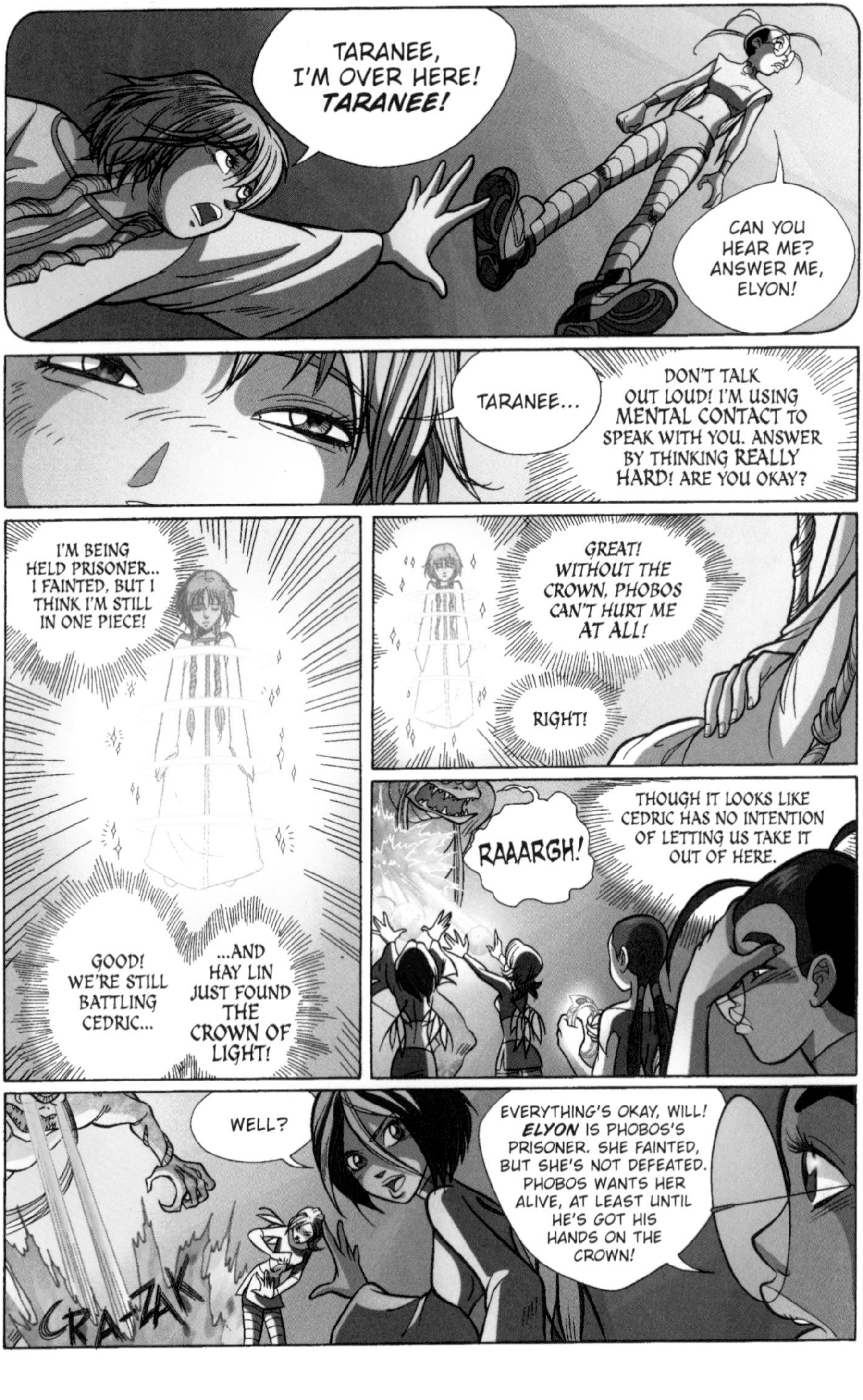
TARANEE, I'M OVER HERE! *TARANEE!*
CAN YOU HEAR ME? ANSWER ME, ELYON!
TARANEE...
DON'T TALK OUT LOUD! I'M USING MENTAL CONTACT TO SPEAK WITH YOU. ANSWER BY THINKING REALLY HARD! ARE YOU OKAY?
I'M BEING HELD PRISONER... I FAINTED, BUT I THINK I'M STILL IN ONE PIECE!
GOOD! WE'RE STILL BATTLING CEDRIC...
...AND HAY LIN JUST FOUND THE CROWN OF LIGHT!
GREAT! WITHOUT THE CROWN, PHOBOS CAN'T HURT ME AT ALL!
RIGHT!
RAAARGH!
THOUGH IT LOOKS LIKE CEDRIC HAS NO INTENTION OF LETTING US TAKE IT OUT OF HERE.
WELL?
EVERYTHING'S OKAY, WILL! *ELYON* IS PHOBOS'S PRISONER. SHE FAINTED, BUT SHE'S NOT DEFEATED. PHOBOS WANTS HER ALIVE, AT LEAST UNTIL HE'S GOT HIS HANDS ON THE CROWN!
CRA-ZAK

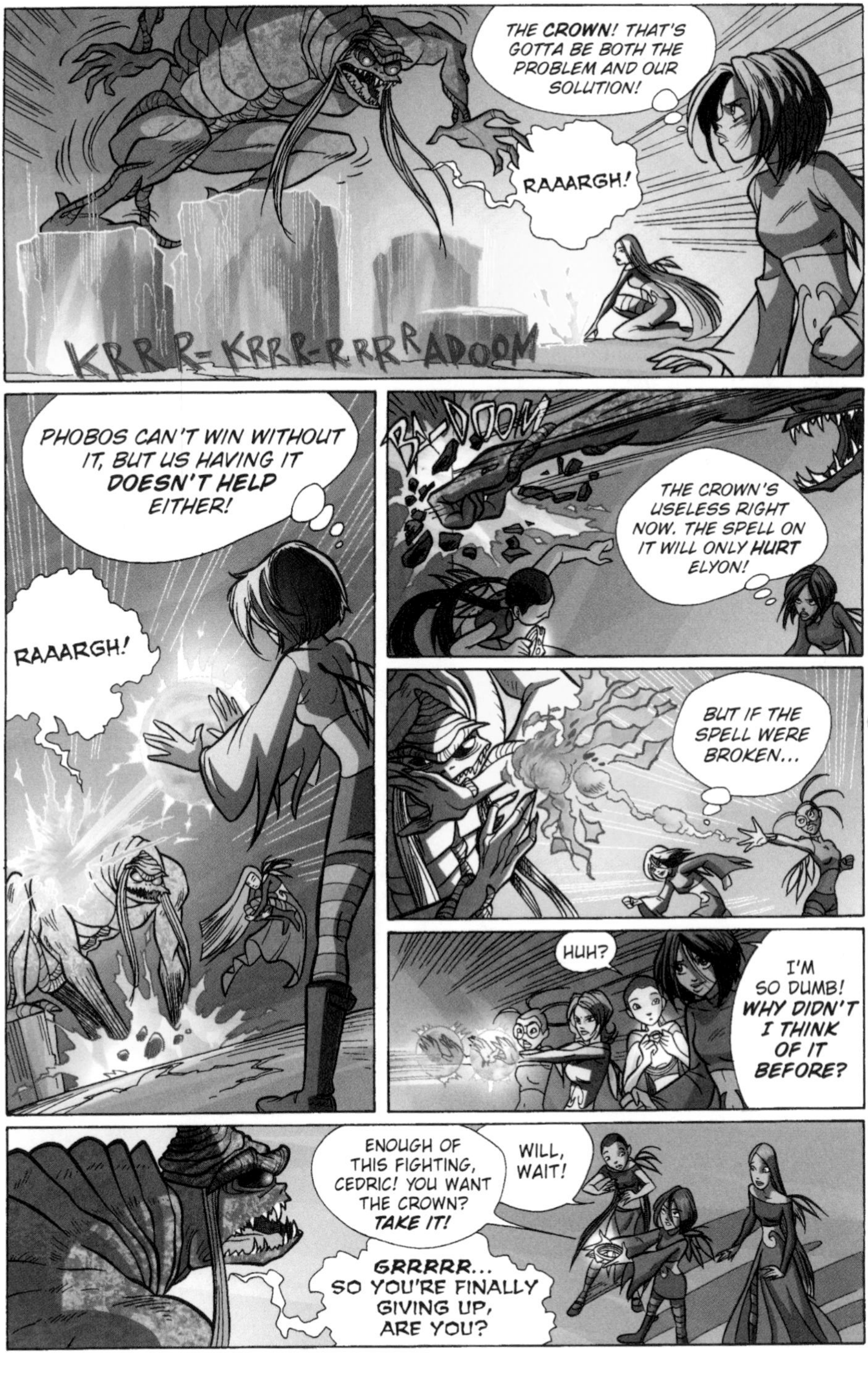
THE CROWN! THAT'S GOTTA BE BOTH THE PROBLEM AND OUR SOLUTION!
RAAARGH!
KRRR-KRRR-RRRRADOOM
PHOBOS CAN'T WIN WITHOUT IT, BUT US HAVING IT DOESN'T HELP EITHER!
RAAARGH!
THE CROWN'S USELESS RIGHT NOW. THE SPELL ON IT WILL ONLY HURT ELYON!
BUT IF THE SPELL WERE BROKEN...
HUH?
I'M SO DUMB! WHY DIDN'T I THINK OF IT BEFORE?
ENOUGH OF THIS FIGHTING, CEDRIC! YOU WANT THE CROWN? TAKE IT!
WILL, WAIT!
GRRRRR... SO YOU'RE FINALLY GIVING UP, ARE YOU?

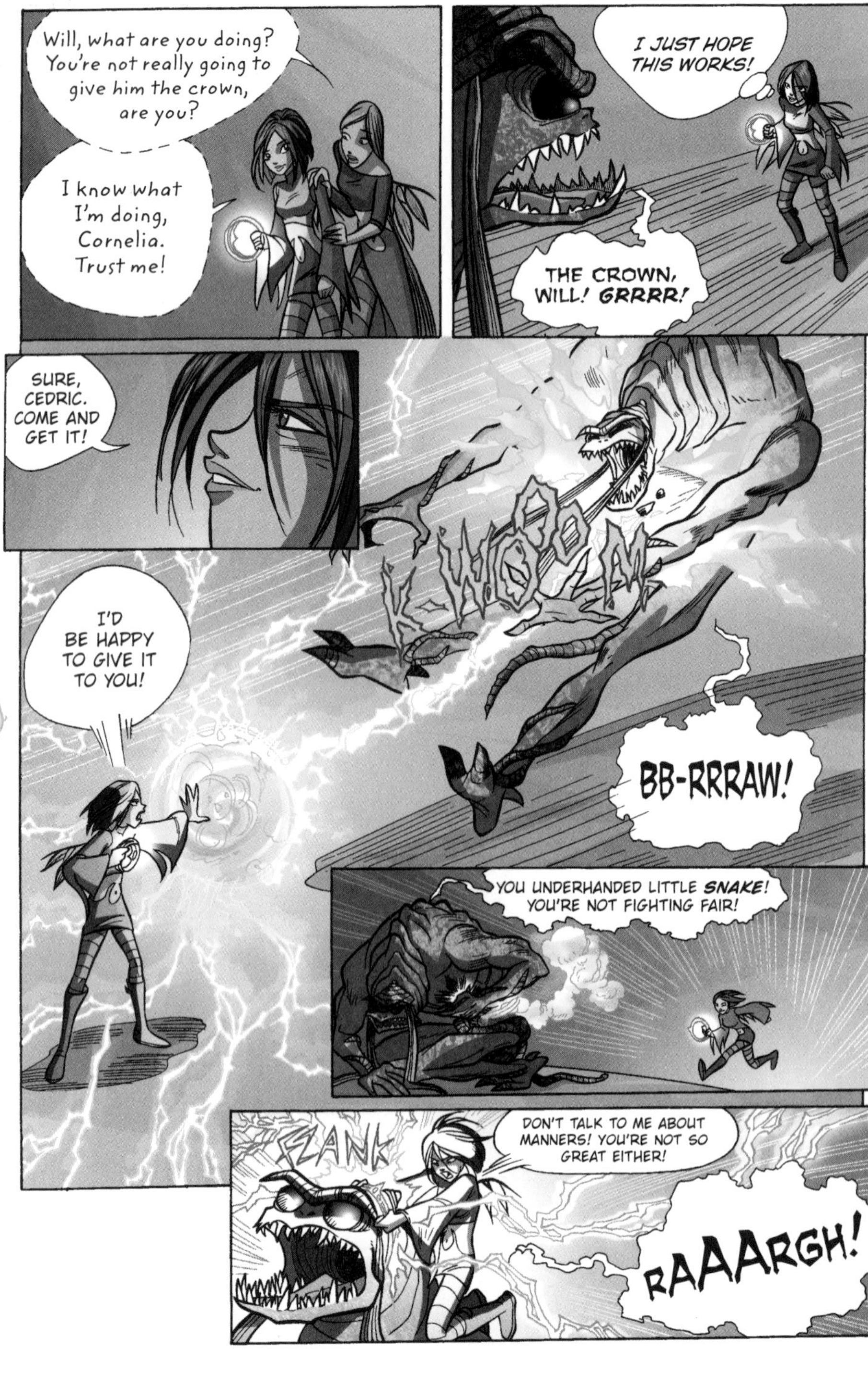
Will, what are you doing? You're not really going to give him the crown, are you?
I know what I'm doing, Cornelia. Trust me!
I JUST HOPE THIS WORKS!
THE CROWN, WILL! GRRRR!
SURE, CEDRIC. COME AND GET IT!
K-WOOOM
I'D BE HAPPY TO GIVE IT TO YOU!
BB-RRRAW!
YOU UNDERHANDED LITTLE SNAKE! YOU'RE NOT FIGHTING FAIR!
DON'T TALK TO ME ABOUT MANNERS! YOU'RE NOT SO GREAT EITHER!
CLANK
RAAARGH!

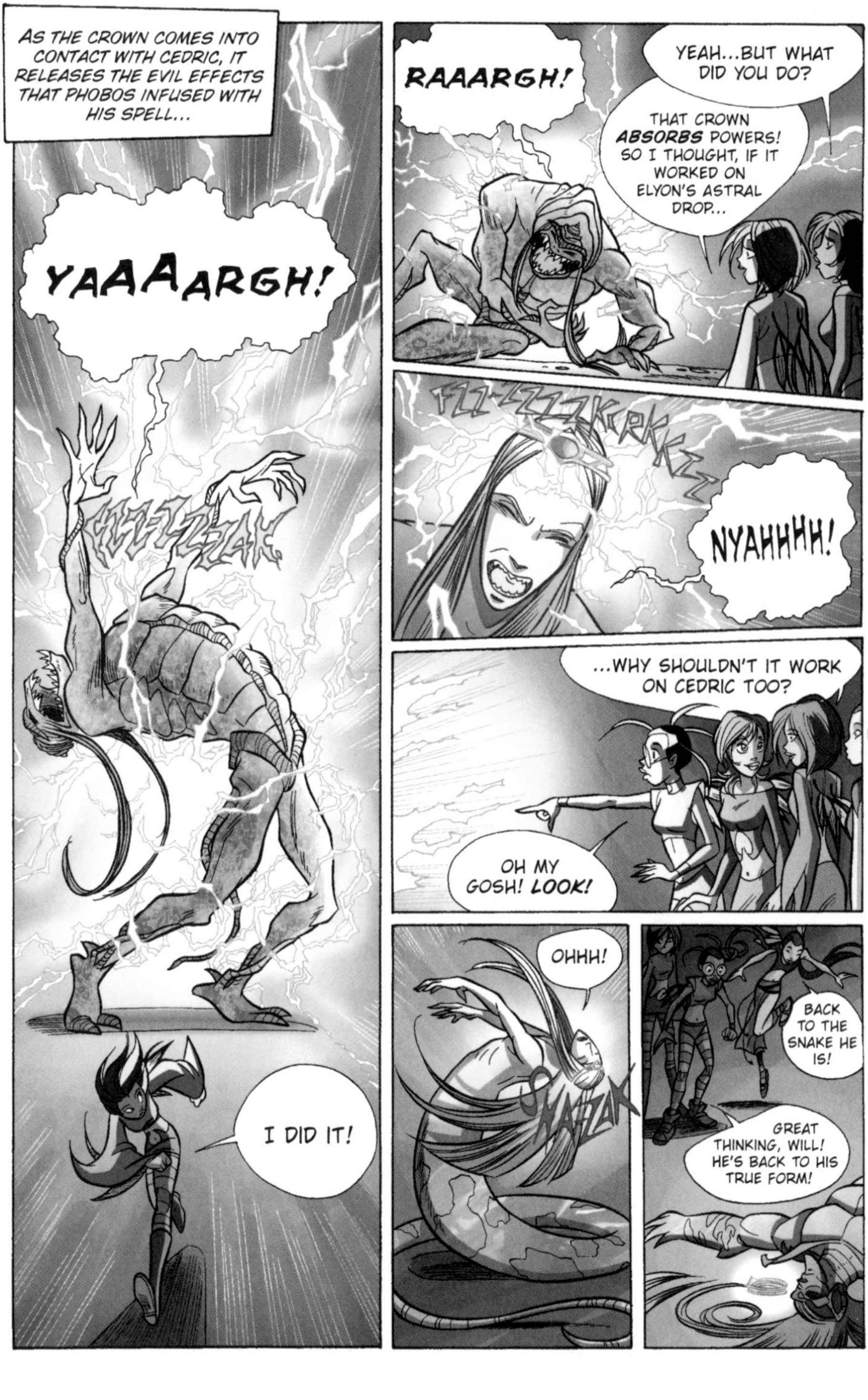
AS THE CROWN COMES INTO CONTACT WITH CEDRIC, IT RELEASES THE EVIL EFFECTS THAT PHOBOS INFUSED WITH HIS SPELL...
YAAAARGH!
I DID IT!
RAAARGH!
YEAH...BUT WHAT DID YOU DO?
THAT CROWN ABSORBS POWERS! SO I THOUGHT, IF IT WORKED ON ELYON'S ASTRAL DROP...
NYAHHHH!
...WHY SHOULDN'T IT WORK ON CEDRIC TOO?
OH MY GOSH! LOOK!
OHHH!
BACK TO THE SNAKE HE IS!
GREAT THINKING, WILL! HE'S BACK TO HIS TRUE FORM!

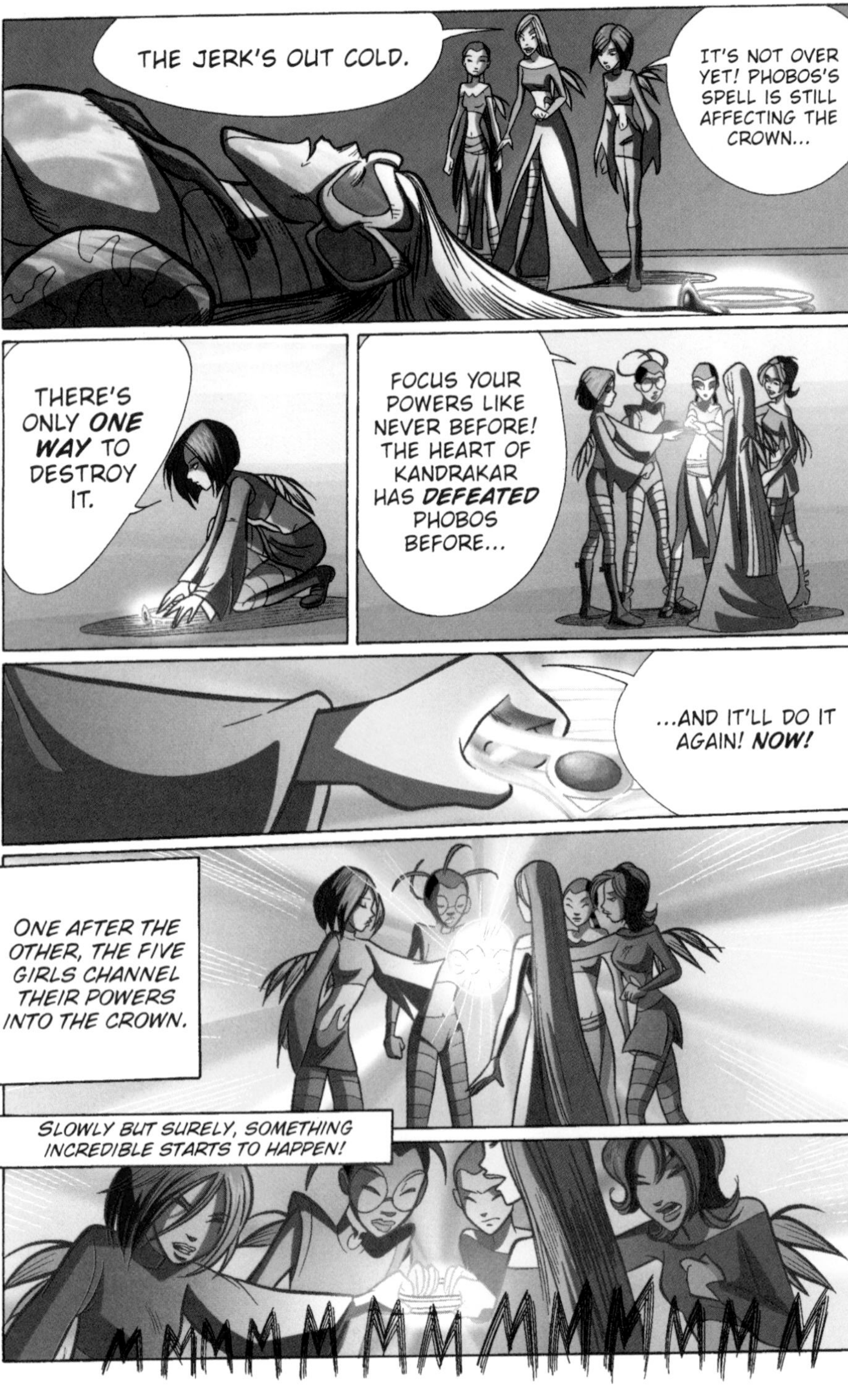
THE JERK'S OUT COLD.
IT'S NOT OVER YET! PHOBOS'S SPELL IS STILL AFFECTING THE CROWN...
THERE'S ONLY ONE WAY TO DESTROY IT.
FOCUS YOUR POWERS LIKE NEVER BEFORE! THE HEART OF KANDRAKAR HAS DEFEATED PHOBOS BEFORE...
...AND IT'LL DO IT AGAIN! NOW!
ONE AFTER THE OTHER, THE FIVE GIRLS CHANNEL THEIR POWERS INTO THE CROWN.
SLOWLY BUT SURELY, SOMETHING INCREDIBLE STARTS TO HAPPEN!
MMMMMMMMMMMMMMMMM

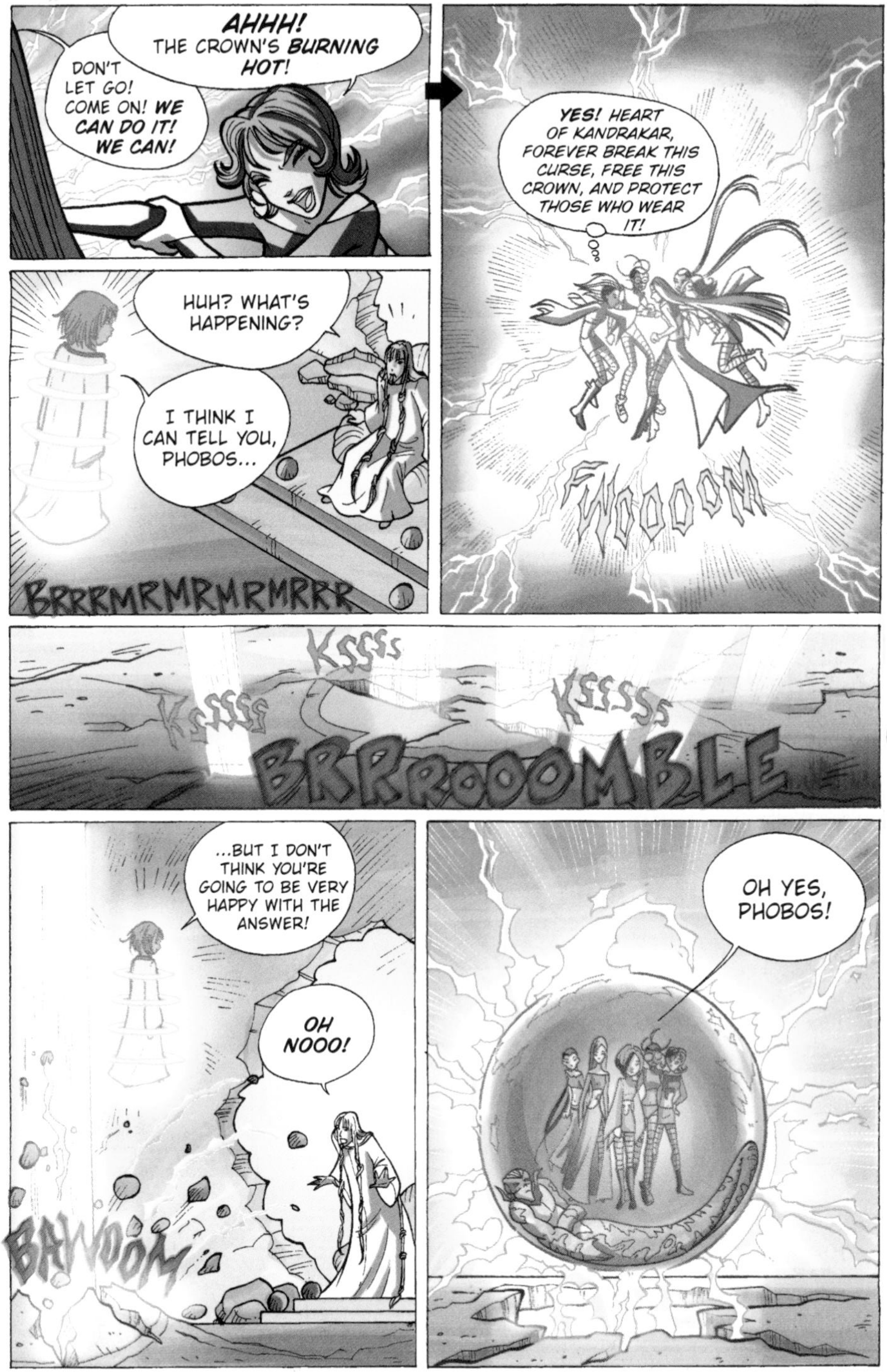
AHHH! THE CROWN'S BURNING HOT!
DON'T LET GO! COME ON! WE CAN DO IT! WE CAN!
YES! HEART OF KANDRAKAR, FOREVER BREAK THIS CURSE, FREE THIS CROWN, AND PROTECT THOSE WHO WEAR IT!
FWOOOOM
HUH? WHAT'S HAPPENING?
I THINK I CAN TELL YOU, PHOBOS...
BRRRMRMRMRMRRR
KSSSS
KSSSSS
KSSSSS
BRRROOOMBLE
...BUT I DON'T THINK YOU'RE GOING TO BE VERY HAPPY WITH THE ANSWER!
OH NOOO!
BAWOOM
OH YES, PHOBOS!

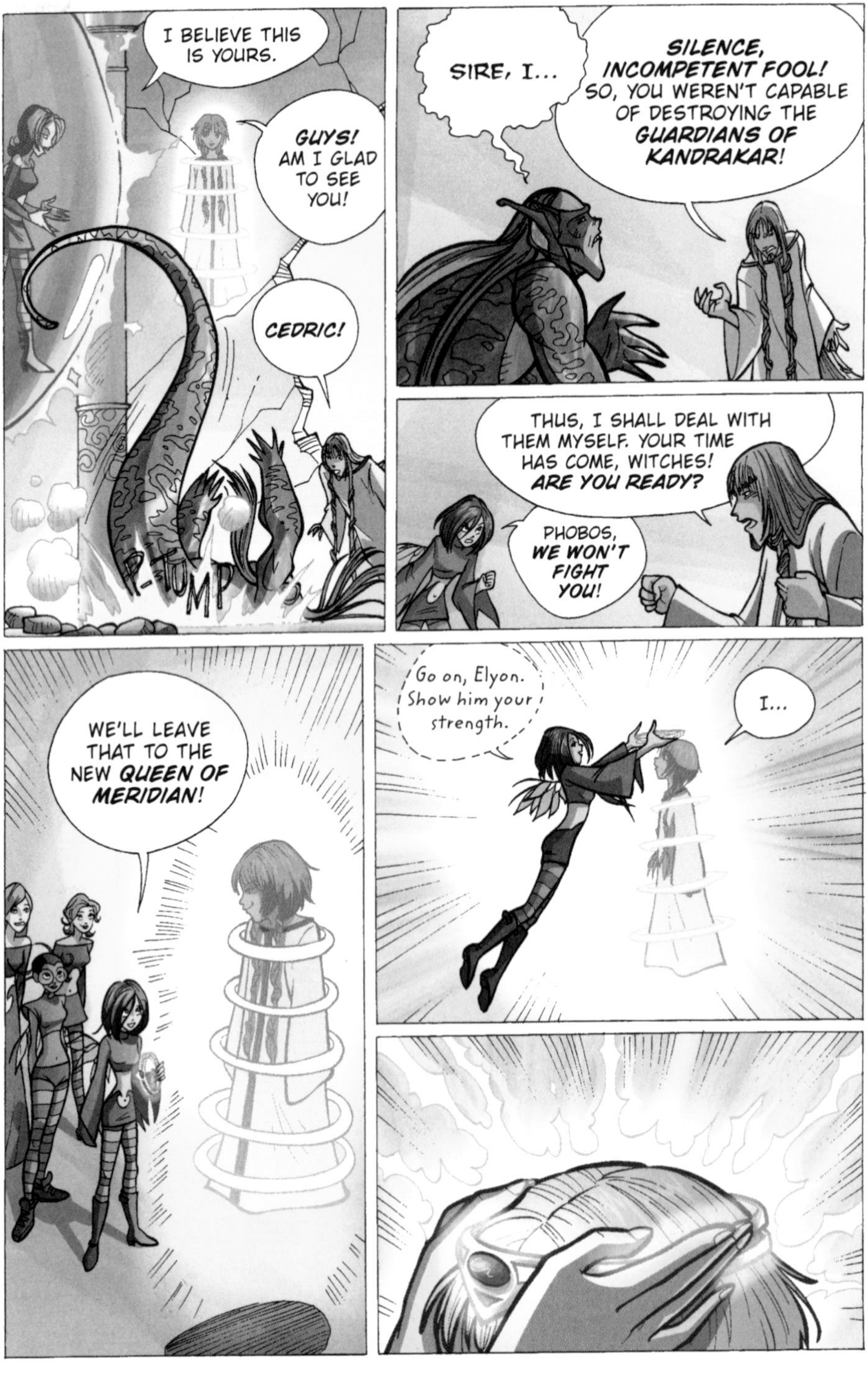

I BELIEVE THIS IS YOURS.
GUYS! AM I GLAD TO SEE YOU!
CEDRIC!
P-TUMP
SIRE, I...
SILENCE, INCOMPETENT FOOL! SO, YOU WEREN'T CAPABLE OF DESTROYING THE GUARDIANS OF KANDRAKAR!
THUS, I SHALL DEAL WITH THEM MYSELF. YOUR TIME HAS COME, WITCHES! ARE YOU READY?
PHOBOS, WE WON'T FIGHT YOU!
WE'LL LEAVE THAT TO THE NEW QUEEN OF MERIDIAN!
Go on, Elyon. Show him your strength.
I...

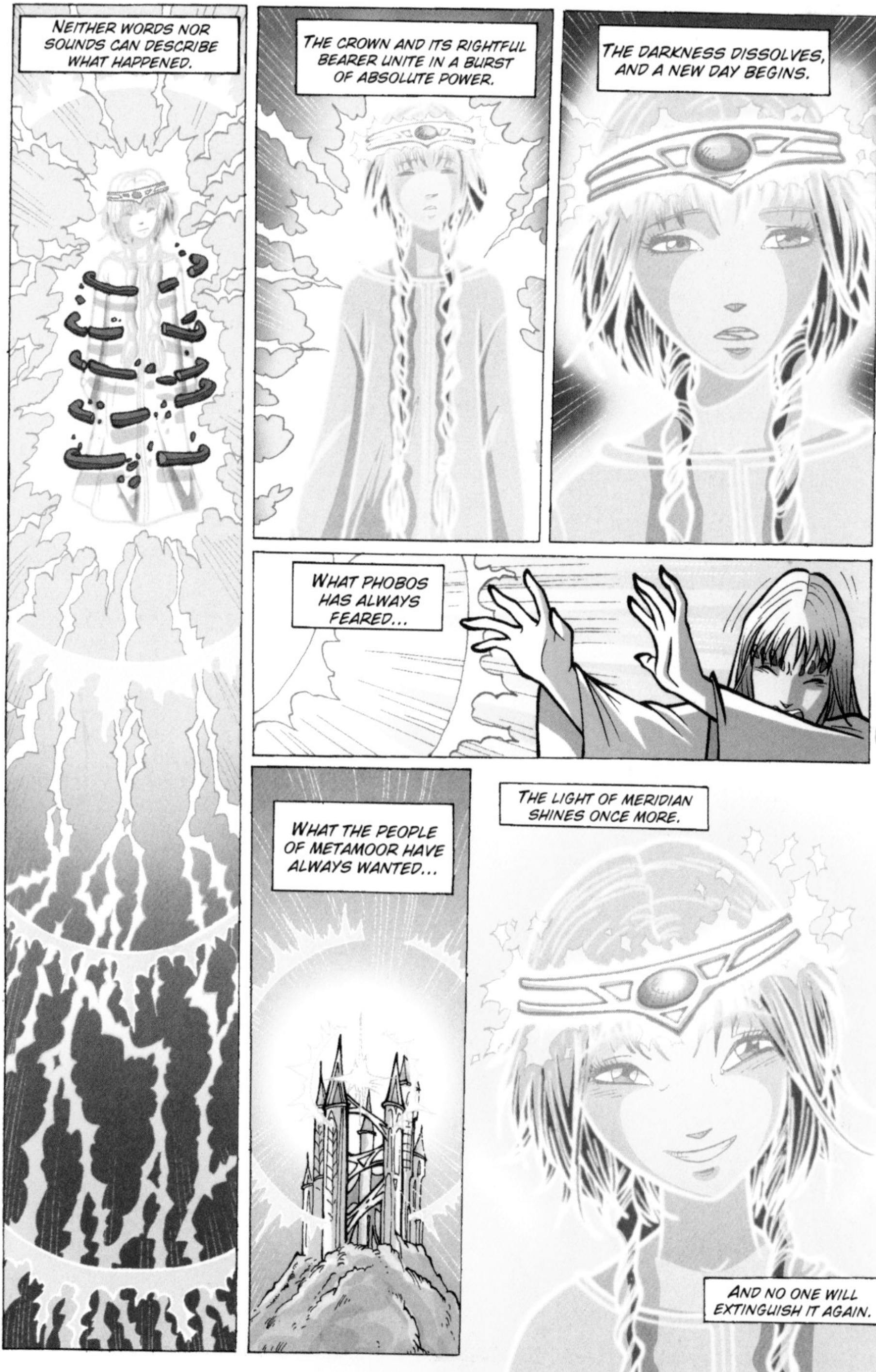

NEITHER WORDS NOR SOUNDS CAN DESCRIBE WHAT HAPPENED.
THE CROWN AND ITS RIGHTFUL BEARER UNITE IN A BURST OF ABSOLUTE POWER.
THE DARKNESS DISSOLVES, AND A NEW DAY BEGINS.
WHAT PHOBOS HAS ALWAYS FEARED...
WHAT THE PEOPLE OF METAMOOR HAVE ALWAYS WANTED...
THE LIGHT OF MERIDIAN SHINES ONCE MORE.
AND NO ONE WILL EXTINGUISH IT AGAIN.

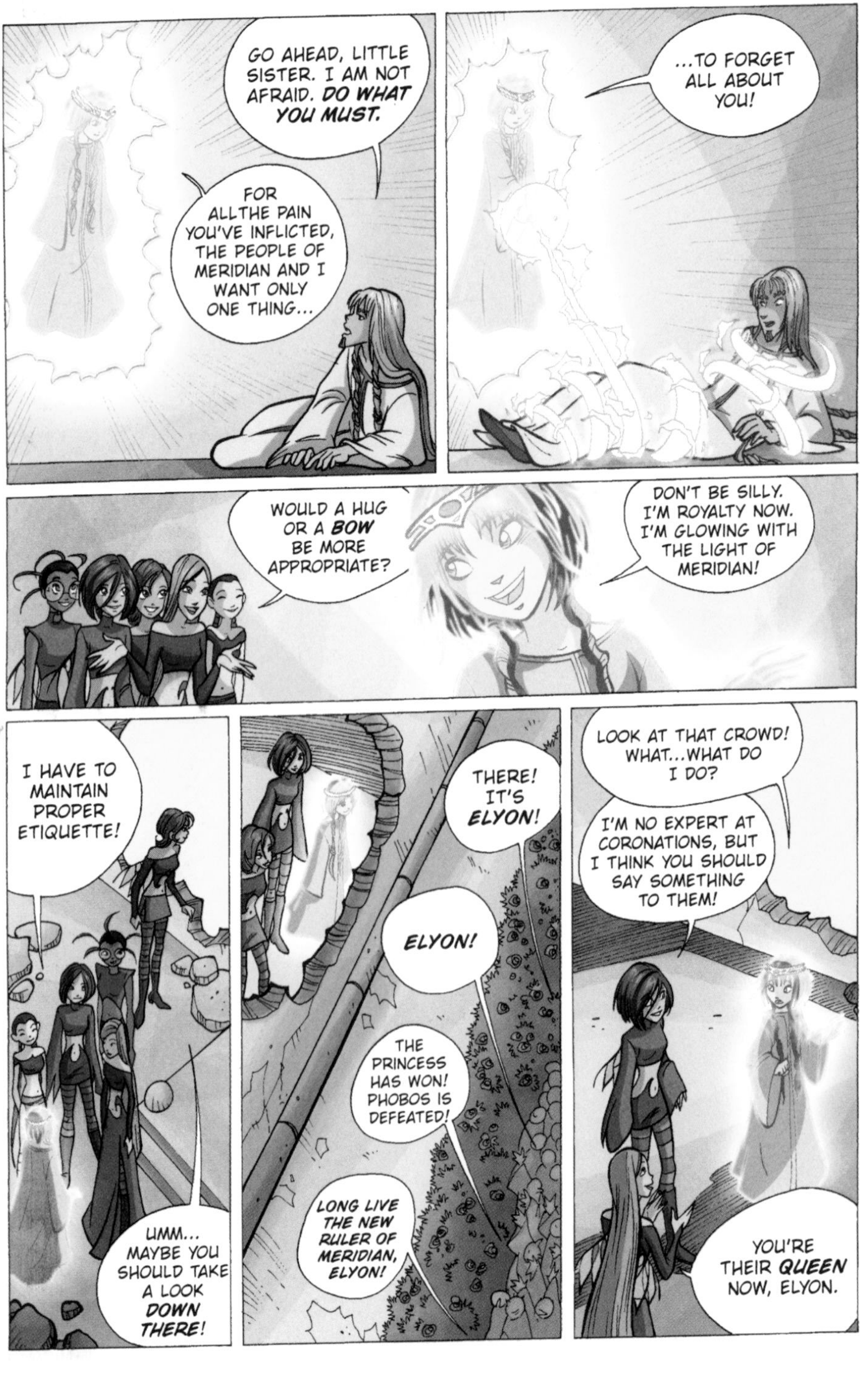
GO AHEAD, LITTLE SISTER. I AM NOT AFRAID. DO WHAT YOU MUST.
FOR ALLTHE PAIN YOU'VE INFLICTED, THE PEOPLE OF MERIDIAN AND I WANT ONLY ONE THING...
...TO FORGET ALL ABOUT YOU!
WOULD A HUG OR A BOW BE MORE APPROPRIATE?
DON'T BE SILLY. I'M ROYALTY NOW. I'M GLOWING WITH THE LIGHT OF MERIDIAN!
I HAVE TO MAINTAIN PROPER ETIQUETTE!
UMM... MAYBE YOU SHOULD TAKE A LOOK DOWN THERE!
THERE! IT'S ELYON!
ELYON!
THE PRINCESS HAS WON! PHOBOS IS DEFEATED!
LONG LIVE THE NEW RULER OF MERIDIAN, ELYON!
LOOK AT THAT CROWD! WHAT...WHAT DO I DO?
I'M NO EXPERT AT CORONATIONS, BUT I THINK YOU SHOULD SAY SOMETHING TO THEM!
YOU'RE THEIR QUEEN NOW, ELYON.

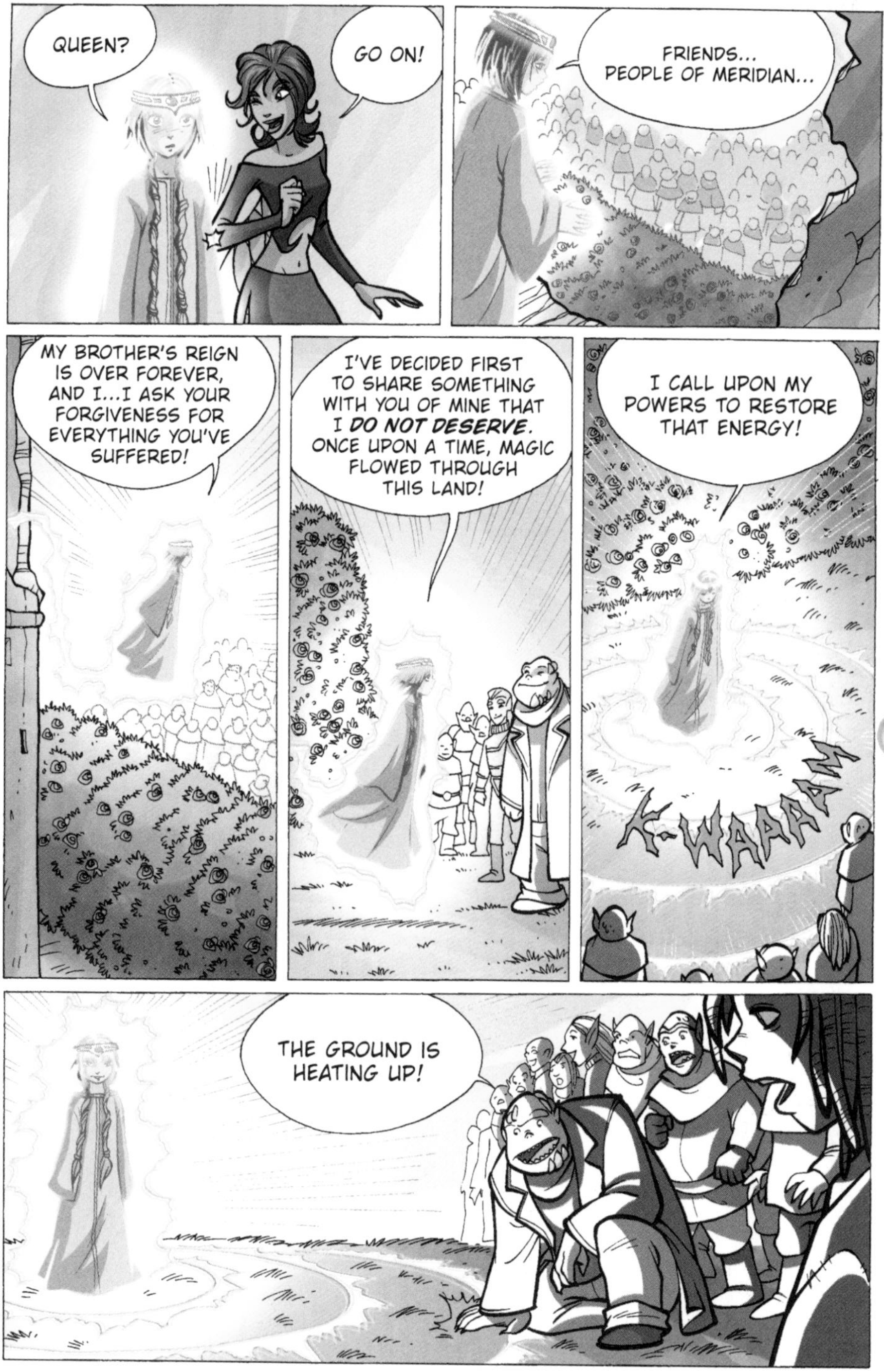
QUEEN?
GO ON!
FRIENDS... PEOPLE OF MERIDIAN...
MY BROTHER'S REIGN IS OVER FOREVER, AND I...I ASK YOUR FORGIVENESS FOR EVERYTHING YOU'VE SUFFERED!
I'VE DECIDED FIRST TO SHARE SOMETHING WITH YOU OF MINE THAT I DO NOT DESERVE. ONCE UPON A TIME, MAGIC FLOWED THROUGH THIS LAND!
I CALL UPON MY POWERS TO RESTORE THAT ENERGY!
K-WAAAM
THE GROUND IS HEATING UP!

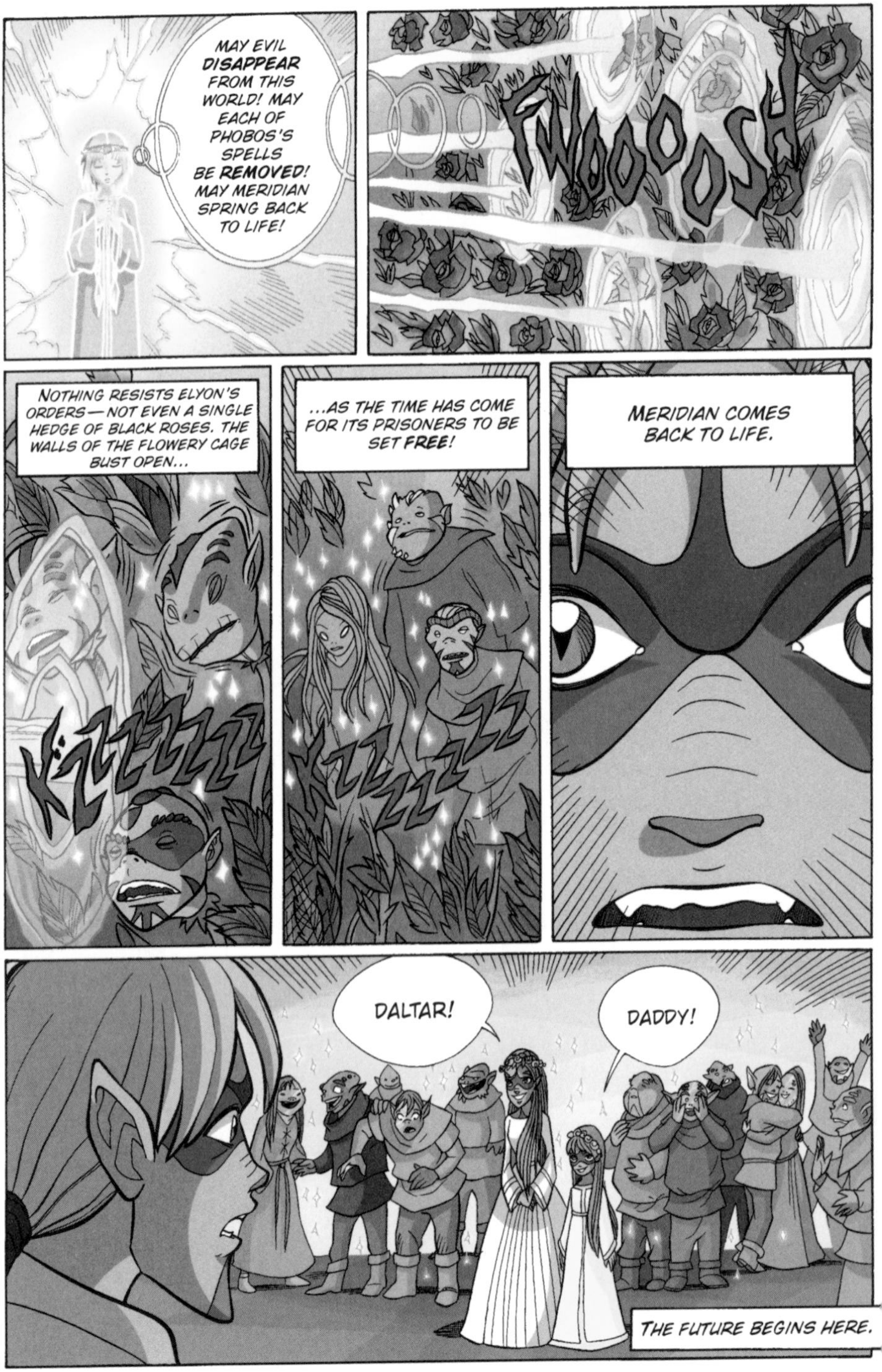

MAY EVIL DISAPPEAR FROM THIS WORLD! MAY EACH OF PHOBOS'S SPELLS BE REMOVED! MAY MERIDIAN SPRING BACK TO LIFE!
FWOOOOSH
NOTHING RESISTS ELYON'S ORDERS—NOT EVEN A SINGLE HEDGE OF BLACK ROSES. THE WALLS OF THE FLOWERY CAGE BUST OPEN...
KZZZZZZZ
...AS THE TIME HAS COME FOR ITS PRISONERS TO BE SET FREE!
KZZZZZZZ
MERIDIAN COMES BACK TO LIFE.
DALTAR!
DADDY!
THE FUTURE BEGINS HERE.

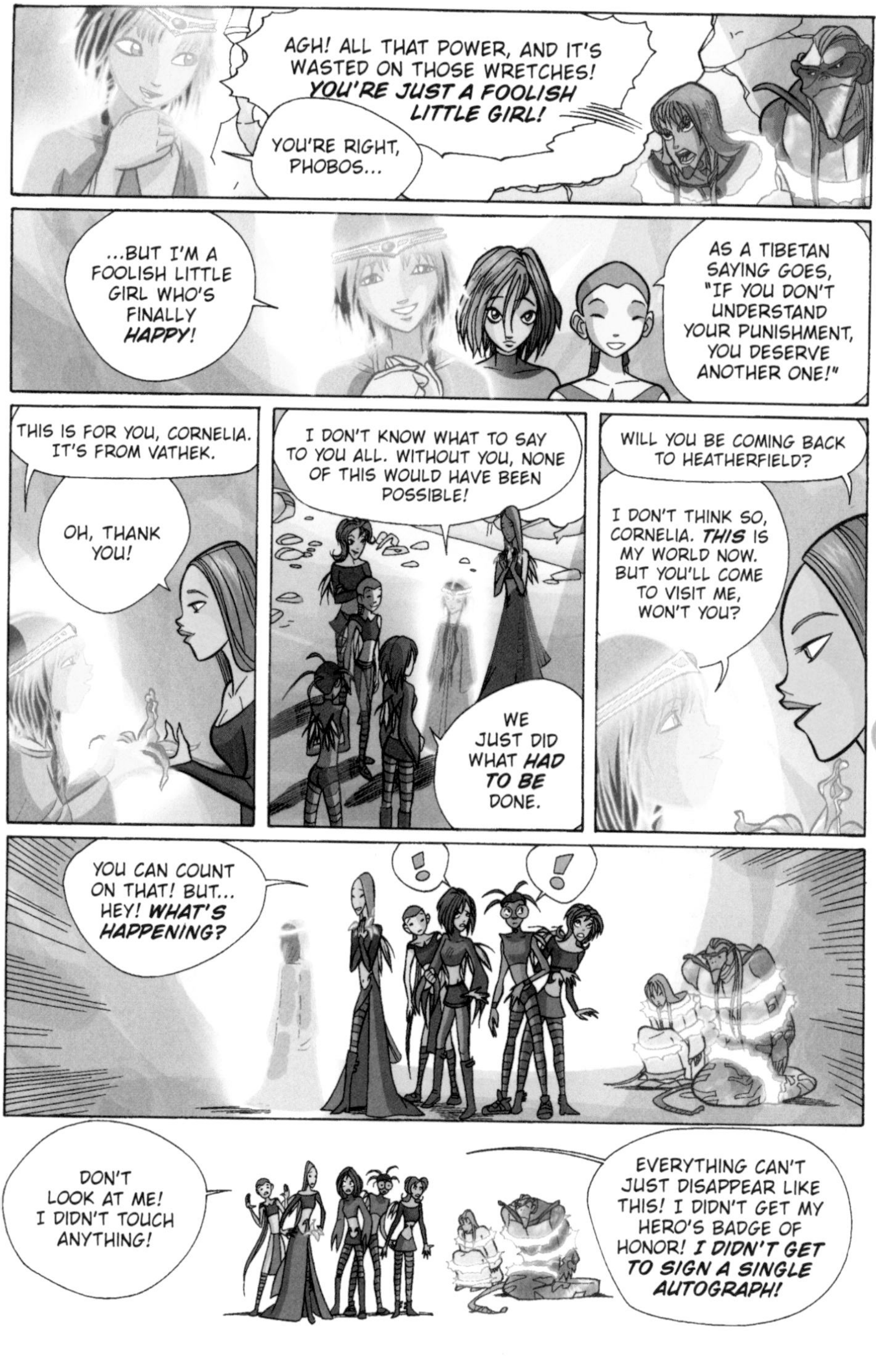

AGH! ALL THAT POWER, AND IT'S WASTED ON THOSE WRETCHES! YOU'RE JUST A FOOLISH LITTLE GIRL!
YOU'RE RIGHT, PHOBOS...
...BUT I'M A FOOLISH LITTLE GIRL WHO'S FINALLY HAPPY!
AS A TIBETAN SAYING GOES, "IF YOU DON'T UNDERSTAND YOUR PUNISHMENT, YOU DESERVE ANOTHER ONE!"
THIS IS FOR YOU, CORNELIA. IT'S FROM VATHEK.
OH, THANK YOU!
I DON'T KNOW WHAT TO SAY TO YOU ALL. WITHOUT YOU, NONE OF THIS WOULD HAVE BEEN POSSIBLE!
WE JUST DID WHAT HAD TO BE DONE.
WILL YOU BE COMING BACK TO HEATHERFIELD?
I DON'T THINK SO, CORNELIA. THIS IS MY WORLD NOW. BUT YOU'LL COME TO VISIT ME, WON'T YOU?
YOU CAN COUNT ON THAT! BUT... HEY! WHAT'S HAPPENING?
!
!
DON'T LOOK AT ME! I DIDN'T TOUCH ANYTHING!
EVERYTHING CAN'T JUST DISAPPEAR LIKE THIS! I DIDN'T GET MY HERO'S BADGE OF HONOR! I DIDN'T GET TO SIGN A SINGLE AUTOGRAPH!

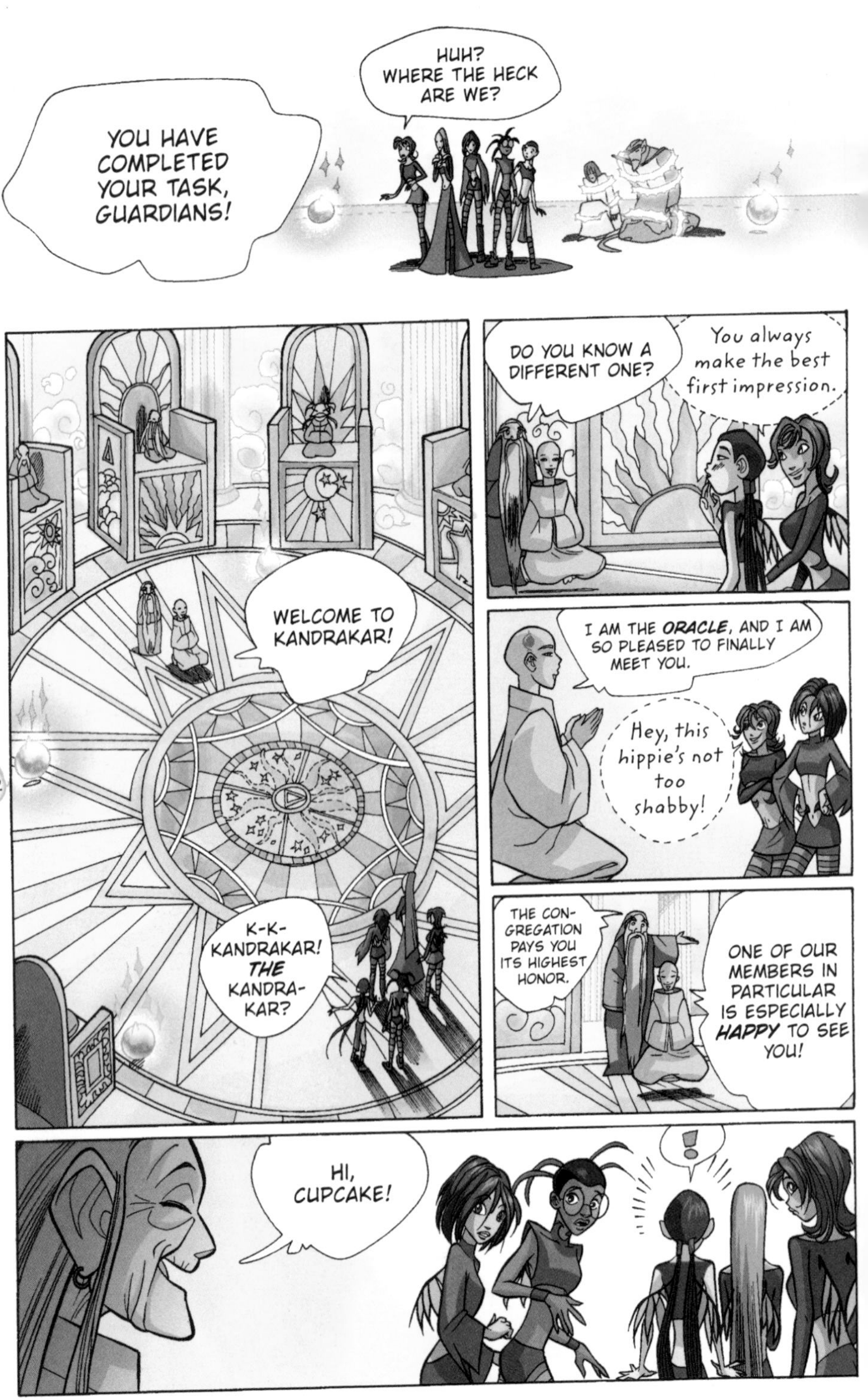
YOU HAVE COMPLETED YOUR TASK, GUARDIANS!
HUH? WHERE THE HECK ARE WE?
WELCOME TO KANDRAKAR!
K-K-KANDRAKAR! *THE* KANDRA-KAR?
DO YOU KNOW A DIFFERENT ONE?
You always make the best first impression.
I AM THE *ORACLE*, AND I AM SO PLEASED TO FINALLY MEET YOU.
Hey, this hippie's not too shabby!
THE CON-GREGATION PAYS YOU ITS HIGHEST HONOR.
ONE OF OUR MEMBERS IN PARTICULAR IS ESPECIALLY *HAPPY* TO SEE YOU!
HI, CUPCAKE!
!

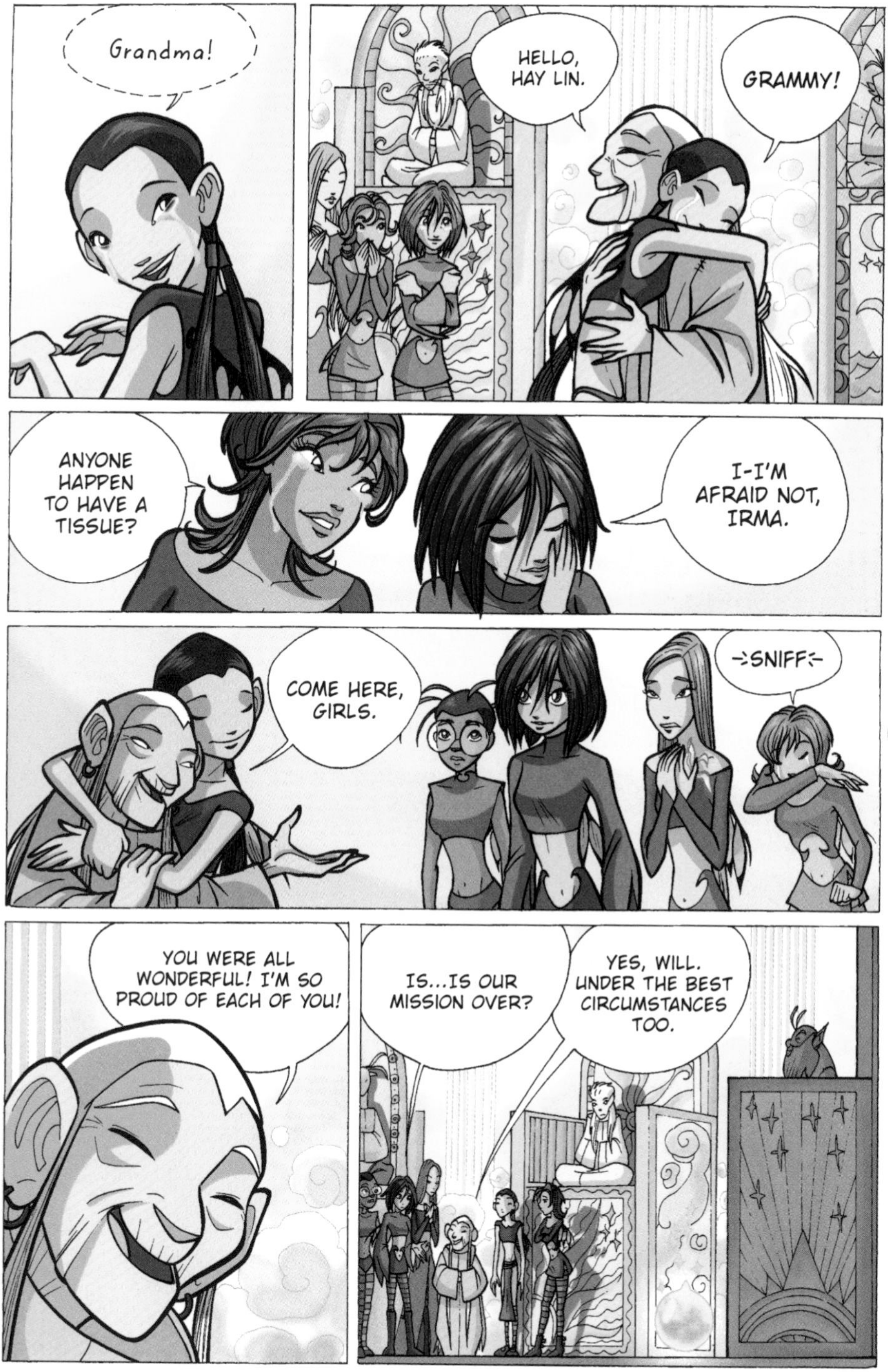
Grandma!
HELLO, HAY LIN.
GRAMMY!
ANYONE HAPPEN TO HAVE A TISSUE?
I-I'M AFRAID NOT, IRMA.
COME HERE, GIRLS.
SNIFF
YOU WERE ALL WONDERFUL! I'M SO PROUD OF EACH OF YOU!
IS...IS OUR MISSION OVER?
YES, WILL. UNDER THE BEST CIRCUMSTANCES TOO.

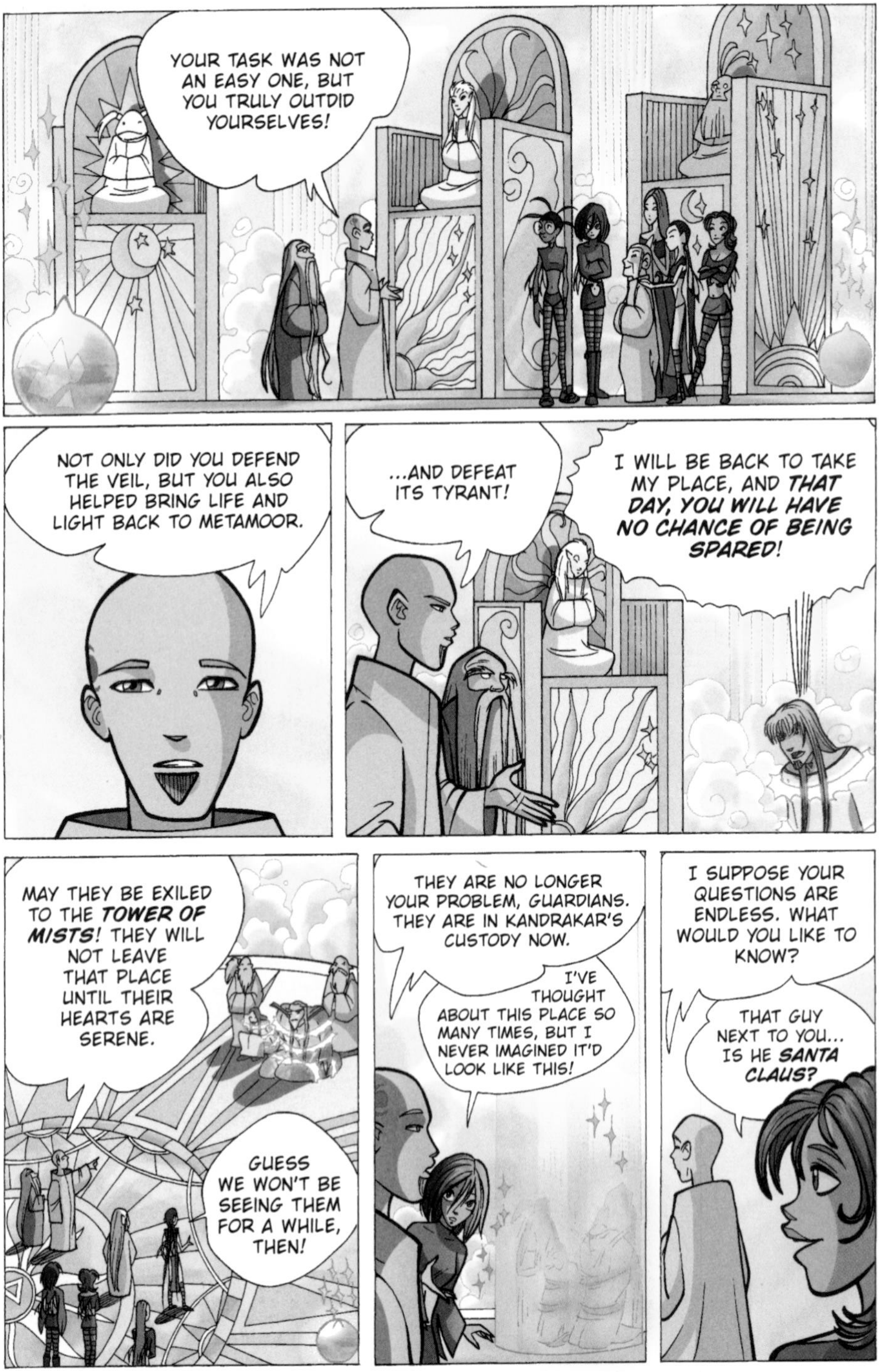
YOUR TASK WAS NOT AN EASY ONE, BUT YOU TRULY OUTDID YOURSELVES!
NOT ONLY DID YOU DEFEND THE VEIL, BUT YOU ALSO HELPED BRING LIFE AND LIGHT BACK TO METAMOOR.
...AND DEFEAT ITS TYRANT!
I WILL BE BACK TO TAKE MY PLACE, AND THAT DAY, YOU WILL HAVE NO CHANCE OF BEING SPARED!
MAY THEY BE EXILED TO THE TOWER OF MISTS! THEY WILL NOT LEAVE THAT PLACE UNTIL THEIR HEARTS ARE SERENE.
GUESS WE WON'T BE SEEING THEM FOR A WHILE, THEN!
THEY ARE NO LONGER YOUR PROBLEM, GUARDIANS. THEY ARE IN KANDRAKAR'S CUSTODY NOW.
I'VE THOUGHT ABOUT THIS PLACE SO MANY TIMES, BUT I NEVER IMAGINED IT'D LOOK LIKE THIS!
I SUPPOSE YOUR QUESTIONS ARE ENDLESS. WHAT WOULD YOU LIKE TO KNOW?
THAT GUY NEXT TO YOU... IS HE SANTA CLAUS?

EXCUSE ME?

UM...DON'T MIND HER. THERE ARE SO MANY THINGS WE'D LIKE TO KNOW THAT WE'RE NOT SURE WHERE TO START!

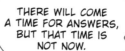

THERE WILL COME A TIME FOR ANSWERS, BUT THAT TIME IS NOT NOW.

EVEN THOUGH THIS PART OF YOUR MISSION IS OVER, YOU WILL *CONTINUE* TO BE OUR GUARDIANS...

...AND YOU WILL ONE DAY HAVE THE POWER TO FIND THE ANSWERS TO EVERYTHING *ON YOUR OWN!*

BUT, SIR!

WE MAY NEED YOUR HELP AGAIN IN THE FUTURE. BE VIGILANT AND HEED OUR CALL!

YOUR POWERS WILL DEFEND NOT ONLY YOUR WORLD BUT ALL WORLDS UNDER THE WATCHFUL EYE OF KANDRAKAR!

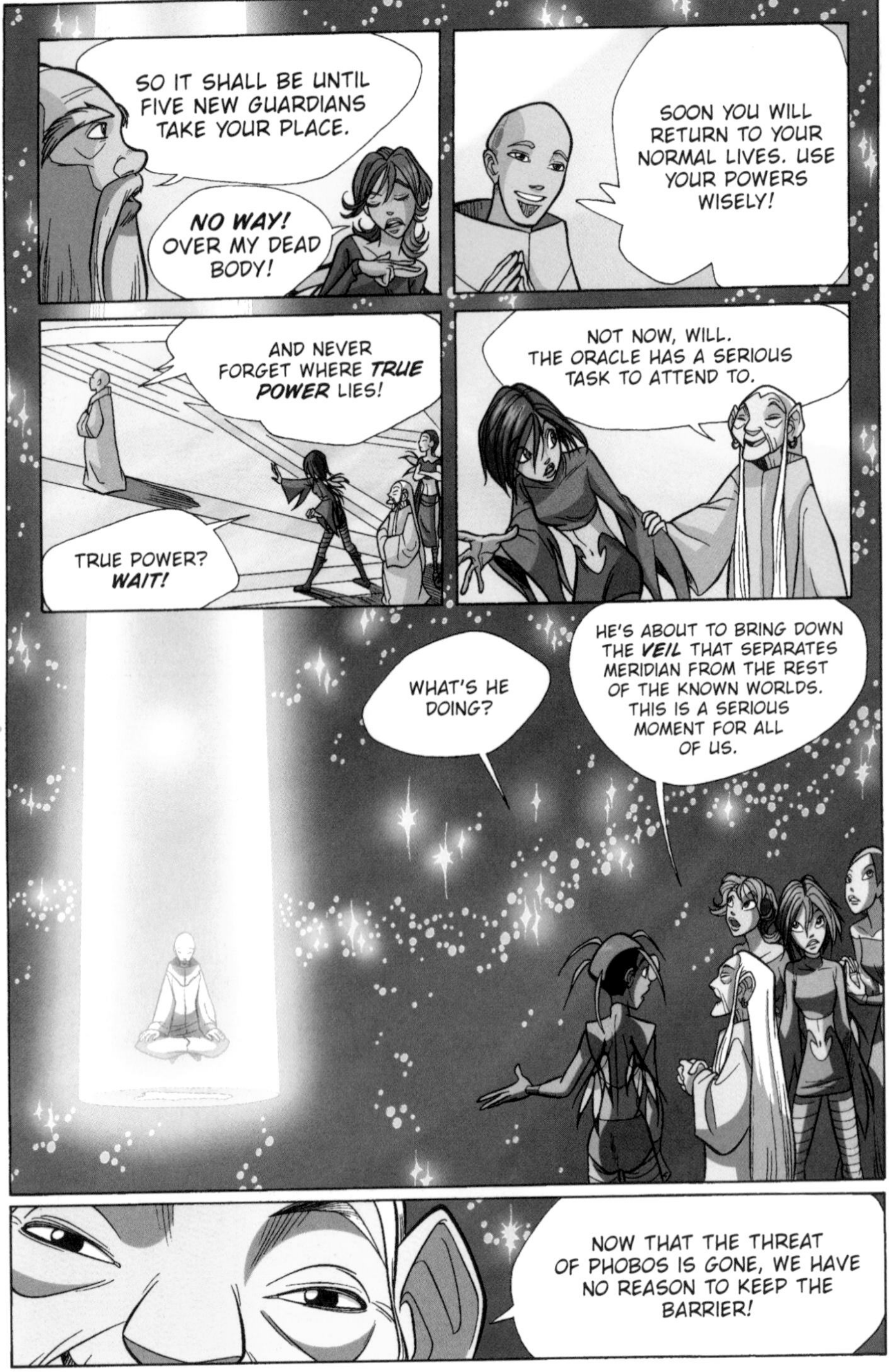

SO IT SHALL BE UNTIL FIVE NEW GUARDIANS TAKE YOUR PLACE.
NO WAY! OVER MY DEAD BODY!
SOON YOU WILL RETURN TO YOUR NORMAL LIVES. USE YOUR POWERS WISELY!
AND NEVER FORGET WHERE TRUE POWER LIES!
TRUE POWER? WAIT!
NOT NOW, WILL. THE ORACLE HAS A SERIOUS TASK TO ATTEND TO.
WHAT'S HE DOING?
HE'S ABOUT TO BRING DOWN THE VEIL THAT SEPARATES MERIDIAN FROM THE REST OF THE KNOWN WORLDS. THIS IS A SERIOUS MOMENT FOR ALL OF US.
NOW THAT THE THREAT OF PHOBOS IS GONE, WE HAVE NO REASON TO KEEP THE BARRIER!

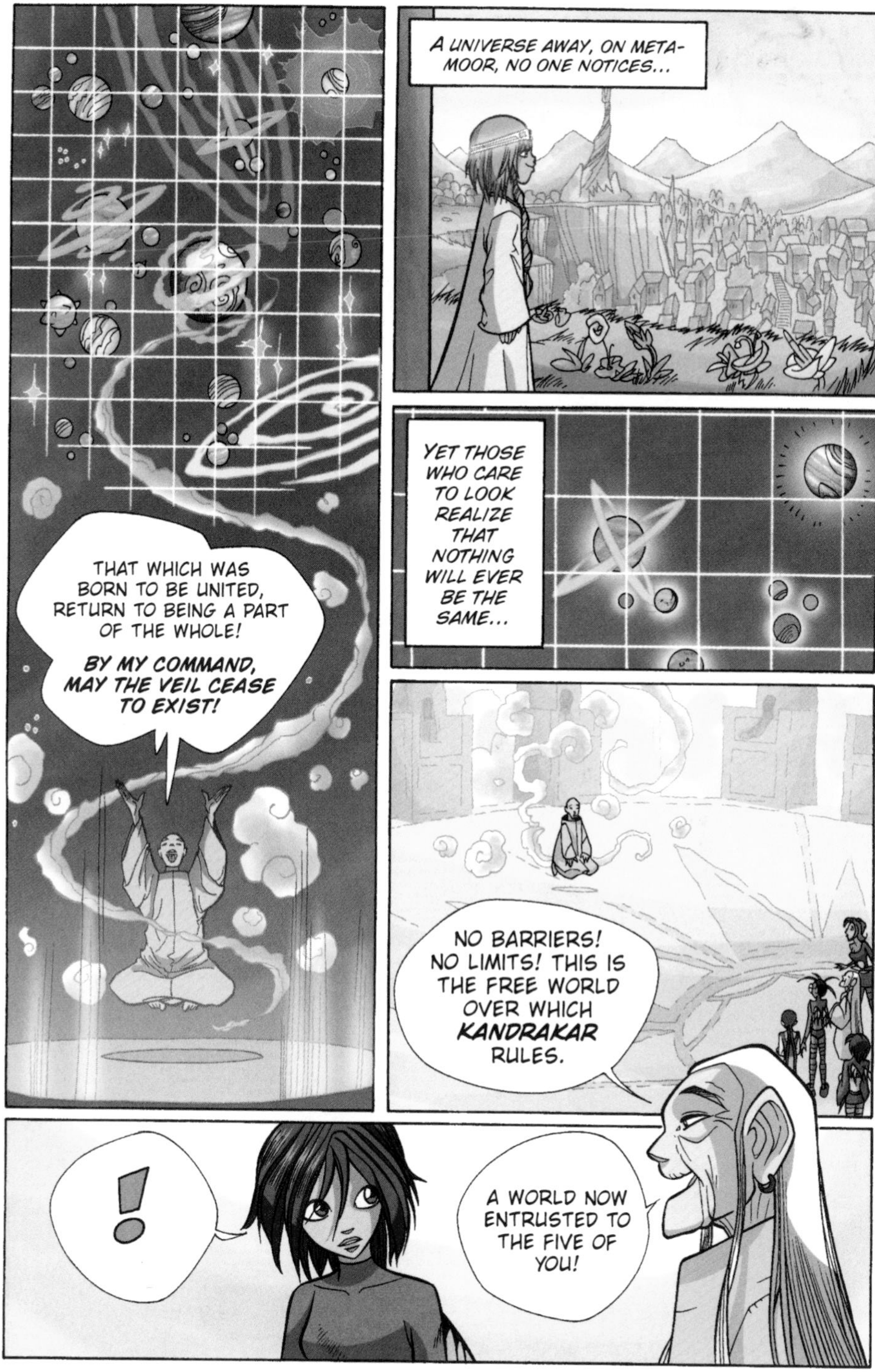
THAT WHICH WAS BORN TO BE UNITED, RETURN TO BEING A PART OF THE WHOLE!
BY MY COMMAND, MAY THE VEIL CEASE TO EXIST!
A UNIVERSE AWAY, ON META-MOOR, NO ONE NOTICES...
YET THOSE WHO CARE TO LOOK REALIZE THAT NOTHING WILL EVER BE THE SAME...
NO BARRIERS! NO LIMITS! THIS IS THE FREE WORLD OVER WHICH KANDRAKAR RULES.
!
A WORLD NOW ENTRUSTED TO THE FIVE OF YOU!

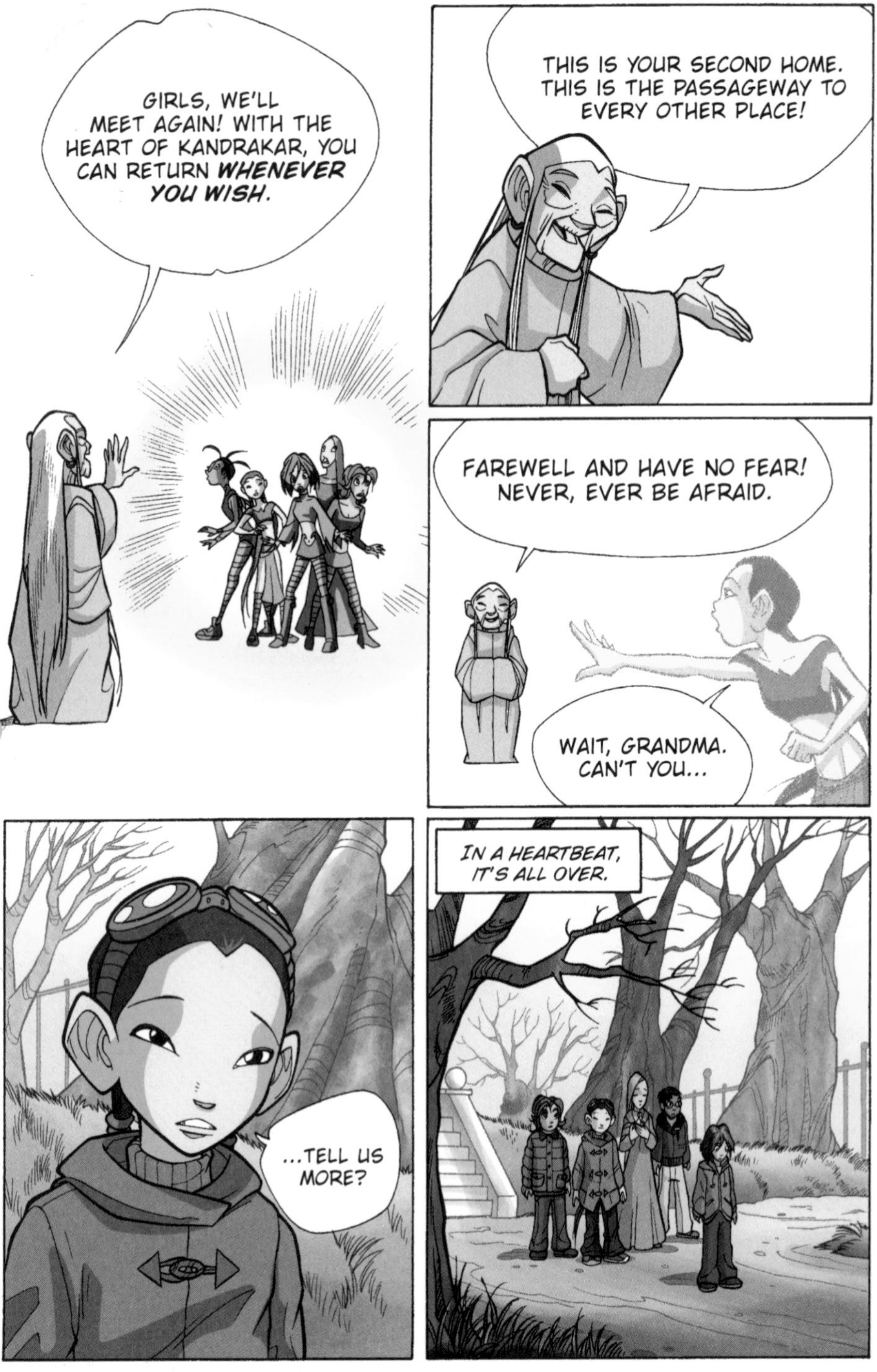
GIRLS, WE'LL MEET AGAIN! WITH THE HEART OF KANDRAKAR, YOU CAN RETURN **WHENEVER YOU WISH**.
THIS IS YOUR SECOND HOME. THIS IS THE PASSAGEWAY TO EVERY OTHER PLACE!
FAREWELL AND HAVE NO FEAR! NEVER, EVER BE AFRAID.
WAIT, GRANDMA. CAN'T YOU...
...TELL US MORE?
IN A HEARTBEAT, IT'S ALL OVER.

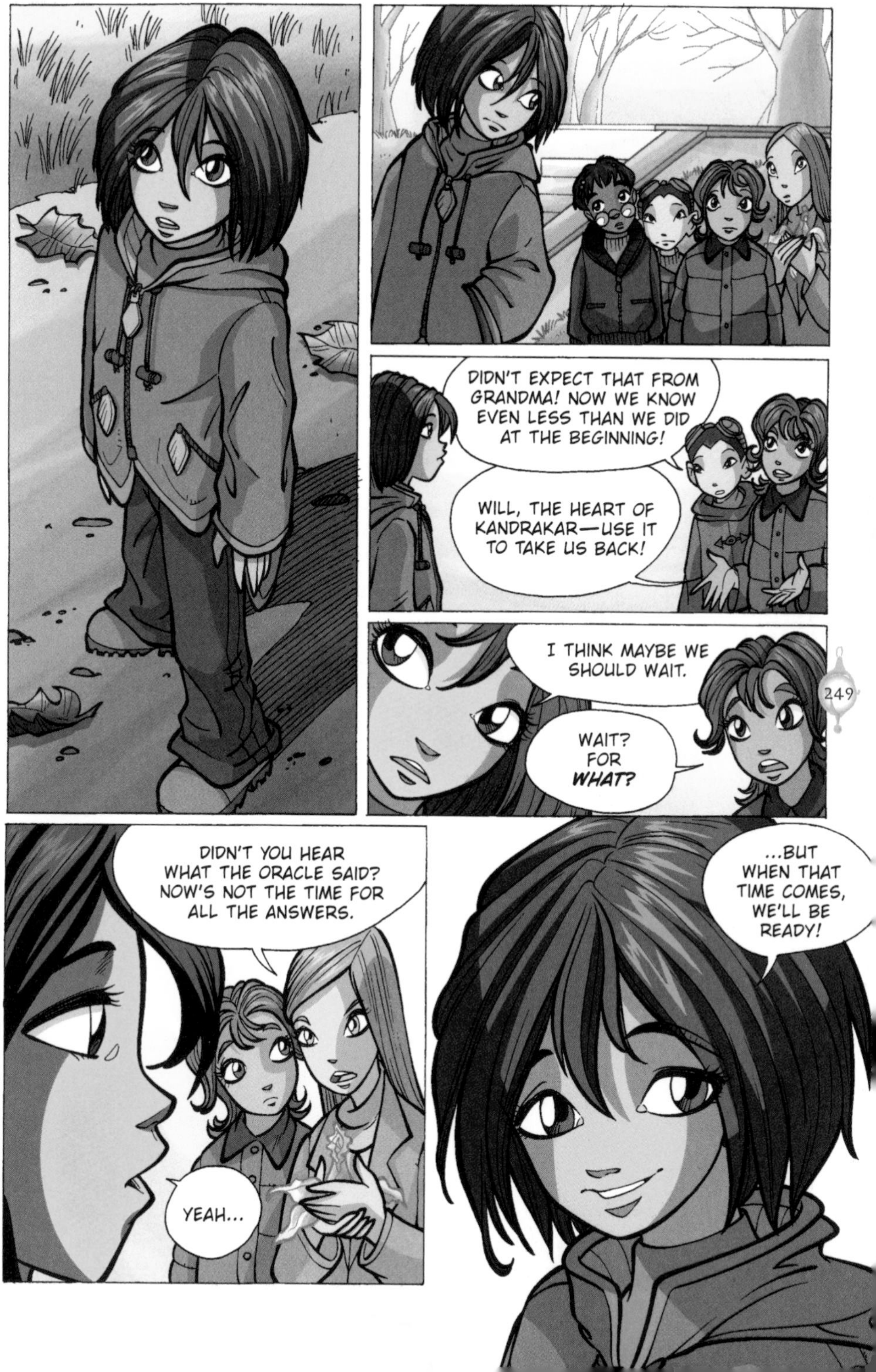
DIDN'T EXPECT THAT FROM GRANDMA! NOW WE KNOW EVEN LESS THAN WE DID AT THE BEGINNING!
WILL, THE HEART OF KANDRAKAR—USE IT TO TAKE US BACK!
I THINK MAYBE WE SHOULD WAIT.
WAIT? FOR *WHAT?*
DIDN'T YOU HEAR WHAT THE ORACLE SAID? NOW'S NOT THE TIME FOR ALL THE ANSWERS.
YEAH...
...BUT WHEN THAT TIME COMES, WE'LL BE READY!

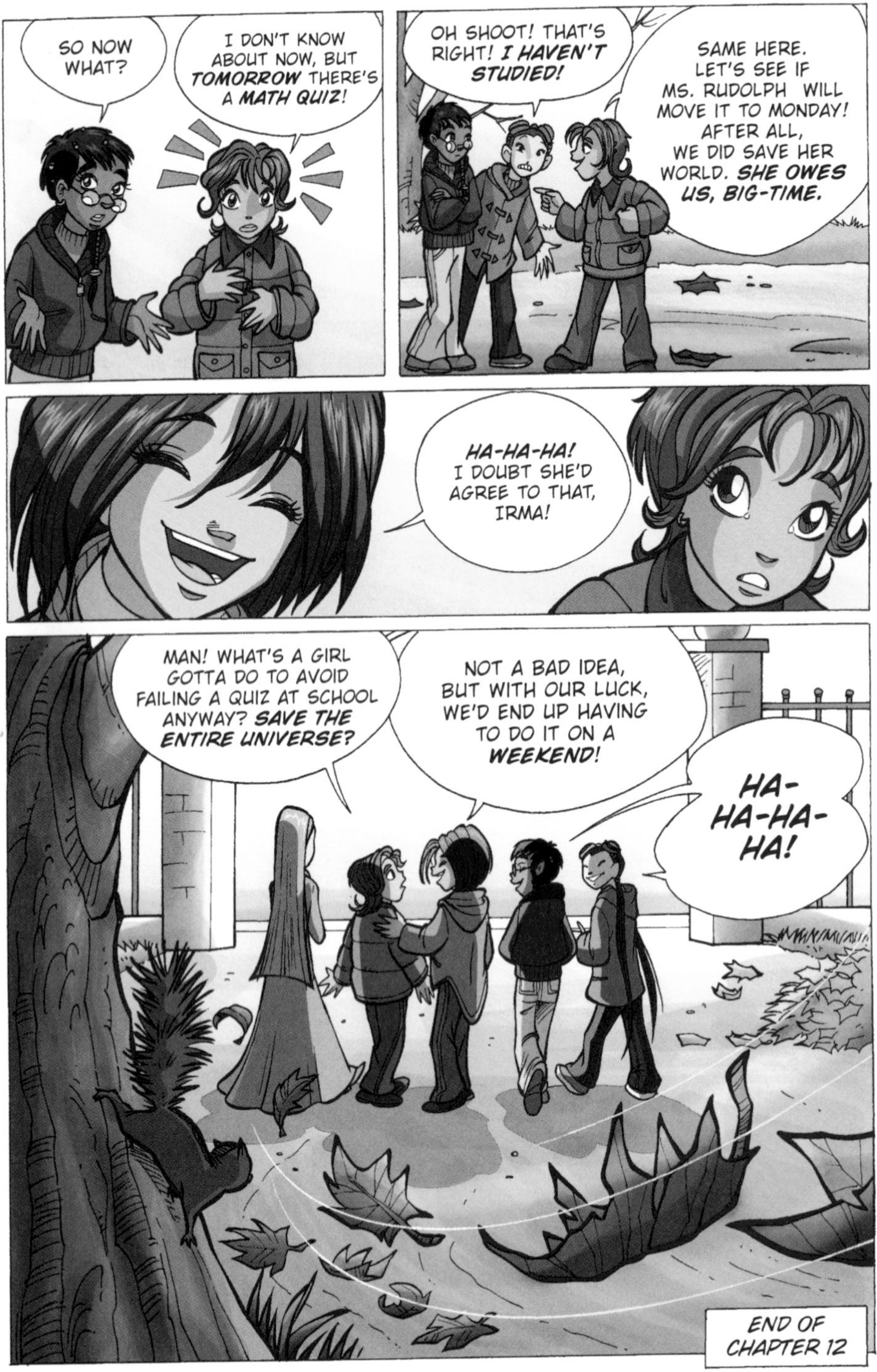

SO NOW WHAT?
I DON'T KNOW ABOUT NOW, BUT TOMORROW THERE'S A MATH QUIZ!
OH SHOOT! THAT'S RIGHT! I HAVEN'T STUDIED!
SAME HERE. LET'S SEE IF MS. RUDOLPH WILL MOVE IT TO MONDAY! AFTER ALL, WE DID SAVE HER WORLD. SHE OWES US, BIG-TIME.
HA-HA-HA! I DOUBT SHE'D AGREE TO THAT, IRMA!
MAN! WHAT'S A GIRL GOTTA DO TO AVOID FAILING A QUIZ AT SCHOOL ANYWAY? SAVE THE ENTIRE UNIVERSE?
NOT A BAD IDEA, BUT WITH OUR LUCK, WE'D END UP HAVING TO DO IT ON A WEEKEND!
HA-HA-HA-HA!
END OF CHAPTER 12

Read on in Volume 4!

ASTONISHED BY...

Elyon

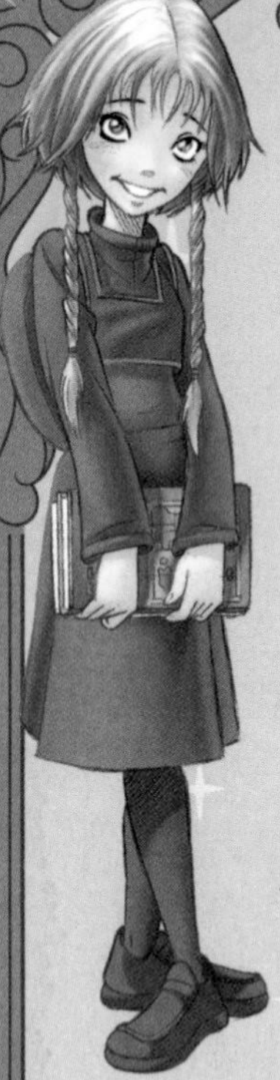

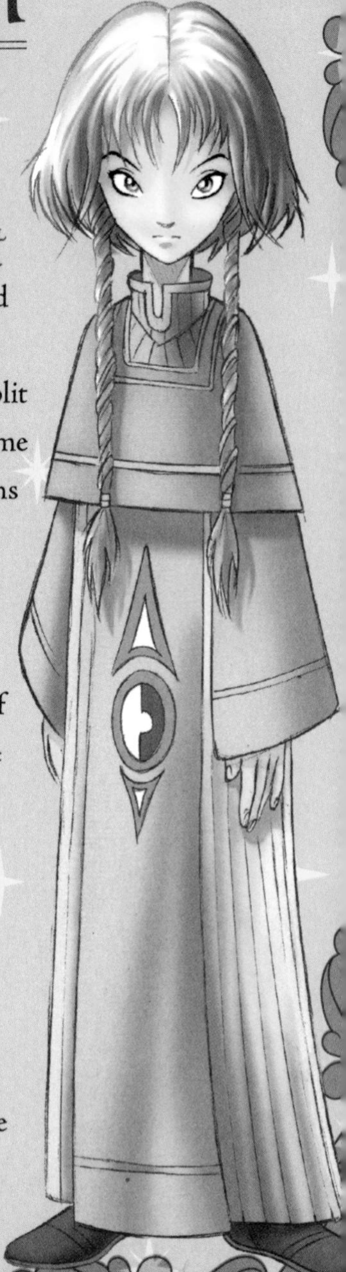

Almost **14** years old, Scorpio, born **October 31**

She was **Cornelia's best friend** until she encountered Cedric and suddenly went to Metamoor. Since then, she has split with the other girls and has become the worst enemy of the Guardians of Kandrakar.

From Cedric, she learned the people of Metamoor expected her to become the **Light of Meridian**, future ruler of that realm where the female offspring of the royal line become sovereign. Her brother, **Phobos**, is the regent in the interim and is looking forward to Elyon's rule (according to Cedric).

Elyon uses **negative" magical powers**. They have nothing to do with nature, but they come from the energy of the world and control matter.

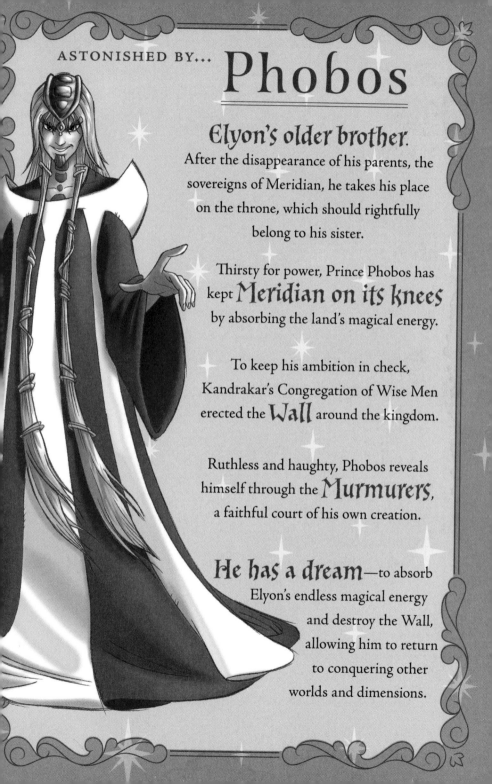

Phobos

Elyon's older brother.

After the disappearance of his parents, the sovereigns of Meridian, he takes his place on the throne, which should rightfully belong to his sister.

Thirsty for power, Prince Phobos has kept **Meridian on its knees** by absorbing the land's magical energy.

To keep his ambition in check, Kandrakar's Congregation of Wise Men erected the **Wall** around the kingdom.

Ruthless and haughty, Phobos reveals himself through the **Murmurers**, a faithful court of his own creation.

He has a dream—to absorb

Elyon's endless magical energy and destroy the Wall, allowing him to return to conquering other worlds and dimensions.

ASTONISHED BY...

Cedric

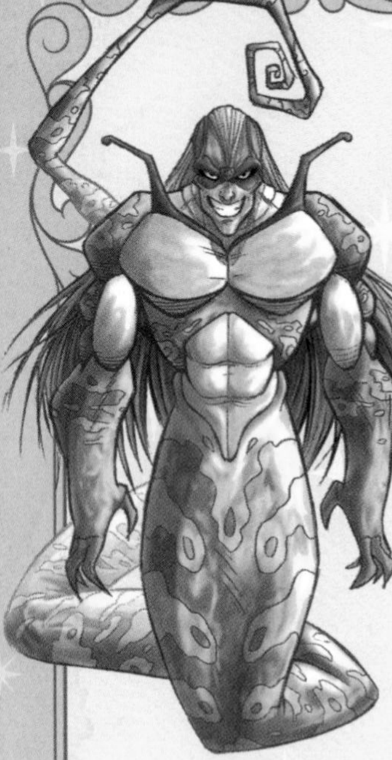

Prince Phobos's right hand man. His other, human identity is a **bookseller in Heatherfield.**

He's one of the monstrous, faithful assistants to Phobos.

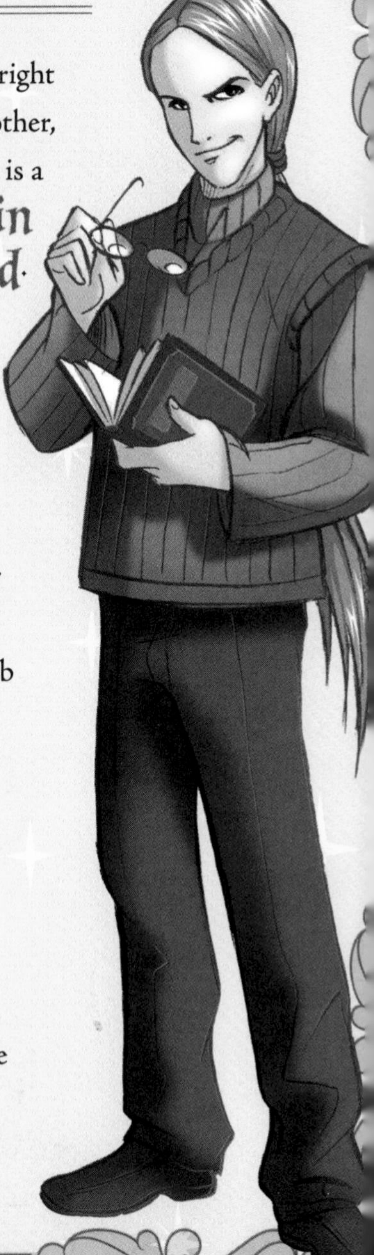

His **antique bookstore,** Ye Olde Book Shop, was the cover for Elyon's investigations with his aide Vathek (who then partnered with Caleb as part of the Meridian rebels).

Like every Metamoor resident, Cedric can change his appearance; he's actually "**reptilian.**"

His only ambition is to be a part of the **Court of Murmurers,** reporting to the Prince of Meridian.

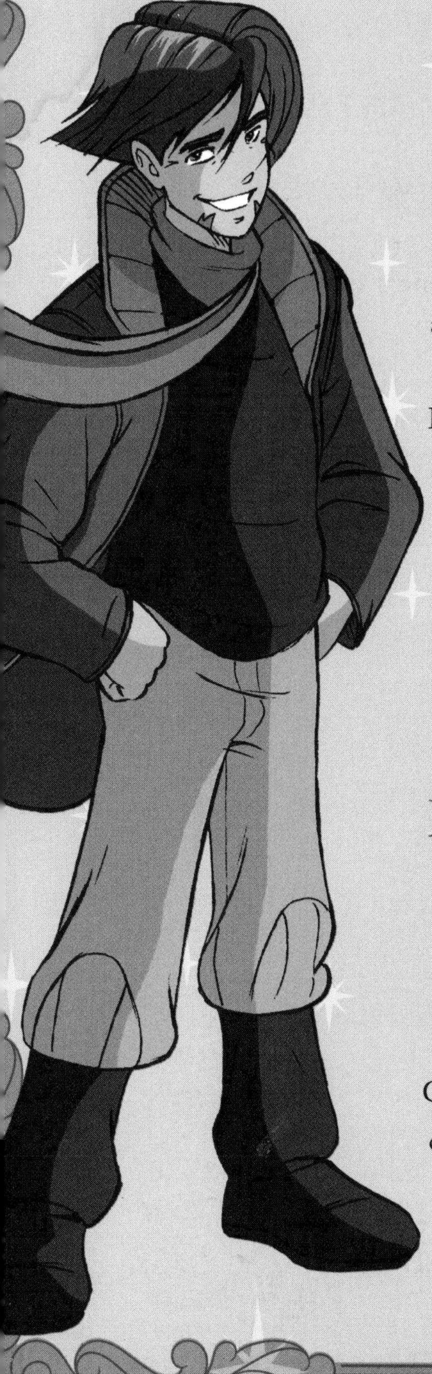

ASTONISHED BY...

Caleb

Caleb is the young leader of the **Rebels of Meridian**, a clandestine organization seeking the end to Prince Phobos's reign. Its base (also used for other people revolting) lies in the city's infinite underground.

His faithful lieutenant is **Vathek**, who, upon leaving Cedric's loyalty, has completely converted to the rebels' cause.

Born as a Murmurer, Caleb developed a will and a conscience that led him to rebel against the control of his creator, Phobos.

Caleb is the love of **Cornelia's** dreams. The future of their love is still up in the air...

Part I. The Twelve Portals • Volume 3

Series Created by Elisabetta Gnone
Comic Art Direction: Alessandro Barbucci, Barbara Canepa

W.I.T.C.H.: The Graphic Novel, Part I: The Twelve Portals © Disney Enterprises, Inc.

English translation © 2017 by Disney Enterprises, Inc.

JY
1290 Avenue of the Americas
New York, NY 10104

Visit us at yenpress.com
facebook.com/yenpress
twitter.com/yenpress
yenpress.tumblr.com
instagram.com/yenpress

First JY Edition: October 2017

JY is an imprint of Yen Press, LLC.
The JY name and logo are trademarks of Yen Press, LLC.

The publisher is not responsible for websites (or their content) that are not owned by the publisher.

Library of Congress Control Number: 2017950917

ISBNs:
978-0-316-47699-7 (paperback)
978-0-316-41508-8 (ebook)

10 9 8 7 6 5 4 3 2 1

LSC-C

Printed in the United States of America

Cover Art by Daniela Vetro
Colors by Marco Colletti

Translation Assistance by Eva Martina Allione
Lettering by Katie Blakeslee

THE FOUR DRAGONS

Concept by Francesco Artibani and Giulia Conti
Script by Giulia Conti
Pencils and Layout by Federico Bartolucci
Art Supervision by Graziano Barbaro
Inks by Marina Baggio and Roberta Zanotta
Title Page Art by Graziano Barbaro
with Colors by Andrea Cagol

A BRIDGE BETWEEN TWO WORLDS

Concept and Script by Bruno Enna
Layout by Ettore Gula
Pencils by Paolo Campinoti
Inks by Marina Baggio and Roberta Zanotta
Title Page Art by Ettore Gula with Colors by Andrea Cagol

THE CROWN OF LIGHT

Concept and Script by Francesco Artibani
Layout by Gianluca Panniello
Pencils by Manuela Razzi
Inks by Marina Baggio and Roberta Zanotta
Color Direction by Francesco Legramandi
Title Page Art by Manuela Razzi with Colors by Andrea Cagol

SO BE IT FOREVER

Concept and Script by Francesco Artibani
Art by Donald Soffritti with Assistance by Daniela Vetro
Inks by Marina Baggio and Roberta Zanotta
Color Direction by Francesco Legramandi
Title Page Art by Daniela Vetro with Colors by Marco Collet